from Dorothy La Mar

*The Grass Is Singing*
*This Was the Old Chief's Country* (stories)
*Five* (short novels)
*Retreat to Innocence*
*The Habit of Loving* (stories)
*In Pursuit of the English*
*Going Home*
*Fourteen Poems*
*The Golden Notebook*
*A Man and Two Women* (stories)
*African Stories*
*Particularly Cats*
*Briefing for a Descent Into Hell*
*The Temptation of Jack Orkney and Other Stories*
*The Summer Before the Dark*
*A Small Personal Voice*
*Memoirs of a Survivor*

CHILDREN OF VIOLENCE:
*Martha Quest*
*A Proper Marriage*
*A Ripple from the Storm*
*Landlocked*
*The Four-Gated City*

# STORIES

# DORIS LESSING

# STORIES

ALFRED · A · KNOPF
NEW YORK
1978

THIS IS A BORZOI BOOK
PUBLISHED BY ALFRED A. KNOPF, INC.

The stories in this book were taken from the following previously
published anthologies:

A Man and Two Women, Copyright © 1958, 1962, 1963 by Doris
Lessing. Reprinted by permission of Simon & Schuster, a division
of Gulf & Western Corporation.

The Habit of Loving, Copyright © 1975 by Doris Lessing. Reprinted by permission of Thomas Y. Crowell, Publishers.

The Temptation of Jack Orkney and Other Stories, Copyright ©
1963, 1964, 1968, 1969, 1971, 1972 by Doris Lessing. Published
in 1972 by Alfred A. Knopf, Inc.

Five, first published in Great Britain by Michael Joseph Ltd.
1953, Copyright © Doris Lessing 1953.

Library of Congress Cataloging in Publication Data
Lessing, Doris May, 1919–
Stories.
I. Title.
PZ3.L56684St      1978      [PR6023.E833]      823'.9'14
ISBN 0–394–50009–1
77–20709

Manufactured in the United States of America
First Edition

# Contents

# STORIES

# The Habit of Loving

In 1947 George wrote again to Myra, saying that now the war was well over she should come home and marry him. She wrote back from Australia, where she had gone with her two children in 1943 because there were relations there, saying she felt they had drifted apart; she was no longer sure she wanted to marry George. He did not allow himself to collapse. He cabled her the air fare and asked her to come over and see him. She came, for two weeks, being unable to leave the children for longer. She said she liked Australia; she liked the climate; she did not like the English climate any longer; she thought England was, very probably, played out; and she had become used to missing London. Also, presumably, to missing George Talbot.

For George this was a very painful fortnight. He believed it was painful for Myra, too. They had met in 1938, had lived together for five years, and had exchanged for four years the letters of lovers separated by fate. Myra was certainly the love of his life. He had believed he was of hers until now. Myra, an attractive woman made beautiful by the suns and beaches of Australia, waved goodbye at the airport, and her eyes were filled with tears.

George's eyes, as he drove away from the airport, were dry. If one person has loved another truly and wholly, then it is more than love that collapses when one side of the indissoluble partnership turns away with a tearful goodbye. George dismissed the taxi early and walked through St. James's Park. Then it seemed too small for him, and he went to the Green

Park. Then he walked into Hyde Park and through to Kensington Gardens. When the dark came and they closed the great gates of the park he took a taxi home. He lived in a block of flats near the Marble Arch. For five years Myra had lived with him there, and it was here he had expected to live with her again. Now he moved into a new flat near Covent Garden. Soon after that he wrote Myra a very painful letter. It occurred to him that he had often received such letters, but had never written one before. It occurred to him that he had entirely underestimated the amount of suffering he must have caused in his life. But Myra wrote him a sensible letter back, and George Talbot told himself that now he must finally stop thinking about Myra.

Therefore he became rather less of a dilettante in his work than he had been recently, and he agreed to produce a new play written by a friend of his. George Talbot was a man of the theatre. He had not acted in it for many years now; but he wrote articles, he sometimes produced a play, he made speeches on important occasions and was known by everyone. When he went into a restaurant people tried to catch his eye, and he often did not know who they were. During the four years since Myra had left, he had had a number of affairs with young women round and about the theatre, for he had been lonely. He had written quite frankly to Myra about these affairs, but she had never mentioned them in her letters. Now he was very busy for some months and was seldom at home; he earned quite a lot of money, and he had a few more affairs with women who were pleased to be seen in public with him. He thought about Myra a great deal, but he did not write to her again, nor she to him, although they had agreed they would always be great friends.

One evening in the foyer of a theatre he saw an old friend of his he had always admired, and he told the young woman he was with that that man had been the most irresistible man of his generation—no woman had been able to resist him. The young woman stared briefly across the foyer and said, "Not really?"

When George Talbot got home that night he was alone, and he looked at himself with honesty in the mirror. He was sixty, but he did not look it. Whatever had attracted women to him in the past had never been his looks, and he was not much changed: a stoutish man, holding himself erect, grey-haired, carefully brushed, well-dressed. He had not paid much attention to his face since those many years ago when he had been an actor; but now he had an uncharacteristic fit of vanity and remembered that Myra had admired his mouth, while his wife had loved his eyes. He took to taking glances at himself in foyers and restaurants where there were mirrors, and he saw himself as unchanged. He was becoming conscious, though, of a discrepancy between that suave exterior and what he felt. Beneath his ribs his heart had become swollen and soft and painful, a monstrous area of sympathy playing enemy to what he had been. When people made jokes he was often unable to laugh; and his manner of talking, which was light and allusive and dry, must have changed, because more than once old friends asked him if he was depressed, and they no longer smiled appreciatively as he told his stories. He gathered he was not being good company. He understood he might be ill, and he went to the doctor. The doctor said there was nothing wrong with his heart, he had thirty years of life in him yet—luckily, he added respectfully, for the British theatre.

George came to understand that the word "heartache" meant that a person could carry a heart that ached around with him day and night for, in his case, months. Nearly a year now. He would wake in the night, because of the pressure of pain in his chest; in the morning he woke under a weight of grief. There seemed to be no end to it; and this thought jolted him into two actions. First, he wrote to Myra a tender, carefully phrased letter, recalling the years of their love. To this he got, in due course, a tender and careful reply. Then he went to see his wife. With her he was, and had been for many years, good friends. They saw each other often, but not so often now the children were grownup; perhaps once or twice a year, and they never quarrelled.

His wife had married again after they divorced, and now she was a widow. Her second husband had been a member of Parliament, and she worked for the Labour Party, and she was on a Hospital Advisory Committee and on the Board of Directors of a progressive school. She was fifty, but did not look it. On this afternoon she was wearing a slim grey suit and grey shoes, and her grey hair had a wave of white across the front which made her look distinguished. She was animated, and very happy to see George; and she talked about some deadhead on her hospital committee who did not see eye to eye with the progressive minority about some reform or other. They had always had their politics in common, a position somewhere left of center in the Labour Party. She had sympathised with his being a pacifist in the First World War—he had been for a time in prison because of it; he had sympathised with her militant feminism. Both had helped the strikers in 1926. In the Thirties, after they were divorced, she had helped with money when he went on tour with a company acting Shakespeare to people on the dole, or hunger-marching.

Myra had not been at all interested in politics, only in her children. And in George, of course.

George asked his first wife to marry him again, and she was so startled that she let the sugar tongs drop and crack a saucer. She asked what had happened to Myra, and George said: "Well, dear, I think Myra forgot about me during those years in Australia. At any rate, she doesn't want me now." When he heard his voice saying this it sounded pathetic, and he was frightened, for he could not remember ever having to appeal to a woman. Except to Myra.

His wife examined him and said briskly: "You're lonely, George. Well, we're none of us getting any younger."

"You don't think you'd be less lonely if you had me around?"

She got up from her chair in order that she could attend to something with her back to him, and she said that she intended to marry again quite soon. She was marrying a man considerably younger than herself, a doctor who was in the progressive minority at her hospital. From her voice George understood that she was both proud and ashamed of this marriage, and that was why she was hiding her face from him. He congratulated her and asked her if there wasn't perhaps a chance for him yet? "After all, dear, we were happy together, weren't we? I've never really understood why that marriage ever broke up. It was you who wanted to break it up."

"I don't see any point in raking over that old business," she said, with finality, and returned to her seat opposite him. He envied her very much, looking young with her pink and scarcely lined face under that brave lock of deliberately whitened hair.

"But dear, I wish you'd tell me. It doesn't do any harm now, does it? And I always wondered. . . . I've often thought about it and wondered." He could hear the pathetic note in his voice again, but he did not know how to alter it.

"You wondered," she said, "when you weren't occupied with Myra."

"But I didn't know Myra when we got divorced."

"You knew Phillipa and Georgina and Janet and Lord knows who else."

"But I didn't care about them."

She sat with her competent hands in her lap, and on her face was a look he remembered seeing when she told him she would divorce him. It was bitter and full of hurt. "You didn't care about me either," she said.

"But we were happy. Well, I was happy . . ." he trailed off, being pathetic against all his knowledge of women. For, as he sat there, his old rake's heart was telling him that if only he could find them, there must be the right words, the right tone. But whatever he said came out in this hopeless, old dog's voice, and he knew that this voice could never defeat the gallant and crusading young doctor. "And I did care about you. Sometimes I think you were the only woman in my life."

At this she laughed. "Oh, George, don't get maudlin now, please."

"Well, dear, there was Myra. But when you threw me over there was bound to be Myra, wasn't there? There were two women, you and then Myra. And I've never never understood why you broke it all up when we seemed to be so happy."

"You didn't care for me," she said again. "If you had, you would never have come home from Phillipa, Georgina, Janet, *et al.*, and said calmly, just as if it didn't matter to me in the least, that you had been with them in Brighton or wherever it was."

"But if I had cared about them I would never have told you."

She was regarding him incredulously, and her face was flushed. With what? Anger? George did not know.

"I remember being so proud," he said pathetically, "that we had solved this business of marriage and all that sort of thing. We had such a good marriage that it didn't matter, the little flirtations. And I always thought one should be able to tell the truth. I always told you the truth, didn't I?"

"Very romantic of you, dear George," she said dryly; and soon he got up, kissed her fondly on the cheek, and went away.

He walked for a long time through the parks, hands behind his erect back, and he could feel his heart swollen and painful in his side. When the gates shut, he walked through the lighted streets he had lived in for fifty years of his life, and he was remembering Myra and Molly, as if they were one woman, merging into each other, a shape of warm easy intimacy, a shape of happiness walking beside him. He went into a little restaurant he knew well, and there was a girl sitting there who knew him because she had heard him lecture once on the state of the British theatre. He tried hard to see Myra and Molly in her face, but he failed; and he paid for her coffee and his own and went home by himself. But his flat was unbearably empty, and he left it and walked down by the Embankment for a couple of hours to tire himself, and there must have been a colder wind blowing than he knew, for next day he woke with a pain in his chest which he could not mistake for heartache.

He had 'flu and a bad cough, and he stayed in bed by himself and did not ring up the doctor until the fourth day, when he was getting lightheaded. The doctor said it must be the hospital at once. But he would not go to the hospital. So the doctor said he must have day and night nurses. This he submitted to until the cheerful friendliness of the nurses saddened him beyond bearing, and he asked the doctor to ring up his wife, who would find someone to look after him who would be sympathetic. He was hoping that Molly would come herself to nurse him, but when she arrived he did not like to mention it, for she was busy with preparations for her new marriage. She promised to find him someone who would not wear a uniform and make jokes. They naturally had many friends in common; and she rang up an old flame of his in the theatre who said she knew of a girl who was looking for a secretary's job to tide her over a patch of not working, but who didn't really mind what she did for a few weeks.

So Bobby Tippett sent away the nurses and made up a bed for herself in his study. On the first day she sat by George's bed sewing. She wore a full dark skirt and a demure printed blouse with short frills at the wrist, and George watched her sewing and already felt much better. She was a small, thin, dark girl, probably Jewish, with sad black eyes. She had a way of letting her sewing lie loose in her lap, her hands limp over it; and her eyes fixed themselves, and a bloom of dark introspection came over them. She sat very still at these moments, like a small china figure of a girl sewing. When she was nursing George, or letting in his many visitors, she put on a manner of cool and even languid charm; it was the extreme good manners of heartlessness, and at first George was chilled: but then he saw through the pose; for whatever world Bobby Tippett had been born into he did not think it was the English class to which these manners belonged. She replied with a "yes," or a "no," to questions about herself; he gathered that her parents were dead, but there was a married sister she saw sometimes; and for the rest she had lived around and about London, mostly by herself, for ten or more years. When he asked her if she had not been lonely, so much by herself, she drawled, "Why, not at all, I don't mind being alone." But he saw her as a small, brave child, a waif against London, and was moved.

He did not want to be the big man of the theatre; he was afraid of evoking the impersonal admiration he was only too accustomed to; but soon he was asking her questions about her career, hoping that this might be the point of her enthusiasm. But she spoke lightly of small parts, odd jobs, scene-painting and understudying, in a jolly good-little-trouper's voice; and he could not see that he had come any closer to her at all. So at last he did what he had tried to avoid and, sitting up against his pillows like a judge or an impresario, he said: "Do something for me, dear. Let me see you." She went next door like an obedient child, and came back in tight black trousers, but still in her demure little blouse, and stood on the carpet before him, and went into a little song-and-dance act. It wasn't bad. He had seen a hundred worse. But he was very moved; he saw her now above all as the little urchin, the gamin, boy-girl and helpless. And utterly touching. "Actually," she said, "this is half of an act. I always have someone else."

There was a big mirror that nearly filled the end wall of the large, dark room. George saw himself in it, an elderly man sitting propped up on pillows watching the small doll-like figure standing before him on the carpet. He saw her turn her head towards her reflection in the darkened mirror, study it, and then she began to dance with her own reflection, dance against it, as it were. There were two small, light figures dancing in George's room; there was something uncanny in it. She began singing, a little broken song in stage cockney, and George felt that she was expecting the other figure in the mirror to sing with her; she was singing at the mirror as if she expected an answer.

"That's very good, dear," he broke in quickly, for he was upset, though he did not know why. "Very good indeed." He was relieved when she broke off and came away from the mirror, so that the uncanny shadow of her went away.

"Would you like me to speak to someone for you, dear? It might help. You know how things are in the theatre," he suggested apologetically.

"I don't maind if I dew," she said in the stage cockney of her act; and for a moment her face flashed into a mocking, reckless, gaminlike charm. "Perhaps I'd better change back into my skirt?" she suggested. "More natural-like for a nurse, ain't it?"

But he said he liked her in her tight black trousers, and now she always wore them, and her neat little shirts; and she moved about the flat as a charming feminine boy, chattering to him about the plays she had had small parts in and about the big actors and actresses and producers she had spoken to, who were, of course, George's friends or, at least, equals. George sat up against his pillows and listened and watched, and his heart ached. He remained in bed longer than there was need, because he did not want her to go. When he transferred himself to a big chair, he said: "You mustn't think you're bound to stay here, dear, if there's somewhere else you'd rather go." To which she replied, with a wide flash of her black eyes, "But I'm resting, darling, resting. I've nothing better to do with myself." And then: "Oh aren't I awful, the things wot I sy?"

"But you do like being here? You don't mind being here with me, dear?" he insisted.

There was the briefest pause. She said: "Yes, oddly enough I do like it." The "oddly enough" was accompanied by a quick, half-laughing, almost flirtatious glance; and for the first time in many months the pressure of loneliness eased around George's heart.

Now it was a happiness to him because when the distinguished ladies and gentlemen of the theatre or of letters came to see him, Bobby became a cool, silky little hostess; and the instant they had gone she relapsed into urchin charm. It was a proof of their intimacy. Sometimes he took her out to dinner or to the theatre. When she dressed up she wore bold,

fashionable clothes and moved with the insolence of a mannequin; and George moved beside her, smiling fondly, waiting
for the moment when the black, reckless, freebooting eyes
would flash up out of the languid stare of the woman presenting
herself for admiration, exchanging with him amusement at her
posing, amusement at the world; promising him that soon,
when they got back to the apartment, by themselves, she would
again become the dear little girl or the gallant, charming waif.

Sometimes, sitting in the dim room at night, he would let his
hand close over the thin point of her shoulder; sometimes, when
they said goodnight, he bent to kiss her, and she lowered her
head, so that his lips encountered her demure, willing forehead.

George told himself that she was unawakened. It was a
phrase that had been the prelude to a dozen warm discoveries
in the past. He told himself that she knew nothing of what she
might be. She had been married, it seemed—she dropped this
information once, in the course of an anecdote about the
theatre; but George had known women in plenty who after
years of marriage had been unawakened. George asked her to
marry him; and she lifted her small sleek head with an animal's
startled turn and said: "Why do you want to marry me?"

"Because I like being with you, dear. I love being with you."

"Well, I like being with you." It had a questioning sound. She
was questioning herself? "Strainge," she said in cockney, laughing. "Strainge but trew."

The wedding was to be a small one, but there was a lot about
it in the papers. Recently several men of George's generation
had married young women. One of them had fathered a son at
the age of seventy. George was flattered by the newspapers, and
told Bobby a good deal about his life that had not come up
before. He remarked, for instance, that he thought his generation had been altogether more successful about this business of
love and sex than the modern generation. He said, "Take my
son, for instance. At his age I had had a lot of affairs and knew
about women; but there he is, nearly thirty, and when he stayed
here once with a girl he was thinking of marrying I know for a
fact they shared the same bed for a week and nothing ever
happened. She told me so. Very odd it all seems to me. But it
didn't seem odd to her. And now he lives with another young
man and listens to that long-playing record thing of his, and

he's engaged to a girl he takes out twice a week, like a schoolboy. And there's my daughter, she came to me a year after she was married, and she was in an awful mess, really awful. . . . It seems to me your generation are very frightened of it all. I don't know why."

"Why my generation?" she asked, turning her head with that quick listening movement. "It's not my generation."

"But you're nothing but a child," he said fondly.

He could not decipher what lay behind the black, full stare of her sad eyes as she looked at him now; she was sitting cross-legged in her black glossy trousers before the fire, like a small doll. But a spring of alarm had been touched in him and he didn't dare say any more.

"At thirty-five, I'm the youngest child alive," she sang, with a swift sardonic glance at him over her shoulder. But it sounded gay.

He did not talk to her again about the achievements of his generation.

After the wedding he took her to a village in Normandy where he had been once, many years ago, with a girl called Eve. He did not tell her he had been there before.

It was spring, and the cherry trees were in flower. The first evening he walked with her in the last sunlight under the white-flowering branches, his arm around her thin waist, and it seemed to him that he was about to walk back through the gates of a lost happiness.

They had a large comfortable room with windows which overlooked the cherry trees and there was a double bed. Madame Cruchot, the farmer's wife, showed them the room with shrewd, non-commenting eyes, said she was always happy to shelter honeymoon couples, and wished them a good night.

George made love to Bobby, and she shut her eyes, and he found she was not at all awkward. When they had finished, he gathered her in his arms, and it was then that he returned simply, with an incredulous awed easing of the heart, to a happiness which—and now it seemed to him fantastically ungrateful that he could have done—he had taken for granted for so many years of his life. It was not possible, he thought, holding her compliant body in his arms, that he could have been by himself, alone, for so long. It had been intolerable. He held her silent breathing body, and he stroked her back and thighs, and his hands remembered the emotions of nearly fifty years of loving. He could feel the memoried emotions of his life flooding through his body, and his heart swelled with a joy it seemed to him he had never known, for it was a compound of a dozen loves.

He was about to take final possession of his memories when she turned sharply away, sat up, and said: "I want a fag. How about yew?"

"Why, yes, dear, if you want."

They smoked. The cigarettes finished, she lay down on her back, arms folded across her chest, and said, "I'm sleepy." She closed her eyes. When he was sure she was asleep, he lifted himself on his elbow and watched her. The light still burned, and the curve of her cheek was full and soft, like a child's. He touched it with the side of his palm, and she shrank away in her sleep, but clenched up, like a fist; and her hand, which was white and unformed, like a child's hand, was clenched in a fist on the pillow before her face.

George tried to gather her in his arms, and she turned away from him to the extreme edge of the bed. She was deeply asleep, and her sleep was unsharable. George could not endure it. He got out of bed and stood by the window in the cold spring night air, and saw the white cherry trees standing under the white moon, and thought of the cold girl asleep in her bed. He was there in the chill moonlight until the dawn came; in the morning he had a very bad cough and could not get up. Bobby was charming, devoted, and gay. "Just like old times, me nursing you," she commented, with a deliberate roll of her black eyes. She asked Madame Cruchot for another bed, which she placed in the corner of the room, and George thought it was quite reasonable she should not want to catch his cold; for he did not allow himself to remember the times in his past when quite serious illness had been no obstacle to the sharing of the dark; he decided to forget the sensualities of tiredness, or of fever, or of the extremes of sleeplessness. He was even beginning to feel ashamed.

For a fortnight the Frenchwoman brought up magnificent meals, twice a day, and George and Bobby drank a great deal of red wine and of calvados and made jokes with Madame Cruchot about getting ill on honeymoons. They returned from Normandy rather earlier than had been arranged. It would be better for George, Bobby said, at home, where his friends could drop in to see him. Besides, it was sad to be shut indoors in springtime, and they were both eating too much.

On the first night back in the flat, George waited to see if she would go into the study to sleep, but she came to the big bed in her pyjamas, and for the second time he held her in his arms for the space of the act, and then she smoked, sitting up in bed and looking rather tired and small and, George thought, terribly young and pathetic. He did not sleep that night. He did not dare move out of bed for fear of disturbing her, and he was afraid to drop off to sleep for fear his limbs remembered the habits of a lifetime and searched for hers. In the morning she woke smiling, and he put his arms around her, but she kissed him with small gentle kisses and jumped out of bed.

That day she said she must go and see her sister. She saw her sister often during the next few weeks and kept suggesting that George should have his friends around more than he did. George asked why didn't the sister come to see her here, in the flat? So one afternoon she came to tea. George had seen her briefly at the wedding and disliked her, but now for the first time he had a spell of revulsion against the marriage itself. The sister was awful—a commonplace, middleaged female from some suburb. She had a sharp, dark face that poked itself inquisitively into the corners of the flat, pricing the furniture, and a thin acquisitive nose bent to one side. She sat, on her best behaviour, for two hours over the teacups, in a mannish navy blue suit, a severe black hat, her brogued feet set firmly side by side before her; and her thin nose seemed to be carrying on a silent, satirical conversation with her sister about George. Bobby was being cool and well-mannered, as it were, deliberately tired of life, as she always was when guests were there, but George was sure this was simply on his account. When the sister had gone, George was rather querulous about her; but Bobby said, laughing, that of course she had known George wouldn't like Rosa; she *was* rather ghastly; but then who had suggested inviting her? So Rosa came no more, and Bobby went out to meet her for a visit to the pictures, or for shopping. Meanwhile, George sat alone and thought uneasily about Bobby, or visited his old friends. A few months after they returned from Normandy, someone suggested to George that perhaps he was ill. This made George think about it, and he realised he was not far from being ill. It was because he could not sleep. Night after night he lay beside Bobby, after her cheerfully affectionate submission to him; and he saw the soft curve of her cheek on the pillow, the long dark lashes lying close and flat. Never had anything in his life moved him so deeply as that childish cheek, the shadow of those lashes. A small crease in one cheek seemed to him the signature of emotion; and the lock of black glossy hair falling across her forehead filled his throat with tears. His nights were long vigils of locked tenderness.

Then one night she woke and saw him watching her.

"What's the matter?" she asked, startled. "Can't you sleep?"

"I'm only watching you, dear," he said hopelessly.

She lay curled up beside him, her fist beside her on the pillow, between him and her. "Why aren't you happy?" she asked suddenly; and as George laughed with a sudden bitter irony, she sat up, arms around her knees, prepared to consider this problem practically.

"This isn't marriage; this isn't love," he announced. He sat up beside her. He did not know that he had never used that tone to her before. A portly man, his elderly face flushed with sorrow, he had forgotten her for the moment, and he was speaking across her from his past, resurrected in her, to his past. He was dignified with responsible experience and the warmth of a lifetime's responses. His eyes were heavy, satirical, and condemning. She rolled herself up against him and said with a small smile, "Then show me, George."

"Show you?" he said, almost stammering. "Show you?" But he held her, the obedient child, his cheek against hers, until she slept; then a too close pressure of his shoulder on hers caused her to shrink and recoil from him away to the edge of the bed.

In the morning she looked at him oddly, with an odd sad little respect, and said, "You know what, George? You've just got into the habit of loving."

"What do you mean, dear?"

She rolled out of bed and stood beside it, a waif in her white pyjamas, her black hair ruffled. She slid her eyes at him and smiled. "You just want something in your arms, that's all. What do you do when you're alone? Wrap yourself around a pillow?"

He said nothing; he was cut to the heart.

"My husband was the same," she remarked gaily. "Funny

thing is, he didn't care anything about me." She stood considering him, smiling mockingly. "Strainge, ain't it?" she commented and went off to the bathroom. That was the second time she had mentioned her husband.

That phrase, "the habit of loving," made a revolution in George. It was true, he thought. He was shocked out of himself, out of the instinctive response to the movement of skin against his, the pressure of a breast. It seemed to him that he was seeing Bobby quite newly. He had not really known her before. The delightful little girl had vanished, and he saw a young woman toughened and wary because of defeats and failures he had never stopped to think of. He saw that the sadness that lay behind the black eyes was not at all impersonal; he saw the first sheen of grey lying on her smooth hair; he saw that the full curve of her cheek was the beginning of the softening into middleage. He was appalled at his egotism. Now, he thought, he would really know her, and she would begin to love him in response to it.

Suddenly, George discovered in himself a boy whose existence he had totally forgotten. He had been returned to his adolescence. The accidental touch of her hand delighted him; the swing of her skirt could make him shut his eyes with happiness. He looked at her through the jealous eyes of a boy and began questioning her about her past, feeling that he was slowly taking possession of her. He waited for a hint of emotion in the drop of her voice, or a confession in the wrinkling of the skin by the full, dark, comradely eyes. At night, a boy again, reverence shut him into ineptitude. The body of George's sensuality had been killed stone dead. A month ago he had been a man vigorous with the skilled harbouring of memory; the long use of his body. Now he lay awake beside this woman, longing—not for the past, for that past had dropped away from him, but dreaming of the future. And when he questioned her, like a jealous boy, and she evaded him, he could see it only as the locked virginity of the girl who would wake in answer to the worshipping boy he had become.

But still she slept in a citadel, one fist before her face.

Then one night she woke again, roused by some movement of his. "What's the matter *now*, George?" she asked, exasperated.

In the silence that followed, the resurrected boy in George died painfully.

"Nothing," he said. "Nothing at all." He turned away from her, defeated.

It was he who moved out of the big bed into the narrow bed in the study. She said with a sharp, sad smile, "Fed up with me, George? Well I can't help it, you know. I didn't ever like sleeping beside someone very much."

George, who had dropped out of his work lately, undertook to produce another play, and was very busy again; and he became drama critic for one of the big papers and was in the swim and at all the first nights. Sometimes Bobby was with him, in her startling, smart clothes, being amused with him at the whole business of being fashionable. Sometimes she stayed at home. She had the capacity of being by herself for hours, apparently doing nothing. George would come home from some crowd of people, some party, and find her sitting cross-legged before the fire in her tight trousers, chin in hand, gone off by herself into some place where he was now afraid to try and follow. He could not bear it again, putting himself in a position where he might hear the cold, sharp words that showed she had never had an inkling of what he felt, because it was not in her nature to feel it. He would come in late, and she would make them both some tea; and they would sit hand in hand before the fire, his flesh and memories quiet. Dead, he thought. But his heart ached. He had become so used to the heavy load of loneliness in his chest that when, briefly, talking to an old friend, he became the George Talbot who had never known Bobby, and his heart lightened and his oppression went, he would look about him, startled, as if he had lost something. He felt almost lightheaded without the pain of loneliness.

He asked Bobby if she weren't bored, with so little to do, month after month after month, while he was so busy. She said no, she was quite happy doing nothing. She wouldn't like to take up her old work again.

"I wasn't ever much good, was I?" she said.

"If you'd enjoy it, dear, I could speak to someone for you."

She frowned at the fire but said nothing. Later he suggested it again, and she sparked up with a grin and: "Well, I don't maind if I dew. . . ."

So he spoke to an old friend, and Bobby returned to the theatre, to a small act in a little intimate revue. She had found somebody, she said, to be the other half of her act. George was very busy with a production of *Romeo and Juliet*, and did not have time to see her at rehearsal, but he was there on the night *The Offbeat Revue* opened. He was rather late and stood at the back of the gimcrack little theatre, packed tight with fragile little chairs. Everything was so small that the well-dressed audience looked too big, like oversize people crammed in a box. The tiny stage was left bare, with a few black-and-white posters stuck here and there, and there was one piano. The pianist was good, a young man with black hair falling limp over his face, playing as if he were bored with the whole thing. But he played very well. George, the man of the theatre, listened to the first number, so as to catch the mood, and thought, Oh Lord, not again. It was one of the songs from the First World War, and he could not stand the flood of easy emotion it aroused. He refused to feel. Then he realised that the emotion was, in any case, blocked; the piano was mocking the song; There's a Long, Long Trail was being played like a five-finger exercise; and Keep the Home Fires Burning and Tipperary followed, in the same style, as if the piano were bored. People were beginning to chuckle, they had caught the mood. A young blond man with a moustache and wearing the uniform of 1914 came in and sang fragments of the songs, like a corpse singing; and then George understood he was supposed to be one of the dead of that war singing. George felt all his responses blocked, first because he could not allow himself to feel any emotion from that time at all—it was too painful; and then because of the five-finger exercise style, which contradicted everything, all pain or protest, leaving nothing, an emptiness. The show went on; through the Twenties, with bits of popular songs from that time, a number about the General Strike, which reduced the whole thing to the scale of marionettes without passion, and then on to the Thirties. George saw it was a sort of potted history, as it were—Noël Coward's falsely heroic view of his time parodied. But it wasn't even that. There was no emotion, nothing. George did not know what he was supposed to feel. He looked curiously at the faces of the people around him and saw that the older people looked puzzled, affronted, as if the show were an insult to them. But the younger people were in the mood of the thing. But what mood? It was the parody of a parody. When the Second World War was evoked by Run Rabbit Run, played like *Lohengrin*, while the soldiers in the uniforms of the time mocked their own understated heroism from the other side of death, then George could not stand it. He did not look at the stage at all. He was waiting for Bobby to come on, so he could say that he had seen her. Meanwhile he smoked and watched the face of a very young man near him; it was a pale, heavy, flaccid face, but it was responding, it seemed from a habit of rancour, to everything that went on on the stage. Suddenly, the young face lit into sarcastic delight, and George looked at the stage. On it were two urchins, identical, it seemed, in tight black glossy trousers, tight crisp white shirts. Both had short black hair, neat little feet placed side by side. They were standing together, hands crossed loosely before them at the waist, waiting for the music to start. The man at the piano, who had a cigarette in the corner of his mouth, began playing something very sentimental. He broke off and looked with sardonic enquiry at the urchins. They had not moved. They shrugged and rolled their eyes at him. He played a marching song, very loud and pompous. The urchins twisted a little and stayed still. Then the piano broke fast and sudden into a rage of jazz. The two puppets on the stage began a furious movement, their limbs clashing with each other and with the music, until they fell into poses of helpless despair while the music grew louder and more desperate. They tried again, whirling themselves into a frenzied attempt to keep up with the music. Then, two waifs, they turned their two small white sad faces at each other, and, with a formal nod, each took a phrase of music from the fast flood of sound that had already swept by them, held it, and began to sing. Bobby sang her bad stage-cockney phrases, meaningless, jumbled up, flat, hopeless; the other urchin sang drawling languid phrases from the upperclass jargon of the moment. They looked at each other, offering the phrases, as it were, to see if they would be accepted. Meanwhile, the hard, cruel, hurtful music went on. Again the two went limp and helpless, unwanted, unaccepted. George, outraged and hurt, asked himself again: What am I feeling? What am I supposed to be feeling? For that insane nihilistic music demanded some opposition, some statement of affirmation, but the two urchins, half-boy, half-girl, as alike as twins (George had to watch Bobby carefully so as not to confuse her with "the other half of her act"), were not even trying to resist the music. Then, after a long, sad immobility, they changed roles. Bobby took the languid jaw-writhing part of a limp young man, and the other waif sang false-cockney phrases in a cruel copy of a woman's voice. It was the parody of a parody. George stood tense, waiting for a resolution. His nature demanded that now, and quickly, for the limp sadness of the turn was unbearable, the two false urchins should flash out in some sort of rebellion. But there was nothing. The jazz went on like hammers; the whole room shook—stage, walls, ceiling —and it seemed the people in the room jigged lightly and helplessly. The two children on the stage twisted their limbs into the wilful mockery of a stage convention, and finally stood side by side, hands hanging limp, heads lowered meekly, twitching a little while the music rose into a final crashing discord and the lights went out. George could not applaud. He saw that the damp-faced young man next to him was clapping wildly, while his lank hair fell all over his face. George saw that the older people were all, like himself, bewildered and insulted.

When the show was over, George went backstage to fetch Bobby. She was with "the other half of the act," a rather good-looking boy of about twenty, who was being deferential to the impressive husband of Bobby. George said to her: "You were very good, dear, very good indeed." She looked smilingly at him, half-mocking, but he did not know what it was she was mocking now. And she had been good. But he never wanted to see it again.

The revue was a success and ran for some months before it was moved to a bigger theatre. George finished his production of *Romeo and Juliet*, which, so the critics said, was the best London had seen for many years, and refused other offers of work. He did not need the money for the time being, and besides, he had not seen very much of Bobby lately.

But of course now she was working. She was at rehearsals several times a week, and away from the flat every evening. But George never went to her theatre. He did not want to see the sad, unresisting children twitching to the cruel music.

It seemed Bobby was happy. The various little parts she had played with him—the urchin, the cool hostess, the dear child —had all been absorbed into the hard-working female who cooked him his meals, looked after him, and went out to her theatre giving him a friendly kiss on the cheek. Their relationship was most pleasant and amiable. George lived beside this good friend, his wife Bobby, who was doing him so much credit in every way, and ached permanently with loneliness.

One day he was walking down the Charing Cross Road, looking into the windows of bookshops, when he saw Bobby strolling up the other side with Jackie, the other half of her act. She looked as he had never seen her: her dark face was alive with animation, and Jackie was looking into her face and laughing. George thought the boy very handsome. He had a warm gloss of youth on his hair and in his eyes; he had the lithe, quick look of a young animal.

George was not jealous at all. When Bobby came in at night, gay and vivacious, he knew he owed this to Jackie and did not mind. He was even grateful to him. The warmth Bobby had for "the other half of the act" overflowed towards him; and for some months Myra and his wife were present in his mind, he saw and felt them, two loving presences, young women who loved George, brought into being by the feeling between Jackie and Bobby. Whatever that feeling was.

*The Offbeat Revue* ran for nearly a year, and then it was coming off, and Bobby and Jackie were working out another act. George did not know what it was. He thought Bobby needed a rest, but he did not like to say so. She had been tired recently, and when she came in at night there was strain beneath her gaiety. Once, at night, he woke to see her beside his bed. "Hold me for a little, George," she asked. He opened his arms and she came into them. He lay holding her, quite still. He had opened his arms to the sad waif, but it was an unhappy woman lying in his arms. He could feel the movement of her lashes on his shoulder, and the wetness of tears.

He had not lain beside her for a long time—years, it seemed. She did not come to him again.

"You don't think you're working too hard, dear?" he asked once, looking at her strained face; but she said briskly, "No, I've got to have something to do, can't stand doing nothing."

One night it was raining hard, and Bobby had been feeling sick that day, and she did not come home at her usual time. George became worried and took a taxi to the theatre and asked the doorman if she was still there. It seemed she had left some time before. "She didn't look too well to me, sir," volunteered the doorman, and George sat for a time in the taxi, trying not to worry. Then he gave the driver Jackie's address;

he meant to ask him if he knew where Bobby was. He sat limp in the back of the taxi, feeling the heaviness of his limbs, thinking of Bobby ill.

The place was in a mews, and he left the taxi and walked over rough cobbles to a door which had been the door of stables. He rang, and a young man he didn't know let him in, saying yes, Jackie Dickson was in. George climbed narrow, steep, wooden stairs slowly, feeling the weight of his body, while his heart pounded. He stood at the top of the stairs to get his breath, in a dark which smelled of canvas and oil and turpentine. There was a streak of light under a door; he went towards it, knocked, heard no answer, and opened it. The scene was a high, bare, studio sort of place, badly lighted, full of pictures, frames, junk of various kinds. Jackie, the dark, glistening youth, was seated cross-legged before the fire, grinning as he lifted his face to say something to Bobby, who sat in a chair, looking down at him. She was wearing a formal dark dress and jewellery, and her arms and neck were bare and white. She looked beautiful, George thought, glancing once, briefly, at her face, and then away; for he could see on it an emotion he did not want to recognise. The scene held for a moment before they realised he was there and turned their heads, with the same lithe movement of disturbed animals, to see him standing there in the doorway. Both faces froze. Bobby looked quickly at the young man, and it was in some kind of fear. Jackie looked sulky and angry.

"I've come to look for you, dear," said George to his wife. "It was raining and the doorman said you seemed ill."

"It's very sweet of you," she said and rose from the chair, giving her hand formally to Jackie, who nodded with bad grace at George.

The taxi stood in the dark, gleaming rain, and George and Bobby got into it and sat side by side, while it splashed off into the street.

"Was that the wrong thing to do, dear?" asked George, when she said nothing.

"No," she said.

"I really did think you might be ill."

She laughed. "Perhaps I am."

"What's the matter, my darling? What is it? He was angry, wasn't he? Because I came?"

"He thinks you're jealous," she said shortly.

"Well, perhaps I am rather," said George.

She did not speak.

"I'm sorry, dear, I really am. I didn't mean to spoil anything for you."

"Well, that's certainly *that*," she remarked, and she sounded impersonally angry.

"Why? But why should it be?"

"He doesn't like—having things asked of him," she said, and he remained silent while they drove home.

Up in the warmed, comfortable old flat, she stood before the fire, while he brought her a drink. She smoked fast and angrily, looking into the fire.

"Please forgive me, dear," he said at last. "What is it? Do you love him? Do you want to leave me? If you do, of course you must. Young people should be together."

She turned and stared at him, a black strange stare he knew well.

"George," she said, "I'm nearly forty."

"But darling, you're a child still. At least, to me."

"And he," she went on, "will be twenty-two next month. I'm old enough to be his mother." She laughed, painfully. "Very painful, maternal love . . . or so it seems . . . but then how should I know?" She held out her bare arm and looked at it. Then, with the fingers of one hand she creased down the skin of that bare arm toward the wrist, so that the ageing skin lay in creases and folds. Then, setting down her glass, her cigarette held between tight, amused, angry lips, she wriggled her shoulders out of her dress, so that it slipped to her waist, and she looked down at her two small, limp, unused breasts. "Very painful, dear George," she said, and shrugged her dress up quickly, becoming again the formal woman dressed for the world. "He does not love me. He does not love me at all. Why should he?" She began singing:

> "He does not love me
> With a love that is trew. . . ."

Then she said, in stage cockney, "Repeat; I could 'ave bin 'is muvver, see?" And with the old rolling derisive black flash of her eyes she smiled at George.

George was thinking only that this girl, his darling, was

suffering now what he had suffered, and he could not stand it. She had been going through this for how long now? But she had been working with that boy for nearly two years. She had been living beside him, George, and he had had no idea at all of her unhappiness. He went over to her, put his old arms around her, and she stood with her head on his shoulder and wept. For the first time, George thought, they were together. They sat by the fire a long time that night, drinking, smoking, and her head was on his knee and he stroked it, and thought that now, at last, she had been admitted into the world of emotion and they would learn to be really together. He could feel his strength stirring along his limbs for her. He was still a man, after all.

Next day she said she would not go on with the new show. She would tell Jackie he must get another partner. And besides, the new act wasn't really any good. "I've had one little act all my life," she said, laughing. "And sometimes it's fitted in, and sometimes it hasn't."

"What was the new act? What's it about?" he asked her.

She did not look at him. "Oh, nothing very much. It was Jackie's idea, really. . . ." Then she laughed. "It's quite good really, I suppose. . . ."

"But what is it?"

"Well, you see. . . ." Again he had the impression she did not want to look at him. "It's a pair of lovers. We make fun . . . it's hard to explain, without doing it."

"You make fun of love?" he asked.

"Well, you know, all the attitudes . . . the things people say. It's a man and a woman—with music, of course. All the music you'd expect, played offbeat. We wear the same costume as for the other act. And then we go through all the motions. . . . It's rather funny, really . . ." she trailed off, breathless, seeing George's face. "Well," she said, suddenly very savage, "if it isn't all bloody funny, what is it?" She turned away to take a cigarette.

"Perhaps you'd like to go on with it after all?" he asked ironically.

"No. I can't. I really can't stand it. I can't stand it any longer, George," she said, and from her voice he understood she had nothing to learn from him of pain.

He suggested they both needed a holiday, so they went to Italy. They travelled from place to place, never stopping anywhere longer than a day, for George knew she was running away from any place around which emotion could gather. At night he made love to her, but she closed her eyes and thought of the other half of the act; and George knew it and did not care. But what he was feeling was too powerful for his old body; he could feel a lifetime's emotions beating through his limbs, making his brain throb.

Again they curtailed their holiday, to return to the comfortable old flat in London.

On the first morning after their return, she said: "George, you know you're getting too old for this sort of thing—it's not good for you; you look ghastly."

"But, darling, why? What else am I still alive for?"

"People'll say I'm killing you," she said, with a sharp, half-angry, half-amused, black glance.

"But, my darling, believe me . . ."

He could see them both in the mirror; he, an old pursy man, head lowered in sullen obstinacy; she . . . but he could not read her face.

"And perhaps *I'm* getting too old?" she remarked suddenly.

For a few days she was gay, mocking, then suddenly tender. She was provocative, teasing him with her eyes; then she would deliberately yawn and say, "I'm going to sleep. Goodnight George."

"Well of course, my darling, if you're tired."

One morning she announced she was going to have a birthday party; it would be her fortieth birthday soon. The way she said it made George feel uneasy.

On the morning of her birthday she came into his study where he had been sleeping, carrying his breakfast tray. He raised himself on his elbow and gazed at her, appalled. For a moment he had imagined it must be another woman. She had put on a severe navy blue suit, cut like a man's; heavy black-laced shoes; and she had taken the wisps of black hair back off her face and pinned them into a sort of clumsy knot. She was suddenly a middleaged woman.

"But, my darling," he said, "my darling, what have you done to yourself?"

"I'm forty," she said. "Time to grow up."

"But, my darling, I do so love you in your nice clothes. I do so love you being beautiful in your lovely clothes."

She laughed, and left the breakfast tray beside his bed, and went clumping out on her heavy shoes.

That morning she stood in the kitchen beside a very large cake, on which she was carefully placing forty small pink candles. But it seemed only the sister had been asked to the party, for that afternoon the three of them sat around the cake and looked at one another. George looked at Rosa, the sister, in her ugly, straight, thick suit, and at his darling Bobby, all her grace and charm submerged into heavy tweed, her hair dragged back, without makeup. They were two middleaged women, talking about food and buying.

George said nothing. His whole body throbbed with loss.

The dreadful Rosa was looking with her sharp eyes around the expensive flat, and then at George and then at her sister.

"You've let yourself go, haven't you, Bobby?" she commented at last. She sounded pleased about it.

Bobby glanced defiantly at George. "I haven't got time for all this nonsense any more," she said. "I simply haven't got time. We're all getting on now, aren't we?"

George saw the two women looking at him. He thought they had the same black, hard, inquisitive stare over sharp-bladed noses. He could not speak. His tongue was thick. The blood was beating through his body. His heart seemed to be swelling and filling his whole body, an enormous soft growth of pain. He could not hear for the tolling of the blood through his ears. The blood was beating up into his eyes, but he shut them so as not to see the two women.

# The Woman

•─•─•─•─•─•─•─•─•─•─•─•─•─•─•─•─•─•─•─•─•─•─•─•─•─•─•─•─•─•─•─•─•─•─•─•─•─•─•─•─•

The two elderly gentlemen emerged onto the hotel terrace at the same moment. They stopped, and checked movements that suggested they wished to retreat. Their first involuntary glances had been startled, even troubled. Now they allowed their eyes to exchange a long, formal glare of hate, before turning deliberately away from each other.

They surveyed the terrace. A problem! Only one of the tables still remained in sunlight. They stiffly marched towards it, pulled out chairs, seated themselves. At once they opened newspapers and lifted them up like screens.

A pretty waitress came sauntering across to take the orders. The two newspapers remained stationary. Around the edge of one Herr Scholtz ordered warmed wine; from the shelter of the other Captain Forster from England demanded tea—with milk.

When she returned with these fluids, neatly disposed on similar metal trays, both walls of print slightly lowered themselves. Captain Forster, with an aggressive flicker of uneasy blue eyes toward his opponent, suggested that it was a fine evening. Herr Scholtz remarked with warm freemasonry that it was a shame such a pretty girl should not be free to enjoy herself on such an evening. Herr Scholtz appeared to consider that he had triumphed, for his look towards the Englishman was boastful. To both remarks, however, Rosa responded with an amiable but equally perfunctory smile. She strolled away to the balustrade where she leaned indolently, her back to them.

Stirring sugar into tea, sipping wine, was difficult with those stiff papers in the way. First Herr Scholtz, then the Captain, folded his and placed it on the table. Avoiding each other's eyes, they looked away towards the mountains, which, however, were partly blocked by Rosa.

She wore a white blouse, low on the shoulders; a black skirt, with a tiny white apron; smart red shoes. It was at her shoulders that the gentlemen gazed. They coughed, tapped on the table with their fingers, narrowed their eyes in sentimental appreciation at the mountains, looked at Rosa again. From time to time their eyes almost met but quickly slid away. Since they could not fight, civilisation demanded they should speak. Yes, conversation appeared imminent.

A week earlier they had arrived on the same morning and were given rooms at either end of a long corridor. The season was nearly over, the hotel half-empty. Rosa therefore had plenty of time to devote to Herr Scholtz, who demanded it: he wanted bigger towels, different pillows, a glass of water. But soon the bell pealed from the other side of the corridor, and she excused herself and hastened over to Captain Forster, who was also dissatisfied with the existing arrangements for his comfort. Before she had finished with him, Herr Scholtz's bell rang again. Between the two of them Rosa was kept busy until the midday meal, and not once did she suggest by her manner that she had any other desire in this world than to readjust Captain Forster's reading light or bring Herr Scholtz cigarettes and newspapers.

That afternoon Captain Forster happened to open his door; and he found he had a clear view into the room opposite, where Rosa stood at the window smiling, in what seemed to him charming surrender, at Herr Scholtz, who was reaching out a hand towards her elbow. The hand dropped. Herr Scholtz scowled, walked across, indignantly closed his door as if it were the Captain's fault it had been left open. . . . Almost at once the Captain's painful jealousy was eased, for Rosa emerged from that door, smiling with perfect indifference, and wished him good day.

That night, very late, quick footsteps sounded on the floor of the corridor. The two doors gently opened at the same moment; and Rosa, midway between them, smiled placidly at first Herr Scholtz, then the Captain, who gave each other contemptuous looks after she had passed. They both slammed their doors.

Next day Herr Scholtz asked her if she would care to come with him up the funicular on her afternoon off, but unfortunately she was engaged. The day after Captain Forster made the same suggestion.

Finally, there was a repetition of that earlier incident. Rosa was passing along the corridor late at night on her way to her own bed, when those two doors cautiously opened and the two urgent faces appeared. This time she stopped, smiled politely, wished them a very good night. Then she yawned. It was a slight gesture, but perfectly timed. Both gentlemen solaced themselves with the thought that it must have been earned by his rival; for Herr Scholtz considered the Captain ridiculously gauche, while the Captain thought Herr Scholtz's attitude toward Rosa disgustingly self-assured and complacent. They were therefore able to retire to their beds with philosophy.

Since then Herr Scholtz had been observed in conversation with a well-preserved widow of fifty who unfortunately was obliged to retire to her own room every evening at nine o'clock for reasons of health and was, therefore, unable to go dancing with him, as he longed to do. Captain Forster took his tea every afternoon in a cafe where there was a charming waitress who might have been Rosa's sister.

The two gentlemen looked through each other in the dining-room, and each crossed the street if he saw the other approaching. There was a look about them which suggested that they might be thinking Switzerland—at any rate, so late in the season—was not all that it had been.

Gallant, however, they both continued to be; and they might continually be observed observing the social scene of flirtations and failures and successes with the calm authority of those well-qualified by long familiarity with it to assess and make judgements. Men of weight, they were; men of substance; men who expected deference.

And yet . . . here they were seated on opposite sides of that table in the last sunlight, the mountains rising about them, all mottled white and brown and green with melting spring, the

warm sun folding delicious but uncertain arms around them—
and surely they were entitled to feel aggrieved? Captain Forster
—a lean, tall, military man, carefully suntanned, spruced,
brushed—was handsome still, no doubt of it. And Herr Scholtz
—large, rotund, genial, with infinite resources of experience—
was certainly worth more than the tea-time confidences of a
widow of fifty?

Unjust to be sixty on such a spring evening; particularly
hard with Rosa not ten paces away, shrugging her shoulders
in a low-cut embroidered blouse.

And almost as if she were taking a pleasure in the cruelty,
she suddenly stopped humming and leaned forward over the
balustrade. With what animation did she wave and call down
the street, while a very handsome young man below waved
and called back. Rosa watched him stride away, and then she
sighed and turned, smiling dreamily.

There sat Herr Scholtz and Captain Forster gazing at her
with hungry resentful appreciation.

Rosa narrowed her blue eyes with anger and her mouth
went thin and cold, in disastrous contrast with her tenderness
of a moment before. She shot bitter looks from one gentleman
to the other, and then she yawned again. This time it was a
large, contemptuous, prolonged yawn; and she tapped the
back of her hand against her mouth for emphasis and let
out her breath in a long descending note, which, however, was
cut off short as if to say that she really had no time to waste
even on this small demonstration. She then swung past them
in a crackle of starched print, her heels tapping. She went
inside.

The terrace was empty. Gay painted tables, striped chairs,
flowery sun umbrellas—all were in cold shadow, save for the
small corner where the gentlemen sat. At the same moment,
from the same impulse, they rose and pushed the table forward into the last well of golden sunlight. And now they looked
at each other straight and frankly laughed.

"Will you have a drink?" enquired Herr Scholtz in English,
and his jolly smile was tightened by a consciously regretful
stoicism. After a moment's uncertainty, during which Captain
Forster appeared to be thinking that the stoicism was too early
an admission of defeat, he said, "Yes—yes. Thanks, I will."

Herr Scholtz raised his voice sharply, and Rosa appeared

from indoors, ready to be partly defensive. But now Herr
Scholtz was no longer a suppliant. Master to servant, a man
who habitually employed labour, he ordered wine without
looking at her once. And Captain Forster was the picture of
a silky gentleman.

When she reappeared with the wine they were so deep in
good fellowship they might have been saying aloud how foolish
it was to allow the sound companionship of men to be spoiled,
even for a week, on account of the silly charm of women. They
were roaring with laughter at some joke. Or, rather, Herr
Scholtz was roaring, a good stomach laugh from depths of
lusty enjoyment. Captain Forster's laugh was slightly nervous,
emitted from the back of his throat, and suggested that Herr
Scholtz's warm Bavarian geniality was all very well, but that
there were always reservations in any relationship.

It soon transpired that during the war—the First War, be
it understood—they had been enemies on the same sector of
the front at the same time. Herr Scholtz had been wounded in
his arm. He bared it now, holding it forward under the Captain's nose to show the long white scar. Who knew but that
it was the Captain who had dealt that blow—indirectly, of
course—thirty-five years before? Nor was this all. During
the Second War Captain Forster had very nearly been sent to
North Africa, where he would certainly have had the pleasure
of fighting Herr, then Oberstleutnant, Scholtz. As it happened,
the fortunes of war had sent him to India instead. While these
happy coincidences were being established, it was with the
greatest amity on both sides; and if the Captain's laugh tended
to follow Herr Scholtz's just a moment late, it could easily be
accounted for by those unavoidable differences of temperament.
Before half an hour was out, Rosa was despatched for a second
flask of the deep crimson wine.

When she returned with it, she placed the glasses so, the
flasks so, and was about to turn away when she glanced at the
Captain and was arrested. The look on his face certainly invited comment. Herr Scholtz was just remarking, with that
familiar smiling geniality, how much he regretted that the
"accidents of history"—a phrase that caused the Captain's
face to tighten very slightly—had made it necessary for them
to be enemies in the past. In the future, he hoped, they would
fight side by side, comrades in arms against the only possible

foe for either. . . . But now Herr Scholtz stopped, glanced swiftly at the Captain, and after the briefest possible pause, and without a change of tone, went on to say that as for himself he was a man of peace, a man of creation: he caused innumerable tubes of toothpaste to reach the bathrooms of his country, and he demanded nothing more of life than to be allowed to continue to do so. Besides, had he not dropped his war title, the Oberstleutnant, in proof of his fundamentally civilian character?

Here, as Rosa still remained before them, contemplating them with a look that can only be described as ambiguous, Herr Scholtz blandly enquired what she wanted. But Rosa wanted nothing. Having enquired if that was all she could do for the gentlemen, she passed to the end of the terrace and leaned against the balustrade there, looking down into the street where the handsome young man might pass.

Now there was a pause. The eyes of both men were drawn painfully towards her. Equally painful was the effort to withdraw them. Then, as if reminded that any personal differences were far more dangerous than the national ones, they plunged determinedly into gallant reminiscences. How pleasant, said that hearty masculine laughter—how pleasant to sit here in snug happy little Switzerland, comfortable in easy friendship, and after such fighting, such obviously meaningless hostilities! Citizens of the world they were, no less, human beings enjoying civilised friendship on equal terms. And each time Herr Scholtz or the Captain succumbed to that fatal attraction and glanced towards the end of the terrace, he as quickly withdrew his eyes and, as it were, set his teeth to offer another gauge of friendship across the table.

But fate did not intend this harmony to continue.

Cruelly, the knife was turned again. The young man appeared at the bottom of the street and, smiling, waved towards Rosa. Rosa leaned forward, arms on the balustrade, the picture of bashful coquetry, rocking one heel up and down behind her and shaking her hair forward to conceal the frankness of her response.

There she stood, even after he had gone, humming lightly to herself, looking after him. The crisp white napkin over her arm shone in the sunlight; her bright white apron shone; her mass of rough fair curls glowed. She stood there in the last sunlight and looked away into her own thoughts, singing softly as if she were quite alone.

Certainly she had completely forgotten the existence of Herr Scholtz and Captain Forster.

The Captain and the ex-Oberstleutnant had apparently come to the end of their sharable memories. One cleared his throat; the other, Herr Scholtz, tapped his signet ring irritatingly on the table.

The Captain shivered. "It's getting cold," he said, for now they were in the blue evening shadow. He made a movement, as if ready to rise.

"Yes," said Herr Scholtz. But he did not move. For a while he tapped his ring on the table, and the Captain set his teeth against the noise. Herr Scholtz was smiling. It was a smile that announced a new trend in the drama. Obviously. And obviously the Captain disapproved of it in advance. A blatant fellow, he was thinking, altogether too noisy and vulgar. He glanced impatiently towards the inside room, which would be warm and quiet.

Herr Scholtz remarked, "I always enjoy coming to this place. I always come here."

"Indeed?" asked the Captain, taking his cue in spite of himself. He wondered why Herr Scholtz was suddenly speaking German. Herr Scholtz spoke excellent English, learned while he was interned in England during the latter part of the Second World War. Captain Forster had already complimented him on it. His German was not nearly so fluent, no.

But Herr Scholtz, for reasons of his own, was speaking his own language, and rather too loudly, one might have thought. Captain Forster looked at him, wondering, and was attentive.

"It is particularly pleasant for me to come to this resort," remarked Herr Scholtz in that loud voice, as if to an inner listener who was rather deaf, "because of the happy memories I have of it."

"Really?" enquired Captain Forster, listening with nervous attention. Herr Scholtz, however, was speaking very slowly, as if out of consideration for him.

"Yes," said Herr Scholtz. "Of course during the war it was out of bounds for both of us, but now . . ."

The Captain suddenly interrupted: "Actually I'm very fond of it myself. I come here every year it is possible."

Herr Scholtz inclined his head, admitting that Captain Forster's equal right to it was incontestable, and continued, "I associate with it the most charming of my memories—perhaps you would care to . . ."

"But certainly," agreed Captain Forster hastily. He glanced involuntarily towards Rosa—Herr Scholtz was speaking with his eyes on Rosa's back. Rosa was no longer humming. Captain Forster took in the situation and immediately coloured. He glanced protestingly towards Herr Scholtz. But it was too late.

"I was eighteen," said Herr Scholtz very loudly. "Eighteen." He paused, and for a moment it was possible to resurrect, in the light of his rueful reminiscent smile, the delightful, ingenuous bouncing youth he had certainly been at eighteen. "My parents allowed me, for the first time, to go alone for a vacation. It was against my mother's wishes; but my father on the other hand . . ."

Here Captain Forster necessarily smiled, in acknowledgement of that international phenomenon, the sweet jealousy of mothers.

"And here I was, for a ten days' vacation, all by myself—imagine it!"

Captain Forster obligingly imagined it, but almost at once interrupted: "Odd, but I had the same experience. Only I was twenty-five."

Herr Scholtz exclaimed: "Twenty-five!" He cut himself short, covered his surprise, and shrugged as if to say: Well, one must make allowances. He at once continued to Rosa's listening back. "I was in this very hotel. Winter. A winter vacation. There was a woman . . ." He paused, smiling. "How can I describe her?"

But the Captain, it seemed, was not prepared to assist. He was frowning uncomfortably towards Rosa. His expression said quite clearly: Really, *must* you?

Herr Scholtz appeared not to notice it. "I was, even in those days, not backward—you understand?" The Captain made a movement of his shoulders which suggested that to be forward at eighteen was not a matter for congratulation, whereas at twenty-five . . .

"She was beautiful—beautiful," continued Herr Scholtz with enthusiasm. "And she was obviously rich, a woman of the world; and her clothes . . ."

"Quite," said the Captain.

"She was alone. She told me she was here for her health. Her husband unfortunately could not get away, for reasons of business. And I, too, was alone."

"Quite," said the Captain.

"Even at that age I was not too surprised at the turn of events. A woman of thirty . . . a husband so much older than herself . . . and she was beautiful . . . and intelligent. . . . Ah, but she was magnificent!" He almost shouted this, and drained his glass reminiscently towards Rosa's back. "Ah . . ." He breathed gustily. "And now I must tell you. All that was good enough, but now there is even better. Listen. A week passed. And what a week! I loved her as I never loved anyone. . . ."

"Quite," said the Captain, fidgeting.

But Herr Scholtz swept on: "And then one morning I wake, and I am alone." Herr Scholtz shrugged and groaned.

The Captain observed that Herr Scholtz was being carried away by the spirit of his own enjoyment. This tale was by now only half for the benefit of Rosa. That rich dramatic groan—Herr Scholtz might as well be in the theatre, thought the Captain uncomfortably.

"But there was a letter, and when I read it . . ."

"A letter?" interrupted the Captain suddenly.

"Yes, a letter. She thanked me so that the tears came into my eyes. I wept."

One could have sworn that the sentimental German eyes swam with tears, and Captain Forster looked away. With eyes averted he asked nervously, "What was in the letter?"

"She said how she hated her husband. She had married him against her will—to please her parents. In those days, this thing happened. And she had sworn a vow to herself never to have his child. But she wanted a child. . . ."

"*What?*" exclaimed the Captain. He was leaning forward over the table now, intent on every syllable.

This emotion seemed unwelcome to Herr Scholtz, who said blandly, "Yes, that was how it was. That was my good fortune, my friend."

"*When* was that?" enquired the Captain hungrily.

"I beg your pardon?"

"When was it? What year?"

"What year? Does it matter? She told me she had arranged this little holiday on grounds of her bad health, so that she might come by herself to find the man she wanted as the father of her child. She had chosen me. I was her choice. And now she thanked me and was returning to her husband." Herr Scholtz stopped, in triumph, and looked at Rosa. Rosa did not move. She could not possibly have failed to hear every word. Then he looked at the Captain. But the Captain's face was scarlet, and very agitated.

"What was her name?" barked the Captain.

"Her name?" Herr Scholtz paused. "Well, she would clearly have used a false name?" he enquired. As the Captain did not respond, he said firmly: "That is surely obvious, my friend. And I did not know her address." Herr Scholtz took a slow sip of his wine, then another. He regarded the Captain for a moment thoughtfully, as if wondering whether he could be trusted to behave according to the rules, and then continued: "I ran to the hotel manager—no, there was no information. The lady had left unexpectedly, early that morning. No address. I was frantic. You can imagine. I wanted to rush after her, find her, kill her husband, marry her!" Herr Scholtz laughed in amused, regretful indulgence at the follies of youth.

"You *must* remember the year," urged the Captain.

"But—my friend—" began Herr Scholtz after a pause, very annoyed. "What can it matter, after all?"

Captain Forster glanced stiffly at Rosa and spoke in English, "As it happened, the same thing happened to me."

"Here?" enquired Herr Scholtz politely.

"Here."

"In this valley?"

"In this hotel."

"Well," shrugged Herr Scholtz, raising his voice even more, "well, women—women, you know. At eighteen, of course—and perhaps even at twenty-five"—here he nodded indulgently towards his opponent—"even at twenty-five perhaps one takes such things as miracles that happen only to oneself. But at our age—?"

He paused, as if hoping against hope that the Captain might recover his composure.

But the Captain was speechless.

"I tell you, my friend," continued Herr Scholtz, good-humouredly relishing the tale, "I tell you, I was crazy; I thought I would go mad. I wanted to shoot myself; I rushed around the

streets of every city I happened to be in, looking into every face.
I looked at photographs in the papers—actresses, society women;
I used to follow a woman I had glimpsed in the street, thinking
that perhaps this was she at last. But no," said Herr Scholtz
dramatically, bringing down his hand on the table, so that his
ring clicked again, "no, never, never was I successful!"

"What did she look like?" asked the Captain agitatedly in
English, his anxious eyes searching the by now very irritated
eyes of Herr Scholtz.

Herr Scholtz moved his chair back slightly, looked toward
Rosa, and said loudly in German: "Well, she was beautiful, as
I have told you." He paused, for thought. "And she was an
aristocrat."

"Yes, yes," said the Captain impatiently.

"She was tall, very slim, with a beautiful body—beautiful!
She had that black hair, you know, black, black! And black eyes,
and beautiful teeth." He added loudly and spitefully towards
Rosa: "She was not the country bumpkin type, not at all. One
has some taste."

With extreme discomfort the Captain glanced towards the
plump village Rosa. He said, pointedly using English even at
this late stage, "Mine was fair. Tall and fair. A lovely girl.
Lovely!" he insisted with a glare. "Might have been an English
girl."

"Which was entirely to her credit," suggested Herr Scholtz,
with a smile.

"That was in 1913," said the Captain insistently, and then:
"You say she had *black* hair?"

"Certainly, black hair. On that occasion—but that was not
the last time it happened to me." He laughed. "I had three
children by my wife, a fine woman—she is now dead, unfortunately." Again, there was no doubt tears filled his eyes. At the
sight, the Captain's indignation soared. But Herr Scholtz had
recovered and was speaking: "But I ask myself, how many
children in addition to the three? Sometimes I look at a young
man in the streets who has a certain resemblance, and I ask
myself: Perhaps he is my son? Yes, yes, my friend, this is a
question that every man must ask himself, sometimes, is it
not?" He put back his head and laughed wholeheartedly, though
with an undertone of rich regret.

The Captain did not speak for a moment. Then he said, in

English, "It's all very well, but it did happen to me—it *did*." He sounded like a defiant schoolboy, and Herr Scholtz shrugged.

"It happened to me, here. In this hotel."

Herr Scholtz controlled his irritation, glanced at Rosa, and, for the first time since the beginning of this regrettable incident, he lowered his voice to a reasonable tone and spoke English. "Well," he said, in frank irony, smiling gently, with a quiet shrug, "well, perhaps if we are honest we must say that this is a thing that has happened to every man? Or rather, if it did not exist, it was necessary to invent it?"

And now, said his look towards the Captain, and now, for heaven's sake!—for the sake of decency, masculine solidarity, for the sake of our dignity in the eyes of that girl over there, who has so wounded us both—pull yourself together, my friend, and consider what you are saying!

But the Captain was oblivious in memories. "No," he insisted. "No. Speak for yourself. It *did* happen. Here." He paused, and then brought out, with difficulty, "I never married."

Herr Scholtz shrugged, at last, and was silent. Then he called out, "Fräulein, Fräulein—may I pay?" It was time to put an end to it.

Rosa did not immediately turn around. She patted her hair at the back. She straightened her apron. She took her napkin from one forearm and arranged it prettily on the other. Then she turned and came, smiling, towards them. It could at once be seen that she intended her smile to be noticed.

"You wish to pay?" she asked Herr Scholtz. She spoke calmly and deliberately in English, and the Captain started and looked extremely uncomfortable. But Herr Scholtz immediately adjusted himself and said in English, "Yes, I am paying."

She took the note he held out and counted out the change from the small satchel under her apron. Having laid the last necessary coin on the table, she stood squarely in front of them, smiling down equally at both, her hands folded in front of her. At last, when they had had the full benefit of her amused, maternal smile, she suggested in English: "Perhaps the lady changed the color of her hair to suit what you both like best?" Then she laughed. She put back her head and laughed a full, wholehearted laugh.

Herr Scholtz, accepting the defeat with equanimity, smiled a rueful, appreciative smile.

The Captain sat stiffly in his chair, regarding them both with hot hostility, clinging tight to his own, authentic, memories.

But Rosa laughed at him, until with a final swish of her dress she clicked past them both and away off the terrace.

# Through the Tunnel

●··●··●··●··●··●··●··●··●··●··●··●··●··●··●··●··●··●··●··●··●··●··●··●··●··●··●··●··●··●··●··●··●··●··●··●··●··●··●··●··●·●

Going to the shore on the first morning of the vacation, the young English boy stopped at a turning of the path and looked down at a wild and rocky bay, and then over to the crowded beach he knew so well from other years. His mother walked on in front of him, carrying a bright striped bag in one hand. Her other arm, swinging loose, was very white in the sun. The boy watched that white naked arm, and turned his eyes, which had a frown behind them, towards the bay and back again to his mother. When she felt he was not with her, she swung around. "Oh, there you are, Jerry!" she said. She looked impatient, then smiled. "Why, darling, would you rather not come with me? Would you rather—" She frowned, conscientiously worrying over what amusements he might secretly be longing for, which she had been too busy or too careless to imagine. He was very familiar with that anxious, apologetic smile. Contrition sent him running after her. And yet, as he ran, he looked back over his shoulder at the wild bay; and all morning, as he played on the safe beach, he was thinking of it.

Next morning, when it was time for the routine of swimming and sunbathing, his mother said, "Are you tired of the usual beach, Jerry? Would you like to go somewhere else?"

"Oh, no!" he said quickly, smiling at her out of that unfailing impulse of contrition—a sort of chivalry. Yet, walking down the path with her, he blurted out, "I'd like to go and have a look at those rocks down there."

She gave the idea her attention. It was a wild-looking place, and there was no one there; but she said, "Of course, Jerry. When you've had enough, come to the big beach. Or just go straight back to the villa, if you like." She walked away, that bare arm, now slightly reddened from yesterday's sun, swinging. And he almost ran after her again, feeling it unbearable that she should go by herself, but he did not.

She was thinking, Of course he's old enough to be safe without me. Have I been keeping him too close? He mustn't feel he ought to be with me. I must be careful.

He was an only child, eleven years old. She was a widow. She was determined to be neither possessive nor lacking in devotion. She went worrying off to her beach.

As for Jerry, once he saw that his mother had gained her beach, he began the steep descent to the bay. From where he was, high up among red-brown rocks, it was a scoop of moving blueish green fringed with white. As he went lower, he saw that it spread among small promontories and inlets of rough, sharp rock, and the crisping, lapping surface showed stains of purple and darker blue. Finally, as he ran sliding and scraping down the last few yards, he saw an edge of white surf and the shallow, luminous movement of water over white sand, and, beyond that, a solid, heavy blue.

He ran straight into the water and began swimming. He was a good swimmer. He went out fast over the gleaming sand, over a middle region where rocks lay like discoloured monsters under the surface, and then he was in the real sea—a warm sea where irregular cold currents from the deep water shocked his limbs.

When he was so far out that he could look back not only on the little bay but past the promontory that was between it and the big beach, he floated on the buoyant surface and looked for his mother. There she was, a speck of yellow under an umbrella that looked like a slice of orange peel. He swam back to shore, relieved at being sure she was there, but all at once very lonely.

On the edge of a small cape that marked the side of the bay away from the promontory was a loose scatter of rocks. Above them, some boys were stripping off their clothes. They came running, naked, down to the rocks. The English boy swam towards them, but kept his distance at a stone's throw. They were of that coast; all of them were burned smooth dark brown and speaking a language he did not understand. To be with them, of them, was a craving that filled his whole body. He swam a little closer; they turned and watched him with narrowed, alert dark eyes. Then one smiled and waved. It was enough. In a minute, he had swum in and was on the rocks beside them, smiling with a desperate, nervous supplication. They shouted cheerful greetings at him; and then, as he preserved his nervous, uncomprehending smile, they understood that he was a foreigner strayed from his own beach, and they proceeded to forget him. But he was happy. He was with them.

They began diving again and again from a high point into a well of blue sea between rough, pointed rocks. After they had dived and come up, they swam around, hauled themselves up, and waited their turn to dive again. They were big boys—men, to Jerry. He dived, and they watched him; and when he swam around to take his place, they made way for him. He felt he was accepted and he dived again, carefully, proud of himself.

Soon the biggest of the boys poised himself, shot down into the water, and did not come up. The others stood about, watching. Jerry, after waiting for the sleek brown head to appear, let out a yell of warning; they looked at him idly and turned their eyes back towards the water. After a long time, the boy came up on the other side of a big dark rock, letting the air out of his lungs in a sputtering gasp and a shout of triumph. Immediately the rest of them dived in. One moment, the morning seemed full of chattering boys; the next, the air and the surface of the water were empty. But through the heavy blue, dark shapes could be seen moving and groping.

Jerry dived, shot past the school of underwater swimmers, saw a black wall of rock looming at him, touched it, and bobbed up at once to the surface, where the wall was a low barrier he could see across. There was no one visible; under him, in the water, the dim shapes of the swimmers had disappeared. Then one, and then another of the boys came up on the far side of the barrier of rock, and he understood that they had swum through some gap or hole in it. He plunged down again. He could see nothing through the stinging salt water but the blank rock. When he came up the boys were all on the diving rock, preparing to attempt the feat again. And now, in a panic of failure, he yelled up, in English, "Look at me! Look!" and he began splashing and kicking in the water like a foolish dog.

They looked down gravely, frowning. He knew the frown. At moments of failure, when he clowned to claim his mother's attention, it was with just this grave, embarrassed inspection that she rewarded him. Through his hot shame, feeling the pleading grin on his face like a scar that he could never remove, he looked up at the group of big brown boys on the rock and shouted *"Bonjour! Merci! Au revoir! Monsieur, monsieur!"* while he hooked his fingers round his ears and waggled them.

Water surged into his mouth; he choked, sank, came up. The rock, lately weighted with boys, seemed to rear up out of the water as their weight was removed. They were flying down past him now, into the water; the air was full of falling bodies. Then the rock was empty in the hot sunlight. He counted one, two, three . . .

At fifty, he was terrified. They must all be drowning beneath him, in the watery caves of the rock! At a hundred, he stared around him at the empty hillside, wondering if he should yell for help. He counted faster, faster, to hurry them up, to bring them to the surface quickly, to drown them quickly—anything rather than the terror of counting on and on into the blue emptiness of the morning. And then, at a hundred and sixty, the water beyond the rock was full of boys blowing like brown whales. They swam back to the shore without a look at him.

He climbed back to the diving rock and sat down, feeling the hot roughness of it under his thighs. The boys were gathering up their bits of clothing and running off along the shore to another promontory. They were leaving to get away from him. He cried openly, fists in his eyes. There was no one to see him, and he cried himself out.

It seemed to him that a long time had passed, and he swam out to where he could see his mother. Yes, she was still there, a yellow spot under an orange umbrella. He swam back to the big rock, climbed up, and dived into the blue pool among the fanged and angry boulders. Down he went, until he touched the wall of rock again. But the salt was so painful in his eyes that he could not see.

He came to the surface, swam to shore and went back to the villa to wait for his mother. Soon she walked slowly up the path, swinging her striped bag, the flushed, naked arm dangling beside her. "I want some swimming goggles," he panted, defiant and beseeching.

She gave him a patient, inquisitive look as she said casually, "Well, of course, darling."

But now, now, now! He must have them this minute, and no other time. He nagged and pestered until she went with him to a shop. As soon as she had bought the goggles, he grabbed them from her hand as if she were going to claim them for herself, and was off, running down the steep path to the bay.

Jerry swam out to the big barrier rock, adjusted the goggles, and dived. The impact of the water broke the rubber-enclosed vacuum, and the goggles came loose. He understood that he must swim down to the base of the rock from the surface of the water. He fixed the goggles tight and firm, filled his lungs, and floated, face down, on the water. Now he could see. It was as if he had eyes of a different kind—fish eyes that showed everything clear and delicate and wavering in the bright water.

Under him, six or seven feet down, was a floor of perfectly clean, shining white sand, rippled firm and hard by the tides. Two greyish shapes steered there, like long, rounded pieces of wood or slate. They were fish. He saw them nose towards each other, poise motionless, make a dart forward, swerve off, and come around again. It was like a water dance. A few inches above them the water sparkled as if sequins were dropping through it. Fish again—myriads of minute fish, the length of his fingernail—were drifting through the water, and in a moment he could feel the innumerable tiny touches of them against his limbs. It was like swimming in flaked silver. The great rock the big boys had swum through rose sheer out of the white sand—black, tufted lightly with greenish weed. He could see no gap in it. He swam down to its base.

Again and again he rose, took a big chestful of air, and went down. Again and again he groped over the surface of the rock, feeling it, almost hugging it in the desperate need to find the entrance. And then, once, while he was clinging to the black wall, his knees came up and he shot his feet out forward and they met no obstacle. He had found the hole.

He gained the surface, clambered about the stones that littered the barrier rock until he found a big one, and, with this in his arms, let himself down over the side of the rock. He dropped, with the weight, straight to the sandy floor. Clinging tight to the anchor of stone, he lay on his side and looked in under the dark shelf at the place where his feet had gone.

He could see the hole. It was an irregular, dark gap; but he could not see deep into it. He let go of his anchor, clung with his hands to the edges of the hole, and tried to push himself in.

He got his head in, found his shoulders jammed, moved them in sidewise, and was inside as far as his waist. He could see nothing ahead. Something soft and clammy touched his mouth; he saw a dark frond moving against the greyish rock, and panic filled him. He thought of octopuses, of clinging weed. He pushed himself out backward and caught a glimpse, as he retreated, of a harmless tentacle of seaweed drifting in the mouth of the tunnel. But it was enough. He reached the sunlight, swam to shore, and lay on the diving rock. He looked down into the blue well of water. He knew he must find his way through that cave, or hole, or tunnel, and out the other side.

First, he thought, he must learn to control his breathing. He let himself down into the water with another big stone in his arms, so that he could lie effortlessly on the bottom of the sea. He counted. One, two, three. He counted steadily. He could hear the movement of blood in his chest. Fifty-one, fifty-two. . . . His chest was hurting. He let go of the rock and went up into the air. He saw that the sun was low. He rushed to the villa and found his mother at her supper. She said only "Did you enjoy yourself?" and he said "Yes."

All night the boy dreamed of the water-filled cave in the rock, and as soon as breakfast was over he went to the bay.

That night, his nose bled badly. For hours he had been underwater, learning to hold his breath, and now he felt weak and dizzy. His mother said, "I shouldn't overdo things, darling, if I were you."

That day and the next, Jerry exercised his lungs as if everything, the whole of his life, all that he would become, depended upon it. Again his nose bled at night, and his mother insisted on his coming with her the next day. It was a torment to him to waste a day of his careful self-training, but he stayed with her on that other beach, which now seemed a place for small children, a place where his mother might lie safe in the sun. It was not his beach.

He did not ask for permission, on the following day, to go to his beach. He went, before his mother could consider the complicated rights and wrongs of the matter. A day's rest, he discovered, had improved his count by ten. The big boys had made the passage while he counted a hundred and sixty. He had been counting fast, in his fright. Probably now, if he tried, he could get through that long tunnel, but he was not going to try yet. A curious, most unchildlike persistence, a controlled impatience, made him wait. In the meantime, he lay underwater on the white sand, littered now by stones he had brought down from the upper air, and studied the entrance to the tunnel. He knew every jut and corner of it, as far as it was possible to see. It was as if he already felt its sharpness about his shoulders.

He sat by the clock in the villa, when his mother was not near, and checked his time. He was incredulous and then proud to find he could hold his breath without strain for two minutes. The words "two minutes," authorised by the clock, brought close the adventure that was so necessary to him.

In another four days, his mother said casually one morning, they must go home. On the day before they left, he would do it. He would do it if it killed him, he said defiantly to himself. But two days before they were to leave—a day of triumph when he increased his count by fifteen—his nose bled so badly that he turned dizzy and had to lie limply over the big rock like a bit of seaweed, watching the thick red blood flow on to the rock and trickle slowly down to the sea. He was frightened. Supposing he turned dizzy in the tunnel? Supposing he died there, trapped? Supposing—his head went around, in the hot sun, and he almost gave up. He thought he would return to the house and lie down, and next summer, perhaps, when he had another year's growth in him—*then* he would go through the hole.

But even after he had made the decision, or thought he had, he found himself sitting up on the rock and looking down into the water; and he knew that now, this moment, when his nose had only just stopped bleeding, when his head was still sore and throbbing—this was the moment when he would try. If he did not do it now, he never would. He was trembling with fear that he would not go; and he was trembling with horror at the long, long tunnel under the rock, under the sea. Even in the open sunlight, the barrier rock seemed very wide and very heavy; tons of rock pressed down on where he would go. If he died there, he would lie until one day—perhaps not before next year—those big boys would swim into it and find it blocked.

He put on his goggles, fitted them tight, tested the vacuum. His hands were shaking. Then he chose the biggest stone he could carry and slipped over the edge of the rock until half of him was in the cool enclosing water and half in the hot sun. He looked up once at the empty sky, filled his lungs once, twice, and then sank fast to the bottom with the stone. He let it go and began to count. He took the edges of the hole in his hands and drew himself into it, wriggling his shoulders in sidewise as he remembered he must, kicking himself along with his feet.

Soon he was clear inside. He was in a small rock-bound hole filled with yellowish-grey water. The water was pushing him up against the roof. The roof was sharp and pained his back. He pulled himself along with his hands—fast, fast—and used his legs as levers. His head knocked against something; a sharp pain dizzied him. Fifty, fifty-one, fifty-two. . . . He was without light, and the water seemed to press upon him with the weight of rock. Seventy-one, seventy-two. . . There was no strain on his lungs. He felt like an inflated balloon, his lungs were so light and easy, but his head was pulsing.

He was being continually pressed against the sharp roof, which felt slimy as well as sharp. Again he thought of octopuses, and wondered if the tunnel might be filled with weed that could tangle him. He gave himself a panicky, convulsive kick forward, ducked his head, and swam. His feet and hands moved freely, as if in open water. The hole must have widened out. He thought he must be swimming fast, and he was frightened of banging his head if the tunnel narrowed.

A hundred, a hundred and one . . . The water paled. Victory filled him. His lungs were beginning to hurt. A few more strokes and he would be out. He was counting wildly; he said a hundred and fifteen, and then, a long time later, a hundred and fifteen again. The water was a clear jewel-green all around him. Then he saw, above his head, a crack running up through the rock. Sunlight was falling through it, showing the clean, dark rock of the tunnel, a single mussel shell, and darkness ahead.

He was at the end of what he could do. He looked up at the crack as if it were filled with air and not water, as if he could put his mouth to it to draw in air. A hundred and fifteen, he heard himself say inside his head—but he had said that long ago. He must go on into the blackness ahead, or he would drown. His head was swelling, his lungs cracking. A hundred and fifteen, a hundred and fifteen pounded through his head, and he feebly clutched at rocks in the dark, pulling himself forward leaving the brief space of sunlit water behind. He felt he was dying. He was no longer quite conscious. He struggled on in the darkness between lapses into unconsciousness. An immense, swelling pain filled his head, and then the darkness cracked with an explosion of green light. His hands, groping forward, met nothing; and his feet, kicking back, propelled him out into the open sea.

He drifted to the surface, his face turned up to the air. He was gasping like a fish. He felt he would sink now and drown; he could not swim the few feet back to the rock. Then he was clutching it and pulling himself up onto it. He lay face down, gasping. He could see nothing but a red-veined, clotted dark. His eyes must have burst, he thought; they were full of blood. He tore off his goggles and a gout of blood went into the sea. His nose was bleeding, and the blood had filled the goggles.

He scooped up handfuls of water from the cool, salty sea, to splash on his face, and did not know whether it was blood or salt water he tasted. After a time, his heart quieted, his eyes cleared, and he sat up. He could see the local boys diving and playing half a mile away. He did not want them. He wanted nothing but to get back home and lie down.

In a short while, Jerry swam to shore and climbed slowly up the path to the villa. He flung himself on his bed and slept, waking at the sound of feet on the path outside. His mother was coming back. He rushed to the bathroom, thinking she must not see his face with bloodstains, or tearstains, on it. He came out of the bathroom and met her as she walked into the villa, smiling, her eyes lighting up.

"Have a nice morning?" she asked, laying her hand on his warm brown shoulder a moment.

"Oh, yes, thank you," he said.

"You look a bit pale." And then, sharp and anxious, "How did you bang your head?"

"Oh, just banged it," he told her.

She looked at him closely. He was strained; his eyes were glazed-looking. She was worried. And then she said to herself,

Oh, don't fuss! Nothing can happen. He can swim like a fish.
They sat down to lunch together.

"Mummy," he said, "I can stay underwater for two minutes
—three minutes, at least." It came bursting out of him.

"Can you, darling?" she said. "Well, I shouldn't overdo it.
I don't think you ought to swim any more today."

She was ready for a battle of wills, but he gave in at once.
It was no longer of the least importance to go to the bay.

# *Pleasure*

●–●–●–●–●–●–●–●–●–●–●–●–●–●–●–●–●–●–●–●–●–●–●–●–●–●–●–●–●–●–●–●–●–●–●–●–●–●–●–●–●–●–●–●–●–●●

There were two great feasts, or turning points, in Mary Rogers' year. She began preparing for the second as soon as the Christmas decorations were down. This year, she was leafing through a fashion magazine when her husband said, "Dreaming of the sun, old girl?"

"I don't see why not," she said, rather injured. "After all, its been four years."

"I really don't see how we can afford it."

On her face he saw a look that he recognised.

Her friend Mrs. Baxter, the manager's wife, also saw the magazine, and said, "You'll be off to the south of France again, this year, I suppose, now that your daughter won't be needing you." She added those words which in themselves were justification for everything: "We'll stay faithful to Brighton, I expect."

And Mary Rogers said, as she always did: "I can't imagine why anyone takes a holiday in Britain when the same money'd take them to the continent."

For four years she had gone with her daughter and the grandchildren to Cornwall. It sounded a sacrifice on the altar of the family, the way she put it to her friends. But this year the daughter was going to the other grandmother in Scotland, and everyone knew it. Everyone. That is, Mrs. Baxter, Mrs. Justin-Smith, and Mrs. Jones.

Mary Rogers bought gay cottons and spread them over the livingroom. Outside, a particularly grim February held the little Midlands town in a steady shiver. Rain swept the windowpanes. Tommy Rogers saw the cottons and said not a word. But a week later she was fitting a white linen sunsuit before the mirror when he said, "I say, old girl, that shows quite a bit of leg, you know. . . ."

At that moment it was acknowledged that they should go. Also, that the four years had made a difference in various ways. Mary Rogers secretly examined her thighs and shoulders before the glass, and thought they might very well be exposed. But the clothes she made were of the sensible but smart variety. She sewed at them steadily through the evenings of March, April, May, June. She was a good needlewoman. Also, for a few happy months before she married, she had studied fashion designing in London. That had been a different world. In speaking of it now, to the women of her circle—Mrs. Baxter, Mrs. Justin-Smith, and Mrs. Jones—her voice conveyed the degree of difference. And Mrs. Baxter would say, kindly as always, "Ah well, we none of us know what's in store for us when we're young."

They were to leave towards the end of July. A week before, Tommy Rogers produced a piece of paper on which were set out certain figures. They were much lower figures than ever before. "Oh, we'll manage," said Mary vaguely. Her mind was already moving among the scenes of blue sea, blue sky.

"Perhaps we'd better book at the Plaza."

"Oh, surely no need. They know us there."

The evening before they left there was a bridge party in the Baxters' house for the jaunting couple. Tommy Rogers was seen to give his wife an uneasy glance as she said, "With air travel as cheap as it is now, I really can't understand why . . ."

For they had booked by train, of course, as usual.

They successfully negotiated the Channel, a night in a Paris hotel, and the catching of the correct train.

In a few hours they would see the little village on the sea where they had first come twenty-five years ago on their honeymoon. They had chosen it because Mary Hill had met, in those artistic circles which she had enjoyed for, alas, so short a time, a certain well-known stage decorator who had a villa there. During that month of honeymoon, they had spent a happy afternoon at the villa.

As the train approached, she was looking to see the villa, alone on its hill above the sea. But the hill was now thick with little white villas, green-shuttered, red-roofed in the warm southern green.

"The place seems to have grown quite a bit," said Tommy. The station had grown, too. There was a long platform now, and a proper station building. And gazing down towards the sea, they saw a cluster of shops and casinos and cafes. Even four years before, there had been only a single shop, a restaurant, and a couple of hotels.

"Well," said Mary bitterly, "if the place is full of tourists now, it won't be the same at all."

But the sun was shining, the sea tossed and sparkled, and the palm trees stood along the white beach. They carried their suitcases down the slope of the road to the Plaza, feeling at home.

Outside the Plaza, they looked at each other. What had been a modest building was now an imposing one, surrounded by gay awnings and striped umbrellas. "Old Jaques is spreading himself," said Tommy, and they walked up the neat gravel path to the foyer, looking for Jaques, who had welcomed them so often.

At the office, Mary enquired in her stiff, correct French for Monsieur Jaques. The clerk smiled and regretted that Monsieur Jaques had left them three years before. "He knew us well," said Mary, her voice coming aggrieved and shrill. "He always had room for us here."

But certainly there was a room for Madame. Most certainly. At once attendants came hurrying for the suitcases.

"Hold your horses a minute," said Tommy. "Wait. Ask what it costs now."

Mary enquired, casually enough, what the rates now were. She received the information with a lengthening of her heavy jaw, and rapidly transmitted it to Tommy. He glanced, embarrassed, at the clerk, who, recognising a situation, turned tactfully to a ledger and prepared to occupy himself so that the elderly English couple could confer.

They did, in rapid, angry undertones.

"We can't, Mary. It's no good. We'd have to go back at the end of a week."

"But we've always stayed here. . . ."

At last she turned towards the clerk, who was immediately attentive, and said with a stiff smile: "I'm afraid the currency regulations make things difficult for us." She had spoken in English, such was her upset; and it was in English that he replied pleasantly, "I understand perfectly, Madame. Perhaps you would care to try the Belle Vue across the street. There are many English people there."

The Rogerses left, carrying their two suitcases ignominiously down the neat gravelled path, among the gay tables where people already sat at dinner. The sun had gone down. Opposite, the Belle Vue was a glow of lights. Tommy Rogers was not surprised when Mary walked past it without a look. For years, staying at the Plaza, they had felt superior to the Belle Vue. Also, had that clerk not said it was full of English people?

Since this was France, and the season, the Agency was of course open. An attractive mademoiselle deplored that they had not booked rooms earlier.

"We've been here every year for twenty-five years," said Mary, pardonably overlooking the last four, and another stretch of five when the child had been small. "We've never had to book before."

Alas, alas, suggested the mademoiselle with her shoulders and her pretty eyes, what a pity that St. Nichole had become so popular, so attractive. There was no fact she regretted more. She suggested the Belle Vue.

The Rogerses walked the hundred yards back to the Belle Vue, feeling they were making a final concession to fate, only to find it fully booked up. Returning to the Agency, they were informed that there was, happily, one room vacant in a villa on the hillside. They were escorted to it. And now it was the turn of the pretty mademoiselle to occupy herself, not with a ledger, but in examining the view of brilliant stars and the riding lights of ships across the bay, while the Rogerses conferred. Their voices were now not only angry, but high with exasperation. For this room—an extremely small one, at the bottom of a big villa, stone-floored, uncarpeted, with a single large bed of the sort Mary always thought of as French; a wardrobe that was no wardrobe, since it had been filled with shelves; a sink and a small gas stove—they were asked to pay a sum which filled them with disbelief. If they desired hot water, as the English so often do, they would have to heat it in a saucepan on the stove.

But, as the mademoiselle pointed out, turning from her

appreciative examination of the exotic night scene, it would be such an advantage to do one's own cooking.

"I suggest we go back to the Plaza. Better one week of comfort than three of this," said Mary. They returned to the Plaza to find that the room had been taken, and none were available.

It was now nearly ten in the evening, and the infinitely obliging mademoiselle returned them to the little room in the villa, for which they agreed to pay more than they had done four years before for comfort, good food, and hot water in the Plaza. Also, they had to pay a deposit of over ten pounds in case they might escape in the night with the bed, the wardrobe, or the tin spoons, or in case they refused to pay the bills for electricity, gas, and water.

The Rogerses went to bed immediately, worn out with travelling and disappointment.

In the morning Mary announced that she had no intention of cooking on a holiday, and they took *petit déjeuner* at a cafe, paid the equivalent of twelve shillings for two small cups of coffee and two rolls, and changed their minds. They would have to cook in the room.

Preserving their good humour with an effort, they bought cold food for lunch, left it in the room, and prepared themselves for enjoyment. For the sea was blue, blue and sparkling. And the sunshine was hot and golden. And after all, this was the south of France, the prettiest place in Europe, as they had always agreed. And in England now, said the *Daily Telegraph*, it was pouring rain.

On the beach they had another bad moment. Umbrellas stretched six deep, edge to edge, for half a mile along the silvery beach. Bodies lay stretched out, baking in the sun, hundreds to the acre, a perfect bed of heated brown flesh.

"They've ruined the place, ruined it!" cried Mary, as she surveyed the untidy scene. But she stepped heavily down into the sand and unbuttoned her dress. She was revealed to be wearing a heavy black bathing suit; and she did not miss the relieved glance her husband gave her. She felt it to be unfair. There he stood, a tall, very thin, fair man, quite presentable in an absurd bathing slip that consisted of six inches of material held on by a string round his hips. And there *she* was, a heavy firm woman, with clear white flesh—but middleaged, and in a black bathing suit.

She looked about. Two feet away was a mess of tangled brown limbs belonging to half a dozen boys and girls, the girls wearing nothing but colored cotton brassières and panties. She saw Tommy looking at them, too. Then she noticed, eighteen inches to the other side, a vast grey-haired lady, bulging weary pallid flesh out of a white cotton playsuit. Mary gave her a look of happy superiority and lay down flat on the sand, congratulating herself.

All the morning the English couple lay there, turning over and over on the sand like a pair of grilling herrings, for they felt their pale skins to be a shame and a disgrace. When they returned to their room for lunch, it was to find that swarms of small black ants had infested their cold meats. They were unable to mind very much, as it had become evident they had overdone the sunbathing. Both were bright scarlet, and their eyes ached. They lay down in the cool of the darkened room, feeling foolish to be such amateurs—they, who should know better! They kept to their beds that afternoon, and the next day . . . several days passed. Sometimes, when hunger overcame them, Mary winced down to the village to buy cold food —impossible to keep supplies in the room because of the ants. After eating, she hastily washed up in the sink where they also washed. Twice a day, Tommy went reluctantly outside while she washed herself inch by inch in water heated in the saucepan. Then she went outside while he did the same. After these indispensable measures of hygiene, they retired to the much too narrow bed, shrinking away from any chance of contact with each other.

At last the discomfort of the room, as much as their healing flesh, drove them forth again, more cautiously clothed, to the beach. Skin was ripping off them both in long shreds. At the end of a week, however, they had become brown and shining, able to take their places without shame among the other brown and glistening bodies that littered the beach like so many stranded fish.

Day after day the Rogerses descended the steep path to the beach, after having eaten a hearty English breakfast of ham and eggs, and stayed there all morning. All morning they lay, and then all afternoon, but at a good distance from a colony of English, which kept itself to itself some hundreds of yards away.

They watched the children screaming and laughing in the unvarying blue waves. They watched the groups of French adolescents flirt and roll each other over on the sand in a way that Mary, at least, thought appallingly free. Thank heavens her daughter had married young and was safely out of harm's way! Nothing could have persuaded Mary Rogers of the extreme respectability of these youngsters. She suspected them all of shocking and complicated vices. Incredible that, in so few a number of years, they would be sorted by some powerful and comforting social process into these decent, well-fed French couples, each so anxiously absorbed in the welfare of one, or perhaps two small children.

They watched also, with admiration, the more hardened swimmers cleave out through the small waves into the sea beyond the breakwater with their masks, their airtubes, their frog's feet.

They were content.

This is what they had come for. This is what all these hundreds of thousands of people along the coast had come for—to lie on the sand and receive the sun on their heating bodies; to receive, too, in small doses, the hot blue water which dried so stickily on them. The sea was very salty and warm-smelling—smelling of a little more than salt and weed, for beyond the breakwater the town's sewers spilled into the sea, washing back into the inner bay rich deposits which dried on the perfumed oiled bodies of the happy bathers.

This is what they had come for.

Yet, there was no doubt that in the Plaza things had been quite different. There one rose late; lingered over coffee and rolls; descended, or did not descend, to the beach for a couple of hours' sun-worship; returned to a lengthy lunch; slept, bathed again, enjoyed an even more lengthy dinner. That, too, was called a seaside vacation. Now, the beach was really the only place to go. From nine until one, from two until seven, the Rogerses were on it. It was a seaside vacation with a vengeance.

About the tenth day, they realised that half of their time had gone; and Tommy showed his restlessness, his feeling that there should be more to it than this, by diving into one of the new and so terribly expensive shops and emerging with a mask, frog's feet, and airtube. With an apology to Mary for leaving her, he plunged out into the bay, looking like—or so she rather tartly remarked—a spaceman in a children's comic. He did not return for some hours.

"This is better than anything, old girl, you should try it," he said, wading out of the sea with an absorbed excited look. That afternoon she spent on the beach alone, straining her eyes to make out which of the bobbing periscopes in the water was his.

Thus engaged, she heard herself addressed in English: "I always say I am an undersea widow, too." She turned to see a slight girl, clearly English, with pretty fair curls, a neat blue bathing suit, pretty blue eyes, good legs stretched out in the warm sand. An English girl. But her voice was, so Mary decided, passable, in spite of a rather irritating giggle. She relented and, though it was her principle that one did not go to France to consort with the English, said: "Is your husband out there?"

"Oh, I never see him between meals," said the girl cheerfully, and lay back on the sand.

Mary thought that this girl was very similar to herself at that age—only, of course, *she* had known how to make the best of herself. They talked, in voices drugged by sea and sun, until first Tommy Rogers, and then the girl's husband, rose out of the sea. The young man was carrying a large fish speared through the back by a sort of trident. The excitement of this led the four of them to share a square yard of sand for a few minutes, making cautious overtures.

The next day, Tommy Rogers insisted that his wife should don mask and flippers and try the new sport. She was taken out into the bay, like a ship under escort, by the two men and young Betty Clarke. Mary Rogers did not like the suffocating feeling of the mask pressing against her nose. The speed the frog feet lent her made her nervous, for she was not a strong swimmer. But she was not going to appear a coward with that young girl sporting along so easily just in front.

Out in the bay a small island, a mere cluster of warm, red-brown rock, rose from a surf of frisking white. Around the island, a couple of feet below the surface, submerged rocks lay; and all over them floated the new race of frog-people, face down, tridents poised, observing the fish that darted there. As Mary looked back through her goggles to the shore, it seemed very far, and rather commonplace, with the striped umbrellas, the lolling browned bodies, the paddling children. That was the other sea. This was something different indeed. Here were the adventurers and explorers of the sea, who disdained the safe beaches.

Mary lay loose on the surface of the water and looked down. Enormous, this undersea world, with great valleys and boulders, all wavering green in the sun-dappled water. On a dazzling patch of white sand—twenty feet down, it seemed—sprouted green grass as fresh and bright as if it grew on the shore in sunlight. By reaching down her hand she could almost touch it. Farther away, long fronds of weed rocked and swayed, a forest of them. Mary floated over them, feeling with repugnance how they reached up to touch her knees and shoulders with their soft, dragging touch. Underneath her now, a floor of rock, covered with thick growth. Pale grey-green shapes, swelling like balloons, or waving like streamers; delicate whitey-brown flowers and stars, bubbled silver with air; soft swelling udders or bladders of fine white film, all rocking and drifting in the slow undersea movement. Mary was fascinated—a new world, this was. But also repelled. In her ears there was nothing but a splash and crash of surf, and, through it, voices that sounded a long way off. The rocks were now very close below. Suddenly, immediately below her, a thin brown arm reached down, groped in a dark gulf of rock, and pulled out a writhing tangle of grey-dappled flesh. Mary floundered up, slipping painfully on the rocks. She had drifted unknowingly close to the islet; and on the rocks above her stood a group of half-naked bronzed boys, yelling and screaming with excitement as they killed the octopus they had caught by smashing it repeatedly against a great boulder. They would eat it—so Mary heard—for supper. No, it was too much. She was in panic. The loathsome thing must have been six inches below her—she might have touched it! She climbed onto a rock and looked for Tommy, who was lying on a rock fifty feet off, pointing down at something under it, while Francis Clarke dived for it, and then again. She saw him emerge with a small striped fish, while Tommy and Betty Clarke yelled their excitement.

But she looked at the octopus, which was now lying draped over a rock like a limp, fringed, grey rag; she called her husband, handed over the goggles, the flippers and the tube, and swam slowly back to shore.

There she stayed. Nothing would tempt her out again.

That day Tommy bought an underwater fish gun. Mary found herself thinking, first, that it was all very well to spend over five pounds on this bizarre equipment; and then, that they weren't going to have much fun at Christmas if they went on like this.

A couple of days passed. Mary was alone all day. Betty Clarke, apparently, was only a beach widow when it suited her, for she much preferred the red-rock island to staying with Mary. Nevertheless, she did sometimes spend half an hour making conversation, and then, with a flurry of apology, darted off through the blue waves to rejoin the men.

Quite soon, Mary was able to say casually to Tommy, "Only three days to go."

"If only I'd tried this equipment earlier," he said. "Next year I'll know better."

But for some reason the thought of next year did not enchant Mary. "I don't think we ought to come here again," she said. "It's quite spoiled now it's so fashionable."

"Oh well—anywhere, provided there's rocks and fish."

On that next day, the two men and Betty Clarke were on the rock island from seven in the morning until lunchtime, to which meal they grudgingly allowed ten minutes, because it was dangerous to swim on a full stomach. Then they departed again until the darkness fell across the sea. All this time Mary Rogers lay on her towel on the beach, turning over and over in the sun. She was now a warm red-gold all over. She imagined how Mrs. Baxter would say: "You've got yourself a fine tan!" And then, inevitably, "You won't keep it long here, will you?" Mary found herself unaccountably close to tears. What did Tommy see in these people? she asked herself. As for that young man, Francis—she had never heard him make any remark that was not connected with the weights, the varieties, or the vagaries of fish!

That night, Tommy said he had asked the young couple to dinner at the Plaza.

"A bit rash, aren't you?"

"Oh well, let's have a proper meal, for once. Only another two days."

Mary let that "proper meal" pass. But she said, "I shouldn't have thought they were the sort of people to make friends of."

A cloud of irritation dulled his face. "What's the matter with them?"

"In England, I don't think . . ."

"Oh come off it, Mary!"

In the big garden of the Plaza, where four years ago they had eaten three times a day by right, they found themselves around a small table just over the sea. There was an orchestra and more waiters than guests, or so it seemed. Betty Clarke, seen for the first time out of a bathing suit, was revealed to be a remarkably pretty girl. Her thin brown shoulders emerged from a full white frock, which Mary Rogers conceded to be not bad at all; and her wide blue eyes were bright in her brown face. Again Mary thought: If I were twenty—well, twenty-five—years younger, they'd take us for sisters.

As for Tommy, he looked as young as the young couple—it simply wasn't fair, thought Mary. She sat and listened while they talked of judging distances underwater and the advantages of various types of equipment.

They tried to draw her in; but there she sat, silent and dignified. Francis Clarke, she had decided, looked stiff and commonplace in his suit, not at all the handsome young sea god of the beaches. As for the girl, her giggle was irritating Mary.

They began to feel uncomfortable. Betty mentioned London, and the three conscientiously talked about London, while Mary said yes and no.

The young couple lived in Clapham, apparently; and they went into town for a show once a month.

"There's ever such a nice show running now," said Betty. "The one at the Princess."

"We never get to a show these days," said Tommy. "It's five hours by train. Anyway, it's not in my line."

"Speak for yourself," said Mary.

"Oh I know you work in a matinée when you can."

At the irritation in the look she gave him, the Clarkes involuntarily exchanged a glance; and Betty said tactfully, "I like going to the theatre; it gives you something to talk about."

Mary remained silent.

"My wife," said Tommy, "knows a lot about the theatre. She used to be in a theatre set—all that sort of thing."

"Oh how interesting!" said Betty eagerly.

Mary struggled with temptation, then fell. "The man who

did the décor for the show at the Princess used to have a villa here. We visited him quite a bit."

Tommy gave his wife an alarmed and warning look, and said, "I wish to God they wouldn't use so much garlic."

"It's not much use coming to France," said Mary, "if you're going to be insular about food.

"You never cook French at home," said Tommy suddenly. "Why not, if you like it so much?"

"How can I? If I do, you say you don't like your food messed up."

"I don't like garlic either," said Betty, with the air of one confessing a crime. "I must say I'm pleased to be back home where you can get a bit of good plain food."

Tommy now looked in anxious appeal at his wife, but she enquired, "Why don't you go to Brighton or somewhere like that?"

"Give me Brighton any time," said Francis Clarke. "Or Cornwall. You can get damned good fishing off Cornwall. But Betty drags me here. France is overrated, that's what I say."

"It would really seem to be better if you stayed at home."

But he was not going to be snubbed by Mary Rogers. "As for the French," he said aggressively, "they think of nothing but their stomachs. If they're not eating, they're talking about it. If they spent half the time they spend on eating on something worthwhile, they could make something of themselves, that's what I say."

"Such as—catching fish?"

"Well, what's wrong with that? Or . . . for instance . . ." Here he gave the matter his earnest consideration. "Well, there's that government of theirs for instance. They could do something about that."

Betty, who was now flushed under her tan, rolled her blue eyes, and let out a high, confused laugh. "Oh well, you've got to consider what people say. France is so much the rage."

A silence. It was to be hoped the awkward moment was over. But no; for Francis Clarke seemed to think matters needed clarifying. He said, with a sort of rallying gallantry towards his wife, "She's got a bee in her bonnet about getting on."

"Well," cried Betty, "it makes a good impression, you must admit that. And when Mr. Beaker—Mr. Beaker is his boss," she explained to Mary, "when you said to Mr. Beaker at the whist drive you were going to the south of France, he was impressed, you can say what you like."

Tommy offered his wife an entirely disloyal, sarcastic grin.

"A woman should think of her husband's career," said Betty. "It's true, isn't it? And I know I've helped Francie a lot. I'm sure he wouldn't have got that raise if it weren't for making a good impression. Besides, you meet such nice people. Last year, we made friends—well, acquaintance, if you like—with some people who live at Ealing. We wouldn't have, otherwise. He's in the films."

"He's a cameraman," said Francis, being accurate.

"Well, that's films, isn't it? And they asked us to a party. And who do you think was there?"

"Mr. Beaker?" enquired Mary finely.

"How did you guess? Well, they could see, couldn't they? And I wouldn't be surprised if Francis couldn't be buyer, now they know he's used to foreigners. He should learn French, I tell him."

"Can't speak a word," said Francis. "Can't stand it anyway—gabble, gabble, gabble."

"Oh, but Mrs. Rogers speaks it so beautifully," cried Betty.

"She's cracked," said Francis, good-humouredly, nodding to indicate his wife. "She spends half the year making clothes for three weeks' holiday at the sea. Then the other half making Christmas presents out of bits and pieces. That's all she ever does."

"Oh, but it's so nice to give people presents with that individual touch," said Betty.

"If you want to waste your time I'm not stopping you," said Francis. "I'm not stopping you. It's your funeral."

"They're not grateful for what we do for them," said Betty, wrestling with tears, trying to claim the older woman as an ally. "If I didn't work hard, we couldn't afford the friends we got. . . ."

But Mary Rogers had risen from her place. "I think I'm ready for bed," she said. "Goodnight, Mrs. Clarke. Goodnight, Mr. Clarke." Without looking at her husband, she walked away.

Tommy Rogers hastily got up, paid the bill, bade the young couple an embarrassed goodnight, and hurried after his wife. He caught her up at the turning of the steep road up to the villa. The stars were brilliant overhead; the palms waved seductively in the soft breeze. "I say," he said angrily, "that wasn't very nice of you."

"I haven't any patience with that sort of thing," said Mary. Her voice was high and full of tears. He looked at her in astonishment and held his peace.

But next day he went off fishing. For Mary, the holiday was over. She was packing and did not go to the beach.

That evening he said, "They've asked us back to dinner."

"You go. I'm tired."

"I shall go," he said defiantly, and went. He did not return until very late.

They had to catch the train early next morning. At the little station, they stood with their suitcases in a crowd of people who regretted the holiday was over. But Mary was regretting nothing. As soon as the train came, she got in and left Tommy shaking hands with crowds of English people whom, apparently, he had met the night before. At the last minute, the young Clarkes came running up in bathing suits to say goodbye. She nodded stiffly out of the train window and went on arranging the baggage. Then the train started and her husband came in.

The compartment was full and there was an excuse not to talk. The silence persisted, however. Soon Tommy was watching her anxiously and making remarks about the weather, which worsened steadily as they went north.

In Paris there were five hours to fill in.

They were walking beside the river, by the open-air market, when she stopped before a stall selling earthenware.

"That big bowl," she exclaimed, her voice newly alive, "that big red one, there—it would be just right for the Christmas tree."

"So it would. Go ahead and buy it, old girl," he agreed at once, with infinite relief.

# The Witness

In the mornings, when Mr. Brooke had hung his hat carefully on the nail over his desk and arranged his pipe and tobacco at his elbow, he used to turn to the others and say hopefully: "You should have just seen Twister today. He brought my newspaper from the doorstep without dropping it once." Then he looked at the polite, hostile faces; laughed a short, spluttering, nervous laugh; and bent his head to his papers.

Miss Jenkins, the private secretary, kept a peke called Darling; and she had only to mention him for everyone to listen and laugh. As for Richards, he was engaged, and they pulled his leg about it. Every time he went purple and writhed delightedly under his desk. The accountant, Miss Ives, a tart old maid who lived some proud, defiant life of her own, had a garden. When she talked about trees the office grew silent with respect. She won prizes at flower shows. There was no getting past her.

At eight, as they settled down for the day; at eleven, when cups of tea came round, slopped into saucers; at three in the afternoon, when they ate cream cakes—they all had something.

Mr. Brooke had bought his terrier Twister simply so that he could make them notice him sometimes. First it was a canary, but he decided at last canaries couldn't be interesting. Although Miss Jenkins' peke did nothing but eat, she could talk about it every day and get an audience, but then she was a very attractive girl. She wouldn't have been the boss's private secretary if she weren't. Mr. Brooke's dog did everything. He taught it at night, in his room, to beg and balance and wait for sugar. He used to rub its ears gratefully, thinking: It will make them sit up when I tell them he can keep perfectly still for ten minutes by the watch the office gave me when I had worked for them twenty years. He used to say things like that to himself long after he had given up trying to attract their notice.

And, after all, he had not been alone, had not added up figures from eight to four for thirty years, without making something of his own he could live from. He decided to keep the canary, because it took no room and he had come to enjoy its noise. He kept the dog, too, because it was company, of a kind. The real reason why he got rid of neither was because they annoyed his landlady, with whom he bickered continually. After office hours he used to walk home thinking that after supper he would make the dog bark so that she would come in and make a scene. These scenes usually ended in her crying; and then he could say: "I am alone in the world, too, my dear." Sometimes she made him a cup of tea before going to bed, saying bitterly, "If you won't look after yourself I suppose someone must. But don't let that damned dog spill it all over the floor."

After she had gone to bed, and there was no chance of meeting her in the passage, he cut out pictures from magazines, sent off postal orders to addresses he was careful to keep hidden from her inquisitive eyes, and was not in the least ashamed of himself. He was proud of it; it was a gesture of defiance, like getting drunk every Friday. He chose Fridays because on Saturday mornings, when he was really not fit for work, he could annoy Miss Ives by saying: "I went on the loose last night." Then he got through the hours somehow. A man was entitled to something, and he did not care for gardens.

The rest of the week he used to sit quietly at his desk, watching them talk together as if he were simply not there, and wish that Miss Jenkins' dog would get ill, and she would ask him for advice; or that Miss Ives would say: "Do help me with my ledger; I have never seen anyone who could calculate as fast as you"; or that Richards would quarrel with his girl and confide in him. He imagined himself saying: "Women! Of course! You can't tell me anything."

Other times he stood looking out of the window, listening to the talk behind him, pretending not to, pretending he was indifferent. Two stories down in the street, life rushed past. Always, he felt, he had been looking out of windows. He dreamed, often, that two of the cars down below would crash into each other, and that he was the only witness. Police would come stamping up the stairs with notebooks; the typists would ask avidly, "What actually happened, Mr. Brooke?"; the boss would slap him on the shoulder and say: "How lucky you saw it. I don't know what I would do without you." He imagined himself in court, giving evidence. "Yes, your worship, I always look out of the window at that time every day. I make a habit of it. I saw everything. . . ."

But there never was an accident. The police only came once, and that was to talk to Miss Jenkins when her peke got lost; and he hardly saw Mr. Jones except to nod to. It was Miss Ives who was his real boss.

He used to peep through the door of the typists' room, where six girls worked, when the boss went through each morning, and go sick with envious admiration.

Mr. Jones was a large, red-faced man with hair grown white over the ears; and after lunch every day he smelled of beer. Nevertheless, the girls would do anything for him. He would say breezily, "Well, and how's life today?" Sometimes he put his arm round the prettiest and said, "You're too cute to keep long. You'll be getting married. . . ." He said it as if he were handing out medals, something one had to do, part of his job. It's only to make them work harder, thought Mr. Brooke bitterly, surreptitiously shutting the door and listening to how the typewriters started clattering furiously the moment Mr. Jones left. Then he used to go to the washroom and look at his own face in the glass. He had no white hair himself; he was quite a good-looking man, he thought. But if he put his arm round a girl's shoulder he would get his face slapped, he knew that.

It was the year he was fifty-five, retiring age, that Marnie de Kok came into the office as a junior, straight from school. Mr. Brooke did not want to leave off working. He couldn't live on what he had saved; and in any case the office was all he had. For some weeks he looked crumpled up with apprehension; but Mr. Jones said nothing, and after a while he took heart again.

He did not want to think about it; and besides, with Marnie there everything was changed. After one morning there was a different feeling in the office.

She was a girl of eighteen from some little dorp miles away, the youngest of ten children. She had a small plump, fresh face that always had a look of delighted expectation, and a shrill, expressive voice, and was as slim and as quick as a fish. She darted about the place, talking to the staff as if it had never entered her head anyone in the world could not be pleased to waste his time on her account. She shattered the sacred silence of the main office with her gossip about her family; sat on the desks and swung her legs; put vases of flowers among the telephones. And even Miss Ives took off her glasses and watched her. They all watched her; and particularly Mr. Jones, who made plenty of excuses to leave his desk, with the indulgent, amused, faintly ironic smile with which one looks at children, remembering what all that fearlessness and charm is going to come to. As for Mr. Brooke, he couldn't keep his eyes off her. For a while he was afraid to speak, for Marnie, like the others, seemed not to know he was there; and when he did, she looked at him with startled distaste, a look he was used to, though it in no way corresponded with what he felt about himself. She might be my daughter, he said to himself defensively; and he used to ask her with whom she ate lunch, what picture she had seen the night before, as a jealous lover can't resist talking about his mistress, feeling that even to speak about what she has been doing robs it of its danger, makes the extraordinary and wonderful life she leads apart from him in some way his. But Marnie answered shortly, or not at all, wrinkling up her nose.

Even that he found attractive. What was so charming about her was her directness, the simplicity of her responses. She knew nothing of the secret sycophancy of the office that made the typists speak to Mr. Jones in one voice and Miss Ives in another. She treated everyone as if she had known them always. She was as confiding as a child, read her letters out loud, jumped with joy when parcels came from home, and wept when someone suggested gently that there were better ways of doing her work.

For she was catastrophically inefficient. She was supposed to learn filing; but in actual fact she made the tea, slipped over to the teashop across the road ten times a day for cream cakes, and gave people advice about their colds or how to make their dresses.

The other typists, who were, after all, her natural enemies, were taken by surprise and treated her with the tenderest indulgence. It was because it occurred to no one that she could last out the first month. But Miss Ives made out her second paycheck, which was very generous, with a grim face, and snubbed her until she cried.

It was Miss Ives, who was afraid of nothing, who at last walked into Mr. Jones's office and said that the child was impossible and must leave at once. As it was, the files would take months to get straight. No one could find anything.

She came back to her desk looking grimmer than ever, her lips twitching.

She said angrily, "I've kept myself for twenty-seven years this March. I've never had anything. How many women have the qualifications I have? I should have had a pretty face." And then she burst into tears. It was mild hysterics. Mr. Brooke was the first to fuss around with water and handkerchiefs. No one had ever seen Miss Ives cry.

And what about? All Mr. Jones had said was that Marnie was the daughter of an old school friend and he had promised to look after her. If she was no good at filing, then she must be given odd jobs.

"Is this an office or a charitable institution?" demanded Miss Ives. "I've never seen anything like this, never." And then she turned to Mr. Brooke, who was leaning ineffectually over her, and said, "There are other people who should go too. I suppose he was a friend of your father? Getting drunk and making a pig of yourself. Pictures of girls in your desk, and putting grease on your hair in the washrooms . . ."

Mr. Brooke went white, tried to find words, looked helplessly round for support to Miss Jenkins and Richards. They did not meet his eyes. He felt as if they were dealing him invisible blows on the face; but after a few moments Miss Ives put away her handkerchief, picked up her pen with a gesture of endurance, and went back to her ledger. No one looked at Mr. Brooke.

He made himself forget it. She was hysterical, he said. Women would say anything. He knew from what men had told him that there were times you should take no notice of them. An old maid, too, he said spitefully, wishing he could say it aloud, forgetting that she, too, had made of her weakness a strength, and that she could not be hurt long by him, any more than he could by her.

But that was not the only case of hysteria. It seemed extraordinary that for years these people had worked together, making the same jokes, asking after each other's health, borrowing each other's things, and then everything went wrong from one day to the next.

For instance, one of the typists wept with rage all of one morning because Mr. Jones sent back a letter to be retyped. Such a thing had never been known. Such was his manner, as a rule, that a reprimand was almost as warming as praise.

As for Marnie herself, she was like a small child who does not know why it had been slapped. She wandered about the office miserably, sniffing a little, until by chance Mr. Jones saw her and asked what was wrong. She began to cry, and he took her into his room. The door was shut for over an hour while clients waited. When she came out, subdued but cheerful, the typists cold-shouldered her. Then she rushed in to Miss Ives and asked if she could move her desk into the main office, because the other girls were "nasty" to her. Very naturally Miss Ives was unsympathetic, and she cried again, with her head among the papers on Mr. Brooke's desk. It happened to be the nearest.

It was lunch hour. Everyone left but Marnie and Mr. Brooke. The repugnance she felt for this elderly man with the greasy faded hair, the creased white hands, the intimate unpleasant eyes melted in the violence of her misery. She allowed him to stroke her hair. She cried on his shoulder as she had cried on Mr. Jones's shoulder that morning.

"No one likes me," she sobbed.

"Of course everyone likes you."

"Only Mr. Jones likes me."

"But Mr. Jones is the boss . . ." stammered Mr. Brooke, appalled at her incredible ingenuousness. His heart ached for her. He caressed the damp bundle huddled over his desk gently, paternally, wanting only to console her. "If you could just remember this is an office, Marnie."

"I don't want to work in an office. I want to go home. I want my mother. I want Mr. Jones to send me home. He says I can't. He says he will look after me. . . ."

When they heard steps on the stairs Mr. Brooke guiltily slipped back to his corner; and Marnie stood up, sullen and defiant, to face Miss Ives, who ignored her. Marnie dragged her feet across the floor to the typists' room.

"I suppose you have been encouraging her," said Miss Ives. "She needs a good spanking. I'll give it to her myself soon."

"She's homesick," he said.

"What about her stepfather in there?" snapped Miss Ives, jerking her head at Mr. Jones's door.

"He's sorry for her," said Mr. Brooke, defending his own new feeling of protectiveness for the girl.

"Some people have no eyes in their heads," she said unpleasantly. "Taking her to the pictures. Taking her to dinner every night. I suppose that is being sorry for her, too?"

"Yes, it is," said Mr. Brooke hotly. But he was sick with dismay and anger. He wanted to hit Miss Ives, wanted to run into Mr. Jones's room and hit him, wanted to do something desperate. But he sat himself down at his desk and began adding figures. He was behindhand as usual. "Slow but sure, that's what I am," he said to himself, as always, when he saw how the work piled up and he never was level with it. But that afternoon Miss Ives returned him three sheets of calculations and said, "Try to be more accurate, Mr. Brooke, *if* you please."

At four, when Mr. Jones came through the front office on his way home, Marnie was waiting to catch his eyes. He stopped, smiling; then realised the entire staff were watching, and went on, reddening.

Marnie's lips quivered again.

"More rain coming," said Miss Ives acidly.

"Can I take you to your bus stop?" asked Mr. Brooke, defying Miss Ives. There was laughter from the open door of the typists' room. Mr. Brooke had heard that kind of laugh too often, after he had left a room, to care about it now. Marnie tossed her head at Miss Ives. "I should be pleased," she said daintily.

They walked down the stairs, she racing in front, he trying to keep up. She seemed to dance down the street; the sun was shining; it dazzled in her bright hair. Mr. Brooke was panting, smiling, trying to find breath to talk. He knew that above their heads Miss Ives and the others were leaning over the sill and watching them with scornful disgusted faces. He did not care; but when he saw Mr. Jones come out of a shop, as if he had been waiting for Marnie, he stopped guiltily and said: "Goodnight, sir."

Mr. Jones nodded, not looking at him. To Marnie he said, smiling gently, "Feeling happier? Don't worry, you won't be in an office for long. Some lucky man will marry you soon." It was the sort of thing he said to his typists. But not as he said it now.

Marnie laughed, ran up to him, kissed his cheek.

"Well!" said Mr. Jones, looking fatuously pleased. He glared over Marnie's head at Mr. Brooke, who hurried off down the street as if he had been given an order, without looking around. Soon he heard Marnie pattering up behind him.

"You shouldn't have done that," he said reproachfully.

Her face was happy, guileless. "He's like my dad," she said.

At the bus stop Mr. Brooke suddenly could not bear to see her go. He caught her arm and said, "Come to my place and see my dog Twister. You would like him."

She said, "You know, I didn't like you at first. I do now."

"My dog can fetch the newspaper in the morning," he said. "He never tears it."

"I like dogs," she said confidingly, as if it were the most surprising news in the world.

When they reached his room he was so proud, so flustered, that he could only look at her and smile. He unlocked it with shaking hands and dropped the key when he saw the landlady peeping through her window. Marnie picked it up and went before him into his room as if taking possession of it.

"What a nice room," she said. "But it's too small. If you moved your bed . . ."

She darted over to the divan he slept on and pushed it across a corner. Then she patted cushions, moved a chair, and turned to him. "That's much better," she said. "I'm good at this sort of thing. I'm a home girl. That's what my mum says. She didn't want me to come to an office. Dad and Mr. Jones fixed it up."

"Your mother is quite right," said Mr. Brooke devotedly.

It was then she paused to look about her, and it was then her face changed and Mr. Brooke slowly went cold. He saw the room with her eyes, and saw himself, too, as she would see him henceforward.

It was a small room, with patterned wallpaper, all roses and ribbons. The canary hung in the window, the dog's basket was under the bed. There was nothing else of Mr. Brooke in the room that had been inhabited by so many people before him. Except the pictures, which covered most of the wallpaper.

Marnie moved forward slowly, with a queer hunching of her shoulders, as if a draught blew on them, and Mr. Brooke went after her, unconsciously holding out his hands behind her back in appeal.

"I must buy some pictures," he said, trying to sound casual.

There were film stars, bathing beauties, half-nude women all over his walls, dozens of them.

He knew, instinctively, that he should ask for her pity, as she had asked for his. He said: "I can't afford to buy pictures."

But when she turned towards him at last, he knew his expression must be wrong, for she searched his face, and looked as if she had trodden on something unpleasant.

"I had forgotten about them," he cried, truthfully and desperately. Then: "I'm not like that, Marnie, not really."

Her hand swung out and stung his cheek. "You dirty old man," she said. "You dirty, dirty old man."

She ran out of his room, and as she went the landlady came in.

"Baby-snatching?" she said. "You can't have women here, I told you."

"She's my daughter," said Mr. Brooke.

The door slammed. He sat on his bed and looked at the walls, and felt, for just a few moments, old and mean and small. Then he recovered himself and said aloud: "Well, and what do you expect, making me live alone?" He was addressing not only Marnie and the landlady but all the women he had seen in the street, or on the screen, or eating at the next table.

"You wouldn't have stayed, anyway," he muttered at last. He began tearing the pictures off the walls. Then he slowly put them back again. He even cut out a new one from a paper called *Parisian Fancies*, which he had sent for because of an advertisement, and hung it immediately over his bed. "That will give you something to think about," he said to the landlady, whom he could hear stomping about in the next room. Then he went out and got very drunk indeed.

Next morning the landlady saw the picture while he was in

his bath, and told him he must go or she would fetch the police. "Indecent exposure, that's what it is," she said.

"Do you think I care?" said Mr. Brooke.

He was still a little drunk when he reached the office. He walked in aggressively, and at once Miss Ives sniffed and stared at him. She got up immediately and went into Mr. Jones's room. Mr. Jones came out with her and said: "If you do this again, Brooke, you must go. There's a limit to everything."

Through the open door, Mr. Brooke could see Marnie swinging herself round and round in Mr. Jones's big chair, eating sweets.

Towards the middle of the morning Miss Jenkins started to cry and said, "Either she goes or I do."

"Don't worry," said Miss Ives. She nodded her head up and down significantly. "It won't last. Something will happen, one way or the other. Things can't go on like this." Miss Jenkins went home, saying she had a headache. Richards went into Mr. Jones's office for something and came out, too angry to speak. The typewriters were silent next door. No one did any work except Miss Ives. It seemed everyone was waiting.

At lunchtime they all left early. Mr. Brooke stayed in the office. His head ached, his limbs were stiff, and he couldn't face the two flights of stairs. He ate sandwiches and then went to sleep with his head on his desk. When he woke he was still alone. He could not think clearly and wondered for a moment where he was. Then he saw flies gathering over the crumbs on his papers and got up stiffly to fetch a duster. The door into the typists' room was closed. He opened it a few inches and peered cautiously through. He thought for a moment he was still asleep, for there were Marnie and Mr. Jones. His face was buried in her hair, and he was saying, "Please, Marnie, please, please, please . . ." as if he were drunk.

Mr. Brooke stared, his eyes focussing with difficulty. Then Marnie gave a little scream and Mr. Jones jumped up. "Spying!" he said angrily.

Mr. Brooke had lost his breath. His mouth fell open; his hands spread out helplessly. Finally, he said to Marnie, "Why didn't you slap *his* face?"

She ran across the room shouting, "You dirty old man, you dirty old man!"

"He's older than I am."

"You shut up, Brooke," said Mr. Jones.

"He has grownup children. He has grandchildren, Marnie."

Mr. Jones lifted his fist; but at that moment Marnie said triumphantly, "I'm going to marry him. I'm going to get married. So there!" Mr. Jones dropped his arm; and his angry red face became slowly complacent, grateful, adoring.

Mr. Brooke saw that she had said that for the first time; that if he had not entered perhaps she would never have said it.

He looked at Mr. Jones, and out of his knowledge of himself, hated him, but with a small feeling of envious admiration. The confused thought in his mind was: If he had pictures he would be careful to keep them hidden.

After a while he said, half-pityingly, half-spitefully, to Marnie, "You are a silly little girl. You'll be sorry." Then he turned and groped his way out, holding on to the walls.

Later in the afternoon Miss Ives brought him a check. He was dismissed with a bonus of ten pounds. Ten pounds for thirty years' work! He was too numbed to notice it.

"Did you know she was marrying him?" he asked Miss Ives, wanting to see her made angry.

But she sounded pleased. "He told us just now."

"He's older than I am. . . ."

"Serves her right," snapped Miss Ives. "Little fool like that. It's all she's good for. Getting married. That's all these girls think of. She'll learn what men are."

And then she handed him his hat and began gently pushing him to the door. "You'd better go," she said, but not unkindly. "He doesn't want to see you again. He said so. And you look after yourself. You can't go drinking like that, at your age."

Then she shut the door behind him. When he saw he was quite alone in the passage, he began to laugh. He laughed hysterically for some time. Then he went slowly and carefully down the stairs, holding his hat in one hand and his fountain pen in the other. He began to walk down the street, but at the corner he came back, and waited at the foot of the stairs. He wanted to say goodbye to the people he had worked with so long. He could imagine them saying in the typists' room: "What! Old Brooke has gone, has he? I am sorry I didn't have a chance to see him before he left."

# The Day Stalin Died

That day began badly for me with a letter from my aunt in Bournemouth. She reminded me that I had promised to take my Cousin Jessie to be photographed at four that afternoon. So I had; and forgotten all about it. Having arranged to meet Bill at four, I had to telephone him to put it off. Bill was a film writer from the United States who, having had some trouble with an Un-American Activities Committee, was blacklisted, could no longer earn his living, and was trying to get a permit to live in Britain. He was looking for someone to be a secretary to him. His wife had always been his secretary; but he was divorcing her after twenty years of marriage on the grounds that they had nothing in common. I planned to introduce him to Beatrice.

Beatrice was an old friend from South Africa whose passport had expired. Having been named as a communist, she knew that once she went back she would not get out again, and she wanted to stay another six months in Britain. But she had no money. She needed a job. I imagined that Bill and Beatrice might have a good deal in common; but later it turned out that they disapproved of each other. Beatrice said that Bill was corrupt, because he wrote sexy comedies for TV under another name and acted in bad films. She did not think his justification, namely, that a guy has to eat, had anything in its favour. Bill, for his part, had never been able to stand political women. But I was not to know about the incompatibility of my two dear friends; and I spent an hour following Bill through one switchboard after another, until at last I got him in some studio where he was rehearsing for a film about Lady Hamilton. He said it was quite all right, because he had forgotten about the appointment in any case. Beatrice did not have a telephone, so I sent her a telegram.

That left the afternoon free for Cousin Jessie. I was just settling down to work when comrade Jean rang up to say she wanted to see me during lunch hour. Jean was for many years my self-appointed guide or mentor towards a correct political viewpoint. Perhaps it would be more accurate to say she was one of several self-appointed guides. It was Jean who, the day after I had my first volume of short stories published, took the morning off work to come and see me, in order to explain that one of the stories, I forget which, gave an incorrect analysis of the class struggle. I remember thinking at the time that there was a good deal in what she said.

When she arrived that day at lunchtime, she had her sandwiches with her in a paper bag, but she accepted some coffee, and said she hoped I didn't mind her disturbing me, but she had been very upset by something she had been told I had said.

It appeared that a week before, at a meeting, I had remarked that there seemed to be evidence for supposing that a certain amount of dirty work must be going on in the Soviet Union. I would be the first to admit that this remark savoured of flippancy.

Jean was a small, brisk woman with glasses, the daughter of a Bishop, whose devotion to the workingclass was proved by thirty years of work in the Party. Her manner towards me was always patient and kindly. "Comrade," she said, "intellectuals like yourself are under greater pressure from the forces of capitalist corruption than any other type of Party cadre. It is not your fault. But you must be on your guard."

I said I thought I had been on my guard; but nevertheless I could not help feeling that there were times when the capitalist press, no doubt inadvertently, spoke the truth.

Jean tidily finished the sandwich she had begun, adjusted her spectacles, and gave me a short lecture about the necessity for unremitting vigilance on the part of the workingclass. She then said she must go, because she had to be at her office at two. She said that the only way an intellectual with my background could hope to attain to a correct workingclass viewpoint was to work harder in the Party; to mix continually with the workingclass;

and in this way my writing would gradually become a real weapon in the class struggle. She said, further, that she would send me the verbatim record of the Trials in the Thirties, and if I read this, I would find my present vacillating attitude towards Soviet justice much improved. I said I had read the verbatim records a long time ago; and I always did think they sounded unconvincing. She said that I wasn't to worry; a really sound workingclass attitude would develop with time.

With this she left me. I remember that, for one reason and another, I was rather depressed.

I was just settling down to work again when the telephone rang. It was Cousin Jessie, to say she could not come to my flat as arranged, because she was buying a dress to be photographed in. Could I meet her outside the dress shop in twenty minutes? I therefore abandoned work for the afternoon and took a taxi.

On the way the taxi man and I discussed the cost of living, the conduct of the government, and discovered that we had everything in common. Then he began telling me about his only daughter, aged eighteen, who wanted to marry his best friend, aged forty-five. He did not hold with this; had said so; and thereby lost daughter and friend at one blow. What made it worse was that he had just read an article on psychology in the woman's magazine his wife took, from which he had suddenly gathered that his daughter was father-fixated. "I felt real bad when I read that," he said. "It's a terrible thing to come on suddenlike, a thing like that." He drew up smartly outside the dress shop and I got out.

"I don't see why you should take it to heart," I said. "I wouldn't be at all surprised if we weren't all father-fixated."

"That's not the way to talk," he said, holding out his hand for the fare. He was a small, bitter-looking man, with a head like a lemon or like a peanut, and his small blue eyes were brooding and bitter. "My old woman's been saying to me for years that I favoured our Hazel too much. What gets me is, she might have been in the right of it."

"Well," I said, "look at it this way. It's better to love a child too much than too little."

"Love?" he said. "Love, is it? Precious little love or anything else these days, if you ask me, and Hazel left home three months ago with my mate George and not so much as a postcard to say where or how."

"Life's pretty difficult for everyone," I said, "what with one thing and another."

"You can say that," he said.

This conversation might have gone on for some time, but I saw my Cousin Jessie standing on the pavement watching us. I said goodbye to the taxi man and turned, with some apprehension, to face her.

"I saw you," she said. "I saw you arguing with him. It's the only thing to do. They're getting so damned insolent these days. My principle is, tip them sixpence regardless of the distance, and if they argue, let them have it. Only yesterday I had one shouting at my back all down the street because I gave him sixpence. But we've got to stand up to them."

My Cousin Jessie is a tall girl, broad-shouldered, aged about twenty-five. But she looks eighteen. She has light brown hair which she wears falling loose around her face, which is round and young and sharp-chinned. Her wide, light blue eyes are virginal and fierce. She is altogether like the daughter of a Viking, particularly when battling with bus conductors, taxi men, and porters. She and my Aunt Emma carry on permanent guerrilla warfare with the lower orders; an entertainment I begrudge neither of them, because their lives are dreary in the extreme. Besides, I believe their antagonists enjoy it. I remember once, after a set-to between Cousin Jessie and a taxi driver, when she had marched smartly off, shoulders swinging, he chuckled appreciatively and said: "That's a real oldfashioned type, that one. They don't make them like that these days."

"Have you bought your dress?" I asked.

"I've got it on," she said.

Cousin Jessie always wears the same outfit: a well-cut suit, a round-necked jersey, and a string of pearls. She looks very nice in it.

"Then we might as well go and get it over," I said.

"Mummy is coming, too," she said. She looked at me aggressively.

"Oh well," I said.

"But I told her I would *not* have her with me while I was buying my things. I told her to come and pick me up here. I will *not* have her choosing my clothes for me."

"Quite right," I said.

My Aunt Emma was coming towards us from the tearoom at

the corner, where she had been biding her time. She is a very large woman, and she wears navy blue and pearls and white gloves like a policeman on traffic duty. She has a big, heavy-jowled, sorrowful face; and her bulldog eyes are nearly always fixed in disappointment on her daughter.

"There!" she said as she saw Jessie's suit. "You might just as well have had me with you."

"What do you mean?" said Jessie quickly.

"I went in to Renée's this morning and told them you were coming, and I asked them to show you that suit. And you've bought it. You see, I do know your tastes as I know my own."

Jessie lifted her sharp battling chin at her mother, who dropped her eyes in modest triumph and began poking at the pavement with the point of her umbrella.

"I think we'd better get started," I said.

Aunt Emma and Cousin Jessie, sending off currents of angry electricity into the air all around them, fell in beside me, and we proceeded up the street.

"We can get a bus at the top," I said.

"Yes, I think that would be better," said Aunt Emma. "I don't think I could face the insolence of another taxi driver today."

"No," said Jessie, "I couldn't either."

We went to the top of the bus, which was empty, and sat side by side along the two seats at the very front.

"I hope this man of yours is going to do Jessie justice," said Aunt Emma.

"I hope so, too," I said. Aunt Emma believes that every writer lives in a whirl of photographers, press conferences, and publishers' parties. She thought I was the right person to choose a photographer. I wrote to say I wasn't. She wrote back to say it was the least I could do. "It doesn't matter in the slightest anyway," said Jessie, who always speaks in short, breathless, battling sentences, as from an unassuageably painful inner integrity that she doesn't expect anyone else to understand.

It seems that at the boarding house where Aunt Emma and Jessie live, there is an old inhabitant who had a brother who is a TV producer. Jessie had been acting in *Quiet Wedding* with the local Reps. Aunt Emma thought that if there was a nice photograph of Jessie, she could show it to the TV producer when he came to tea with his brother at the boarding house, which he was expected to do any weekend now; and if Jessie proved to be photogenic, the TV producer would whisk her off to London to be a TV star.

What Jessie thought of this campaign I did not know. I never did know what she thought of her mother's plans for her future. She might conform or she might not; but it was always with the same fierce and breathless integrity of indifference.

"If you're going to take that attitude, dear," said Aunt Emma, "I really don't think it's fair to the photographer."

"Oh, Mummy!" said Jessie.

"There's the conductor," said Aunt Emma, smiling bitterly. "I'm not paying a penny more than I did last time. The fare from Knightsbridge to Little Duchess Street is threepence."

"The fares have gone up," I said.

"Not a penny more," said Aunt Emma.

But it was not the conductor. It was two middleaged people, who steadied each other at the top of the stair and then sat down, not side by side, but one in front of the other. I thought this was odd, particularly as the woman leaned forward over the man's shoulder and said in a loud parrot voice: "Yes, and if you turn my goldfish out of doors once more, I'll tell the landlady to turn *you* out. I've warned you before."

The man, in appearance like a damp, grey, squashed felt hat, looked in front of him and nodded with the jogging of the bus.

She said, "And there's fungus on my fish. You needn't think I don't know where it came from."

Suddenly he remarked in a high insistent voice, "There are all those little fishes in the depths of the sea, all those little fishes. We explode all these bombs at them, and we're not going to be forgiven for that, are we, we're not going to be forgiven for blowing up the poor little fishes."

She said, in an amiable voice, "I hadn't thought of that," and she left her seat behind him and sat in the same seat with him.

I had known that the afternoon was bound to get out of control at some point; but this conversation upset me. I was relieved when Aunt Emma restored normality by saying: "*There.* There never used to be people like *that*. It's the Labour government."

"Oh, Mummy," said Jessie, "I'm not in the mood for politics this afternoon."

We had arrived at the place we wanted, and we got down off

the bus. Aunt Emma gave the bus conductor ninepence for the three of us, which he took without comment. "And they're inefficient as well," she said.

It was drizzling and rather cold. We proceeded up the street, our heads together under Aunt Emma's umbrella.

Then I saw a newsboard with the item: STALIN IS DYING. I stopped and the umbrella went jerking up the pavement without me. The newspaperman was an old acquaintance. I said to him, "What's this, another of your sales boosters?" He said: "The old boy's had it, if you ask me. Well, the way he's lived—the way I look at it, he's had it coming to him. Must have the constitution of a bulldozer." He folded up a paper and gave it to me. "The way I look at it is that it doesn't do anyone any good to live that sort of life. Sedentary. Reading reports and sitting at meetings. That's why I like this job—there's plenty of fresh air."

A dozen paces away Aunt Emma and Jessie were standing facing me, huddled together under the wet umbrella. "What's the matter, dear?" shouted Aunt Emma. "Can't you see, she's buying a newspaper," said Jessie crossly.

The newspaperman said, "It's going to make quite a change, with *him* gone. Not that I hold much with the goings-on out there. But they aren't used to democracy much, are they? What I mean is, if people aren't used to something, they don't miss it."

I ran through the drizzle to the umbrella. "Stalin's dying," I said.

"How do you know?" said Aunt Emma suspiciously.

"It says so in the newspaper."

"They said he was sick this morning, but I expect it's just propaganda. I won't believe it till I see it."

"Oh don't be silly, Mummy. How can you *see* it?" said Jessie.

We went on up the street. Aunt Emma said: "What do you think, would it have been better if Jessie had bought a nice pretty afternoon dress?"

"Oh, Mummy," said Jessie, "can't you see she's upset? It's the same for her as it would be for us if Churchill was dead."

"Oh, my *dear!*" said Aunt Emma, shocked, stopping dead. An umbrella spoke scraped across Jessie's scalp, and she squeaked. "Do put that umbrella down now. Can't you see it's stopped raining?" she said irritably, rubbing her head.

Aunt Emma pushed and bundled at the umbrella until it collapsed, and Jessie took it and rolled it up. Aunt Emma, flushed and frowning, looked dubiously at me. "Would you like a nice cup of tea?" she said.

"Jessie's going to be late," I said. The photographer's door was just ahead.

"I do hope this man's going to get Jessie's expression," said Aunt Emma. "There's never been one yet that got her *look*."

Jessie went crossly ahead of us up some rather plushy stairs in a hallway with mauve and gold striped wallpaper. At the top there was a burst of Stravinsky as Jessie masterfully opened a door and strode in. We followed her into what seemed to be a drawingroom, all white and grey and gold. The *Rite of Spring* tinkled a baby chandelier overhead; and there was no point in speaking until our host, a charming young man in a black velvet jacket, switched off the machine, which he did with an apologetic smile.

"I do hope this is the right place," said Aunt Emma. "I have brought my daughter to be photographed."

"Of course it's the right place," said the young man. "How delightful of you to come!" He took my Aunt Emma's white-gloved hands in his own and seemed to press her down onto a large sofa; a pressure to which she responded with a confused blush. Then he looked at me. I sat down quickly on another divan, a long way from Aunt Emma. He looked professionally at Jessie, smiling. She was standing on the carpet, hands linked behind her back, like an admiral on the job, frowning at him.

"You don't look at all relaxed," he said to her gently. "It's really no use at all, you know, unless you are really relaxed all over."

"I'm perfectly relaxed," said Jessie. "It's my cousin here who isn't relaxed."

I said, "I don't see that it matters whether I'm relaxed or not, because it's not me who is going to be photographed." A book fell off the divan beside me on the floor. It was *Prancing Nigger* by Ronald Firbank. Our host dived for it, anxiously.

"Do you read our Ron?" he asked.

"From time to time," I said.

"Personally I never read anything else," he said. "As far as I am concerned he said the last word. When I've read him all through, I begin again at the beginning and read him through again. I don't see that there's any point in anyone ever writing another word after Firbank."

This remark discouraged me, and I did not feel inclined to say anything.

"I think we could all do with a nice cup of tea," he said. "While I'm making it, would you like the gramophone on again?"

"I can't stand modern music," said Jessie.

"We can't all have the same tastes," he said. He was on his way to a door at the back, when it opened and another young man came in with a tea tray. He was as light and lithe as the first, with the same friendly ease of manner. He was wearing black jeans and a purple sweater, and his hair looked like two irregular glossy black wings on his head.

"Ah, bless you, dear!" said our host to him. Then, to us: "Let me introduce my friend and assistant, Jackie Smith. My name you know. Now if we all have a nice cup of tea, I feel that our vibrations might become just a *little* more harmonious."

All this time Jessie was standing-at-ease on the carpet. He handed her a cup of tea. She nodded towards me, saying, "Give it to her." He took it back and gave it to me. "What's the matter, dear?" he asked. "Aren't you feeling well?"

"I am perfectly well," I said, reading the newspaper.

"Stalin is dying," said Aunt Emma. "Or so they would like us to believe."

"Stalin?" said our host.

"That man in Russia," said Aunt Emma.

"Oh, you mean old Uncle Joe. Bless him."

Aunt Emma started. Jessie looked gruffly incredulous.

Jackie Smith came and sat down beside me and read the newspaper over my shoulder. "Well, well," he said. "Well, well, well, well." Then he giggled and said: "Nine doctors. If there were fifty doctors I still wouldn't feel very safe, would you?"

"No, not really," I said.

"Silly old nuisance," said Jackie Smith. "Should have bumped him off years ago. Obviously outlived his usefulness at the end of the war, wouldn't you think?"

"It seems rather hard to say," I said.

Our host, a teacup in one hand, raised the other in a peremptory gesture. "I don't like to hear that kind of thing," he said. "I really don't. God knows, if there's one thing I make a point of never knowing a thing about, it's politics, but during the war Uncle Joe and Roosevelt were absolutely my pin-up boys. But absolutely!"

Here Cousin Jessie, who had neither sat down nor taken a cup of tea, took a stride forward and said angrily: "Look, do you think we could get this *damned* business over with?" Her virginal pink cheeks shone with emotion, and her eyes were brightly unhappy.

"But, my *dear!*" said our host, putting down his cup. "But of course. If you feel like that, of course."

He looked at his assistant, Jackie, who reluctantly laid down the newspaper and pulled the cords of a curtain, revealing an alcove full of cameras and equipment. Then they both thoughtfully examined Jessie. "Perhaps it would help," said our host, "if you could give me an idea what you want it for? Publicity? Dust jackets? Or just for your lucky friends?"

"I don't know and I don't care," said Cousin Jessie.

Aunt Emma stood up and said: "I would like you to catch her expression. It's just a little *look* of hers. . . ."

Jessie clenched her fists at her.

"Aunt Emma," I said, "don't you think it would be a good idea if you and I went out for a little?"

"But my *dear* . . ."

But our host had put his arm around her and was easing her to the door. "There's a duck," he was saying. "You do want me to make a good job of it, don't you? And I never could really do my best, even with the most sympathetic lookers-on."

Again Aunt Emma went limp, blushing. I took his place at her side and took her to the door. As we shut it, I heard Jackie Smith saying: "Music, do you think?" And Jessie: "I *loathe* music." And Jackie again: "We do rather find music helps, you know. . . ."

The door shut and Aunt Emma and I stood at the landing window, looking into the street.

"Has that young man done *you?*" she asked.

"He was recommended to me," I said.

Music started up from the room behind us. Aunt Emma's foot tapped on the floor. "Gilbert and Sullivan," she said. "Well, she can't say she loathes that. But I suppose she would, just to be difficult."

I lit a cigarette. *The Pirates of Penzance* abruptly stopped.

"Tell me, dear," said Aunt Emma, suddenly roguish, "about all the exciting things you are doing."

Aunt Emma always says this; and always I try hard to think

of portions of my life suitable for presentation to Aunt Emma. "What have you been doing today, for instance?" I considered Bill; I considered Beatrice; I considered comrade Jean.

"I had lunch," I said, "with the daughter of a Bishop."

"Did you, dear?" she said doubtfully.

Music again: Cole Porter. "That doesn't sound right to me," said Aunt Emma. "It's modern, isn't it?" The music stopped. The door opened. Cousin Jessie stood there, shining with determination. "It's no good," she said. "I'm sorry, Mummy, but I'm not in the mood."

"But we won't be coming up to London again for another four months."

Our host and his assistant appeared behind Cousin Jessie. Both were smiling rather bravely. "Perhaps we had better all forget about it," said Jackie Smith.

Our host said, "Yes, we'll try again later, when everyone is really themselves."

Jessie turned to the two young men and thrust out her hand at them. "I'm very sorry," she said, with her fierce virgin sincerity. "I'm really terribly sorry."

Aunt Emma went forward, pushed Jessie aside, and shook their hands. "I must thank you both," she said, "for the tea."

Jackie Smith waved my newspaper over the three heads. "You've forgotten this," he said.

"Never mind, you can keep it," I said.

"Oh, bless you, now I can read all the gory details." The door shut on their friendly smiles.

"Well," said Aunt Emma, "I've never been more ashamed."

"I don't care," said Jessie fiercely. "I really couldn't care less."

We descended into the street. We shook each other's hands. We kissed each other's cheeks. We thanked each other. Aunt Emma and Cousin Jessie waved at a taxi. I got on a bus.

When I got home, the telephone was ringing. It was Beatrice. She said she had got my telegram, but she wanted to see me in any case. "Did you know Stalin was dying?" I said.

"Yes, of course. Look, it's absolutely essential to discuss this business on the Copper Belt."

"Why is it?"

"If we don't tell people the truth about it, who is going to?"

"Oh, well, I suppose so," I said.

She said she would be over in an hour. I set out my typewriter and began to work. The telephone rang. It was comrade Jean. "Have you heard the news?" she said. She was crying.

Comrade Jean had left her husband when he became a member of the Labour Party at the time of the Stalin-Hitler Pact, and ever then had been living in bed-sitting-rooms since on bread, butter, and tea, with a portrait of Stalin over her bed.

"Yes, I have," I said.

"It's awful," she said sobbing. "Terrible. They've murdered him."

"Who has? How do you know?" I said.

"He's been murdered by capitalist agents," she said. "It's perfectly obvious."

"He was seventy-three," I said.

"People don't die just like *that*," she said.

"They do at seventy-three," I said.

"We will have to pledge ourselves to be worthy of him," she said.

"Yes," I said, "I suppose we will."

# *Wine*

•··•··•··•··•··•··•··•··•··•··•··•··•··•··•··•··•··•··•··•··•··•··•··•··•··•··•··•··•··•··•··•··•··•··•··•··•··•··•··•

A man and woman walked towards the boulevard from a little hotel in a side street.

The trees were still leafless, black, cold; but the fine twigs were swelling towards spring, so that looking upward it was with an expectation of the first glimmering greenness. Yet everything was calm, and the sky was a calm, classic blue.

The couple drifted slowly along. Effort, after days of laziness, seemed impossible; and almost at once they turned into a cafe and sank down, as if exhausted, in the glass-walled space that was thrust forward into the street.

The place was empty. People were seeking the midday meal in the restaurants. Not all: that morning crowds had been demonstrating, a procession had just passed, and its straggling end could still be seen. The sounds of violence, shouted slogans and singing, no longer absorbed the din of Paris traffic; but it was these sounds that had roused the couple from sleep.

A waiter leaned at the door, looking after the crowds, and he reluctantly took an order for coffee.

The man yawned; the woman caught the infection; and they laughed with an affectation of guilt and exchanged glances before their eyes, without regret, parted. When the coffee came, it remained untouched. Neither spoke. After some time the woman yawned again; and this time the man turned and looked at her critically, and she looked back. Desire asleep, they looked. This remained: that while everything which drove them slept, they accepted from each other a sad irony; they could look at each other without illusion, steady-eyed.

And then, inevitably, the sadness deepened in her till she consciously resisted it; and into him came the flicker of cruelty.

"Your nose needs powdering," he said.

"You need a whipping boy."

But always he refused to feel sad. She shrugged, and, leaving him to it, turned to look out. So did he. At the far end of the boulevard there was a faint agitation, like stirred ants, and she heard him mutter, "Yes, and it still goes on. . . ."

Mocking, she said, "Nothing changes, everything always the same. . . ."

But he had flushed. "I remember," he began, in a different voice. He stopped, and she did not press him, for he was gazing at the distant demonstrators with a bitterly nostalgic face.

Outside drifted the lovers, the married couples, the students, the old people. There the stark trees; there the blue, quiet sky. In a month the trees would be vivid green; the sun would pour down heat; the people would be brown, laughing, bare-limbed. No, no, she said to herself, at this vision of activity. Better the static sadness. And, all at once, unhappiness welled up in her, catching her throat, and she was back fifteen years in another country. She stood in blazing tropical moonlight, stretching her arms to a landscape that offered her nothing but silence; and then she was running down a path where small stones glinted sharp underfoot, till at last she fell spent in a swath of glistening grass. Fifteen years.

It was at this moment that the man turned abruptly and called the waiter and ordered wine.

"What," she said humorously, "already?"

"Why not?"

For the moment she loved him completely and maternally, till she suppressed the counterfeit and watched him wait, fidgeting, for the wine, pour it, and then set the two glasses before them beside the still-brimming coffee cups. But she was again remembering that night, envying the girl ecstatic with moonlight, who ran crazily through the trees in an unsharable desire for—but that was the point.

"What are you thinking of?" he asked, still a little cruel.

"Ohhh," she protested humorously.

"That's the trouble, that's the trouble." He lifted his glass, glanced at her, and set it down. "Don't you want to drink?"

"Not yet."

He left his glass untouched and began to smoke.

These moments demanded some kind of gesture—something slight, even casual, but still an acknowledgement of the separateness of those two people in each of them; the one seen, perhaps, as a soft-staring never-closing eye, observing, always observing, with a tired compassion; the other, a shape of violence that struggled on in the cycle of desire and rest, creation and achievement.

He gave it to her. Again their eyes met in the grave irony, before he turned away, flicking his fingers irritably against the table; and she turned also, to note the black branches where the sap was tingling.

"I remember," he began; and again she said, in protest, "Ohhh!"

He checked himself. "Darling," he said dryly, "you're the only woman I've ever loved." They laughed.

"It must have been this street. Perhaps this cafe—only they change so. When I went back yesterday to see the place where I came every summer, it was a *pâtisserie*, and the woman had forgotten me. There was a whole crowd of us—we used to go around together—and I met a girl here, I think, for the first time. There were recognised places for contacts; people coming from Vienna or Prague, or wherever it was, knew the places— it couldn't be this cafe, unless they've smartened it up. We didn't have the money for all this leather and chromium."

"Well, go on."

"I keep remembering her, for some reason. Haven't thought of her for years. She was about sixteen, I suppose. Very pretty— no, you're quite wrong. We used to study together. She used to bring her books to my room. I liked her, but I had my own girl, only she was studying something else, I forget what." He paused again, and again his face was twisted with nostalgia, and involuntarily she glanced over her shoulder down the street. The procession had completely disappeared; not even the sounds of singing and shouting remained.

"I remember her because . . ." And, after a preoccupied silence: "Perhaps it is always the fate of the virgin who comes and offers herself, naked, to be refused."

"What!" she exclaimed, startled. Also, anger stirred in her. She noted it, and sighed. "Go on."

"I never made love to her. We studied together all that summer. Then, one weekend, we all went off in a bunch. None of us had any money, of course, and we used to stand on the pavements and beg lifts, and meet up again in some village. I was with my own girl, but that night we were helping the farmer get in his fruit, in payment for using his barn to sleep in, and I found this girl Marie was beside me. It was moonlight, a lovely night, and we were all singing and making love. I kissed her, but that was all. That night she came to me. I was sleeping up in the loft with another lad. He was asleep. I sent her back down to the others. They were all together down in the hay. I told her she was too young. But she was no younger than my own girl." He stopped; and after all these years his face was rueful and puzzled. "I don't know," he said. "I don't know why I sent her back." Then he laughed. "Not that it matters, I suppose."

"Shameless hussy," she said. The anger was strong now. "You had kissed her, hadn't you?"

He shrugged. "But we were all playing the fool. It was a glorious night—gathering apples, the farmer shouting and swearing at us because we were making love more than working, and singing and drinking wine. Besides, it was that time: the youth movement. We regarded faithfulness and jealousy and all that sort of thing as remnants of bourgeois morality." He laughed again, rather painfully. "I kissed her. There she was, beside me, and she knew my girl was with me that weekend."

"You kissed her," she said accusingly.

He fingered the stem of his wine glass, looking over at her and grinning. "Yes, darling," he almost crooned at her. "I kissed her."

She snapped over into anger. "There's a girl all ready for love. You make use of her for working. Then you kiss her. You know quite well . . ."

"What do I know quite well?"

"It was a cruel thing to do."

"I was a kid myself. . . ."

"Doesn't matter." She noted, with discomfort, that she was almost crying. "Working with her! Working with a girl of sixteen, all summer!"

"But we all studied very seriously. She was a doctor afterwards, in Vienna. She managed to get out when the Nazis came in, but . . ."

She said impatiently, "Then you kissed her, on *that* night. Imagine her, waiting till the others were asleep, then she climbed up the ladder to the loft, terrified the other man might wake up, then she stood watching you sleep, and she slowly took off her dress and . . ."

"Oh, I wasn't asleep. I pretended to be. She came up dressed. Shorts and sweater—our girls didn't wear dresses and lipstick—more bourgeois morality. I watched her strip. The loft was full of moonlight. She put her hand over my mouth and came down beside me." Again, his face was filled with rueful amazement. "God knows, I can't understand it myself. She was a beautiful creature. I don't know why I remember it. It's been coming into my mind the last few days." After a pause, slowly twirling the wine glass: "I've been a failure in many things, but not with . . ." He quickly lifted her hand, kissed it, and said sincerely: "I don't know why I remember it now, when . . ." Their eyes met, and they sighed.

She said slowly, her hand lying in his: "And so you turned her away."

He laughed. "Next morning she wouldn't speak to me. She started a love affair with my best friend—the man who'd been beside me that night in the loft, as a matter of fact. She hated my guts, and I suppose she was right."

"Think of her. Think of her at that moment. She picked up her clothes, hardly daring to look at you. . . ."

"As a matter of fact, she was furious. She called me all the names she could think of; I had to keep telling her to shut up, she'd wake the whole crowd."

"She climbed down the ladder and dressed again, in the dark. Then she went out of the barn, unable to go back to the others. She went into the orchard. It was still brilliant moonlight. Everything was silent and deserted, and she remembered how you'd all been singing and laughing and making love. She went to the tree where you'd kissed her. The moon was shining on the apples. She'll never forget it, never, never!"

He looked at her curiously. The tears were pouring down her face.

"It's terrible," she said. "Terrible. Nothing could ever make up to her for that. Nothing, as long as she lived. Just when everything was most perfect, all her life, she'd suddenly remember that night, standing alone, not a soul anywhere, miles of damned empty moonlight. . . ."

He looked at her shrewdly. Then, with a sort of humorous, deprecating grimace, he bent over and kissed her and said: "Darling, it's not my fault; it just isn't my fault."

"No," she said.

He put the wine glass into her hands; and she lifted it, looked at the small crimson globule of warming liquid, and drank with him.

# He

**G**oodness! You gave me a start, Mary. . . ."

Mary Brooke was quietly knitting beside the stove. "Thought I'd drop in," she said.

Annie Blake pulled off her hat and flopped a net of bread and vegetables on the table; at the same time her eyes were anxiously inspecting her kitchen: there was an unwashed dish in the sink, a cloth over a chair. "Everything's in such a mess," she said irritably.

Mary Brooke, eyes fixed on her knitting, said, "Eh, sit down. It's clean as can be."

After a hesitation Annie flopped herself into the chair and shut her eyes. "Those stairs . . ." she panted. Then: "Like a cuppa tea, Mary?"

Mary quickly pushed her knitting away and said, "You sit still. I'll do it." She heaved up her large, tired body, filled a kettle from the tap, and set it on the flame. Then, following her friend's anxious glance, she hung the dishcloth where it belonged and shut the door. The kitchen was so clean and neat it could have gone on exhibition. She sat down, reached for her knitting, and knitted without looking at it, contemplating the wall across the room. "He was carrying on like anything last night," she observed.

Annie's drooping lids flew open, her light body straightened. "Yes?" she murmured casually. Her face was tense.

"What can you expect with that type? She doesn't get the beds made before dinnertime. There's dirt everywhere. He was giving it to her proper. Dirty slut, he called her."

"She won't do for him what I did, that's certain," said Annie bitterly.

"Shouting and banging until nearly morning—we all heard it." She counted purl, plain, purl, and added: "Don't last long, do it? Six months he's been with her now?"

"He never lifted his hand to me, *that's* certain," said Annie victoriously. "Never. I've got my pride, if others haven't."

"That's right, love. Two purl. One plain."

"Nasty temper he's got. I'd be up summer and winter at four, cleaning those offices till ten, then cleaning for Mrs. Lynd till dinnertime. Then if he got home and found his dinner not ready, he'd start to shout and carry on—well, I'd say, if you can't wait five minutes, get home and cook it yourself, I'd say. I bring in as much money as you do, don't I? But he never lifted a finger. Bone lazy. Men are all the same."

Mary gave her friend a swift, searching glance, then murmured, "Eh, you can't tell *me*. . . ."

"I'd have the kids and the cleaning and the cooking, and working all day—sometimes when he was unemployed I'd bring in all the money . . . and he wouldn't even put the kettle on for me. Women's work, he said."

"Two purl, plain." But Mary's kindly face seemed to suggest that she was waiting to say something else. "We all know what it is," she agreed at last, patiently.

Annie rose lightly, pulled the shrieking kettle off the flame, and reached for the teapot. Seen from the back, she looked twenty, slim and erect. When she turned with the steaming pot, she caught a glimpse of herself; she set down the pot and went to the mirror. She stood touching her face anxiously. "Look at me!" She pushed a long, sagging curl into position, then shrugged. "Well, who's to care what I look like anyway?"

She began setting out the cups. She had a thin face, sharpened by worry, and small sharp blue eyes. As she sat down, she nervously felt her hair. "I must get the curlers onto my hair," she muttered.

"Heard from the boys?"

Annie's hand fell and clenched itself on the table. "Not a word from Charlie for months. They don't think. . . . He'll turn up one fine day and expect his place laid, if I know my Charlie. Tommy's after a job in Manchester, Mrs. Thomas said. But I had a nice letter from Dick. . . . " Her face softened; her eyes

were soft and reminiscent. "He wrote about his father. Should
he come down and speak to the old so-and-so for me, he said.
I wrote back and said that was no way to speak of his father.
He should respect him, I said, no matter what he's done. It's
not his place to criticise his father, I said."

"You're lucky in your boys, Annie."

"They're good workers, no one can say they aren't. And
they've never done anything they shouldn't. They don't take
after their dad, *that's* certain."

At this, Mary's eyes showed a certain tired irony. "Eh, Annie
—but we all do things we shouldn't." This gaining no response
from the bitter Annie, she added cautiously, "I saw him this
morning in the street."

Annie's cup clattered down into the saucer. "Was he alone?"

"No. But he took me aside—he said I could give you a message if I was passing this way—he might be dropping in this
evening instead of tomorrow with your money, he said. Thurs-
day *she* goes to her mother's—I suppose he thinks while the
cat's away . . ."

Annie had risen, in a panic. She made herself sit down again
and stirred her tea. The spoon tinkled in the cup with the
quivering of her hand. "He's regular with the money, anyway,"
she said heavily. "I didn't have to take him into court. He offered. And I suppose he needn't, now the boys are out keeping
themselves."

"He still feels for you, Annie. . . ." Mary was leaning forward,
speaking in a direct appeal. "He does, really."

"He never felt for anyone but himself," snapped Annie.
"Never."

Mary let a sigh escape her. "Oh, well . . ." she murmured.
"Well, I'll be getting along to do the supper." She stuffed her
knitting into her carryall and said consolingly: "You're lucky.
No one to get after you if you feel like sitting a bit. No one to
worry about but yourself. . . ."

"Oh, don't think I'm wasting any tears over *him*. I'm taking
it easy for the first time in my life. You slave your life out for
your man and your kids. Then off they go, with not so much as
a thank you. Now I can please myself."

"I wouldn't mind being in your place," said Mary loyally. At
the door she remarked, apparently at random, "Your floor's so
clean you could eat off it."

The moment Mary was gone, Annie rushed into her apron and began sweeping. She got down on her knees to polish the floor, and then took off her dress and washed herself at the sink. She combed her dragging wisps of pale hair and did each one up neatly with a pin till her face was surrounded by a ring of little sausages. She put back her dress and sat down at the table. Not a moment too soon. The door opened, and Rob Blake stood there.

He was a thin, rather stooping man, with an air of apology. He said politely, "You busy, Annie?"

"Sit down," she commanded sharply. He stooped loosely in the doorway for a moment, then came forward, minding his feet. Even so, she winced as she saw the dusty marks on the gleaming linoleum. "Take it easy," he said with friendly sarcasm. "You can put up with my dust once a week, can't you?"

She smiled stiffly, her blue eyes fastened anxiously on him, while he pulled out a chair and sat down. "Well, Annie?"

To this conciliatory opening she did not respond. After a moment she remarked, "I heard from Dick. He's thinking of getting married."

"Getting married, now? That puts us on the shelf, don't it?"

"*You*'re not on any shelf that I can see," she snapped.

"Now—Annie . . ." he deprecated, with an appealing smile. She showed no signs of softening. Seeing her implacable face, his smile faded, and he took an envelope from his pocket and pushed it over.

"Thanks," she said, hardly glancing at it. Then that terrible bitterness came crowding up, and he heard the words: "If you can spare it from *her*."

He let that one pass; he looked steadily at his wife, as if seeking a way past that armour of anger. He watched her, passing the tip of his tongue nervously over his lips.

"Some women know how to keep themselves free from kids and responsibilities. They just do this and that, and take up with anyone they please. None of the dirty work for *them*."

He gave a sigh, and was on the point of getting up, when she demanded, "Like a cuppa tea?"

"I wouldn't mind." He let himself sink back again.

While she worked at the stove, her back to him, he was looking around the kitchen; his face had a look of tired, disappointed irony. An ageing man, but with a dogged set to his shoulders. Trying to find the right words, he remarked, "Not so much work for you now, Annie."

But she did not answer. She returned with the two cups and put the sugar into his for him. This wifely gesture encouraged him. "Annie," he began. "Annie—can't we talk this over. . . ." He was stirring the tea clumsily, not looking at it, leaning forward. The cup knocked over. "Oh, look what you've done," she cried out. "Just look at the mess." She snatched up a cloth and wiped the table.

"It's only a drop of tea, Annie," he protested at last, shrinking a little aside from her furious energy.

"Only a drop of tea—I can polish and clean half the day, and then in a minute the place is like a pig sty."

His face darkened with remembered irritation.

"Yes, I've heard," she went on accusingly, "she lets the beds lie until dinner, and the place isn't cleaned from one week to the next."

"At least she cares more for me than she does for a clean floor!" he shouted. Now they looked at each other with hatred.

At this delicate moment there came a shout: "Rob! Rob!"

She laughed angrily. "She's got you where she wants you—waits and spies on you and now she comes after you."

"Rob! You there, Rob?" It was a loud, confident, female voice.

"She sounds just what she is, a proper—"

"Shut up," he interrupted. He was breathing heavily. "You keep that tongue of yours quiet, now."

Her eyes were full of tears, but the blue shone through, bright and vengeful. " 'Rob, Rob'—and off you trot like a little dog."

He got up from the table heavily, as a loud knock came at the door.

Annie's mouth quivered at the insult of it. And *his* first instinct was to stand by her—she could see that. He looked apologetically at her, then went to the door, opened it an inch, and said in a low, furious voice: "Don't you do that, now. Do you hear me!" He shut the door, leaned against it, facing Annie. "Annie," he said again, in an awkward appeal. "Annie . . ."

But she sat at her table, hands folded in a trembling knot before her, her face tight and closed against him.

"Oh, all right!" he said at last despairingly, angry. "You've always got to be in the right about everything, haven't you? That's all that matters to you—if you're in the right. Bloody plaster saint, you are." He went out quickly.

She sat quite still, listening until it was quiet. Then she drew a deep breath and put her two fists to her cheeks, as if trying to keep them still. She was sitting thus when Mary Brooke came in. "You let him go?" she said incredulously.

"And good riddance, too."

Mary shrugged. Then she suggested bravely, "You shouldn't be so hard on him, Annie—give him a chance."

"I'd see him dead first," said Annie through shaking lips. Then: "I'm forty-five, and I might as well be on the dust heap." And then, after a pause, in a remote, cold voice: "We've been together twenty-five years. Three kids. And then he goes off with that . . . with that . . ."

"You're well rid of him, and that's a fact," agreed Mary swiftly.

"Yes, I am, and I know it. . . ." Annie was swaying from side to side in her chair. Her face was stony, but the tears were trickling steadily down, following a path worn from nose to chin. They rolled off and splashed onto her white collar.

"Annie," implored her friend. "Annie . . ."

Annie's face quivered, and Mary was across the room and had her in her arms. "That's right, love, that's right, that's right, love," she crooned.

"I don't know what gets into me," wept Annie, her voice coming muffled from Mary's large shoulder. "I can't keep my wicked tongue still. He's fed up and sick of that—cow, and I drive him away. I can't help it. I don't know what gets into me."

"There now, love, there now, love." The big, fat, comfortable woman was rocking the frail Annie like a baby. "Take it easy, love. He'll be back, you'll see."

"You think he will?" asked Annie, lifting her face up to see if her friend was lying to comfort her.

"Would you like me to go and see if I can fetch him back for you now?"

In spite of her longing, Annie hesitated. "Do you think it'll be all right?" she said doubtfully.

"I'll go and slip in a word when *she's* not around."

"Will you do that, Mary?"

Mary got up, patting at her crumpled dress. "You wait here,

love," she said imploringly. She went to the door and said as she went out: "Take it easy, now, Annie. Give him a chance."

"I go running after him to ask him back?" Annie's pride spoke out of her in a wail.

"Do you want him back or don't you?" demanded Mary, patient to the last, although there was a hint of exasperation now. Annie did not say anything, so Mary went running out.

Annie sat still, watching the door tensely. But vague, rebellious, angry thoughts were running through her head: If I want to keep him, I can't ever say what I think, I can't ever say what's true—I'm nothing to him but a convenience, but if I say so he'll just up and off. . . .

But that was not the whole truth; she remembered the affection in his face, and for a moment the bitterness died. Then she remembered her long hard life, the endless work, work, work—she remembered, all at once, as if she were feeling it now, her aching back when the children were small; she could see him lying on the bed reading the newspaper when she could hardly drag herself. . . . It's all very well, she cried out to herself, it's not right, it just isn't right. . . . A terrible feeling of injustice was gripping her; and it was just this feeling she must push down, keep under, if she wanted him. For she knew finally—and this was stronger than anything else—that without him there would be no meaning in her life at all.

# The Eye of God
# in Paradise

●·○··●··○··●··○··●··○··●··○··●··○··●··○··●··○··●··○··●··○··●··○··●··○··●··○··●··○··●··○··●··○··●··○··●··○··●··○··●··○··●··○··●··○··●··○··●··○··●··○··●··○··●·

O—— in the Bavarian Alps is a charming little village. It is no more charming, however, than ten thousand others; although it is known to an astonishing number of people, some of whom have actually been there, while others have savoured its attractions in imagination only. Pleasure resorts are like film stars and royalty who—or so one hopes—must be embarrassed by the figures they cut in the fantasies of people who have never met them. The history of O—— is fascinating; for this is true of every village. Its location has every advantage, not least that of being so near to the frontier that when finally located on the map it seems to the exuberant holiday-making fancy that one might toss a stone from it into Austria. This is, of course, not the case, since a high wall of mountains forms a natural barrier to any such adventure, besides making it essential that all supplies for O—— and the ten or a dozen villages in the valley above it must come from Germany. This wall of mountains is in fact the reason why O—— is German, and has always been German; although its inhabitants, or so it would seem from the songs and stories they offer the summer and winter visitors on every possible occasion, take comfort from the belief that Austria is at least their spiritual home. And so those holiday-makers who travel there in the hope of finding the attractions of two countries combined are not so far wrong. And there are those who go there because of the name, which is a homely, simple, gentle name, with none of the associations of, let us say, Berchtesgaden, a place in which one may also take one's ease, if one feels so inclined. O—— has never been famous; never has the spotlight of history touched it. It has not been one of those places that no one ever heard of until woken into painful memory, like Seoul, or Bikini, or, for that matter, this same Berchtesgaden, although that is quite close enough for discomfort.

Two holiday-makers who had chosen O—— out of the several hundred winter resorts that clamoured for their patronage were standing in one of the upper streets on the evening of their arrival there. The charming little wooden houses weighted with snow, the delightful little streets so narrow and yet so dignified as to make the great glittering cars seem pretentious and out of place, the older inhabitants in their long dark woollen skirts and heavy clogs, even a sleigh drawn by ribboned horses and full of holiday-makers—all this was attractive, and undeniably what they had come for; particularly as slopes suitable for skiing stretched away on every side. Yet there was no denying that something weighed on them; they were uneasy. And what this thing was does not need to be guessed at, since they had not ceased to express it, and very volubly, since their arrival.

This was a pleasure resort; it existed solely for its visitors. In winter, heavy with snow, and ringing with the shouts of swooping skiers; in summer, garlanded with flowers and filled with the sounds of cowbells—it was all the same: summer and winter dress were nothing but masks concealing the fact that this village had no existence apart from its flux of visitors, which it fed and supplied by means of the single rickety little train that came up from the lowlands of Bavaria, and which in turn it drained of money spent freely on wooden shoes, carved and painted wooden bottles, ironwork, embroidered aprons, ski trousers and sweaters, and those slender curved skis themselves that enabled a thousand earth-plodders to wing over the slopes all through the snow months.

The fact is that for real pleasure a pleasure resort should have no one in it but its legitimate inhabitants, oneself, and perhaps one's friends. Everyone knows it, everyone feels it; and this is the insoluble contradiction of tourism; and perhaps the whole edifice will collapse at that moment when there is not one little town, not one village in the whole of Europe that has not been, as the term is, exploited. No longer will it be possible to drive one's car away into the mountains in search of that unspoiled village, that Old World inn by the stream; for when one arrives most certainly a professional host will hasten out, offering professional hospitality. What then? Will everyone stay at home?

But what of poor, war-denuded Europe whose inhabitants continue to live, a little sullenly perhaps, under the summer and winter eyes of their visitors, eyes that presumably are searching for some quality, some good, that they do not possess themselves, since otherwise why have they travelled so far from themselves in order to examine the lives of other people?

These were the sorts of reflections—which, it must be confessed, could scarcely be more banal—that were being exchanged by our two travellers.

There they stood, outside a little wayside booth, or open shop, that sold not carved bottles or leather aprons but real vegetables and butter and cheese. These goods were being bought by a group of American wives who were stationed here with their husbands as part of the army of occupation. Or, rather, their husbands were part of the machinery which saw to it that American soldiers stationed all over the American zone of occupation could have pleasant holidays in the more attractive parts of Europe.

Between small, green-painted houses, the snow was pitted and rutted in the narrow street, glazed with the newly frozen heat of tramping feet. In places it was stained yellow and mounded with dark horse droppings, and there was a strong smell of urine mingling with the fresh tang of winter cabbage, giving rise to further reflections about the superiority of automobiles over horses—and even, perhaps, of wide streets over narrow ones, for at every moment the two travellers had to step down off the small pavement into the strong-smelling snow to allow happy groups of skiers to pass by; had to stand back again to make room for the cars that were trying to force a passage up to the big hotels where the American soldiers were holidaying with their wives or girls.

There were so many of the great powerful cars, rocking fast and dangerously up over the slippery snow, that it was hard to preserve the illusion of an unspoiled mountain village. And so the two lifted their eyes to the surrounding forests and peaks. The sun had slipped behind the mountains, but had left their snowfields tinted pink and gold, sentinelled by pine groves which, now that the light had gone from them, loomed black and rather sinister, inevitably suggesting wolves, witches, and other creatures from a vanished time—a suggestion, however, tinged with bathos, since it was obvious that wolves or witches would have got short shrift from the mighty creators of those powerful machines. The tinted glitter of the smooth slopes and the black stillness of the woods did their best to set the village in a timelessness not disturbed by the gear and machinery of the travelling cages that lifted clear over intervening valleys to the ledge of a mountain where there was yet another hotel and the amenities of civilisation. And perhaps it was a relief, despite all the intrusions of the machinery of domesticity and comfort, to rest one's eyes on those forests, those mountains, whose savagery seemed so innocent. The year was 1951; and while the inhabitants of the village seemed almost feverishly concerned to present a scene of carefree charm, despite all their efforts the fact which must immediately strike everyone was that most of the people in the streets wore the uniform of the war which was six years past, and that the language most often overheard was American. But it was not possible to stand there, continually being edged this way and that on and off the pavement, with one's eyes fixed determinedly on natural beauty, particularly as the light was going fast and now the houses, shops, and hotels were taking their nocturnal shape and spilling the white pallor of electricity from every door and window, promising warmth, promising certain pleasure. The mountains had massed themselves, black against a luminous sky. Life had left them and was concentrating down in the village. Everywhere came groups of skiers hastening home for the night, and everywhere among them those men and women who proclaimed themselves immediately and at first glance as American. Why? Our two stood there, looking into first one face and then the next, trying to define what it was that set them apart. A goodlooking lot, these policemen of Europe. And well-fed, well-dressed . . . They were distinguished above all, perhaps, by their assurance! Or was this noisy cheerfulness nothing more than the expression of an inner guilt because the task of policing and preserving order earned such attractive holidays? In which case, it was rather to their credit than not.

But when the four Army wives had finished their bargaining at the vegetable and dairy stall and went up the steep street, walking heavily because of their crammed baskets, they so dominated the scene in their well-cut trousers and their bright jackets that the women selling produce and the locals who had been waiting patiently for the four to conclude their shopping seemed almost unimportant, almost like willing extras in a crowd-scene from a film called, perhaps, *Love in the Alps*, or *They Met in the Snow*.

And six years had been enough to still in the hearts of these Germans—for Germans they were, although Austria was no more than a giant's stone-throw away—all the bitterness of defeat? They were quite happy to provide a homely and picturesque background for whatever nationalities might choose to visit them, even if most were American, and many British —as our two conscientiously added, trying not to dissociate themselves from their responsibilities, even though they felt very strongly that the representatives of *their* country were much too naturally modest and tactful to appropriate a scene simply by the fact that they were in it.

It was hard to believe; and the knowledge of the secret angers, or at the very best an ironical patience, that must be burning in the breasts of their hosts, the good people of the village of O——, deepened an uneasiness which was almost (and this was certainly irrational) a guilt which should surely have no place in the emotions of a well-deserved vacation.

Guilt about what? It was absurd.

Yet, from the moment they had arrived on the frontier— the word still came naturally to them both—and had seen the signs in German; had heard the language spoken all around them; had passed through towns whose names were associated with the savage hate and terror of headlines a decade old—from that moment had begun in both the complicated uneasiness of which they were so ashamed. Neither had admitted it to the other; both were regretting they had come. Why—they were both thinking—why submit ourselves, when we are on vacation and won't be able to afford another one for goodness knows how long, to something that must be unpleasant? Why not say simply and be done with it that, for us, Germany is poisoned? We never want to set foot in it again or hear the language spoken or see a sign in German. We simply do not want to think about it; and if we are unjust and lacking in humanity and reason and good sense then—why not? One cannot be expected to be reasonable about everything.

Yet here they were.

The man remarked, after a long silence, "Last time I was here there was nothing of *that*."

Down the other side of the street, pressed close to the wall to avoid a big car that was going by, came a group of five girls in local peasant costume. All day these girls had been serving behind the counters, or in the restaurants, wearing clothes such as girls anywhere in Europe might wear. Now their individual faces had dwindled behind great white starched headdresses. Their bodies were nothing more than supports for the long-sleeved, long-skirted, extinguishing black dresses. The whole costume had something reminiscent of the prim fantasy of the habits of certain orders of nuns. They were plodding resignedly enough— since, after all, they were being well paid for doing this— down over the snow towards one of the big hotels where they would regale the tourists with folk songs before slipping home to change into their own clothes in time to spend an hour or so with their young men.

"Well, never mind, I suppose one does like to see it?" The woman slipped her arm through his.

"Oh, I suppose so, why not?"

They began to walk down the street, leaning on each other because of the slipperiness of the rutted snow.

It hung in the balance whether one or other of them might have said something like: Suppose we all stopped coming? Suppose there were no tourists at all; perhaps they would simply cease to exist? Like actors who devote so much of themselves to acting they have no emotions left over for their own lives but continue to exist in whatever part they are playing. . . .

But neither of them spoke. They turned into the main street of the village, where there were several large hotels and restaurants.

Very easily one of them might have remarked to the other, with a kind of grumbling good humour: It's all very well, all these things we're saying about tourists, but we are tourists ourselves?

Come, come, the other would have replied. Clearly we are tourists on a much higher level than most!

Then they would have both laughed.

But at the same moment they stopped dead, looking at some queer hopping figure that was coming along the pavement over the badly lighted snow. For a moment it was impossible to make out what this great black jumping object could be that was coming fast towards them along the ground. Then they saw it was a man whose legs had been amputated and who was hopping over the snow like a frog, his body swinging and jerking between his heavy arms like the body of some kind of insect.

The two saw the eyes of this man stare up at them as he went hopping past.

At the station that day, when they arrived, two men hacked and amputated by war almost out of humanity, one without arms, his legs cut off at the knee; one whose face was a great scarred eyeless hollow, were begging from the alighting holiday-makers.

"For God's sake," said the man suddenly, as if this were nothing but a continuation of what they had been saying, "for God's sake, let's get out of here."

"Oh, yes," she agreed instantly. They looked at each other, smiling, acknowledging in that smile all that they had not said that day.

"Let's go back. Let's find somewhere in France."

"We shouldn't have come."

They watched the cripple lever himself up over a deep doorstep, dragging his body up behind his arms, using the stump of his body as a support while he reached up with long arms to ring the bell.

"What about the money?" she asked.

"We'll go home when it runs out."

"Good, we'll go back tomorrow."

Instantly they felt gay; they were leaving tomorrow.

They walked along the street, looking at the menus outside the hotels. He said, "Let's go in here. It's expensive, but it's the last night."

It was a big, brown, solid-looking hotel called the Lion's Head; and on the oldfashioned gilded signboard was a great golden lion snarling down at them.

Inside was a foyer, lined with dark, shining wood; there were dark, straight-backed wooden settles around the walls and heavy arrangements of flowers in massive brass tubs. Glass doors opened into the restaurant proper. This was a long room lined with the same gleaming dark wood, and in each corner stood even larger brass tubs crammed with flowers. The table-cloths were heavy white damask; a profusion of cutlery and glass gleamed and glittered. It was a scene of solid middleclass comfort. A waiter showed them to an empty table at one side. The menu was placed between them. They exchanged a grim-ace, for the place was far too expensive for them, particularly as now they were committed to spending so much of their money on fares away and out of Germany into France—a country where they would feel no compulsion at all to make disparaging and ironical remarks about tourists or tourism.

They ordered their dinner and, while they waited, sat examin-ing the other diners. The Americans were not here. Their hotels were the big, new, modern ones at the top of the village. The clientele here was solidly German. Again the two British tourists were conscious of a secret, half-ashamed unease. They looked from one face to another, thinking: Six years ago, what were you doing? And you—and you? We were mortal enemies then; now we sit in the same room, eating together. You were the defeated.

This last was addressed as a reminder to themselves, for no people could have looked less defeated than these. A more solid, sound, well-dressed, comfortable crowd could not be imagined; and they were eating with the easy satisfaction of those who cannot imagine ever being short of a meal. Yet six years ago . . .

The waiter brought two plates of soup, very big plates, monogrammed with the sign of the Lion's Head, so full that they asked him to take them away and divide one portion between the two of them. For they had observed that a single portion (served on large metal dishes) of any dish here was enough for two English stomachs. Not that they were not more than willing to do as well as these people around them—the defeated—whose capacity seemed truly incredible. But one day in this country of hearty eaters had not enlarged their stomachs to German capacity; and now that they were leaving, not later than tomorrow, it was too late.

They consumed their half-portions of very strong meat soup, full of vegetables; and pointed out to each other that, even so, their plates held twice as much as they would in England; and continued to dart curious, half-guilty glances at their fellow diners.

Six years ago these people were living amid ruins, in cellars, behind any scrap of masonry that remained standing. They were half-starved, and their clothes were rags. An entire generation of young men were dead. Six years. A remarkable nation, surely.

The jugged hare came and was eaten with appreciation.

They had ordered pastries with cream; but alas, before they could eat them, they had to restore themselves with strong cups of coffee.

Back in France, they told themselves and each other, they would find themselves at home, at table as well as spiritually. By this time tomorrow, they would be in France. And now, with the last meal over and the bill to pay, came the moment of general reckoning, soon over, and in fact accomplished hastily on the back of an envelope.

To take a train, thirdclass, back to the nearest suitable spot in the French Alps would use up half of their available currency; and it would be a choice of staying out their full three weeks and eating one meal a day—and that a very slender meal—or staying a week and then going home.

They did not look at each other as they reached this final depressing conclusion. They were thinking, of course, that they were mad to leave at all. If to come to Germany was the result of some sort of spiritual quixotry, a symptom of moral philanthropy suitable only for liberal idealists whom—they were convinced—they both despised, then to leave again was simply weak-minded. In fact, their present low-spiritedness was probably due to being overtired, for they had spent two successive nights sitting up on hard wooden train seats, sleeping fitfully on each other's shoulders.

They would have to stay. And now that they reached this conclusion, depression settled on them both; and they looked at the rich Germans who surrounded them with a gloomy hatred which, in their better moments, they would have utterly repudiated.

Just then the waiter came forward, followed by an energetically striding young man apparently fresh from a day's skiing, for his face was flaming scarlet under untidy shags of sandy hair. They did not want him at their table, but the restaurant was now quite full. The waiter left their bill on the tablecloth; and they occupied themselves in finding the right change, under the interested inspection of the young sportsman, who, it seemed, was longing to advise them about money and tips. Resenting his interest, they set themselves to be patient. But the waiter did not return for some time, so busy was he at the surrounding tables; and they watched a party of new arrivals who were settling down at a nearby table that had been reserved for them. There came first a handsome woman in her early middleage, unfastening a shaggy, strong-looking fur coat of the kind worn for winter sports or bad weather outdoors. She flung this open on her chair, making a kind of nest, in which she placed herself, wrapping it closely around her legs. She was wearing a black wool dress, full-skirted and embroidered in bright colors, a dress which flirted with the idea of a peasant naivety. Having arranged herself, she raised her face to greet the rest of her family with a smile that seemed to mock and chide them for taking so long to follow after her. It was a handsome face: she was a fine-looking woman, with her fair curling hair, and a skin bronzed deep with the sun and oil of many weeks of winter sport. Next came a young lad, obviously her son, a very tall, goodlooking, attractive youth, who began teasing her because of her hurry to begin eating. He flashed his white strong teeth at her, and his young blue eyes, until she playfully took his arm and shook him. He protested. Then both, with looks of mock concern because this was a public place, desisted, lowered their voices, and sat laughing while the daughter, a delightfully pretty girl of fifteen or so, and the father, a heavy, good-humoured gentleman, took the two empty chairs. The family party was complete. The waiter was attentive for their order, which was for four tall glasses of beer, which they insisted on having that moment, before they could order or even think of food. The waiter hurried off to fetch the beer, while they settled down to study the menus. And one could be sure that there would be no half-portions for this family, either for financial reasons or because they suffered from limitations of appetite.

Watching this family, it came home to the couple from

Britain that what they were resenting was very likely their sheer capacity for physical enjoyment. Since, like all British people of their type, they spent a great deal of emotional energy on complaining about the inability of their countrymen to experience joy and well-being, they told themselves that what they felt was both churlish and inconsistent. The woman said to the man, in a conciliating, apologetic, almost resigned voice, "They really are extraordinarily goodlooking."

To this he responded with a small ironical grimace; and he returned his attention to the family.

Mother, father, and son were laughing over some joke, while the girl turned a very long tapering glass of beer between thumb and forefinger of a thin, tanned hand so that the frost beads glittered and spun. She was staring out of the family group, momentarily lost to it, a fair, dreaming tendril of a girl with an irregular wedge of a little face. Her eyes wandered over the people at the tables, encountered those of our couple, and lingered in open, bland curiosity. It was a gaze of frank unself-consciousness, almost innocence; the gaze of a protected child who knew she might commit no folly on her own individual account, since the family stood between her and the results of folly. Yet, just then, she chose to be out of the family group; or at least she gazed out of it as one looks through an open door. Her pale, pretty eyes absorbed what she wanted of the British couple, and, at their leisure, moved on to the other diners; and all the time her fingers moved slowly up and down the slim cold walls of her beer glass. The woman, finding in this girl a poetic quality totally lacking from the stolid burghers who filled this room, indicated her to the man by saying: "She's charming." Again he grimaced, as if to say: Every young girl is poetic. And: She'll be her mother in ten years.

Which was true. Already the family had become aware of the infidelity of this, their youngest member; already the handsome mother was leaning over her daughter, rallying her for her dreamy inattention, claiming her by little half-caressing, peremptory exclamations. The solid, kindly father laid his brown and capable hand on the girl's white-wool-covered forearm and bent towards her with solicitude, as if she were sick. The boy put a large forkful of meat into his mouth and ate it ruminantly, watching his sister with an irreverent grin. Then he said in a low tone some word that was clearly an old trumpet for disagreement between them, for she swung her chin towards him petulantly, with a half-reproachful and half-resentful epithet. The brother went on grinning, protective but derisive; the father and mother smiled tenderly at each other because of the brother-and-sister sparring.

No, clearly, this young girl had no chance of escaping from the warm prison of her family; and in a few years she would be a capable, handsome, sensual woman, married to some manufacturer carefully chosen for her by her father. That is, she would be unless another war or economic cataclysm intervened and plunged all her people into the edge-of-disaster hunger-bitten condition from which they had just emerged. Though they did not look as if they had. . . .

Returned full circle to the point of their complicated and irrational dislike, the man and woman raised ironical eyes at each other, and the man said briefly: "Blond beasts."

These two were of another family of mankind from most of the people in the restaurant.

The man was Scotch, small-built, nervous, energetic, with close-springing black hair, white freckled skin, quick, deep blue eyes. He tended to be sarcastic about the English, among whom, of course, he had spent most of his life. He was busy, hard-working, essentially pragmatic, practical, and humane. Yet above and beyond all these admirably useful qualities was something else, expressed in his characteristic little grimace of ironical bitterness, as if he were saying: Well, yes, and then?

As for her, she was small, dark, and watchful, Jewish in appearance and arguably by inheritance, since there had been a Jewish great-grandmother who had escaped from pogrom-loving Poland in the last century and married an Englishman. More potent than the great-grandmother was the fact that her fiancé, a medical student and refugee from Austria, had been killed in the early days of the war flying over this same country in which they now sat and took their holiday. Mary Parrish was one of those people who had become conscious of their claims to being Jewish only when Hitler drew their attention to the possibility they might have some.

She now sat and contemplated the handsome German family and thought: Ten years ago . . . She was seeing them as executioners.

As for the man, who had taken his name, Hamish, from a string of possible names, some of them English, because of another kind of national pride, he had served in his capacity as a doctor on one of the commissions that, after the war, had tried to rescue the debris of humanity the war had left all over Europe.

It was no accident that he had served on this commission. Early in 1939 he had married a German girl, or, rather, a Jewish girl, studying in Britain. In July of that year she had made a brave and foolhardy attempt to rescue some of her family who had so far escaped the concentration camps, and had never been heard of since. She had simply vanished. For all Hamish knew, she was still alive somewhere. She might very well be in this village of O———. Ever since yesterday morning when they entered Germany, Mary had been watching Hamish's anxious, angry, impatient eyes moving, preoccupied, from the face of one woman to another: old women, young women; women on busses, trains, platforms; women glimpsed at the end of a street; a woman at a window. And she could feel him thinking: Well, and if I did see her, I wouldn't recognise her.

And his eyes would move back to hers; she smiled; and he gave his small, bitter, ironical grimace.

They were both doctors, both hard-working and conscientious, both very tired because, after all, while living in Britain has many compensations, it is hard work, this business of maintaining a decent level of life with enough leisure for the pursuits that make life worthwhile, or at least to cultivated people, which they both were, and determined to remain. They were above all, perhaps, tired people.

They were tired and they needed to rest. This was their holiday. And here they sat, knowing full well that they were pouring away energies into utterly useless, irrelevant, and above all, unfair, emotions.

The word "unfair" was one they both used without irony.

She said, "I think one week in France would be better than three here. Let's go. I really do think we should."

He said, "Let's go into one of the smaller villages higher up the valley. They are probably just ordinary mountain villages, not tarted-up like this place."

"We'll go tomorrow," she agreed with relief.

Here they both became alert to the fact that the young man

who had sat down at their table was watching them, at the same time as he heartily chewed a large mouthful of food, and looked for an inlet into their conversation. He was an unpleasant person. Tall, with an unco-ordinated, bony look, his blue eyes met the possibilities of their reaction to him with a steady glare of watchful suspicion out of an ugly face whose skin had a peculiar harsh red texture. The eyes of our couple had been, unknown to them, returning again and again to this remarkable scarlet face, and at the back of their minds they had been thinking professionally: A fool to overheat himself in this strong reflected light up here.

Now, at the same moment, the two doctors realised that the surface of his face was a skin-graft; that the whole highly colored, shiny, patchy surface, while an extraordinarily skilful reconstruction of a face, was nothing but a mask, and what the face had been before must be guessed at. They saw, too, that he was not a young man, but, like themselves, in early middle-age. Instantly pity fought with their instinctive dislike of him; and they reminded themselves that the aggressive glare of the blue eyes was the expression of the pitiful necessity of a wounded creature to defend itself.

He said in stiff but good English, or, rather, American: "I must beg your pardon for interrupting your conversation, and beg leave to introduce myself—Doctor Schröder. I wish to place myself at your service. I know this valley well, and can recommend hotels in the other villages."

He was looking at Hamish, as he had from the time he began speaking, though he gave a small, minimal bow when Mary Parrish introduced herself, and instantly returned his attention to the man.

Both the British couple felt discomfort; but it was hard to say whether this was because of the man's claim on their pity, because of their professional interest in him, which they must disguise, or because of the impolite insistence of his manner.

"That is very kind of you," said Hamish; and Mary murmured that it was very kind. They wondered whether he had heard his "blond beasts." They wondered what other indiscretions they might have committed.

"As it happens," said Doctor Schröder, "I have a very good buddy who runs a guest house at the top of the valley. I was up there this morning, and she has a dandy room to let."

Once again they indicated that it was very kind of him.

"If it is not too early for you, I shall be taking the nine-thirty autobus up the valley tomorrow for a day's skiing, and I shall be happy to assist you."

And now it was necessary to take a stand one way or the other. Mary and Hamish glanced at each other enquiringly; and immediately Doctor Schröder said, with a perceptible increase of tension in his manner, "As you know, at this time in the season, it is hard to find accommodation." He paused, seemed to assure himself of their status by a swift inspection of their clothes and general style, and added: "Unless you can afford one of the big hotels—but they are not of the cheapest."

"Actually," said Mary, trying to make of what he must have heard her say before a simple question of caprice, "actually we were wondering whether we might not go back to France? We are both very fond of France."

But Doctor Schröder was not prepared to take this from them. "If it is a question of skiing, then the weather report announced today that the snow is not as good in the French Alps as it is with us. And, of course, France is much more expensive."

They agreed that this was so; and he continued to say that if they took the empty room at his buddy's guest house it would cost them much less than it would at a German pension, let alone a French pension. He examined their clothes again and remarked, "Of course, it must be hard for you to have such unfortunate restrictions with your travel allowance. Yes, it must be annoying. For people of a good salary and position it must be annoying."

For both these two the restrictions of the travel allowance merely confirmed a fact: they could not have afforded more than the allowance in any case. They realised that Doctor Schröder was quite unable to decide whether they were rich and eccentric English people who notoriously prefer old clothes to new clothes, or whether they were rich people deliberately trying to appear poor, or whether they were poor. In the first two cases they would perhaps be eager to do some trade in currency with him? Was that what he wanted?

It seemed it was; for he immediately said that he would be very happy to lend them a modest sum of dough, in return for which he would be glad if they would do the same for him

when he visited London, which he intended to do very soon.
He fastened the steady glare of his eyes on their faces—or,
rather, on Hamish's face—and said: "Of course, I am prepared
to offer every guarantee." And he proceeded to do so. He was
a doctor attached to a certain hospital in the town of S——
and his salary was regular. If they wished to make independent
enquiries they were welcome to do so.

And now Hamish intervened to make it clear that they could
not afford to spend on this vacation one penny more than the
travel allowance. For a long moment Doctor Schröder did not
believe him. Then he examined their clothes again and openly
nodded.

Now, perhaps, the man would go away?

Not at all. He proceeded to deliver a harangue on the subject
of his admiration for Britain. His love for the entire British
nation, their customs, their good taste, their sportsmanship,
their love of fair play; their history, and their art were the
ruling passions of his life. He went on like this for some
minutes, while the British couple wondered if they ought to
confess that their trade was the same as his. But, if they did,
presumably it would let them in for even closer intimacy. And
by a hundred of the minute signs which suffice for communi-
cation between people who knew each other well, they had
said that they disliked this man intensely and wished only that
he would go away.

But now Doctor Schröder enquired outright what profession
his new friend Mr. Anderson pursued; and when he heard that
they were both doctors, and attached to hospitals whose names
he knew, his expression changed. But subtly. It was not surprise, but rather the look of a prosecutor who has been cross-
examining witnesses and at last got what he wants.

And the British couple were beginning to understand what
it was Doctor Schröder wanted of them. He was talking with
a stiff, brooding passion of resentment about his position and
prospects as a doctor in Germany. For professional people, he
said, Germany was an unkind country. For the business people
—yes. For the artisans—yes. The workers were all millionaires
these days, yes sir! Better far to be a plumber or an electrician
than a doctor. The ruling dream of his life was to make his
way to Britain, and there become an honoured and—be it
understood—a well-paid member of his profession.

Here Doctors Anderson and Parrish pointed out that foreign doctors were not permitted to practise in Britain. They might lecture; they might study; but they might not practise. Not unless, added Doctor Parrish, possibly reacting to the fact that not once had this man done more than offer her the barest minimum of politeness until he had recognised that she, as well as Hamish, was a doctor and therefore possibly of use to him—not unless they were refugees, and even then they must take the British examinations.

Doctor Schröder did not react to the word "refugee."

He returned to a close cross-examination about their salaries and prospects, dealing first with Mary's, and then, in more detail, with Hamish's. At last, in response to their warning that for him to become a doctor in Britain would be much more difficult than he seemed to think, he replied that in this world everything was a question of pulling strings. In short, he intended they should pull strings for him. It was the most fortunate occurrence of his life that he had happened to meet them that evening, the happiest and the best-timed. . . .

At this, the eyes of the British couple met on a certain suspicion. Ten minutes later in the talk it emerged that he knew the lady who ran the house where they had taken a room, and therefore he probably had heard from her that she had a British doctor as a lodger. Very likely he had arranged with the waiter to be put at their table. For he must know the people of the village well: he had been coming for his winter holidays to O—— since he was a small child—Doctor Schröder held out his hand below table-level to show how small. Yes, all those years of winters O—— had known Doctor Schröder, save for the years of war, when he was away serving his country.

There was a small stir in the restaurant. The family were rising, gathering their wraps, and departing. The lady first, her shaggy brown coat slung over her handsome shoulders, her rosy lower lip caught by her white teeth as she searched for her belongings she might have forgotten. Then she extended her smile, so white against the clear brown skin, and waited for her son to take her by the shoulder and propel her, while she laughed, protesting, to the door. There, when it opened, she shivered playfully, although it was only the door to the vestibule. Behind her came the pretty, rather languid girl; then the stout authoritative father, shepherding his family away and out to the snow-cold air. The family vanished, leaving their table a mess of empty glasses, plates, broken bread, cheeses, fruit, wine. The waiter cleared the table with a look as if he found it a privilege.

The British couple also rose and said to Doctor Schröder that they would think over his suggestion and perhaps let him know in the morning. His thin-skinned shiny face tilted up at them, and levelled into an affronted mask as he stood up and said, "But I understood all arrangements were made."

And how had they got themselves into this position, where they could not exercise simple freedom of choice without upsetting this extremely dislikable person? But they knew how. It was because he was a wounded man, a cripple; because they knew that his fixed aggression was part of his laudable determination not to let that shockingly raw face drive him into self-pity and isolation. They were doctors, and they were reacting above all to the personality of a cripple. When they said that they were tired and intended to go to bed early, and he replied instantly, insulted, that he would be happy to accompany them to a certain very pleasant place of entertainment, they knew that they could bring themselves to do no more than say they could not afford it.

They knew he would immediately offer to be their host. He did, and they politely refused as they would refuse an ordinary acquaintance, and were answered by the man who could tolerate no refusal, because if he once accepted a refusal, he would be admitting to himself that his face put him outside simple human intercourse.

Doctor Schröder, who had spent all the winter holidays of his life in this valley, naturally knew the proprietor of the hotel where he proposed to take them; and he guaranteed them a pleasant and relaxing evening while he fixed on them a glare of suspicious hate.

They walked together under the snow-weighted eaves of the houses, over snow rutted by the hundred enormous American cars which had rocked over it that day, to the end of the street where there was a hotel whose exterior they had already inspected earlier that day and rejected on the grounds that anything inside it must necessarily be too expensive for them. Immediately outside, on the seared snow, sat the man without legs they had seen earlier. Or rather he stood, his head level with their hips, looking as if he were buried to hip-level in the snow, holding out a cloth cap to them. His eyes had the same bold, watchful glare as those of Doctor Schröder.

Doctor Schröder said, "It's a disgrace that these people should be allowed to behave like this. It makes a bad impression on our visitors." And he led the British couple past the cripple with a look of angry irritation.

Inside was a long room sheltered by glass on two sides from the snow which could be seen spinning down through the areas of yellow light conquered from the black mass of the darkness by the room and its warmth and its noise and its people. It was extraordinarily pleasant to enter this big room, so busy with pleasure, and to see the snow made visible only during its passage through the beams from the big windows, as if the wildness of the mountain valley had been admitted just so far as would give the delight of contrast to the guests who could see savagery as a backdrop of pretty, spinning white flakes.

There was a small band, consisting of piano, clarinet, and drum, playing the kind of jazz that makes a pleasant throb, like a blood-beat, behind conversation.

The family had moved themselves from the table in the restaurant to a table here and sat as before in a close group. The British couple found an empty table near them, which Doctor Schröder approved; and when the waiter came knew they had been right—the drinks were very expensive and this was not a place where one might lightly sip one drink for a whole evening while richer people drank seriously. One was expected to drink; people were drinking, although a small beer cost nearly ten shillings. They saw, too, that Doctor Schröder's boast that he had special privileges here because he was a friend of the proprietor was untrue. His passport here, as everywhere else, was his raw, shiny face. When the proprietor glanced towards him during his hospitable passage among the tables, he did so with a nod and a smile, but it was a smile that had the over-kindness of controlled hostility. And his eyes lingered briefly on the British couple, who, after this inspection, were forced to feel that everyone else in this place was German. The Americans were in their own rich hotels; the impoverished British in the cheap guest houses; this place was for wealthy Germans. And the British couple wondered at the insistence of

Doctor Schröder in bringing them here. Was it possible that
he really believed he had a special place in the heart of the
proprietor? Yes, it was; he kept smiling and nodding after
the turned back of the fat host, as if to say: You see, he
knows me; then smiling at them, proud of his achievement.
For which he was prepared to pay heavily in actual money. He
counted out the price of the drinks with the waiter with a
painful care for the small change of currency that they understood very well. What recompense could they possibly give
this man; what was he wanting so badly? Was it really only
that he wanted to live and work in Britain?

Again Doctor Schröder began to talk, and again of his admiration for their country, leaning across the table, looking
into their faces, as if this was a message of incalculable importance to them both.

He was interrupted by the clarinet player who stood up,
took a note from the regular ground-throb of the music, and
began to develop a theme of his own from it. Couples went
on to a small area of shiny floor not occupied by tables, and
which was invaded at every moment by the hurrying waiters
with their trays of drinks. They were dancing, these people,
for the pleasure not of movement, but of contact. A dozen or
a score of men and women, seemingly held upright by the
pressure of the seated guests around them, idled together,
loosely linked, smiling, sceptical, good-natured with the practice
of pleasure.

Immediately the dancing was broken up because the group
of folk singers had come in at the big glass entrance door, in
their demure conventual dress, and now stood by the band
waiting.

The woman at the next table gave a large cheerful shrug
and said, "This is the fifth time. This is my fifth home-evening."
People turned to smile at the words *heimat-abend*, indulgent
with the handsome woman and her look of spoiled enjoyment.
Already one of the folk singers was moving among the tables
to collect their fee, which was high; and already the rich Papa
was thrusting towards the girl a heap of money, disdaining
the change with a shake of his head—change, however, which
she did not seem in any urgency to give him. When she reached
the table where our couple sat with Doctor Schröder, Hamish
paid, and not with good grace. After all, the prices were high

enough here without having to pay more for folk songs which
one did not necessarily want to listen to at all.

When the girl had made her rounds and collected her money,
she rejoined the group, which formed itself together near the
band and sang, one after another, songs of the valley, in which
yodelling figured often and loudly, earning loud applause.

It was clear that Doctor Schröder, who listened to the group
with a look of almost yearning nostalgia, did not feel its
intrusion as an irritant at all. Folk songs, his expression said,
were something he could listen to all night. He clapped often
and glanced at his guests, urging them to share his sentimental
enjoyment.

At last the group left; the clarinet summoned the dancers to
the tiny floor; and Doctor Schröder resumed his hymn of love
for Britain. Tragic, he said, having stated and restated the
theme of praise—tragic that these two countries had ever had
to fight at all. Tragic that natural friends should have been
divided by the machinations of interested and sinister groups.
The British couple's eyes met ironically over the unspoken
phrase "international Jewry," and even with the consciousness
of being pedantic, if not unfair. But Doctor Schröder did not
believe in the unstated. He said that international Jewry had
divided the two natural masters of Europe, Germany and
Britain; and it was his passionate belief that in the future these
two countries should work together for the good of Europe
and thus, obviously, of the whole world. Doctor Schröder had
had good friends, friends who were almost brothers, killed on
the fronts where British and German troops had been manoeu-
vred into hostility; and he grieved over them even now as one
does for sacrificed victims.

Doctor Schröder paused, fixed them with the glare of his
eyes, and said: "I wish to tell you that I, too, was wounded;
perhaps you have not noticed. I was wounded on the Russian
front. My life was despaired of. But I was saved by the skill
of our doctors. My entire face is a witness to the magnificent
skill of our German doctors."

The British couple hastened to express their surprise and
congratulations. Oddly enough, they felt a lessened obligation
toward compassion because of Doctor Schröder's grotesque and
touching belief that his face was nearly normal enough to be
unnoticed. He said that the surface of his face had burned off

when a tank beside him had exploded into pieces, showering him with oil. He had fought for three years with the glorious armies of his country all over the Ukraine. He spoke like a survivor from the Grande Armée to fellow admirers of "The Other," inviting and expecting interested congratulation. "Those Russians," he said, "are savages. Barbarians. No one would believe the atrocities they committed. Unless you had seen it with your own eyes, you would not believe the brutality the Russians are capable of."

The British couple, now depressed into silence, and even past the point where they could allow their eyes to meet in ironical support of each other, sat watching the languidly revolving dancers.

Doctor Schröder said insistently, "Do you know that those Russians would shoot at our soldiers as they walked through the streets of a village? An ordinary Russian peasant, if he got the chance, would slaughter one of our soldiers? And even the women—I can tell you cases of Russian women murdering our soldiers after pretending to be buddies with them."

Mary and Hamish kept their peace and wondered how Doctor Schröder had described to himself the mass executions, the hangings, the atrocities of the German Army in Russia. They did not wonder long, for he said, "We were forced to defend ourselves. Yes, I can tell you that we had to defend ourselves against the savagery of those people. The Russians are monsters."

Mary Parrish roused herself to say, "Not such monsters, perhaps, as the Jews?" And she tried to catch and hold the fanatic eyes of their host with her own. He said, "Ah, yes, we had many enemies." His eyes, moving fast from Hamish's face to Mary's, paused and wavered. It occurred to him perhaps that they were not entirely in accordance with him. For a second his ugly, blistered mouth twisted in what might have been doubt. He said politely, "Of course, our Führer went too far in his zeal against our enemies. But he understood the needs of our country."

"It is the fate of great men," said Hamish, in the quick sarcastic voice that was the nearest he ever got to expressed anger, "to be misunderstood by the small-minded."

Doctor Schröder was now unmistakably in doubt. He was silent, examining their faces with his eyes, into which all the expression of his scarred face was concentrated, while they suffered the inner diminishment and confusion that happen when the assumptions on which one bases one's life are attacked. They were thinking dubiously that this was the voice of madness. They were thinking that they knew no one in Britain who would describe it as anything else. They were thinking that they were both essentially, self-consciously, of that element in their nation dedicated to not being insular, to not falling into the errors of complacency; and they were, at this moment, feeling something of the despair that people like them had felt ten, fifteen years ago, watching the tides of madness rise while the reasonable and the decent averted their eyes. At the same time, they were feeling an extraordinary but undeniable reluctance to face the fact that Doctor Schröder might represent any more than himself. No, they were assuring themselves, this unfortunate man is simply a cripple, scarred mentally as well as physically, a bit of salvage from the last war.

At this moment the music again stopped, and there was an irregular clapping all over the room; clearly there was to be a turn that the people there knew and expected.

Standing beside the piano was a small, smiling man who nodded greetings to the guests. He was dark, quick-eyed, with an agreeable face that the British couple instinctively described as "civilised." He nodded to the pianist, who began to improvise an accompaniment to his act; he was half-singing, half-talking the verse of a song or ballad about a certain general whose name the British couple did not recognise. The accompaniment was a steady, military-sounding thump-thump against which the right hand wove fragments of Deutschland Uber Alles and the Horst Wessel Song. The refrain was: "And now he sits in Bonn."

The next verse was about an admiral, also now sitting in Bonn.

The British couple understood that the song consisted of the histories of a dozen loyal German militarists who had been over-zealous in their devotion to their Führer; had been sentenced by the Allied courts of justice to various terms of imprisonment, or to death; "and now they sat in Bonn."

All that was fair enough. It sounded like a satire on Allied policy in Germany, which—so both these conscientious people knew and deplored—tended to be over-generous to the ex-murderers of the Nazi regime. What could be more heartening than to find their own view expressed there, in this comfortable resort of the German rich? And what more surprising?

They looked at Doctor Schröder and saw his eyes gleaming with pleasure. They looked back at the urbane, ironical little singer, who was performing with the assurance of one who knows himself to be perfectly at one with his audience, and understood that this was the type of ballad adroitly evolved to meet the needs of an occupied people forced to express themselves under the noses of a conqueror. True that the American Army was not here, in this room, this evening; but even if they had been, what possible exception could they have taken to the words of this song?

It was a long ballad, and when it was ended there was very little applause. Singer and audience exchanged with each other smiles of discreet understanding, and the little man bowed this way and that. He then straightened himself, looked at the British couple, and bowed to them. It was as if the room caught its breath. Only when they looked at Doctor Schröder's face, which showed all the malicious delight of a child who had thumbed his nose behind teacher's back, did they understand what a demonstration of angry defiance that bow had been. And they understood, with a sinking of the heart, the depths of furious revengeful humiliation which made such a very slight gesture so extremely satisfying to these rich burgesses, who merely glanced discreetly, smiling slightly, at these conquerors in their midst—conquerors who were so much shabbier than they were, so much more worn and tired—and turned away, exchanging glances of satisfaction, to their batteries of gleaming glasses filled with wine and with beer.

And now Mary and Hamish felt that this demonstration, which presumably Doctor Schröder had shared in, perhaps even invited, released them from any obligation to him; and they looked at him with open dislike, indicating that they wished to leave.

Besides, the waiter stood beside them, showing an open insolence that was being observed and admired by the handsome matron and her husband and her son; the girl was, as usual, dreaming some dream of her own and not looking at anyone in particular. The waiter bent over them, put his hands on their still half-filled glasses, and asked what they would have.

Hamish and Mary promptly drank what remained of their beer and rose. Doctor Schröder rose with them. His whole knobby, ugly body showed agitation and concern. Surely they weren't going? Surely, when the evening was just beginning, and very soon they would have the privilege of hearing again the talented singer who had just retired, but only for a short interval. Did they realise that he was a famous artist from M——, a man who nightly sang to crammed audiences, who was engaged by the management of this hotel, alas, only for two short weeks of the winter season?

This was either the most accomplished insolence or another manifestation of Doctor Schröder's craziness. For a moment the British couple wondered if they had made a mistake and had misunderstood the singer's meaning. But one glance around the faces of the people at the near tables was enough: each face expressed a discreetly hidden smile of satisfaction at the rout of the enemy—routed by the singer, and by the waiter, their willing servant who was nevertheless at this moment exchanging democratic grins of pleasure with the handsome matron.

Doctor Schröder was mad, and that was all there was to it. He both delighted in the little demonstration of hostility and, in some involved way of his own, wanted them to delight in it —probably out of brotherly love for him. And now he was quite genuinely agitated and hurt because they were going.

The British couple went out, past the smiling band, past the conscious waiter, while Doctor Schröder followed. They went down the iced steps of the hotel and stopped by the legless man, who was still rooted in the snow like a plant, where Hamish gave him all the change he had, which amounted to the price of another round of drinks had they stayed in the big warm room.

Doctor Schröder watched this and said at once, with indignant reproach, "You should not do this. It is not expected. Such people should be locked away." All his suspicion had returned; they must, obviously, be rich, and they had been lying to him.

Mary and Hamish went without speaking down the snow-soft street, through a faint fall of white snow; and Doctor

Schröder came striding behind them, breathing heavily. When they reached the door of the little house where they had a room, he ran around them and stood facing them, saying hurriedly, "And so I shall see you tomorrow at the autobus, nine-thirty."

"We will get in touch with you," said Hamish politely, which, since they did not know his address, and had not asked for it, was as good as dismissing him.

Doctor Schröder leaned toward them, examining their faces with his gleaming, suspicious eyes. He said, "I will attend you in the morning," and left them.

They let themselves in and ascended the shallow wooden stairs to their room in silence. The room was low and comfortable, gleaming with well-polished wood. There was an old-fashioned rose-patterned jug and basin on the washstand and an enormous bed laden with thick eiderdowns. A great, shining, blue-tiled stove filled half a wall. Their landlady had left a note pinned to one of the fat pillows, demanding politely that they should leave, in their turn, a note for her outside their door, saying at what hour they wished to receive their breakfast tray. She was the widow of the pastor. She now lived by letting this room to the summer and winter visitors. She knew this couple were not married because she had had, by regulation, to take down particulars from their passports. She had said nothing of any disapproval she might have felt. The gods of the tourist trade must not be offended by any personal prejudice she might hold; and she must have prejudices, surely, as the widow of a man of God, even against a couple so obviously respectable as this one?

Mary said, "I wish she'd turn us out in a fit of moral indignation. I wish someone would have a fit of moral indignation about something, instead of everything simmering and festering in the background."

To which he replied, with the calm of a practical man, "We will get up extremely early and leave this valley before our friend Doctor Fascist can see us. I don't think I could bear to exchange even one more word with him." He wrote a short note to the widow of the pastor, demanding breakfast for seven o'clock; left it outside the door; and, thus well-organised, invited Mary to come to bed and stop worrying.

They got into bed and lay side by side. This was not a night when their arms could hold any comfort for each other. This was a night when they were not a couple, they were two people. Their dead were in the room with them—if Lise, his wife, could be called dead. For how were they to know? War above all breeds a knowledge of the fantastic, and neither of them heard one of the extraordinary and impossible stories of escape, coincidence, and survival without thinking: Perhaps Lise is alive somewhere after all. And the possible aliveness of Hamish's dead wife had kept alive the image of the very young medical student who, being a medical student, had no right to risk himself in the air at all; but who had in fact taken wing out of his furious misery and anger because of the Nazis and had crashed in flames a year later. These two, the pretty and vivacious Lise and the gallant and crusading airman, stood by the enormous, eiderdown-weighted bed and said softly: You must include us, you must include us.

And so it was a long time before Mary and Hamish slept.

Both awoke again in the night, aware of the snow-sheen on the windowpanes, listening to the soft noises of the big porcelain stove which sounded as if there were a contented animal breathing beside them in the room. Now they thought that they were leaving this valley because, out of some weakness of character apparently inherent in both of them, they had put themselves in a position where, if they took a room higher up the valley, it would have to be a room chosen for them by Doctor Schröder, since they could not bring themselves to be finally rude to him because of that scarred face of his.

No, they preferred to conclude that Doctor Schröder summed up in his personality and being everything they hated in this country, Germany, the great catalyst and mirror of Europe: summed it up and presented it to them direct and unambiguously, in such a way that they must reject or accept it.

Yet how could they do either? For to meet Doctor Schröder at all made it inevitable that these two serious and conscience-driven people must lie awake and think: One nation is not very different from another. . . . (For if one did not take one's stand on this proposition where did one end?) And therefore it followed that they must think: What in Britain corresponds to Doctor Schröder? What unpleasant forces are this moment simmering in the sewers of our national soul that might explode suddenly into shapes like Doctor Schröder? Well, then? And what deplorable depths of complacency there must be in

us both that we should feel so superior to Doctor Schröder—
that we should wish only that he might be pushed out of sight
somewhere, like a corpse in a house full of living people; or
masked like a bad smell; or exorcised like an evil spirit?

Were they or were they not on vacation? They were; and
therefore exempt by definition from lying awake and thinking
about the last war; lying awake and worrying about the possible
next war; lying awake and wondering what perverse masochism
had brought them here at all.

At the dead and silent hour of four, when not a light glimmered anywhere in the village, they were both awake, lying
side by side in the great feather-padded bed, discussing Doctor
Schröder in depth. They analysed him politically, psychologically, and medically—particularly medically—and at such
length that when the maid came in with their early breakfast
they were extremely reluctant to wake up. But they forced
themselves to wake, to eat and to dress, and then went downstairs where their landlady was drinking coffee in her kitchen.
They put their problem to her. Yesterday they had agreed to stay
with her for a week. Today they wanted to leave. Since it was
the height of the season, presumably she would let her room today? If not, of course they would be delighted to pay what they
were morally bound to do.

Frau Stohr dismissed the subject of payment as irrelevant.
At this time of the year her bell rang a dozen times a day with
enquiries for rooms by people who had arrived at the station
and hoped, usually over-optimistically, to find empty rooms in
the village. Frau Stohr was upset that her two guests wished
to leave. They were not comfortable? They were badly served?

They hastened to assure her that the place was everything
they wanted. At the moment they felt it was. Frau Stohr was
the most pleasant sight in an early morning after a night of
conscience-searching. She was a thin and elderly lady, her
white hair drawn back into a tight knot which was stuck
through with stiff utilitarian pins almost the size of knitting
needles. Her face was severe, but tranquil and kindly. She
wore a long, full, black woollen skirt, presumably a practical
descendant of the great woollen skirts of the local peasant
costume. She wore a long-sleeved striped woollen blouse fastened high at the throat with a gold brooch.

They found it very hard to say that they wanted to leave

the valley the day after arriving in it. The rectitude of this admirable old lady made it difficult. So they said they had decided to take a room farther up the valley where the snow slopes organised for skiing would be closer to the villages. For, above all, they did not want to hurt Frau Stohr's national feelings; they intended to slip quietly down to the station and take the first train away from the place, away and out of Germany into France.

Frau Stohr instantly agreed. She had always thought it more suitable for the serious skiers to find homes farther up the valley. But there were people who came to the winter sports not for the sport, but for the atmosphere of the sport. As for herself, she never tired of seeing the young people at their tricks on the snow. Of course, when she had been a girl, it was not a question of tricks at all; skis were simply a means of getting from one place to another quickly . . . but now, of course, all that had changed, and someone like herself who had been almost born on skis, like all the children of the valley, would find it embarrassing to stand on skis again with nothing to show in the way of jumps and turns. Of course, at her age she seldom left the house, and so she did not have to expose her deficiencies. But her two guests, being serious skiers, must be feeling frustrated, knowing that all the long runs, and the big ski lifts were at the head of the valley. Luckily she knew of a lady in the last village of the valley who had a free room and would be just the person to look after them.

Here she mentioned the name of the lady recommended by Doctor Schröder the night before, and it was extraordinary how this name, yesterday associated with every kind of unpleasantness, became attractive and reassuring, simply because it came from the lips of Frau Stohr.

Mary and Hamish exchanged looks and came to a decision without speaking. In the sober light of early morning, all the very sound arguments against leaving the valley returned to them. And after all, Doctor Schröder was staying in O—— itself, and not in the village thirty miles up the valley. At worst he might come and visit them.

Frau Stohr offered to telephone Frau Länge, who was a good woman and an unfortunate one. Her husband had been killed in the last war. Here Frau Stohr smiled at them with the gentle tolerance of the civilised who take it for granted that war between nations need not destroy their common humanity and understanding. Yes, yes, as long as men were so stupid there would be wars and, afterwards, widows like poor Frau Länge, who had lost not only her husband but her two sons, and now lived alone with her daughter, taking in lodgers.

Frau Stohr and the British couple, united on the decent common ground of the international humanitarian conscience, smiled at each other, thinking compassionately of Frau Länge. Then Frau Stohr went to the telephone and engaged the room on behalf of her two guests, for whom she was prepared to vouch personally. Then they settled the bill, thanked each other, and separated—Mary and Hamish with their cases in their hands and their skis over their shoulders towards the bus stop, and Frau Stohr to her knitting and her cup of coffee in her big heated kitchen.

It was a clear morning, the sun sparkling pinkly over the slopes of snow where the pine trees stood up, stiff and dark. The first bus of the day was just leaving, and they found places in it. They sat behind two small, pigtailed blond girls who saw nobody else in the bus, but held each other's hands and sang one folk song after another in small, clear voices. Everyone in the bus turned to smile with affectionate indulgence at them. The bus climbed slowly up and up, along the side of the snow-filled valleys; and as the skiing villages came into sight, one after another, the bus stopped, shedding some passengers and taking on others, but always full; up and up while the two small girls sang, holding hands, looking earnestly into each other's faces, so as to be sure they were keeping time, and never once repeating a song.

The British couple thought it unlikely that they could find, in their own country, two small girls who could sing, without repeating themselves, for two solid hours of a bus journey, even if their British stiff-lippedness would allow them to open their mouths in public in the first place. These two singing children comforted Mary and Hamish quite remarkably. This was the real Germany—rather oldfashioned, a bit sentimental, warm, simple, kindly. Doctor Schröder and what he stood for was an unlucky and not very important phenomenon. Everything they had felt yesterday was the result of being overtired. Now they examined the pleasant villages through which they passed with anticipation, hoping that the one they were committed to would be equally as full of modest wooden chalets and apparently inexpensive restaurants.

It was. At the very head of the valley where the mountain barrier beyond which lay Innsbruck rose tall and impregnable, there was a small village, as charming as all the others. Here, somewhere, was the house of Frau Länge. They made enquiries at a hotel and were directed. A path ran off from the village up-hill among the pine woods to a small house about a mile away. The isolation of this house appealed naturally to the instincts of the British couple, who trudged towards it over cushions of glittering snow, feeling grateful to Frau Stohr. The path was nar-row, and they had constantly to stand aside while skiers in bright clothes whizzed past them, laughing and waving. The proficiency of the sun-bronzed gods and goddesses of the snow-fields discouraged Mary and Hamish, and perhaps half the attraction of that isolated house was that they could make their tame flights over the snow in comparative privacy.

The house was square, small, wooden; built on a low mound of snow in a space surrounded by pine woods. Frau Länge was waiting for them at her front door, smiling. For some reason they had imagined her in the image of Frau Stohr; but she was a good twenty years younger, a robust, straw-headed, red-cheeked woman wearing a tight scarlet sweater and a tight, bright blue skirt. Behind her was a girl, obviously her daughter, a healthy, brown, flaxen-haired girl. Both women occupied themselves with a frank and intensive examination of their new guests for the space of time it took them to cross the snow to the house. The room they were given was at the front of the house, looking away from the village up into a side valley. It was a room like the one they had occupied for the one night at Frau Stohr's: low, large, gleaming with waxed wood, and warmed by an enormous tiled stove. Frau Länge took their passports to write down their particulars, and when she returned them it was with a change of manner which made Mary Parrish and Hamish Anderson know they had been accepted into a free-masonry with their hostess. She said, while her frankly vulgar blue eyes continued a minute examination of them and their belongings, that her dear aunt Frau Stohr, who was not really her aunt, just a second cousin, called Aunt out of respect for her age and position as widow of the pastor, had spoken for them; that she had every confidence in any person recommended from that quarter. And she had heard, too, from dear Doctor Schröder, who was an old friend, a friend of many years, ah— what a brave man. Did they notice his face? Yes, truly? Did they know that for two years he had lain in hospital while a new face was moulded for him and covered with skin taken from his thighs? Poor man. Yes, it was the barbarity of those Russians that was responsible for Doctor Schröder's face. Here she gave an exaggerated sigh and a shrug and left them.

They reminded themselves that they had hardly slept for three nights of their precious holiday, and this doubtless accounted for their present lack of enthusiasm for the idea of putting on skis. They went to sleep and slept the day through; that evening they were served a heavy meal in the livingroom by Frau Länge herself, who stood chatting to them until they asked her to sit down. Which she did, and proceeded to cross-examine them about the affairs of the British royal family. It was impossible to exaggerate the degree of enthusiasm aroused in Frau Länge by the royal family. She followed every move made by any member of it through a dozen illustrated papers. She knew what they all ate, how they liked things cooked, and how served. She knew the type of corset favoured by the Queen, the names of the doctors attending her, the methods of up-bringing planned for the royal children, the favourite colours of the two royal Elizabeths and the royal Margaret.

The British couple, who were by temperament republicans and who would have described themselves as such had the word not, at that time, been rather *vieux jeu*, acquired an impressive amount of information about "their" royal family, and felt inadequate, for they were unable to answer any of her questions.

To escape from Frau Länge they went back to their room. They discovered that this house was not at all as isolated as it had seemed during the day when the pine trees had concealed from them buildings farther up the little side valley. Lights sparkled in the trees, and it seemed that there were at least two large hotels less than half a mile away. Music streamed towards them across the dark snow.

In the morning they found there were two American hotels; that is, hotels specifically for the recreation of American troops. Frau Länge used the word "American" with a mixture of admiration and hatred. And she took it for granted that they, who were after all partners with the Americans (and the Russians, of course) in this business of policing the defeated country, should share this emotion with her. It was because they shared with her, Frau Länge, the quality of not being rich.

"Ah," she said, with a false and hearty shrug of her shoulders, a false humility in her voice, "it is a terrible thing, the way they come here and behave as if they owned our country." And she stood at the window, while the British couple ate their breakfast, watching the American soldiers and their wives and their girl friends swooping past down the slopes; and on her face was a bitter envy, an admiring spite, as if she were thinking: Yes? Then wait and see!

Later that day they saw the daughter standing displayed on her doorstep in well-cut ski trousers and sweater, like a girl in a poster, looking at the American soldiers. And they heard her call out, every time a single man went past: "Yank-ee." The soldier would look up and wave, and she waved back shouting: "I love you, Buddy." At last one came over; and the two went off on skis, down to the village.

Frau Länge, who had seen them watching, said, "Ach, these young girls, I was one myself." She waited until they smiled their tolerant complicity—and waited in such a way they felt they could do no less, seeing that their passports proved they had no right to different standards; and said, "Yes, when one is young one is foolish. I remember how I fell in love with every man I saw. Ach, yes, it was so. I was living in Munich when I was a girl. Yes, youth has no discrimination. I was in love with our Führer, yes, it is true. And before that in love with a communist leader who lived in our street. And now I tell my Lili it is lucky that she falls in love with the American Army, because she is in love with democracy." Frau Länge giggled and sighed.

At all the heavy meals she served them—sausage and sauerkraut and potatoes; sauerkraut, potatoes, and beef stew—she stood by them, talking, or sat modestly at the other end of the polished wood table, one plump forearm resting before her, one hand stroking and arranging her bright yellow hair, and talked and talked. She told them the history of her life while they ate. Her mother died of hunger in the First World War. Her father was a carpenter. Her elder brother was a political; he was a Social Democrat, and so she had been a Social Democrat, too.

And then he had been a communist; and so she voted for the communists, God forgive her. And then there came the Führer; and her brother told her he was a good man, and so she became a Nazi. Of course, she was very young and foolish in those days. She told them, giggling, how she had stood in those vast crowds while the Führer spoke, shrieking with enthusiasm. "For my brother was in the uniform, yes, and he was so goodlooking, you would never believe it."

The British couple remembered listening on the radio to the sound of those fanatic crowds roaring and yelling approval to the dedicated, hysterical, drum-beating voice; they watched Frau Länge and imagined her a young girl, sweating and scarlet-faced, yelling with the thousands, arm in arm with her girl friend, who was of course in love with the uniformed brother. Then, afterwards cooling her sore throat with beer in a cafe, she would perhaps have giggled with the girl friend at the memory of her intoxication. Or perhaps she had not giggled. At any rate, she had married and come here to the mountains and had three children.

And now her man was dead, killed on the front near Stalingrad. And one son had been killed in North Africa, and another at Avranches. And when her Lili leaned out of the window giggling and waving at a passing American soldier she giggled and said, with a glance at the British couple, "Lucky for us we aren't in the Russian zone, because if so Lili would have loved a Russki." And Lili giggled and leaned farther out of the window and waved and called, "Buddy, I love you."

Frau Länge, conscious perhaps that the continued politeness of her British guests need not necessarily mean agreement, would sometimes straighten her shoulders into prim self-righteousness, look in front of her with lowered and self-conscious eyelids, and say with a murmuring shocked rectitude: "Yes, Lili, say what you like, but we are lucky this time to have English people as guests. They are people like ourselves who have suffered from this terrible war. And they will go back home and tell their friends what we suffer because our country is divided. For it is clear they are shocked. They did not know of the humiliations we have to undergo."

At this Mary Parrish and Hamish Anderson would say nothing at all, but politely passed each other the salt or the dumplings and shortly afterwards excused themselves and went to their room. They were sleeping a good deal, for, after all, they were people kept permanently short of sleep. And they ate heartily if not well. They skied a little and lay often in the sun, acquiring a layer of brown that they would lose within a week of returning to London. They were feeling rested. They were in a lethargy of physical contentment. They listened to Frau Länge, accepted her scolding because of their total ignorance of the manners and habits of the royal families of Europe, watched the daughter go off with this U.S. soldier or that; and when Doctor Schröder arrived one afternoon to take coffee with Frau Länge, they were happy to join the party. Frau Länge had explained to them that it was the dream of Doctor Schröder's life to reach the United States. Unfortunately, every attempt he had made to do this had failed. It was, perhaps, easy for them to arrange a visa for Doctor Schröder from London? No? It was difficult there, too? Ach, if she were a young woman she too would go to the United States; that was the country of the future, was it not? She did not blame Doctor Schröder that he wished so much to go there. And if she were in a position to assist him, they must believe her that she would, for friends should always help each other.

They had decided that it was Frau Länge's plan to marry Lili to the doctor. But it seemed Lili did not share this idea, for although she knew he was coming, she did not appear that evening. And perhaps Frau Länge was not altogether sorry, for while the word "flirtation" could hardly be used of a relationship like this one, it was extremely amiable. Frau Länge sighed a great deal, her silly blue eyes fastened on the terrible shining mask of her friend's face, saying, "*Ach, mein Gott, mein Gott, mein Gott!*" while Doctor Schröder accepted the tribute like a film star bored with flattery, making polite gestures of repudiation with one hand, using the other to eat with. He stayed the night, ostensibly on the old sofa in the kitchen.

In the morning he woke Mary and Hamish at seven to say that unfortunately he was leaving the valley because he was due to take up his duties at the hospital, that he was delighted to have been of service to them, that he hoped they would arrange their return journey so as to pass through the city where his hospital was, and asked for their assurances that they would.

The departure of Doctor Schröder brought it home to them that their own vacation would end in a week and that they were bored, or on the point of becoming bored. They had much better rouse themselves, leave the snow mountains, and go down to one of the cities below, take a cheap room, and make an effort to meet some ordinary people. By this they meant neither the rich industrialists who frequented this valley, nor people like Frau Stohr, who were manifestly something left over from an older and more peaceful time; nor like Frau Länge and her daughter Lili; nor like Doctor Schröder. Saying goodbye to Frau Länge was almost painless for, as she said instantly, a day never passed without at least one person knocking on her door and asking for a room because, as everyone in the village knew, she gave good value for money. This was true: Frau Länge was a natural landlady; she had given them far more than had been contracted for in the way of odd cups of coffee and above all in hours of fraternal conversation. But at last she accepted their plea that they wanted to spend a week in their professional guise, seeing hospitals and making contact with their fellow doctors. "In that case," she said at once, "it is lucky that you know Doctor Schröder, for there could be no better person to show you everything that you need to see." They said that they would look up Doctor Schröder the moment they arrived, if they should happen to pass through his town, and with this the goodbyes were made.

They made the journey by bus down the long winding valley to the mother village, O——, caught the little rickety train, spent another uncomfortable night sitting up side by side on the hard wooden benches, and at last reached the city of Z——, where they found a small room in a cheap hotel. And now they were pledged to contact ordinary people and widen their view of present-day Germany. They took short walks through the streets of the city, surrounded by ordinary people, looked into their faces, as tourists do, made up stories about them, and got into brief conversation from which they made large generalisations. And, like every earnest tourist, they indulged in fantasies of how they would stop some pleasant-faced person in the street and say: We are ordinary people, completely representative of the people of our country. You are obviously an ordinary person, representative of yours. Please divulge and unfold yourself to us, and we will do the same.

Whereupon this pleasant-faced person would let out an exclamation of delight, strike his forehead with his fist and say:

But my friends! There is nothing I would like better. With which he would take them to his house, flat, or room; and a deathless friendship would begin, strong enough to outlast any international misunderstandings, accidents, incidents, wars, or other phenomena totally undesired by the ordinary people on both sides.

They did not contact Doctor Schröder, since they had taken good care not to choose the town he was working in. But from time to time they thought how pleasant it would have been if Doctor Schröder had not been such an utterly disgusting person; if he had been a hard-working, devoted, idealistic doctor like themselves, who could initiate them into the medical life of Germany, or at least, of one city, without politics entering their intercourse at all.

Thinking wistfully along these lines led them into a course of action foreign to their naturally diffident selves. It so happened that about a year before, Doctor Anderson had got a letter from a certain Doctor Kroll, who was attached to a hospital just outside the city of Z——, congratulating him on a paper he had published recently and enclosing a paper of his own which dealt with a closely related line of research. Hamish remembered reading Doctor Kroll's paper and diagnosing it as typical of the work put out by elderly and established doctors who are no longer capable of ploughing original furrows in the field of medicine but, because they do not wish to seem as if they have lost all interest in original research, from time to time put out a small and harmless paper which amounts to an urbane comment on the work of other people. In short, Doctor Anderson had despised the paper sent to him by his colleague in Germany and had done no more than write him a brief letter of thanks. Now he remembered the incident and told Mary Parrish about it, and both wondered if they might telephone Doctor Kroll and introduce themselves. When they decided that they should, it was with a definite feeling that they were confessing a defeat. Now they were going to be professional people, nothing more. The "ordinary people" had totally eluded them. Conversations with three workmen (on busses), two housewives (in cafes), a businessman (on a train), two waiters and two maids (at the hotel) had left them dissatisfied. None of these people had come out with the final, pithy, conclusive statement about modern Germany that they so badly needed. In fact none of them had said more than what their counterparts in Britain would have done. The nearest to a political comment any one of them had made was the complaint by one of the maids that she did not earn enough money and would very likely go to England where, she understood, wages were much higher.

No, contact with that real, sound, oldfashioned, healthy Germany, as symbolised by the two little girls singing on the bus, had failed them. But certainly it must be there. Something which was a combination of the rather weary irony of the refugees both had known, the bitter affirmation of the songs of Bertolt Brecht, the fighting passion of a Dimitrov (though of course Dimitrov was not a German), the innocence of the little girls, the crashing chords of Beethoven's Fifth. These qualities were fused in their minds into the image of a tired, sceptical, sardonic, but tough personage, a sort of civilised philosopher prepared at any moment to pick up a rifle and fight for the good and the right and the true. But they had not met anyone remotely like this. As for the two weeks up in the valley, they had simply wiped them out. After all, was it likely that a valley given up wholly to the pursuit of pleasure, and all the year round at that, could be representative of anything but itself?

They would simply accept the fact that they had failed, and ring up Doctor Kroll, and spend the remaining days of their vacation acquiring information about medicine. They rang up Doctor Kroll, who, rather to their surprise, remembered the interesting correspondence he had had with Doctor Anderson and invited them to spend the next morning with him. He sounded not at all like the busy head of a hospital, but more like a host. Having made this arrangement, Doctors Parrish and Anderson were on the point of going out to find some cheap restaurant—for their reserve of money was now very small indeed—when Doctor Schröder was announced to them. He had travelled that afternoon all the way from S—— especially to greet them, having heard from his buddy Frau Länge that they were here. In other words, he must have telephoned or wired Frau Länge, who knew their address since she was forwarding letters for them; his need for them was so great that he had also travelled all the way from S——, an expensive business, as he did not hesitate to point out.

The British couple, once again faced with the scarred face

and bitter eyes of Doctor Schröder, once again felt a mixture of loathing and compassion and limply made excuses because they had chosen to stop in this town and not in S——. They said they could not possibly afford to spend the evening, as he wanted to do, in one of the expensive restaurants; refused to go as his guests, since he had already spent so much money on coming to meet them; and compromised on an agreement to drink beer with him. This they did in various beer cellars where the cohorts of the Führer used to gather in the old days. Doctor Schröder told them this in a way that could be taken either as if he were pointing out a tourist attraction or as if he were offering them the opportunity to mourn a lost glory with him. His manner towards them now fluctuated between hostility and a self-abasing politeness. They, for their part, maintained their own politeness, drank their beer, occasionally caught each other's eye, and suffered through an evening which, had it not been for Doctor Schröder, might have been a very pleasant one. From time to time he brought the conversation around to the possibilities of his working in Britain; and they repeated their warnings, until at last, although he had not mentioned the United States, they explained that getting visas to live in that part of the world would be no easier in Britain than it was here. Doctor Schröder was not at all discomposed when they showed that they were aware of his real objective. Not at all; he behaved as if he had told them from the start that the United States was his ideal country. Just as if he had never sung songs of praise to Britain, he now disparaged Britain as part of Europe, which was dead and finished, a parasite on the healthy body of America. Quite obviously all people of foresight would make their way to America—he assumed that they, too, had seen this obvious truth, and had possibly already made their plans? Of course he did not blame anyone for looking after himself first, that was a rule of nature; but friends should help each other. And who knew but that once they were all in America Doctor Schröder might be in a position to help Doctors Anderson and Parrish? The wheel of chance might very well bring such a thing to pass. Yes, it was always advisable in this world to plan well ahead. As for himself, he was not ashamed to admit that it was his first principle; that was why he was sitting this evening in the city of Z——, at their service. That was why he had arranged a day's leave from his own hospital—not the easiest thing to do, this, since he had just returned from a fortnight's holiday—in order to be their guide around the hospitals of Z——.

Mary and Hamish, after a long stunned silence, said that his kindness to them was overwhelming. But unfortunately they had arranged to spend tomorrow with Doctor Kroll of such-and-such a hopsital.

The eyes of Doctor Schröder showed a sudden violent animation. The shiny stretched mask of his face deepened its scarlet and, after a wild angry flickering of blue light at the name Kroll, the eyes settled into a steady, almost anguished glare of enquiry.

It appeared that at last they had hit upon, quite by chance, the way to silence Doctor Schröder.

"Doctor Kroll," he said, with the sigh of a man who, after long searching, finds the key. "Doctor Kroll. I see. Yes."

At last he had placed them. It seemed that Doctor Kroll's status was so high, and therefore, presumably, their status also, that he could not possibly aspire to any equality with them. Perfectly understandable that they did not need to emigrate to America, being the close friends of Doctor Kroll. His manner became bitter, brooding, and respectful, and at the most suggested that they might have said, nearly three weeks ago on that first evening in O——, that they were intimates of Doctor Kroll, thereby saving him all this anguish and trouble and expense.

Doctor Kroll, it emerged, was a man loaded with honours and prestige, at the very height of his profession. Of course, it was unfortunate that such a man should be afflicted in the way he was. . . .

And how was Doctor Kroll afflicted?

Why, didn't they know? Surely, they must! Doctor Kroll was for six months in every year a voluntary patient in his own hospital—yes, that was something to admire, was it not?— that a man of such brilliance should, at a certain point in every year, hand over his keys to his subordinates and submit to seeing a door locked upon himself, just as, for the other six months, he locked doors on other people. It was very sad, yes. But of course they must know all this quite well, since they had the privilege of Doctor Kroll's friendship.

Mary and Hamish did not like to admit that they had not

known it was a mental hospital that Doctor Kroll administered. If they did, they would lose the advantage of their immunity from Doctor Schröder, who had, obviously, already relinquished them entirely to a higher sphere. Meanwhile, since his evening was already wasted, and there was time to fill in, he was prepared to talk.

By the time the evening had drawn to a close in a beer cellar where one drank surrounded by great wooden barrels from which the beer was drawn off direct into giant-sized mugs—the apotheosis of all beer cellars—they had formed an image of Doctor Kroll as a very old, Lear-like man, proud and bitter in the dignified acceptance of his affliction; and although neither of them had any direct interest in the problems of the mentally sick, since Mary Parrish specialised in small children and Hamish Anderson in geriatrics, they were sympathetically looking forward to meeting this courageous old man.

The evening ended without any unpleasantness because of the invisible presence of Doctor Kroll. Doctor Schröder returned them to the door of their hotel, shook their hands, and wished them a happy conclusion to their vacation. The violent disharmony of his personality had been swallowed entirely by the self-abasing humility into which he had retreated, with which he was consoling himself. He said that he would look them up when he came to London, but it was merely conventional. He wished them a pleasant reunion with Doctor Kroll and strode off through the black, cold, blowing night towards the railway station, springing on his long lean legs like a black-mantled grasshopper—a hooded, bitter, energetic shape whirled about by flurries of fine white snow that glittered in the street lights like blown salt or sand.

Next morning it was still snowing. The British couple left their hotel early to find the right bus stop, which was at the other end of the city in a poor suburb. The snow fell listlessly from a low grey sky, and fine shreds of dingy snow lay sparse on the dark earth. The bombs of the recent war had laid the streets here flat for miles around. The streets were etched in broken outlines, and the newly laid railway lines ran clean and shining through them. The station had been bombed, and there was a wooden shed doing temporary duty until another could be built. A dark-wrapped, dogged crowd stood bunched around the bus stop. Nearby a mass of workmen were busy on a new building that rose fine and clean and white out of the miles of damaged houses. They looked like black and energetic insects at work against the stark white of the walls. The British couple stood hunching their cold shoulders and shifting their cold feet with the German crowd, and watched the builders. They thought that it was the bombs of their country which had created this havoc; thought of the havoc created in their country by the bombs of the people they now stood shoulder to shoulder with, and sank back slowly into a mood of listless depression. The bus was a long time coming. It seemed to grow colder. From time to time people drifted past to the station shed or added themselves to the end of the bus queues, or a woman went past with a shopping basket. Behind the ruined buildings rose the shapes and outlines of the city that had been destroyed and the outlines of the city that would be rebuilt. It was as if they stood solid among the ruins and ghosts of dead cities and cities not yet born. And Hamish's eyes were at work again on the faces of the people about them, fixed on the face of an old shawled woman who was passing; and it seemed as if the crowd, like the streets, became transparent and fluid, for beside them, behind them, among them stood the dead. The dead of two wars peopled the ruined square and jostled the living, a silent snow-bound multitude.

The silence locked the air. There was a low, deep thudding that seemed to come from under the earth. It was from a machine at work on the building site. The machine, low in the dirty snow, lifted black grappling arms like a wrestler or like someone in prayer; and the sound of its labouring travelled like a sensation of movement through the cold earth, as if the soil were hoarsely breathing. And the workmen swarmed and worked around the machine and over the steep sides of the new building. They were like children playing with bricks. Half an hour before a giant of a man in black jackboots had strode past their block building and carelessly kicked it down. Now the children were building it again, under the legs of a striding race of great black-booted giants. At any moment another pair of trampling black legs might come straddling over the building and down it would go, down into ruin, to the accompaniment of crashing thunder and bolts of lightning. All over the soil of patient Europe, soil soaked again and again by blood, soil broken again and again by angry metal, the small figures were at work, building their bright new houses among the shells and the ruins of war; and in their eyes was the shadow from the great marching jackbooted feet, and beside each of them, beside every one of them, their dead, the invisible, swarming, memoried dead.

The crowd continued to wait. The machine kept up its hoarse breathing. From time to time a shabby bus came up, a few people climbed in, the bus went off, and more people came dark-clothed through the thinly falling snow to join the crowd, which was very similar to a British crowd in its stolid disciplined quality of patience.

At last a bus with the number they had been told to look for drew up, and they got into it with a few other people. The bus was half-empty. Almost at once it left the city behind. Doctor Kroll's hospital, like so many of the similar hospitals in Britain, was built well outside the city boundaries so that the lives of healthy people might not be disturbed by thoughts of those who had to retreat behind the shelter of high walls. The way was straight on a good narrow road, recently rebuilt, over flat black plains streaked and spotted with snow. The quiet, windless air was full of fine particles of snow that fell so slowly it seemed that the sky was falling, as if the slow weight of the snow dragged the grey covering over the black flat plains down to the earth. They travelled forward in a world without colour.

Doctor Kroll's hospital made itself visible a long way off over the plain. It consisted of a dozen or more dark, straight buildings set at regular angles to each other, like the arrangements of the sheds in the concentration camps of the war. Indeed, at a distance, the resemblance to the mechanical order of a concentration camp was very great; but as the bus drew nearer the buildings grew and spread into their real size and surrounded themselves with a regular pattern of lawns and shrubs.

The bus set them down outside a heavy iron gate; and at the entrance of the main building, which was high and square, they were welcomed by a doctor whose enthusiasm was expressly delegated from Doctor Kroll, who was impatiently waiting for them upstairs. They went up several staircases and along many corridors, and thought that whatever bleak impression this place might give from the outside, great care had been given to banishing bleakness from within. The walls were all covered by bright pictures, which there was no time to examine now, as

they hurried after their busy guide; flowers stood on high pedestals at every turning of the corridor, and the walls and ceiling
and woodwork were painted in clean white and blue. They were
thinking sympathetically of the storm-driven Lear whom they
were so soon to meet, as they passed through these human and
pleasant corridors; they were even thinking that perhaps it was
an advantage to have as director of a mental hospital a man
who knew what it was like to spend time inside it as a victim.
But their guide remarked, "This is, of course, the administrative
block and the doctors' quarters. Doctor Kroll will be happy to
show you the hospital itself later."

With this he shook them by the hand, nodded a goodbye and
went, leaving them outside the half-open door of what looked
like a middleclass livingroom.

A hearty voice called out that they must come in; and they
went into a suite of two rooms, half-divided by sheets of sliding
glass, brightly lighted, pleasantly furnished, and with nothing
in it reminiscent of an office but a single small desk in the
farther of the two rooms. Behind the desk sat a handsome man
of late middleage who was rising to greet them. It occurred to
them, much too late, that this must be Doctor Kroll; and so their
greetings, because they were shocked, were much less enthusiastic than his. His greetings were in any case much more like a
host's than a colleague's. He was apparently delighted to see
them and pressed them to sit down while he ordered them some
coffee. This he did by going to the house telephone on the desk
in the room beyond the pane of glass; and the two looked at
each other, exchanging surprise, and then, finally, pleasure.

Doctor Knoll was, to begin with, extremely distinguished, and
they remembered something Doctor Schröder had said the night
before, to the effect that he came from an old and respected
family; that he was, in short, an aristocrat. They had to accept
the word when looking at Doctor Kroll himself, even though they
could not conceivably take it from Doctor Schröder. Doctor Kroll
was rather tall and managed to combine heaviness and leanness
in a remarkable way, for while he was a man of whom one instinctively wondered how much he must weigh when he stood
on a scale, he was not fat, or even plump. But he was heavy; and
his face, which had strong and prominent bones, carried a
weight of large-pored flesh. Yet one would have said, because of
the prominent dome of pale forehead and because of the large,

commanding nose, and because of the deep dark lively eyes, that it was a lean face. And his movements were not those of a heavy man; he had quick impatient gestures and his large, handsome hands were in constant movement. He returned, smiling, from giving orders about the coffee, sat down in an easy chair opposite the two British doctors, and proceeded to entertain them in the most urbane and pleasant way in the world. He spoke admirable English, he knew a good deal about Britain, and he now discussed the present state of affairs in Britain with assurance.

His admiration for Britain was immense. And this time the British couple were flattered. This was something very different from hearing praise from that appalling Doctor Schröder. Until the coffee came, and while they were drinking it, and for half an hour afterwards, they discussed Britain and its institutions. The British couple listened to a view of Britain that they disagreed with profoundly, but without irritation, since it was natural that a man like this should hold conservative ideas. Doctor Kroll believed that a limited monarchy was the best guarantee against disorder and was, in fact, the reason for the well-known British tolerance, which was a quality he admired more than any other. Speaking as a German, and therefore peculiarly equipped to discuss the dangers of anarchy, he would say that the best thing the Allied Armies could have done would have been to impose upon Germany a royal family, created, if necessary, from the shreds and fragments of the unfortunately dwindling royal families of Europe. Further, he believed that this should have been done at the end of the First World War, at the Treaty of Versailles. When Britain, usually so perspicacious in matters of this kind, had left Germany without a royal safeguard, they had made the worst mistake of their history. For a royal family would have imposed good conduct and respect for institutions and made an upstart like Hitler impossible.

At this point the eyes of the British pair met again, though briefly. There was no doubt that to hear Hitler described as an upstart revived some of the sensations they felt when listening to Doctor Schröder or Frau Länge. A few seconds later they heard him being referred to as a mongrel upstart, and unease definitely set in, beneath the well-being induced by the good coffee and their liking for their host.

Doctor Kroll developed his theme for some time, darting his

lively and intelligent glances at them, offering them more coffee, offering them cigarettes, and demanded from them an account of how the Health Service worked in Britain. He took it for granted that neither would approve of a scheme which gave people something for nothing, and he commiserated with them for their subjection to state tyranny. They ventured to point out to him certain advantages they felt it had; and at last he nodded and admitted that a country as stable and well-ordered as their own might very well be able to afford extravagant experiments that would wreck other countries—his own, for instance. But he did feel disturbed when he saw their country, which he regarded as the bulwark of decency against socialism in Europe, giving in to the mob.

Here they suggested that they did not want to take up more of his time than was necessary; he must be very busy. For surely the director of such a large hospital could not possibly afford to devote so much time to every foreign doctor who wished to see over it? Or could it be his devotion to Britain that made him so ready to devote his time to them?

At any rate, he seemed disappointed at being reminded of what they had come for. He even sighed and sat silent a little, so that Doctor Anderson, out of politeness, mentioned the paper he had received from him so that they might, if Doctor Kroll wished it, discuss the subject of their research. But Doctor Kroll merely sighed again and said that these days he had very little time for original work; such was the penalty one must pay for accepting the burdens of administration. He rose, all his animation gone, and invited them to step into the other room beyond the glass panel where he would collect his keys. So the three of them went into the inner drawingroom, which was an office because of the desk and the telephone; and there Mary Parrish's attention was drawn to a picture on the wall above the desk. At a distance of six or eight feet it was a gay fresh picture of a cornfield painted from root-vision, or field-mouse view. The sheaves of corn rose startlingly up, bright and strong, mingled with cornflowers and red poppies, as if one were crouching in the very center of a field. But as one walked toward the picture it vanished, it became a confusion of bright paint. It was finger-painted. The surface of the canvas was as rough as a ploughed field. Mary Parrish walked up to it, into the bright paint, took a few steps back, and back again; and, behold, the picture recreated itself, the cornfield strong and innocent, with something of the sensual innocence of Renoir's pictures. She was so absorbed that she started when Doctor Kroll dropped a heavy hand on her shoulder and demanded, Was she fond of painting? Instantly both she and Hamish assured him that they were enthusiastically fond of pictures.

Doctor Kroll dropped back on the surface of his very neat desk —so neat one could not help wondering how much it was used— the very large black bunch of keys he had removed from it; and he stood in front of the cornfield picture, his hand on Mary's shoulder.

"This," he said, "is what I am really interested in. Yes, yes; this, you must agree, is more interesting than medicine."

They agreed, since they had just understood that this was the artist in person. Doctor Kroll proceeded to take out from a large cupboard set into the wall a thick stack of pictures, all finger-painted, all with the rough staring surface of thick paint, all of which created themselves at ten paces into highly organised and original pictures.

Soon both rooms were full of pictures that leaned against chairs, tables, walls and along the sliding glass panels. Doctor Kroll, his fine hands knotted together in anxiety because of their possible reception of his work, followed them around as they gazed at one picture after another. It became evident that the pictures separated themselves into two categories. There were those, like the cornfield, done in bright clear colors, very fresh and lyrical. Then there were those which, close up, showed grim rutted surfaces of dirty black, grey, white, a sullen green and— recurring again and again—a characteristic sullen shade of red, a dark, lightless, rusty red like old blood. These pictures were all extraordinary and macabre, of graveyards and skulls and corpses, of war scenes and bombed buildings and screaming women and houses on fire with people falling from burning windows like ants into flames. It was quite extraordinary how, in the space of a few seconds, these two conventional and pretty rooms had been transformed by these pictures into an exhibition of ghoulishness, particularly as the scenes of the pictures were continually vanishing altogether into areas of thick paint that had been smeared, rubbed, piled, worked all over the canvas an inch or so thick by the handsome fingers of Doctor Kroll. Standing at six feet from one picture, the proper distance to view the work of Doctor Kroll, the picture they had been examining five moments before, and which they had now moved away from, lost its meaning and disintegrated into a surface of jumbled and crusted color. They were continually stepping forward or stepping back from chaos into moments of brief, clear, startling illumination. And they could not help wondering if Doctor Kroll was gifted with a peculiar vision of his own, a vision perhaps of his fingertips, which enabled him to *see* his work as he stood up against it, rubbing and plastering the thick paint onto the canvas; they even imagined him as a monster with arms six feet long, standing back from his canvas as he worked on it like a clambering spider. The quality of these pictures was such that, as they examined them, they could not help picturing the artist as a monster, a maniac, or kind of gifted insect. Yet, turning to look at Doctor Kroll, there he stood, a handsome man who was the very essence of everything that was conservative, correct, and urbane.

Mary, at least, was feeling a little giddy. She sought out the battling blue eyes of her partner, Hamish, and understood that he felt the same. For this was an exact repetition of their encounter with Doctor Schröder with his scarred face that demanded compassion. In saying what they thought of his work to Doctor Kroll, they must remember that they were speaking to a man who gallantly and bravely volunteered to hand the keys of sanity over to a subordinate and retired into madness for six months of the year, when, presumably, he painted these horrible pictures, whose very surfaces looked like the oozing, shredding substance of decomposing flesh.

Meanwhile, there he stood beside them, searching their faces anxiously.

They said, in response to his appeal, that this was obviously a real and strong talent. They said that his work was striking and original. They said they were deeply impressed.

He stood silent, not quite smiling, but with a quizzical look behind the fine eyes. He was judging them. He knew what they were feeling and was condemning them, in the same way as the initiated make allowances for the innocent.

Doctor Anderson remarked that it must be admitted that the pictures were rather strong? Not to everybody's taste, perhaps? Perhaps rather savage?

Doctor Kroll, smiling urbanely, replied that life tended sometimes to be savage. Yes, that was his experience. He deepened his smile and indicated the cornfield on the wall behind his desk and said that he could see Doctor Anderson preferred pictures like that one?

Doctor Anderson took his stand, and very stubbornly, on the fact that he preferred that picture to any of the others he had seen.

Mary Parrish moved to stand beside Doctor Anderson and joined him in asserting that to her mind this picture was entirely superior to all the others; she preferred the few bright pictures, all of which seemed to her to be loaded with a quality of sheer joy, a sensuous joy, to the others which seemed to her—if he didn't mind her saying so—simply horrible.

Doctor Kroll turned his ironical, dark gaze from one face to the other and remarked: "So." And again, accepting their bad taste: "So."

He remarked, "I am subject to fits of depression. When I am depressed, naturally enough, I paint these pictures." He indicated the lightless pictures of his madness. "And when I am happy again, and when I have time—for, as I have said, I am extremely busy—I paint pictures such as these. . . ." His gesture towards the cornfield was impatient, almost contemptuous. It was clear that he had hung the joyous cornfield on the wall of his reception room because he expected all his guests or visiting colleagues to have the bad taste to prefer it.

"So," he said again, smiling dryly.

At which, Mary Parrish—since he was conveying a feeling of total isolation—said quickly, "But we are very interested. We would love to see some more, if you have time."

It seemed that he needed very much to hear her say this. For the ironical condemnation left his face and was succeeded by the pathetic anxiety of the amateur artist to be loved for his work. He said that he had had two exhibitions of his paintings, that he had been misunderstood by the critics, who had praised the paintings he did not care for, so that he would never again expose himself publicly to the stupidity of critics. He was dependent for sympathy on the understanding minority, some of them chance visitors to his hospital; some of them even—if they did not mind his saying so—inmates of it. He would, for two such delightful guests as his visitors from England, be happy to show more of his work.

With this he invited them to step into a passage behind his office. Its walls were covered from floor to ceiling with pictures. Also the walls of the passage beyond it.

It was terrifying to think of the energy this man must have when he was "depressed." Corridor after corridor opened up, the walls all covered with canvases loaded with thick, crusted paint. Some of the corridors were narrow, and it was impossible to stand far enough back for the pictures to compose themselves. But it seemed that Doctor Kroll was able to see what his hands had done even when he was close against the canvas. He would lean into a big area of thick, dry paint from which emerged fragmentarily a jerky branch that looked like a bombed tree, or a bit of cracked bone, or a tormented mouth, and say: "I call this picture 'Love.' " Or Victory, or Death; for he liked this kind of title. "See? See that house there? See how I've put the church?" And the two guests gazed blankly at the smears of paint and wondered if perhaps this canvas represented the apotheosis of his madness and had no form in it at all. But if they stepped back against the opposite wall as far as they could, and leaned their heads back to gain an extra inch of distance, they could see that there was a house or a church. The house was also a skull; and the dead grey walls of the church oozed rusty blood, or spilled a gout of blood over the sills of its windows, or its door ejected blood like a person's mouth coughing blood.

Depression again weighed on the pair, who, following after the dignified back of Doctor Kroll as he led them into yet another picture-filled corridor, instinctively reached for each other's hands, reached for the warm contact of healthy flesh.

Soon their host led them back into the office, where he offered them more coffee. They refused politely but asked to see his hospital. Doctor Kroll carelessly agreed. It was not, his manner suggested, that he did not take his hospital seriously, but that he would much rather, now he had been given the privilege of a visit from these rarely sympathetic people, share with them his much higher interests: his love for their country, his art. But he would nevertheless escort them around the hospital.

Again he took up the great bundle of black keys and went before them down the corridor they had first entered by. Now they saw that the pictures they had noticed then were all by him; these were the pictures he despised and hung for public view. But as they passed through a back door into a courtyard he paused, held up his keys, smiling, and indicated a small picture by the door. The picture was of the keys. From a scramble of whitey-grey paint came out, very black and hard and shining, a great jangling bunch of keys that also looked like bells, and, from certain angles, like staring eyes. Doctor Kroll shared a smile with them as if to say: An interesting subject?

The three doctors went across a courtyard into the first block, which consisted of two parallel very long wards, each filled with small, tidy, white beds that had a chair and a locker beside them. On the beds sat, or leaned, or lay, the patients. Apart from the fact that they tended to be listless and staring, there was nothing to distinguish this ward from the ward of any public hospital. Doctor Kroll exchanged brisk greetings with certain of his patients; discouraged an old man who grasped his arm as he passed and said that he had a momentous piece of news to tell him which he had heard that moment over his private wireless station, and which affected the whole course of history; and passed on smiling through this building into the next. There was nothing new here. This block, like the last, had achieved the ultimate in reducing several hundred human beings into complete identity with each other. Doctor Kroll said, almost impatiently, that if you had seen one of these wards you had seen them all, and took off at a tangent across a courtyard to another of these regular blocklike buildings which was full of women. It occurred to the British pair that the two buildings on the other side of the court had men in them only; and they asked Doctor Kroll if he kept the men in the line of buildings on one side of the court, and the women on the other—for there was a high wire fence down the court, with a door in it that he opened and locked behind him. "Why, that is so," said Doctor Kroll indifferently.

"Do the men and the women meet—in the evenings, perhaps?"

"Meet? No."

"Not at social evenings? At dances perhaps? At some meals during the week?"

Here Doctor Kroll turned and gave his guests a tolerant smile. "My friends," he said, "sex is a force destructive enough even when kept locked up. Do you suggest that we should mix the sexes in a place like this, where it is hard enough to keep people quiet and unexcited?"

Doctor Anderson remarked that in progressive mental hospitals in Britain it was a policy to allow men and women to mix together as much as was possible. For what crime were these poor people being punished, he enquired hotly, that they were treated as if they had taken perpetual vows of celibacy?

Doctor Parrish noted that the word "progressive" fell very flat in this atmosphere. Such was the power of Doctor Kroll's conservative personality that it sounded almost eccentric.

"So?" commented Doctor Kroll. "So the administrators of your English hospitals are prepared to give themselves so much unnecessary trouble?"

"Do the men and the women never meet?" insisted Doctor Parrish.

Doctor Kroll said tolerantly that at night they behaved like naughty schoolchildren and passed each other notes through the wire.

The British couple fell back on their invincible politeness and felt their depression inside them like a fog. It was still snowing lightly through the heavy grey air.

Having seen three buildings all full of women of all ages, lying and sitting about in the listlessness of complete idleness, they agreed with Doctor Kroll it was enough; they were prepared to end their tour of inspection. He said that they must return with him for another cup of coffee, but first he had to make a short visit, and perhaps they would be kind enough to accompany him. He led the way to another building set rather apart from others, whose main door he opened with an enormous key from his bunch of keys. As soon as they were inside it became evident that this was the children's building. Doctor Kroll was striding down the main passage, calling aloud for some attendant, who appeared to take instructions.

Meanwhile, Mary Parrish, doctor who specialised in small children, finding herself at the open door of a ward, looked in, and invited Doctor Anderson to do the same. It was a very large room, very clean, very fresh, with barred windows. It was full of cots and small beds. In the centre of the room a five-year-old child stood upright against the bars of a cot. His arms were confined by a straitjacket, and because he could not prevent himself from falling, he was tied upright against the bars with a cord. He was glaring around the room, glaring and grinding his teeth. Never had Mary seen such a desperate, wild, suffering little creature as this one. Immediately opposite the child sat a very large tow-headed woman, dressed in heavy striped grey material, like a prison dress, knitting as comfortably as if she were in her kitchen.

Mary was speechless with horror at the sight. She could feel Hamish stiff and angry beside her.

Doctor Kroll came back down the passage, saw them, and said amiably: "You are interested? So? Of course, Doctor Parrish, you said children are your field. Come in, come in." He led the way into the room, and the fat woman stood up respectfully as he entered. He glanced at the straitjacketed child and moved past it to the opposite wall, where there were a line of small beds, placed head to foot. He pulled back the coverings one after another, showing a dozen children aged between a year and six years—armless children, limbless children, children with enormous misshapen heads, children with tiny heads and monstrous bodies. He pulled the coverings off, one after another, replacing them as soon as Mary Parrish and Hamish Anderson had seen what he was showing them, and remarked: "Modern drugs are a terrible thing. Now these horrors are kept alive. Before, they died of pneumonia."

Hamish said, "The theory is, I believe, that medical science advances so fast that we should keep even the most apparently hopeless people alive in case we find something that can save them?"

Doctor Kroll gave them the ironical smile they had seen before, and said, "Yes, yes, yes. That is the theory. But for my part . . ."

Mary Parrish was watching the imprisoned little boy, who glared from a flushed wild face, straining his small limbs inside the thick stuff of the straitjacket. She said, "In Britain straitjackets are hardly ever used. Certainly not for children."

"So?" commented Doctor Kroll. "So? But sometimes it is for the patient's own good."

He advanced towards the boy and stood before the bars of the cot, looking at him. The child glared back like a wild animal into the eyes of the big doctor. "This one bites if you go too near him," commented Doctor Kroll; and with a nod of his head invited them to follow him out.

"Yes, yes," he remarked, unlocking the big door and locking

it behind them, "there are things we cannot say in public, but we may agree in private that there are many people in this hospital who would be no worse for a quick and painless death."

Again he asked that they would excuse him, and he strode off to have a word with another doctor, who was crossing the court in his white coat, with another big bunch of black keys in his hand.

Hamish said, "This man told us that he has directed this hospital for thirty years."

"Yes, I believe he did."

"So he was here under Hitler."

"The mongrel upstart, yes."

"And he would not have kept his job unless he had agreed to sterilise Jews, serious mental defectives, and communists. Did you remember?"

"No, I'd forgotten."

"So had I."

They were silent a moment, thinking of how much they had liked, how much they still liked, Doctor Kroll.

"Any Jew or mental defective or communist unlucky enough to fall into Doctor Kroll's hands would have been forcibly sterilised. And the very ill would have been killed outright."

"Not necessarily," she objected feebly. "After all, perhaps he refused. Perhaps he was strong enough to refuse."

"Perhaps."

"After all, even under the worst governments there are always people in high places who use their influence to protect weak people."

"Perhaps."

"And he might have been one."

"We should keep an open mind?" he enquired, quick and sarcastic. They stood very close together under the cold snow in a corner of the grey courtyard. Twenty paces away, behind walls and locked doors, a small boy, naked save for a straitjacket and tied to bars like an animal, was grinding his teeth and glaring at the fat knitting wardress.

Mary Parrish said miserably, "We don't know, after all. We shouldn't condemn anyone without knowing. For all we know he might have saved the lives of hundreds of people."

At this point Doctor Kroll came back, swinging his keys.

Hamish enquired blandly, "It would interest us very much to know if Hitler's regime made any difference to you professionally?"

Doctor Kroll considered this question as he strolled along beside them. "Life was easy for no one during that time," he said.

"But as regards medical policy?"

Doctor Kroll gave this question his serious thought, and said, "No, they did not interfere very much. Of course, on certain questions, the gentlemen of the Nazi regime had sensible ideas."

"Such as? For instance?"

"Oh, questions of hygiene? Yes, one could call them questions of social hygiene." He had led them to the door of the main building, and now he said: "You will, I hope, join me in a cup of coffee before you leave? Unless I can persuade you to stay and have a meal with us?"

"I think we should catch our bus back to town," said Hamish, speaking firmly for both of them. Doctor Kroll consulted his watch. "Your bus will not be passing for another twenty minutes." They accompanied him back through the picture-hung corridors to his office.

"And I would like so much to give you a memento of your visit," he said, smiling at them both. "Yes, I would like that. No, wait for one minute; I want to show you something."

He went to the wall cupboard and took out a flat object wrapped in a piece of red silk. He unwrapped the silk and brought forth another picture. He set this picture against the side of the desk and invited them to stand back and look at it. They did so, already prepared to admire it, for it was a product of one of the times when he was not depressed. It was a very large picture, done in clear blues and greens, the picture of a forest—an imaginary forest with clear streams running through it, a forest where impossibly brilliant birds flew, and full of plants and trees created in Doctor Kroll's mind. It was beautiful, full of joy and tranquillity and light. But in the centre of the sky glared a large black eye. It was an eye remote from the rest of the picture; and obviously what had happened was that Doctor Kroll had painted his fantasy forest, and then afterwards, looking at it during some fit of misery, had painted in that black, condemnatory, judging eye.

Mary Parrish stared back at the eye and said, "It's lovely; it's a picture of paradise." She felt uncomfortable at using the word "paradise" in the presence of Hamish, who by temperament was critical of words like these.

But Doctor Kroll smiled with pleasure, and laid his heavy hand on her shoulder, and said: "You understand. Yes, you understand. That picture is called 'The Eye of God in Paradise.' You like it?"

"Very much," she said, afraid that he was about to present that picture to her. For how could they possibly transport such a big picture all the way back to Britain and what would she do with it when she got there? For it would be dishonest to paint out the black, wrathful eye: one respected, naturally, an artist's conception even if one disagreed with it. And she could not endure to live with that eye, no matter how much she liked the rest of the picture.

But it seemed that Dr. Kroll had no intention of parting with the picture itself, which he wrapped up again in its red silk and hid in the cupboard. He took from a drawer a photograph of the picture and offered it to her, saying, "If you really like my picture—and I can see that you do, for you have a real feeling, a real understanding—then kindly take this as a souvenir of a happy occasion."

She thanked him, and both she and Hamish looked with polite gratitude at the photograph. Of course it gave no idea at all of the original. The subtle blues and greens had gone, were not hinted at; and even the softly waving grasses, trees, plants, foliage were obliterated. Nothing remained but a reproduction of crude crusts of paint, smeared thick by the fingers of Doctor Kroll, from which emerged the hint of a branch, the suggestion of a flower. Nothing remained except the black, glaring eye, the eye of a wrathful and punishing God. It was the photograph of a roughly scrawled eye, as a child might have drawn it— as, so Mary could not help thinking, that unfortunate strait- jacketed little boy might have drawn the eye of God, or of Doctor Kroll, had he been allowed to get his arms free and use them.

The thought of that little boy hurt her; it was still hurting Hamish, who stood politely beside her. She knew that the moment they could leave this place and get on to the open road where the bus passed would be the happiest of her life.

They thanked Doctor Kroll profoundly for his kindness, insisted they were afraid they might miss their bus, said goodbye, and promised letters and an exchange of medical papers of interest to them all—promised, in short, eternal friendship.

Then they left the big building and Doctor Kroll and emerged into the cold February air. Soon the bus came and picked them up, and they travelled back over the flat black plain to the city terminus.

The terminus was exactly as it had been four or five hours before. Under the low grey sky lay the black chilled earth, the ruins of streets, the already softening shapes of bomb craters, the big new shining white building covered with the energetic shapes of the workers. The bus queue still waited patiently, huddled into dark, thick clothes, while a thin bitter snow drifted down, down, hardly moving, as if the sky itself were slowly falling.

Mary Parrish took out the photograph and held it in her chilly gloved hand.

The black angry eye glared up at them.

"Tear it up," he said.

"No," she said.

"Why not? What's the use of keeping the beastly thing?"

"It wouldn't be fair," she said seriously, returning it to her handbag.

"Oh, *fair*," he said bitterly, with an impatient shrug.

They moved off side by side to the bus stop where they would catch a bus back to their hotel. Their feet crunched sharply on the hard earth. The stillness, save for the small shouts of the men at work on the half-finished building, save for the breathing noise of the machine, was absolute. And this queue of people waited like the other across the square, waited eternally, huddled up, silent, patient, under the snow; listening to the silence, under which seemed to throb from the depths of the earth the memory of the sound of marching feet, of heavy, black-booted, marching feet.

# The Other Woman

Rose's mother was killed one morning crossing the street to do her shopping. Rose was fetched from work, and a young policeman, awkward with sympathy, asked questions and finally said: "You ought to tell your dad, miss, he ought to know." It had struck him as strange that she had not suggested it, but behaved as if the responsibility for everything must of course be hers. He thought Rose was too composed to be natural. Her mouth was set and there was a strained look in her eyes. He insisted; Rose sent a message to her father; but when he came she put him straight into bed with a cup of tea. Mr. Johnson was a plump, fair little man, with wisps of light hair lying over a rosy scalp, and blue, candid, trustful eyes. Then she came back to the kitchen and her manner told the policeman that she expected him to leave. From the door he said diffidently: "Well, I'm sorry, miss, I'm real sorry. A terrible thing—you can't rightly blame the lorry-driver, and your mum—it wasn't her fault either." Rose turned her white, shaken face, her cold and glittering eyes towards him and said tartly: "Being sorry doesn't mend broken bones." That last phrase seemed to take her by surprise, for she winced, her face worked in a rush of tears, and then she clenched her jaw again. "Them lorries," she said heavily, "them machines, they ought to be stopped, that's what I think." This irrational remark encouraged the policeman: it was nearer to the tears, the emotion that he thought would be good for her. He remarked encouragingly: "I daresay, miss, but we couldn't do without them, could we now?" Rose's face did not change. She said politely: "Yes?"

It was sceptical and dismissing; that monosyllable said finally: You keep your opinions, I'll keep mine. It examined and dismissed the whole machine age. The young policeman, still lingering over his duty, suggested: "Isn't there anybody to come and sit with you? You don't look too good, miss, and that's a fact."

"There isn't anybody," said Rose briefly, and added: "I'm all right." She sounded irritated, and so he left. She sat down at the table and she was shocked at herself for what she had said. She thought: I ought to tell George. . . . But she did not move. She stared vaguely around the kitchen, her mind dimly churning around several ideas. One was that her father had taken it hard, she would have her hands full with him. Another, that policeman, officials—they were all nosey-parkers, knowing what was best for everybody. She found herself staring at a certain picture on the wall, and thinking: Now I can take that picture down. Now she's gone I can do what I like. She felt a little guilty, but almost at once she briskly rose and took the picture down. It was of a battleship in a stormy sea, and she hated it. She put it away in a cupboard. Then the white empty square on the wall troubled her, and she replaced it by a calendar with yellow roses on it. Then she made herself a cup of tea and began cooking her father's supper, thinking: I'll wake him up and make him eat, do him good to have a bite of something hot.

At supper her father asked: "Where's George?" Her face closed against him in irritation and she said: "I don't know." He was surprised and shocked, and he protested: "But Rosie, you ought to tell him, it's only right." Now, it was against this knowledge that she had been arming herself all day; but she knew that sooner or later she must tell George, and when she had finished the washing-up she took a sheet of writing paper from the drawer of her dresser and sat down to write. She was as surprised at herself as her father was: Why didn't she want to tell George? Her father said, with the characteristic gentle protest: "But Rosie, why don't you give him a ring at the factory? They'd give him the message." Rose made as if she had not heard. She finished the letter, found some coppers in her bag for a stamp, and went out to post it. Afterwards she found herself thinking of George's arrival with reluctance that deserved the name of fear. She could not understand herself, and soon went to bed in order to lose herself in sleep. She dreamed of the lorry that had killed her mother; she dreamed, too, of an enormous black machine, relentlessly moving its great arms back and forth, back and forth, in a way that was menacing to Rose.

George found the letter when he returned from work the following evening. His first thought was: Why couldn't she have got killed next week, after we were married, instead of now? He was shocked at the cruel selfish idea. But he and Rose had been going together now for three years, and he could not help feeling that it was cruel fate to cloud their wedding with this terrible, senseless death. He had not liked Rose's mother: he thought her a fussy and domineering woman; but to be killed like that, all of a sudden, in her vigorous fifties—He thought suddenly: Poor little Rosie, she'll be upset bad, and there's her dad, he's just like a big baby; I'd better get to her quick. He was putting the letter in his pocket when it struck him: Why did she write? Why didn't she telephone to the works? He looked at the letter and saw that Mrs. Johnson had been killed as long ago as yesterday morning. At first he was too astonished to be angry; then he was extraordinarily angry. "What!" he muttered, "why the hell—what's she doing?" He was a member of the family, wasn't he?—or as good as. And she wrote him stiff little letters, beginning *Dear George*, and ending *Rose*—no love, not even a sincerely. But underneath the anger he was deeply dismayed. He was remembering that there had been a listlessness, an apathy about her recently that could almost be taken as indifference. For instance, when he took her to see the two rooms that would be their home she made all kinds of objections instead of being as delighted as he was. "Look at all those stairs," she had said, "it's so high up," and so on. You might almost think she wasn't keen on marrying him—but this idea was unsupportable, and he abandoned it quickly. He remembered that at the beginning, three years ago, she had pleaded for them to marry at once; she didn't mind taking a chance, she had said; lots of people got married on less money than they had. But he was a cautious man and had talked her into waiting for some kind of security. That's where he made his mistake; he decided now he should have taken her at a word and married her straight off, and then . . . He hastened across London to comfort Rose; and all the time his thoughts of her were uneasy and aggrieved; and he felt as anxious as a lost child.

When he entered the kitchen it was with no clear idea of what to expect; but he was surprised to find her seated at her usual place at the table, her hands folded before her, pale, heavy-lidded, but quite composed. The kitchen was spotless and there was a smell of soapsuds and clean warmth. Evidently the place had just been given a good scrub.

Rose turned heavy eyes on him and said: "It was good of you to come over, George."

He had been going to give her a comforting kiss, but this took him by surprise. His feeling of outrage deepened. "Hey," he said, accusingly. "What's all this, Rosie, why didn't you let me know?"

She looked upset, but said evasively: "It was all over so quickly, and they took her away—there didn't seem no point in getting you disturbed too."

George pulled out a chair and sat opposite her. He had thought that there was nothing new to learn about Rose, after three years. But now he was giving her troubled and apprehensive glances; she seemed a stranger. In appearance she was small and dark, rather too thin. She had a sharp, pale face, with irregular prettiness about it. She usually wore a dark skirt and a white blouse. She would sit up at night to wash and iron the blouse so that it would always be fresh. This freshness, the neatness, was her strongest characteristic. "You look as if you could be pulled through a hedge backwards and come out with every hair in order," he used to tease her. To which she might reply: "Don't make me laugh. How could I?" She would be quite serious; and at such moments he might sigh, humorously, admitting that she had no sense of humour. But really he liked her seriousness, her calm practicality; he relied on it. Now he said, rather helplessly: "Don't take on, Rosie, everything's all right."

"I'm not taking on," she replied unnecessarily, looking quietly at him or, rather, through him, with an air of patient waiting. He was now more apprehensive than angry. "How's your dad?" he asked.

"I've put him to bed with a nice cup of tea."

"How's he taking it?"

She seemed to shrug. "Well, he's upset, but he's getting over it now."

And now for the life of him, he could think of nothing to say. The clock's ticking seemed very loud, and he shifted his feet noisily. After a long silence he said aggressively: "This won't make any difference to us; it'll be all right next week, Rosie?"

He knew that it wasn't all right when, after a further pause, she turned her eyes towards him with a full, dark, vague stare: "Oh well, I don't know. . . ."

"What do you mean?" he challenged quickly, leaning across at her, forcibly, so that she might be made to respond: "What do you mean, Rosie, let us have it now."

"Well—there's Dad," she replied, with that maddening vagueness.

"You mean we shan't get married?" he shouted angrily. "Three years, Rosie . . ." As her silence persisted: "Your dad can live with us. Or—he might get married again—or something."

Suddenly she laughed, and he winced: her moments of rough humour always disconcerted him. At the same time they pained him because they seemed brutal. "You mean to say," she said, clumsily jeering, "you mean you hope he gets married again, even if no one else'd ever think of it." But her eyes were filled with tears. They were lonely and self-sufficing tears. He slowly fell back into his chair, letting his hands drop loosely. He simply could not understand it. He could not understand her. It flashed into his mind that she intended not to marry him at all, but this was too monstrous a thought, and he comforted himself: She'll be all right tomorrow, it's the shock, that's all. She liked her ma, really, even though they scrapped like two cats. He was just going to say: "Well, if I can't do anything I'll be getting along; I'll come and see you tomorrow," when she asked him carefully, as if it were an immense effort for her to force her attention on to him: "Would you like a cuppa tea?"

"Rose!" he shouted miserably.

"What?" She sounded unhappy but stubborn; and she was unreachable, shut off from him behind a barrier of—what? He did not know. "Oh, go to hell then," he muttered, and got up and stamped out of the kitchen. At the door he gave her an appealing glance, but she was not looking at him. He slammed the door hard. Afterwards he thought guiltily: She's upset, and then I treat her bad.

But Rose did not think of him when he had gone. She remained where she was for some time, looking vaguely at the calendar with the yellow roses. Then she got up, washed her hands, hung her apron on the hook behind the door, as usual, and went to bed. "That's over," she said to herself, meaning George. She began to cry. She knew she would not marry him—

rather, *could* not marry him. She did not know why this was impossible or why she was crying: she could not understand her own behaviour. Up till so few hours before she had been going to marry George, live with him in the little flat: everything was settled. Yet, from the moment she had heard the shocked voices saying outside in the street: "Mrs. Johnson's dead, she's been killed"—from that moment, or so it seemed now, it had become impossible to marry George. One day he had meant everything to her, he represented her future, and the next, he meant nothing. The knowledge was shocking to her; above all she prided herself on being a sensible person; the greatest praise she could offer was: "You've got sense," or "I like people to behave proper, no messing about." And what she felt was not sensible, therefore, she could not think too closely about. She cried for a long time, stifling her sobs so that her father could not hear them where he lay through the wall. Then she lay awake and stared at the square of light that showed chimney-pots and the dissolving yellowish clouds of a rainy London dawn, scolding herself scornfully: What's the good of crying? while she mopped up the tears that rose steadily under her lids and soaked down her cheeks to the already damp pillow.

Next morning when her father asked over breakfast cups: "Rosie, what are you going to do about George?" she replied calmly, "It's all right, he came last night and I told him."

"You told him what?" He spoke cautiously. His round, fresh face looked troubled, the clear, rather childlike blue eyes were not altogether approving. His workmates knew him as a jaunty, humorous man with a warm, quick laugh and ingrained opinions about life and politics. In his home he was easy and uncritical. He had been married for twenty-five years to a woman who had outwardly let him do as he pleased while taking all the responsibility on herself. He knew this. He used to say of his wife: "Once she's got an idea into her head you might as well whistle at a wall!" And now he was looking at his daughter as he had at the mother. He did not know what she had planned, but he knew nothing he said would make any difference.

"Everything's all right, Dad," Rosie said quietly.

I daresay, he thought; but what's it all about? He asked: "You don't have to get ideas into your head about not getting married. I'm easy." Without looking at him she filled his cup with the strong, brown, sweet tea he loved, and said again: "It's all right."

He persisted: "You don't want to make any mistakes now, Rosie, you're upset, and you want to give yourself time to have a good think about things."

To this there was no reply at all. He sighed and took his newspaper to the fire. It was Sunday. Rose was cooking the dinner when George came in. Jem, the father, turned his back on the couple, having nodded at George, thus indicating that as far as he was concerned they were alone. He was thinking: George's a good bloke, she's a fool if she gives him up.

"Well, Rosie?" said George, challengingly, the misery of the sleepless night bursting out of him.

"Well, what?" temporised Rose, wiping dishes. She kept her head lowered and her face was pale and set hard. Confronted thus, with George's unhappiness, her decision did not seem so secure. She wanted to cry. She could not afford to cry now, in front of him. She went to the window so that her back might be turned to him. It was a deep basement, and she looked up at the rubbish-can and railings showing dirty black against the damp, grey houses opposite. This had been her view of the world since she could remember. She heard George saying, uncertainly: "You marry me on Wednesday, the way we fixed it, and your dad'll be all right; he can stay here or live with us, just as you like."

"I'm sorry," said Rose after a pause.

"But why, Rosie, why?"

Silence. "I don't know," she muttered. She sounded obstinate but unhappy. Grasping this moment of weakness in her, he laid his hand on her shoulder and appealed: "Rosie girl, you're upset, that's all it is." But she tensed her shoulder against him and then, since his hand remained there, jerked herself away and said angrily: "I'm sorry. It's no good. I keep telling you."

"Three years," he said slowly, looking at her in amazed anger. "Three years! And now you throw me over."

She did not reply at once. She could see the monstrousness of what she was doing and could not help herself. She had loved him then. Now he exasperated her. "I'm not throwing you over," she said defensively.

"So you're not!" he shouted in derision, his face clenched in pain and rage. "What are you doing then?"

"I don't know," she said helplessly.

He stared at her, suddenly swore under his breath and went

to the door: "I'm not coming back," he said, "you're just playing the fool with me, Rosie. You shouldn't've treated me like this. No one'd stand for it, and I'm not going to." There was no sound from Rose, and so he went out.

Jem slowly let down the paper and remarked: "You want to think what you're doing, Rosie."

She did not reply. The tears were pouring down her face, but she wiped them impatiently away and bent to the oven. Later that day Jem watched her secretly over the top of the paper. There was a towel-rail beside the dresser. She was un-screwing it and moving it to a different position. She rolled the dresser itself into the opposite corner and then shifted various ornaments on the mantelpiece. Jem remembered that over each of these things she had bickered with her mother: the women could not agree about where the dresser would stand best, or the height of the towel-rail. So now Rose was having her own way, thought Jem, amazed at the sight of his daughter's quiet but determined face. The moment her mother was dead she moved everything to suit herself. . . . Later she made tea and sat down opposite him, in her mother's chair. Women, thought Jem, half-humorous, half-shocked at the per-sistence of the thing. And she was throwing over a nice, decent chap just because of—what? At last he struggled and accepted it; he knew she would have her way. Also, at the bottom of his heart, he was pleased. He would never have put any pressure on her to give up marriage, but he was glad that he did not have to move, that he could stay in his old ways without disturbance. She's still young, he comforted himself; there's plenty of time for her to marry.

A month later they heard George had married someone else. Rose had a pang of regret, but it was the kind of regret one feels for something inevitable, that could not have been other-wise. When they met in the street, she said "Hullo, George," and he gave her a curt, stiff nod. She even felt a little hurt because he would not let bygones be; that he felt he had to store resentment. If she could greet him nicely as a friend, then it was unkind of him to treat her coldly. . . . She glanced with covert interest at the girl who was his wife, and waited for a greeting; but the girl averted her face and stared coldly away. She knew about Rose; she knew she had got George on the rebound.

This was in 1938. The rumours and the fear of war were still more an undercurrent in people's minds than a part of their thinking. Vaguely, Rose and her father expected that everything would continue as it was. About four months after Mother's death, Jem said one day: "Why don't you give up your work now. We can manage without what you earn, if we're careful."

"Yes?" said Rose, in the sceptical way which already told him his pleading was wasted. "You've got too much," he persisted. "Cleaning and cooking, then out all day at work."

"Men," she said simply, with a good-natured but dismissing sniff.

"There's no sense in it," he protested, knowing he was wasting his breath. His wife had insisted on working until Rose was sixteen and could take her place. "Women should be independent," she had said. And now Rose was saying: "I like to be independent."

Jem said: "Women. They say all women want is a man to keep them, but you and your mother, you go on as if I'm trying to do you out of something when I say you mustn't work."

"Women here and women there," said Rose. "I don't know about *women*. All I know is what I think."

Jem was that old type of Labour man who has been brought up in the trade union movement. He went to meetings once or twice a week, and sometimes his friends came in for a cup of tea and an argument. For years he had been saying to his wife: "If they paid you proper, it'd be different. You work ten hours a day, and it's all for the bosses." Now he used the argument on Rose, and she said: "Oh, politics, I'm not interested." Her father said: "You're as stubborn as a mule, like your mother."

"Then I am," said Rose, good-humouredly. She would have said she had not "got on" with her mother; she had had to fight to become independent of that efficient and possessive woman. But in this she agreed with her: it had been instilled into her ever since she could remember, that women must look after themselves. Like her mother, she was indulgent about the trade union meetings, as if they were a childish amusement that men should be allowed; and she voted Labour to please him, as her mother had done. And every time her father

pleaded with her to give up her job at the bakery she inexorably
replied: "Who knows what might happen? It's silly not to be
careful." And so she continued to get up early in order to clean
the basement kitchen and the two little rooms over it that
was their home; then she made the breakfast and went out to
shop. Then she went to the bakery, and at six o'clock came
back to cook supper for her father. At weekends she had a
grand clean-up of the whole place, and cooked puddings and
cakes. They were in bed most nights by nine. They never went
out. They listened to the radio while they ate, and they read
the newspapers. It was a hard life, but Rose did not think of
it as hard. If she had ever used words like "happiness," she
would have said she was happy. Sometimes she thought wistfully, not of George, but of the baby his wife was going to have.
Perhaps, after all, she had made a terrible mistake? Then
she squashed the thought and comforted herself: There's
plenty of time, there's no hurry, I couldn't leave Dad now.

When the war started, she accepted it fatalistically while
her father was deeply upset. His vision of the future had been
the old socialist one: everything would slowly get better and
better; and one day the working man would get into power by
the automatic persuasion of commonsense, and then—but his
picture of that time was not so clear. Vaguely he thought of a
house with a little garden and a holiday by the sea once a year.
The family had never been able to afford a proper holiday. But
the war cut right across this vision.

"Well, what did you expect?" asked Rose satirically.

"What do you mean?" he demanded aggressively. "If Labour'd
been in, it wouldn't have happened."

"Maybe, maybe not."

"You're just like your mother," he complained again. "You
haven't got any logic."

"Well, you've been going to meetings for years and years,
and you make resolutions, and you talk, but there's a war just
the same." She felt as if this ended the argument. She felt,
though she could never have put it into words, that there was a
deep basic insecurity, that life itself was an enemy to be
placated and humoured, liable at any moment to confront her,
or people like her, with death or destitution. The only sensible
thing to do was to gather together every penny that came along

and keep it safe. When her mother had been alive, she paid thirty shillings of the two pounds a week she earned towards the housekeeping. Now that thirty shillings went straight into the post office. When the newspapers and the wireless blared war and horror at her, she thought of that money, and it comforted her. It didn't amount to much, but if something happened . . . What that *something* might be, she did not clearly know. But life was terrible, there was no justice—had not her own mother been killed by a silly lorry crossing the street she had crossed every day of her life for twenty-five years . . . that just proved it. And now there was a war, and all sorts of people were going to be hurt, all for nothing—that proved it too, if it needed any proof. Life was frightening and dangerous—therefore, put money into the post office; hold on to your job, work, and—put money into the post office.

Her father sat over the wireless set, bought newspapers, argued with his cronies, trying to make sense of the complicated, cynical movements of power politics, while the familiar pattern of life dissolved into the slogans and noise of war, and the streets filled with uniforms and rumours. "It's all Hitler," he would say aggressively to Rose.

"Maybe, maybe not."

"Well, he started it, didn't he?"

"I'm not interested who started it. All I know is, ordinary people don't want war. And there's war all the time. They make me sick if you want to know—and you men make me sick, too. If you were young enough, you'd be off like the rest of them," she said accusingly.

"But Rosie," he said, really shocked, "Hitler's got to be stopped, hasn't he?"

"Hitler," she said scornfully. "Hitler and Churchill and Stalin and Roosevelt—they all make me sick, if you want to know. And that goes for your Attlee too."

"Women haven't got any logic," he said, in despair.

So they came not to discuss the war at all, they merely suffered it. Slowly, Rose came to use the same words and slogans as everyone else; and like everyone else, with deep sad knowledge that it was all talk, and what was really happening in the world was something vast and terrible, beyond her comprehension; and perhaps it was wonderful too, if she only knew—

but she could never hope to understand. Better get on with the job, live as best she could, try not to be afraid and—put money in the post office.

Soon she switched to a job in a munitions factory. She felt she ought to do something for the war, and also she was paid much better than in the bakery. She did fire-watching too. Often she was up till three or four and then woke at six to clean and cook. Her father continued as a bricklayer and did fire-watching three or four nights a week. They were both permanently tired and sad. The war went on, month after month, year after year, food was short, it was hard to keep warm, the search-lights wheeled over the dark wilderness of London, the bombs fell screaming, and the black-out was like a weight on their minds and spirits. They listened to the news, read the news-papers, with the same look of bewildered but patient courage; and it seemed as if the war was a long, black, noisome tunnel from which they would never emerge.

In the third year Jem fell off a ladder one cold, foggy morn-ing and injured his back. "It's all right, Rosie," he said. "I can get back to work all right."

"You're not working," she said flatly. "You're sixty-seven. That's enough now, you've been working since you was four-teen."

"There won't be enough coming in every week."

"Won't there?" she said triumphantly. "You used to go on at me for working. Aren't you glad now? With your bit of pen-sion and what I get, I can still put some away every week if I try. Funny thing," she said reflectively, not without grim humour: "It was two pounds a week when there was peace, and I was supposed to be grateful for it. Comes a war and they pay you like you was a queen. I'm getting seven pounds a week now, one way and another. So you take things easy, and if I find you back to work, with your back as it is, and your rheu-matism, you'll catch it from me, I'm telling you."

"It's not easy for me to sit at home, with the war and all," he said uneasily.

"Well, did you make the war? No! You have some sense now."

Now things were not so hard for Rose, because when Jem could get out of bed he cleaned the rooms for her and there was a cup of tea waiting when she came in at night. But there was an emptiness in her and she could not pretend to herself there was not. One day she saw George's wife in the street with a little girl of about four, and stopped her. The girl was hostile, but Rose said hurriedly: "I wanted to know, how's George?" Rather unwillingly came the reply: "He's all right, so far, he's in North Africa." She held the child to her as she spoke, as if for comfort, and tears came into Rose's eyes. The two women stood hesitating on the pavement; then Rose said appealingly: "It must be hard for you." "Well, it'll be over some day—when they've stopped playing soldiers" was the grim reply; and at this Rose smiled in sympathy and the women suddenly felt friendly towards each other. "Come over some time if you like," said George's wife, slowly; and Rose said quickly: "I'd like to ever so much."

So Rose got into the habit of going over once a week to the rooms that had originally been got ready for herself. She went because of the little girl, Jill. She was secretly asking herself now: Did I make a mistake then? Should I have married George? But even as she asked the question she knew it was futile: she could have behaved in no other way; it was one of those irrational, emotional things that seem so slight and meaningless, but are so powerful. And yet, time was passing, she was nearly thirty, and when she looked in the mirror she was afraid. She was very thin now, nothing but a white-faced shrimp of a girl, with lank, tired, stringy black hair. Her sombre dark eyes peered anxiously back at her over hollowed and bony cheeks. "It's because I work so hard," she comforted herself. "No sleep, that's what it is, and the bad food, and those chemicals in the factory . . . it'll be better after the war." It was a question of endurance; somehow she had to get through the war, and then everything would be all right. Soon she looked forward all week to the Sunday night when she went over to George's wife with a little present for Jill. When she lay awake at night, she thought not of George, nor of the men she met at the factory who might have become interested in her, but of children. What with the war and all the men getting killed, she sometimes worried, perhaps it's too late. There won't be any left by the time they've finished killing them all off. But if her father could have managed for himself before, he could not now; he was really dependent on her. So she always pushed away her fears and longings with the thought: When the war's over, we can eat and sleep again, and then I'll look better, and then perhaps . . .

Not long before the war ended, Rose came home late one night, dragging her feet tiredly along the dark pavement, thinking that she had forgotten to buy anything for supper. She turned into her street, was troubled by a feeling that something was wrong, looked down towards the house where she lived, and stopped dead. There were heaps of smoking rubble showing against the reddish glare of fire.

At first she thought: I must have come to the wrong street in the black-out. Then she understood and began to run towards her home, clutching her handbag tightly, holding the scarf under her chin. At the edge of the street was a deep crater. She nearly fell into it, but righted herself and walked stumblingly among bomb refuse and tangling wires. Where her gate had been she stopped. A group of people were standing there. "Where's my father?" she demanded angrily. "Where is he?" A young man came forward and said, "Take it easy, miss." He laid a hand on her shoulder. "You live here? I think your dad was an unlucky one." The words brought no conviction to her and she stared at him, frowning. "What have you done with him?" she asked, accusingly. "They took him away, miss." She stood passively, then she heavily lifted her head and looked around her. In this part of the street all the houses were gone. She pushed her way through the people and stood looking down at the steps to the basement door. The door was hanging loose from the frame, but the glass of the window was whole. "It's all right," she said half-aloud. She took a key from her handbag and slowly descended the steps over a litter of bricks. "Miss, miss," called the young man, "you can't go down there." She made no reply, but fitted the key into the door and tried to turn it. It would not turn, so she pushed the door; it swung in on its one remaining hinge and she went inside. The place looked as it always did, save that the ornaments on the mantelpiece had been knocked to the floor. It was half-lit from the light of burning houses over the street. She was slowly picking up the ornaments and putting them back when a hand was laid on her arm. "Miss," said a compassionate voice, "you can't stay down here."

"Why shouldn't I?" she retorted, with a flash of stubbornness.

She looked upwards. There was a crack across the ceiling and dust was still settling through the air. But a kettle was boiling on the stove. "It's all right," she announced. "Look, the gas is still working. If the gas is all right then things isn't too bad, that stands to reason, doesn't it now?"

"You've got the whole weight of the house lying on that ceiling," said the man dubiously.

"The house has always stood over the ceiling, hasn't it," she said, with a tired humour that surprised him. He could not see what was funny, but she was grinning heavily at the joke. "So nothing's changed," she said, airily. But there was a look on her face that worried him, and she was trembling in a hard, locked way, as if her muscles were held rigid against the weakness of her flesh. Sudden spasmodic shudders ran through her, and then she shut her jaw hard to stop them. "It's not safe," he protested again, and she obediently gazed around to see. The kettle and the pans stood as they had ever since she could remember; the cloth on the table was one her mother had embroidered, and through the cracked window she could see the black, solid shape of the dust-can, though beyond it there were no silhouettes of grey houses, only grey sky spurting red flame. "I think it's all right," she said, stolidly. And she did. She felt safe. This was her home. She lifted the kettle and began making tea. "Have a cup?" she enquired, politely. He did not know what to do. She took her cup to the table, blew off the thick dust and began stirring in sugar. Her trembling made the spoon tinkle against the cup.

"I'll be back," he announced suddenly, and went out, meaning to fetch someone who would know how to talk to her. But now there was no one outside. They had all gone over to the burning houses; and after a little indecision he thought: I'll come back later, she's all right for the moment. He helped with the others over at the houses until very late, and he was on his way home when he remembered: That kid, what's she doing? Almost, he went straight home. He had not had his clothes off for nights, he was black and grimy, but he made the effort and returned to the basement under the heap of rubble. There was a faint glow beneath the ruin and, peering low, he saw two candles on the table, while a small figure sat sewing beside them. Well I'll be . . . he thought, and went in. She was darning socks. He went beside her and said: "I've come to see if you're all right." Rose worked on her sock and replied calmly: "Yes, of course I'm all right, but thanks for dropping in." Her eyes were enormous, with a wild look, and her mouth was trembling like that of an old woman. "What are you doing?" he asked, at a loss. "What do you think?" she said, tartly. Then she looked wonderingly at the sock which was stretched across her palm and shuddered. "Your dad's sock?" he said carefully; and she gave him an angry glance and began to cry. That's better, he thought, and went forward and made her lean against him while he said aloud: "Take it easy, take it easy, miss." But she did not cry for long. Almost at once she pushed him away and said: "Well there's no need to let the socks go to waste. They'll do for someone."

"That's right, miss." He stood hesitantly beside her and after a moment she lifted her head and looked at him. For the first time she saw him. He was a slight man, of middle height, who seemed young because of the open, candid face, though his hair was greying. His pleasant grey eyes rested compassionately on her and his smile was warm. "Perhaps you'd like them," she suggested. "And there's his clothes, too—he didn't have anything very special, but he always looked after his things." She began to cry again, this time more quietly, with small, shuddering sobs. He sat gently beside her, patting her hand as it lay on the table, repeating, "Take it easy, miss, take it easy, it's all right." The sound of his voice soothed her and soon she came to an end, dried her eyes and said in a matter-of-fact voice: "There, I'm just silly, what's the use of crying?" She got up, adjusted the candles so that they would not gutter over the cloth, and said: "Well we might as well have a cup of tea." She brought him one, and they sat drinking in silence. He was watching her curiously; there was something about her that tugged at his imagination. She was such an indomitable little figure sitting there staring out of sad, tired eyes, under the ruins of her home, like a kind of waif. She was not pretty, he decided, looking at the small, thin face, at the tired locks of black hair lying tidily beside it. He felt tender towards her; also he was troubled by her. Like everyone who lived through the big cities during the war, he knew a great deal about nervous strain; about shock; he could not have put words around what he knew, but he felt there was still something very wrong with Rosie; outwardly, however, she seemed sensible, and so he suggested: "You'd better get yourself some sleep. It'll be morning soon."

"I've got to be getting to work. I'm working an early shift."

He said: "If you feel like it," thinking it might be better for her to work. And so he left her, and went back home to get some sleep.

That next evening he came by expecting to find her gone, and saw her sitting at the table, in the yellow glow from the candles, her hands lying idly before her, staring at the wall. Everything was very tidy, and the dust had been removed. But the crack in the ceiling had perceptibly widened. "Hasn't anyone been to see you?" he asked carefully. She replied evasively: "Oh, some old nosey-parkers came and said I mustn't stay." "What did you tell them?" She hesitated, and then said: "I said I wasn't staying here, I was with some friends." He scratched his head, smiling ruefully: he could imagine the scene. "These old nosey-parkers," she went on resentfully, "interfering, telling people what to do."

"You know miss, I think they were right, you ought to move out."

"I'm staying here," she announced defiantly, with unmistakable fear. "Nothing's getting me out. Not all the king's horses."

"I don't expect they could spare the king's horses," he said, trying to make her laugh; but she replied seriously, after considering it: "Well, even if they could." He smiled tenderly at her literal-mindedness, and suggested on an impulse: "Come to the pictures with me, doesn't do any good to sit and mope."

"I'd like to, but it's Sunday, see?"

"What's the matter with Sunday?"

"Every Sunday I go and see a friend of mine who has a little girl . . ." She began to explain; and then she stopped and went pale. She scrambled to her feet and said: "Oh, oh I never thought . . ."

"What's wrong, what's up?"

"Perhaps that bomb got them too, they were along this street —oh dear, oh dear, I never came to think—I'm wicked, that's what I am. . . ." She had taken up her bag and was frantically wrapping her scarf around her head.

"Here, miss, don't go rushing off—I can find out for you, perhaps I know—what was her name?"

She told him. He hesitated for a moment and then said: "You're having bad luck, and that's a fact. She was killed the same time."

"She?" asked Rose quickly.

"The mother was killed, the kid's all right, it was playing in another room."

Rose slowly sat down, thinking deeply, her hand still holding the scarf together at her chin. Then she said: "I'll adopt her, that's what I'll do."

He was surprised that she showed no sort of emotion at the death of the woman, her friend. "Hasn't the kid got a dad?" he asked. "He's in North Africa," she said. "Well, he'll come back after the war, he might not want you to adopt the kid." But she was silent, and her face was hard with determination. "Why this kid in particular?" he asked. "You'll have kids of your own one day."

She said evasively: "She's a nice kid, you should see her." He left it. He could see that there was something there too deep for him to grasp. Again he suggested: "Come to the pictures and take your mind off things." Obediently she rose and placed herself at his disposal, as it were. Walking along the streets, she turned this way and that at a touch of his hand, but in spirit she was not with him. He knew that she sat through the film without seeing it. She's in a bad way, he said helplessly to himself. It's time she snapped out of it.

But Rose was thinking only of Jill. Her whole being was now concentrated on the thought of the little girl. Tomorrow she would find out where she was. Some nosey-parkers would have got hold of her—that was certain; they were always bossing other people. She would take Jill away from them and look after her—they could stay in the basement until the house got rebuilt. . . . Rose was awake all night, dreaming of Jill; and next day she did not go to work. She went in search of the child. She found her grandmother had taken her. She had never thought of the grandmother, and the discovery was such a shock that she came back to the basement not knowing how she walked or what she did. The fact that she could not have the child seemed more terrible than anything else; it was as if she had been deprived maliciously of something she had a right to; something had been taken away from her—that was how she felt.

Jimmie came that night. He was asking himself why he

kept returning, what it would come to; and yet he could not keep away. The image of Rose, the silent, frightened little girl—which was how he saw her—stayed with him all day. When he entered the basement she was sitting as usual by the candles, staring before her. He saw with dismay that she had made no effort to clean the place, and that her hair was untidy. This last fact seemed worse than anything.

He sat beside her, as usual, and tried to think of some way to make her snap out of it. At last he remarked: "You ought to be making some plans to move, Rose." At this she irritably shrugged her shoulders. She wished he would stop pestering her with this sort of reminder. At the same time she was glad to have him there. She would have liked him to stay beside her silently; his warm friendliness wrapped her about like a blanket, but she could never relax into it because there was a part of her mind alert against him for fear of what he might say.

She was afraid, really, that he might talk of her father. Not once had she allowed herself to think of it—her father's death, as it must have been. She said to herself the words: My father's dead, just as she had once said to herself: My mother's dead. Never had she allowed those words to form into images of death. If they had been ordinary deaths, deaths one could understand, it would have been different. People dying of illness or age, in bed; and then the neighbours coming, and then the funeral—that was understandable, that would have been different. But not the senselessness of a black bomb falling out of the sky, dropped by a nice young man in an aeroplane, not the silly business of a lorry running someone over—no, she could not bear to think of it. Underneath the surface of living was a black gulf, full of senseless horror. All day, at the factory (where she helped to make other bombs) or in the basement at night, she made the usual movements, said the expected things, but never allowed herself to think of death. She said: "My father's been killed," in a flat, ordinary voice, without letting pictures of death arise into her mind.

And now here was Jimmie, who had come into her life just when she needed his warmth and support most; and even this was two-faced, because it was the same Jimmie who made these remarks, forcing her to think . . . she would not think, she refused to respond. Jimmie noticed that whenever he made a remark connected in any way with the future, or even with the war, a blank nervous look came onto her face and she turned away her eyes. He did not know what to do. For that evening he left it, and came back next day. This was the sixth day after the bomb, and he saw that the crack in the ceiling was bulging heavily downwards from the weight on top of it, and when a car passed, bits of plaster flaked down in a soft white rain. It was really dangerous. He had to do something. And still she sat there, her hands lying loosely in front of her, staring at the wall. He decided to be cruel. His heart was hammering with fright at what he was going to do; but he announced in a loud and cheerful voice: "Rose, your father's dead, he's not going to come back."

She turned her eyes vaguely towards him; it seemed as if she had not heard at all. But he had to go on now. "Your dad's had it," he said brightly. "He's copped it. He's dead as a doornail, and it's no use staying here."

"How do you know?" she asked faintly. "Sometimes there are mistakes. Sometimes people come back, don't they?"

This was much worse than he had thought. "He won't come back. I saw him myself."

"No," she protested, sharply drawing breath.

"Oh, yes I did. He was lying on the pavement, smashed to smithereens." He was waiting for her face to change. So far, it was obstinate, but her eyes were fixed on him like a scared rabbit's. "Nothing left," he announced, jauntily, "his legs were gone—nothing there at all, and he didn't have a head left either. . . ."

And now Rose got to her feet with a sudden angry movement, and her eyes were small and black. "You—" she began. Her lips shook. Jimmie remained seated. He was trying to look casual, even jaunty. He was forcing himself to smile. Underneath, he was very frightened. Supposing this was the wrong thing? Supposing she went clean off her rocker . . . supposing . . . He passed his tongue quickly over his lips and glanced at her to see how she was. She was still staring at him. But now she seemed to hate him. He wanted to laugh from fright. But he stood up and with an appearance of deliberate brutality, said: "Yes, Rosie girl, that's how it is, your dad's nothing but a bleeding corpse—that's good, bleeding!" And now, he thought, I've done it properly! "You—" began Rose again, her face contracted with hatred. "You—" And such a stream of foul language came

from her mouth that it took him by surprise. He had expected
her to cry, to break down. She shouted and raved at him, lifting
her fists to batter at his chest. Gently holding her off, he said
silently to himself, giving himself courage: Ho, ho, Rosie my
girl, what language, naughty, naughty! Out loud he said, with
uneasy jocularity: "Hey, take it easy, it's not my fault now. . . ."
He was surprised at her strength. The quiet, composed, neat little Rose was changed into a screaming hag, who scratched and
kicked and clawed. "Get out of here, you—" and she picked up
a candlestick and threw it at him. Holding his arm across his
face, he retreated backwards to the door, gave it a kick with his
heel, and went out. There he stood, waiting, with a half-rueful,
half-worried smile on his face, listening. He was rubbing the
scratches on his face with his handkerchief. At first there was
silence, then loud sobbing. He straightened himself slowly. I
might have hurt her bad, talking like that, he thought; perhaps
she'll never get over it. But he felt reassured; instinctively he
knew he had done the right thing. He listened to the persistent
crying for a while, and then wondered: Yes, but what do I do
now? Should I go back again now, or wait a little? And more
persistent than these worries was another: And what then? If
I go back now, I'll let myself in for something and no mistake.
He slowly retreated from Rose's door, down the damaged street,
to a pub at the corner, which had not been hit. Must have a
drink and a bit of a think. . . . Inside the pub he leaned quietly
by the counter, glass in hand, his grey eyes dark with worry. He
heard someone say: "Well, handsome, and what's been biting
you?" He looked up, smiling, and saw Pearl. He had known her
for some time—nothing serious; they exchanged greetings
and bits of talk over the counter when he dropped in. He liked
Pearl, but now he wanted to be left alone. She lingered and said,
again: "How's your wife?" He frowned quickly, and did not
reply. She made a grimace as if to say: Well, if you don't want
to be sociable I'm not going to force you! But she remained
where she was, looking at him closely. He was thinking: I
shouldn't have started it, I shouldn't have taken her on. No
business of mine what happened to her. . . . And then, unconsciously straightening himself, with a small, desperate smile
that was also triumphant: You're in trouble again, my lad,
you're in for it now! Pearl remarked in an offhand way: "You'd
better get your face fixed up—been in a fight?" He lifted his

hand to his face and it came away covered with blood. "Yes," he said, grinning, "with a spitfire." She laughed, and he laughed with her. The words presented Rose to him in a new way. Proper little spitfire, he said to himself, caressing his cheek. Who would have thought Rose had all that fire in her? Then he set down the glass, straightened his tie, wiped his cheek with his handkerchief, nodded to Pearl with his debonair smile, and went out. Now he did not hesitate. He went straight back to the basement.

Rose was washing clothes in the sink. Her face was swollen and damp with crying, but she had combed her hair. When she saw him, she went red, trying to meet his eyes, but could not. He went straight over to her and put his arms around her. "Here, Rosie, don't get all worked up now." "I'm sorry," she said, with prim nervousness, trying to smile. Her eyes appealed to him. "I don't know what came over me, I don't really."

"It's all right, I'm telling you."

But now she was crying from shame. "I never use them words. Never. I didn't know I knew them. I'm not like that. And now you'll think . . ." He gathered her to him and felt her shoulders shaking. "Now, don't you waste any more time thinking about it. You were upset—well, I wanted you to be upset. I did it on purpose, don't you see, Rosie? You couldn't go on like that, pretending to yourself." He kissed the part of her cheek that was not hidden in his shoulder. "I'm sorry, I'm ever so sorry," she wept, but she sounded much better.

He held her tight and made soothing noises. At the same time he had the feeling of a man sliding over the edge of a dangerous mountain. But he could not stop himself now. It was much too late. She said, in a small voice: "You were quite right, I know you were. But it was just that I couldn't bear to think. I didn't have anybody but Dad. It's been him and me together for ever so long. I haven't got anybody at all. . . ." The thought came into her mind and vanished: Only George's little girl. She belongs to me by rights.

Jimmie said indignantly: "Your dad—I'm not saying anything against him, but it wasn't right to keep you here looking after him. You should have got out and found yourself a nice husband and had kids." He did not understand why, though only for a moment, her body hardened and rejected him. Then she relaxed and said submissively: "You mustn't say anything against my dad."

"No," he agreed, mildly, "I won't." She seemed to be waiting. "I haven't got anything now," she said, and lifted her face to him. "You've got me," he said at last, and he was grinning a little from sheer nervousness. Her face softened, her eyes searched his, and she still waited. There was a silence, while he struggled with commonsense. It was far too long a silence, and she was already reproachful when he said: "You come with me, Rosie, I'll look after you."

And now she collapsed against him again and wept: "You do love me, don't you, you do love me?" He held her and said: "Yes, of course I love you." Well, that was true enough. He did. He didn't know why, there wasn't any sense in it, she wasn't even pretty, but he loved her. Later she said: "I'll get my things together and come to where you live."

He temporised, with an anxious glance at the ominous ceiling: "You stay here for a bit. I'll get things fixed first."

"Why can't I come now?" She looked on in a horrified, caged way around the basement as if she couldn't wait to get out of it—she, who had clung so obstinately to its shelter.

"You just trust me now, Rosie. You pack your things, like a good girl. I'll come back and fetch you later." She clutched his shoulders and looked into his face and pleaded: "Don't leave me here long—that ceiling—it might fall." It was as if she had only just noticed it. He comforted her, put her persuasively away from him, and repeated he would be back in half an hour. He left her sorting out her belongings in worried haste, her eyes fixed on the ceiling.

And now what was he going to do? He had no idea. Flats—they weren't so hard to find, with so many people evacuated; yes, but here it was after eleven at night, and he couldn't even lay hands on the first week's rent. Besides, he had to give his wife some money tomorrow. He walked slowly through the damaged streets, in the thick dark, his hands in his pockets, thinking: Now you're in a fix. Jimmie boy, you're properly in a fix.

About an hour later his feet took him back. Rose was seated at the table, and on it were two cardboard boxes and a small suitcase—her clothes. Her hands were folded together in front of her.

"It's all right?" she enquired, already on her feet.

"Well, Rosie, it's like this—" He sat down and tried for the right words. "I should've told you. I haven't got a place really."

"You've got no place to sleep?" she enquired incredulously. He avoided her eyes and muttered: "Well, there's complications." He caught a glimpse of her face and saw there—pity! It made him want to swear. Hell, this was a mess, and what was he to do? But the sorrowful warmth of her face touched him and, hardly knowing what he was doing, he let her put her arms around him, while he said: "I was bombed out last week."

"And you were looking after me, and you had no place yourself?" she accused him tenderly.

"We'll be all right. We'll find a place in the morning," he said.

"That's right, we'll have our own place and—can we get married soon?" she enquired shyly, going pink.

At this, he laid his face against hers, so that she could not look at him, and said: "Let's get a place first, and we can fix everything afterwards."

She was thinking. "Haven't you got no money?" she enquired diffidently, at last. "Yes, but not the cash. I'll have it later." He was telling himself again: You're properly in the soup, Jimmie, in—the—soup!

"I've got two hundred pounds in the post office," she offered, smiling with shy pride, as she fondled his hair. "And there's the furniture from here—it's not hurt by the bomb a bit. We can furnish nicely."

"I'll give it back to you later," he said desperately.

"When you've got it. Besides, my money is yours now," she said, smiling tenderly at him. "*Ours.*" She tasted the word delicately, inviting him to share her pleasure in it.

Jimmie was essentially a man who knew people, got around, had irons in the fire and strings to pull; and by next afternoon he had found a flat. Two rooms and a kitchen, a cupboard for the coal, hot and cold water, and a share of the bathroom downstairs. Cheap, too. It was the top of an old house, and he was pleased that one could see trees from Battersea Park over the tops of the buildings opposite. Rose'll like it, he thought. He was happy now. All last night he had lain on the floor beside her in the ruinous basement, under the bulging ceiling, consumed by dubious thoughts; now these had vanished, and he was optimistic. But when Rose came up the stairs with her packages she went straight to the window and seemed to shrink back. "Don't you like it, Rosie?" "Yes, I like it, but . . ." Soon she laughed and said, apologetically: "I've always lived underneath—I mean, I'm not used to being so high up." He kissed her and teased her and she laughed too. But several times he noticed that she looked unhappily down from the window and quickly came away, with a swift, uncertain glance around at the empty rooms. All her life she had lived underground, with busses and cars rumbling past above eye-level, the weight of the big old house heavy over her, like the promise of protection. Now she was high above streets and houses, and she felt unsafe. Don't be silly, she told herself. You'll get used to it. And she gave herself to the pleasure of arranging furniture, putting things away. She took a hundred pounds of her money out of the post office and bought—but what she bought was chiefly for him. A chest for his clothes: she teased him because he had so many; a small wireless set; and finally a desk for him to work on, for he had said he was studying for an engineering degree of some kind. He asked her why she bought nothing for herself, and she said, defensively, that she had plenty. She had arranged the new flat to look like her old home. The table stood the same way, the calendar with yellowing roses hung on the wall, and she worked happily beside her stove, making the same movements she had used for years; for the cupboard, the drying-line and the drain-ing-board had been fixed exactly as they had been "at home." Unconsciously, she still used the phrase. "Here," he protested, "isn't this home now?" She said seriously: "Yes, but I can't get used to it." "Then you'd better get used to it," he complained, and then kissed her to make amends for his resentment. When this had happened several times, he let out: "Anyway, the base-ment's fallen in. I passed today, and it's filled with bricks and stuff." He had intended not to tell her. She shrank away from him and went quite white. "Well, you knew it wasn't going to stay for long," he said. She was badly shaken. She could not bear to think of her old home gone; she could imagine it, the great beams slanting into it, filled with dirty water—she imagined it and shut out the vision forever. She was quiet and listless all that day, until he grew angry with her. He was quite often angry. He would protest when she bought things for him. "Don't you like it?" she would enquire, looking puzzled. "Yes, I like it fine, but . . ." And later she was hurt because he seemed reluctant to use the chest, or the desk.

There were other points where they did not understand each other. About four weeks after they moved in she said: "You aren't much of a one for home, are you?" He said, in genuine astonishment: "What do you mean? I'm stuck here like . . ." He stopped, and put a cigarette in his mouth to take the place of speech. From his point of view he had turned over a new leaf; he was a man who hated to be bound, to spend every evening the same way; and now he came to Rose most evenings straight from work, ate supper with her, paid her sincere compliments on her cooking, and then—well, there was every reason why he should come, he would be a fool not to! He was consumed by secret pride in her. Fancy Rose, a girl like her, living with her old man all these years, like a girl shut into a convent, or not much better—you'd think there was something wrong with a girl who got to be thirty before having a man in her bed! But there was nothing wrong with Rose. And at work he'd think of their nights and laugh with deep satisfaction. She was all right, Rose was. And then slowly, a doubt began to eat into the pride. It wasn't natural that she'd been alone all those years. Besides, she was a good-looker. He laughed when he remembered that he thought her quite ugly at first. Now that she was happy, and in a place of her own and warmed through with love, she was really pretty. Her face had softened, she had a delicate colour in her thin cheeks, and her eyes were deep and welcoming. It was like coming home to a little cat, all purring and pliable. And when he took her to the pictures he walked proudly by her, conscious of the other men's glances at her. And yet he was the first man who had the sense to see what she could be? Hmm, not likely, it didn't make sense.

He talked to Rose, and suddenly the little cat showed its sharp and unpleasant claws. "What is it you want to know?" she demanded coldly, after several clumsy remarks from him. "Well, Rosie—it's that bloke George, you said you were going to marry him when you were a kid still?"

"What of it?" she said, giving him a cool glance.

"You were together a long time?"

"Three years," she said flatly.

"Three years!" he exclaimed. He had not thought of anything so serious. "Three years is a long time."

She looked at him with a pleading reproach that he entirely failed to understand. As far as she was concerned the delight

Jimmie had given her completely cancelled out anything she had known before. George was less than a memory. When she told herself that Jimmie was the first man she had loved, it was true, because that was how she felt. The fact that he could now question it, doubting himself, weakened the delight, made her unsure not only of him but of herself. How could he destroy their happiness like this! And into the reproach came contempt. She looked at him with heavy critical eyes; and Jimmie felt quite wild with bewilderment and dismay—she could look at him like that!—then that proved she had been lying when she said he was the first—if she had said so. . . . "But Rosie," he blustered, "it stands to reason. Engaged three years, and you tell me . . ."

"I've never told you anything," she pointed out, and got up from the table and began stacking the dishes ready for washing.

"Well, I've a right to know, haven't I?" he cried out, unhappily.

But this was very much a mistake. "Right?" she enquired in a prim, disdainful voice. She was no longer Rose, she was something much older. She seemed to be hearing her mother speaking. "Who's talking about rights?" She dropped the dishes neatly into the hot, soapy water and said: "Men! I've never asked you what you did before me. And I'm not interested either, if you want to know. And what I did if I did anything doesn't interest you neither." Here she turned on the tap so that the splashing sound made another barrier. Her ears filled with the sound of water, she thought: Men, they always spoil everything. She had forgotten George, he didn't exist. And now Jimmie brought him to life and made her think of him. Now she was forced to wonder: Did I love him as much then? Was it the same as this? And if her happiness with George had been as great as now it was with Jimmie, then that very fact seemed to diminish love itself and make it pathetic and uncertain. It was as if Jimmie were doing it on purpose to upset her. That, at any rate, was how she felt.

But across the din of the running water Jimmie shouted: "So I'm not interested, is that it?"

"No, you'd better not be interested," she announced, and looked stonily before her, while her hands worked among the hot slippery plates. "So that's how it is?" he shouted, again furiously.

To which she did not reply. He remained leaning at the table, calling Rose names under his breath, but at the same time conscious of bewilderment. He felt that all his possessive masculinity was being outraged and flouted; there was, however, no doubt that she felt as badly treated as he did. As she did not relent he went to her and put his arms around her. It was necessary for him to destroy this aloof and wounded-looking female and restore the loving, cosy woman. He began to tease: "Spitfire, little cat, that's what you are." He pulled her hair and held her arms to her sides so that she could not dry the plates. She remained unresponsive. Then he saw that the tears were running down her immobile and stubborn cheeks, and in a flush of triumph picked her up and carried her over to the bed. It was all quite easy, after all.

But maybe not so easy, because late that night, in a studiously indifferent voice, Rose enquired from the darkness at his side: "When are we going to get married?" He stiffened. He had forgotten—or almost—about this. Hell, wasn't she satisfied? Didn't he spend all his evenings here? He might just as well be married, seeing what she expected of him. "Don't you trust me, Rosie?" he enquired at last. "Yes, I trust you," she said, rather doubtfully, and waited. "There's reasons why I can't marry you just now." She remained silent, but her silence was like a question hanging in the dark between them. He did not reply, but turned and kissed her. "I love you, Rosie, you know that, don't you?" Yes, she knew that; but about a week later he left her one morning saying: "I can't come tonight, Rosie. I've got to put in some work on this exam." He saw her glance at the desk she had bought him and which he had never used. "I'll be along tomorrow as usual," he said quickly, wanting to escape from the troubled, searching eyes.

She asked suddenly: "Your wife getting anxious about you?"

He caught his breath and stared at her: "Who told you?" She laughed derisively. "Well, who told you?"

"No one told me," she said, with contempt.

"Then I must have been talking in my sleep," he muttered, anxiously.

She laughed loudly: " 'Someone told me.' 'Talking in your sleep'—you must think I'm stupid." And with a familiar, maddening gesture, she turned away and picked up a dishcloth.

"Leave the dishes alone; they're clean, anyway," he shouted.

"Don't shout at me like that."

"Rose," he appealed after a moment, "I was going to tell you, I just couldn't tell you—I tried to, often."

"Yes?" she said laconically. That "yes" of hers always exasperated him. It was like a statement of rock-bottom disbelief, a basic indifference to himself and the world of men. It was as if she said: There's only one person I can rely on—myself.

"Rosie, she won't divorce me, she won't give me my freedom." These dramatic words were supplied straight to his tongue by the memory of a film he had seen the week before. He felt ashamed of himself. But her face had changed. "You should have told me," she said; and once again he was disconcerted because of the pity in her voice. She had instinctively turned to him with a protective movement. Her arms went around him and he let his head sink on her shoulder with that old feeling that he was being swept away, that he had no control over the things he did and said. Hell, he thought, even while he warmed to her tenderness: to hell with it. I never meant to get me and Rosie into this fix. In the meantime she held him comfortingly, bending her face to his hair, but there was a rigidity in her pose that told him she was still waiting. At last she said: "I want to have kids. I'm not getting any younger." He tightened his arms around her waist while he thought: I never thought of that. For he had two children of his own. Then he thought: She's right. She should have kids. Remember how she got worked up over that other kid in the blitz? Women need to have kids. He thought of her with his child, and pride stirred in him. He realised he would be pleased if she got pregnant, and felt even more at sea. Rose said: "Ask her again, Jimmie. Make her divorce you. I know women get spiteful and that about divorces, but if you talk to her nice—" He miserably promised that he would. "You'll ask her tonight?" she insisted. "Well . . ." The fact was, that he had not intended to go home tonight. He wanted to have an evening to himself—go to the pub, see some of his pals, even work for an hour or so. "Weren't you going home tonight?" she asked, incredulously, seeing his face. "No, I meant it. I want to do some work. I've got to get this exam, Rosie. I know I can take it if I work a little. And then I'm qualified. Just now I'm not one thing and I'm not the other." She accepted this with a sigh, then pleaded: "Go home tomorrow then and ask her."

"But tomorrow I want to come and see you, Rosie, don't you want me?" She sighed again, not knowing that she did, and smiled: "You're nothing but a baby, Jimmie." He began coaxing: "Come on, be nice, Rosie, give me a kiss." He felt it was urgently necessary for him to have her warm and relaxed and loving again before he could leave her with a quiet mind. And so she was—but not entirely. There was a thoughtful line across her forehead and her mouth was grave and sad. Oh, to hell with it, he thought, as he went off. To hell with them all.

The next evening he went to Rose anxiously. He had drunk himself gay and debonair in the pub, he had flirted a little with Pearl, talked sarcastically about women and marriage, and finally gone home to sleep. He had breakfast with his family, avoided his wife's sardonic eye, and went off to work with a bad hangover. At the factory, as always, he became absorbed in what he was doing. It was a small factory which made precision instruments. He was highly skilled, but in status an ordinary workman. He knew, had known for a long time, that with little effort he could easily take an examination which would lift him into the middleclasses as far as money was concerned. It was the money he cared about, not the social aspect of it. For years his wife had been nagging at him to better himself, and he answered impatiently because, for her, what mattered was to outdo their neighbours. This he despised. But she was right for the wrong reasons. It was a question of devoting a year of evenings to study. What was a year of one's life? Nothing. And he had always found examinations easy. That day, at the factory, he had decided to tell Rose that she would not see as much of him in future. He swore angrily to himself that she must understand a man had a duty to himself. He was only forty, after all. . . . And yet, even while he spoke firmly to himself and to the imaginary Rose, he saw a mental picture of the desk she had bought him that stood unused in the livingroom of the flat. "Well, who's stopping you from working?" she would enquire, puzzled. Genuinely puzzled, too. But he could not work in that flat, he knew that; although in the two months before he had met Rose he was working quite steadily in his evenings. That day he was cursing the fate that had linked him with Rose; and by evening he was hurrying to her as if some terrible thing might happen if he were not there by supper time. He was expecting her to be cold and distant, but she fell into his arms as if he had been away for weeks. "I missed you," she said, clinging to him. "I was so lonely without you."

"It was only one night," he said, jauntily, already reassured.

"You were gone two nights last week," she said, mournfully. At once he felt irritated. "I didn't know you counted them up," he said, trying to smile. She seemed ashamed that she had said it. "I just get lonely," she said, kissing him guiltily. "After all . . ."

"After all what?" His voice was aggressive.

"It's different for you," she defended herself. "You've got— other things." Here she evaded his look. "But I go to work, and then I come home and wait for you. There's nothing but you to look forward to." She spoke hastily, as if afraid to annoy him, and then she put her arms around his neck and kissed him coaxingly and said: "I've cooked you something you like—can you smell it?" And she was the warm and affectionate woman he wanted her to be. Later he said: "Listen, Rosie girl, I've got to tell you something. That exam—I must start working for it." She said, gaily, at once: "But I told you already, you can work here at the desk and I'll sew while you work, and it'll be lovely." The idea seemed to delight her, but his heart chilled at it. It seemed to him quite insulting to their romantic love that she should not mind his working, that she should suggest prosaic sewing—just like a wife. He spent the next few evenings with her, newly in love, absorbed in her. And he felt hurt when she suggested hurriedly—for she was afraid of a rebuff—"If you want to work tonight, I don't mind, Jimmie." He said laughing: "Oh, to hell with work, you're the only work I want." She was flattered, but the thoughtful line was marked deep across her forehead. About a fortnight after his wife was first mentioned, she delicately enquired: "Have you asked her about the divorce?"

He turned away, saying evasively, "She wouldn't listen just now." He was not looking at her, but he could feel her heavy, questioning look on him. His irritation was so strong that he had to make an effort to control it. Also he was guilty, and that guilt he could understand even less than the irritation. He all at once became very gay, so that his mood infected her, and they were giggling and laughing like two children. "You're just conventional, that's what you are," he said, pulling her hair. "Conventional?" she tasted the big word doubtfully. "Women always want to get married. What do you want to get married for? Aren't we happy? Don't we love each other? Getting married would just spoil it." But theoretical statements like these always confused Rose. She would consider each of them separately, with a troubled face, rather respectful of the intellectual minds that had formulated them. And while she considered them, the current of her emotions ran steadily and deep, unconnected with words. From the gulf of love in which she was sunk she murmured, fondly: "Oh, you—you just talk and talk." "Men are polygamous," he said gaily, "it's a fact, scientists say so." "What are women then?" she asked, keeping her end up. "They aren't polygamous." She considered this seriously, as was her way, and said doubtfully: "Yes?" "Hell," he expostulated, half-seriously, half-laughing, "you're telling me you're polygamous?" But Rose moved uneasily, with a laugh, away from him. To connect a word like "polygamous," reeking as it did of the "nosey-parkers" who were, she felt, her chief enemy in life, with herself, was too much to ask of her. Silence. "You're thinking of George," he suddenly shouted, jealously. "I wasn't doing any such thing," she said, indignantly. Her genuine indignation upset him. He always hated it when she was serious. As far as he was concerned, he had just been teasing her—he thought.

Once she said: "Why do you always look cross when I say what I think about something?" Now, that surprised him—didn't she always say what she thought? "I don't get cross, Rosie, but why do you take everything so serious?" To this she remained silent, in the darkness. He could see the small, thoughtful face turned away from him, lit by the bleak light from the window. The thoughtfulness seemed to him like a reproach. He liked her childish and responsive. "Don't I make you happy, Rose?" He sounded miserable. "Happy?" she said, testing the word. Then she unexpectedly laughed and said: "You talk so funny sometimes you make me laugh." "I don't see what's funny, you've no sense of humour, that's what's wrong with you." But instead of responding to his teasing voice, she thought it over and said seriously: "Well, I laugh at things, don't I? I must be laughing at something then. My dad used to say I hadn't any sense of humour. I used to say to him, 'How do you know what I laugh at isn't as funny as what you laugh at?'" He said, wryly, after a moment, "When you laugh, it's like you're not laughing at all, it's something nasty." "I don't know what you mean." "I ask you if you're happy and you laugh—what's funny about being happy?" Now he was really resentful. Again she meditated about it, instead of responding—as he had hoped —with a laugh or some reassurance that he made her perfectly happy. "Well, it stands to reason," she concluded, "people who talk about happy or unhappy, and then the long words—and the things you say, women are like this, and men are like that, and polygamous and all the rest—well . . ." "Well?" he demanded. "Well, it just seems funny to me," she said lamely. For she could have found no words at all for what she felt, that deep knowledge of the dangerousness and the sadness of life. Bombs fell on old men, lorries killed people, and the war went on and on, and the nights when he did not come to her she would sit by herself, crying for hours, not knowing why she was crying, looking down from the high window at the darkened, ravaged streets—a city dark with the shadow of war.

In the early days of their love Jimmie had loved best the hours of tender, aimless, frivolous talk. But now she was, it seemed, always grave. And she questioned him endlessly about his life, about his childhood. "Why do you want to know?" he would enquire, unwilling to answer. And then she was hurt. "If you love someone, you want to know about them, it stands to reason." So he would give simple replies to her questions, the facts, not the spirit, which she wanted. "Was your mum good to you?" she would ask, anxiously. "Did she cook nice?" She wanted him to talk about the things he had felt; but he would reply, shortly: "Yes" or "Not bad."

"Why don't you want to tell me?" she would ask, puzzled.

He repeated that he didn't mind telling her; but all the same he hated it. It seemed to him that no sooner had one of those long companionable silences fallen, in which he could drift off into a pleasant dream, than the questions began. "Why didn't you join up in the war?" she asked once. "They wouldn't have me, that's why." "You're lucky," she said fiercely. "Lucky nothing, I tried over and over. I wanted to join."

And then, to her obstinate silence he said: "You're queer. You've got all sorts of ideas. You talk like a pacifist; it's not right when there's a war on."

"Pacifist!" she cried angrily. "Why do you use all these silly words? I'm not anything."

"You ought to be careful, Rosie, if you go saying things like that where people can hear you, they'll think you're against the war, you'll get into trouble."

"Well, I am against the war, I never said I wasn't."

"But Rosie—"

"Oh shut up. You make me sick. You all make me sick. Everybody just talks and talks, and those fat old so-and-so's talking away in Parliament, they just talk so they can't hear themselves think. Nobody knows anything and they pretend they do. Leave me alone, I don't want to listen." He was silent. To this Rose he had nothing to say. She was a stranger to him. Also, he was shocked: he was a talker who liked picking up phrases from books and newspapers and using them in a verbal game. But she, who could not use words, who was so deeply inarticulate, had her own ideas and stuck to them. Because he used words so glibly, she tried to become a citizen of his country— out of love for him and because she felt herself lacking. She would sit by the window with the newspapers and read earnestly, line by line, having first overcome her instinctive shrinking from the language of violence and hatred that filled them. But the war news, the slogans, just made her exhausted and anxious. She turned to the more personal. WAR TAKES TOLL OF MARRIAGE, she would read. WAR DISRUPTS HOMES. Then she dropped the paper and sat looking before her, her brow puzzled. That headline was about her, Rose. And again, she would read the divorces; some judge would pronounce: "This unscrupulous woman broke up a happy marriage and . . ." Again the paper dropped while Rose frowned and thought. That meant herself. She was one of those bad women. She was The Other Woman. She might even be that ugly thing, A Co-Respondent. . . . But she didn't feel like that. It didn't make sense. So she stopped reading the newspapers; she simply gave up trying to understand.

She felt she was not on an intellectual level with Jimmie, so instinctively she fell back on her feminine weapons—much to his relief. She was all at once very gay, and he fell easily into the mood. Neither of them mentioned his wife for a time. It was their happiest time. After love, lying in the dark, they talked aimlessly, watching the sky change through moods of cloud and rain and tinted light, watching the searchlights. They took no notice of raids or danger. The war was nearly over, and they spoke as if it had already ended. "If we was killed now, I shouldn't mind," she said, seriously, one night when the bombs were bad. He said: "We're not going to get killed, they can't kill us." It sounded a simple statement of fact: their love and happiness was proof enough against anything. But she said again, earnestly: "Even if we was killed, it wouldn't matter. I don't see how anything afterwards could be as good as this, now."

"Ah, Rosie, don't be so serious always."

It was not long before they quarrelled again—because she was so serious. She was asking questions again about his past. She was trying to find out why the Army wouldn't have him. He would never tell her. And then he said, impatiently, one night: "Well, if you must know, I've got ulcers. . . . Ah for God's sake, Rosie, don't fuss, I can't stand being fussed." For she had given a little cry and was holding him tight. "Why didn't you tell me? I haven't been cooking the proper things for you."

"Rose, for crying out aloud, don't go on."

"But if you've got ulcers you must be fed right, it stands to reason." And next evening when she served him some milk pudding, saying anxiously: "This won't hurt your stomach," he flared up and said, "I told you, Rosie, I won't have you coddling me." Her face was loving and stubborn and she said: "But you've got no sense. . . ."

"For the last time, I'm not going to put up with it."

She turned away, her mouth trembling, and he went to her and said desperately: "Now don't take on Rosie, you mean it nicely, but I don't like it, that's why I didn't tell you before. Get it?" She responded to him, listlessly, and he found himself thinking angrily: I've got two wives, not one. . . . They were both dismayed and unhappy because their happiness was so precarious it could vanish overnight just because of a little thing like ulcers and milk pudding.

A few days later he ate in heavy silence through the supper she had provided, and then sarcasm broke out of him: "Well, Rosie, you've decided to humour me, that's what it is." The meal had consisted of steamed fish, baked bread, and very weak tea, which he hated. She looked uncomfortable, but said obstinately: "I went to a friend of mine who's a chemist at the corner, and he told me what it was right for you to eat." Involuntarily he got up, his face dark with fury. He hesitated, then he went out, slamming the door.

He stood moodily in the pub, drinking. Pearl came across and said: "What's eating you tonight?" Her tone was light, but her eyes were sympathetic. The sympathy irritated him. He ground out: "Women!" slammed down his glass and turned to go. "Doesn't cost you anything to be polite," she said tartly, and he replied: "Doesn't cost you anything to leave me alone." Outside he hesitated a moment, feeling guilty. Pearl had been a friend for so long, and she had a soft spot for him—also, she knew about his wife, and about Rose, and made no comment, seemed not to condemn. She was a nice girl, Pearly was—he went back and said, hastily: "Sorry, Pearl, didn't mean it." Without waiting for a reply he left again, and this time set off for home.

The woman he called his wife looked up from her sewing and asked briefly: "What do you want now?"

"Nothing." He sat down, picked up a paper and pretended to read, conscious of her glances. They were not hostile. They had gone a long way beyond that, and the fact that she seemed scarcely interested in him was a relief after Rose's persistent, warm curiosity—like loving white fingers strangling him, he thought involuntarily. "Want something to eat?" she enquired at last.

"What have you got?" he enquired cautiously, thinking of the tasteless steamed fish and baked bread he had just been offered.

"Help yourself," she returned, and he went to the cupboard on the landing, filled a plate with bread and mustard pickles and cheese, and came back to the room where she was. She glanced at his plate, but made no comment. After a while he asked sarcastically: "Aren't you going to tell me I shouldn't eat pickles?"

"Couldn't care less," she returned equably. "If you want to kill yourself, it's your funeral." At this he laughed loudly, and she joined him. Later, she asked: "Staying here the night?"

"If you don't mind." At this she gave a snort of derisive laughter, got up and said: "Well, I'm off to bed. You can't have the sofa because the kids have got a friend and he's got it. You'll have to put a blanket and a cushion on the floor."

"Thanks," he said, indifferently. "How are the kids?" he enquired, as an afterthought.

"Fine—if you're interested."

"I asked, didn't I?" he replied, without heat. All this conversation had been conducted quietly, indifferently, and the undercurrent was almost amiable. An outsider would have said they hardly knew each other. When she had gone he took a blanket from a drawer, wrapped it round his legs, and settled himself in a chair. He had meant to think about himself and Rose, but instead he dropped off at once. He left the house early, before anyone was awake. All day at the factory he thought: About Rose, what must I do about Rose? After work he went instinctively to the pub. Pearl stood quietly behind the counter, showing him by her manner that she was not holding last night's bad humour against him. He meant to have one drink and go, but he had three. He liked Pearl's cheerful humour. She told him that her young man was playing about with another girl, and added, as if it hardly concerned her: "There's plenty of fish in the sea after all."

"That's right," he said, non-committally.

"Well, we all have our troubles," she said, with a half-humorous sigh.

"Yes—for all they're worth." At this he felt a pang of guilt because he had been thinking of Rose. Pearl was giving him a keen look. Then she said: "I didn't say he hadn't been worth it. But now that other girl's getting all the benefit. . . ." Here she laughed grimly.

He liked this cheerful philosophy, and could not prevent himself saying: "He's got no sense, turning you up." He looked with appreciation at her crown of bright yellow curls, at her shapely body. Her eyes brightened, and he said goodnight quickly, and left. He mustn't get mixed up with Pearl now, he was thinking.

It was after eight. Usually he was with Rose by seven. He lagged down the street, thinking of what he would say to her, and entered the flat with a blank mind. For some reason he was very tired. Rose had eaten by herself, cleared the table, and now sat beside it, frowning over a newspaper. "What are you reading?" he asked, for something to break the ice. Looking over her shoulder he saw that she had marked a column headed: SURPLUS WOMEN PRESENT PROBLEM TO CHURCHES. He was surprised.

"That's what I am, a surplus woman," she said, and gave that sudden, unexpected laugh.

"What's funny?" he asked, uncomfortably.

"I've a right to laugh if I want," she retorted. "Better than cry-ing, anyhow."

"Oh, Rose," he said helplessly. "Oh, Rose, stop it now. . . ." She burst into tears and clung to him. But this was not the end, and he knew it. Later that night she said: "I want to tell you something . . ." and he thought: Now I'm for it—whatever it is.

"You were home last night, weren't you?"

"Yes," he said, alertly.

A pause and then she asked: "What did she say?"

"About what?" It was a fact that he did not immediately understand her. "*Jimmie*," she said incredulously, under her breath, and he said: "Rosie, it's no good, I told you that before."

She did not immediately reply, but when she did her voice was very bitter: "Well, I see how it is now."

"You don't see at all," he said sarcastically.

"Well, then, tell me?" He was silent. Her silence was like a persistent question. Again he felt as if the warm, soft fingers were wrapping around him. He felt suffocated. "There's nothing to explain, I just can't help it." A pause, and then she said in the flat, laconic way he hated: "Yes?" That was all. For the time being, at least. A week later she said, calmly: "I went to see Jill's granny today."

His heart faltered and he thought: Now what? "Well?" he enquired.

"George was killed last month. In Italy."

He felt triumph, then he said guiltily: "I'm sorry." She waved this away and said: "I told her granny that I want to adopt Jill."

"But Rose . . ." Then he saw her face and quailed.

"I want kids," she said fiercely. He dropped his gaze.

"Her granny won't give her up."

"I'm not so sure. At first she said no, then she thought it over a bit. She's getting old now—eighty next year. She thinks per-haps Jill'd be better with me."

"You want to have the kid *here*?" he asked, incredulously. "Why shouldn't I? You're working all day." She was silent; he looked at her—and slowly coloured.

"Listen a minute," she began, persuasively—not unpleasantly at all, though every word wounded Jimmie. "I furnished this place. It was my furniture and my money. And I've got a hundred still in the post office in case of accidents—I'll need it; now the war's over we won't be earning so much money, if I know anything. So far, I've not been . . ." But here her instinctive delicacy overcame her, and she could not go on. She wanted to say that she paid for the food, paid for everything. Lately, even the rent. One week he had said, apologetically, that he hadn't the cash, and that if she could do it this once—but now it was a regular thing.

"You want me to give you the money so you can stay here with the kid?" he enquired, cautiously. She was blushing with embarrassment. "No, no," she said, quickly. "Listen. If you can just pay the rent—that would be enough. I could get a part-time job, just the mornings. Jill goes to school now, and I'd manage somehow."

He digested this silently. He was thinking, unbelievingly: She wants to have a kid here, a kid's always in the way—that means she can't love me any more. He said slowly: "Well, Rosie, if that's what you want, then go ahead."

Her face cleared into vivid happiness and she came running to him in the old way and kissed him and said: "Oh, Jimmie; oh, Jimmie. . . ." He held her and thought, bitterly, that all this joy was not because of him; all she cared about was the kid—women! But at the back of his mind were two other thoughts: First, that he did not know how he would find the money to pay the rent unless he passed that examination soon, and the other was that the authorities would never let Rose have Jill.

Next evening Rose was despondent. "Did you see the officials?" he asked at last.

"Yes." She would not look at him. She was staring helpless down from the window.

"Wasn't it any good?"

"They said I must prove myself a fit and proper person. So I said that I was. I told them I'd known Jill since she was born. I said I knew her mother and father."

"That's true enough," he could not help interjecting, jealously. She gave him a cold look and said: "Don't start that now. I told them her granny was too old, and I could easily look after her."

"Well then?"

She was silent; then, wringing her hands unconsciously, she cried out: "They wasn't nice, they wasn't nice to me at all. There were two of them, a woman and a man. They said: How could I support Jill? I said I could get money. They said I must show them papers and things. . . ." She was silently crying now, but she did not come to him. She stayed at the window, her back turned, shutting him out of her sorrow. "They asked me, how could a working girl look after a child, and I said I'd do it easy, and they said, did I have a husband. . . ." Here she leaned her head against the wall and sobbed bitterly. After a time he said: "Well, Rosie, it looks as if I'm no good for you. Perhaps you'd better give me up and get yourself a proper husband." At this she jerked her head up, looked incredulously at him and cried: "Jimmie! How could I give you up. . . ." He went to her, thinking, in relief: She loves me better after all. He meant: better than the child.

It seemed that Rose had accepted her defeat. For some days she talked sorrowfully about those "nosey-parkers" at the Council. She was even humorous, though in the way that made him uneasy. "I'll go to them," she said, smiling grimly. "I'll go and I'll say: I can't help being a surplus woman. Don't blame me, blame the war, it's not my fault that they keep killing all the men off in their silly wars. . . ."

And then his jealousy grew unbearable and he said: "You love Jill better than me." She laughed in amazement, and said: "Don't be a baby, Jimmie." "Well, you must. Look how you go on and on about that kid. It's all you think about."

"There isn't no sense in you being jealous of Jill."

"Jealous," he said, roughly. "Who says I'm jealous?"

"Well, if you're not, what are you then?"

Oh, go to hell, go to hell, he muttered to himself, as he put his arms around her. Aloud he said: "Come on Rosie girl, come on, stop being like this; be like you used to be, can't you?"

"I'm not any different," she said patiently, submitting to his caresses with a sigh.

"So you're not any different," he said, exasperatedly. Then, controlling himself with difficulty he coaxed: "Rosie, Rosie, don't you love me a little. . . ."

For the truth was, he was becoming obsessed with the difference in Rose. He thought of her continuously as she had been. It was like dreaming of another woman, she was so changed now. At work, busy with some job that needed all his attention, he would start as if stung, and mutter: "Rose—oh, to hell with her!" He was remembering, with anguish, how she had run across the room to welcome him, how responsive she had been, how affectionate. He thought of her patient kindliness now, and wanted to swear. After work he would go straight to the flat, reaching it even before she did. The lights would be out, the rooms cold, like a reminder of how Rose had changed. She would come in, tired, laden with string bags, to find him seated at the table staring at her, his eyes black with jealousy. "This place is as cold as a street-corner," he would say angrily. She looked at him, sighed, then said, reasonably: "But Jimmie, look, here's where I keep the sixpences for the gas—why don't you light the fire?" Then he would go to her, holding down her arms as he kissed her, and she would say: "Just leave me a minute, Jimmie. I must get the potatoes on or there'll be no supper."

"Can't the potatoes wait a minute?"

"Let me get my arms free, Jimmie." He held them, so she would carefully reach them out from under the pressure of his grip, and put the string bags on the table. Then she would turn to kiss him. He noticed that she would be glancing worriedly at the curtains, which had not been drawn, or at the rubbish-pail, which had not been emptied. "You can't even kiss me until you've done all the housework," he cried, sullenly. "All right then, you tip me the wink when you've got a moment to spare and you don't mind being kissed."

To this she replied, listlessly but patiently: "Jimmie, I come straight from work and there's nothing ready, and before you didn't come so early."

"So now you're complaining because I come straight here. Before, you complained because I dropped in for a drink somewhere first."

"I never complained."

"You sulked, even if you didn't complain."

"Well, Jimmie," she said, after a sorrowful pause, as she peeled the potatoes. "If I went to drink with a boyfriend you wouldn't like it either."

"That means Pearl, I suppose. Anyway, it's quite different."

"Why is it different?" she asked, reasonably. "I don't like to go to pubs by myself, but if I did I don't see why not; I don't see why men should do one thing and women another."

These sudden lapses into feminism always baffled him. They seemed so inconsistent with her character. He left that point and said: "You're jealous of Pearl, that's what it is."

He wanted her, of course, to laugh, or even quarrel a little, so the thing could be healed by kisses, but she considered it, thoughtfully, and said: "You can't help being jealous if you love someone."

"Pearl!" he snorted. "I've known her for years. Besides, who told you?"

"You always think that nobody ever notices things," she said, sadly. "You're always so surprised."

"Well, how did you know?"

"People always tell you things."

"And you believe *people*."

A pause. Then: "Oh, Jimmie, I don't want to quarrel all the time, there isn't any sense in it." This sad helplessness satisfied him, and he was able to take her warmly in his arms. "I don't mean to quarrel either," he murmured.

But they quarrelled continuously. Every conversation was bound to end, it seemed, either in Pearl or in George. Or their tenderness would lapse into tired silence, and he would see her staring quietly away from him, thinking. "What are you getting so serious about now, Rosie?" "I was thinking about Jill. Her granny's too old. Jill's shut up in that kitchen all day—just think, those old nosey-parkers say I'm not a fit person for Jill, but at least I'd take her for walks on Sundays. . . ."

"You want Jill because of George," he would grind out, gripping her so tight she had to ease her arms free. "Oh, stop it, Jimmie, stop it."

"Well, it's true."

"If you want to think it, I can't stop you." Then the silence of complete estrangement.

After some weeks of this he went back to the pub one evening. "Hullo, stranger," said Pearl. Her eyes shone welcomingly over at him.

"I've been busy, one way or another," he said.

"I bet," she said, satirically, challenging him with her look.

He could not resist it. "Women," he said, "women." And he took a long drain from his glass.

"Don't you talk that way to me," she said, with a short laugh. "My boyfriend's just got himself married. Didn't so much as send me an invite to the wedding."

"He doesn't know what's good for him."

Her wide, blue eyes swung around and rested obliquely on

him before she lowered them to the glasses she was rinsing. "Perhaps there are others who don't neither."

He hesitated and said: "Maybe, maybe not." Caution held him back. Yet they had been flirting cheerfully for so long, out of sheer good nature. The new hesitation was dangerous in itself, and gave depth to their casual exchanges. He thought to himself: Careful, Jimmie boy, you're off again if you're not careful. He decided he should go to another pub. Yet he came back, every evening, for he looked forward to the moment when he stood in the doorway, and then she saw him, and her eyes warmed to him as she said lightly: "Hullo, handsome, what trouble have you been getting yourself into today?" He got into the way of staying for an hour or more, instead of the usual half hour. He leaned quietly against the counter, his coat collar turned up round his face, while his grey eyes rested appreciatively on Pearl. Sometimes she grew self-conscious and said: "Your eyes need a rest," and he replied, coolly: "If you don't want people to look at you, better buy yourself another jumper." He would think, with a sense of disloyalty: Why doesn't Rosie buy herself one like that? But Rose always wore her plain, dark skirts and her neat blouses, pinned at the throat with a brooch.

Afterwards he climbed the stairs to the flat thinking anxiously: Perhaps today she'll be like she used to be? He would expectantly open the door, thinking: Perhaps she'll smile when she sees me and come running over. . . .

But she would be at the stove, or seated at the table waiting, and she gave him that tired, patient smile before beginning to dish up the supper. His disappointment dragged down his spirits, but he forced himself to say: "Sorry I'm late, Rosie." He braced himself for a reproach, but it never came, though her eyes searched him anxiously, then lowered as if afraid he might see a reproach in them.

"That's all right," she replied, carefully, setting the dishes down and pulling out the chair for him.

Always, he could not help looking to see if she was still "fussing" about the food. But she was taking trouble to hide the precautions she took to feed him sensibly. Sometimes he would probe sarcastically: "I suppose your friend the chemist said that peas were good for ulcers—how about a bit of fried onions, Rose?"

"I'll make you some tomorrow," she would reply. And she

averted her eyes, as if she were wincing, when he pulled the pickle bottle towards him and heaped mustard pickle over his fish. "You only live once," he remarked, jocularly.

"That's right." And then, in a prepared voice: "It's your stomach, after all."

"That's what I always said." To himself he said: Might be my bloody wife. For his wife had come to say at last: "It's your stomach, if you want to die ten years too soon. . . ."

If he had attacks of terrible pain in the night, after a plateful of fried onions, or chips thick with tomato sauce, he would lie rigid beside her, concealing it, just as he had with his wife. Women fussing! Fussing women!

He asked himself continually why he did not break it off. A dozen times he had said to himself: That's enough now, it's no good; she doesn't love me, anyway. Yet by evening he was back at the pub, flirting tentatively with Pearl, until the time came when he could delay no longer. And back he went, as if dragged, to Rose. He could not understand it. He was behaving badly— and he could not help himself; he should be studying for his exam—and he couldn't bring himself to study; it would be so easy to make Rose happy—and he couldn't take the decisive step; he should decide not to return to Pearl in the evenings, and he could not keep away. What was it all about? Why did people just go on doing things, as if they were dragged along against their will, even against what they enjoyed?

One Saturday evening Rose said: "Tomorrow I won't be here."

He clutched at her hand and demanded: "Why not? Where are you going?"

"I'm going to take Jill out all day and then have supper with her granny."

Breathing quickly, his lips set hard, he brought out: "No time for me any more, eh?"

"Oh, Jimmie, have some sense."

Next morning he lay in bed and watched her dress to go out. She was smiling, her face soft with pleasure. She kissed him consolingly before she left, and said: "It's only on Sundays, Jimmie."

So it's going to be every Sunday, he thought, miserably.

In the evening he went to the pub. It was Pearl's evening off. He had thought of asking her along to the pictures, but he didn't know where she lived. He went to his home. The children were in bed and his wife had gone to see a neighbour. He felt as if everyone had let him down. At last he went back to the flat and waited for Rose. When she came he sat quietly, an angry little smile on his face, while she chatted animatedly about Jill. In bed he turned his back on her and lay gazing at the greyish light at the window. It couldn't go on, he thought; what was the point of it? Yet he was back next evening as usual.

Next Sunday she asked him to go with her to see Jill.

"What the hell!" he exclaimed, indignantly.

She was hurt. "Why not, Jimmie? She's so sweet. She's such a good girl. She's got long golden ringlets."

"I suppose George had long yellow ringlets, too," he said, sardonically.

She looked at him blankly, shrugged, and said no more. When she had gone he went to Pearl's house—for he had asked for the address—and took her to the pictures. They were careful and polite with each other. She watched him secretly: his face was tight with worry; he was thinking of Rose with that damned brat—she was happy with Jill, when she couldn't even raise a smile for him! When he said goodnight Pearl drawled out: "Do you even know what the film was called?"

He laughed uncomfortably and said: "Sorry, Pearl, got things on my mind."

"Thanks for the information." But she was not antagonistic; she sounded sympathetic. He was grateful for her understanding. He hastily kissed her cheek and said: "You're a nice kid, Pearl." She flushed and quickly put her arms around his neck and kissed him again. Afterwards he thought, uneasily: If I just lifted my little finger I could have her.

At home Rose was cautious with him and did not mention Jill until he did. She was afraid of him. He saw it, and it made him half-wild with frustration. Anyone'd think that he was cruel to her! "For crying out loud, Rose," he pleaded, "what's the matter with you, why can't you be nice to me?"

To which she sighed and asked in a dry, tired voice: "I suppose Pearl is nice to you?"

"Hell, Rosie, I have to do something when you're away."

"I asked you to come with me, didn't I?"

They were now on the verge of some crisis, and both knew it, and for several days they were treating each other almost like strangers, for fear of an explosion. They hardly dared let their eyes meet.

On the following Saturday evening Rose enquired: "Made a date with Pearl for tomorrow?"

He was going to deny it, but she went on implacably: "Things can't go on like this, Jimmie." He was silent, and then she asked suddenly: "Jimmie, did you ever ask your wife to divorce you?"

He exploded: "Hell, Rosie, are you going back to that now?"

"I suppose you are thinking it's not my affair and I'm interfering," she said, and laughed with that unexpected, grim humour of hers.

Rose went off to Jill in the morning without another word to him. As for him, he went to Pearl. The girl was gentle with him: "If you don't feel like the pictures, you don't have to take me," she said, sympathetically. So they went to a cafe and he said, abruptly: "You know, Pearl, it's no good getting to like me; women think I'm poison when they get to know me better." He was grinning savagely and his hands were clenched. She reached out, took one of them and said: "It's for me to say what I want, isn't it?"

"Don't say I didn't warn you," he said at random, putting his arm around her, feeling that he had, by this remark, absolved himself of all responsibility for Pearl. He was thinking of Rose. She'd be back home by now. Well, it'd do her good not to find him there. She just took him for granted, and it was a fact. But after a restless five minutes he said: "I'd better be going along." When he left her, Pearl said: "I love you, Jimmie, don't forget that. I'd do anything for you, anything. . . ." She ran into the house, and he saw she was crying. She loves me, at any rate, he thought, thinking angrily of Rose. Slowly he climbed the long, dark stairs. He was very tired again. I must get some sleep, he mused, dimly; this can't go on, it wears a man out, I'll go straight to bed and sleep.

But he opened the door on the bright light; she was already in, seated at the table. She was still in her best clothes: a neat, grey suit, white blouse, brooch; and her hair looked as if she had just combed it. Her face was what held him: she looked tight-lipped, determined, even triumphant. What's up? he thought.

"Don't go to bed straight away," she said—for he was throwing off his shoes and coat. "There's something we've got to do."

"It'd better be pretty important," he said. "I'm dead on my feet."

"For once you'd better stay on your feet." This brutal note was new and astonishing from Rose.

"What's going on?"

"You'll see in a minute."

He almost ignored her and went to bed: but at last he compromised by pushing the pillows against the wall and leaning on them. "Wake me up when the mystery's ripe," he said, and dropped off at once.

Rose remained at the table in a stiff attitude, watching the door and listening. The day before she had made a decision. Or rather, a decision had been made for her. It had come into her head: Why not write and ask? She'll know. . . . At first the idea had shocked her. It was a terrible thing to do, contrary to what she felt to be the right way to behave. And yet from the moment it entered her head, the idea gathered strength until she could think of nothing else. At last she sat down and wrote:

Dear Mrs. Pearson, I am writing to you on a matter which is personal to us both, and I hope it gives no offence, because I am not writing in that spirit. I am Rose Johnson, and your husband has been courting me two years since before the war stopped. He says you live separate and you won't divorce him. I want things to be straight and proper now, and I've been thinking perhaps if we have a little talk, things will be straight. If this meets with your approval, Jimmie will be home tomorrow night, ten or so, and we could all three have a talk. Believing me, I mean no trouble or offence.

This letter she carried herself to the house and dropped through the letter slot. Afterwards, she could not go away. She walked guiltily up the street, and then down, her eyes fixed on the windows. That was where *she* lived. Her heart was so heavy with jealous love it was as if her very feet were weighted. That was where Jimmie had lived with *her*. That was where his children lived. She hoped to get a glimpse of them, and looked searchingly at some children playing in the street, trying to find his eyes, his features in their faces. There was a little boy she thought might be his son, and she found herself smiling at the child, her eyes filled with tears. Then finally, she walked past the house and thought: If only it'd come to an end, I can't bear it no longer, I can't bear it. . . .

There were footsteps, Rose half-rose to open the door, but they went past. Later, when she had given up hope, there were steps again, and they stopped at the door. Now the moment had come, Rose was faint with anxiety and could hardly cross the floor. She thought: I mustn't wake Jimmie, he's so tired. She opened the door with an instinctive gesture of warning towards the sleeping man. Mrs. Pearson glanced at him, smiled in a tight-lipped fashion, and came in, making her heels click loudly. Rose had created for herself many pictures of this envied woman, Jimmie's wife. She had imagined her, for some reason, fair, frail, pretty—rather like Pearl, whom she had seen in the street once. But she was not like that at all. She was a big square woman, heavy on her feet. Her face was square and good-humoured, her brown eyes calm and direct. Her dark, greying hair was tightly waved, too close around her head for the big features. "Well," she said in a normal voice, with a good-humoured nod at Rose, "the prisoner's sleeping before the execution."

"Oh, no," breathed Rose, in dismay: "It's not like that at all."

Mrs. Pearson looked curiously at her, shrugged, and laid her bag on the table. "Thanks for the letter," she said. "It's about time you found out."

"Found out what?" asked Rose quickly.

Jimmie stirred, looked blankly over at the women and then scrambled quickly to his feet. "What the hell?" he asked, involuntarily. And then, very angry: "What are you poking your nose in for?"

"She asked me to come," said his wife, quietly. She sat down. "Come and sit down, Jimmie, and let's talk it over."

He looked quite baffled. Then he, too, shrugged, lit a cigarette and came to the table. "O.K., get it over," he said jauntily. He glanced incredulously at Rose. She could do this to him, he thought, hurt to the very bone—and she says she loves me. . . . He was set hard against Rose, hard against his wife. . . . Well, let them do as they liked.

"Now listen, Jimmie," said his wife, reasonably as to a child, "it seems you've been telling this poor child a lot of lies." He sat tight and said nothing. She waited, then went on, looking at Rose: "This is the truth. We've been married ten years. We've got two kids. We were happy at first—well, nothing unusual in that. Then he got fed up. Nothing unusual in that either. In any case, he's not a man who can settle to anything. I used to be unhappy, and then I got used to it. I thought: Well, we can't change our natures. Jimmie doesn't mean any harm, he just drifts into everything. Then the war started, and you know how things were. I was working night-shifts, and he too, and there was a girl at his factory, and they got together." She paused, looking at Jimmie like a presiding judge, but he said nothing. He smoked, looking down at the table with a small, angry smile. "I got fed up and said we'd better separate. Then he came running back and said it wouldn't happen again, he didn't really want a divorce." Jimmie stirred, opened his mouth to say something then shut it again. "You were going to say?" enquired his wife, pleasantly. "Nothing. Go on, enjoy yourself."

"Isn't it true?"

He shrugged, she waited and then went on: "So everything was all right for a month or so. And he started up with the girl again. . . ."

"Pearl?" Rose suddenly asked.

He snorted derisively: "Pearl, that's all she can think of."

"Who's Pearl?" asked Mrs. Pearson, alertly. "She's a new one on me."

"Never mind," said Rose. "Go on."

"But this time I'd had enough. I said either me or her." Addressing Rose, excluding Jimmie, she said: "If there's one thing he can't do, it's make up his mind to anything."

"Yes," agreed Rose, involuntarily. Then she flushed and looked guiltily at Jimmie.

"Go on, enjoy yourselves," he said, sarcastically.

"*We* haven't been enjoying ourselves. *You* have."

"That's what you think."

"Oh, have it your own way. You always do. But now I'm talking to Rose. When I said either her or me, he got into a proper state. The root of the matter was, he wanted both of us. Men are naturally bigamists, he said."

"Yes," said Rose again, quickly.

"Oh, for crying out aloud, can't you two ever take a joke. It was a joke. What did you think? I wanted to be married to two women at once? One's enough."

"You have been married to two women at once," said his

wife, tartly. "Whether you liked it or not. Or as good as." The two women were looking at each other, smiling grimly. Jimmie glanced at them, got up and went to the window. "Let me know when you've finished," he said.

Rose made an impulsive movement towards him. "Oh, sit down; the trouble with you is you're too soft with him. I was too."

From the window Jimmie said: "Soft as concrete." To Rose he made a gesture indicating his wife: "Just take a good look at her and see how soft she is." Rose looked, flushed, and said: "Jimmie, I didn't mean anything nasty for you."

"You didn't?" That was contemptuous.

"Well," said Mrs. Pearson, loudly, interrupting this exchange: "At last I got the pip and divorced him."

Rose drew her breath. Her eyes were frantic. "You're *divorced*?" She stared at Jimmie, waiting for him to deny it, but he kept his back turned. "Jimmie, it isn't true, is it?"

Mrs. Pearson, with rough kindness, "Now don't get upset, Rose. It's time you knew what's what. We got divorced three years ago. I got the kids, and he's supposed to pay me two pounds a week for them. But if the other girl thought he was going to marry her she made a mistake. He was courting me for three years and then I had to put my foot down. He said he couldn't live without me, but at the registry he looked like a man being executed."

Jimmie said, in cold fury: "If you want to know the truth, she wouldn't marry me, she married someone else."

"I daresay. She learned some sense, I expect. You never told her you were married, and she got shocked into her senses when she found out."

"Go on," said Rose, "I want to hear the end of it."

"There wasn't any end, that's the point. After the divorce Jimmie was popping in and out as if he belonged in the house. 'Here,' I used to say, 'I thought we were divorced.' But if he was short of a place to sleep, or he wanted somewhere to read, or his ulcers was bad, he'd drop in for a meal or the use of the sofa. And he still does," she concluded.

Rose was crying now. "Why did you lie to me, Jimmie," she implored, gazing at his impervious back. "Why? You didn't have to lie to *me*."

He said miserably: "What was the use, Rosie? I have to pay

two pounds a week to her. I couldn't do that and give you a proper home too."

Rose gave a helpless sort of gesture and sat silently, while the tears ran steadily down. Mrs. Pearson watched her, not unkindly. "What's the use of crying?" she enquired. "He's no good to you. And you say he's got another woman already! Who's this Pearl?"

Rose said: "He takes her to the pictures and she wants to marry him."

"How the hell do you know?" he asked, turning around and facing them at last.

Rose glanced pleadingly at him and said softly: "But Jimmie, everybody knows."

"I suppose you've been down talking to Pearl," he said, contemptuously. "Women!"

"Of course I didn't." She was shocked. "I wouldn't do no such thing. But everyone knows about it."

"Who's everyone this time?"

"Well, there's my friend at the shop at the corner, who keeps my bit extra for me when there's biscuits or something going. He told me Pearl was crazy for you, and he said people said you were going to marry her."

"Jesus," he said simply, sitting on the bed. "Women."

"Just like him," commented Mrs. Pearson dryly. "He always thinks he's the invisible man. He can just carry on in broad daylight and no one'll notice what he's doing. He's always surprised when they do. He was going out with that other girl for months, and the whole factory knew it, but when I mentioned it he thought I'd had a private detective on him."

"Well," said Rose, helplessly, at last. "I don't know, I really don't."

Mrs. Pearson said again, with that rough warmth: "Now don't you mind too much, Rosie. You're well out of it, believe me."

Rosie's lips trembled again. Mrs. Pearson got up, sat by her and patted her shoulders. "There now," she said, as Rose collapsed. "Now don't take on. There, there," she soothed, while over Rose's head she gave her husband a deadly look. Jimmie was sitting on the edge of the bed, smoking, looking badly shaken. What he was thinking was: That Rose could do this to me—how could she do it to me?

"I haven't got nothing," wailed Rose. "I haven't got anything or anybody anywhere."

Mrs. Pearson went on patting. Her face was thoughtful. She made soothing noises, and then she asked suddenly, out of the blue: "Listen, Rose, how'd you like to come and live with me?"

Rose stopped crying from the shock, lifted her face and said: "What did you say?"

"I expect you're surprised." Mrs. Pearson looked surprised at herself. "I just thought of it—I'm starting a cake shop next month. I saved a bit during the war. I was looking for someone to help me with it. You could live in my place if you like. It's only got three rooms and a kitchen, but we'd manage."

"The house isn't yours?"

Mrs. Pearson laughed: "I suppose my lord told you he owned the whole house? Not on your life. I've got the basement."

"The basement," said Rose, intently.

"Well, it's warm and dry and in one piece, more than can be said for most basements."

"It's safer, too," said Rose, slowly.

"Safer?"

"If there's bombing or something."

"I suppose so," said Mrs. Pearson, rather puzzled at this. Rose was gazing eagerly into her face. "You've got the kids," said Rose, slowly.

"They're no trouble, really. They're at school."

"I didn't mean that—could I have a kid—no, listen, I'd be wanting to adopt a kid if I came to you. If I lived with you I'd be a fit and proper person and those nosey-parkers would let me have her."

"You want to adopt a kid?" said Mrs. Pearson, rather put out. She glanced at Jimmie, who said: "You say things about me—but look at her. She was engaged to a man, and he was killed and all she thinks about is his kid."

"Jimmie—" began Rose, in protest. But Mrs. Pearson asked: "Hasn't the kid got a mother?"

"The blitz," said Rose, simply.

After a pause Mrs. Pearson said thoughtfully: "I suppose there's no reason why not."

Rose's face illuminated. "Mrs. Pearson," she prayed, "Mrs. Pearson—if I could have Jill, if only I could have Jill . . ."

Mrs. Pearson said dryly: "I can't see me cluttering myself up

with kids if I didn't have to. You wouldn't catch me marrying
and getting kids if I had my chance over again, but it takes all
sorts to make a world."

"Then it'd be all right?"

Mrs. Pearson hesitated: "Yes, why not?"

Jimmie gave a short laugh. "Women," he said. "Women."

"You can talk," said his wife.

Rose looked shyly at him. "What are you going to do now?"
she asked.

"A fat lot you care," he said, bitterly.

"He's going to marry Pearl, I don't think," commented his
wife.

Rose said slowly: "You ought to marry Pearl, you know, Jimmie. You did really ought to marry her. It's not right. You
shouldn't make her unhappy, like me."

Jimmie stood before them, hands in pockets, trying to look
nonchalant. He was slowly nodding his head as if his worst sus-
picions were being confirmed. "So now you've decided to marry
me off," he said, savagely.

"Well, Jimmie," said Rose, "she loves you, everyone knows
that, and you've been taking her out and giving her ideas—and
—and—you could have this flat now, I don't want it. You'd
better have it, anyway; you can't get flats now the war's finished. And you and Pearl could live here." She sounded as if
she were pleading for herself.

"For crying out loud," said Jimmie, astonished, gazing at her.

Mrs. Pearson was looking shrewdly at him. "You know, Jimmie, it's not a bad idea, Rose is quite right."

"Wha-a-at? You too?"

"It's about time you stopped messing around. You messed
around with Rose here, and I told you time and time again, you
should either marry her or not, I said."

"You *knew* about me?" said Rosie, dazedly.

"Well, no harm in that," said Mrs. Pearson, impatiently. "Be
your age, Rose. Of course I knew. When he came home I used to
say to him: Now do right by that poor girl. You can't expect her
to go hanging about, missing her chances, just to give you an
easy life and somewhere to play nicely at nights."

"I told Rose," he said, abruptly. "I told her often enough I
wasn't good enough for her, I said."

"I bet you did," said his wife, shortly.

"Didn't I, Rose?" he asked her.

Rose was silent. Then she shrugged. "I just don't understand," she said at last. And then, after a pause: "I suppose you're just made that way." And then, after a longer pause: "But you ought to marry Pearl now."

"Just to please you, I suppose!" He turned challengingly to his wife: "And you, too, I suppose. You want to see me safely tied up to someone, don't you?"

"No one's going to marry me, stuck with two kids," said his wife. "I don't see why you shouldn't be tied too, if we're going to look at it that way."

"And you can't see why I shouldn't marry Pearl when I've got to pay you two pounds a week?"

Mrs. Pearson said on an impulse: "If you marry Pearl, I'll let you off the two pounds. I'm going to make a good thing out of my cake shop, I expect, and I won't need your bit."

"And if I don't marry her, then I must go on paying you the two pounds?"

"Fair enough," she said, calmly.

"Blackmail," he said bitterly. "Blackmail, that's what it is."

"Call it what you like." She got up and lifted her handbag from the table. "Well, Rose," she said. "All this has been sudden, spur-of-the-moment sort of thing. Perhaps you'd like to think about it. I'm not one for rushing into things myself, in the usual way. I wouldn't like you to come and then be sorry after."

Rose had unconsciously risen and was standing by her. "I'll come with you now, if it's all right. I'll get my things tomorrow. I wouldn't want to stay here tonight." She glanced at Jimmie, then averted her face.

"She's afraid of staying here with me," said Jimmie with bitter triumph.

"Quite right. I know you." She mimicked his voice: *"Don't go back on me, Rose, don't you trust me?"*

Rose winced and muttered: "Don't do that."

"Oh, I know him, I know him. And you'd have to put chains on him and drag him to the registry. It's not that he doesn't want to marry you. I expect he does, when all's said. But it just kills him to make up his mind."

"Staying with me, Rosie?" asked Jimmie, suddenly—the gambler playing his last card. He watched her bright eyes, waiting, almost sure of his power to make her stay.

Rose looked unhappily from him to Mrs. Pearson.

Mrs. Pearson watched her with a half-smile; that smile seemed to say: I'm not implicated, settle it for yourself, it makes no difference to me. But aloud she said: "You're a fool if you stay, Rosie."

"Let her decide," said Jimmie, quietly. He was thinking: If she cares anything she'll stay with me, she'll stand by me. Rose gazed pitifully at him and wavered. It flashed across her mind: He's just trying to prove something to his wife, he doesn't really want me at all. But she could not take her eyes away. There he sat, upright but easy, his hair ruffled lightly on his forehead, his handsome grey eyes watching her. She thought, wildly: Why does he just sit there waiting? If he loved me he'd come across and put his arms around me and ask nicely to stay with him, and I would—if he'd only do that. . . .

But he remained quiet, challenging her to move; and slowly the tension shifted and Rose drooped away from him with a sigh. She turned to Mrs. Pearson. He couldn't really love her or he wouldn't have just sat there—that's what she felt.

"I'll come with you," she said, heavily.

"That's a sensible girl, Rose."

Rose followed the older woman with dragging feet.

"You won't regret it," said Mrs. Pearson. "Men—they're more trouble than they're worth, when all is said. Women have to look after themselves these days, because if they don't, no one will."

"I suppose so," said Rose, reluctantly. She stood hesitating at the door, looking hopefully at Jimmie. Even now—she thought —even now, if he said one word she'd run back to him and stay with him.

But he remained motionless, with that bitter little smile about his mouth.

"Come on, Rose," said Mrs. Pearson. "Come, if you're coming. We'll miss the underground."

And Rose followed her. She was thinking, dully: I'll have Jill, that's something. And by the time she grows up perhaps there won't be wars and bombs and things, and people won't act silly any more.

# One off the Short List

•·•··•··•··•··•··•··•··•··•··•··•··•··•··•··•··•··•··•··•··•··•··•··•··•··•··•··•··•··•··•··•··•··•··•··•··•··•··•··•··•··•··•··•··•··•·•

**W**hen he had first seen Barbara Coles, some years before, he only noticed her because someone said: "That's Johnson's new girl." He certainly had not used of her the private erotic formula: *Yes, that one.* He even wondered what Johnson saw in her. She won't last long, he remembered thinking as he watched Johnson, a handsome man, but rather flushed with drink, flirting with some unknown girl while Barbara stood by a wall looking on. He thought she had a sullen expression.

She was a pale girl, not slim, for her frame was generous, but her figure could pass as good. Her straight yellow hair was parted on one side in a way that struck him as gauche. He did not notice what she wore. But her eyes were all right, he remembered: large, and solidly green, square-looking because of some trick of the flesh at their corners. Emeraldlike eyes in the face of a schoolgirl, or young schoolmistress who was watching her lover flirt and would later sulk about it.

Her name sometimes cropped up in the papers. She was a stage decorator, a designer, something on those lines.

Then a Sunday newspaper had a competition for stage design and she won it. Barbara Coles was one of the "names" in the theatre, and her photograph was seen about. It was always serious. He remembered having thought her sullen.

One night he saw her across the room at a party. She was talking with a well-known actor. Her yellow hair was still done on one side, but now it looked sophisticated. She wore an emerald ring on her right hand that seemed deliberately to invite comparison with her eyes. He walked over and said: "We have met before, Graham Spence." He noted, with discomfort, that he sounded abrupt. "I'm sorry, I don't remember, but how do you do?" she said, smiling. And continued her conversation.

He hung around a bit, but soon she went off with a group of people she was inviting to her home for a drink. She did not invite Graham. There was about her an assurance, a carelessness, that he recognised as the signature of success. It was then, watching her laugh as she went off with her friends, that he used the formula: *Yes, that one.* And he went home to his wife with enjoyable expectation, as if his date with Barbara Coles were already arranged.

His marriage was twenty years old. At first it had been stormy, painful, tragic—full of partings, betrayals and sweet reconciliations. It had taken him at least a decade to realise that there was nothing remarkable about this marriage that he had lived through with such surprise of the mind and the senses. On the contrary, the marriages of most of the people he knew, whether they were first, second or third attempts, were just the same. His had run true to form even to the serious love affair with the young girl for whose sake he had *almost* divorced his wife—yet at the last moment had changed his mind, letting the girl down so that he must have her for always (not unpleasurably) on his conscience. It was with humiliation that he had understood that this drama was not at all the unique thing he had imagined. It was nothing more than the experience of everyone in his circle. And presumably in everybody else's circle too?

Anyway, round about the tenth year of his marriage he had seen a good many things clearly, a certain kind of emotional adventure went from his life, and the marriage itself changed.

His wife had married a poor youth with a great future as a writer. Sacrifices had been made, chiefly by her, for that future. He was neither unaware of them, nor ungrateful; in fact he felt permanently guilty about it. He at last published a decently successful book, then a second, which now, thank God, no one remembered. He had drifted into radio, television, book reviewing.

He understood he was not going to make it; that he had become—not a hack, no one could call him that—but a member of that army of people who live by their wits on the fringes of

the arts. The moment of realisation was when he was in a pub
one lunchtime near the B.B.C. where he often dropped in to
meet others like himself: he understood that was why he went
there—they *were* like him. Just as that melodramatic marriage
had turned out to be like everyone else's—except that it had
been shared with one woman instead of with two or three—so
it had turned out that his unique talent, his struggles as a writer
had led him here, to this pub and the half-dozen pubs like it,
where all the men in sight had the same history. They all had
their novel, their play, their book of poems, a moment of fame,
to their credit. Yet here they were, running television programmes about which they were cynical (to each other or to
their wives) or writing reviews about other people's books. Yes,
that's what he had become, an impresario of other people's
talent. These two moments of clarity, about his marriage and
about his talent, had roughly coincided; and (perhaps not by
chance) had coincided with his wife's decision to leave him for
a man younger than himself who had a future, she said, as a
playwright. Well, he had talked her out of it. For her part, she had
to understand he was not going to be the T. S. Eliot or Graham
Greene of our time—but after all, how many were? She must
finally understand this, for he could no longer bear her awful
bitterness. For his part, he must stop coming home drunk at five
in the morning, and starting a new romantic affair every six
months which he took so seriously that he made her miserable
because of her implied deficiencies. In short he was to be a good
husband. (He had always been a dutiful father.) And she a
good wife. And so it was: the marriage became stable, as they
say.

The formula: *Yes, that one* no longer implied a necessarily
sexual relationship. In its more mature form, it was far from
being something he was ashamed of. On the contrary, it expressed a humorous respect for what he was, for his real talents
and flair, which had turned out to be not artistic after all, but
to do with emotional life, hard-earned experience. It expressed
an ironical dignity, a proving to himself not only: I can be
honest about myself, but also: I have earned the best in *that*
field whenever I want it.

He watched the field for the women who were well known in
the arts, or in politics; looked out for photographs, listened for
bits of gossip. He made a point of going to see them act, or dance,

or orate. He built up a not unshrewd picture of them. He would either quietly pull strings to meet a woman or—more often, for there was a gambler's pleasure in waiting—bide his time until he met her in the natural course of events, which was bound to happen sooner or later. He would be seen out with her a few times in public, which was in order, since his work meant he had to entertain well-known people, male and female. His wife always knew, he told her. He might have a brief affair with this woman, but more often than not it was the appearance of an affair. Not that he didn't get pleasure from other people envying him—he would make a point, for instance, of taking this woman into the pubs where his male colleagues went. It was that his real pleasure came when he saw her surprise at how well she was understood by him. He enjoyed the atmosphere he was able to set up between an intelligent woman and himself: a humorous complicity which had in it much that was unspoken, and which almost made sex irrelevant.

Onto the list of women with whom he planned to have this relationship went Barbara Coles. There was no hurry. Next week, next month, next year, they would meet at a party. The world of well-known people in London is a small one. Big and little fishes, they drift around, nose each other, flirt their fins, wriggle off again. When he bumped into Barbara Coles, it would be time to decide whether or not to sleep with her.

Meanwhile he listened. But he didn't discover much. She had a husband and children, but the husband seemed to be in the background. The children were charming and well brought up, like everyone else's children. She had affairs, they said; but while several men he met sounded familiar with her, it was hard to determine whether they had slept with her, because none directly boasted of her. She was spoken of in terms of her friends, her work, her house, a party she had given, a job she had found someone. She was liked, she was respected, and Graham Spence's self-esteem was flattered because he had chosen her. He looked forward to saying in just the same tone: "Barbara Coles asked me what I thought about the set and I told her quite frankly. . . ."

Then by chance he met a young man who did boast about Barbara Coles; he claimed to have had the great love affair with her, and recently at that; and he spoke of it as something generally known. Graham realised how much he had already become involved with her in his imagination because of how perturbed he was now, on account of the character of this youth, Jack Kennaway. He had recently become successful as a magazine editor—one of those young men who, not as rare as one might suppose in the big cities, are successful from sheer impertinence, effrontery. Without much talent or taste, yet he had the charm of his effrontery. "Yes, I'm going to succeed, because I've decided to; yes, I may be stupid, but not so stupid that I don't know my deficiencies. Yes, I'm going to be successful because you people with integrity, et cetera, et cetera, simply don't believe in the possibility of people like me. You are too cowardly to stop me. Yes, I've taken your measure and I'm going to succeed because I've got the courage not only to be unscrupulous but to be quite frank about it. And besides, you admire me; you must, or otherwise you'd stop me. . . ." Well, that was young Jack Kennaway, and he shocked Graham. He was a tall, languishing young man, handsome in a dark melting way, and, it was quite clear, he was either asexual or homosexual. And this youth boasted of the favours of Barbara Coles; boasted, indeed, of her love. Either she was a raving neurotic with a taste for neurotics; or Jack Kennaway was a most accomplished liar; or she slept with anyone. Graham was intrigued. He took Jack Kennaway out to dinner in order to hear him talk about Barbara Coles. There was no doubt the two were pretty close—all those dinners, theatres, weekends in the country—Graham Spence felt he had put his finger on the secret pulse of Barbara Coles; and it was intolerable that he must wait to meet her; he decided to arrange it.

It became unnecessary. She was in the news again, with a run of luck. She had done a successful historical play, and immediately afterwards a modern play, and then a hit musical. In all three, the sets were remarked on. Graham saw some interviews in newspapers and on television. These all centred around the theme of her being able to deal easily with so many different styles of theatre; but the real point was, of course, that she was a woman, which naturally added piquancy to the thing. And now Graham Spence was asked to do a half-hour radio interview with her. He planned the questions he would ask her with care, drawing on what people had said of her, but above all on his instinct and experience with women. The interview was to be at nine-thirty at night; he was to pick her up at six from the theatre where she was currently at work, so that there would be time, as the letter from the B.B.C. had put it, "for you and Miss Coles to get to know each other."

At six he was at the stage door, but a message from Miss Coles said she was not quite ready, could he wait a little. He hung about, then went to the pub opposite for a quick one, but still no Miss Coles. So he made his way backstage, directed by voices, hammering, laughter. It was badly lit, and the group of people at work did not see him. The director, James Poynter, had his arm around Barbara's shoulders. He was newly well known, a carelessly goodlooking young man reputed to be intelligent. Barbara Coles wore a dark blue overall, and her flat hair fell over her face so that she kept pushing it back with the hand that had the emerald on it. These two stood close, side by side. Three young men, stagehands, were on the other side of a trestle which had sketches and drawings on it. They were studying some sketches. Barbara said, in a voice warm with energy: "Well, so I thought if we did *this*—do you see, James? What do you think, Steven?" "Well, love," said the young man she called Steven, "I see your idea, but I wonder if . . ." "I think you're right, Babs," said the director. "Look," said Barbara, holding one of the sketches towards Steven, "look, let me show you." They all leaned forward, the five of them, absorbed in the business.

Suddenly Graham couldn't stand it. He understood he was shaken to his depths. He went off-stage, and stood with his back against a wall in the dingy passage that led to the dressing rooms. His eyes were filled with tears. He was seeing what a long way he had come from the crude, uncompromising, admirable young egomaniac he had been when he was twenty. That group of people there—working, joking, arguing, yes, that's what he hadn't known for years. What bound them was the democracy of respect for each other's work, a confidence in themselves and in each other. They looked like people banded together against a world which they—no, not despised, but which they measured, understood, would fight to the death, out of respect for what *they* stood for, for what *it* stood for. It was a long time since he felt part of that balance. And he understood that he had seen Barbara Coles when she was most herself, at ease with a group of people she worked with. It was then, with the tears drying on his eyelids, which felt old and ironic, that he decided he would sleep with Barbara Coles. It was a necessity for him. He went back through the door onto the stage, burning with this single determination.

The five were still together. Barbara had a length of blue gleaming stuff which she was draping over the shoulder of Steven, the stagehand. He was showing it off, and the others watched. "What do you think, James?" she asked the director. "We've got that sort of dirty green, and I thought . . ." "Well," said James, not sure at all, "well, Babs, well . . ."

Now Graham went forward so that he stood beside Barbara, and said: "I'm Graham Spence, we've met before." For the second time she smiled socially and said: "Oh, I'm sorry, I don't remember." Graham nodded at James, whom he had known, or at least had met off and on, for years. But it was obvious James didn't remember him either.

"From the B.B.C.," said Graham to Barbara, again sounding abrupt, against his will. "Oh I'm sorry, I'm so sorry, I forgot all about it. I've got to be interviewed," she said to the group. "Mr. Spence is a journalist." Graham allowed himself a small smile ironical of the word "journalist," but she was not looking at him. She was going on with her work. "We should decide tonight," she said. "Steven's right." "Yes, I am right," said the stagehand. "She's right, James, we need that blue with that sludge-green everywhere." "James," said Barbara, "James, what's wrong with it? You haven't said." She moved forward to James, passing Graham. Remembering him again, she became contrite. "I'm sorry," she said, "we can none of us agree. Well, look"—she turned to Graham—"you advise us, we've got so involved with it that . . ." At which James laughed, and so did the stagehands. "No, Babs," said James, "of course Mr. Spence can't advise. He's just this moment come in. We've got to decide. Well I'll give you till tomorrow morning. Time to go home, it must be six by now."

"It's nearly seven," said Graham, taking command.

"It isn't!" said Barbara, dramatic. "My God, how terrible, how appalling, how could I have done such a thing. . . ." She was laughing at herself. "Well, you'll have to forgive me, Mr. Spence, because you haven't got any alternative."

They began laughing again: this was clearly a group joke. And now Graham took his chance. He said firmly, as if he were her director, in fact copying James Poynter's manner with her: "No, Miss Coles, I won't forgive you, I've been kicking my heels for nearly an hour." She grimaced, then laughed and accepted it. James said: "There, Babs, that's how you ought to be treated. We spoil you." He kissed her on the cheek, she kissed him on both his, the stagehands moved off. "Have a good evening, Babs," said James, going, and nodding to Graham. Who stood concealing his pleasure with difficulty. He knew, because he had had the courage to be firm, indeed, peremptory, with Barbara, that he had saved himself hours of manoeuvring. Several drinks, a dinner—perhaps two or three evenings of drinks and dinners—had been saved because he was now on this footing with Barbara Coles, a man who could say: No, I won't forgive you, you've kept me waiting.

She said: "I've just got to . . ." and went ahead of him. In the passage she hung her overall on a peg. She was thinking, it seemed, of something else, but seeing him watching her, she smiled at him, companionably: he realised with triumph it was the sort of smile she would offer one of the stagehands, or even James. She said again: "Just one second . . ." and went to the stage-door office. She and the stage doorman conferred. There was some problem. Graham said, taking another chance: "What's the trouble, can I help?"—as if he could help, as if he expected to be able to. "Well . . ." she said, frowning. Then, to the man: "No, it'll be all right. Goodnight." She came to Graham. "We've got ourselves into a bit of a fuss because half the set's in Liverpool and half's here and—but it will sort itself out." She stood, at ease, chatting to him, one colleague to another. All this was admirable, he felt; but there would be a bad moment when they emerged from the special atmosphere of the theatre into the street. He took another decision, grasped her arm firmly, and said: "We're going to have a drink before we do anything at all, it's a terrible evening out." Her arm felt resistant, but remained within his. It was raining outside, luckily. He directed her, authoritative: "No, not that pub, there's a nicer one around the corner." "Oh, but I like this pub," said Barbara, "we always use it."

Of course you do, he said to himself. But in that pub there would be the stagehands, and probably James, and he'd lose contact with her. He'd become a *journalist* again. He took her firmly out of danger around two corners, into a pub he picked at random. A quick look around—no, they weren't there. At least, if there were people from the theatre, she showed no sign.

She asked for a beer. He ordered her a double Scotch, which she accepted. Then, having won a dozen preliminary rounds already, he took time to think. Something was bothering him—what? Yes, it was what he had observed backstage, Barbara and James Poynter. Was she having an affair with him? Because if so, it would all be much more difficult. He made himself see the two of them together, and thought with a jealousy surprisingly strong: *Yes, that's it.* Meantime he sat looking at her, seeing himself look at her, *a man gazing in calm appreciation at a woman:* waiting for her to feel it and respond. She was examining the pub. Her white woollen suit was belted, and had a not unprovocative suggestion of being a uniform. Her flat yellow hair, hastily pushed back after work, was untidy. Her clear white skin, without any colour, made her look tired. Not very exciting, at the moment, thought Graham, but maintaining his appreciative pose for when she would turn and see it. He knew what she would see: he was relying not only on the "warm, kindly" beam of his gaze, for this was merely a reinforcement of the impression he knew he made. He had black hair, a little greyed. His clothes were loose and bulky—masculine. His eyes were humorous and appreciative. He was not, never had been, concerned to lessen the impression of being settled, dependable: the husband and father. On the contrary, he knew women found it reassuring.

When she at last turned, she said, almost apologetic: "Would you mind if we sat down? I've been lugging great things around all day." She had spotted two empty chairs in a corner. So had he, but rejected them, because there were other people at the table. "But my dear, of course!" They took the chairs, and then Barbara said: "If you'll excuse me a moment." She had remembered she needed makeup. He watched her go off, annoyed with himself. She was tired; and he could have understood, protected, sheltered. He realised that in the other pub, with the people she had worked with all day, she would not have thought: I must make myself up, I must be on show. That was for outsiders. She had not, until now, considered Graham an outsider, because of his taking his chance to seem one of the working group in the theatre; but now he had thrown this opportunity away. She returned armoured. Her hair was sleek, no longer defenceless. And she had made up her eyes. Her eyebrows were untouched, pale gold streaks above the brilliant green eyes whose lashes were blackened. Rather good, he thought, the contrast. Yes, but the moment had gone when he could say: Did you know you had a smudge on your cheek? Or—my dear girl—pushing her hair back with the edge of a brotherly hand. In fact, unless he was careful, he'd be back at starting point.

He remarked: "That emerald is very cunning," smiling into her eyes.

She smiled politely, and said: "It's not cunning, it's an accident; it was my grandmother's." She flirted her hand lightly by her face, though, smiling. But that was something she had done before, to a compliment she had had before, and often. It was all social, she had become social entirely. She remarked: "Didn't you say it was half past nine we had to record?"

"My dear Barbara, we've got two hours. We'll have another drink or two, then I'll ask you a couple of questions, then we'll drop down to the studio and get it over, and then we'll have a comfortable supper."

"I'd rather eat now, if you don't mind. I had no lunch, and I'm really hungry."

"But my dear, of course." He was angry. Just as he had been surprised by his real jealousy over James, so now he was thrown off balance by his anger: he had been counting on the long quiet dinner afterwards to establish intimacy. "Finish your drink and I'll take you to Nott's." Nott's was expensive. He glanced at her assessingly as he mentioned it. She said: "I wonder if you know Butler's? It's good and it's rather close." Butler's was good, and it was cheap, and he gave her a good mark for liking it. But Nott's it was going to be. "My dear, we'll get into a taxi and be at Nott's in a moment, don't worry."

She obediently got to her feet: the way she did it made him understand how badly he had slipped. She was saying to herself: Very well, he's like that, then all right, I'll do what he wants and get it over with. . . .

Swallowing his own drink, he followed her, and took her arm in the pub doorway. It was polite within his. Outside it drizzled. No taxi. He was having bad luck now. They walked in silence to the end of the street. There Barbara glanced into a side street where a sign said: BUTLER's. Not to remind him of it, on the contrary, she concealed the glance. And here she was, entirely at his disposal; they might never have shared the comradely moment in the theatre.

They walked half a mile to Nott's. No taxis. She made conversation: this was, he saw, to cover any embarrassment he might feel because of a half-mile walk through rain when she was tired. She was talking about some theory to do with the theatre, with designs for theatre building. He heard himself saying, and repeatedly: "Yes, yes, yes." He thought about Nott's, how to get things right when they reached Nott's. There he took the headwaiter aside, gave him a pound, and instructions. They were put in a corner. Large Scotches appeared. The menus were spread. "And now, my dear," he said, "I apologise for dragging you here, but I hope you'll think it's worth it."

"Oh, it's charming, I've always liked it. It's just that . . ." She stopped herself saying: It's such a long way. She smiled at him, raising her glass, and said: "It's one of my very favourite places, and I'm glad you dragged me here." Her voice was flat with tiredness. All this was appalling; he knew it; and he sat thinking how to retrieve his position. Meanwhile she fingered the menu. The headwaiter took the order, but Graham made a gesture which said: Wait a moment. He wanted the Scotch to take effect before she ate. But she saw his silent order; and, without annoyance or reproach, leaned forward to say, sounding patient: "Graham, please, I've got to eat; you don't want me drunk when you interview me, do you?"

"They are bringing it as fast as they can," he said, making it sound as if she were greedy. He looked neither at the headwaiter nor at Barbara. He noted in himself, as he slipped further and further away from contact with her, a cold determination growing in him—one apart from, apparently, any conscious act of will—that come what may, if it took all night, he'd be in her bed before morning. And now, seeing the small pale face, with the enormous green eyes, it was for the first time that he imagined her in his arms. Although he had said: *Yes, that one*, weeks ago, it was only now that he imagined her as a sensual experience. Now he did, so strongly that he could only glance at her, and then away towards the waiters who were bringing food.

"Thank the Lord," said Barbara, and all at once her voice was gay and intimate. "Thank heavens. Thank every power that is. . . ." She was making fun of her own exaggeration; and, as he saw, because she wanted to put him at his ease after his boorishness over delaying the food. (She hadn't been taken in, he saw, humiliated, disliking her.) "Thank all the gods of Nott's," she went on, "because if I hadn't eaten inside five minutes I'd have died, I tell you." With which she picked up her knife and fork and began on her steak. He poured wine, smiling with her, thinking that *this* moment of closeness he would not throw away. He watched her frank hunger as she ate, and thought: Sensual—it's strange I hadn't wondered whether she would be or not.

"Now," she said, sitting back, having taken the edge off her hunger, "let's get to work."

He said: "I've thought it over very carefully—how to present you. The first thing seems to me, we must get away from that old chestnut: Miss Coles, how extraordinary for a woman to be so versatile in her work. . . . I hope you agree?" This was his trump card. He had noted, when he had seen her on television, her polite smile when this note was struck. (The smile he had seen so often tonight.) This smile said: All right, if you *have* to be stupid, what can I do?

Now she laughed and said: "What a relief. I was afraid you were going to do the same thing."

"Good, now you eat and I'll talk."

In his carefully prepared monologue he spoke of the different styles of theatre she had shown herself mistress of, but not directly: he was flattering her on the breadth of her experience; the complexity of her character, as shown in her work. She ate, steadily, her face showing nothing. At last she asked: "And how did you plan to introduce this?"

He had meant to spring that on her as a surprise, something like: Miss Coles, a surprisingly young woman for what she has accomplished (she was thirty? thirty-two?) and a very attractive one. . . . Perhaps I can give you an idea of what she's like if I say she could be taken for the film star Marie Carletta. . . . The Carletta was a strong earthy blonde, known to be intellectual. He now saw he could not possibly say this: he could imagine her cool look if he did. She said: "Do you mind if we get away from all that—my manifold talents, et cetera. . . ." He felt himself stiffen with annoyance, particularly because this was not an accusation; he saw she did not think him worth one. She had assessed him: This is the kind of man who uses this kind of flattery and therefore . . . It made him angrier that she did not even trouble to say: Why did you do exactly what you promised you wouldn't? She was being invincibly polite, trying to conceal her patience with his stupidity.

"After all," she was saying, "it is a stage designer's job to design what comes up. Would anyone take, let's say, Johnnie Cranmore" (another stage designer) "onto the air or television and say: 'How very versatile you are because you did that musical about Java last month and a modern play about Irish labourers this'?"

He battened down his anger. "My dear Barbara, I'm sorry. I didn't realise that what I said would sound just like the mixture as before. So what shall we talk about?"

"What I was saying as we walked to the restaurant: can we get away from the personal stuff?"

Now he almost panicked. Then, thank God, he laughed from nervousness, for she laughed and said: "You didn't hear one word I said."

"No, I didn't. I was frightened you were going to be furious because I made you walk so far when you were tired."

They laughed together, back to where they had been in the theatre. He leaned over, took her hand, kissed it. He said: "Tell me again." He thought: Damn, now she's going to be earnest and intellectual.

But he understood he had been stupid. He had forgotten himself at twenty—or, for that matter, at thirty; forgotten one could live inside an idea, a set of ideas, with enthusiasm. For in talking about her ideas (also the ideas of the people she worked with) for a new theatre, a new style of theatre, she was as she had been with her colleagues over the sketches or the blue material. She was easy, informal, almost chattering. This was how, he remembered, one talked about ideas that were a breath of life. The ideas, he thought, were intelligent enough; and he would agree with them, with her, if he believed it mattered a damn one way or another, if any of these enthusiasms mattered a damn. But at least he now had the key; he knew what to do. At the end of not more than half an hour, they were again two professionals, talking about ideas they shared, for he remembered caring about all this himself once. *When? How many years ago was it that he had been able to care?*

At last he said: "My dear Barbara, do you realise the impossible position you're putting me in? Margaret Ruyen who runs this programme is determined to do you personally; the poor woman hasn't got a serious thought in her head."

Barbara frowned. He put his hand on hers, teasing her for the

frown: "No, wait, trust me, we'll circumvent her." She smiled.
In fact Margaret Ruyen had left it all to him, had said nothing
about Miss Coles.

"They aren't very bright—the brass," he said. "Well, never
mind: we'll work out what we want, do it, and it'll be a *fait
accompli*."

"Thank you, what a relief. How lucky I was to be given you
to interview me." She was relaxed now, because of the whisky,
the food, the wine, above all because of this new complicity
against Margaret Ruyen. It would all be easy. They worked out
five or six questions, over coffee, and took a taxi through rain
to the studios. He noted that the cold necessity to have her, to
make her, to beat her down, had left him. He was even seeing
himself, as the evening ended, kissing her on the cheek and going home to his wife. This comradeship was extraordinarily
pleasant. It was balm to the wound he had not known he carried
until that evening, when he had had to accept the justice of the
word "journalist." He felt he could talk forever about the state
of the theatre, its finances, the stupidity of the government, the
philistinism of . . .

At the studios he was careful to make a joke so that they
walked in on the laugh. He was careful that the interview began
at once, without conversation with Margaret Ruyen; and that
from the moment the green light went on, his voice lost its easy
familiarity. He made sure that not one personal note was struck
during the interview. Afterwards, Margaret Ruyen, who was
pleased, came forward to say so; but he took her aside to say
that Miss Coles was tired and needed to be taken home at once:
for he knew this must look to Barbara as if he were squaring a
producer who had been expecting a different interview. He led
Barbara off, her hand held tight in his against his side. "Well,"
he said, "we've done it, and I don't think she knows what hit
her."

"Thank you," she said, "it really was pleasant to talk about
something sensible for once."

He kissed her lightly on the mouth. She returned it, smiling.
By now he felt sure that the mood need not slip again, he could
hold it.

"There are two things we can do," he said. "You can come
to my club and have a drink. Or I can drive you home and you
can give me a drink. I have to go past you."

"Where do you live?"

"Wimbledon." He lived, in fact, at Highgate; but she lived in Fulham. He was taking another chance, but by the time she found out, they would be in a position to laugh over his ruse.

"Good," she said. "You can drop me home then. I have to get up early." He made no comment. In the taxi he took her hand; it was heavy in his, and he asked: "Does James slave-drive you?"

"I didn't realise you knew him—no, he doesn't."

"Well I don't know him intimately. What's he like to work with?"

"Wonderful," she said at once. "There's no one I enjoy working with more."

Jealousy spurted in him. He could not help himself: "Are you having an affair with him?"

She looked: What's it to do with you? but said: "No, I'm not."

"He's very attractive," he said, with a chuckle of worldly complicity. She said nothing, and he insisted: "If I were a woman I'd have an affair with James."

It seemed she might very well say nothing. But she remarked: "He's married."

His spirits rose in a swoop. It was the first stupid remark she had made. It was a remark of such staggering stupidity that . . . he let out a humouring snort of laughter, put his arm around her, kissed her, said: "My dear little Babs."

She said: "Why Babs?"

"Is that the prerogative of James. And of the stagehands?" he could not prevent himself adding.

"I'm only called that at work." She was stiff inside his arm.

"My dear Barbara, then . . ." He waited for her to enlighten and explain, but she said nothing. Soon she moved out of his arm, on the pretext of lighting a cigarette. He lit it for her. He noted that his determination to lay her, and at all costs, had come back. They were outside her house. He said quickly: "And now, Barbara, you can make me a cup of coffee and give me a brandy." She hesitated; but he was out of the taxi, paying, opening the door for her. The house had no lights on, he noted. He said: "We'll be very quiet so as not to wake the children."

She turned her head slowly to look at him. She said, flat, replying to his real question: "My husband is away. As for the children, they are visiting friends tonight." She now went ahead of him to the door of the house. It was a small house, in a terrace of small and not very pretty houses. Inside a little, bright, intimate hall, she said: "I'll go and make some coffee. Then, my friend, you must go home because I'm very tired."

The "my friend" struck him deep, because he had become vulnerable during their comradeship. He said, gabbling: "You're annoyed with me—oh, please don't, I'm sorry."

She smiled, from a cool distance. He saw, in the small light from the ceiling, her extraordinary eyes. "Green" eyes are hazel, are brown with green flecks, are even blue. Eyes are chequered, flawed, changing. Hers were solid green, but really, he had never seen anything like them before. They were like very deep water. They were like—well, emeralds; or the absolute clarity of green in the depths of a tree in summer. And now, as she smiled almost perpendicularly up at him, he saw a darkness come over them. Darkness swallowed the clear green. She said: "I'm not in the least annoyed." It was as if she had yawned with boredom. "And now I'll get the things . . . in there." She nodded at a white door and left him. He went into a long, very tidy white room that had a narrow bed in one corner, a table covered with drawings, sketches, pencils. Tacked to the walls with drawing pins were swatches of coloured stuffs. Two small chairs stood near a low round table: an area of comfort in the working room. He was thinking: I wouldn't like it if my wife had a room like this. I wonder what Barbara's husband . . . ? He had not thought of her till now in relation to her husband, or to her children. Hard to imagine her with a frying pan in her hand, or, for that matter, cosy in the double bed.

A noise outside: he hastily arranged himself, leaning with one arm on the mantelpiece. She came in with a small tray that had cups, glasses, brandy, coffeepot. She looked abstracted. Graham was on the whole flattered by this: it probably meant she was at ease in his presence. He realised he was a little tight and rather tired. Of course, she was tired too; that was why she was vague. He remembered that earlier that evening he had lost a chance by not using her tiredness. Well now, if he were intelligent . . . She was about to pour coffee. He firmly took the coffeepot out of her hand, and nodded at a chair. Smiling, she obeyed him. "That's better," he said. He poured coffee, poured brandy, and pulled the table towards her. She watched him. Then he took her hand, kissed it, patted it, laid it down gently. Yes, he thought, I did that well.

Now, a problem. He wanted to be closer to her, but she was fitted into a damned silly little chair that had arms. If he were to sit by her on the floor . . . ? But no, for him, the big bulky reassuring man, there could be no casual gestures, no informal postures. Suppose I scoop her out of the chair onto the bed? He drank his coffee as he plotted. Yes, he'd carry her to the bed, but not yet.

"Graham," she said, setting down her cup. She was, he saw with annoyance, looking tolerant. "Graham, in about half an hour I want to be in bed and asleep."

As she said this, she offered him a smile of amusement at this situation—man and woman manoeuvring, the great comic situation. And with part of himself he could have shared it. Almost, he smiled with her, laughed. (Not till days later he exclaimed to himself: Lord what a mistake I made, not to share the joke with her then: that was where I went seriously wrong.) But he could not smile. His face was frozen, with a stiff pride. Not because she had been watching him plot—the amusement she now offered him took the sting out of that—but because of his revived determination that he was going to have his own way, he was going to have her. He was not going home. But he felt that he held a bunch of keys, and did not know which one to choose.

He lifted the second small chair opposite to Barbara, moving aside the coffee table for this purpose. He sat in this chair, leaned forward, took her two hands, and said: "My dear, don't make me go home yet, don't, I beg you." The trouble was, nothing had happened all evening that could be felt to lead up to these words and his tone—simple, dignified, human being pleading with human being for surcease. He saw himself leaning forward, his big hands swallowing her small ones; he saw his face, warm with the appeal. And he realised he had meant the words he used. They were nothing more than what he felt. He wanted to stay with her because she wanted him to, because he was her colleague, a fellow worker in the arts. He needed this desperately. But she was examining him, curious rather than surprised, and from a critical distance. He heard himself saying: "If James were here, I wonder what you'd do?" His voice was aggrieved; he saw the sudden dark descend over her eyes, and she said: "Graham, would you like some more coffee before you go?"

He said: "I've been wanting to meet you for years. I know a good many people who know you."

She leaned forward, poured herself a little more brandy, sat back, holding the glass between her two palms on her chest. An odd gesture: Graham felt that this vessel she was cherishing between her hands was herself. A patient, long-suffering gesture. He thought of various men who had mentioned her. He thought of Jack Kennaway, wavered, panicked, said: "For instance, Jack Kennaway."

And now, at the name, an emotion lit her eyes—what was it? He went on, deliberately testing this emotion, adding to it: "I had dinner with him last week—oh, quite by chance!—and he was talking about you."

"Was he?"

He remembered he had thought her sullen, all those years ago. Now she seemed defensive, and she frowned. He said: "In fact he spent most of the evening talking about you."

She said in short, breathless sentences, which he realised were due to anger: "I can very well imagine what he says. But surely you can't think I enjoy being reminded that . . ." She broke off, resenting him, he saw, because he forced her down on to a level she despised. But it was not his level either: it was all her fault, all hers! He couldn't remember not being in control of a situation with a woman for years. Again he felt like a man teetering on a tightrope. He said, trying to make good use of Jack Kennaway, even at this late hour: "Of course, he's a charming boy, but not a man at all."

She looked at him, silent, guarding her brandy glass against her breasts.

"Unless appearances are totally deceptive, of course." He could not resist probing, even though he knew it was fatal.

She said nothing.

"Do you know you are supposed to have had the great affair with Jack Kennaway?" he exclaimed, making this an amused expostulation against the fools who could believe it.

"So I am told." She set down her glass. "And now," she said, standing up, dismissing him. He lost his head, took a step forward, grabbed her in his arms, and groaned: "Barbara!"

She turned her face this way and that under his kisses. He snatched a diagnostic look at her expression—it was still patient. He placed his lips against her neck, groaned "Barbara" again, and waited. She would have to do something. Fight free, respond, something. She did nothing at all. At last she said: "For the Lord's sake, Graham!" She sounded amused: he was again being offered amusement. But if he shared it with her, it would be the end of this chance to have her. He clamped his mouth over hers, silencing her. She did not fight him off so much as blow him off. Her mouth treated his attacking mouth as a woman blows and laughs in water, puffing off waves or spray with a laugh, turning aside her head. It was a gesture half-annoyance, half-humour. He continued to kiss her while she moved her head and face about under the kisses as if they were small attacking waves.

And so began what, when he looked back on it afterwards, was the most embarrassing experience of his life. Even at the time he hated her for his ineptitude. For he held her there for what must have been nearly half an hour. She was much shorter than he, he had to bend, and his neck ached. He held her rigid, his thighs on either side of hers, her arms clamped to her side in a bear's hug. She was unable to move, except for her head. When his mouth ground hers open and his tongue moved and writhed inside it, she still remained passive. And he could not stop himself. While with his intelligence he watched this ridiculous scene, he was determined to go on, because sooner or later her body must soften in wanting his. And he could not stop because he could not face the horror of the moment when he set her free and she looked at him. And he hated her more, every moment. Catching glimpses of her great green eyes, open and dismal beneath his, he knew he had never disliked anything more than those "jewelled" eyes. They were repulsive to him. It occurred to him at last that even if by now she wanted him, he wouldn't know it, because she was not able to move at all. He cautiously loosened his hold so that she had an inch or so leeway. She remained quite passive. As if, he thought derisively, she had read or been told that the way to incite men maddened by lust was to fight them. He found he was thinking: Stupid cow, so you imagine I find you attractive, do you? You've got the conceit to think that!

The sheer, raving insanity of this thought hit him, opened his arms, his thighs, and lifted his tongue out of her mouth. She stepped back, wiping her mouth with the back of her hand, and stood dazed with incredulity. The embarrassment that lay in wait for him nearly engulfed him, but he let anger postpone it. She said positively apologetic, even, at this moment, humorous: "You're crazy, Graham. What's the matter, are you drunk? You don't seem drunk. You don't even find me attractive."

The blood of hatred went to his head and he gripped her again. Now she had got her face firmly twisted away so that he could not reach her mouth, and she repeated steadily as he kissed the parts of her cheeks and neck that were available to him: "Graham, let me go, do let me go, Graham." She went on saying this; he went on squeezing, grinding, kissing and licking. It might go on all night: it was a sheer contest of wills, nothing else. He thought: It's only a really masculine woman who wouldn't have given in by now out of sheer decency of the flesh! One thing he knew, however: that she would be in that bed, in his arms, and very soon. He let her go, but said: "I'm going to sleep with you tonight, you know that, don't you?"

She leaned with hand on the mantelpiece to steady herself. Her face was colourless, since he had licked all the makeup off. She seemed quite different: small and defenceless with her large mouth pale now, her smudged green eyes fringed with gold. And now, for the first time, he felt what it might have been supposed (certainly by her) he felt hours ago. Seeing the small damp flesh of her face, he felt kinship, intimacy with her, he felt intimacy of the flesh, the affection and good humour of sensuality. He felt she was flesh of his flesh, his sister in the flesh. He felt desire for her, instead of the will to have her; and because of this, was ashamed of the farce he had been playing. Now he desired simply to take her into bed in the affection of his senses.

She said: "What on earth am I supposed to do? Telephone for the police, or what?" He was hurt that she still addressed the man who had ground her into sulky apathy; she was not addressing *him* at all.

She said: "Or scream for the neighbours, is that what you want?"

The gold-fringed eyes were almost black, because of the depth of the shadow of boredom over them. She was bored and weary to the point of falling to the floor, he could see that.

He said: "I'm going to sleep with you."

"But how can you possibly want to?"—a reasonable, a civilised demand addressed to a man who (he could see) she believed would respond to it. She said: "You know I don't want to, and I know you don't really give a damn one way or the other."

He was stung back into being the boor because she had not the intelligence to see that the boor no longer existed; because she could not see that this was a man who wanted her in a way which she must respond to.

There she stood, supporting herself with one hand, looking small and white and exhausted, and utterly incredulous. She was going to turn and walk off out of simple incredulity, he could see that. "Do you think I don't mean it?" he demanded, grinding this out between his teeth. She made a movement—she was on the point of going away. His hand shot out on its own volition and grasped her wrist. She frowned. His other hand grasped her other wrist. His body hove up against hers to start the pressure of a new embrace. Before it could, she said: "Oh Lord, no, I'm not going through all that again. Right, then."

"What do you mean—right, then?" he demanded.

She said: "You're going to sleep with me. O.K. Anything rather than go through that again. Shall we get it over with?"

He grinned, saying in silence: "No darling, oh no you don't, I don't care what words you use, I'm going to have you now and that's all there is to it."

She shrugged. The contempt, the weariness of it, had no effect on him, because he was now again hating her so much that wanting her was like needing to kill something or someone.

She took her clothes off, as if she were going to bed by herself: her jacket, skirt, petticoat. She stood in white bra and panties, a rather solid girl, brown-skinned still from the summer. He felt a flash of affection for the brown girl with her loose yellow hair as she stood naked. She got into bed and lay there, while the green eyes looked at him in civilised appeal: Are you really going through with this? Do you have to? Yes, his eyes said back: I do have to. She shifted her gaze aside, to the wall, saying silently: Well, if you want to take me without any desire at all on my part, then go ahead, if you're not ashamed. He was not ashamed, because he was maintaining the flame of hate for her which he knew quite well was all that stood between him and shame. He took off his clothes, and got into bed beside her. As he did so, knowing he was putting himself in the position of raping a woman who was making it elaborately clear he bored her, his flesh subsided completely, sad, and full of reproach because a few moments ago it was reaching out for his sister whom he could have made happy. He lay on his side by her, secretly at work on himself, while he supported himself across her body on his elbow, using the free hand to manipulate her breasts. He saw that she gritted her teeth against his touch. At least she could not know that after all this fuss he was not potent.

In order to incite himslf, he clasped her again. She felt his smallness, writhed free of him, sat up and said: "Lie down."

While she had been lying there, she had been thinking: The only way to get this over with is to make him big again, otherwise I've got to put up with him all night. His hatred of her was giving him a clairvoyance: he knew very well what went on through her mind. She had switched on, with the determination to *get it all over with*, a sensual good humour, a patience. He lay down. She squatted beside him, the light from the ceiling blooming on her brown shoulders, her flat fair hair falling over her face. But she would not look at his face. Like a bored, skilled wife, she was; or like a prostitute. She administered to him, she was setting herself to please him. Yes, he thought, she's sensual, or she could be. Meanwhile she was succeeding in defeating the reluctance of his flesh, which was the tender token of a possible desire for her, by using a cold skill that was the result of her contempt for him. Just as he decided: Right, it's enough, now I shall have her properly, she made him come. It was not a trick, to hurry or cheat him; what defeated him was her transparent thought: Yes, that's what he's worth.

Then, having succeeded, and waited for a moment or two, she stood up, naked, the fringes of gold at her loins and in her armpits speaking to him a language quite different from that of her green, bored eyes. She looked at him and thought, showing it plainly: What sort of man is it who . . . He watched the slight movement of her shoulders: a just-checked shrug. She went out of the room: then the sound of running water. Soon she came back in a white dressing-gown, carrying a yellow towel. She handed him the towel, looking away in politeness as he used it. "Are you going now?" she enquired hopefully, at this point.

"No, I'm not." He believed that now he would have to start fighting her again, but she lay down beside him, not touching him (he could feel the distaste of her flesh for his) and he thought: Very well, my dear, but there's a lot of the night left yet. He said aloud: "I'm going to have you properly tonight." She said nothing, lay silent, yawned. Then she remarked consolingly, and he could have laughed outright from sheer surprise: "Those were hardly conducive circumstances for making love." She was *consoling* him. He hated her for it. A proper little slut: I force her into bed, she doesn't want me, but she still has to make me feel good, like a prostitute. But even while he hated her he responded in kind, from the habit of sexual generosity. "It's because of my admiration for you, because . . . after all, I was holding in my arms one of the thousand women."

A pause. "The thousand?" she enquired, carefully.

"The thousand especial women."

"In Britain or in the world? You choose them for their brains, their beauty—what?"

"Whatever it is that makes them outstanding," he said, offering her a compliment.

"Well," she remarked at last, inciting him to be amused again, "I hope that at least there's a short list you can say I am on, for politeness' sake."

He did not reply for he understood he was sleepy. He was still telling himself that he must stay awake when he was slowly waking and it was morning. It was about eight. Barbara was not there. He thought: My God! What on earth shall I tell my wife? Where was Barbara? He remembered the ridiculous scenes of last night and nearly succumbed to shame. Then he thought, reviving anger: If she didn't sleep beside me here I'll never forgive her. . . . He sat up, quietly, determined to go through the house until he found her and, having found her, to possess her, when the door opened and she came in. She was fully dressed in a green suit, her hair done, her eyes made up. She carried a tray of coffee, which she set down beside the bed. He was conscious of his big loose hairy body, half uncovered. He said to himself that he was not going to lie in bed, naked, while she was dressed. He said: "Have you got a gown of some kind?" She handed him, without speaking, a towel, and said: "The bathroom's second on the left." She went out. He followed, the towel around him. Everything in this house was gay, intimate— not at all like her efficient working room. He wanted to find out where she had slept, and opened the first door. It was the kitchen, and she was in it, putting a brown earthenware dish into the oven. "The next door," said Barbara. He went hastily past the second door, and opened (he hoped quietly) the third. It was a cupboard full of linen. "This door," said Barbara, behind him.

"So all right then, where did you sleep?"

"What's it to do with you? Upstairs, in my own bed. Now, if you have everything, I'll say goodbye. I want to get to the theatre."

"I'll take you," he said at once.

He saw again the movement of her eyes, the dark swallowing the light in deadly boredom. "I'll take you," he insisted.

"I'd prefer to go by myself," she remarked. Then she smiled: "However, you'll take me. Then you'll make a point of coming right in, so that James and everyone can see—that's what you want to take me for, isn't it?"

He hated her, finally, and quite simply, for her intelligence; that not once had he got away with anything, that she had been watching, since they had met yesterday, every movement of his campaign for her. However, some fate or inner urge over which he had no control made him say sentimentally: "My dear, you must see that I'd like at least to take you to your work."

"Not at all, have it on me," she said, giving him the lie direct. She went past him to the room he had slept in. "I shall be leaving in ten minutes," she said.

He took a shower, fast. When he returned, the workroom was already tidied, the bed made, all signs of the night gone. Also, there were no signs of the coffee she had brought in for him. He did not like to ask for it, for fear of an outright refusal. Besides, she was ready, her coat on, her handbag under her arm. He went, without a word, to the front door, and she came after him, silent.

He could see that every fibre of her body signalled a simple message: Oh God, for the moment when I can be rid of this boor! She was nothing but a slut, he thought.

A taxi came. In it she sat as far away from him as she could. He thought of what he should say to his wife.

Outside the theatre she remarked: "You could drop me here, if you liked." It was not a plea, she was too proud for that. "I'll take you in," he said, and saw her thinking: Very well, I'll go through with it to shame him. He was determined to take her in and hand her over to her colleagues, he was afraid she would give him the slip. But far from playing it down, she seemed determined to play it his way. At the stage door, she said to the doorman: "This is Mr. Spence, Tom—do you remember, Mr. Spence from last night?" "Good morning, Babs," said the man, examining Graham, politely, as he had been ordered to do.

Barbara went to the door to the stage, opened it, held it open for him. He went in first, then held it open for her. Together they walked into the cavernous, littered, badly lit place and she called out: "James, James!" A man's voice called out from the front of the house: "Here, Babs, why are you so late?"

The auditorium opened before them, darkish, silent, save for an early-morning busyness of charwomen. A vacuum cleaner roared, smally, somewhere close. A couple of stagehands stood looking up at a drop which had a design of blue-and-green spirals. James stood with his back to the auditorium, smoking. "You're late, Babs," he said again. He saw Graham behind her, and nodded. Barbara and James kissed. Barbara said, giving allowance to every syllable: "You remember Mr. Spence from last night?" James nodded: How do you do? Barbara stood beside him, and they looked together up at the blue-and-green backdrop. Then Barbara looked again at Graham, asking silently: All right now, isn't that enough? He could see her eyes, sullen with boredom.

He said: "Bye, Babs. Bye, James. I'll ring you, Babs." No response, she ignored him. He walked off slowly, listening for what might be said. For instance: Babs, for God's sake, what are you doing with him? Or she might say: Are you wondering about Graham Spence? Let me explain.

Graham passed the stagehands, who, he could have sworn, didn't recognise him. Then at last he heard James's voice to Barbara: "It's no good, Babs, I know you're enamoured of that particular shade of blue, but do have another look at it, there's a good girl. . . ." Graham left the stage, went past the office where the stage doorman sat reading a newspaper. He looked up, nodded, went back to his paper. Graham went to find a taxi, thinking: I'd better think up something convincing, then I'll telephone my wife.

Luckily he had an excuse not to be at home that day, for this evening he had to interview a young man (for television) about his new novel.

# A Woman on a Roof

It was during the week of hot sun, that June.

Three men were at work on the roof, where the leads got so hot they had the idea of throwing water on to cool them. But the water steamed, then sizzled; and they made jokes about getting an egg from some woman in the flats under them, to poach it for their dinner. By two it was not possible to touch the guttering they were replacing, and they speculated about what workmen did in regularly hot countries. Perhaps they should borrow kitchen gloves with the egg? They were all a bit dizzy, not used to the heat; and they shed their coats and stood side by side squeezing themselves into a foot-wide patch of shade against a chimney, careful to keep their feet in the thick socks and boots out of the sun. There was a fine view across several acres of roofs. Not far off a man sat in a deck chair reading the newspapers. Then they saw her, between chimneys, about fifty yards away. She lay face down on a brown blanket. They could see the top part of her: black hair, a flushed solid back, arms spread out.

"She's stark naked," said Stanley, sounding annoyed.

Harry, the oldest, a man of about forty-five, said: "Looks like it."

Young Tom, seventeen, said nothing, but he was excited and grinning.

Stanley said: "Someone'll report her if she doesn't watch out."

"She thinks no one can see," said Tom, craning his head all ways to see more.

At this point the woman, still lying prone, brought her two hands up behind her shoulders with the ends of a scarf in them, tied it behind her back, and sat up. She wore a red scarf tied around her breasts and brief red bikini pants. This being the first day of the sun she was white, flushing red. She sat smoking, and did not look up when Stanley let out a wolf whistle. Harry said: "Small things amuse small minds," leading the way back to their part of the roof, but it was scorching. Harry said: "Wait, I'm going to rig up some shade," and disappeared down the skylight into the building. Now that he'd gone, Stanley and Tom went to the farthest point they could to peer at the woman. She had moved, and all they could see were two pink legs stretched on the blanket. They whistled and shouted but the legs did not move. Harry came back with a blanket and shouted: "Come on, then." He sounded irritated with them. They clambered back to him and he said to Stanley: "What about your missus?" Stanley was newly married, about three months. Stanley said, jeering: "What about my missus?"—preserving his independence. Tom said nothing, but his mind was full of the nearly naked woman. Harry slung the blanket, which he had borrowed from a friendly woman downstairs, from the stem of a television aerial to a row of chimney-pots. This shade fell across the piece of gutter they had to replace. But the shade kept moving, they had to adjust the blanket, and not much progress was made. At last some of the heat left the roof, and they worked fast, making up for lost time. First Stanley, then Tom, made a trip to the end of the roof to see the woman. "She's on her back," Stanley said, adding a jest which made Tom snicker, and the older man smile tolerantly. Tom's report was that she hadn't moved, but it was a lie. He wanted to keep what he had seen to himself: he had caught her in the act of rolling down the little red pants over her hips, till they were no more than a small triangle. She was on her back, fully visible, glistening with oil.

Next morning, as soon as they came up, they went to look. She was already there, face down, arms spread out, naked except for the little red pants. She had turned brown in the night. Yesterday she was a scarlet-and-white woman, today she was a brown woman. Stanley let out a whistle. She lifted her head, startled, as if she'd been asleep, and looked straight over at them. The sun was in her eyes, she blinked and stared, then she dropped her head again. At this gesture of indifference, they all three, Stanley, Tom, and old Harry, let out whistles and yells. Harry was doing it in parody of the younger men, making fun of them, but he was also angry. They were all angry because of her utter indifference to the three men watching her.

"Bitch," said Stanley.

"She should ask us over," said Tom, snickering.

Harry recovered himself and reminded Stanley: "If she's married, her old man wouldn't like that."

"Christ," said Stanley virtuously, "if my wife lay about like that, for everyone to see, I'd soon stop her."

Harry said, smiling: "How do you know, perhaps she's sunning herself at this very moment?"

"Not a chance, not on our roof." The safety of his wife put Stanley into a good humour, and they went to work. But today it was hotter than yesterday; and several times one or the other suggested they should tell Matthew, the foreman, and ask to leave the roof until the heat wave was over. But they didn't. There was work to be done in the basement of the big block of flats, but up here they felt free, on a different level from ordinary humanity shut in the streets or the buildings. A lot more people came out on to the roofs that day, for an hour at midday. Some married couples sat side by side in deck chairs, the women's legs stockingless and scarlet, the men in vests with reddening shoulders.

The woman stayed on her blanket, turning herself over and over. She ignored them, no matter what they did. When Harry went off to fetch more screws, Stanley said: "Come on." Her roof belonged to a different system of roofs, separated from theirs at one point by about twenty feet. It meant a scrambling climb from one level to another, edging along parapets, clinging to chimneys, while their big boots slipped and slithered, but at last they stood on a small square projecting roof looking straight down at her, close. She sat smoking, reading a book. Tom thought she looked like a poster, or a magazine cover, with the blue sky behind her and her legs stretched out. Behind her a great crane at work on a new building in Oxford Street swung its black arm across roofs in a great arc. Tom imagined himself at work on the crane, adjusting the arm to swing over and pick her up and swing her back across the sky to drop her near him.

They whistled. She looked up at them, cool and remote, then went on reading. Again, they were furious. Or, rather, Stanley was. His sun-heated face was screwed into a rage as he whistled again and again, trying to make her look up. Young Tom stopped whistling. He stood beside Stanley, excited, grinning; but he felt as if he were saying to the woman: Don't associate me with *him*, for his grin was apologetic. Last night he had thought of the unknown woman before he slept, and she had been tender with him. This tenderness he was remembering as he shifted his feet by the jeering, whistling Stanley, and watched the indifferent, healthy brown woman a few feet off, with the gap that plunged to the street between them. Tom thought it was romantic, it was like being high on two hilltops. But there was a shout from Harry, and they clambered back. Stanley's face was hard, really angry. The boy kept looking at him and wondered why he hated the woman so much, for by now he loved her.

They played their little games with the blanket, trying to trap shade to work under; but again it was not until nearly four that they could work seriously, and they were exhausted, all three of them. They were grumbling about the weather by now. Stanley was in a thoroughly bad humour. When they made their routine trip to see the woman before they packed up for the day, she was apparently asleep, face down, her back all naked save for the scarlet triangle on her buttocks. "I've got a good mind to report her to the police," said Stanley, and Harry said: "What's eating you? What harm's she doing?"

"I tell you, if she was my wife!"

"But she isn't, is she?" Tom knew that Harry, like himself, was uneasy at Stanley's reaction. He was normally a sharp young man, quick at his work, making a lot of jokes, good company.

"Perhaps it will be cooler tomorrow," said Harry.

But it wasn't; it was hotter, if anything, and the weather forecast said the good weather would last. As soon as they were on the roof, Harry went over to see if the woman was there, and Tom knew it was to prevent Stanley going, to put off his bad humour. Harry had grownup children, a boy the same age as Tom, and the youth trusted and looked up to him.

Harry came back and said: "She's not there."

"I bet her old man has put his foot down," said Stanley, and Harry and Tom caught each other's eyes and smiled behind the young married man's back.

Harry suggested they should get permission to work in the basement, and they did, that day. But before packing up Stanley said: "Let's have a breath of fresh air." Again Harry and Tom smiled at each other as they followed Stanley up to the roof, Tom in the devout conviction that he was there to protect the woman from Stanley. It was about five-thirty, and a calm, full sunlight lay over the roofs. The great crane still swung its black arm from Oxford Street to above their heads. She was not there. Then there was a flutter of white from behind a parapet, and she stood up, in a belted, white dressing-gown. She had been there all day, probably, but on a different patch of roof, to hide from them. Stanley did not whistle; he said nothing, but watched the woman bend to collect papers, books, cigarettes, then fold the blanket over her arm. Tom was thinking: If they weren't here, I'd go over and say . . . what? But he knew from his nightly dreams of her that she was kind and friendly. Perhaps she would ask him down to her flat? Perhaps . . . He stood watching her disappear down the skylight. As she went, Stanley let out a shrill derisive yell; she started, and it seemed as if she nearly fell. She clutched to save herself, they could hear things falling. She looked straight at them, angry. Harry said, facetiously: "Better be careful on those slippery ladders, love." Tom knew he said it to save her from Stanley, but she could not know it. She vanished, frowning. Tom was full of a secret delight, because he knew her anger was for the others, not for him.

"Roll on some rain," said Stanley, bitter, looking at the blue evening sky.

Next day was cloudless, and they decided to finish the work in the basement. They felt excluded, shut in the grey cement basement fitting pipes, from the holiday atmosphere of London in a heat wave. At lunchtime they came up for some air, but while the married couples, and the men in shirt-sleeves or vests, were there, she was not there, either on her usual patch of roof or where she had been yesterday. They all, even Harry, clambered about, between chimney-pots, over parapets, the hot leads stinging their fingers. There was not a sign of her. They took off their shirts and vests and exposed their chests, feeling their feet sweaty and hot. They did not mention the woman. But Tom felt alone again. Last night she had him into her flat: it was big and had fitted white carpets and a bed with a padded white leather head-board. She wore a black filmy negligée and her kindness to Tom thickened his throat as he remembered it. He felt she had betrayed him by not being there.

And again after work they climbed up, but still there was nothing to be seen of her. Stanley kept repeating that if it was as hot as this tomorrow he wasn't going to work and that's all there was to it. But they were all there next day. By ten the temperature was in the middle seventies, and it was eighty long before noon. Harry went to the foreman to say it was impossible to work on the leads in that heat; but the foreman said there was nothing else he could put them on, and they'd have to. At midday they stood, silent, watching the skylight on her roof open, and then she slowly emerged in her white gown, holding a bundle of blanket. She looked at them, gravely, then went to the part of the roof where she was hidden from them. Tom was pleased. He felt she was more his when the other men couldn't see her. They had taken off their shirts and vests, but now they put them back again, for they felt the sun bruising their flesh. "She must have the hide of a rhino," said Stanley, tugging at guttering and swearing. They stopped work, and sat in the shade, moving around behind chimney stacks. A woman came to water a yellow window box opposite them. She was middleaged, wearing a flowered summer dress. Stanley said to her: "We need a drink more than them." She smiled and said: "Better drop down to the pub quick, it'll be closing in a minute." They exchanged pleasantries, and she left them with a smile and a wave.

"Not like Lady Godiva," said Stanley. "She can give us a bit of a chat and a smile."

"You didn't whistle at *her*," said Tom, reproving.

"Listen to him," said Stanley, "you didn't whistle, then?"

But the boy felt as if he hadn't whistled, as if only Harry and Stanley had. He was making plans, when it was time to knock off work, to get left behind and somehow make his way over to the woman. The weather report said the hot spell was due to break, so he had to move quickly. But there was no chance of being left. The other two decided to knock off work at four, because they were exhausted. As they went down, Tom quickly climbed a parapet and hoisted himself higher by pulling his weight up a chimney. He caught a glimpse of her lying on her back, her knees up, eyes closed, a brown woman lolling in the sun. He slipped and clattered down, as Stanley looked for information: "She's gone down," he said. He felt as if he had protected her from Stanley, and that she must be grateful to him. He could feel the bond between the woman and himself.

Next day, they stood around on the landing below the roof, reluctant to climb up into the heat. The woman who had lent Harry the blanket came out and offered them a cup of tea. They accepted gratefully, and sat around Mrs. Pritchett's kitchen an hour or so, chatting. She was married to an airline pilot. A smart blonde, of about thirty, she had an eye for the handsome sharp-faced Stanley; and the two teased each other while Harry sat in a corner, watching, indulgent, though his expression reminded Stanley that he was married. And young Tom felt envious of Stanley's ease in badinage; felt, too, that Stanley's getting off with Mrs. Pritchett left his romance with the woman on the roof safe and intact.

"I thought they said the heat wave'd break," said Stanley, sullen, as the time approached when they really would have to climb up into the sunlight.

"You don't like it, then?" asked Mrs. Pritchett.

"All right for some," said Stanley. "Nothing to do but lie about as if it was a beach up there. Do you ever go up?"

"Went up once," said Mrs. Pritchett. "But it's a dirty place up there, and it's too hot."

"Quite right too," said Stanley.

Then they went up, leaving the cool neat little flat and the friendly Mrs. Pritchett.

As soon as they were up they saw her. The three men looked at her, resentful at her ease in this punishing sun. Then Harry said, because of the expression on Stanley's face: "Come on, we've got to pretend to work, at least."

They had to wrench another length of guttering that ran beside a parapet out of its bed, so that they could replace it. Stanley took it in his two hands, tugged, swore, stood up. "Fuck it," he said, and sat down under a chimney. He lit a cigarette. "Fuck them," he said. "What do they think we are, lizards? I've got blisters all over my hands." Then he jumped up and climbed over the roofs and stood with his back to them.

He put his fingers either side of his mouth and let out a shrill whistle. Tom and Harry squatted, not looking at each other, watching him. They could just see the woman's head, the beginnings of her brown shoulders. Stanley whistled again. Then he began stamping with his feet, and whistled and yelled and screamed at the woman, his face getting scarlet. He seemed quite mad, as he stamped and whistled, while the woman did not move, she did not move a muscle.

"Barmy," said Tom.

"Yes," said Harry, disapproving.

Suddenly the older man came to a decision. It was, Tom knew, to save some sort of scandal or real trouble over the woman. Harry stood up and began packing tools into a length of oily cloth. "Stanley," he said, commanding. At first Stanley took no notice, but Harry said: "Stanley, we're packing it in, I'll tell Matthew."

Stanley came back, cheeks mottled, eyes glaring.

"Can't go on like this," said Harry. "It'll break in a day or so. I'm going to tell Matthew we've got sunstroke, and if he doesn't like it, it's too bad." Even Harry sounded aggrieved, Tom noted. The small, competent man, the family man with his grey hair, who was never at a loss, sounded really off balance. "Come on," he said, angry. He fitted himself into the open square in the roof, and went down, watching his feet on the ladder. Then Stanley went, with not a glance at the woman. Then Tom, who, his throat beating with excitement, silently promised her on a backward glance: Wait for me, wait, I'm coming.

On the pavement Stanley said: "I'm going home." He looked white now, so perhaps he really did have sunstroke. Harry went off to find the foreman, who was at work on the plumbing of some flats down the street. Tom slipped back, not into the building they had been working on, but the building on whose roof the woman lay. He went straight up, no one stopping him. The skylight stood open, with an iron ladder leading up. He emerged on to the roof a couple of yards from her. She sat up, pushing back her black hair with both hands. The scarf across her breasts bound them tight, and brown flesh bulged around it. Her legs were brown and smooth. She stared at him in silence. The boy stood grinning, foolish, claiming the tenderness he expected from her.

"What do you want?" she asked.

"I . . . I came to . . . make your acquaintance," he stammered, grinning, pleading with her.

They looked at each other, the slight, scarlet-faced excited boy, and the serious, nearly naked woman. Then, without a word, she lay down on her brown blanket, ignoring him.

"You like the sun, do you?" he enquired of her glistening back.

Not a word. He felt panic, thinking of how she had held him in her arms, stroked his hair, brought him where he sat, lordly, in her bed, a glass of some exhilarating liquor he had never tasted in life. He felt that if he knelt down, stroked her shoulders, her hair, she would turn and clasp him in her arms.

He said: "The sun's all right for you, isn't it?"

She raised her head, set her chin on two small fists. "Go away," she said. He did not move. "Listen," she said, in a slow reasonable voice, where anger was kept in check, though with difficulty; looking at him, her face weary with anger, "if you get a kick out of seeing women in bikinis, why don't you take a sixpenny bus ride to the Lido? You'd see dozens of them, without all this mountaineering."

She hadn't understood him. He felt her unfairness pale him. He stammered: "But I like you, I've been watching you and . . ."

"Thanks," she said, and dropped her face again, turned away from him.

She lay there. He stood there. She said nothing. She had simply shut him out. He stood, saying nothing at all, for some minutes. He thought: She'll have to say something if I stay. But the minutes went past, with no sign of them in her, except in the tension of her back, her thighs, her arms—the tension of waiting for him to go.

He looked up at the sky, where the sun seemed to spin in heat; and over the roofs where he and his mates had been earlier. He could see the heat quivering where they had worked. And they expect us to work in these conditions! he thought, filled with righteous indignation. The woman hadn't moved. A bit of hot wind blew her black hair softly; it shone, and was iridescent. He remembered how he had stroked it last night.

Resentment of her at last moved him off and away down the ladder, through the building, into the street. He got drunk then, in hatred of her.

Next day when he woke the sky was grey. He looked at the wet grey and thought, vicious: Well, that's fixed you, hasn't it now? That's fixed you good and proper.

The three men were at work early on the cool leads, sur-rounded by damp drizzling roofs where no one came to sun themselves, black roofs, slimy with rain. Because it was cool now, they would finish the job that day, if they hurried.

# How I Finally
# Lost My Heart

It would be easy to say that I picked up a knife, slit open my side, took my heart out, and threw it away; but unfortunately it wasn't as easy as that. Not that I, like everyone else, had not often wanted to do it. No, it happened differently, and not as I expected.

It was just after I had had a lunch and a tea with two different men. My lunch partner I had lived with for (more or less) four and seven-twelfths years. When he left me for new pastures, I spent two years, or was it three, half-dead, and my heart was a stone, impossible to carry about, considering all the other things weighing on one. Then I slowly, and with difficulty, got free, because my heart cherished a thousand adhesions to my first love—though from another point of view he could be legitimately described as either my second *real* love (my father being the first) or my third (my brother intervening).

As the folk song has it:

> *I have loved but three men in my life,*
> *My father, my brother, and the man that*
> *took my life.*

But if one were going to look at the thing from outside, without insight, he could be seen as (perhaps, I forget) the thirteenth, but to do that means disregarding the inner emotional truth. For we all know that those affairs or entanglements one has between *serious* loves, though they may number dozens and stretch over years, *don't really count.*

This way of looking at things creates a number of unhappy people, for it is well known that what doesn't really count for me might very well count for you. But there is no way of getting over this difficulty, for a *serious* love is the most important business in life, or nearly so. At any rate, most of us are engaged in looking for it. Even when we are in fact being very serious indeed with one person we still have an eighth of an eye cocked in case some stranger unexpectedly encountered might turn out to be even more serious. We are all entirely in agreement that we are in the right to taste, test, sip and sample a thousand people on our way to the *real* one. It is not too much to say that in our circles tasting and sampling is probably the second most important activity, the first being earning money. Or to put it another way, if you are serious about this thing, you go on laying everybody that offers until something clicks and you're all set to go.

I have digressed from an earlier point: that I regarded this man I had lunch with (we call him A) as my first love; and still do, despite the Freudians, who insist on seeing my father as A and possibly my brother as B, making my (real) first love C. And despite, also, those who might ask: What about your two husbands and all those affairs?

What about them? I did not *really* love them, the way I loved A.

I had lunch with him. Then, quite by chance, I had tea with B. When I say B, here, I mean my *second* serious love, not my brother, or the little boys I was in love with between the ages of five and fifteen, if we are going to take fifteen (arbitrarily) as the point of no return . . . which last phrase is in itself a pretty brave defiance of the secular arbiters.

In between A and B (my count) there were a good many affairs, or samples, but they didn't score. B and I *clicked*, we went off like a bomb, though not quite as simply as A and I had clicked, because my heart was bruised, sullen, and suspicious because of A's throwing me over. Also there were all those ligaments and adhesions binding me to A still to be loosened, one by one. However, for a time B and I got on like a house on fire, and then we came to grief. My heart was again a ton weight in my side.

*If this were a stone in my side, a stone,*
*I could pluck it out and be free. . . .*

Having lunch with A, then tea with B, two men who between
them had consumed a decade of my precious years (I am not
counting the test or trial affairs in between) and, it is fair
to say, had balanced all the delight (plenty and intense) with
misery (oh Lord, Lord)—moving from one to the other, in
the course of an afternoon, conversing amiably about this and
that, with meanwhile my heart giving no more than slight
reminiscent tugs, the fish of memory at the end of a long slack
line . . .

To sum up, it was salutary.

Particularly as that evening I was expecting to meet C, or
someone who might very well turn out to be C; though I don't
want to give too much emphasis to C, the truth is I can hardly
remember what he looked like, but one can't be expected to
remember the unimportant ones one has sipped or tasted in
between. But after all, he might have turned out to be C, we
might have *clicked*, and I was in that state of mind (in which
we all so often are) of thinking: He might turn out to be the
one. (I use a woman's magazine phrase deliberately here, instead of saying, as I might: *Perhaps it will be serious.*)

So there I was (I want to get the details and atmosphere
right) standing at a window looking into a street (Great Portland Street, as a matter of fact) and thinking that while I
would not dream of regretting my affairs, or experiences, with
A and B (it is better to have loved and lost than never to have
loved at all), my anticipation of the heart because of spending an
evening with a possible C had a certain unreality, because there
was no doubt that both A and B had caused me unbelievable
pain. Why, therefore, was I looking forward to C? I should rather
be running away as fast as I could.

It suddenly occurred to me that I was looking at the whole
phenomenon quite inaccurately. My (or perhaps I am permitted to say our?) way of looking at it is that one must search
for an A, or a B, or a C or a D with a certain combination of
desirable or sympathetic qualities so that one may click, or
spontaneously combuŝt: or to put it differently, one needs a
person who, like a saucer of water, allows one to float off on
him/her, like a transfer. But this wasn't so at all. Actually one

carries with one a sort of burning spear stuck in one's side, that one waits for someone else to pull out; it is something painful, like a sore or a wound, that one cannot wait to share with someone else.

I saw myself quite plainly in a moment of truth: I was standing at a window (on the third floor) with A and B (to mention only the mountain peaks of my emotional experience) behind me, a rather attractive woman, if I may say so, with a mellowness that I would be the first to admit is the sad harbinger of age, but is attractive by definition, because it is a testament to the amount of sampling and sipping (I nearly wrote "simpling" and "sapping") I have done in my time. . . . There I stood, brushed, dressed, red-lipped, kohl-eyed, all waiting for an evening with a possible C. And at another window overlooking (I think I am right in saying) Margaret Street, stood C, brushed, washed, shaved, smiling: an attractive man (I think), and *he* was thinking: Perhaps she will turn out to be D (or A or 3 or ? or %, or whatever symbol he used). We stood, separated by space, certainly, in identical conditions of pleasant uncertainty and anticipation, and we both held our hearts in our hands, all pink and palpitating and ready for pleasure and pain, and we were about to throw these hearts in each other's face like snowballs, or cricket balls (How's that?) or, more accurately, like great bleeding wounds: "Take my wound." Because the last thing one ever thinks at such moments is that he (or she) will say: Take *my* wound, please remove the spear from *my* side. No, not at all; one simply expects to get rid of one's own.

I decided I must go to the telephone and say, C!—You know that joke about the joke-makers who don't trouble to tell each other jokes, but simply say Joke 1 or Joke 2, and everyone roars with laughter, or snickers, or giggles appropriately. . . . Actually one could reverse the game by guessing whether it was Joke C(b) or Joke A(d) according to what sort of laughter a person made to match the silent thought. . . . Well, C (I imagined myself saying), the analogy is for our instruction: Let's take the whole thing as read or said. Let's not lick each other's sores; let's keep our hearts to ourselves. Because just consider it, C, how utterly absurd—here we stand at our respective windows with our palpitating hearts in our hands. . . .

At this moment, dear reader, I was forced simply to put

down the telephone with an apology. For I felt the fingers of my left hand push outwards around something rather large, light, and slippery—hard to describe this sensation, really. My hand is not large, and my heart was in a state of inflation after having had lunch with A, tea with B, and then looking forward to C. . . . Anyway, my fingers were stretching out rather desperately to encompass an unknown, largish, lightish object, and I said: Excuse me a minute, to C, looked down, and there was my heart, in my hand.

I had to end the conversation there.

For one thing, to find that one has achieved something so often longed for, so easily, is upsetting. It's not as if I had been trying. To get something one wants simply by accident—no, there's no pleasure in it, no feeling of achievement. So to find myself heart-whole, or, more accurately, heart-less, or at any rate, rid of the damned thing, and at such an awkward moment, in the middle of an imaginary telephone call with a man who might possibly turn out to be C—well, it was irritating rather than not.

For another thing, a heart, raw and bleeding and fresh from one's side is not the prettiest sight. I'm not going into that at all. I was appalled, and indeed embarrassed that *that* was what had been loving and beating away all those years, because if I'd had any idea at all—well, enough of that.

My problem was how to get rid of it.

Simple,  you'll say, drop it into the waste bucket.

Well, let me tell you, that's what I tried to do. I took a good look at this object, nearly  died with embarrassment, and walked over to the rubbish-can, where I tried to let it roll off my fingers. It wouldn't. It was stuck. There was my heart, a large red pulsing bleeding repulsive object, stuck to my fingers. What was I going to do? I sat down, lit a cigarette (with one hand, holding the matchbox between my knees), held my hand with the heart stuck on it over the side of the chair so that it could drip into a bucket, and considered.

> If this were a stone in my hand, a stone,
> I could throw it over a tree. . . .

When I had finished the cigarette, I carefully unwrapped some tin foil of the kind used to wrap food in when cooking, and I fitted a sort of cover around my heart. This was absolutely and urgently necessary. First, it was smarting badly. After all, it had spent some forty years protected by flesh and ribs, and the air was too much for it. Secondly, I couldn't have any Tom, Dick and Harry walking in and looking at it. Thirdly, I could not look at it for too long myself, it filled me with shame. The tin foil was effective, and indeed rather striking. It is quite pliable and now it seemed as if there were a stylised heart balanced on my palm, like a globe, in glittering, silvery substance. I almost felt I needed a sceptre in the other hand to balance it. . . . But the thing was, there is no other word for it, in bad taste. I then wrapped a scarf around hand and tin-foiled heart, and felt safer. Now it was a question of pretending to have hurt my hand until I could think of a way of getting rid of my heart altogether, short of amputating my hand.

Meanwhile I telephoned (really, not in imagination) C, who now would never be C. I could feel my heart, which was stuck so close to my fingers that I could feel every beat or tremor, give a gulp of resigned grief at the idea of this beautiful experience now never to be. I told him some idiotic lie about having 'flu. Well, he was all stiff and indignant, but concealing it urbanely, as I would have done, making a joke but allowing a tiny barb of sarcasm to rankle in the last well-chosen phrase. Then I sat down again to think out my whole situation.

There I sat.

What was I going to do?

There I sat.

I am going to have to skip about four days here, vital enough in all conscience, because I simply cannot go heartbeat by heartbeat through my memories. A pity, since I suppose this is what this story is about; but in brief: I drew the curtains, I took the telephone off the hook, I turned on the lights, I took the scarf off the glittering shape, then the tin foil; then I examined the heart. There were two-fifths of a century's experience to work through, and before I had even got through the first night, I was in a state hard to describe. . . .

> Or if I could pull the nerves from my skin
> A quick red net to drag through a sea for fish. . . .

By the end of the fourth day I was worn out. By no act of will, or intention, or desire, could I move that heart by a fraction— on the contrary, it was not only stuck to my fingers, like a sucked boiled sweet, but was actually growing to the flesh of my fingers and my palm.

I wrapped it up again in tin foil and scarf, and turned out the lights and pulled up the blinds and opened the curtains. It was about ten in the morning, an ordinary London day, neither hot nor cold nor clear nor clouded nor wet nor fine. And while the street is interesting, it is not exactly beautiful, so I wasn't looking at it so much as waiting for something to catch my attention while thinking of something else.

Suddenly I heard a tap-tap-tapping that got louder, sharp and clear, and I knew before I saw her that this was the sound of high heels on a pavement though it might just as well have been a hammer against stone. She walked fast opposite my window and her heels hit the pavement so hard that all the noises of the street seemed absorbed into that single tap-tap-clang-clang. As she reached the corner at Great Portland Street two London pigeons swooped diagonally from the sky very fast, as if they were bullets aimed to kill her; and then as they saw her they swooped up and off at an angle. Meanwhile she had turned the corner. All this has taken time to write down, but the thing happening took a couple of seconds: the woman's body hitting the pavement bang-bang through her heels then sharply turning the corner in a right angle; and the pigeons making another acute angle across hers and intersecting it in a fast swoop of displaced air. Nothing to all that, of course, nothing—she had gone off down the street, her heels tip-tapping, and the pigeons landed on my windowsill and began cooing. All gone, all vanished, the marvellous exact co-ordination of sound and movement, but it had happened, it had made me happy and exhilarated, I had no problems in this world, and I realised that the heart stuck to my fingers was quite loose. I couldn't get it off altogether, though I was tugging at it under the scarf and the tin foil, but almost.

I understood that sitting and analysing each movement or pulse or beat of my heart through forty years was a mistake. I was on the wrong track altogether: this was the way to attach my red, bitter, delighted heart to my flesh for ever and ever. . . .

*Ha! So you think I'm done! You think. . . .*
*Watch, I'll roll my heart in a mesh of rage*
*And bounce it like a handball off*
*Walls, faces, railings, umbrellas and pigeons' backs. . . .*

No, all that was no good at all; it just made things worse. What I must do is to take myself by surprise, as it were, the way I was taken by surprise over the woman and the pigeons and the sharp sounds of heels and silk wings.

I put on my coat, held my lumpy scarfed arm across my chest, so that if anyone said: What have you done with your hand? I could say: I've banged my finger in the door. Then I walked down into the street.

It wasn't easy to go among so many people, when I was worried that they were thinking: What has that woman done to her hand? because that made it hard to forget myself. And all the time it tingled and throbbed against my fingers, reminding me.

Now I was out, I didn't know what to do. Should I go and have lunch with someone? Or wander in the park? Or buy myself a dress? I decided to go to the Round Pond, and walk around it by myself. I was tired after four days and nights without sleep. I went down into the underground at Oxford Circus. Midday. Crowds of people. I felt self-conscious, but of course need not have worried. I swear you could walk naked down the street in London and no one would even turn round.

So I went down the escalator and looked at the faces coming up past me on the other side, as I always do; and wondered, as I always do, how strange it is that those people and I should meet by chance in such a way, and how odd that we would never see each other again, or, if we did, we wouldn't know it. And I went on to the crowded platform and looked at the faces as I always do, and got into the train, which was very full, and found a seat. It wasn't as bad as at rush hour, but all the seats were filled. I leaned back and closed my eyes, deciding to sleep a little, being so tired. I was just beginning to doze off when I heard a woman's voice muttering, or rather, declaiming:

> "A gold cigarette case, well, that's a nice thing,
>   isn't it, I must say, a gold case, yes. . . ."

There was something about this voice which made me open my eyes: on the other side of the compartment, about eight persons away, sat a youngish woman, wearing a cheap green cloth coat, gloveless hands, flat brown shoes, and lisle stockings. She must be rather poor—a woman dressed like this is a rare sight, these days. But it was her posture that struck me. She was sitting half-twisted in her seat, so that her head was turned over her left shoulder, and she was looking straight at the stomach of an elderly man next to her. But it was clear she was not seeing it: her young staring eyes were sightless, she was looking inwards.

She was so clearly alone, in the crowded compartment, that it was not as embarrassing as it might have been. I looked around, and people were smiling, or exchanging glances, or winking, or ignoring her, according to their natures, but she was oblivious of us all.

She suddenly aroused herself, turned so that she sat straight in her seat, and directed her voice and her gaze to the opposite seat:

> *"Well so that's what you think, you think that,*
> *you think that do you, well, you think I'm just going*
> *to wait at home for you, but you gave her a gold*
> *case and . . ."*

And with a clockwork movement of her whole thin person, she turned her narrow pale-haired head sideways over her left shoulder, and resumed her stiff empty stare at the man's stomach. He was grinning uncomfortably. I leaned forward to look along the line of people in the row of seats I sat in, and the man opposite her, a young man, had exactly the same look of discomfort which he was determined to keep amused. So we all looked at her, the young, thin, pale woman in her private drama of misery, who was so completely unconscious of us that she spoke and thought out loud. And again, without particular warning or reason, in between stops, so it wasn't that she was disturbed from her dream by the train stopping at Bond Street, and then jumping forward again, she twisted her body frontways, and addressed the seat opposite her (the young man had got off, and a smart grey-curled matron had got in):

> *"Well I know about it now, don't I, and if you come*
> *in all smiling and pleased well then I know, don't*
> *I, you don't have to tell me, I know, and I've said*
> *to her, I've said, I know he gave you a gold cigarette*
> *case. . . ."*

At which point, with the same clockwork impulse, she stopped, or was checked, or simply ran out, and turned herself half-around to stare at the stomach—the same stomach, for the middleaged man was still there. But we stopped at Marble Arch and he got out, giving the compartment, rather than the people in it, a tolerant half-smile which said: I am sure I can trust you to realise that this unfortunate woman is stark staring mad. . . .

His seat remained empty. No people got in at Marble Arch, and the two people standing waiting for seats did not want to sit by her to receive her stare.

We all sat, looking gently in front of us, pretending to ourselves and to each other that we didn't know the poor woman was mad and that in fact we ought to be doing something about it. I even wondered what I should say: Madam, you're mad—shall I escort you to your home? Or: Poor thing, don't go on like that, it doesn't do any good, you know—just leave him, that'll bring him to his senses. . . .

And behold, after the interval that was regulated by her inner mechanism had elapsed, she turned back and said to the smart matron who received this statement of accusation with perfect self-command:

> "*Yes, I know! Oh yes! And what about my
> shoes, what about them, a golden cigarette
> case is what she got, the filthy bitch,
> a golden case. . . .*"

Stop. Twist. Stare. At the empty seat by her.

Extraordinary. Because it was a frozen misery, how shall I put it? A passionless passion—we were seeing unhappiness embodied; we were looking at the essence of some private tragedy—rather, Tragedy. There was no emotion in it. She was like an actress doing Accusation, or Betrayed Love, or Infidelity, when she has only just learned her lines and is not bothering to do more than get them right.

And whether she sat in her half-twisted position, her unblinking eyes staring at the greenish, furry, ugly covering of the train seat, or sat straight, directing her accusation to the smart woman opposite, there was a frightening immobility about her—yes, that was why she frightened us. For it was clear that she might very well (if the inner machine ran down) stay silent, forever, in either twisted or straight position, or at any point between them—yes, we could all imagine her, frozen perpetually in some arbitrary pose. It was as if we watched the shell of some woman going through certain predetermined motions.

For *she* was simply not there. *What* was there, who she was, it was impossible to tell, though it was easy to imagine her thin, gentle little face breaking into a smile in total forgetfulness of what she was enacting now. She did not know she was in a train between Marble Arch and Queensway, nor that she was publicly accusing her husband or lover, nor that we were looking at her.

And we, looking at her, felt an embarrassment and shame that was not on her account at all. . . .

Suddenly I felt, under the scarf and the tin foil, a lightening of my fingers, as my heart rolled loose.

I hastily took it off my palm, in case it decided to adhere there again, and I removed the scarf, leaving balanced on my knees a perfect stylised heart, like a silver heart on a Valentine card, though of course it was three-dimensional. This heart was not so much harmless, no that isn't the word, as artistic, but in very bad taste, as I said. I could see that the people in the train, now looking at me and the heart, and not at the poor madwoman, were pleased with it.

I got up, took the four or so paces to where she was, and laid the tin-foiled heart down on the seat so that it received her stare.

For a moment she did not react, then with a groan or a mutter of relieved and entirely theatrical grief, she leaned forward, picked up the glittering heart, and clutched it in her arms, hugging it and rocking it back and forth, even laying her cheek against it, while staring over its top at her husband as if to say: Look what I've got, I don't care about you and your cigarette case, I've got a silver heart.

I got up, since we were at Notting Hill Gate, and, followed by the pleased congratulatory nods and smiles of the people left behind, I went out onto the platform, up the escalators, into the street, and along to the park.

No heart. No heart at all. What bliss. What freedom . . .

> *Hear that sound? That's laughter, yes.*
> *That's me laughing, yes, that's me.*

# A Man and Two Women

•–•–•–•–•–•–•–•–•–•–•–•–•–•–•–•–•–•–•–•–•–•–•–•–•–•–•–•–•–•–•–•–•–•–•–•–•

Stella's friends the Bradfords had taken a cheap cottage in Essex for the summer, and she was going down to visit them. She wanted to see them, but there was no doubt there was something of a letdown (and for them too) in the English cottage. Last summer Stella had been wandering with her husband around Italy; had seen the English couple at a cafe table, and found them sympathetic. They all liked each other, and the four went about for some weeks, sharing meals, hotels, trips. Back in London the friendship had not, as might have been expected, fallen off. Then Stella's husband departed abroad, as he often did, and Stella saw Jack and Dorothy by herself. There were a great many people she might have seen, but it was the Bradfords she saw most often, two or three times a week, at their flat or hers. They were at ease with each other. Why were they? Well, for one thing they were all artists—in different ways. Stella designed wallpapers and materials; she had a name for it.

The Bradfords were real artists. He painted, she drew. They had lived mostly out of England in cheap places around the Mediterranean. Both from the North of England, they had met at art school, married at twenty, had taken flight from England, then returned to it, needing it, then off again: and so on, for years, in the rhythm of so many of their kind, needing, hating, loving England. There had been seasons of real poverty, while they lived on pasta or bread or rice, and wine and fruit and sunshine, in Majorca, southern Spain, Italy, North Africa.

A French critic had seen Jack's work, and suddenly he was

successful. His show in Paris, then one in London, made money; and now he charged in the hundreds where a year or so ago he charged ten or twenty guineas. This had deepened his contempt for the values of the markets. For a while Stella thought that this was the bond between the Bradfords and herself. They were so very much, as she was, of the new generation of artists (and poets and playwrights and novelists) who had one thing in common, a cool derision about the racket. They were so very unlike (they felt) the older generation with their Societies and their Lunches and their salons and their cliques: their atmosphere of connivance with the snobberies of success. Stella, too, had been successful by a fluke. Not that she did not consider herself talented; it was that others as talented were unfêted, and unbought. When she was with the Bradfords and other fellow spirits, they would talk about the racket, using each other as yardsticks or fellow consciences about how much to give in, what to give, how to use without being used, how to enjoy without becoming dependent on enjoyment.

Of course Dorothy Bradford was not able to talk in quite the same way, since she had not yet been "discovered"; she had not "broken through." A few people with discrimination bought her unusual delicate drawings, which had a strength that was hard to understand unless one knew Dorothy herself. But she was not at all, as Jack was, a great success. There was a strain here, in the marriage, nothing much; it was kept in check by their scorn for their arbitrary rewards of "the racket." But it was there, nevertheless.

Stella's husband had said: "Well, I can understand that, it's like me and you—you're creative, whatever that may mean, I'm just a bloody TV journalist." There was no bitterness in this. He was a good journalist, and besides he sometimes got the chance to make a good small film. All the same, there was that between him and Stella, just as there was between Jack and his wife.

After a time Stella saw something else in her kinship with the couple. It was that the Bradfords had a close bond, bred of having spent so many years together in foreign places, dependent on each other because of their poverty. It had been a real love marriage; one could see it by looking at them. It was now. And Stella's marriage was a real marriage. She understood she enjoyed being with the Bradfords because the two couples

were equal in this. Both marriages were those of strong, passionate, talented individuals; they shared a battling quality that
strengthened them, not weakened them.

The reason why it had taken Stella so long to understand this
was that the Bradfords had made her think about her own marriage, which she was beginning to take for granted, sometimes
even found exhausting. She had understood, through them,
how lucky she was in her husband; how lucky they all were.
No marital miseries; nothing of (what they saw so often in
friends) one partner in a marriage victim to the other, resenting
the other; no claiming of outsiders as sympathisers or allies in
an unequal battle.

There had been a plan for these four people to go off again to
Italy or Spain, but then Stella's husband departed, and Dorothy
got pregnant. So there was the cottage in Essex instead, a bad
second choice, but better, they all felt, to deal with a new baby
on home ground, at least for the first year. Stella, telephoned by
Jack (on Dorothy's particular insistence, he said), offered and
received commiserations on its being only Essex and not
Majorca or Italy. She also received sympathy because her husband had been expected back this weekend, but had wired to
say he wouldn't be back for another month, probably—there
was trouble in Venezuela. Stella wasn't really forlorn; she didn't
mind living alone, since she was always supported by knowing
her man would be back. Besides, if she herself were offered the
chance of a month's "trouble" in Venezuela, she wouldn't hesitate, so it wasn't fair . . . fairness characterised their relationship. All the same, it was nice that she could drop down (or up)
to the Bradfords, people with whom she could always be herself,
neither more nor less.

She left London at midday by train, armed with food unobtainable in Essex: salamis, cheeses, spices, wine. The sun
shone, but it wasn't particularly warm. She hoped there would
be heating in the cottage, July or not.

The train was empty. The little station seemed stranded in
a green nowhere. She got out, cumbered by bags full of food. A
porter and a stationmaster examined, then came to succour her.
She was a tallish, fair woman, rather ample; her soft hair,
drawn back, escaped in tendrils, and she had great helpless-
looking blue eyes. She wore a dress made in one of the materials
she had designed. Enormous green leaves laid hands all over

"Yes," said Jack, with a brief reluctant look at her.

"All right, don't worry," she said, replying aloud as she often did to things that Jack had not said aloud.

"Good," he said.

Stella thought of how she had seen Dorothy, in the hospital room, with the new baby. She had sat up in bed, in a pretty bed-jacket, the baby beside her in a basket. He was restless. Jack stood between basket and bed, one large hand on his son's stomach. "Now, you just shut up, little bleeder," he had said, as he grumbled. Then he had picked him up, as if he'd been doing it always, held him against his shoulder, and, as Dorothy held her arms out, had put the baby into them. "Want your mother, then? Don't blame you."

That scene, the ease of it, the way the two parents were together, had, for Stella, made nonsense of all the months of Dorothy's self-questioning. As for Dorothy, she had said, parodying the expected words but meaning them: "He's the most beautiful baby ever born. I can't imagine why I didn't have him before."

"There's the cottage," said Jack. Ahead of them was a small labourer's cottage, among full green trees, surrounded by green grass. It was painted white, had four sparkling windows. Next to it a long shed or structure that turned out to be a greenhouse.

"The man grew tomatoes," said Jack. "Fine studio now."

The car came to rest under another tree.

"Can I just drop in to the studio?"

"Help yourself." Stella walked into the long, glass-roofed shed. In London Jack and Dorothy shared a studio. They had shared huts, sheds, any suitable building, all around the Mediterranean. They always worked side by side. Dorothy's end was tidy, exquisite, Jack's lumbered with great canvases, and he worked in a clutter. Now Stella looked to see if this friendly arrangement continued, but as Jack came in behind her he said: "Dorothy's not set herself up yet. I miss her, I can tell you."

The greenhouse was still partly one: trestles with plants stood along the ends. It was lush and warm.

"As hot as hell when the sun's really going, it makes up. And Dorothy brings Paul in sometimes, so he can get used to a decent climate young."

Dorothy came in, at the far end, without the baby. She had

recovered her figure. She was a small dark woman, with neat, delicate limbs. Her face was white, with scarlet rather irregular lips, and black glossy brows, a little crooked. So while she was not pretty, she was lively and dramatic-looking. She and Stella had their moments together, when they got pleasure from contrasting their differences, one woman so big and soft and blond, the other so dark and vivacious.

Dorothy came forward through shafts of sunlight, stopped, and said: "Stella, I'm glad you've come." Then forward again, to a few steps off, where she stood looking at them. "You two look good together," she said, frowning. There was something heavy and over-emphasised about both statements, and Stella said: "I was wondering what Jack had been up to."

"Very good, I think," said Dorothy, coming to look at the new canvas on the easel. It was of sunlit rocks, brown and smooth, with blue sky, blue water, and people swimming in spangles of light. When Jack was in the south, he painted pictures that his wife described as "dirt and grime and misery"—which was how they both described their joint childhood background. When he was in England he painted scenes like these.

"Like it? It's good, isn't it?" said Dorothy.

"Very much " said Stella. She always took pleasure from the contrast between Jack's outward self—the small, self-contained little man who could have vanished in a moment into a crowd of factory workers in, perhaps Manchester, and the sensuous bright pictures like these.

"And you?" asked Stella.

"Having a baby's killed everything creative in me—quite different from being pregnant," said Dorothy, but not complaining of it. She had worked like a demon while she was pregnant.

"Have a heart," said Jack, "he's only just got himself born."

"Well, I don't care," said Dorothy. "That's the funny thing, I *don't* care." She said this flat, indifferent. She seemed to be looking at them both again from a small troubled distance. "You two look good together," she said, and again there was the small jar.

"Well, how about some tea?" said Jack, and Dorothy said at once: "I made it when I heard the car. I thought better inside, it's not really hot in the sun." She led the way out of the greenhouse, her white linen dress dissolving in lozenges of yellow light from the glass panes above, so that Stella was reminded of the white limbs of Jack's swimmers disintegrating under sunlight in his new picture. The work of these two people was always reminding one of each other, or each other's work, and in all kinds of ways: they were so much married, so close.

The time it took to cross the space of rough grass to the door of the little house was enough to show Dorothy was right: it was really chilly in the sun. Inside two electric heaters made up for it. There had been two little rooms downstairs, but they had been knocked into one fine lowceilinged room, stone-floored, whitewashed. A tea table, covered with a purple checked cloth, stood waiting near a window where flowering bushes and trees showed through clean panes. Charming. They adjusted the heaters and arranged themselves so they could admire the English countryside through glass. Stella looked for the baby; Dorothy said: "In the pram at the back." Then she asked: "Did yours cry a lot?"

Stella laughed and said again: "I'll try to remember."

"We expect you to guide and direct, with all your experience," said Jack.

"As far as I can remember, she was a little demon for about three months, for no reason I could see, then suddenly she became civilised."

"Roll on the three months," said Jack.

"Six weeks to go," said Dorothy, handling teacups in a languid indifferent manner Stella found new in her.

"Finding it tough going?"

"I've never felt better in my life," said Dorothy at once, as if being accused.

"You look fine."

She looked a bit tired, nothing much; Stella couldn't see what reason there was for Jack to warn her. Unless he meant the languor, a look of self-absorption? Her vivacity, a friendly aggressiveness that was the expression of her lively intelligence, was dimmed. She sat leaning back in a deep airchair, letting Jack manage things, smiling vaguely.

"I'll bring him in in a minute," she remarked, listening to the silence from the sunlit garden at the back.

"Leave him," said Jack. "He's quiet seldom enough. Relax, woman, and have a cigarette."

He lit a cigarette for her, and she took it in the same vague way, and sat breathing out smoke, her eyes half-closed.

"Have you heard from Philip?" she asked, not from politeness, but with sudden insistence.

"Of course she has, she got a wire," said Jack.

"I want to know how she feels," said Dorothy. "How do you feel, Stell?" She was listening for the baby all the time.

"Feel about what?"

"About his not coming back."

"But he is coming back, it's only a month," said Stella, and heard, with surprise, that her voice sounded edgy.

"You see?" said Dorothy to Jack, meaning the words, not the edge on them.

At this evidence that she and Philip had been discussed, Stella felt, first, pleasure: because it was pleasurable to be understood by two such good friends; then she felt discomfort, remembering Jack's warning.

"See what?" she asked Dorothy, smiling.

"That's enough now," said Jack to his wife in a flash of stubborn anger, which continued the conversation that had taken place.

Dorothy took direction from her husband, and kept quiet a moment, then seemed impelled to continue: "I've been thinking it must be nice, having your husband go off, then come back. Do you realise Jack and I haven't been separated since we married? That's over ten years. Don't you think there's something awful in two grown people stuck together all the time like Siamese twins?" This ended in a wail of genuine appeal to Stella.

"No, I think it's marvellous."

"But you don't mind being alone so much?"

"It's not *so* much; it's two or three months in a year. Well of course I mind. But I enjoy being alone, really. But I'd enjoy it too if we were together all the time. I envy you two." Stella was surprised to find her eyes wet with self-pity because she had to be without her husband another month.

"And what does he think?" demanded Dorothy. "What does Philip think?"

Stella said: "Well, I think he likes getting away from time to time—yes. He likes intimacy, he enjoys it, but it doesn't come as easily to him as it does to me." She had never said this before because she had never thought about it. She was annoyed with herself that she had had to wait for Dorothy to prompt her. Yet she knew that getting annoyed was what she must not do, with the state Dorothy was in, whatever it was. She glanced at Jack for guidance, but he was determinedly busy on his pipe.

"Well, I'm like Philip," announced Dorothy. "Yes, I'd love it if Jack went off sometimes. I think I'm being stifled being shut up with Jack day and night, year in year out."

"Thanks," said Jack, short but good-humoured.

"No, but I mean it. There's something humiliating about two adult people never for one second out of each other's sight."

"Well," said Jack, "when Paul's a bit bigger, you buzz off for a month or so and you'll appreciate me when you get back."

"It's not that I don't appreciate you, it's not that at all," said Dorothy, insistent, almost strident, apparently fevered with restlessness. Her languor had quite gone, and her limbs jerked and moved. And now the baby, as if he had been prompted by his father's mentioning him, let out a cry. Jack got up, forestalling his wife, saying: "I'll get him."

Dorothy sat, listening for her husband's movements with the baby, until he came back, which he did, supporting the infant sprawled against his shoulder with a competent hand. He sat down, let his son slide on to his chest, and said: "There now, you shut up and leave us in peace a bit longer." The baby was looking up into his face with the astonished expression of the newly born, and Dorothy sat smiling at both of them. Stella understood that her restlessness, her repeated curtailed movements, meant that she longed—more, needed—to have the child in her arms, have its body against hers. And Jack seemed to feel this, because Stella could have sworn it was not a conscious decision that made him rise and slide the infant into his wife's arms. Her flesh, her needs, had spoken direct to him without words, and he had risen at once to give her what she wanted. This silent instinctive conversation between husband and wife made Stella miss her own husband violently, and with resentment against fate that kept them apart so often. She ached for Philip.

Meanwhile Dorothy, now the baby was sprawled softly against her chest, the small feet in her hand, seemed to have lapsed into good humour. And Stella, watching, remembered something she really had forgotten: the close, fierce physical tie between herself and her daughter when she had been a tiny baby. She saw this bond in the way Dorothy stroked the small head that trembled on its neck as the baby looked up into his mother's face. Why, she remembered it was like being in love, having a new baby. All kinds of forgotten or unused instincts woke in Stella. She lit a cigarette, took herself in hand; set herself to enjoy the other woman's love affair with her baby instead of envying her.

The sun, dropping into the trees, struck the windowpanes; and there was a dazzle and a flashing of yellow and white light into the room, particularly over Dorothy in her white dress and the baby. Again Stella was reminded of Jack's picture of the white-limbed swimmers in sun-dissolving water. Dorothy shielded the baby's eyes with her hand and remarked dreamily: "This is better than any man, isn't it, Stell? Isn't it better than any man?"

"Well—no," said Stella laughing. "No, not for long."

"If you say so, you should know . . . but I can't imagine ever . . . Tell me, Stell, does your Philip have affairs when he's away?"

"For God's sake!" said Jack, angry. But he checked himself.

"Yes, I am sure he does."

"Do you mind?" asked Dorothy, loving the baby's feet with her enclosing palm.

And now Stella was forced to remember, to think about having minded, minding, coming to terms, and the ways in which she now did not mind.

"I don't think about it," she said.

"Well, I don't think I'd mind," said Dorothy.

"Thanks for letting me know," said Jack, short despite himself. Then he made himself laugh.

"And you, do you have affairs while Philip's away?"

"Sometimes. Not really."

"Do you know, Jack was unfaithful to me this week," remarked Dorothy, smiling at the baby.

"That's *enough*," said Jack, really angry.

"No it isn't enough, it isn't. Because what's awful is, I don't care."

"Well why should you care, in the circumstances?" Jack turned to Stella. "There's a silly bitch Lady Edith lives across that field. She got all excited, real live artists living down her lane. Well Dorothy was lucky, she had an excuse in the baby, but I had to go to her silly party. Booze flowing in rivers, and the most incredible people—you know. If you read about them in a novel, you'd never believe . . . but I can't remember much after about twelve."

"Do you know what happened?" said Dorothy. "I was feeding the baby, it was terribly early. Jack sat straight up in bed and said: 'Jesus, Dorothy, I've just remembered, I screwed that silly bitch Lady Edith on her brocade sofa.'"

Stella laughed. Jack let out a snort of laughter. Dorothy laughed, an unscrupulous chuckle of appreciation. Then she said seriously: "But that's the point, Stella—the thing is, I don't care a tuppenny damn."

"But why should you?" asked Stella.

"But it's the first time he ever has, and surely I should have minded?"

"Don't you be too sure of that," said Jack, energetically puffing his pipe. "Don't be too sure." But it was only for form's sake, and Dorothy knew it, and said: "Surely I should have cared, Stell?"

"No. You'd have cared if you and Jack weren't so marvellous together. Just as I'd care if Philip and I weren't. . . ." Tears came running down her face. She let them. These were her good friends; and besides, instinct told her tears weren't a bad thing, with Dorothy in this mood. She said, sniffing: "When Philip gets home, we always have a flaming bloody row in the first day or two, about something unimportant, but what it's really about, and we know it, is that I'm jealous of any affair he's had and vice versa. Then we go to bed and make up." She wept, bitterly, thinking of this happiness, postponed for a month, to be succeeded by the delightful battle of their day-to-day living.

"Oh Stella," said Jack. "Stell . . ." He got up, fished out a handkerchief, dabbed her eyes for her. "There, love, he'll be back soon."

"Yes, I know. It's just that you two are so good together and whenever I'm with you I miss Philip."

"Well, I suppose we're good together?" said Dorothy, sounding surprised. Jack, bending over Stella with his back to his wife, made a warning grimace, then stood up and turned, commanding the situation. "It's nearly six. You'd better feed Paul. Stella's going to cook supper."

"Is she? How nice," said Dorothy. "There's everything in the kitchen, Stella. How lovely to be looked after."

"I'll show you our mansion," said Jack.

Upstairs were two small white rooms. One was the bedroom, with their things and the baby's in it. The other was an overflow room, jammed with stuff. Jack picked up a large leather folder off the spare bed and said: "Look at these, Stell." He stood at the window, back to her, his thumb at work in his pipe bowl, looking into the garden. Stella sat on the bed, opened the folder and at once exclaimed: "When did she do these?"

"The last three months she was pregnant. Never seen anything like it, she just turned them out one after the other."

There were a couple of hundred pencil drawings, all of two bodies in every kind of balance, tension, relationship. The two bodies were Jack's and Dorothy's, mostly unclothed, but not all. The drawings startled, not only because they marked a real jump forward in Dorothy's achievement, but because of their bold sensuousness. They were a kind of chant, or exaltation about the marriage. The instinctive closeness, the harmony of Jack and Dorothy, visible in every movement they made towards or away from each other, visible even when they were not together, was celebrated here with a frank, calm triumph.

"Some of them are pretty strong," said Jack, the northern workingclass boy reviving in him for a moment's puritanism.

But Stella laughed, because the prudishness masked pride: some of the drawings were indecent.

In the last few of the series the woman's body was swollen in pregnancy. They showed her trust in her husband, whose body, commanding hers, stood or lay in positions of strength and confidence. In the very last Dorothy stood turned away from her husband, her two hands supporting her big belly, and Jack's hands were protective on her shoulders.

"They are marvellous," said Stella.

"They are, aren't they."

Stella looked, laughing, and with love, towards Jack; for she saw that his showing her the drawings was not only pride in his wife's talent, but that he was using this way of telling Stella not to take Dorothy's mood too seriously. And to cheer himself up. She said, impulsively: "Well that's all right then, isn't it?"

"What? Oh yes, I see what you mean, yes, I think it's all right."

"Do you know what?" said Stella, lowering her voice. "I think Dorothy's guilty because she feels unfaithful to you."

"*What*?"

"No, I mean, with the baby, and that's what it's all about."

He turned to face her, troubled, then slowly smiling. There was the same rich unscrupulous quality of appreciation in that smile as there had been in Dorothy's laugh over her husband and Lady Edith. "You think so?" They laughed together, irrepressibly and loudly.

"What's the joke?" shouted Dorothy.

"I'm laughing because your drawings are so good," shouted Stella.

"Yes, they are, aren't they?" But Dorothy's voice changed to flat incredulity: "The trouble is, I can't imagine how I ever did them, I can't imagine ever being able to do it again."

"Downstairs," said Jack to Stella, and they went down to find Dorothy nursing the baby. He nursed with his whole being, all of him in movement. He was wrestling with the breast, thumping Dorothy's plump pretty breast with his fists. Jack stood looking down at the two of them, grinning. Dorothy reminded Stella of a cat, half-closing her yellow eyes to stare over her kittens at work on her side, while she stretched out a paw where claws sheathed and unsheathed themselves, making a small rip-rip-rip on the carpet she lay on.

"You're a savage creature," said Stella, laughing.

Dorothy raised her small vivid face and smiled. "Yes, I am," she said, and looked at the two of them calm, and from a distance, over the head of her energetic baby.

Stella cooked supper in a stone kitchen, with a heater brought by Jack to make it tolerable. She used the good food she had brought with her, taking trouble. It took some time, then the three ate slowly over a big wooden table. The baby was not asleep. He grumbled for some minutes on a cushion on the floor, then his father held him briefly, before passing him over, as he had done earlier, in response to his mother's need to have him close.

"I'm supposed to let him cry," remarked Dorothy. "But why should he? If he were an Arab or an African baby he'd be plastered to my back."

"And very nice too," said Jack. "I think they come out too soon into the light of day; they should just stay inside for about eighteen months, much better all around."

"Have a heart," said Dorothy and Stella together, and they all laughed; but Dorothy added, quite serious: "Yes, I've been thinking so too."

This good nature lasted through the long meal. The light went cool and thin outside; and inside they let the summer dusk deepen, without lamps.

"I've got to go quite soon," said Stella, with regret.

"Oh, no, you've got to stay!" said Dorothy, strident. It was sudden, the return of the woman who made Jack and Dorothy tense themselves to take strain.

"We all thought Philip was coming. The children will be back tomorrow night, they've been on holiday."

"Then stay till tomorrow, I *want* you," said Dorothy, petulant.

"But I can't," said Stella.

"I never thought I'd want another woman around, cooking in my kitchen, looking after me, but I do," said Dorothy, apparently about to cry.

"Well, love, you'll have to put up with me," said Jack.

"Would you mind, Stell?"

"Mind *what*?" asked Stella, cautious.

"Do you find Jack attractive?"

"Very."

"Well I know you do. Jack, do you find Stella attractive?"

"Try me," said Jack, grinning; but at the same time signalling warnings to Stella.

"Well, then!" said Dorothy.

"A *ménage à trois*?" asked Stella, laughing. "And how about my Philip? Where does he fit in?"

"Well, if it comes to that, I wouldn't mind Philip myself," said Dorothy, knitting her sharp black brows and frowning.

"I don't blame you," said Stella, thinking of her handsome husband.

"Just for a month, till he comes back," said Dorothy. "I tell you what, we'll abandon this silly cottage, we must have been mad to stick ourselves away in England in the first place. The three of us'll just pack up and go off to Spain or Italy with the baby."

"And what else?" enquired Jack, good-natured at all costs, using his pipe as a safety valve.

"Yes, I've decided I approve of polygamy," announced Dorothy. She had opened her dress and the baby was nursing again, quietly this time, relaxed against her. She stroked his head, softly, softly, while her voice rose and insisted at the other two people: "I never understood it before, but I do now. I'll be the senior wife, and you two can look after me."

"Any other plans?" enquired Jack, angry now. "You just drop in from time to watch Stella and me have a go, is that it? Or are you going to tell us when we can go off and do it, give us your gracious permission?"

"Oh I don't care what you do, that's the point," said Dorothy, sighing, sounding forlorn, however.

Jack and Stella, careful not to look at each other, sat waiting.

"I read something in the newspaper yesterday, it struck me," said Dorothy, conversational. "A man and two women living together—here, in England. They are both his wives, they consider themselves his wives. The senior wife has a baby, and the younger wife sleeps with him—well, that's what it looked like, reading between the lines."

"You'd better stop reading between lines," said Jack. "It's not doing you any good."

"No, I'd like it," insisted Dorothy. "I think our marriages are silly. Africans and people like that, they know better, they've got some sense."

"I can just see you if I did make love to Stella," said Jack.

"Yes!" said Stella, with a short laugh, which, against her will, was resentful.

"But I wouldn't mind," said Dorothy, and burst into tears.

"Now, Dorothy, that's enough," said Jack. He got up, took the baby, whose sucking was mechanical now, and said: "Now listen, you're going right upstairs and you're going to sleep. This little stinker's full as a tick, he'll be asleep for hours, that's my bet."

"I don't feel sleepy," said Dorothy, sobbing.

"I'll give you a sleeping pill, then."

Then started a search for sleeping pills. None to be found.

"That's just like us," wailed Dorothy, "we don't even have a sleeping pill in the place. . . . Stella, I wish you'd stay, I really do. Why can't you?"

"Stella's going in just a minute, I'm taking her to the station," said Jack. He poured some Scotch into a glass, handed it to his wife and said: "Now drink that, love, and let's have an end of it. I'm getting fed-up." He sounded fed-up.

Dorothy obediently drank the Scotch, got unsteadily from her chair and went slowly upstairs. "Don't let him cry," she demanded, as she disappeared.

"Oh you silly bitch!" he shouted after her. "When have I let him cry? Here, you hold on a minute," he said to Stella, handing her the baby. He ran upstairs.

Stella held the baby. This was almost for the first time, since she sensed how much another woman's holding her child made Dorothy's fierce new possessiveness uneasy. She looked down at the small, sleepy, red face and said softly: "Well, you're causing a lot of trouble, aren't you?"

Jack shouted from upstairs: "Come up a minute, Stell." She went up, with the baby. Dorothy was tucked up in bed, drowsy from the Scotch, the bedside light turned away from her. She looked at the baby, but Jack took it from Stella.

"Jack says I'm a silly bitch," said Dorothy, apologetic, to Stella.

"Well, never mind, you'll feel different soon."

"I suppose so, if you say so. All right, I *am* going to sleep," said Dorothy, in a stubborn, sad little voice. She turned over, away from them. In the last flare of her hysteria she said: "Why don't you two walk to the station together? It's a lovely night."

"We're going to," said Jack, "don't worry."

She let out a weak giggle, but did not turn. Jack carefully deposited the now sleeping baby in the bed, about a foot from Dorothy. Who suddenly wriggled over until her small, defiant white back was in contact with the blanketed bundle that was her son.

Jack raised his eyebrows at Stella: but Stella was looking at mother and baby, the nerves of her memory filling her with sweet warmth. What right had this woman, who was in possession of such delight, to torment her husband, to torment her friend, as she had been doing—what right had she to rely on their decency as she did?

Surprised by these thoughts, she walked away downstairs,

and stood at the door into the garden, her eyes shut, holding herself rigid against tears.

She felt a warmth on her bare arm—Jack's hand. She opened her eyes to see him bending towards her, concerned.

"It'd serve Dorothy right if I did drag you off into the bushes. . . ."

"Wouldn't have to drag me," he said; and while the words had the measure of facetiousness the situation demanded, she felt his seriousness envelop them both in danger.

The warmth of his hand slid across her back, and she turned towards him under its pressure. They stood together, cheeks touching, scents of skin and hair mixing with the smells of warmed grass and leaves.

She thought: What is going to happen now will blow Dorothy and Jack and that baby sky-high; it's the end of my marriage; I'm going to blow everything to bits. There was almost uncontrollable pleasure in it.

She saw Dorothy, Jack, the baby, her husband, and two half-grown children, all dispersed, all spinning downwards through the sky like bits of debris after an explosion.

Jack's mouth was moving along her cheek towards her mouth, dissolving her whole self in delight. She saw, against closed lids, the bundled baby upstairs, and pulled back from the situation, exclaiming energetically: "Damn Dorothy, damn her, damn her, I'd like to kill her. . . ."

And he, exploding into reaction, said in a low furious rage: "Damn you both! I'd like to wring both your bloody necks. . . ."

Their faces were at a foot's distance from each other, their eyes staring hostility. She thought that if she had not the vision of the helpless baby they would now be in each other's arms—generating tenderness and desire like a couple of dynamos, she said to herself, trembling with dry anger.

"I'm going to miss my train if I don't go," she said.

"I'll get your coat," he said, and went in, leaving her defenceless against the emptiness of the garden.

When he came out, he slid the coat around her without touching her, and said: "Come on, I'll take you by car." He walked away in front of her to the car, and she followed meekly over rough lawn. It really was a lovely night.

# A Room

When I first came into this flat
of four small boxlike rooms, the bedroom was painted pale pink,
except for the fireplace wall, which had a fanciful pink-and-blue
paper. The woodwork was a dark purple, almost black. This
paint is sold by a big decorating shop in the West End and is
called Bilberry.

Two girls had the flat before me. Very little money, obviously,
because the carpeting was going into holes and the walls were
decorated with travel posters. The woman upstairs told me
they often had parties that lasted all night. "But I liked to hear
them, I enjoy the sounds of life." She was reproachful. I don't
have parties often enough for her. The girls left no forwarding
address, following the tradition for this flat. Over the years it
has often happened that the bell rings and people ask for "Angus
Ferguson—I thought he lived here?" And the Maitlands? And
Mrs. Dowland? And the young Caitsbys? All these people, and
probably many others, have lived in this flat, and departed
leaving nothing behind. I know nothing about them, nor does
anyone else in the building, though some of them have lived
here for years.

I found the pink too assertive, and after several mistakes
settled on white walls, leaving the plum-colour, or Bilberry,
woodwork. First I had grey curtains, then blue ones. My bed is
under the window. There is a desk, which I had meant to write
on, but it is always too cluttered with papers. So I write in the
livingroom or on the kitchen table. But I spend a lot of time in
the bedroom. Bed is the best place for reading, thinking, or do-

ing nothing. It is my room; it is where I feel I live, though the shape is bad and there are things about it that can never be anything but ugly. For instance, the fireplace was of iron—a bulging, knobbed, ornamented black. The girls had left it as it was, using a small gas heater in the opening. Its heavy ugliness kept drawing my eyes towards it; and I painted a panel from the ceiling downwards in the dark plum colour, so that the fireplace and the small thick shelf over it would be absorbed. On either side of the panel, since I could not have the whole wall in plum, which at night looks black, were left two panels of the absurd wallpaper which has bright people like birds in pink-and-blue cages. The fireplace seemed less obtrusive, but my fire is a gas fire, a square solid shape of bronze, brought from an earlier flat where it did not look too bad. But it does not fit here at all. So the whole wall doesn't work, it fails to come off.

Another wall, the one beside my bed, is also deformed. Over the bed swells a grainy irregular lump two or more feet across. Someone—Angus Ferguson? The Maitlands? Mrs. Dowland? —attempted to replace falling plaster and made a hash of it. No professional plasterer could have got away with such a protuberance.

On the whole, this wall gives me pleasure: it reminds me of the irregular whitewashed walls of another house I lived in once. Probably I chose to paint this room white because I wanted to have the whitewashed lumpy walls of that early house repeated here in London?

The ceiling is a ceiling: flat, white, plain. It has a plaster border which is too heavy for the room and looks as if it might fall off easily. The whole building has a look of solid ugliness, but it was built cheap, and is not solid at all. For instance, walls, tapped, sound hollow; the plaster, when exposed, at once starts to trickle as if the walls were of loose sand held together by wallpaper. I can hear anything that goes on over my head, where the old woman who likes to hear a bit of life lives with her husband. She is Swedish, gives Swedish lessons. She dresses prettily, and looks a dear respectable old thing. Yet she is quite mad. Her door has four heavy, specially fitted locks inside, as well as bolts and bars. If I knock she opens the door on a chain four inches long and peers through to make sure that I (or they) will not attack her. Inside is a vision of neatness and order. She spends all day cleaning and arranging. When she can't find anything more to do in her flat she posts notices on the stairs saying: "Any person who drops rubbish on these stairs will be reported to the Authorities!" Then she visits every flat in turn (there are eight identical flats, one above the other) and says confidingly: "Of course the notice isn't meant for you."

Her husband works for an export firm and is away a good deal. When she expects him back, she dresses as carefully as a bride and goes off to meet him, blushing. On the nights he comes back from his trips the bed creaks over my head, and I hear them giggling.

They are an orderly couple, bed at eleven every night, up every morning at nine. As for myself, my life has no outward order and I like having them up there. Sometimes, when I've worked late, I hear them getting up and I think through my sleep or half-sleep: Good, the day's started, has it? And I drift back to semiconsciousness blended with their footsteps and the rattling of cups.

Sometimes, when I sleep in the afternoons, which I do because afternoon sleep is more interesting than night sleep, she takes a nap too. I think of her and of myself lying horizontally above each other, as if we were on two shelves.

When I lie down after lunch there is nothing unplanned about it. First I must feel the inner disturbance or alertness that is due to over-stimulation, or being a little sick or very tired. Then I darken the room, shut all the doors so the telephone won't wake me (though its distant ringing can be a welcome dream-progenitor) and I get into bed carefully, preserving the mood. It is these sleeps which help me with my work, telling me what to write or where I've gone wrong. And they save me from the fever of restlessness that comes from seeing too many people. I always drift off to sleep in the afternoons with the interest due to a long journey into the unknown, and the sleep is thin and extraordinary and takes me into regions hard to describe in a waking state.

But one afternoon there was no strange journey, nor was there useful information about my work. The sleep was so different from usual that for some time I thought I was awake.

I had been lying in the semidark, the curtains, of varying shades of dark blue, making a purply-moving shade. Outside it was a busy afternoon. I could hear sounds from the market underneath, and there was angry shouting, a quarrel of some kind, a man's voice and a woman's. I was looking at the fireplace and thinking how ugly it was, wondering what sort of person had deliberately chosen such a hideous shape of black iron. Though of course I had painted it over. Yes, whether I could afford it or not, I must get rid of the square bronze gas fire and find a prettier one. I saw the bronze shape had gone; there was a small black iron grate and a small fire in it, smoking. The smoke was coming into the room, and my eyes were sore.

The room was different; I felt chilled and estranged from myself as I looked. The walls had a paper whose general effect was a dingy brown, but looking closely at it I saw a small pattern of brownish-yellow leaves and brown stems. There were stains on it. The ceiling was yellowish and shiny from the smoke. There were some shreds of pinky-brown curtains at the windows with a tear in one so that the bottom edge hung down.

I was no longer lying on the bed, but sitting by the fire across the room, looking at the bed and at the window. Outside a shrill quarrel went on, the voices rising up from the street. I felt cold, I was shivering, and my eyes watered. In the little grate sat three small lumps of shiny coal, smoking dismally. Under me was a cushion or a folded coat, something like that. The room seemed much larger. Yes, it was a largish room. A chest of brown-varnished wood stain stood by the bed, which was low, a good foot lower than mine. There was a red army blanket stretched across the bed's foot. The recesses on either side of the fireplace had shallow wooden shelves down them, holding folded clothes, old magazines, crockery, a brown teapot. These things conveyed an atmosphere of thin poverty.

I was alone in the room, though someone was next door. I could hear sounds that made me unhappy, apprehensive. From upstairs a laugh, hostile to me. Was the old Swedish lady laughing? With whom? Had her husband come back suddenly?

I was desolate with loneliness that felt it would never be assuaged, no one would ever come to comfort me. I sat and looked at the bed which had the cheap red blanket on it that suggested illness, and sniffed because the smoke was tearing at the back of my throat. I was a child, I knew that. And that there was a war, something to do with war, war had something to do with this dream or memory—*whose*? I came back to my own room, lying on my bed, with silence upstairs and next door. I was alone in the flat, watching my soft dark blue curtains softly moving. I was filled with misery.

I left my pretty bedroom and made myself tea; then returned to draw the curtains and let the light in. I switched on the gas heater, which came up hot and red, driving the memory of cold away; and I looked behind its bronze efficiency into a grate that had not had coals in it, I knew, for years.

I have tried to dream myself back into that other room which is under this room, or beside it, or in it, or existing in someone's memory. Which war was it? Whose was the chilly poverty? And I would like to know more about the frightened little child. He (or she) must have been very small for the room to look so big. So far I have failed. Perhaps it was the quarrel outside in the street that . . . that *what*? And why?

# England versus England

I think I'll be off," said Charlie. "My things are packed." He had made sure of getting his holdall ready so that his mother wouldn't. "But it's early," she protested. Yet she was already knocking red hands together to rid them of water while she turned to say goodbye: she knew her son was leaving early to avoid the father. But the back door now opened and Mr. Thornton came in. Charlie and his father were alike: tall, over-thin, big-boned. The old miner stooped, his hair had gone into grey wisps, and his hollow cheeks were coal-pitted. The young man was still fresh, with jaunty fair hair and alert eyes. But there were scoops of strain under his eyes.

"You're alone," said Charlie involuntarily, pleased, ready to sit down again. The old man was not alone. Three men came into view behind him in the light that fell into the yard from the door, and Charlie said quickly: "I'm off, Dad, it's goodbye till Christmas." They all came crowding into the little kitchen, bringing with them the spirit of facetiousness that seemed to Charlie his personal spiteful enemy, like a poltergeist always standing in wait somewhere behind his right shoulder. "So you're back to the dreaming spires," said one man, nodding goodbye. "Off to t'palaces of learning," said another. Both were smiling. There was no hostility in it, or even envy, but it shut Charlie out of his family, away from his people. The third man, adding his tribute to this, the most brilliant son of the village, said: "You'll be coming back to a right Christmas with us, then, or will you be frolicking with t'lords and t'earls you're the equal of now?"

"He'll be home for Christmas," said the mother sharply. She turned her back on them, and dropped potatoes one by one from a paper bag into a bowl.

"For a day or so, any road," said Charlie, in obedience to the prompting spirit. "That's time enough to spend with t'hewers of wood and t'drawers of water." The third man nodded, as if to say: That's right! and put back his head to let out a relieved bellow. The father and the other two men guffawed with him. Young Lennie pushed and shoved Charlie encouragingly and Charlie jostled back, while the mother nodded and smiled because of the saving horseplay. All the same, he had not been home for nearly a year, and when they stopped laughing and stood waiting for him to go, their grave eyes said they were remembering this fact.

"Sorry I've not had more time with you, son," said Mr. Thornton, "but you know how 'tis."

The old miner had been union secretary, was now chairman, and had spent his working life as miners' representative in a dozen capacities. When he walked through the village, men at a back door, or a woman in an apron, called: "Just a minute, Bill," and came after him. Every evening Mr. Thornton sat in the kitchen, or in the parlour when the television was claimed by the children, giving advice about pensions, claims, work rules, allowances; filling in forms; listening to tales of trouble. Ever since Charlie could remember, Mr. Thornton had been less his father than the father of the village. Now the three miners went into the parlour, and Mr. Thornton laid his hand on his son's shoulder, and said: "It's been good seeing you," nodded, and followed them. As he shut the door he said to his wife: "Make us a cup of tea, will you, lass?"

"There's time for a cup, Charlie," said the mother, meaning there was no need for him to rush off now, when it was unlikely any more neighbours would come in. Charlie did not hear. He was watching her slosh dirty potatoes about under the running tap while with her free hand she reached for the kettle. He went to fetch his raincoat and his holdall, listening to the nagging inner voice which he hated, but which he felt as his only protection against the spiteful enemy outside: "I can't stand it when my father apologises to me—he was apologising to me for not seeing more of me. If he wasn't as he is, better than anyone else in the village, and our home the only house with real books in it, I wouldn't be at Oxford, I wouldn't have done well at school, so it cuts both ways." The words "cuts both ways" echoed uncannily in his inner ear, and he felt queasy, as if the earth he stood on was shaking. His eyes cleared on the sight of his mother, standing in front of him, her shrewd, non-judging gaze on his face. "Eh, lad," she said, "you don't look any too good to me." "I'm all right," he said hastily, and kissed her, adding: "Say my piece to the girls when they come in." He went out, with Lennie behind him.

The two youths walked in silence past fifty crammed lively brightly lit kitchens whose doors kept opening as the miners came in from the pit for their tea. They walked in silence along the fronts of fifty more houses. The fronts were all dark. The life of the village, even now, was in the kitchens where great fires roared all day on the cheap coal. The village had been built in the Thirties by the company, now nationalised. There were two thousand houses, exactly alike, with identical patches of carefully tended front garden, and busy back yards. Nearly every house had a television aerial. From every chimney poured black smoke.

At the bus stop Charlie turned to look back at the village, now a low hollow of black, streaked and spattered with sullen wet lights. He tried to isolate the gleam from his own home, while he thought how he loved his home and how he hated the village. Everything about it offended him, yet as soon as he stepped inside his kitchen he was received into warmth. That morning he had stood on the front step and looked out on lines of grey stucco houses on either side of grey tarmac; on grey ugly lampposts and greyish hedges, and beyond to the grey minetip and the neat black diagram of the minehead.

He had looked, listening while the painful inner voice lectured: "There's nothing in sight, not one object or building anywhere, that is beautiful. Everything is so ugly and mean and graceless that it should be bulldozed into the earth and out of the memory of man." There was not even a cinema. There was a post office, and attached to it a library that had romances and war stories. There were two miners' clubs for drinking. And there was television. These were the amenities for two thousand families.

When Mr. Thornton stood on his front step and looked forth he smiled with pride and called his children to say: "You've never seen what a miners' town can be like. You couldn't even imagine the conditions. Slums, that's what they used to be. Well, we've put an end to all that. . . . Yes, off you go to Doncaster, I suppose, dancing and the pictures—that's all you can think about. And you take it all for granted. Now, in our time . . ."

And so when Charlie visited his home he was careful that none of his bitter criticisms reached words, for above all, he could not bear to hurt his father.

A group of young miners came along for the bus. They wore smartly shouldered suits, their caps set at angles, and scarves flung back over their shoulders. They greeted Lennie, looked to see who the stranger was, and when Lennie said: "This is my brother," they nodded and turned quickly to board the bus. They went upstairs, and Lennie and Charlie went to the front downstairs. Lennie looked like them, with a strong cloth cap and a jaunty scarf. He was short, stocky, strong—"built for t'pit," Mr. Thornton said. But Lennie was in a foundry in Doncaster. No pit for him, he said. He had heard his father coughing through all the nights of his childhood, and the pit wasn't for him. But he had never said this to his father.

Lennie was twenty. He earned seventeen pounds a week, and wanted to marry a girl he had been courting for three years now. But he could not marry until the big brother was through college. The father was still on the coal face, when by rights of age he should have been on the surface, because he earned four pounds a week more on the face. The sister in the office had wanted to be a school-teacher, but at the moment of decision all the extra money of the family had been needed for Charlie. It cost them two hundred pounds a year for his extras at Oxford. The only members of the family not making sacrifices for Charlie were the schoolgirl and the mother.

It was half an hour on the bus, and Charlie's muscles were set hard in readiness for what Lennie might say, which must be resisted. Yet he had come home thinking: Well, at least I can talk it out with Lennie, I can be honest with him.

Now Lennie said facetiously, but with an anxious loving inspection of his brother's face: "And what for do we owe the pleasure of your company, Charlie boy? You could have knocked us all down with a feather when you said you were coming this weekend."

Charlie said angrily: "I got fed with t'earls and t'dukes."

"Eh," said Lennie quickly, "but you didn't need to mind *them*, they didn't mean to rile you."

"I know they didn't."

"Mum's right," said Lennie, with another anxious but carefully brief glance, "you're not looking too good. What's up?"

"What if I don't pass t'examinations," said Charlie in a rush.

"Eh, but what is this, then? You were always first in school. You were the best of everyone. Why shouldn't you pass, then?"

"Sometimes I think I won't," said Charlie lamely, but glad he had let the moment pass.

Lennie examined him again, this time frankly, and gave a movement like a shrug. But it was a hunching of the shoulders against a possible defeat. He sat hunched, his big hands on his knees. On his face was a small critical grin. Not critical of Charlie, not at all, but of life.

His heart beating painfully with guilt, Charlie said: "It's not as bad as that, I'll pass." The inner enemy remarked softly: "I'll pass, then I'll get a nice pansy job in a publisher's office with the other wet-nosed little boys, or I'll be a sort of clerk. Or I'll be a teacher—I've no talent for teaching, but what's that matter? Or I'll be on the management side of industry, pushing people like Lennie around. And the joke is, Lennie's earning more than I shall for years." The enemy behind his right shoulder began satirically tolling a bell and intoned: "Charlie Thornton, in his third year at Oxford, was found dead in a gas-filled bed-sitting-room this morning. He had been overworking. Death from natural causes." The enemy added a loud rude raspberry and fell silent. But he was waiting: Charlie could feel him there waiting.

Lennie said: "Seen a doctor, Charlie boy?"

"Yes. He said I should take it easy. That's why I came home."

"No point killing yourself working."

"No, it's not serious, he just said I must take it easy."

Lennie's face remained grave. Charlie knew that when he got home he would say to the mother: "I think Charlie's got summat on his mind." And his mother would say (while she stood shaking chips of potato into boiling fat): "I expect sometimes he wonders is the grind worth it. And he sees you earning, when he isn't." She would say, after a silence during which they exchanged careful looks: "It must be hard for him, coming here, everything different, then off he goes, everything different again."

"Shouldn't worry, Mum."

"I'm not worrying. Charlie's all right."

The inner voice enquired anxiously: "If she's on the spot about the rest, I suppose she's right about the last bit too—*I suppose I am all right?*"

But the enemy behind his right shoulder said: "A man's best friend is his mother, she never lets a thing pass."

Last year he had brought Jenny down for a weekend, to satisfy the family's curiosity about the posh people he knew these days. Jenny was a poor clergyman's daughter, bookish, a bit of a prig, but a nice girl. She had easily navigated the complicated currents of the weekend, while the family waited for her to put on "side." Afterwards Mrs. Thornton had said, putting her finger on the sore spot: "That's a right nice girl. She's a proper mother to you, and that's a fact." The last was not a criticism of the girl, but of Charlie. Now Charlie looked with envy at Lennie's responsible profile and said to himself: Yes, he's a man. He has been for years, since he left school. Me, I'm a proper baby, and I've got two years over him.

For above everything else, Charlie was made to feel, every time he came home, that these people, his people, were serious; while he and the people with whom he would now spend his life (if he passed the examination) were not serious. He did not believe this. The inner didactic voice made short work of any such idea. The outer enemy could, and did, parody it in a hundred ways. His family did not believe it, they were proud of him. Yet Charlie felt it in everything they said and did. They protected him. They sheltered him. And above all, they still paid for him. At his age, his father had been working in the pit for eight years.

Lennie would be married next year. He already talked of a family. He, Charlie (if he passed the examination), would be running around licking people's arses to get a job, Bachelor of Arts, Oxford, and a drug on the market.

They had reached Doncaster. It was raining. Soon they would pass where Doreen, Lennie's girl, worked. "You'd better get off here," Charlie said. "You'll have all that drag back through the wet." "No, s'all right, I'll come with you to the station."

There were another five minutes to go. "I don't think it's right, the way you get at Mum," Lennie said, at last coming to the point.

"But I haven't said a bloody word," said Charlie, switching without having intended it into his other voice, the middleclass voice which he was careful never to use with his family except in joke. Lennie gave him a glance of surprise and reproach and said: "All the same. She feels it."

"But it's bloody ridiculous." Charlie's voice was rising. "She stands in that kitchen all day, pandering to our every whim, when she's not doing housework or making a hundred trips a day with that bloody coal. . . ." In the Christmas holidays, when Charlie had visited home last, he had fixed up a bucket on the frame of an old pram to ease his mother's work. This morning he had seen the contrivance collapsed and full of rainwater in the back yard. After breakfast Lennie and Charlie had sat at the table in their shirt-sleeves watching their mother. The door was open into the back yard. Mrs. Thornton carried a shovel whose blade was nine inches by ten, and was walking back and forth from the coalhole in the yard, through the kitchen, into the parlour. On each inward journey, a small clump of coal balanced on the shovel. Charlie counted that his mother walked from the coalhole to the kitchen fire and the parlour fire thirty-six times. She walked steadily, the shovel in front, held like a spear in both hands, and her face frowned with purpose. Charlie had dropped his head on to his arms and laughed soundlessly until he felt Lennie's warning gaze and stopped the heave of his shoulders. After a moment he had sat up, straight-faced. Lennie said: "Why do you get at Mum, then?" Charlie said: "But I haven't said owt." "No, but she's getting riled. You always show what you think, Charlie boy." As Charlie did not respond to this appeal—for far more than present charity—Lennie went on: "You can't teach an old dog new tricks." "Old! She's not fifty!"

Now Charlie said, continuing the early conversation: "She goes on as if she were an old woman. She wears herself out with nothing—she could get through all the work she has in a couple of hours if she organised herself. Or if just for once she told us where to get off."

"What'd she do with herself then?"

"Do? Well, she could do something for herself. Read. Or see friends. Or something."

"She feels it. Last time you went off she cried."

"She *what?*" Charlie's guilt almost overpowered him, but the inner didactic voice switched on in time and he spoke through it: "What right have we to treat her like a bloody servant? Betty likes her food this way and that way, and Dad won't eat this and that, and she stands there and humours the lot of us—like a servant."

"And who was it last night said he wouldn't have fat on his meat and changed it for hers?" said Lennie smiling, but full of reproach.

"Oh, I'm just as bad as the rest of you," said Charlie, sounding false. "It makes me wild to see it," he said, sounding sincere. Didactically he said: "All the women in the village—they take it for granted. If someone organised them so they had half a day to themselves sometimes, they'd think they were being insulted—they can't stop working. Just look at Mum, then. She comes into Doncaster to wrap sweets two or three times a week —well, she actually loses money on it, by the time she's paid bus fares. I said to her, 'You're actually losing money on it,' and she said: 'I like to get out and see a bit of life.' A bit of life! Wrapping sweets in a bloody factory. Why can't she just come into town of an evening and have a bit of fun without feeling she has to pay for it by wrapping sweets, sweated bloody labour? And she actually loses on it. It doesn't make sense. They're human beings, aren't they? Not just . . ."

"Not just what?" asked Lennie angrily. He had listened to Charlie's tirade, his mouth setting harder, his eyes narrowing. "Here's the station," he said in relief. They waited for the young miners to clatter down and off before going forward themselves. "I'll come with you to your stop," said Charlie; and they crossed the dark, shiny, grimy street to the opposite stop for the bus which would take Lennie back to Doreen.

"It's no good thinking we're going to change, Charlie boy."

"Who said change?" said Charlie excitedly; but the bus had come, and Lennie was already swinging onto the back. "If you're in trouble just write and say," said Lennie, and the bell pinged and his face vanished as the lit bus was absorbed by the light-streaked drizzling darkness.

There was half an hour before the London train. Charlie stood with the rain on his shoulders, his hands in his pockets, wondering whether to go after his brother and explain—what? He bolted across the street to the pub near the station. It was run by an Irishman who knew him and Lennie. The place was still empty, being just after opening time.

"It's you, then," said Mike, drawing him a pint of bitter without asking. "Yes, it's me," said Charlie, swinging himself up onto a stool.

"And what's in the great world of learning?"

"Oh Jesus, *no!*" said Charlie. The Irishman blinked, and Charlie said quickly: "What have you gone and tarted this place up for?"

The pub had been panelled in dark wood. It was ugly and comforting. Now it had half a dozen bright wallpapers and areas of shining paint, and Charlie's stomach moved again, light filled his eyes, and he set his elbows hard down for support, and put his chin on his two fists.

"The youngsters like it," said the Irishman. "But we've left the bar next door as it was for the old ones."

"You should have a sign up: Age This Way," said Charlie. "I'd have known where to go." He carefully lifted his head off his fists, narrowing his eyes to exclude the battling colours of the wallpapers, the shine of the paint.

"You look bad," said the Irishman. He was a small, round, alcoholically cheerful man who, like Charlie, had two voices. For the enemy—that is, all the English whom he did not regard as a friend, which meant people who were not regulars—he put on an exaggerated brogue which was bound, if he persisted, to lead to the political arguments he delighted in. For friends like Charlie he didn't trouble himself. He now said: "All work and no play."

"That's right," said Charlie. "I went to the doctor. He gave me a tonic and said I am fundamentally sound in wind and limb. 'You are sound in wind and limb,' he said," said Charlie, parodying an upperclass English voice for the Irishman's pleasure.

Mike winked, acknowledging the jest, while his professionally humorous face remained serious. "You can't burn the candle at both ends," he said in earnest warning.

Charlie laughed out. "That's what the doctor said. 'You can't burn the candle at both ends,' he said."

This time, when the stool he sat on, and the floor beneath the stool, moved away from him, and the glittering ceiling dipped and swung, his eyes went dark and stayed dark. He shut them and gripped the counter tight. With his eyes still shut, he said facetiously: "It's the clash of cultures, that's what it is. It makes me lightheaded." He opened his eyes and saw from the Irishman's face that he had not said these words aloud.

He said aloud: "Actually the doctor was all right, he meant well. But Mike, I'm not going to make it, I'm going to fail."

"Well, it won't be the end of the world."

"*Jesus*. That's what I like about you, Mike, you take a broad view of life."

"I'll be back," said Mike, going to serve a customer.

A week ago Charlie had gone to the doctor with a cyclostyled leaflet in his hand. It was called "A Report Into the Increased Incidence of Breakdown Among Undergraduates." He had underlined the words: "Young men from workingclass and lower-middleclass families on scholarships are particularly vulnerable. For them, the gaining of a degree is obviously crucial. In addition they are under the continuous strain of adapting themselves to middleclass mores that are foreign to them. They are victims of a clash of standards, a clash of cultures, divided loyalties."

The doctor, a young man of about thirty, provided by the college authorities as a sort of father figure to advise on work problems, personal problems and (as the satirical alter ego took pleasure in pointing out) on clash-of-culture problems, glanced once at the pamphlet and handed it back. He had written it. As, of course, Charlie had known. "When are your examinations?" he asked. *Getting to the root of the matter, just like Mum*, remarked the malevolent voice from behind Charlie's shoulder.

"I've got five months, doctor, and I can't work and I can't sleep."

"For how long?"

"It's been coming on gradually." *Ever since I was born*, said the enemy.

"I can give you sedatives and sleeping pills, of course, but that's not going to touch what's really wrong."

*Which is all this unnatural mixing of the classes. Doesn't do, you know. People should know their place and stick to it.* "I'd like some sleep pills, all the same."

"Have you got a girl?"

"Two."

The doctor paid out an allowance of man-of-the-world sympathy, then shut off his smile and said: "Perhaps you'd be better with one?"

*Which, my mum figure or my lovely bit of sex?* "Perhaps I would, at that."

"I could arrange for you to have talks with a psychiatrist— well, not if you don't want," he said hastily, for the alter ego had exploded through Charlie's lips in a horselaugh and: "What can the trick cyclist tell me I don't know?" He roared with laughter, flinging his legs up; and an ashtray went circling around the room on its rim. Charlie laughed, watched the ashtray, and thought: There, I knew all the time it was a poltergeist sitting there behind my shoulder. I swear I never touched that damned ashtray.

The doctor waited until it circled near him, stopped it with his foot, picked it up, laid it back on the desk. "It's no point your going to him if you feel like that."

*All avenues explored, all roads charted.*

"Well now, let's see, have you been to see your family recently?"

"Last Christmas. No, doctor, it's not because I don't want to, it's because I can't work there." *You try working in an atmosphere of trade union meetings and the telly and the pictures in Doncaster. You try it, doc. And besides all my energies go into not upsetting them. Because I do upset them. My dear doc, when we scholarship boys jump our class, it's not we who suffer, it's our families. We are an expense, doc. And besides— write a thesis, I'd like to read it. . . . Call it: Long-term effects on workingclass or lower-middleclass family of a scholarship child whose existence is a perpetual reminder that they are nothing but ignorant non-cultured clods. How's that for a thesis, doc? Why, I do believe I could write it myself.*

"If I were you, I'd go home for a few days. Don't try to work at all. Go to the pictures. Sleep and eat and let them fuss over you. Get this prescription made up and come and see me when you get back."

"Thanks, doc, I will." *You mean well.*

The Irishman came back to find Charlie spinning a penny, so intent on this game that he did not see him. First he spun it with his right hand, anti-clockwise, then with his left, clock-wise. The right hand represented his jeering alter ego. The left hand was the didactic and rational voice. The left hand was able to keep the coin in a glittering spin for much longer than the right.

"You ambidextrous?"

"Yes, always was."

The Irishman watched the boy's frowning, teeth-clenched concentration for a while, then removed the untouched beer and poured him a double whisky. "You drink that and get on the train and sleep."

"Thanks, Mike. Thanks."

"That was a nice girl you had with you last time."

"I've quarrelled with her. Or rather, she's given me the boot. And quite right too."

After the visit to the doctor Charlie had gone straight to Jenny. He had guyed the interview while she sat, gravely listen-ing. Then he had given her his favourite lecture on the crass and unalterable insensibility of anybody anywhere born middle-class. No one but Jenny ever heard this lecture. She said at last: "You *should* go and see a psychiatrist. No, don't you see, it's not fair."

"Who to, me?"

"No, me. What's the use of shouting at me all the time? You should be saying these things to him."

*"What?"*

"Well, surely you can see that. You spend all your time lecturing me. You make use of me, Charles." (She always called him Charles.)

What she was really saying was: You should be making love to me, not lecturing me. Charlie did not really like making love to Jenny. He forced himself when her increasingly tart and accusing manner reminded him that he ought to. He had another girl, whom he disliked, a tall crisp middleclass girl called Sally. She called him, mocking: Charlie boy. When he had slammed out of Jenny's room, he had gone to Sally and fought his way into her bed. Every act of sex with Sally was a slow, cold subjugation of her by him. That night he had said, when she lay at last, submissive, beneath him: "Horny-handed son of toil wins by his unquenched virility beautiful daughter of the moneyed classes. And doesn't she love it."

"Oh yes I do, Charlie boy."

"I'm nothing but a bloody sex symbol."

"Well," she murmured, already self-possessed, freeing herself, "that's all I am to you." She added defiantly, showing that she did care, and that it was Charlie's fault: "And I couldn't care less."

"Dear Sally, what I like about you is your beautiful honesty."

"Is that what you like about me? I thought it was the thrill of beating me down."

Charlie said to the Irishman: "I've quarrelled with everyone I know in the last weeks."

"Quarrelled with your family too?"

"*No*," he said, appalled, while the room again swung around him. "Good Lord no," he said in a different tone—grateful. He added savagely: "How could I? I can never say anything to them I really think." He looked at Mike to see if he had actually said these words aloud. He had, because now Mike said: "So you know how I feel. I've lived thirty years in this mucking country, and if you arrogant sods knew what I'm thinking half the time."

"Liar. You say whatever you think, from Cromwell to the Black and Tans and Casement. You never let up. But it's not hurting yourself to say it."

"Yourself, is it?"

"Yes. But it's all insane. Do you realise how insane it all is, Mike? There's my father. Pillar of the workingclass. Labour Party, trade union, the lot. But I've been watching my tongue not to say I spent last term campaigning about—he takes it for granted even *now* that the British should push the wogs around."

"You're a great nation," said the Irishman. "But it's not your personal fault, so drink up and have another."

Charlie drank his first Scotch, and drew the second glass towards him. "Don't you see what I mean?" he said, his voice rising excitedly. "Don't you see that it's all *insane*? There's my mother, her sister is ill and it looks as if she'll die. There are two kids, and my mother'll take them both. They're nippers, three and four, it's like starting a family all over again. She thinks nothing of it. If someone's in trouble, she's the mug, every time. But there she sits and stays: 'Those juvenile offenders ought to be flogged until they are senseless.' She read it in the papers and so she says it. She said it to me and I kept my mouth shut. And they're all alike."

"Yes, but you're not going to change it, Charlie, so drink up."

A man standing a few feet down the bar had a paper sticking out of his pocket. Mike said to him: "Mind if I borrow your paper for the winners, sir?"

"Help yourself."

Mike turned the paper over to the back page. "I had five quid on today," he said. "Lost it. Lovely bit of horseflesh, but I lost it."

"Wait," said Charlie excitedly, straightening the paper so he could see the front page. WARDROBE MURDERER GETS SECOND CHANCE, it said. "See that?" said Charlie. "The Home Secretary says he can have another chance; they can review the case, he says."

The Irishman read, cold-faced. "So he does," he said.

"Well, I mean to say, there's some decency left, then. I mean if the case can be reviewed it shows they do *care* about something at least."

"I don't see it your way at all. It's England versus England, that's all. Fair play all round, but they'll hang the poor sod on the day appointed as usual." He turned the newspaper and studied the race news.

Charlie waited for his eyes to clear, held himself steady with one hand flat on the counter, and drank his second double. He pushed over a pound note, remembering it had to last three days, and that now he had quarrelled with Jenny there was no place for him to stay in London.

"No, it's on me," said Mike. "I asked you. It's been a pleasure seeing you, Charlie. And don't take the sins of the world on your personal shoulders, lad, because that doesn't do anyone any good, does it, now?"

"See you at Christmas, Mike, and thanks."

He walked carefully out into the rain. There was no solitude to be had on the train that night, so he chose a compartment with one person in it, and settled himself in a corner before looking to see who it was he had with him. It was a girl. He saw then that she was pretty, and then that she was upperclass. Another Sally, he thought, sensing danger, seeing the cool, self-sufficient little face. Hey, there, Charlie, he said to himself, keep yourself in order, or you've had it. He carefully located himself: *he*, Charlie, was now a warm, whisky-comforted belly, already a little sick. Close above it, like a silent loud-speaker, was the source of the hectoring voice. Behind his shoulder waited his grinning familiar. *He must keep them all apart.* He tested the didactic voice: "It's not her fault, poor bitch, victim of the class system, she can't help she sees everyone under her like dirt. . . ." But the alcohol was working strongly and meanwhile his familiar was calculating: "She's had a good look, but can't make me out. My clothes are right, my haircut's on the line, but there's something that makes her wonder. She's waiting for me to speak, then she'll make up her mind. Well, first I'll get her, and then I'll speak."

He caught her eyes and signalled an invitation, but it was an aggressive invitation, to make it as hard for her as he could. After a bit, she smiled at him. Then he roughened his speech to the point of unintelligibility and said: " 'Appen you'd like t'window up? What wi' t'rain and t'wind and all."

"What?" she said sharply, her face lengthening into such a comical frankness of shock that he laughed out, and afterwards enquired impeccably: "Actually it is rather cold, isn't it? Wouldn't you like to have the window up?" She picked up a magazine and shut him out, while he watched, grinning, the blood creep up from her neat suit collar to her hair-line.

The door slid back; two people came in. They were a man and his wife, both small, crumpled in face and flesh, and dressed in their best for London. There was a fuss and a heaving of suitcases and murmured apologies because of the two superior young people. Then the woman, having settled herself in a corner, looked steadily at Charlie, while he thought: Deep calls to deep, *she* knows who I am all right; she's not foxed by the trimmings. He was right, because soon she said familiarly: "Would you put the window up for me, lad? It's a rare cold night and no mistake."

Charlie put up the window, not looking at the girl, who was

hiding behind the magazine. Now the woman smiled, and the man smiled too, because of her ease with the youth.

"You comfortable like that, Father?" she asked.

"Fair enough," said the husband on the stoical note of the confirmed grumbler.

"Put your feet up beside me, any road."

"But I'm all right, lass," he said bravely. Then, making a favour of it, he loosened his laces, eased his feet inside too new shoes, and set them on the seat beside his wife.

She, for her part, was removing her hat. It was of shapeless grey felt, with a pink rose at the front. Charlie's mother owned just such a badge of respectability, renewed every year or so at the sales. Hers was always blueish felt, with a bit of ribbon or coarse net, and she would rather be seen dead than without it in public.

The woman sat fingering her hair, which was thin and greying. For some reason, the sight of her clean pinkish scalp shining through the grey wisps made Charlie wild with anger. He was taken by surprise, and again summoned himself to himself, making the didactic voice lecture: "The working woman of these islands enjoys a position in the family superior to that of the middleclass woman, et cetera, et cetera, et cetera." This was an article he had read recently, and he continued to recite from it, until he realised the voice had become an open sneer, and was saying: "Not only is she the emotional bulwark of the family, but she is frequently the breadwinner as well, such as wrapping sweets at night, sweated labour for pleasure, anything to get out of the happy home for a few hours."

The fusion of the two voices, the nagging inside voice, and the jeer from the dangerous force outside terrified Charlie, and he told himself hastily: You're drunk, that's all; now keep your mouth shut, for God's sake.

The woman was asking him: "Are you feeling all right?"

"Yes, I'm all right," he said carefully.

"Going all the way to London?"

"Yes, I'm going all the way to London."

"It's a long drag."

"Yes, it's a long drag."

At this echoing dialogue, the girl lowered her magazine to give him a sharp contemptuous look, up and down. Her face was now smoothly pink, and her small pink mouth was judging.

"You have a mouth like a rosebud," said Charlie, listening horrified to these words emerging from him.

The girl jerked up the magazine. The man looked sharply at Charlie, to see if he had heard aright, and then at his wife, for guidance. The wife looked doubtfully at Charlie, who offered her a slow desperate wink. She accepted it, and nodded at her husband: boys will be boys. They both glanced warily at the shining face of the magazine.

"We're on our way to London too," said the woman.

"So you're on your way to London."

Stop it, he told himself. He felt a foolish slack grin on his face, and his tongue was thickening in his mouth. He shut his eyes, trying to summon Charlie to his aid, but his stomach was rolling, warm and sick. He lit a cigarette for support, watching his hands at work. "Lily-handed son of learning wants a manicure badly," commented a soft voice in his ear; and he saw the cigarette poised in a parody of a cad's gesture between displayed nicotined fingers. Charlie, smoking with poise, sat preserving a polite, sarcastic smile.

He was in the grip of terror. He was afraid he might slide off the seat. He could no longer help himself.

"London's a big place, for strangers," said the woman.

"But it makes a nice change," said Charlie, trying hard.

The woman, delighted that a real conversation was at last under way, settled her shabby old head against a leather bulge, and said: "Yes, it does make a nice change." The shine on the leather confused Charlie's eyes; he glanced over at the magazine, but its glitter, too, seemed to invade his pupils. He looked at the dirty floor for comfort, and said: "It's good for people to get a change now and then."

"Yes, that's what I tell my husband, don't I, Father? It's good for us to get away now and then. We have a married daughter in Streatham."

"It's a great thing, family ties."

"Yes, but it's a drag," said the man. "Say what you like, but it is. After all, I mean, when all is said and done." He paused, his head on one side, with a debating look, waiting for Charlie to take it up.

Charlie said: "There's no denying it, say what you like, I mean, there's no doubt about *that*." And he looked interestedly at the man for his reply.

The woman said: "Yes, but the way I look at it, you've got to get *out* of yourself sometimes, look at it that way."

"It's all very well," said the husband, on a satisfied but grumbling note, "but if you're going to do that, well, for a start-off, it's an expense."

"If you don't throw a good penny after a bad one," said Charlie judiciously. "I mean, what's the point?"

"Yes, that's it," said the woman excitedly, her old face animated. "That's what I say to Father, what's the point if you don't sometimes let yourself go?"

"I mean, life's bad enough as it is," said Charlie, watching the magazine slowly lower itself. It was laid precisely on the seat. The girl now sat, two small brown-gloved hands in a ginger-tweeded lap, staring him out. Her blue eyes glinted into his, and he looked quickly away.

"Well, I can see that right enough," said the man, "but there again, you've got to know where to stop."

"That's right," said Charlie, "you're dead right."

"I know it's all right for some," said the man, "I know that, but if you're going to do that, you've got to consider. That's what I think."

"But Father, you know you enjoy it, once you're there and Joyce has settled you in your corner with your own chair and your cup to yourself."

"Ah," said the man, nodding heavily, "but it's not as easy as that, now, is it? Well, I mean, that stands to reason."

"Ah," said Charlie, shaking his head, feeling it roll heavily in the socket of his neck, "but if you're going to consider at all, then what's the point? I mean, what I think is, for a start-off, there's no doubt about it."

The woman hesitated, started to say something, but let her small bright eyes falter away. She was beginning to colour.

Charlie went on compulsively, his head turning like a clockwork man's: "It's what you're used to, that's what I say, well I mean. *Well*, and there's another thing, when all is said and done, and after all, if you're going to take one thing with another . . ."

"Stop it," said the girl, in a sharp high voice.

"It's a question of principle," said Charlie, but his head had stopped rolling and his eyes had focussed.

"If you don't stop I'm going to call the guard and have you put in another compartment," said the girl. To the old people she said in a righteous scandalised voice: "Can't you see he's laughing at you? Can't you see?" She lifted the magazine again.

The old people looked suspiciously at Charlie, dubiously at each other. The woman's face was very pink and her eyes bright and hot.

"I think I am going to get forty winks," said the man, with general hostility. He settled his feet, put his head back, and closed his eyes.

Charlie said: "Excuse me," and scrambled his way to the corridor over the legs of the man, then the legs of the woman, muttering: "Excuse me, excuse me, I'm sorry."

He stood in the corridor, his back jolting slightly against the shifting wood of the compartment's sides. His eyes were shut, his tears running. Words, no longer articulate, muttered and jumbled somewhere inside him, a stream of frightened protesting phrases.

Wood slid against wood close to his ear, and he heard the softness of clothed flesh on wood.

"If it's that bloody little bint I'll kill her," said a voice, small and quiet, from his diaphragm.

He opened his murderous eyes on the woman. She looked concerned.

"I'm sorry," he said, stiff and sullen, "I'm sorry, I didn't mean . . ."

"It's all right," she said, and laid her two red hands on his crossed quivering forearms. She took his two wrists, and laid his arms gently down by his sides. "Don't take on," she said, "it's all right, it's all right, son."

The tense rejection of his flesh caused her to take a step back from him. But there she stood her ground and said: "Now look, son, there's no point taking on like that, well, is there? I mean to say, you've got to take the rough with the smooth, and there's no other way of looking at it."

She waited, facing him, troubled but sure of herself.

After a while Charlie said: "Yes, I suppose you're right."

She nodded and smiled, and went back into the compartment. After a moment, Charlie followed her.

# Two Potters

•··•··•··•··•··•··•··•··•··•··•··•··•··•··•··•··•··•··•··•··•··•··•··•··•··•··•··•··•··•··•··•··•··•··•··•

I have only known one potter in this country, Mary Tawnish, and she lives out of London in a village where her husband is a school-teacher. She seldom comes to town, and I seldom leave it, so we write.

The making of pots is not a thing I often think of, so when I dreamed about the old potter it was natural to think of Mary. But it was difficult to tell her; there are two kinds of humanity, those who dream and those who don't, and both tend to despise, or to tolerate, the other. Mary Tawnish says, when others relate their dreams: "I've never had a dream in my life." And adds, to soften or placate: "At least, I don't remember. They say it's a question of remembering?"

I would have guessed her to be a person who would dream a good deal, I don't know why.

A tall woman, and rather large, she has bright brown clustering hair, and brown eyes that give the impression of light, though not from their surface: it is not a "bright" or "brilliant" glance. She looks at you, smiling or not, but always calm, and there is an impression of light, which seems caught in the structure of colour in the iris, so sometimes her eyes look yellow, set off by smooth brown eyebrows.

A large, slow-moving woman, with large white slow hands. And a silent one—she is a listener.

Her life has been a series of dramas: a childhood on the move with erratic parents, a bad first marriage, a child that died, lovers, but none lasting; then a second marriage to William Tawnish who teaches physics and biology. He is a quick, biting, bitter little man with whom she has three half-grown children.

More than once I have told her story, without comment, in order to observe the silent judgement: Another misfit, another unhappy soul, only to see the judger confounded on meeting her, for there was never a woman less fitted by nature for discord or miseries. Or so it would seem. So it seems she feels herself, for she disapproves of other people's collisions with themselves, just as if her own life had nothing to do with her.

The first dream about the potter was simple and short. Once upon a time . . . there was a village or a settlement, not in England, that was certain, for the scene was of a baked red-dust bareness. Low rectangular structures, of simple baked mud, also reddish-brown, were set evenly on the baked soil, yet because some were roofless and others in the process of crumbling, and others half-built, there was nothing finished or formed about this place. And for leagues and leagues, in all directions, the great plain, of reddish earth, and in the middle of the plain the settlement that looked as if it were hastily moulded by a great hand out of wet clay, allowed to dry, and left there. It seemed uninhabited, but in an empty space among the huts, all by himself, working away on a primitive potter's wheel turned by foot, was an old man. He wore a garment of coarse sacking over yellowish and dusty limbs. One bare foot was set in the dust near me, the cracked toes spread and curled. He had a bit of yellow straw stuck in close grizzling hair.

When I woke from this dream I was rested and excited, in spite of the great dried-up plain and the empty settlement one precarious stage from the dust. In the end I sat down and wrote to Mary Tawnish, although I could hear her flat comment very clearly: Well, that's interesting. Our letters are usually of the kind known as "keeping in touch." First I enquired about her children, and about William, and then I told the dream: "For some reason I thought of you. I did know a man who made pots in Africa. The farmer he worked for discovered he had a talent for potmaking (it seemed his tribe were potters by tradition), because when they made bricks for the farm, this man, Elija, slipped little dishes and bowls into the kiln to bake with the bricks. The farmer used to pay him a couple of shillings a week extra, and sold the dishes to a dealer in the city. He made simple things, not like yours. He had no wheel, of course. He didn't use colour. His things were a darkish yellow, because of the kind of soil on that farm. A bit monotonous after a bit. And they broke easily. If you come up to London give me a ring. . . ."

She didn't come, but soon I had a letter with a postscript: "What an interesting dream, thanks so much for telling me."

I dreamed about the old potter again. There was the great, flat, dust-beaten reddish plain, ringed by very distant blue-hazed mountains, so far away they were like mirages, or clouds, or low-lying smoke. There was the settlement. And there the old potter, sitting on one of his own upturned pots, one foot set firmly in the dust, and the other moving the wheel; one palm shaping the clay, the other shedding water which glittered in the low sullen glare in flashes of moving light on its way to the turning wet clay. He was extremely old, his eyes faded and of the same deceiving blue as the mountains. All around him, drying in rows on a thin scattering of yellow straw, were pots of different sizes. They were all round. The huts were rectangular, the pots round. I looked at these two different manifestations of the earth, separated by shape; and then through a gap in the huts to the plain. No one in sight. It seemed no one lived there. Yet there sat the old man, with the hundreds of pots and dishes drying in rows on the straw, dipping his hand into an enormous jar of water and scattering drops that smelled sweet as they hit the dust and pitted it.

Again I thought of Mary. But they had nothing in common, that poor old potter who had no one to buy his work, and Mary who sold her strange coloured bowls and jugs to the big shops in London. I wondered what the old potter would think of Mary's work—particularly what he'd think of a square flat dish I'd bought from her, coloured a greenish-yellow. The square had, as it were, slipped out of whack, and the surface is rough, with finger marks left showing. I serve cheese on it. The old man's jars were for millet, I knew that, or for soured milk.

I wrote and told Mary the second dream, thinking: Well, if it bores or irritates her, it's too bad. This time she rang me up. She wanted me to go down to one of the shops which had been slow in making a new order. Weren't her things selling? she wanted to know. She added she was getting a fellow feeling for the old potter; he didn't have any customers either, from the size of his stock. But it turned out that the shop had sold all

Mary's things, and had simply forgotten to order more.

I waited, with patient excitement, for the next instalment, or unfolding, of the dream.

The settlement was now populated, indeed, teeming, and it was much bigger. The low flat rooms of dull earth had spread over an area of some miles. They were not separated now, but linked. I walked through a system of these rooms. They were roughly the same size, but set at all angles to each other so that, standing in one, it might have one, two, three doors, leading to a corresponding number of mud rooms. I walked for something like half a mile through low dark rooms without once needing to cross a roofless space, and when I emerged in the daylight, there was the potter, and beyond him a marketplace. But a poor one. From out of his great jars, women, wearing the same sort of yellowish sacking as he, sold grain and milk to dusty, smallish, rather listless people. The potter worked on, under heavy sunlight, with his rows and rows of clay vessels drying on the glinting yellow straw. A very small boy crouched by him, watching every movement he made. I saw how the water shaken from the old fingers on the whirling pot flew past it and spattered the small intent poverty-shaped face with its narrowed watching eyes. But the face received the water unflinching, probably unnoticed.

Beyond the settlement stretched the plain. Beyond that, the thin, illusory mountains. Over the red flat plain drifted small shadows: they were from great birds wheeling and banking and turning.

I wrote to Mary and she wrote back that she was glad the old man had some customers at last, she had been worried about him. As for her, she thought it was time he used some colour, all that red dust was depressing. She said she could see the settlement was short of water, since I hadn't mentioned a well, let alone a river, only the potter's great brimming jar which reflected the blue sky, the sun, the great birds. Wasn't a diet of milk and millet bad for people? Here she broke off to say she supposed I couldn't help all this, it was my nature, and "Apropos, isn't it time your poor village had a storyteller at least? How bored the poor things must be!"

I wrote back to say I was not responsible for this settlement, and whereas if I had my way, it would be set in groves of fruit trees and surrounded by whitening cornfields, with a river full of splashing brown children. I couldn't help it, that's how things were in this place, wherever it was.

One day in a shop I saw a shelf of her work and noticed that some of them were of smooth, dully shining brown, like polished skin—jars, and flat round plates. Our village potter would have known these, nothing to surprise him here. All the same, there was a difference between Mary's consciously simple vessels and the simplicity of the old potter. I looked at them and thought: Well, my dear, that's not going to get you very far. . . . But I would have found it hard to say exactly what I meant, and in fact I bought a plate and a jar, and they gave me great pleasure, thinking of Mary and the old potter linked in them, between my hands.

Quite a long time passed. When I dreamed again, all the plain was populated. The mountains had come closer in, reaching up tall and blue into blue sky, circumscribing the plain. The settlements, looked at from the height of the mountain tops, seemed like patches of slightly raised surface on the plain. I understood their nature and substance: a slight raising of the dust here and there, like the frail patterning of raindrops hitting dry dust, pitting it, then the sun coming out swiftly to dry the dust. The resulting tiny fragile patterned crust of dried dust—that gives, as near as I can, the feeling the settlements gave me, viewed from the mountains. Except that the raised dried crusts were patterned in rectangles. I could see the tiny patternings all over the plain. I let myself down from the mountains, through the great birds that wheeled and floated, and descended to the settlement I knew. There sat the potter, the clay curving under his left hand as he flicked water over it from his right. It was all going on as usual—I was reassured by his being there, creating his pots. Nothing much had changed, though so much time had passed. The low flat monotonous dwellings were the same, though they had crumbled to dust and raised themselves from it a hundred times since I had been here last. No green yet, no river. A scum-covered creek had goats grazing beside it, and the millet grew in straggly patches, flattened and brown from drought. In the marketplace were pinkish fruits, lying in heaps by the soft piles of millet, on woven straw mats. I didn't know the fruit: it was small, about plum-size, smooth-skinned, and I felt it had a sharp pulpy taste. Pinky-yellow skins lay scattered in the dust. A man passed me, with a low slinking movement of the hips, holding his sacklike garment in position at his side with the pressure of an elbow, staring in front of him over the pink fruit which he pressed against sharp yellow teeth.

I wrote and told Mary the plain was more populated, but that things hadn't improved much, except for the fruit. But it was astringent, I wouldn't care for it myself.

She wrote back to say she was glad she slept so soundly, she would find such dreams depressing.

I said there was nothing depressing about it. I entered the dream with pleasure, as if listening to a storyteller say: Once upon a time . . .

But the next was discouraging, I woke depressed. I stood by the old potter in the marketplace, and for once his hands were still, the wheel at rest. His eyes followed the movements of the people buying and selling, and his mouth was bitter. Beside him, his vessels stood in rows on the warm glinting straw. From time to time a woman came picking her way along the rows, bending to narrow her eyes at the pots. Then she chose one, dropped a coin in the potter's hand, and bore it off over her shoulder.

I was inside the potter's mind and I knew what he was thinking. He said: "Just once, Lord, just once, just once!" He put his hand down into a patch of hot shade under the wheel and lifted on his palm a small clay rabbit which he held out to the ground. He sat motionless, looking at the sky, then at the rabbit, praying: "Please, Lord, just once." But nothing happened.

I wrote Mary that the old man was tired with long centuries of making pots whose life was so short: the litter of broken pots under the settlement had raised its level twenty feet by now, and every pot had come off his wheel. He wanted God to breathe life into his clay rabbit. He had hoped to see it lift up its long red-veined ears, to feel its furry feet on his palm, and watch it hop down and off among the great earthenware pots, sniffing at them and twitching its ears—a live thing among the forms of clay.

Mary said the old man was getting above himself. She said further: "Why a *rabbit*? I simply don't *see* a rabbit. What use would a rabbit be? Do you realise that apart from goats (you say they have milk), and those vultures overhead, they have no animals at all? Wouldn't a cow be better than a rabbit?"

I wrote: "I can't do anything about that place when I'm

dreaming it, but when I'm awake, why not? Right then, the rabbit hopped off the old man's hand into the dust. It sat twitching its nose and throbbing all over, the way rabbits do. Then it sprang slowly off and began nibbling at the straw, while the old man wept with happiness. Now what have you to say? If I say there was a rabbit, a rabbit there was. Besides, that poor old man deserves one, after so long. God could have done so much, it wouldn't have cost Him anything."

I had no reply to that letter, and I stopped dreaming about the settlement. I knew it was because of my effrontery in creating that rabbit, inserting myself into the story. Very well, then . . . I wrote to Mary: "I've been thinking: suppose it had been you who'd dreamed about the potter—all right, all right, just suppose it. Now. Next morning you sat at the breakfast table, your William at one end, and the children between eating cornflakes and drinking milk. You were rather silent. (Of course you usually are.) You looked at your husband and you thought: What on earth would he say if I told him what I'm going to do? You said nothing, presiding at the table; then you sent the children off to school, and your husband to his classes. Then you were alone and when you'd washed the dishes and put them away, you went secretly into the stone-floored room where your wheel and the kiln are, and you took some clay and you made a small rabbit and you set it on a high shelf behind some finished vases to dry. You didn't want anyone to see that rabbit. One day, a week later, when it was dry, you waited until your family was out of the house, then you put your rabbit on your palm, and you went into a field, and you knelt down and held the rabbit out to the grass, and you waited. You didn't pray, because you don't believe in God, but you wouldn't have been in the least surprised if that rabbit's nose had started to twitch and its long soft ears stood up. . . ."

Mary wrote: "There aren't any rabbits any more, had you forgotten myxomatosis? Actually I did make some small rabbits recently, for the children, in blue and green glaze, because it occurred to me the two youngest haven't seen a rabbit out of a picture book. Still, they're coming back in some parts, I hear. The farmers will be angry."

I wrote: "Yes, I had forgotten. Well then . . . sometimes at evening, when you walk in the fields, you think: How nice to see a rabbit lift his paws and look at us. You remember the rotting little corpses of a few years back. You think: *I'll try again*. Meantime, you're nervous of what William will say, he's such a rationalist. Well of course, so are we, but he wouldn't even play a little. I may be wrong, but I think you're afraid of William catching you out, and you are careful not to be caught. One sunny morning you take it out onto the field and . . . all right, all right then, it *doesn't* hop away. You can't decide whether to lay your clay rabbit down among the warm grasses (it's a sunny day) and let it crumble back into the earth, or whether to bake it in your kiln. You haven't baked it, it's even rather damp still: the old potter's rabbit was wet, just before he held it out into the sun he sprinkled water on it, I saw him.

"Later you decide to tell your husband. Out of curiosity? The children are in the garden, you can hear their voices, and William sits opposite you reading the newspaper. You have a crazy impulse to say: I'm going to take my rabbit into the field tonight and pray for God to breathe life into it, a field without rabbits is empty. Instead you say: 'William, I had a dream last night. . . .' First he frowns, a quick frown, then he turns those small quick sandy-lashed intelligent eyes on you, taking it all in. To your surprise, instead of saying: 'I don't remember your ever dreaming,' he says: 'Mary, I didn't know you disapproved of the farmers killing off their rabbits.' You say: 'I didn't disapprove. I'd have done the same, I suppose.' The fact that he's not reacted with sarcasm or impatience, as he might very well, makes you feel guilty when you lift the clay rabbit down, take it out to a field and set it in a hedge, its nose pointing out towards some fresh grass. That night William says, casual: 'You'll be glad to hear the rabbits are back. Basil Smith shot one in his field—the first for eight years, he says. Well, I'm glad myself, I've missed the little beggars.' You are delighted. You slip secretly into a cold misty moonlight and you run to the hedge and of course the rabbit is gone. You stand, clutching your thick green stole around you, because it's cold, shivering, but delighted, delighted! Though you know quite well one of your children, or someone else's child, has slipped along this hedge, seen the rabbit, and taken it off to play with."

Mary wrote: "Oh all right, if you say so, so it is. But I must tell you, if you are interested in *facts*, that the only thing that has happened is that Dennis (the middle one) put his blue rabbit out in a hedge for a joke near the Smiths' gate, and Basil

Smith shot it to smithereens one dusk thinking it was real. He used to lose a small fortune every year to rabbits, he didn't think it was a funny joke at all. Anyway, why don't you come down for a weekend?"

The Tawnishes live in an old farmhouse on the edge of the village. There is a great garden, with fruit trees, roses—everything. The big house and the three boys mean a lot of work, but Mary spends all the time she can in the shed that used to be a dairy where she pots. I arrived to find them in the kitchen, having lunch. Mary nodded to me to sit down. William was in conflict with the middle boy, Dennis, who was, as the other two boys kept saying, "showing off." Or, rather, he was in that torment of writhing self-consciousness that afflicts small boys sometimes, rolling his eyes while he stuttered and wriggled, his whole sandy freckled person scarlet and miserable.

"Well I did I did I did I did I did. . . ." He paused for breath, his eyes popping, and his older brother chanted: "No you didn't, you didn't, you didn't."

"Yes I did I did I did I did. . . ."

And the father said, brisk but irritated: "Now then, Dennis, use your loaf, you couldn't have, because it is obvious you have *not.*"

"But I did I did I did I did. . . ."

"Well, then, you had better go out of the room until you come to your senses and are fit company for rational people," said his father, triumphantly in the right.

The child choked on his battling breath, and ran howling out into the garden. Where, after a minute, the older boy followed, ostensibly to control him.

"He did what?" I asked.

"Who knows?" said Mary. There she sat, at the head of the table, bright-eyed and smiling, serving apple pie and custard, a dark changeling in the middle of her gingery, freckled family.

Her husband said, brisk: "What do you mean, who knows? You know quite well."

"It's his battle with Basil Smith," said Mary to me. "Ever since Basil Smith shot at his blue rabbit and broke it, there's been evil feeling on both sides. Dennis claims that he set fire to the Smith farmhouse last night."

"*What?*"

Mary pointed through a low window, where the Smiths' house showed, two fields away, like a picture in a frame.

William said: "He's hysterical and he's got to stop it."

"Well," said Mary, "if Basil shot my blue rabbit I'd want to burn his house down too. It seems quite reasonable to me."

William let out an exclamation of rage, checked himself because of my presence, shot fiery glances all round, and went out, taking the youngest boy with him.

"Well," said Mary. "Well . . ." She smiled. "Come into the pottery, I've got something to show you." She went ahead along a stone passage, a tall, lazy-moving woman, her bright brown hair catching the light. As we passed an open window, there was a fearful row of shrieks, yells, blows; and we saw the three boys rolling and tussling in the grass, while William danced futilely around them shouting: "Stop it, stop it at once!" Their mother proceeded, apparently uninterested, into the potting room.

This held the potting apparatus, and a great many jars, plates, and jugs of all colours and kinds, ranged on shelves. She lifted down a creature from a high shelf, and set it before me. Then she left it with me, while she bent to attend to the kiln.

It was yellowish-brown, a sort of rabbit or hare, but with ears like neither—narrower, sharp, short, like the pointed unfolding shoots of a plant. It had a muzzle more like a dog's than a rabbit's; it looked as if it did not eat grass—perhaps insects and beetles? Yellowish eyes were set on the front of its head. Its hind legs were less powerful than a rabbit's, or hare's; and I saw its talents were for concealment, not for escaping enemies in great pistoning leaps. It rested on short, stubby hind legs, with front paws held up in a queer, twisted, almost affected posture, head turned to one side, and ears furled around each other. It looked as if it had been wound up like a spring, and had half-unwound. It looked like a strangely shaped rock, or like the harsh twisted plants that sometimes grow on rocks.

Mary came back and stood by me, her head slightly on one side, with her characteristic small patient smile that nevertheless held a sweet concealed exasperation.

"Well," she said, "there it is."

I hesitated, because it was not the creature I had seen on the old potter's palm.

"What was an English rabbit doing there at all?" she asked.

"I didn't say it was an English rabbit."

But of course, she was right: this animal was far more in keeping with the dried mud houses, the dusty plain, than the pretty furry rabbit I had dreamed.

I smiled at Mary, because she was humouring me, as she humoured her husband and her children. For some reason I thought of her first husband and her lovers, two of whom I had known. At moments of painful crisis, or at parting, had she stood thus—a calm, pretty woman, smiling her sweetly satirical smile, as if to say: "Well, make a fuss if you like, it's got nothing at all to do with me"? If so, I'm surprised that one of them didn't murder her.

"Well," I said at last, "thanks. Can I take this thing, whatever it is?"

"Of course. I made it for you. You must admit, it may not be pretty, but it's more likely to be *true*."

I accepted this, as I had to; and I said: "Well, thanks for coming down to our level long enough to play games with us."

At which there was a flash of yellow light from her luminous eyes, while her face remained grave, as if amusement, or acknowledgement of the *truth*, could only be focussed in her thus, through a change of light in her irises.

A few minutes later, the three boys and the father came round this part of the house in a whirlwind of quarrelling energy. The aggrieved Dennis was in tears, and the father almost beside himself. Mary, who until now had remained apart from it all, gave an exclamation, slipped on a coat, and said: "I can't stand this. I'm going to talk to Basil Smith."

She went out, and I watched her cross the fields to the other house.

Meanwhile Dennis, scarlet and suffering, came into the pottery in search of his mother. He whirled about, looking for her, then grabbed my creature, said: "Is that for me?", snatched it possessively to him when I said: "No, it's for me," set it down when I told him to, and stood breathing like a furnace, his freckles like tea leaves against his skin.

"Your mother's gone to see Mr. Smith," I said.

"He shot my rabbit," he said.

"It wasn't a real rabbit."

"But he thought it was a real rabbit."

"Yes, but you knew he would think so, and that he'd shoot at it."

"He killed it!"

"You wanted him to!"

At which he let out a scream and danced up and down like a mad boy, shouting: "I didn't I didn't I didn't I didn't. . . ."

His father, entering on this scene, grabbed him by his flailing arms, fought the child into a position of tensed stillness, and held him there, saying, in a frenzy of incredulous commonsense: "I've never—in—my—life—heard—such—lunacy!"

Now Mary came in, accompanied by Mr. Smith, a large, fair, youngish man, with a sweet open face, which was uncomfortable now, because of what he had agreed to do.

"Let that child go," said Mary to her husband. Dennis dropped to the floor, rolled over, and lay face down, heaving with sobs.

"Call the others!"

Resignation itself, William went to the window, and shouted: "Harry, John, Harry, John, come here at once, your mother wants you!" He then stood, with folded arms, a defeated philosopher, grinning angrily while the two other children came in and stood waiting by the door.

"Now," said Mary. "Get up, Dennis."

Dennis got up, his face battered with suffering, and looked with hope towards his mother.

Mary looked at Basil Smith.

Who said, careful to get the words right: "I am very sorry that I killed your rabbit."

The father let out a sharp outraged breath, but kept quiet at a glance from his wife.

The chest of Dennis swelled and sank—in one moment there would be a storm of tears.

"Dennis," said Mary, "say after me: 'Mr. Smith, I'm very sorry I set fire to your house.'"

Dennis said in a rush, to get it out in time: "Mr. Smith I'm very sorry I set fire to your . . . to your . . . to your . . ." He sniffed and heaved, and Mary said firmly: "*House*, Dennis."

"House," said Dennis, in a wail. He then rushed at his mother, buried his head in her waist, and stood howling and wrestling, while she laid large hands on his ginger head and smiled over it at Mr. Basil Smith.

"Dear God," said her husband, letting his folded arms drop

dramatically, now the ridiculous play was over. "Come and have a drink, Basil."

The men went off. The two other children stood silent and abashed, because of the force of Dennis's emotion, for which they clearly felt partly responsible. Then they slipped out to play. The house was tranquil again, save for Dennis's quietening sobs. Soon Mary took the boy up to his room to sleep it off. I stayed in the great, stone-floored pottery, looking at my strange twisted animal, and at the blues and greens of Mary's work all around the walls.

Supper was early and soon over. The boys were silent, Dennis too limp to eat. Bed was prescribed for everyone. William kept looking at his wife, his mouth set under his ginger moustache, and he could positively be heard thinking: Filling them full of this nonsense while I try to bring them up reasonable human beings! But she avoided his eyes, and sat calm and remote, serving mashed potatoes and brown stew. It was only when we had finished the washing-up that she smiled at him—her sweet, amused smile. It was clear they needed to be alone. I said I wanted an early night and left them: he had gone to touch her before I was out of the room.

Next day, a warm summer Sunday, everyone was relaxed, the old house peaceful. I left that evening, with my clay creature, and Mary said smiling, humouring me: "Let me know how things go on with your place, wherever it is." But I had her beautiful animal in my suitcase, so I did not mind being humoured.

That night, at home, I went into the marketplace, and up to the old potter, who stilled his wheel when he saw me coming. The small boy lifted his frowning attentive eyes from the potter's hands and smiled at me. I held out Mary's creature. The old man took it, screwed up his eyes to examine it, nodded. He held it in his left hand, scattered water on it with his right, held his palm down towards the littered dust, and the creature jumped off it and away, with quick, jerky movements, not stopping until it was through the huts, clear of the settlement, and against a small outcrop of jagged brown rocks where it raised its front paws and froze in the posture Mary had created for it. Overhead an eagle or a hawk floated by, looked down, but failed to see Mary's creature, and floated on, up and away into the great blue spaces over the flat dry plain to the mountains. I heard the wheel creak; the old man was back at work. The small boy crouched, watching, and the water flung by the potter's right hand sprayed the bowl he was making and the child's face, in a beautiful curving spray of glittering light.

# Between Men

The chair facing the door was covered in coffee-brown satin. Maureen Jeffries wore dark brown silk tights and a white ruffled shirt. She would look a delectable morsel in the great winged chair. No sooner was she arranged in it, however, than she got out again (with a pathetic smile of which she was certainly unconscious) and sat less dramatically in the corner of a yellow settee. Here she remained some minutes, thinking that after all, her letter of invitation had said, jocularly (she was aware the phrase had an arch quality she did not altogether like): "Come and meet the new me!"

What was new was her hairstyle, that she was a stone lighter in weight, that she been dowered afresh by nature (a word she was fond of) with delicacy of complexion. There was no doubt all this would be better displayed in the big brown chair: she made the change back again.

The second time she removed herself to the yellow settee was out of decency, a genuine calculation of kindness. To ask Peggy Bayley to visit her at all *was* brave of her, she had needed to swallow pride. But Peggy would not be able to compete with the ruffled lace shirt and all that it set off, and while this would be so precisely because of her advantages—that she was married, comfortably, to Professor Bayley (whose mistress she, Maureen, had been for four years)—nevertheless there was no need to rub in her, Maureen's, renewed and indeed incredible attractiveness, even though it had been announced by the words: "the new me."

Besides, her attractiveness was all that she, Maureen, had to face the world with again, and why not display it to the wife of Professor Bayley, who had not married herself, but had married Peggy instead? Though (she whispered it to herself, fierce and bitter) if she had tricked Tom Bayley into it, put pressure on him, as Peggy had, no doubt she would be Mrs. Bayley. . . . She would go back to the brown chair.

But if *she* had tricked Tom into it, then it would have served her right, as it certainly served Peggy right, if from the start of this marriage Tom Bayley had insisted on a second bachelor flat into which she, Maureen, was never allowed to go, just as Peggy was not. She, Maureen, would have refused marriage on such terms, she must give herself credit for that; in fact, her insistence on fidelity from Tom, a natural philanderer, was doubtless the reason for his leaving her for Peggy. So on the whole she did not really envy Peggy, who had achieved marriage when she was already nearly forty with the eminent and attractive professor at the price of knowing from the start she would not be the only woman in his life; and knowing, moreover, she had achieved marriage by the oldest trick in the world. . . .

At this point Maureen left the brown chair for the third time, found the yellow settee obvious, and sat on the floor, in the grip of self-disgust. She was viewing the deterioration of her character, even while she was unable to stop the flow of her bitter thoughts about Peggy. Viewing herself clear-sightedly had, in fact, been as much her occupation for the last six months of semi-retreat as losing a stone and regaining her beauty.

Which she had: she was thirty-nine and she had never been more attractive. The tomboy who had left home in Iowa for the freedoms of New York had been lovely, as every fairly endowed young girl is lovely, but what she was now was the product of twenty years of work on herself. And other people's work too. . . . She was a small, round, white-skinned, big-brown-eyed black-haired beauty, but her sympathy, her softness, her magnetism were the creation of the loves of a dozen intelligent men. No, she did not envy her eighteen-year-old self at all. But she did envy, envied every day more bitterly, that young girl's genuine independence, largeness, scope, and courage.

It had been six months ago when her most recent—and, she

had hoped, her final—lover, Jack Boles, had left her, and left her in pieces, that it had occurred to her that twenty—indeed, only ten—years ago *she* had discarded lovers, *she* had been the one to say, as Jack had said—embarrassed and guilty, but not more than he could easily come to terms with—"I'm sorry, forgive me, I'm off." And—and this was the point—she had never calculated the consequences to herself, had taken money from no man, save what she considered she had earned, had remained herself always. (In her time with Jack she had expressed opinions not her own to please him: he was a man who disliked women disagreeing with him.) Above all, she had never given a moment's thought to what people might say. But when Jack threw her over, after an affair which was publicised through the newspapers for months ("Famous film director shares flat in Cannes with the painter Maureen Jeffries"), she had thought first of all: I'll be a laughingstock. She had told everyone, with reason, that he would marry her. Then she thought: But he stayed with me less than a year; no one has got tired of me before so quickly. Then: The woman he has thrown me over for is not a patch on me, and she can't even cook. Then back again to the beginning: People must be laughing at me.

Self-contempt poisoned her, particularly as she was unable to let Jack go, but pursued him with telephone calls, letters, reproaches, reminders that he had promised marriage. She spoke of what she had given him, did everything in fact that she despised most in women. Above all, she had not left this flat whose rent he had recently paid for five years. What it amounted to was, he was buying her off with the lease of this flat.

And instead of walking right out of it with her clothes (she was surely entitled to those?) she was still here, making herself beautiful and fighting down terror.

At eighteen, leaving her father's house (he was a post-office clerk), she had had her sex and her courage. Not beauty. For like many other professional beauties, women who spend their lives with men, she was not beautiful at all. What she had was a focussed sex, her whole being aware and sharpened by sex, that made her seem beautiful. Now, twenty years later, after being the mistress of eleven men, all of them eminent or at least potentially eminent, she had her sex, and her courage. *But—* since she had never put her own talent, painting, first, but always the career of whichever man she was living with, and out of an instinct of generosity which was probabbly the best thing in her—she now could not earn a living. At least, not in the style she had been used to.

Since she had left home, she had devoted her talents, her warmth, her imagination to an art teacher (her first lover), two actors (then unknown, now world-famous), a choreographer; a writer; another writer; then, crossing the Atlantic to Europe, a film director (Italy), an actor (France), a writer (London), Professor Tom Bayley (London), Jack Boles, film director (London). Who could say how much of her offered self, her continually poured-forth devotion to their work, was responsible for their success? (As she demanded of herself fiercely, weeping, in the dark hours.)

She now had left her sympathy, her charm, her talents for dress and décor, a minor talent for painting (which did not mean she was not a discriminating critic of other people's work), the fact she was a perfect cook, and her abilities in bed, which she knew were outstanding.

And the moment she stepped out of this flat, she would step out, also, of the world of international money and prestige. To what? Her father, now living in a rooming house in Chicago? No, her only hope was to find another man as eminent and lustrous as the others, for she could no longer afford the unknown geniuses, the potential artists. This is what she was waiting for, and why she remained in the luxurious flat, which must serve as a base; and why she despised herself so painfully; and why she had invited Peggy Bayley to visit her. One: she needed to bolster herself up by seeing this woman, whose career (as the mistress of well-known men) had been similar to hers, and who was now well married. Second: she was going to ask her help. She had gone carefully through the list of her ex-lovers, written to three, and drawn three friendly but unhelpful letters. She had remained, officially, a "friend" of Tom Bayley; but she knew better than to offend his wife by approaching him except with her approval. She would ask Peggy to ask Tom to use his influence to get her a job of the kind that would enable her to meet the right sort of man.

When the doorbell rang, and she had answered it, she went hastily to the big brown chair, this time out of bravado, even honesty. She was appealing to the wife of a man whose very publicised mistress she had been; and she did not wish to soften the difficulties of it by looking less attractive than she could; even though Peggy would enter with nothing left of her own beauty; for three years of marriage with Professor Bayley had turned her into a sensible, goodlooking woman, the sleek feline quality gone that had led *her* from Cape Town to Europe as a minor actress, which career she had given up, quite rightly, for the one she was born for.

But Peggy Bayley entered, as it were, four years back: if Maureen was small, delicate, luscious, then Peggy's mode was to be a siren: Maureen jerked herself up, saw Peggy push pale hair off a brown cheek with a white ringed hand and slide her a a green-eyed mocking smile. She involuntarily exclaimed: "Tom's ditched you!"

Peggy laughed—her voice, like Maureen's, was the husky voice of the sex-woman—and said: "How did you guess!" At which she turned, her hips angled in a mannequin's pose, letting her gold hair fall over her face, showing off a straight green linen dress that owed everything to a newly provocative body. Not a trace left of the sensible healthy housewife of the last three years: she, like Maureen, was once again focussed behind her sexuality, poised on it, vibrating with it.

She said: "We both of us *look* very much the better for being ditched!"

Now, with every consciousness of how she looked, she appropriated the yellow settee in a coil of femininity, and said: "Give me a drink and don't look so surprised. After all, I suppose I could have seen it coming?" This was a query addressed to— a fellow conspirator? No. Victim? No. Fellow artisan—yes. Maureen realised that the only-just-under-the-surface hostility that had characterised their meetings when Peggy was with Tom Bayley had vanished entirely. But she was not altogether happy yet about this flow of comradeship. Frowning, she got out of the brown satin chair, a cigarette clumsy between her lips. She remembered that the frown and the dangling cigarette belonged to the condition of *a woman sure of a man*; her instincts were, then, to lie to Peggy, and precisely because she did not like to admit, even now, long after the fact, just how badly she was alone? She poured large brandies, and asked: "Who did he leave you for?"

Peggy said: "I left him," and kept her green eyes steady on

Maureen's face to make her accept it, despite the incredulity she saw there.

"No, really, it's true—of course, there were women all the time, that's why he insisted on the hidey-hole in Chelsea. . . ." Maureen definitely smiled now, to remind her of how often she had *not* acknowledged the reason for the hidey-hole. It had been "Bill's study, where he can get away from dreary domesticity." Peggy accepted the reminder with a small honest smile that nevertheless had impatience: Well of course I told lies and played little games, don't we all?—that's what the smile said; and Maureen's dislike of herself made her say aloud, so as to put an end to her silent rancorous criticism of Peggy: "Well, all right, then. But you did force him to marry you." She had taken three large gulps of brandy. Whereas she had drunk far too much in the months after Jack had left her, during the last weeks her diet had forbidden her alcohol, and she was out of practice. She felt herself already getting tight, and she said: "If I'm going to get tight, then you've got to too."

"I was drunk every day and night for two months," said Peggy, again with the level green look. "But you can't drink if you want to keep pretty."

Maureen went back to the brown chair, looked at Peggy through coiling blue smoke, and said: "I was drunk all the time for—it was ages. It was disgusting. I couldn't stop."

Peggy said: "Well all right, we've finished with that. But the point was, not the other women—we discussed his character thoroughly when we married and . . ." Here she stopped to acknowledge Maureen's rather sour smile, and said: "It's part of our role, isn't it, to thoroughly discuss their characters?" At this, both women's eyes filled with tears, which both blinked away. Another barrier had gone down.

Peggy said: "I came here to show myself off, because of your boasting little letter—I've been watching you patronise me since I married Tom, being dull and ordinary—I wanted *you* to see the new me! . . . God knows why one loses one's sex when one's settled with a man."

They both giggled suddenly, rolling over, Peggy on her yellow linen, Maureen on her glossy brown. Then at the same moment, they had to fight back tears.

"No," said Maureen, sitting up, "I'm not going to cry, oh no! I've stopped crying, there's not the slightest point."

"Then let's have some more to drink," and Peggy handed over her glass.

They were both tight, already; since both were in any case on the edge of themselves with fasting.

Maureen half-filled both glasses with brandy, and asked: "Did you really leave him?"

"Yes."

"Then you've got better reason to like yourself than I have. I fought, and I made scenes, and when I think of it now . . ." She took a brandy gulp, looked around the expensive room, and said: "And I'm still living on him now and that's what's so horrible."

"Well, don't cry, dear," said Peggy. The brandy was slurring her, making her indolent. The "dear" made Maureen shrink. It was the meaningless word of the theatre and film people, which was all right, even enjoyable, with the theatre and film people, but it was only one step from . . .

"*Don't*," said Maureen, sharp. Peggy widened her long green eyes in a "charming" way, then let them narrow into the honesty of her real nature, and laughed.

"I see your point," she said. "Well, we'd better face it, hadn't we? We're not so far off, are we?"

"*Yes*," said Maureen. "I've been thinking it out. If we had married them, that marriage certificate, you know, well then, we'd have felt quite all right to take money, in return for everything, everything, everything!" She put her face down and sobbed.

"Shut up," said Peggy. But it sounded because of her tightness like "Shhrrrp."

"No," said Maureen, sitting up and sniffing. "It's true. I've never taken money—I mean I've never taken anything more than housekeeping money and presents of clothes—have you?" Peggy was not looking at her, so she went on: "All right, but I'll take a guess that Tom Bayley's the first man you've taken a settlement from, or alimony—isn't that so? And that's because you were married to him."

"I suppose so. I told myself I wouldn't, but I have."

"And you don't really feel bad about it, just because of that marriage certificate?"

Peggy turned her glass round and round between long soft fingers and at length nodded: I suppose so.

"Yes. Of course. And all the fun we've both made about that marriage certificate in our time. But the point is, taking money when you're married doesn't make you *feel* like a tart. With all the men I've been with, I've always had to argue with myself; I've said, Well, how much would he have to pay for what I do for him—cooking and the housekeeping and the interior decoration and the advice? A fortune! So there's no need for me to feel badly about living in his flat and taking clothes. But I did feel bad, always. But if Jack had married me, living in this bloody flat of his wouldn't make me feel like a bloody tart." She burst into savage angry tears, stopped herself, breathed deeply, and sat silent, breathing deep. Then she got up, refilled her glass and Peggy's, and sat down. The two women sat in silence, until at last Maureen said: "Why did you leave him?"

"When he married me we both thought I was pregnant. . . . No, it's true. I know what you and everyone else said, but it was true. I had no periods for three months, and then I was very ill; they said it was a miscarriage."

"He wants children?"

"Didn't he with you?"

"No."

"Then he's changed. He wants them badly."

"Jack wouldn't hear of children, wouldn't hear of them, but that little bitch he's ditched me for . . . I hear you're great friends with them?" She meant Jack and the girl for whom she was thrown over.

Peggy said: "Jack is a great friend of Tom's." This was very dry, and Maureen said: "Yes. Yes! All Jack's friends—I cooked for them, I entertained them, but do you know not one of them has even rung me up since he left me? They were *his* friends, not mine."

"Exactly. Since I left Tom I haven't seen either Jack or his new girl. They visit Tom."

"I suppose one of Tom's girls got pregnant?"

"Yes. He came to me and told me. I knew what I was supposed to do, and did it. I said: Right, you can have your divorce."

"Then you've got your self-respect, at least."

Peggy turned her glass round, looking into it; it slopped over onto the yellow linen. Both women watched the orange stain spread, without moving, in an aesthetic interest.

"No, I haven't," said Peggy. "Because I said: 'You can have

your divorce, but you've got to give me so much money, or else I'll sue you for infidelity—I've got the evidence a thousand times over.' "

"How much?"

Peggy coloured, took a gulp of brandy and said: "I'm going to get forty pounds a month alimony. It's a lot for him—he's a professor, not a film director."

"He can't afford it?"

"No. He told me he must give up his hidey-hole. I said: 'Too bad.' "

"What's she like?"

"Twenty-seven. An art student. She's pretty and sweet and dumb."

"But she's pregnant."

"Yes."

"You've never had a baby?"

"No. But I've had several abortions and miscarriages."

The two women looked frankly at each other, their faces bitter.

"Yes," said Maureen. "I've had five abortions and one of them was by one of those old women. I don't even use anything, and I don't get pregnant. . . . How did you like Jack's new girl?"

"I liked her," said Peggy, apologetically.

"She's an intellectual," said Maureen: it sounded like "intelleshual."

"Yes."

"Ever so bright and well-informed." Maureen battled a while with her better self, won the battle, and said: "But *why?* She's attractive, but she's such a schoolgirl; she's a nice bright clever little schoolgirl with nice bright little clothes."

Peggy said: "Stop it. Stop it at once."

"Yes," said Maureen. But she added, out of her agonised depths: "And she can't even cook!"

And now Peggy laughed, flinging herself back and spilling more brandy from her drunken hand. After a while, Maureen laughed too.

Peggy said: "I was thinking, how many times have wives and mistresses said about us: Peggy's such a bore, Maureen's so obvious."

"I can hear them: Of course, they're very pretty, and of

course they can dress well, and they're marvellous cooks, and I suppose they're good in bed, but what have they *got*?"

"Stop it," said Peggy.

Both women were now drunk. It was getting late. The room was full of shadow, its white walls fading into blue heights, the glossy chairs, tables, rugs, sending out deep gleams of light.

"Shall I turn on the light?"

"Not yet." Peggy now got up herself to refill her glass. She said: "I hope she has the sense not to throw up her job."

"Who, Jack's redheaded bitch?"

"Who else? Tom's girl is all right, she's actually pregnant."

"You're right. But I bet she does, I bet Jack's trying to make her give it up."

"I know he is. Just before I left Tom—before he threw me over—your Jack and she were over to dinner. Jack was getting at her for her column, he was sniping at her all evening—he said it was a leftwing society hostess's view of politics. A left-wing bird's-eye view, he said."

"He hated me painting," said Maureen. "Every time I said I wanted a morning to paint, he made jibes about Sunday painters. I'd serve him his breakfast, and go up to the studio—well, it's the spare room, really. First he'd shout up funny cracks, then he'd come up and say he was hungry. He'd start being hungry at eleven in the morning. Then if I didn't come down and cook, he'd make love. Then we'd talk about his work. We'd talk about his bloody films all day and half the night. . . ." Maureen's voice broke into a wail: "It's all so unfair, so unfair, so unfair . . . they were all like that. I'm not saying I'd have been a great painter, but I might have been something. Something of my own. . . . Not one of those men did anything but make fun, or patronise me . . . all of them, in one way or another. And of course, one always gives in, because one cares more for . . ."

Peggy who had been half-asleep, drooping over her settee, sat up and said: "Stop it, Maureen. What's the good of it?"

"But it's true. I've spent twenty years of my life, eighteen hours a day, bolstering up some man's ambition. Well, isn't it true?"

"It's true, but stop it. We chose it."

"Yes. And if that silly red-haired bitch gives up her job, she'll get what she deserves."

"She'll be where we are."

"But Jack says he's going to marry her."

"Tom married me."

"He was intrigued by that clever little redheaded mind of hers. All those bright remarks about politics. But now he's doing everything he can to stop her column. Not that it would be any loss to the nation, but she'd better watch out, oh yes, she had. . . ." Maureen wove her brandy glass back and forth in front of hypnotised eyes.

"Which is the other reason I came to see you."

"You didn't come to see the new me?"

"It's the same thing."

"Well?"

"How much money have you got?"

"Nothing."

"How long is the lease for this flat?" Maureen held up the fingers of one hand. "Five years? Then sell the lease."

"Oh I couldn't."

"Oh yes you could. It would bring you in about two thousand, I reckon. We could take a flat somewhere less expensive."

"*We* could?"

"And I've got forty pounds a month. Well, then."

"Well then what?" Maureen was lying practically flat in the big chair, her white lace shirt ruffled up around her breasts, so that a slim brown waist and diaphragm showed above the tight brown trousers. She held her brandy glass in front of her eyes and moved it back and forth, watching the amber liquid slopping in the glass. From time to time the brandy fell on her brown stomach flesh and she giggled.

Peggy said: "If we don't do something, I've got to go back to my parents in Outshoorn—they're ostrich farmers. I was the bright girl that escaped. Well, I'll never make an actress. So I'll be back living out my life among the sugar-bushes and the ostriches. And where will you be?"

"Ditto, ditto." Maureen now wriggled her soft brown head sideways and let brandy drip into her mouth.

"We're going to open a dress shop. If there's one thing we both really understand, it's how to dress."

"Good idea."

"What city would you fancy?"

"I fancy Paris."

"We couldn't compete in Paris."

"No, can't compete in . . . How about Rome? I've got three ex-lovers in Rome."

"They're not much good when it comes to trouble."

"No good at all."

"Better stay in London."

"Better stay in London. Like another drink?"

"Yes. Yesssh."

"I'lll get-get-itit."

"Next time, we musn't go to bed without the marriage sher-tificate."

"A likely shtory."

"But it's against my prinshiples, bargaining."

"Oh I know, I know."

"Yesh."

"Perhaps we'd better be leshbians, what do you think?"

Peggy got up, with difficulty, came to Maureen, and put her hand on Maureen's bare diaphragm. "Doesh that do anything for you?"

"Not a thing."

"I fanshy men myself," said Peggy, returning to her settee, where she sat with a bump, spilling liquor.

"Me too, and a fat lot of good it duz ush."

"Next time, we don't give up our jobs, we stick with the dress shop."

"Yessh. . . ."

A pause. Then Peggy sat up, and focussed. She was pervaded by an immense earnestness. "Listen," she said. "No, damn it, lishen, that's what I mean to shay all the time, I really mean it."

"I do too."

"No. No giving it up the firsht time a m-m-man appearsh. Damn it, I'm drunk, but I mean it. . . . No, Maureen, I'm not going to shtart a dresh shop unless that's undershtood from the shtart. We musht, we *musht* agree to that, work firsht, or elshe, or *else* you know where we're going to end up." Peggy brought out the last in a rush, and lay back, satisfied.

Maureen now sat up, earnest, trying to control her tongue: "But . . . what . . . we are both *good* at, itsh, it's bolshtering up some damned genus, genius."

"Not any more. Oh no. You've got to *promish* me, Maureen, promish me, or *elshe* . . ."

"All right, I promish."
"Good."
"Have another drink?"
"Lovely brandy, lovely lovely lovely blandy."
"Lovely brandy . . ."

# *Our Friend Judith*

●•●•●•●•●•●•●•●•●•●•●•●•●•●•●•●•●•●•●•●•●•●•●•●•●•●•●•●•●•●•●•●•●•●•●•●•●•●•●•●•●•●•●•●•●

I stopped inviting Judith to meet people when a Canadian woman remarked, with the satisfied fervour of one who has at last pinned a label on a rare specimen: "She is, of course, one of your typical English spinsters."

This was a few weeks after an American sociologist, having elicited from Judith the facts that she was fortyish, unmarried, and living alone, had enquired of me: "I suppose she has given up?" "Given up what?" I asked; and the subsequent discussion was unrewarding.

Judith did not easily come to parties. She would come after pressure, not so much—one felt—to do one a favour, but in order to correct what she believed to be a defect in her character. "I really ought to enjoy meeting new people more than I do," she said once. We reverted to an earlier pattern of our friendship: odd evenings together, an occasional visit to the cinema, or she would telephone to say: "I'm on my way past you to the British Museum. Would you care for a cup of coffee with me? I have twenty minutes to spare."

It is characteristic of Judith that the word "spinster," used of her, provoked fascinated speculation about other people. There are my aunts, for instance: aged seventy-odd, both unmarried, one an ex-missionary from China, one a retired matron of a famous London hospital. These two old ladies live together under the shadow of the cathedral in a country town. They devote much time to the Church, to good causes, to letter writing with friends all over the world, to the grandchildren and the great-grandchildren of relatives. It would be a mistake, however, on entering a house in which nothing has been moved for fifty years, to diagnose a condition of fossilised late-Victorian integrity. They read every book reviewed in the *Observer* or the *Times*, so that I recently got a letter from Aunt Rose enquiring whether I did not think that the author of *On the Road* was not —perhaps?—exaggerating his difficulties. They know a good deal about music, and write letters of encouragement to young composers they feel are being neglected—"You must understand that anything new and original takes time to be understood." Well-informed and critical Tories, they are as likely to despatch telegrams of protest to the Home Secretary as letters of support. These ladies, my aunts Emily and Rose, are surely what is meant by the phrase "English spinster." And yet, once the connection has been pointed out, there is no doubt that Judith and they are spiritual cousins, if not sisters. Therefore it follows that one's pitying admiration for women who have supported manless and uncomforted lives needs a certain modification?

One will, of course, never know; and I feel now that it is entirely my fault that I shall never know. I had been Judith's friend for upwards of five years before the incident occurred which I involuntarily thought of—stupidly enough—as the first time Judith's mask slipped.

A mutual friend, Betty, had been given a cast-off Dior dress. She was too short for it. Also she said: "It's not a dress for a married woman with three children and a talent for cooking. I don't know why not, but it isn't." Judith was the right build. Therefore one evening the three of us met by appointment in Judith's bedroom, with the dress. Neither Betty nor I was surprised at the renewed discovery that Judith was beautiful. We had both often caught each other, and ourselves, in moments of envy when Judith's calm and severe face, her undemonstratively perfect body, succeeded in making everyone else in a room or a street look cheap.

Judith is tall, small-breasted, slender. Her light brown hair is parted in the centre and cut straight around her neck. A high straight forehead, straight nose, a full grave mouth are setting for her eyes, which are green, large and prominent. Her lids are very white, fringed with gold, and moulded close over the eyeball, so that in profile she has the look of a staring gilded mask. The dress was of dark green glistening stuff, cut straight, with a sort of loose tunic. It opened simply at the throat. In it Judith could of course evoke nothing but classical images. Diana, perhaps, back from the hunt, in a relaxed moment? A rather intellectual wood nymph who had opted for an afternoon in the British Museum Reading Room? Something like that. Neither Betty nor I said a word, since Judith was examining herself in a long mirror, and must know she looked magnificent.

Slowly she drew off the dress and laid it aside. Slowly she put on the old cord skirt and woollen blouse she had taken off. She must have surprised a resigned glance between us, for she then remarked, with the smallest of mocking smiles: "One surely ought to stay in character, wouldn't you say?" She added, reading the words out of some invisible book, written not by her, since it was a very vulgar book, but perhaps by one of us: "It does everything *for* me, I must admit."

"After seeing you in it," Betty cried out, defying her, "I can't bear for anyone else to have it. I shall simply put it away." Judith shrugged, rather irritated. In the shapeless skirt and blouse, and without makeup, she stood smiling at us, a woman at whom forty-nine out of fifty people would not look twice.

A second revelatory incident occurred soon after. Betty telephoned me to say that Judith had a kitten. Did I know that Judith adored cats? "No, but of course she would," I said.

Betty lived in the same street as Judith and saw more of her than I did. I was kept posted about the growth and habits of the cat and its effect on Judith's life. She remarked for instance that she felt it was good for her to have a tie and some responsibility. But no sooner was the cat out of kittenhood than all the neighbours complained. It was a tomcat, ungelded, and making every night hideous. Finally the landlord said that either the cat or Judith must go, unless she was prepared to have the cat "fixed." Judith wore herself out trying to find some person, anywhere in Britain, who would be prepared to take the cat. This person would, however, have to sign a written statement not to have the cat "fixed." When Judith took the cat to the vet to be killed, Betty told me she cried for twenty-four hours.

"She didn't think of compromising? After all, perhaps the cat might have preferred to live, if given the choice?"

"Is it likely I'd have the nerve to say anything so sloppy to Judith? It's the nature of a male cat to rampage lustfully about, and therefore it would be morally wrong for Judith to have the cat fixed, simply to suit her own convenience."

"She said that?"

"She wouldn't have to *say* it, surely?"

A third incident was when she allowed a visiting young American, living in Paris, the friend of a friend and scarcely known to her, to use her flat while she visited her parents over Christmas. The young man and his friends lived it up for ten days of alcohol and sex and marijuana, and when Judith came back it took a week to get the place clean again and the furniture mended. She telephoned twice to Paris, the first time to say that he was a disgusting young thug and if he knew what was good for him he would keep out of her way in the future; the second time to apologise for losing her temper. "I had a choice either to let someone use my flat, or to leave it empty. But having chosen that you should have it, it was clearly an un-warrantable infringement of your liberty to make any conditions at all. I do most sincerely ask your pardon." The moral aspects of the matter having been made clear, she was irritated rather than not to receive letters of apology from him—fulsome, embarrassed, but above all, baffled.

It was the note of curiosity in the letters—he even suggested coming over to get to know her better—that irritated her most. "What do you suppose he means?" she said to me. "He lived in my flat for ten days. One would have thought that should be enough, wouldn't you?"

The facts about Judith, then, are all in the open, unconcealed, and plain to anyone who cares to study them; or, as it became plain she feels, to anyone with the intelligence to interpret them.

She has lived for the last twenty years in a small two-roomed flat high over a busy West London street. The flat is shabby and badly heated. The furniture is old, was never anything but ugly, is now frankly rickety and fraying. She has an income of two hundred pounds a year from a dead uncle. She lives on this and what she earns from her poetry, and from lecturing on poetry to night classes and extramural university classes.

She does not smoke or drink, and eats very little, from preference, not self-discipline.

She studied poetry and biology at Oxford, with distinction.

She is a Castlewell. That is, she is a member of one of the academic upper-middleclass families, which have been producing for centuries a steady supply of brilliant but sound men and women who are the backbone of the arts and sciences in Britain. She is on cool good terms with her family, who respect her and leave her alone.

She goes on long walking tours, by herself, in such places as Exmoor or West Scotland.

Every three or four years she publishes a volume of poems.

The walls of her flat are completely lined with books. They are scientific, classical and historical; there is a great deal of poetry and some drama. There is not one novel. When Judith says: "Of course I don't read novels," this does not mean that novels have no place, or a small place, in literature; or that people should not read novels; but that it must be obvious she can't be expected to read novels.

I had been visiting her flat for years before I noticed two long shelves of books, under a window, each shelf filled with the works of a single writer. The two writers are not, to put it at the mildest, the kind one would associate with Judith. They are mild, reminiscent, vague and whimsical. Typical English *belles-lettres*, in fact, and by definition abhorrent to her. Not one of the books in the two shelves has been read; some of the pages are still uncut. Yet each book is inscribed or dedicated to her: gratefully, admiringly, sentimentally and, more than once, amorously. In short, it is open to anyone who cares to examine these two shelves, and to work out dates, to conclude that Judith from the age of fifteen to twenty-five had been the beloved young companion of one elderly literary gentleman, and from twenty-five to thirty-five the inspiration of another.

During all that time she had produced her own poetry, and the sort of poetry, it is quite safe to deduce, not at all likely to be admired by her two admirers. Her poems are always cool and intellectual; that is their form, which is contradicted or supported by a gravely sensuous texture. They are poems to read often; one has to, to understand them.

I did not ask Judith a direct question about these two eminent but rather fusty lovers. Not because she would not have answered, or because she would have found the question impertinent, but because such questions are clearly unnecessary. Having those two shelves of books where they are, and books she could not conceivably care for, for their own sake, is publicly giving credit where credit is due. I can imagine her thinking the thing over, and deciding it was only fair, or perhaps honest, to place the books there; and this despite the fact that she would not care at all for the same attention to be paid to her. There is something almost contemptuous in it. For she certainly despises people who feel they need attention.

For instance, more than once a new emerging wave of "modern" young poets have discovered her as the only "modern" poet among their despised and well-credited elders. This is because, since she began writing at fifteen, her poems have been full of scientific, mechanical and chemical imagery. This is how she thinks, or feels.

More than once has a young poet hastened to her flat, to claim her as an ally, only to find her totally and by instinct unmoved by words like "modern," "new," "contemporary." He has been outraged and wounded by her principle, so deeply rooted as to be unconscious, and to need no expression but a contemptuous shrug of the shoulders, that publicity seeking or to want critical attention is despicable. It goes without saying that there is perhaps one critic in the world she has any time for. He has sulked off, leaving her on her shelf, which she takes it for granted is her proper place, to be read by an appreciative minority.

Meanwhile she gives her lectures, walks alone through London, writes her poems, and is seen sometimes at a concert or a play with a middleaged professor of Greek, who has a wife and two children.

Betty and I had speculated about this professor, with such remarks as: Surely she must sometimes be lonely? Hasn't she ever wanted to marry? What about that awful moment when one comes in from somewhere at night to an empty flat?

It happened recently that Betty's husband was on a business trip, her children visiting, and she was unable to stand the empty house. She asked Judith for a refuge until her own home filled again.

Afterwards Betty rang me up to report: "Four of the five nights Professor Adams came in about ten or so."

"Was Judith embarrassed?"

"Would you expect her to be?"

"Well, if not embarrassed, at least conscious there was a situation?"

"No, not at all. But I must say I don't think he's good enough for her. He can't possibly understand her. He calls her Judy."

"Good God."

"Yes. But I was wondering. Suppose the other two called her Judy—'little Judy'—imagine it! Isn't it awful? But it does rather throw a light on Judith?"

"It's rather touching."

"I suppose it's touching. But *I* was embarrassed—oh, not because of the situation. Because of how she was, with him. 'Judy, is there another cup of tea in that pot?' And she, rather daughterly and demure, pouring him one."

"Well yes, I can see how you felt."

"Three of the nights he went to her bedroom with her—very casual about it, because she was being. But he was not there in the mornings. So I asked her. You know how it is when you ask her a question. As if you've been having long conversations on that very subject for years and years, and she is merely continuing where you left off last. So when she says something surprising, one feels such a fool to be surprised?"

"Yes. And then?"

"I asked her if she was sorry not to have children. She said yes, but one couldn't have everything."

"One can't have everything, she said?"

"Quite clearly feeling she *has* nearly everything. She said she thought it was a pity, because she would have brought up children very well."

"When you come to think of it, she would, too."

"I asked about marriage, but she said on the whole the role of a mistress suited her better."

"She used the word 'mistress'?"

"You must admit it's the accurate word."

"I suppose so."

"And then she said that while she liked intimacy and sex and everything, she enjoyed waking up in the morning alone and *her own person.*"

"Yes, *of course.*"

"Of course. But now she's bothered because the professor would like to marry her. Or he feels he ought. At least, he's getting all guilty and obsessive about it. She says she doesn't see the point of divorce, and anyway, surely it would be very hard on his poor old wife after all these years, particularly after bringing up two children so satisfactorily. She talks about his wife as if she's a kind of nice old charwoman, and it wouldn't be *fair* to sack her, you know. Anyway. What with one thing and another. Judith's going off to Italy soon in order *to collect herself.*"

"But how's she going to pay for it?"

"Luckily the Third Programme's commissioning her to do some arty programmes. They offered her a choice of The Cid— El Thid, you know—and the Borgias. Well, the Borghese, then. And Judith settled for the Borgias."

"The Borgias," I said, "*Judith?*"

"Yes, quite. I said that too, in that tone of voice. She saw my point. She says the epic is right up her street, whereas the Renaissance has never been on her wave length. Obviously it couldn't be, all the magnificence and cruelty and *dirt*. But of course chivalry and a high moral code and all those idiotically noble goings-on are right on her wave length."

"Is the money the same?"

"Yes. But is it likely Judith would let money decide? No, she said that one should always choose something new, that isn't up one's street. Well, because it's better for her character, and so on, to get herself unsettled by the Renaissance. She didn't say *that*, of course."

"Of course not."

Judith went to Florence; and for some months postcards informed us tersely of her doings. Then Betty decided she must go by herself for a holiday. She had been appalled by the discovery that if her husband was away for a night she couldn't sleep; and when he went to Australia for three weeks, she stopped living until he came back. She had discussed this with him, and he had agreed that if she really felt the situation to be serious, he would despatch her by air, to Italy, in order to recover her self-respect. As she put it.

I got this letter from her: "It's no use, I'm coming home. I might have known. Better face it, once you're really married you're not fit for man nor beast. And if you remember what I used to be like! *Well!* I moped around Milan. I sunbathed in Venice, then I thought my tan was surely worth something, so I was on the point of starting an affair with another lonely soul, but I lost heart, and went to Florence to see Judith. She wasn't there. She'd gone to the Italian Riviera. I had nothing better to do, so I followed her. When I saw the place I wanted

to laugh, it's so much not Judith, you know, all those palms
and umbrellas and gaiety at all costs and ever such an orna-
mental blue sea. Judith is in an enormous stone room up on the
hillside above the sea, with grape vines all over the place. You
should see her, she's got beautiful. It seems for the last fifteen
years she's been going to Soho every Saturday morning to buy
food at an Italian shop. I must have looked surprised, because
she explained she liked Soho. I suppose because all that dreary
vice and nudes and prostitutes and everything prove how right
she is to be as she is? She told the people in the shop she was
going to Italy, and the *signora* said, what a coincidence, she
was going back to Italy too, and she did hope an old friend like
Miss Castlewell would visit her there. Judith said to me: 'I felt
lacking, when she used the word friend. Our relations have
always been formal. Can you understand it?' she said to me.
'For fifteen years,' I said to her. She said: 'I think I must feel
it's a kind of imposition, don't you know, expecting people to
feel friendship for one.' *Well.* I said: 'You ought to understand
it, because you're like that yourself.' 'Am I?' she said. 'Well,
think about it,' I said. But I could see she didn't want to think
about it. Anyway, she's here, and I've spent a week with her.
The widow Maria Rineiri inherited her mother's house, so she
came home, from Soho. On the ground floor is a tatty little
*rosticceria* patronised by the neighbours. They are all working
people. This isn't tourist country, up on the hill. The widow lives
above the shop with her little boy, a nasty little brat of about
ten. Say what you like, the English are the only people who know
how to bring up children, I don't care if that's insular. Judith's
room is at the back, with a balcony. Underneath her room is the
barber's shop, and the barber is Luigi Rineiri, the widow's
younger brother. Yes, I was keeping him until the last. He is
about forty, tall dark handsome, a great *bull,* but rather a sweet
fatherly bull. He has cut Judith's hair and made it lighter. Now
it looks like a sort of gold helmet. Judith is all brown. The
widow Rineiri has made her a white dress and a green dress.
They fit, for a change. When Judith walks down the street to
the lower town, all the Italian males take one look at the golden
girl and melt in their own oil like ice cream. Judith takes all
this in her stride. She sort of acknowledges the homage. Then
she strolls into the sea and vanishes into the foam. She swims
five miles every day. *Naturally.* I haven't asked Judith whether

she has collected herself, because you can see she hasn't. The widow Rineiri is matchmaking. When I noticed this I wanted to laugh, but luckily I didn't because Judith asked me, really wanting to know: 'Can you see me married to an Italian barber?' (Not being snobbish, but stating the position, so to speak.) 'Well yes,' I said, 'you're the only woman I know who I can see married to an Italian barber.' Because it wouldn't matter who she married, she'd always be her *own person*. 'At any rate, for a time,' I said. At which she said, asperously: 'You can use phrases like for a time in England but not in Italy.' Did you ever see England, at least London, as the home of licence, liberty and free love? No, neither did I, but of course she's right. Married to Luigi it would be the family, the neighbours, the church and the *bambini*. All the same she's thinking about it, believe it or not. Here she's quite different, all relaxed and free. She's melting in the attention she gets. The widow mothers her and makes her coffee all the time, and listens to a lot of good advice about how to bring up that nasty brat of hers. Unluckily she doesn't take it. Luigi is crazy for her. At mealtimes she goes to the *trattoria* in the upper square and all the workmen treat her like a goddess. Well, a film star then. I said to her, you're mad to come home. For one thing her rent is ten bob a week, and you eat *pasta* and drink red wine till you bust for about one and sixpence. No, she said, it would be nothing but self-indulgence to stay. Why? I said. She said, she's got nothing to stay for. (Ho ho.) And besides, she's done her research on the Borghese, though so far she can't see her way to an honest presentation of the facts. What made these people tick? she wants to know. And so she's only staying because of the cat. I forgot to mention the cat. This is a town of cats. The Italians here love their cats. I wanted to feed a stray cat at the table, but the waiter said no; and after lunch, all the waiters came with trays crammed with leftover food and stray cats came from everywhere to eat. And at dark when the tourists go in to feed and the beach is empty—you know how empty and forlorn a beach is at dusk?—well cats appear from everywhere. The beach seems to move, then you see it's cats. They go stalking along the thin inch of grey water at the edge of the sea, shaking their paws crossly at each step, snatching at the dead little fish, and throwing them with their mouths up on to the dry sand. Then they scamper after them. You've never seen such a snarling and fighting. At dawn when the fishing boats come in to the empty beach, the cats are there in dozens. The fishermen throw them bits of fish. The cats snarl and fight over it. Judith gets up early and goes down to watch. Sometimes Luigi goes too, being tolerant. Because what he really likes is to join the evening promenade with Judith on his arm around and around the square of the upper town. Showing her off. Can you *see* Judith? But she does it. Being tolerant. But she smiles and enjoys the attention she gets, there's no doubt of it.

"She has a cat in her room. It's a kitten really, but it's pregnant. Judith says she can't leave until the kittens are born. The cat is too young to have kittens. Imagine Judith. She sits on her bed in that great stone room, with her bare feet on the stone floor, and watches the cat, and tries to work out why a healthy uninhibited Italian cat always fed on the best from the *rosticceria* should be neurotic. Because it is. When it sees Judith watching it gets nervous and starts licking at the roots of its tail. But Judith goes on watching, and says about Italy that the reason why the English love the Italians is because the Italians make the English feel superior. They have no discipline. And that's a despicable reason for one nation to love another. Then she talks about Luigi and says he has no sense of guilt, but a sense of sin; whereas she has no sense of sin but she has guilt. I haven't asked her if this has been an insuperable barrier, because judging from how she looks, it hasn't. She says she would rather have a sense of sin, because sin can be atoned for, and if she understood sin, perhaps she would be more at home with the Renaissance. Luigi is very healthy, she says, and not neurotic. He is a Catholic of course. He doesn't mind that she's an atheist. His mother has explained to him that the English are all pagans, but good people at heart. I suppose he thinks a few smart sessions with the local priest would set Judith on the right path for good and all. Meanwhile the cat walks nervously around the room, stopping to lick, and when it can't stand Judith watching it another second, it rolls over on the floor, with its paws tucked up, and rolls up its eyes, and Judith scratches its lumpy pregnant stomach and tells it to relax. It makes *me* nervous to see her, it's not like her, I don't know why. Then Luigi shouts up from the barber's shop, then he comes up and stands at the door laughing, and Judith laughs, and the widow says: Children, enjoy yourselves. And off they go, walking down to the town eating ice cream. The cat follows them. It won't let Judith out of its sight, like a dog. When she swims miles out to sea, the cat hides under a beach hut until she comes back. Then she carries it back up the hill, because that nasty little boy chases it. *Well.* I'm coming home tomorrow thank God, to my dear old Billy, I was mad ever to leave him. There is something about Judith and Italy that has upset me, I don't know what. The point is, what on earth can Judith and Luigi *talk* about? Nothing. How can they? And of course it doesn't matter. So I turn out to be a prude as well. See you next week."

It was my turn for a dose of the sun, so I didn't see Betty. On my way back from Rome I stopped off in Judith's resort and walked up through narrow streets to the upper town, where, in the square with the vine-covered *trattoria* at the corner, was a house with ROSTICCERIA written in black paint on a cracked wooden board over a low door. There was a door curtain of red beads, and flies settled on the beads. I opened the beads with my hands and looked into a small dark room with a stone counter. Loops of salami hung from metal hooks. A glass bell covered some plates of cooked meats. There were flies on the salami and on the glass bell. A few tins on the wooden shelves, a couple of pale loaves, some wine casks and an open case of sticky pale green grapes covered with fruit flies seemed to be the only stock. A single wooden table with two chairs stood in a corner, and two workmen sat there, eating lumps of sausage and bread. Through another bead curtain at the back came a short, smoothly fat, slender-limbed woman with greying hair. I asked for Miss Castlewell, and her face changed. She said in an offended, offhand way: "Miss Castlewell left last week." She took a white cloth from under the counter, and flicked at the flies on the glass bell. "I'm a friend of hers," I said, and she said: "*Si*," and put her hands palm down on the counter and looked at me, expressionless. The workmen got up, gulped down the last of their wine, nodded and went. She *ciao*'d them; and looked back at me. Then, since I didn't go, she called: "Luigi!" A shout came from the back room, there was a rattle of beads, and in came first a wiry sharp-faced boy, and then Luigi. He was tall, heavy-shouldered, and his black rough hair was like a cap, pulled low over his brows. He looked good-natured, but at the moment uneasy. His sister said something, and he stood beside her, an ally, and confirmed: "Miss Castlewell went away."

I was on the point of giving up, when through the bead curtain that screened off a dazzling light eased a thin tabby cat. It was ugly and it walked uncomfortably, with its back quarters bunched up. The child suddenly let out a "Ssssss" through his teeth, and the cat froze. Luigi said something sharp to the child, and something encouraging to the cat, which sat down, looked straight in front of it, then began frantically licking at its flanks. "Miss Castlewell was offended with us," said Mrs. Rineiri suddenly, and with dignity. "She left early one morning. We did not expect her to go." I said: "Perhaps she had to go home and finish some work."

Mrs. Rineiri shrugged, then sighed. Then she exchanged a hard look with her brother. Clearly the subject had been discussed, and closed forever.

"I've known Judith a long time," I said, trying to find the right note. "She's a remarkable woman. She's a poet." But there was no response to this at all. Meanwhile the child, with a fixed bared-teeth grin, was staring at the cat, narrowing his eyes. Suddenly he let out another "Sssssss" and added a short high yelp. The cat shot backwards, hit the wall, tried desperately to claw its way up the wall, came to its senses and again sat down and began its urgent, undirected licking at its fur. This time Luigi cuffed the child, who yelped in earnest, and then ran out into the street past the cat. Now that the way was clear the cat shot across the floor, up onto the counter, and bounded past Luigi's shoulder and straight through the bead curtain into the barber's shop, where it landed with a thud.

"Judith was sorry when she left us," said Mrs. Rineiri uncertainly. "She was crying."

"I'm sure she was."

"And so," said Mrs. Rineiri, with finality, laying her hands down again, and looking past me at the bead curtain. That was the end. Luigi nodded brusquely at me, and went into the back. I said goodbye to Mrs. Rineiri and walked back to the lower town. In the square I saw the child, sitting on the running board of a lorry parked outside the *trattoria*, drawing in the dust with his bare toes, and directing in front of him a blank, unhappy stare.

I had to go through Florence, so I went to the address Judith had been at. No, Miss Castlewell had not been back. Her papers and books were still here. Would I take them back with me to

England? I made a great parcel and brought them back to England.

I telephoned Judith and she said she had already written for the papers to be sent, but it was kind of me to bring them. There had seemed to be no point, she said, in returning to Florence.

"Shall I bring them over?"

"I would be very grateful, of course."

Judith's flat was chilly, and she wore a bunchy sage-green woollen dress. Her hair was still a soft gold helmet, but she looked pale and rather pinched. She stood with her back to a single bar of electric fire—lit because I demanded it—with her legs apart and her arms folded. She contemplated me.

"I went to the Rineiris' house."

"Oh. Did you?"

"They seemed to miss you."

She said nothing.

"I saw the cat too."

"Oh. Oh, I suppose you and Betty discussed it?" This was with a small unfriendly smile.

"Well, Judith, you must see we were likely to?"

She gave this her consideration and said: "I don't understand why people discuss other people. Oh—I'm not criticising you. But I don't see why you are so interested. I don't understand human behaviour and I'm not particularly interested."

"I think you should write to the Rineiris."

"I wrote and thanked them, of course."

"I don't mean that."

"You and Betty have worked it out?"

"Yes, we talked about it. We thought we should talk to you, so you should write to the Rineiris."

"Why?"

"For one thing, they are both very fond of you."

"Fond," she said smiling.

"Judith, I've never in my life felt such an atmosphere of being let down."

Judith considered this. "When something happens that shows one there is really a complete gulf in understanding, what is there to say?"

"It could scarcely have been a complete gulf in understanding. I suppose you are going to say we are being interfering?"

Judith showed distaste. "That is a very stupid word. And it's a stupid idea. No one can interfere with me if I don't let them. No, it's that I don't understand people. I don't understand why you or Betty should care. Or why the Rineiris should, for that matter," she added with the small tight smile.

"Judith!"

"If you've behaved stupidly, there's no point in going on. You put an end to it."

"What happened? Was it the cat?"

"Yes, I suppose so. But it's not important." She looked at me, saw my ironical face, and said: "The cat was too young to have kittens. That is all there was to it."

"Have it your way. But that is obviously not all there is to it."

"What upsets me is that I don't understand at all why I was so upset then."

"What happened? Or don't you want to talk about it?"

"I don't give a damn whether I talk about it or not. You really do say the most extraordinary things, you and Betty. If you want to know, I'll tell you. What does it matter?"

"I would like to know, of course."

"*Of course!*" she said. "In your place I wouldn't care. Well, I think the essence of the thing was that I must have had the wrong attitude to that cat. Cats are supposed to be independent. They are suppposed to go off by themselves to have their kittens. This one didn't. It was climbing up on to my bed all one night and crying for attention. I don't like cats on my bed. In the morning I saw she was in pain. I stayed with her all that day. Then Luigi—he's the brother, you know."

"Yes."

"Did Betty mention him? Luigi came up to say it was time I went for a swim. He said the cat should look after itself. I blame myself very much. That's what happens when you submerge yourself in somebody else."

Her look at me was now defiant; and her body showed both defensiveness and aggression. "Yes. It's true. I've always been afraid of it. And in the last few weeks I've behaved badly. It's because I let it happen."

"Well, go on."

"I left the cat and swam. It was late, so it was only for a few minutes. When I came out of the sea the cat had followed me and had had a kitten on the beach. That little beast Michele— the son, you know?—well, he always teased the poor thing, and now he had frightened her off the kitten. It was dead, though. He held it up by the tail and waved it at me as I came out of the sea. I told him to bury it. He scooped two inches of sand away and pushed the kitten in—on the beach, where people are all day. So I buried it properly. He had run off. He was chasing the poor cat. She was terrified and running up the town. I ran too. I caught Michele and I was so angry I hit him. I don't believe in hitting children. I've been feeling beastly about it ever since."

"You were angry."

"It's no excuse. I would never have believed myself capable of hitting a child. I hit him very hard. He went off, crying. The poor cat had got under a big lorry parked in the square. Then she screamed. And then a most remarkable thing happened. She screamed just once, and all at once cats just materialised. One minute there was just one cat, lying under a lorry, and the next, dozens of cats. They sat in a big circle around the lorry, all quite still, and watched my poor cat."

"Rather moving," I said.

"Why?"

"There is no evidence one way or the other," I said in inverted commas, "that the cats were there out of concern for a friend in trouble."

"No," she said energetically. "There isn't. It might have been curiosity. Or anything. How do we know? However, I crawled under the lorry. There were two paws sticking out of the cat's back end. The kitten was the wrong way round. It was stuck. I held the cat down with one hand and I pulled the kitten out with the other." She held out her long white hands. They were still covered with fading scars and scratches. "She bit and yelled, but the kitten was alive. She left the kitten and crawled across the square into the house. Then all the cats got up and walked away. It was the most extraordinary thing I've ever seen. They vanished again. One minute they were all there, and then they had vanished. I went after the cat, with the kitten. Poor little thing, it was covered with dust—being wet, don't you know. The cat was on my bed. There was another kitten coming, but it got stuck too. So when she screamed and screamed I just pulled it out. The kittens began to suck. One kitten was very big. It was a nice fat black kitten. It must have hurt her. But she suddenly bit out—snapped, don't you know, like a reflex action, at the back of the kitten's head. It died, just like that. Extraordinary, isn't it?" she said, blinking hard, her lips quivering. "She was its mother, but she killed it. Then she ran off the bed and went downstairs into the shop under the counter. I called to Luigi. You know, he's Mrs. Rineiri's brother."

"Yes, I know."

"He said she was too young, and she was badly frightened and very hurt. He took the alive kitten to her but she got up and walked away. She didn't want it. Then Luigi told me not to look. But I followed him. He held the kitten by the tail and he banged it against the wall twice. Then he dropped it into the rubbish heap. He moved aside some rubbish with his toe, and put the kitten there and pushed rubbish over it. Then Luigi said the cat should be destroyed. He said she was badly hurt and it would always hurt her to have kittens."

"He hasn't destroyed her. She's still alive. But it looks to me as if he were right."

"Yes, I expect he was."

"What upset you—that he killed the kitten?"

"Oh no, I expect the cat would if he hadn't. But that isn't the point, is it?"

"What is the point?"

"I don't think I really know." She had been speaking breathlessly, and fast. Now she said slowly: "It's not a question of right or wrong, is it? Why should it be? It's a question of what one is. That night Luigi wanted to go promenading with me. For him, that was *that*. Something had to be done, and he'd done it. But I felt ill. He was very nice to me. He's a very good person," she said, defiantly.

"Yes, he looks it."

"That night I couldn't sleep. I was blaming myself. I should never have left the cat to go swimming. Well, and then I decided to leave the next day. And I did. And that's all. The whole thing was a mistake, from start to finish."

"Going to Italy at all?"

"Oh, to go for a holiday would have been all right."

"You've done all that work for nothing? You mean you aren't going to make use of all that research?"

"No. It was a mistake."

"Why don't you leave it a few weeks and see how things are then?"

"Why?"

"You might feel differently about it."

"What an extraordinary thing to say. Why should I? Oh, you mean, time passing, healing wounds—that sort of thing? What an extraordinary idea. It's always seemed to me an extraordinary idea. No, right from the beginning I've felt ill at ease with the whole business, not myself at all."

"Rather irrationally, I should have said."

Judith considered this, very seriously. She frowned while she thought it over. Then she said: "But if one cannot rely on what one feels, what can one rely on?"

"On what one thinks, I should have expected you to say."

"Should you? Why? Really, you people are all very strange. I don't understand you." She turned off the electric fire, and her face closed up. She smiled, friendly and distant, and said: "I don't really see any point at all in discussing it."

# *Each Other*

•–••–••–••–••–••–••–••–••–••–••–••–••–••–••–••–••–••–••–••–••–••–••–••–••–••–••–••–••–••–••–••–••–•

I suppose your brother's coming again?"

"He might."

He kept his back bravely turned while he adjusted tie, collar, and jerked his jaw this way and that to check his shave. Then, with all pretexts used, he remained rigid, his hand on his tie knot, looking into the mirror past his left cheek at the body of his wife, which was disposed prettily on the bed, weight on its right elbow, its two white forearms engaged in the movements obligatory for filing one's nails. He let his hand drop and demanded: "What do you mean, he *might*?" She did not answer, but held up a studied hand to inspect five pink arrows. She was a thin, very thin, dark girl of about eighteen. Her pose, her way of inspecting her nails, her pink-striped nightshirt which showed long, thin, white legs—all her magazine attitudes were an attempt to hide an anxiety as deep as his; for her breathing, like his, was loud and shallow.

He was not taken in. The lonely fever in her black eyes, the muscles showing rodlike in the flesh of her upper arm, made him feel how much she wanted him to go; and he thought, sharp because of the sharpness of his need for her: There's something unhealthy about her, yes. . . . The word caused him guilt. He accepted it, and allowed his mind, which was over-alert, trying to pin down the cause of his misery, to add: Yes, not clean, dirty. But this fresh criticism surprised him, and he remembered her obsessive care of her flesh, hair, nails, and the long hours spent in the bath. *Yes, dirty,* his rising aversion insisted.

Armed by it, he was able to turn, slowly, to look at her direct, instead of through the cold glass. He was a solid, well set up, brushed, washed young man who had stood several inches shorter than she at the wedding a month ago, but with confidence in the manhood which had mastered her freakish adolescence. He now kept on her the pressure of a blue stare both appealing (of which he was not aware) and aggressive—which he meant as a warning. Meanwhile he controlled a revulsion which he knew would vanish if she merely lifted her arms towards him.

"What do you mean, he *might?*" he said again.

After some moments of not answering, she said, languid, turning her thin hand this way and that: "I said, he might."

This dialogue echoed, for both of them, not only from five minutes before; but from other mornings, when it had been as often as not unspoken. They were on the edge of disaster. But the young husband was late. He looked at his watch, a gesture which said, but unconvincingly, bravado merely: I go out to work while you lie there. . . . Then he about-turned, and went to the door, slowing on his way to it. Stopped. Said: "Well, in that case I shan't be back to supper."

"Suit yourself," she said, languid. She now lay flat on her back, and waved both hands in front of her eyes to dry nail varnish which, however, was three days old.

He said loudly: "Freda! I mean it. I'm not going to . . ." He looked both trapped and defiant; but intended to do everything, obviously, to maintain his self-respect, his masculinity, in the face of—but what? Her slow smile across at him was something (unlike everything else she had done since waking that morning) she was quite unaware of. She surely could not be aware of the sheer brutality of her slow, considering, contemptuous smile? For it had invitation in it; and it was this, the unconscious triumph there, that caused him to pale, to begin a stammering: "Fre-Fre-Fred-Freda . . ." but give up, and leave the room. Abruptly though quietly, considering the force of his horror.

She lay still, listening to his footsteps go down, and the front door closing. Then, without hurrying, she lifted her long thin white legs that ended in ten small pink shields, over the edge of the bed, and stood on them by the window, to watch her husband's well-brushed head jerking away along the pavement. This was a suburb of London, and he had to get to the City, where he was a clerk-with-prospects: and most of the other people down there were on their way to work. She watched him and them, until at the corner he turned, his face lengthened with anxiety. She indolently waved, without smiling. He stared back, as if at a memory of nightmare; so she shrugged and removed herself from the window, and did not see his frantically too late wave and smile.

She now stood, frowning, in front of the long glass in the new wardrobe: a very tall girl, stooped by her height, all elbows and knees, and even more ridiculous because of the short nightshirt. She stripped this off over her head, taking assurance in a side-glance from full-swinging breasts and a rounded waist; then slipped on a white negligée that had frills all down it and around the neck, from which her head emerged, poised. She now looked much better, like a model, in fact. She brushed her short gleaming black hair, stared at length into the deep anxious eyes, and got back into bed.

Soon she tensed, hearing the front door open, softly; and close, softly again. She listened, as the unseen person also listened and watched; for this was a two-roomed flatlet, converted in a semidetached house. The landlady lived in the flatlet below this one on the ground floor; and the young husband had taken to asking her, casually, every evening, or listening, casually, to easily given information, about the comings and goings in the house and the movements of his wife. But the steps came steadily up towards her, the door opened, very gently, and she looked up, her face bursting into flower as in came a very tall, lank, dark young man. He sat on the bed beside his sister, took her thin hand in his thin hand, kissed it, bit it lovingly, then bent to kiss her on the lips. Their mouths held while two pairs of deep black eyes held each other. Then she shut her eyes, took his lower lip between her teeth, and slid her tongue along it. He began to undress before she let him go; and she asked, without any of the pertness she used for her husband: "Are you in a hurry this morning?"

"Got to get over to a job in Exeter Street."

An electrician, he was not tied to desk or office.

He slid naked into bed beside his sister, murmuring: "Olive Oyl."

Her long body was pressed against his in a fervour of gratitude for the love name, for it had never received absolution from her husband as it did from this man; and she returned, in as loving a murmur: "Popeye." Again the two pairs of eyes stared into each other at an inch or so's distance. His, though deep in bony sockets like hers, were prominent there, the eyeballs rounded under thin, already crinkling, bruised-looking flesh. Hers, however, were delicately outlined by clear white skin, and he kissed the perfected copies of his own ugly eyes, and said, as she pressed towards him: "Now, now, Olive Oyl, don't be in such a hurry, you'll spoil it."

"No, we won't."

"*Wait*, I tell you."

"All right then . . ."

The two bodies, deeply breathing, remained still a long while. Her hand, on the small of his back, made a soft, circular pressing motion, bringing him inwards. He had his two hands on her hipbones, holding her still. But she succeeded, and they joined, and he said again: "Wait now. Lie still." They lay absolutely still, eyes closed.

After a while he asked suddenly: "Well, did he last night?"

"Yes."

His teeth bared against her forehead and he said: "I suppose you made him."

"Why *made* him?"

"You're a pig."

"All right then, how about Alice?"

"Oh her. Well, she screamed and said: 'Stop. Stop.'"

"Who's a pig, then?"

She wriggled circularly, and he held her hips still, tenderly murmuring: "No, no, no, no."

Stillness again. In the small bright bedroom, with the suburban sunlight outside, new green curtains blew in, flicking the too large, too new furniture, while the long white bodies remained still, mouth to mouth, eyes closed, united by deep soft breaths.

But his breathing deepened; his nails dug into the bones of

her hips, he slid his mouth free and said: "How about Charlie, then?"

"He made me scream too," she murmured, licking his throat, eyes closed. This time it was she who held his loins steady, saying: "No, no, no, you'll spoil it."

They lay together, still. A long silence, a long quiet. Then the fluttering curtains roused her, her foot tensed, and she rubbed it delicately up and down his leg. He said, angry: "Why did you spoil it then? It was just beginning."

"It's much better afterwards if it's really difficult." She slid and pressed her internal muscles to make it more difficult, grinning at him in challenge, and he put his hands around her throat in a half-mocking, half-serious pressure to stop her, simultaneously moving in and out of her with exactly the same emulous, taunting but solicitous need she was showing—to see how far they both could go. In a moment they were pulling each other's hair, biting, sinking between thin bones, and then, just before the explosion, they pulled apart at the same moment, and lay separate, trembling.

"We only just made it," he said, fond, uxorious, stroking her hair.

"Yes. Careful now, Fred."

They slid together again.

"Now it will be just perfect," she said, content, mouth against his throat.

The two bodies, quivering with strain, lay together, jerking involuntarily from time to time. But slowly they quietened. Their breathing, jagged at first, smoothed. They breathed together. They had become one person, abandoned against and in each other, silent and gone.

A long time, a long time, a long . . .

A car went past below in the usually silent street, very loud, and the young man opened his eyes and looked into the relaxed gentle face of his sister.

"Freda."

"Ohhh."

"Yes, I've got to go, it must be nearly dinnertime."

"Wait a minute."

"No, or we'll get excited again, we'll spoil everything."

They separated gently, but the movements both used, the two

hands gentle on each other's hips, easing their bodies apart, were more like a fitting together. Separate, they lay still, smiling at each other, touching each other's face with fingertips, licking each other's eyelids with small cat licks.

"It gets better and better."

"Yes."

"Where did you go this time?"

"You know."

"Yes."

"Where did you go?"

"You know. Where you were."

"Yes. Tell me."

"Can't."

"I know. Tell me."

"With you."

"Yes."

"Are we one person, then?"

"Yes."

"Yes."

Silence again. Again he roused himself.

"Where are you working this afternoon?"

"I told you. It's a baker's shop in Exeter Street."

"And afterwards?"

"I'm taking Alice to the pictures."

She bit her lips, punishing them and him, then sunk her nails into his shoulder.

"Well my darling, I just make her, that's all, I make her come, she wouldn't understand anything better."

He sat up, began dressing. In a moment he was a tall sober youth in a dark blue sweater. He slicked down his hair with the young husband's hairbrushes, as if he lived here, while she lay naked, watching.

He turned and smiled, affectionate and possessive, like a husband. There was something in her face, a lost desperation, that made his harden. He crouched beside her, scowling, baring his teeth, gently fitting his thumb on her windpipe, looking straight into her dark eyes. She breathed hoarsely, and coughed. He let his thumb drop.

"What's that for, Fred?"

"You swear you don't do that with Charlie?"

"How could I?"

"What do you mean? You could show him."

"But why? Why do you think I want to? Fred!"

The two pairs of deep eyes, in bruised flesh, looked lonely with uncertainty into each other.

"How should I know what you want?"

"You're stupid," she said suddenly, with a small maternal smile.

He dropped his head, with a breath like a groan, onto her breasts, and she stroked his head gently, looking over it at the wall, blinking tears out of her eyes. She said: "He's not coming home to supper tonight, he's angry."

"Is he?"

"He keeps talking about you. He asked today if you were coming."

"Why, does he guess?" He jerked his head up off the soft support of her bosom, and stared, his face bitter, into hers. "Why? You haven't been stupid now, have you?"

"No, but Fred . . . but after you've been with me I suppose I'm different. . . ."

"Oh Christ!" He jumped up, desperate, beginning movements of flight, anger, hate, escape—checking each one. "What do you want, then? You want me to make you come, then? Well, that's easy enough, isn't it, if that's all you want. All right then, lie down and I'll do it, and I'll make you come till you cry, if that's all . . ." He was about to strip off his clothes; but she shot up from the bed, first hastily draping herself in her white frills, out of an instinct to protect what they had. She stood by him, as tall as he, holding his arms down by his sides. "Fred, Fred, Fred, darling, my sweetheart, don't spoil it, don't spoil it now when . . ."

"When what?"

She met his fierce look with courage, saying steadily: "Well, what do you expect, Fred? He's not stupid, is he? I'm not a . . . He makes love to me, well, he is my husband, isn't he? And . . . well, what about you and Alice, you do the same, it's normal, isn't it? Perhaps if you and I didn't have Charlie and Alice for coming, we wouldn't be able to do it our way, have you thought of that?"

"Have I thought of that! Well, what do you think?"

"Well, it's normal, isn't it?"

"Normal," he said, with horror, gazing into her loving face for reassurance against the word. "Normal, is it? Well, if you're

going to use words like that . . ." Tears ran down his face, and
she kissed them away in a passion of protective love.

"Well, why did you say I must marry him? I didn't want to,
you said I should."

"I didn't think it would spoil us."

"But it hasn't, has it, Fred? Nothing could be like us. How
could it? You know that from Alice, don't you, Fred?" Now
she was anxiously seeking for his reassurance. They stared at
each other; then their eyes closed, and they laid their cheeks together and wept, holding down each other's amorous hands, for
fear that what they were might be cheapened by her husband,
his girl.

He said: "What were you beginning to say?"

"When?"

"Just now. You said, don't spoil it now *when*."

"I get scared."

"Why?"

"Suppose I get pregnant? Well, one day I must, it's only fair,
he wants kids. Suppose he leaves me—he gets in the mood to
leave me, like today. Well, he feels something . . . it stands to
reason. It doesn't matter how much I try with him, you know he
feels it. . . . Fred?"

"What?"

"There isn't any law against it, is there?"

"Against what?"

"I mean, a brother and sister can share a place, no one would
say anything."

He stiffened away from her: "You're crazy."

"Why am I? Why, Fred?"

"You're just not thinking, that's all."

"What are we going to do, then?"

He didn't answer, and she sighed, letting her head lie on his
shoulder beside his head, so that he felt her open eyes and their
wet lashes on his neck.

"We can't do anything but go on like this, you've got to see
that."

"Then I've got to be nice to him, otherwise he's going to
leave me, and I don't blame him."

She wept, silently; and he held her, silent.

"It's so hard—I just wait for when you come, Fred, and I have
to pretend all the time."

They stood silent, their tears drying, their hands linked. Slowly they quieted, in love and in pity, in the same way that they quieted in their long silences when the hungers of the flesh were held by love on the edge of fruition so long that they burned out and up and away into a flame of identity.

At last they kissed, brother-and-sister kisses, gentle and warm.

"You're going to be late, Fred. You'll get the sack."

"I can always get another job."

"I can always get another husband. . . ."

"Olive Oyl . . . but you look really good in that white nay-gleejay."

"Yes, I'm just the type that's no good naked, I need clothes."

"That's right—I must go."

"Coming tomorrow?"

"Yes. About ten?"

"Yes."

"Keep him happy, then. Ta-ta."

"Look after yourself—look after yourself, my darling, look after yourself. . . ."

# Homage for Isaac Babel

The day I had promised to take Catherine down to visit my young friend Philip at his school in the country, we were to leave at eleven, but she arrived at nine. Her blue dress was new, and so were her fashionable shoes. Her hair had just been done. She looked more than ever like a pink-and-gold Renoir girl who expects everything from life.

Catherine lives in a white house overlooking the sweeping brown tides of the river. She helped me clean up my flat with a devotion which said that she felt small flats were altogether more romantic than large houses. We drank tea, and talked mainly about Philip, who, being fifteen, has pure stern tastes in everything from food to music. Catherine looked at the books lying around his room, and asked if she might borrow the stories of Isaac Babel to read on the train. Catherine is thirteen. I suggested she might find them difficult, but she said: "Philip reads them, doesn't he?"

During the journey I read newspapers and watched her pretty frowning face as she turned the pages of Babel, for she was determined to let nothing get between her and her ambition to be worthy of Philip.

At the school, which is charming, civilised, and expensive, the two children walked together across green fields, and I followed, seeing how the sun gilded their bright friendly heads turned towards each other as they talked. In Catherine's left hand she carried the stories of Isaac Babel.

After lunch we went to the pictures. Philip allowed it to be seen that he thought going to the pictures just for the fun of it was not worthy of intelligent people, but he made the concession, for our sakes. For his sake we chose the more serious of the two films that were showing in the little town. It was about a good priest who helped criminals in New York. His goodness, however, was not enough to prevent one of them from being sent to the gas chamber; and Philip and I waited with Catherine in the dark until she had stopped crying and could face the light of a golden evening.

At the entrance of the cinema the doorman was lying in wait for anyone who had red eyes. Grasping Catherine by her suffering arm, he said bitterly: "Yes, why are you crying? He had to be punished for his crime, didn't he?" Catherine stared at him, incredulous. Philip rescued her by saying with disdain: "Some people don't know right from wrong even when it's *demonstrated* to them." The doorman turned his attention to the next red-eyed emerger from the dark; and we went on together to the station, the children silent because of the cruelty of the world.

Finally Catherine said, her eyes wet again: "I think it's all absolutely beastly, and I can't bear to think about it." And Philip said: "But we've got to think about it, don't you see, because if we don't it'll just go on and *on*, don't you see?"

In the train going back to London I sat beside Catherine. She had the stories open in front of her, but she said: "Philip's awfully lucky. I wish I went to that school. Did you notice that girl who said hullo to him in the garden? They must be great friends. I wish my mother would let me have a dress like that, it's *not* fair."

"I thought it was too old for her."

"Oh, *did* you?"

Soon she bent her head again over the book, but almost at once lifted it to say: "Is he a very famous writer?"

"He's a marvellous writer, brilliant, one of the very best."

"Why?"

"Well, for one thing he's so simple. Look how few words he uses, and how strong his stories are."

"I see. Do you know him? Does he live in London?"

"Oh no, he's dead."

"Oh. Then why did you—I thought he was alive, the way you talked."

"I'm sorry, I suppose I wasn't thinking of him as dead."

"When did he die?"

"He was murdered. About twenty years ago, I suppose."

"*Twenty years.*" Her hands began the movement of pushing the book over to me, but then relaxed. "I'll be fourteen in November," she stated, sounding threatened, while her eyes challenged me.

I found it hard to express my need to apologise, but before I could speak, she said, patiently attentive again: "You said he was murdered?"

"Yes."

"I expect the person who murdered him felt sorry when he discovered he had murdered a famous writer."

"Yes, I expect so."

"Was he old when he was murdered?"

"No, quite young really."

"Well, that was bad luck, wasn't it?"

"Yes, I suppose it was bad luck."

"Which do you think is the very best story here? I mean, in your honest opinion, the very very best one."

I chose the story about killing the goose. She read it slowly, while I sat waiting, wishing to take it from her, wishing to protect this charming little person from Isaac Babel.

When she had finished, she said: "Well, some of it I don't understand. He's got a funny way of looking at things. Why should a man's legs in boots look like *girls*?" She finally pushed the book over at me, and said: "I think it's all morbid."

"But you have to understand the kind of life he had. First, he was a Jew in Russia. That was bad enough. Then his experience was all revolution and civil war and . . ."

But I could see these words bouncing off the clear glass of her fiercely denying gaze; and I said: "Look, Catherine, why don't you try again when you're older? Perhaps you'll like him better then?"

She said gratefully: "Yes, perhaps that would be best. After all, Philip is two years older than me, isn't he?"

A week later I got a letter from Catherine.

Thank you very much for being kind enough to take me to visit Philip at his school. It was the most lovely day in my whole life. I am extremely grateful to you for taking me. I have been thinking about the Hoodlum Priest. That was a film which demonstrated to me beyond any shadow of doubt that Capital Punishment is a Wicked Thing, and I shall never forget what I learned that afternoon, and the lessons of it will be with me all my life. I have been meditating about what you said about Isaac Babel, the famed Russian short story writer, and I now see that the conscious simplicity of his style is what makes him, beyond the shadow of a doubt, the great writer that he is, and now in my school compositions I am endeavouring to emulate him so as to learn a conscious simplicity which is the only basis for a really brilliant writing style. Love, Catherine. P.S. Has Philip said anything about my party? I wrote but he hasn't answered. Please find out if he is coming or if he just forgot to answer my letter. I hope he comes, because sometimes I feel I shall die if he doesn't. P.P.S. Please don't tell him I said anything, because I should die if he knew. Love, Catherine.

# Outside the Ministry

•–••–••–••–••–••–••–••–••–••–••–••–••–••–••–••–••–••–••–••–••–••–••–••–••–••–••–••–••–••–••–••–•

$\mathbf{A}$s Big Ben struck ten, a young man arrived outside the portals of the Ministry, and looked sternly up and down the street. He brought his wrist up to eye-level and frowned at it, the very picture of a man kept waiting, a man who had expected no less. His arm dropped, elbow flexed stiff, hand at mid-thigh-level, palm downwards, fingers splayed. There the hand made a light movement, balanced from the wrist, as if sketching an arpeggio, or saying goodbye to the pavement—or greeting it? An elegant little gesture, full of charm, given out of an abundant sense of style to the watching world. Now he changed his stance, and became a man kept waiting, but maintaining his dignity. He was well-dressed in a dark suit which, with a white shirt and a small grey silk bow tie that seemed positively to wish to fly away altogether, because of the energy imparted to it by his person, made a conventional enough pattern of colour—dark grey, light grey, white. But his black glossy skin, setting off this soberness, made him sparkle, a dandy—he might just as well have been wearing a rainbow.

Before he could frown up and down the street again, another young African crossed the road to join him. They greeted each other, laying their palms together, then shaking hands; but there was a conscious restraint in this which the first seemed to relish, out of his innate sense of drama, but made the second uneasy.

"Good morning, Mr. Chikwe."

"Mr. Mafente! Good morning!"

Mr. Mafente was a large smooth young man, well-dressed

too, but his clothes on him were conventional European clothes, suit, striped shirt, tie; and his gestures had none of the inbuilt delighting self-parody of the other man's. He was suave, he was dignified, he was calm; and this in spite of a situation which Mr. Chikwe's attitude (magisterial, accusing) said clearly was fraught with the possibilities of evil.

Yet these two had known each other for many years; had worked side by side, as the political situation shifted, in various phases of the Nationalist movement; had served prison sentences together; had only recently become enemies. They now (Mr. Chikwe dropped the accusation from his manner for this purpose) exchanged news from home, gossip, information. Then Mr. Chikwe marked the end of the truce by a change of pose, and said, soft and threatening: "And where is your great leader? Surely he is very late?"

"Five minutes only," said the other, smiling.

"Surely when at last we have achieved this great honour, an interview with Her Majesty's Minister, the least we can expect is punctuality from the great man?"

"I agree, but it is more than likely that Her Majesty's Minister will at the last moment be too occupied to see us, as has happened before."

The faces of both men blazed with shared anger for a moment: Mr. Chikwe even showed a snarl of white teeth.

They recovered themselves together and Mr. Mafente said: "And where is your leader? Surely what applies to mine applies to yours also?"

"Perhaps the reasons for their being late are different? Mine is finishing his breakfast just over the road there and yours is— I hear that the night before last your Mr. Devuli was observed very drunk in the home of our hospitable Mrs. James?"

"Possibly, I was not there."

"I hear that the night before that he passed out in the hotel before some unsympathetic journalists and had to be excused."

"It is possible, I was not there."

Mr. Chikwe kept the full force of his frowning stare on Mr. Mafente's bland face as he said softly: "Mr. Mafente!"

"Mr. Chikwe?"

"Is it not a shame and a disgrace that your movement, which, though it is not mine, nevertheless represents several thousand people (not millions, I am afraid, as your publicity men claim)—is it not a pity that this movement is led by a man who is never sober?"

Mr. Mafente smiled, applauding this short speech which had been delivered with a grace and an attack wasted, surely, on a pavement full of London office workers and some fat pigeons. He then observed, merely: "Yet it is Mr. Devuli who is recognised by Her Britannic Majesty's Minister?"

Mr. Chikwe frowned.

"And it is Mr. Devuli who is recognised by those honourable British philanthropic movements—the Anti-Imperialist Society, the Movement for Pan-African Freedom, and Freedom for British Colonies?"

Here Mr. Chikwe bowed, slightly, acknowledging the truth of what he said, but suggesting at the same time its irrelevance.

"I hear, for instance," went on Mr. Mafente, "that the Honourable Member of Parliament for Sutton North-West refused to have your leader on his platform on the grounds that he was a dangerous agitator with leftwing persuasions?"

Here both men exchanged a delighted irrepressible smile— that smile due to political absurdity. (It is not too much to say that it is for the sake of this smile that a good many people stay in politics.) Mr. Chikwe even lifted a shining face to the grey sky, shut his eyes, and while offering his smile to the wet heavens lifted both shoulders in a shrug of scorn.

Then he lowered his eyes, his body sprang into a shape of accusation and he said: "Yet you have to agree with me, Mr. Mafente—it is unfortunate that such a man as Mr. Devuli should be so widely accepted as a national representative, while the virtues of Mr. Kwenzi go unacknowledged."

"We all know the virtues of Mr. Kwenzi," said Mr. Mafente, and his accent on the word "we," accompanied by a deliberately cool glance into the eyes of his old friend, made Mr. Chikwe stand silent a moment, thinking. Then he said softly, testing it: "Yes, yes, yes. And—well, Mr. Mafente?"

Mr. Mafente looked into Mr. Chikwe's face, with intent, while he continued the other conversation: "Nevertheless, Mr. Chikwe, the situation is as I've said."

Mr. Chikwe, responding to the look, not the words, came closer and said: "Yet situations do not have to remain unchanged?" They looked deeply into each other's face as Mr.

Mafente enquired, almost mechanically: "Is that a threat, perhaps?"

"It is a political observation. . . . Mr. Mafente?"

"Mr. Chikwe?"

"This particular situation could be changed very easily."

"Is that so?"

"You know it is so."

The two men were standing with their faces a few inches from
each other, frowning with the concentration necessary for the
swift mental balancing of a dozen factors: so absorbed were
they that clerks and typists glanced uneasily at them, and then,
not wishing to be made uneasy, looked away again.

But here they felt approaching a third, and Mr. Mafente repeated quickly: "Is that a threat, perhaps?" in a loud voice, and
both young men turned to greet Devuli, a man ten or more years
older than they, large, authoritative, impressive. Yet even at this
early hour he had a look of dissipation, for his eyes were red
and wandering, and he stood upright only with difficulty.

Mr. Mafente now fell back a step to take his place half a pace
behind his leader's right elbow; and Mr. Chikwe faced them
both, unsmiling.

"Good morning to you, Mr. Chikwe," said Mr. Devuli.

"Good morning to you, Mr. Devuli. Mr. Kwenzi is just finishing his breakfast, and will join us in good time. Mr. Kwenzi was
working all through the night on the proposals for the new
constitution."

As Mr. Devuli did not answer this challenge, but stood, vague,
almost swaying, his red eyes blinking at the passersby, Mr.
Mafente said for him: "We all admire the conscientiousness of
Mr. Kwenzi." The "we" was definitely emphasised, the two young
men exchanged a look like a nod, while Mr. Mafente tactfully
held out his right forearm to receive the hand of Mr. Devuli.
After a moment the leader steadied himself, and said in a threatening way that managed also to sound like a grumble: "I, too,
know all the implications of the proposed constitution, Mr.
Chikwe."

"I am surprised to hear it, Mr. Devuli, for Mr. Kwenzi, who
has been locked up in his hotel room for the last week, studying
it, says that seven men working for seventy-seven years couldn't
make sense of the constitution proposed by Her Majesty's Honourable Minister."

Now they all three laughed together, relishing absurdity, until Mr. Chikwe reimposed a frown and said: "And since these proposals are so complicated, and since Mr. Kwenzi understands them as well as any man with mere human powers could, it is our contention that it is Mr. Kwenzi who should speak for our people before the Minister."

Mr. Devuli held himself upright with five fingers splayed out on the forearm of his lieutenant. His red eyes moved sombrely over the ugly façade of the Ministry, over the faces of passing people, then, with an effort, came to rest on the face of Mr. Chikwe. "But I am the leader, I am the leader acknowledged by all, and therefore I shall speak for our country."

"You are not feeling well, Mr. Devuli?"

"No, I am not feeling well, Mr. Chikwe."

"It would perhaps be better to have a man in full possession of himself speaking for our people to the Minister?" (Mr. Devuli remained silent, preserving a fixed smile of general benevolence.) "Unless, of course, you expect to feel more in command of yourself by the time of"—he brought his wrist smartly up to his eyes, frowned, dropped his wrist—"ten-thirty A.M., which hour is nearly upon us?"

"No, Mr. Chikwe, I do not expect to feel better by then. Did you not know, I have severe stomach trouble?"

"You have stomach trouble, Mr. Devuli?"

"You did not hear of the attempt made upon my life when I was lying helpless with malaria in the Lady Wilberforce Hospital in Nkalolele?"

"Really, Mr. Devuli, is that so?"

"Yes, it is so, Mr. Chiwke. Some person bribed by my enemies introduced poison into my food while I was lying helpless in hospital. I nearly died that time, and my stomach is still unrecovered."

"I am extremely sorry to hear it."

"I hope that you are. For it is a terrible thing that political rivalry can lower men to such methods."

Mr. Chikwe stood slightly turned away, apparently delighting in the flight of some pigeons. He smiled, and enquired: "Perhaps not so much political rivalry as the sincerest patriotism, Mr. Devuli? It is possible that some misguided people thought the country would be better off without you."

"It must be a matter of opinion, Mr. Chikwe."

The three men stood silent: Mr. Devuli supported himself un-obtrusively on Mr. Mafente's arm; Mr. Mafente stood waiting; Mr. Chikwe smiled at pigeons.

"Mr. Devuli?"

"Mr. Chikwe?"

"You are of course aware that if you agree to the Minister's proposals for this constitution civil war may follow?"

"My agreement to this constitution is because I wish to avert bloodshed."

"Yet when it was announced that you intended to agree, seri-ous rioting started in twelve different places in our unfortunate country."

"Misguided people—misguided by your party, Mr. Chikwe."

"I remember, not twelve months ago, that when you were accused by the newspapers of inciting to riot, your reply was that the people had minds of their own. But of course that was when you refused to consider the constitution."

"The situation has changed, perhaps?"

The strain of this dialogue was telling on Mr. Devuli: there were great beads of crystal sweat falling off his broad face, and he mopped it with the hand not steadying him, while he shifted his weight from foot to foot.

"It is your attitude that has changed, Mr. Devuli. You stood for one man, one vote. Then overnight you became a supporter of the weighted vote. That cannot be described as a situation changing, but as a political leader changing—*selling out*." Mr. Chikwe whipped about like an adder and spat these two last words at the befogged man.

Mr. Mafente, seeing that his leader stood silent, blinking, re-marked quietly for him: "Mr. Devuli is not accustomed to reply-ing to vulgar abuse, he prefers to remain silent." The two young men's eyes consulted; and Mr. Chikwe said, his face not four inches from Mr. Devuli's: "It is not the first time a leader of our people has taken the pay of the whites and has been disowned by our people."

Mr. Devuli looked to his lieutenant, who said: "Yet it is Mr. Devuli who has been summoned by the Minister, and you should be careful, Mr. Chikwe—as a barrister you should know the law: a difference of political opinion is one thing, slander is another."

"As, for instance, an accusation of poisoning?"

Here they all turned, a fourth figure had joined them. Mr.

Kwenzi, a tall, rather stooped, remote man, stood a few paces off, smiling. Mr. Chikwe took his place a foot behind him, and there were two couples, facing each other.

"Good morning, Mr. Devuli."

"Good morning, Mr. Kwenzi."

"It must be nearly time for us to go in to the Minister," said Mr. Kwenzi.

"I do not think that Mr. Devuli is in any condition to represent us to the Minister," said Mr. Chikwe, hot and threatening. Mr. Kwenzi nodded. He had rather small direct eyes, deeply inset under his brows, which gave him an earnest focussed gaze which he was now directing at the sweat-beaded brow of his rival.

Mr. Devuli blurted, his voice rising: "And who is responsible? Who? The whole world knows of the saintly Mr. Kwenzi, the hard-working Mr. Kwenzi, but who is responsible for my state of health?"

Mr. Chikwe cut in: "No one is responsible for your state of health but yourself, Mr. Devuli. If you drink two bottles of hard liquor a day, then you can expect your health to suffer for it."

"The present health of Mr. Devuli," said Mr. Mafente, since his chief was silent, biting his lips, his eyes red with tears as well as with liquor, "is due to the poison which nearly killed him some weeks ago in the Lady Wilberforce Hospital in Nkalolele."

"I am sorry to hear that," said Mr. Kwenzi mildly. "I trust the worst is over?"

Mr. Devuli was beside himself, his face knitting with emotion, sweat drops starting everywhere, his eyes roving, his fists clenching and unclenching.

"I hope," said Mr. Kwenzi, "that you are not suggesting I or my party had anything to do with it?"

"Suggest!" said Mr. Devuli. "*Suggest*? What shall I tell the Minister? That my political opponents are not ashamed to poison a helpless man in hospital? Shall I tell him that I have to have my food tasted, like an Eastern potentate? No, I cannot tell him such things—I am helpless there too, for he would say, 'Black savages, stooping to poison, what else can you expect?'"

"I doubt whether he would say that," remarked Mr. Kwenzi. "His own ancestors considered poison an acceptable political weapon, and not so very long ago either."

But Mr. Devuli was not listening. His chest was heaving, and he sobbed out loud. Mr. Mafente let his ignored forearm drop by his side, and stood away a couple of paces, gazing sombrely at his leader. After this sorrowful inspection, which Mr. Kwenzi and Mr. Chikwe did nothing to shorten, he looked long at Mr. Chikwe, and then at Mr. Kwenzi. During this three-sided silent conversation, Mr. Devuli, like a dethroned king in Shakespeare, stood to one side, his chest heaving, tears flowing, his head bent to receive the rods and lashes of betrayal.

Mr. Chikwe at last remarked: "Perhaps you should tell the Minister that you have ordered a bulletproof vest like an American gangster? It would impress him no doubt with your standing among our people?" Mr. Devuli sobbed again, and Mr. Chikwe continued: "Not that I do not agree with you—the vest is advisable, yes. The food tasters are not enough. I have heard our young hotheads talking among themselves and you would be wise to take every possible precaution."

Mr. Kwenzi, frowning, now raised his hand to check his lieutenant: "I think you are going too far, Mr. Chikwe, there is surely no need . . ."

At which Mr. Devuli let out a great groan of bitter laughter, uncrowned king reeling under the wet London sky, and said: "Listen to the good man, he knows nothing, no—he remains upright while his seconds do his dirty work, listen to the saint!"

Swaying, he looked for Mr. Mafente's forearm, but it was not there. He stood by himself, facing three men.

Mr. Kwenzi said: "It is a very simple matter, my friends. Who is going to speak for our people to the Minister? That is all we have to decide now. I must tell you that I have made a very detailed study of the proposed constitution and I am quite sure that no honest leader of our people could accept it. Mr. Devuli, I am sure you must agree with me—it is a very complicated set of proposals, and it is more than possible there may be implications you have overlooked?"

Mr. Devuli laughed bitterly: "Yes, it is possible."

"Then we are agreed?"

Mr. Devuli was silent.

"I think we are all agreed," said Mr. Chikwe, smiling, looking at Mr. Mafente, who after a moment gave a small nod, and then turned to face his leader's look of bitter accusation.

"It is nearly half past ten," said Mr. Chikwe. "In a few minutes we must present ourselves to Her Majesty's Minister."

The two lieutenants, one threatening, one sorrowful, looked at Mr. Devuli, who still hesitated, grieving, on the pavement's edge. Mr. Kwenzi remained aloof, smiling gently.

Mr. Kwenzi at last said: "After all, Mr. Devuli, you will certainly be elected, certainly we can expect that, and with your long experience the country will need you as Minister. A minister's salary, even for our poor country, will be enough to recompense you for your generous agreement to stand down now."

Mr. Devuli laughed—bitter, resentful, scornful.

He walked away.

Mr. Mafente said: "But Mr. Devuli, Mr. Devuli, where are you going?"

Mr. Devuli threw back over his shoulder: "Mr. Kwenzi will speak to the Minister."

Mr. Mafente nodded at the other two, and ran after his former leader, grabbed his arm, turned him around. "Mr. Devuli, you must come in with us, it is quite essential to preserve a united front before the Minister."

"I bow to superior force, gentlemen," said Mr. Devuli, with a short sarcastic bow, which, however, he was forced to curtail: his stagger was checked by Mr. Mafente's tactful arm.

"Shall we go in?" said Mr. Chikwe.

Without looking again at Mr. Devuli, Mr. Kwenzi walked aloofly into the Ministry, followed by Mr. Devuli, whose left hand lay on Mr. Mafente's arm. Mr. Chikwe came last, smiling, springing off the balls of his feet, watching Mr. Devuli.

"And it is just half past ten," he observed, as a flunkey came forward to intercept them. "Half past ten to the second. I think I can hear Big Ben itself. Punctuality, as we all know, gentlemen, is the cornerstone of that efficiency without which it is impossible to govern a modern state. Is it not so, Mr. Kwenzi? Is it not so, Mr. Mafente? Is it not so, Mr. Devuli?"

# Dialogue

●•●•●•●•●•●•●•●•●•●•●•●•●•●•●•●•●•●•●•●•●•●•●•●•●•●•●•●•●•●•●•●•●•●•●•●•●•●

The building she was headed for, no matter how long she delayed among the shops, stalls, older houses on the pavements, stood narrow and glass-eyed, six or eight stories higher than this small shallow litter of buildings which would probably be pulled down soon, as uneconomical. The new building, economical, whose base occupied the space, on a corner lot, of three small houses, two laundries and a grocer's, held the lives of a hundred and sixty people at forty families of four each, one family to a flat. Inside this building was an atmosphere both secretive and impersonal, for each time the lift stopped, there were four identical black doors, in the same positions exactly as the four doors on the nine other floors, and each door insisted on privacy.

But meanwhile she was standing on a corner watching an old woman in a print dress buy potatoes off a stall. The man selling vegetables said: "And how's the rheumatism today, Ada?" and Ada replied (so it was not *her* rheumatism): "Not so bad, Fred, but it's got him flat on his back, all the same." Fred said: "It attacks my old woman between the shoulders if she doesn't watch out." They went on talking about the rheumatism as if it were a wild beast that sunk claws and teeth into their bodies but which could be coaxed or bribed with heat or bits of the right food, until at last she could positively see it, a jaguarlike animal crouched to spring behind the brussels sprouts. Opposite was a music shop which flooded the whole street with selections from opera, but the street wasn't listening. Just outside the shop a couple of youngsters in jerseys and jeans, both with thin vulnerable necks and untidy shocks of hair, one dark, one fair, were in earnest conversation.

A bus nosed to a standstill; half a dozen people got off; a man passed and said: "What's the joke?" He winked, and she realised she had been smiling.

Well-being, created because of the small familiar busyness of the street, filled her. Which was of course why she had spent so long, an hour now, loitering around the foot of the tall building. This irrepressible good nature of the flesh, felt in the movement of her blood like a greeting to pavements, people, a thin drift of cloud across pale blue sky, she checked, or rather tested, by a deliberate use of the other vision on the scene: the man behind the neat arrangements of coloured vegetables had a stupid face, he looked brutal; the future of the adolescents holding their position outside the music-shop door against the current of pressing people could only too easily be guessed at by the sharply aggressive yet forlorn postures of shoulders and loins; Ada, whichever way you looked at her, was hideous, repulsive, with her loose yellowing flesh and her sour-sweat smell. Et cetera, et cetera. Oh yes, et cetera, on these lines, indefinitely, if she chose to look. Squalid, ugly, pathetic. . . . *And what of it?* insisted her blood, for even now she was smiling, while she kept the other vision sharp as knowledge. She could feel the smile on her face. Because of it, people going past would offer jokes, comments, stop to talk, invite her for drinks or coffee, flirt, tell her the stories of their lives. She was forty this year, and her serenity was a fairly recent achievement. Wrong word: it had not been tried for; but it seemed as if years of pretty violent emotion, one way or another, had jelled or shaken into a joy which welled up from inside her independent of the temporary reactions—pain, disappointment, loss—for it was stronger than they. Well, would it continue? Why should it? It might very well vanish again, without explanation, as it had come. Possibly this was a room in her life; she had walked into it, found it furnished with joy and well-being, and would walk through and out again into another room, still unknown and unimagined. She had certainly never imagined this one, which was a gift from Nature? Chance? Excess? . . . A bookshop had a tray of dingy books outside it, and she rested her hand on their limp backs and loved them. Instantly she looked at the word "love," which her palm, feeling delight at the contact, had chosen, and said to herself: Now it's enough, it's time for me to go in.

She looked at the vegetable stall, and entered the building, holding the colours of growth firm in her *heart* (word at once censored, though that was where she felt it). The lift was a brown cubicle brightly lit and glistening, and it went up fast. Instead of combatting the sink and sway of her stomach, she submitted to nausea; and arrived at the top landing giddy; and because of this willed disco-ordination of her nerves the enclosed cream-and-black glossiness of the little space attacked her with claustrophobia. She rang quickly at door 39. Bill stood aside as she went in, receiving her kiss on his cheekbone, which felt damp against her lips. He immediately closed the door behind her so that he could lean on it, using the handle for a support. Still queasy from the lift, she achieved, and immediately, a moment's oneness with him who stood giddily by the door.

But she was herself again (*herself* examined and discarded) at once; and while he still supported himself by the door, she went to sit in her usual place on a long benchlike settee that had a red blanket over it. The flat had two rooms, one very small and always darkened by permanently drawn midnight blue curtains, so that the narrow bed with the books stacked up the wall beside it was in a suffocating shadow emphasised by a small yellow glow from the bed lamp. This bedroom would have caused her to feel (he spent most of his time in it) at first panic of claustrophobia, and then a necessity to break out or let in light, open the walls to the sky. How long would her amiability of the blood survive in that? Not long, she thought, but she would never know, since nothing would make her try the experiment. As for him, this second room in which they both sat in their usual positions, she watchful on the red blanket, he in his expensive chair which looked surgical, being all black leather and chromium and tilting all ways with his weight, was the room that challenged him, because of its openness—he needed the enclosed dark of the bedroom. It was large, high, had airy white walls, a clear black carpet, the dark red settee, his machinelike chair, more books. But one wall was virtually all window: it was window from knee height to ceiling, and the squalors of this part of London showed as if from an aeroplane; the flat was so high, or seemed so, because what was beneath was so uniformly low. Here, around this room (in which, if she was alone, her spirits always spread into delight), winds clutched and shook and tore. To stand at those windows, staring straight back at sky, at wind, at cloud, at sun, was to her a release. To him, a terror. Therefore she had not gone at once to the windows; it would have destroyed the moment of equality over their shared giddiness—hers from the lift, his from illness. Though not going had another danger, that he might know why she had refrained from enjoying what he knew she enjoyed, and think her too careful of him?

He was turned away from the light. Now, perhaps conscious that she was looking at him, he swivelled the chair so he could face the sky. No, this was not one of his good days, though at first she had thought his paleness was due to his dark blue sweater, whose tight high neck isolated and presented his head. It was a big head, made bigger because of the close-cut reddish hair that fitted the back of the skull like fur, exposing a large pale brow, strong cheekbones, chin, a face where every feature strove to dominate, where large calm green eyes just held the balance with a mouth designed, apparently, only to express the varieties of torment. A single glance from a stranger (or from herself before she had known better) would have earned him: big, strong, healthy, confident man. Now, however, she knew the signs, could, after glancing around a room, say: Yes, you and you and you . . . Because of the times she had been him, achieved his being. But *they*, looking at her, would never claim her as one of them, because being him in split seconds and intervals had not marked her, could not; her nerves were too firmly grounded in normality. (*Normality?*) But she was another creature from them, another species, almost. To be envied? She thought so. But if she did not think them enviable, why had she come here, why did she always come? Why had she deliberately left behind the happiness (word defiantly held on to, despite them) she felt in the streets? Was it that she believed the pain in this room was more real than the happiness? Because of the courage behind it? She might herself not be able to endure the small dark-curtained room which would force her most secret terrors; but she respected this man who lived on the exposed platform swaying in the clouds (which is how his nerves felt it) —and from choice?

Doctors, friends, herself—everyone who knew enough to say

—pronounced: the warmth of a family, marriage if possible, comfort, other people. Never isolation, never loneliness, not the tall wind-battered room where the sky showed through two walls. But he refused commonsense. "It's no good skirting around what I am, I've got to crash right through it, and if I can't, whose loss is it?"

Well, she did not think she was strong enough to crash right through what she most feared, even though she had been born healthy, her nerves under her own command.

"Yes, but you have a choice. I haven't, unless I want to become a little animal living in the fur of other people's warmth."

(So went the dialogue.)

But he had a choice too: there were a hundred ways in which *they*, the people whom she could now recognise from their eyes in a crowd, could hide themselves. Not everyone recognised them, she would say; how many people do we know (men and women, but more men than women) enclosed in marriages, which are for safety only, or attached to other people's families, stealing (if you like) security? But theft means not giving back in exchange or kind, and these men and women, the solitary ones, do give back, otherwise they wouldn't be so welcome, so needed—so there's no need to talk about hanging on to the warmth of belly fur, like a baby kangaroo; it's a question of taking one thing, and giving back another.

"Yes, but I'm not going to pretend, I will not, it's not what I am—I can't and it's your fault that I can't."

This meant that he had been the other, through her, just as she had, through him.

"My dear, I don't understand the emotions, except through my intelligence; 'normality' never meant anything to me until I knew you. Now all right, I give in. . . ."

This was sullen. With precisely the same note of sullenness she used to censor the words her healthy nerves supplied like "love," "happiness," "myself," "health." All right, this sullenness meant: I'll pay you your due, I have to, my intelligence tells me I must. I'll even be you, but briefly, for so long as I can stand it.

Meanwhile they were—not talking—but exchanging information. She had seen X and Y and Z, been to this place, read that book.

He had read so-and-so, seen X and Y, spent a good deal of his time listening to music.

"Do you want me to go away?"

"No, stay."

This very small gift made her happy; refusing to examine the emotion, she sat back, curled up her legs, let herself be comfortable. She smoked. He put on some jazz. He listened to it inert, his body not flowing into it; there was a light sweat on his big straining forehead. (This meant he had wanted her to stay not out of warmth, but for need of somebody there. She sat up straight again, pushed away the moment's delight.) She saw his eyes were closed. His face, mouth tight in an impersonal determination to endure, looked asleep, or—

"Bill," she said quick, in appeal.

Without opening his eyes, he smiled, giving her sweetness, friendship, and the irony, without bitterness, due from one kind of creature to another.

"It's all right," he said.

The piano notes pattered like rain before a gust of wind that swept around the corner of the building. White breaths of cloud were blown across the thin blue air. The drum shook, hissed, steadily, like her blood pumping the beat, and a wild flute danced a sky sign in the rippling smoke of a jet climbing perpendicular from sill to ceiling. But what did he hear, see, feel, sitting eyes closed, palm hard on the armrest for support? The record stopped. He opened his eyes; they resolved themselves out of a knot of inward difficulty, and rested on the wall opposite him, while he put out his hand to stop the machine. Silence now.

He closed his eyes again. She discarded the cross talk in her flesh of music, wind, cloud, raindrops patterning grass and earth, and tried to see—first the room, an insecure platform in height, tenacious against storm and rocking foundations; then a certain discordance of substance that belonged to his vision; then herself, as he saw her—at once she felt a weariness of the spirit, like a cool sarcastic wink from a third eye, seeing them both, two little people, him and herself, as she had seen the vegetable seller, the adolescents, the woman whose husband had rheumatism. Without charity she saw them, sitting there together in silence on either side of the tall room, and the eye seemed to expand till it filled the universe with disbelief and negation.

Now she admitted the prohibited words "love," "joy" (et cetera), and gave them leave to warm her, for not only could she not bear the world without them, she needed them to disperse her anger against him: Yes, yes, it's all very well, but how could the play go on, how could it, if it wasn't for me, the people like me? We create you in order that you may use us, and consume us; and with our willing connivance; but it doesn't do to despise . . .

He said, not surprising her that he did, since their minds so often moved together: "You are more split than I am, do you know that?"

She thought: If I were not split, if one-half (if that is the division) were not able to move in your world, even if only for short periods, then I would not be sitting here, you would not want me.

He said: "I wasn't criticising. Not at all. Because you have the contact. What more do you want?"

"Contact," she said, looking at the cold word.

"Yes. Well, it's everything."

"How can you sit there, insisting on the things you insist on, and say it's everything?"

"If that's what you are, then *be* it."

"Just one thing or the other?"

"Yes."

"Why? It's true that what I think contradicts what I feel, but . . ."

"But?"

"All right, it's all meaningless, with my mind I know it, it's an accident, it's a freak, but all the same, everything gives me pleasure all the time. Why should it be a contradiction, why should it?"

"You don't see it as a contradiction?"

"No."

"You're living on the fat of your ancestors, the fat of their belief, that's all."

"Possibly, but why should I care?"

"A fly buzzing in the sun," he said. His smile was first wry and tender, then full of critical dislike. The criticism, the coldness of it, hurt her, and she felt tears rise. So today she could not stay long, because tears were not allowed, they were part of the other argument, or fight, a personal one, played out (or fought out), finished.

She was blinking her eyes dry, without touching them, so that he would not see she wanted to cry, when he said: "Suppose that *I* am the future?"

A long silence, and she thought: Possibly, possibly.

"It seems to me that I am. Suppose the world fills more and more with people like me, then—"

"The little flies will have to buzz louder."

He laughed, short but genuine. She thought, I don't care what you say, that laugh is stronger than anything. She sat in silence for the thousandth time, *willing* it to be stronger, feeling herself to be a centre of life, or warmth, with which she would fill this room.

He sat, smiling, but in an inert, heavy way, his limbs seeming, even from where she sat across the room, cold and confused. She went to him, squatted on her knees by his chair, lifted his hand off the black leather arm-piece, and felt it heavy with cold. It gave her hand a squeeze more polite than warm, and she gripped it firmly, willing life to move down her arm through her hand into his. Closing her eyes, she now made herself remember, with her flesh, what she had discarded (almost contemptuous) on the pavement—the pleasure from the touch of faded books, pleasure from the sight of ranked fruit and vegetables. Discoloured print, shut between limp damp cotton, small voices to be bought for sixpence or ninepence, became a pulse of muttering sound, a pulse of vitality, like the beating colours of oranges, lemons and cabbages, gold and green, a dazzle, a vibration in the eyes—she held her breath, willed, and made life move down into his hand. It lay warmer and more companionable in hers. After a while he opened his eyes and smiled at her; sadness came into the smile, then a grimness, and she kissed his cheek and went back to her place on the rough blanket. "Flies," she said.

He was not looking at her. She thought: Why do I do it? These girls who come through here for a night, or two nights, because he needs their generous naivety, give him no less. I, or one of them, it makes no difference. "I'd like a drink," she said.

He hesitated, hating her drinking at all, but he poured her one, while she said silently (feeling adrift, without resources, and cold through every particle of herself): All right, but in the days when our two bodies together created warmth (flies, if you like, but I don't feel it), I wouldn't have asked for a drink. She was thinking: And suppose it is yours that is the intoxication and not mine? when he remarked: "Sometimes when I've been alone here a couple of days I wonder if I'm not tipsy on sheer . . ." He laughed, in an intellectual pleasure at an order of ideas she was choosing not to see.

"The delight of nihilism?"

"Which of course you don't feel, ever!"

She saw that this new aggressiveness, this thrust of power and criticism (he was now moving about the room, full of energy( was in fact her gift to him; and she said, suddenly bitter: "Flies don't feel, they buzz."

The bitterness, being the note of the exchange they could not allow themselves, made her finish her few drops of liquor, making a new warmth in her stomach where she had needed a spark of warmth.

He said: "For all that, it seems to me I'm nearer the truth than you are."

The word "truth" did not explode into meaning: it sounded hard and self-defined, like a stone; she let it lie between them, setting against it the pulse that throbbed in the soft place by the ankle bone—her feet being stretched in front of her, so she could see them.

He said: "It seems to me that the disconnected like me must see more clearly than you people. Does that sound ridiculous to you? I've thought about it a great deal, and it seems to me you are satisfied with too little."

She thought: I wish he would come over here, sit by me on this blanket, and put his arm around me—that's all. That's all and that's all. She was very tired. Of course I'm tired—it's all the buzzing I have to do. . . .

Without warning, without even trying, she slipped into being him, his body, his mind. She looked at herself and thought: This little bundle of flesh, this creature who will respond and warm, lay its head on my shoulder, feel happiness—how unreal, how vulgar, and how meaningless!

She shook herself away from him, up and away from the settee. She went to the window.

"What are you doing?"

"Enjoying your view."

The sky was clear, it was evening, and far below in the streets the lights had come on, making small yellow pools and gleams on pavements where the tiny movement of people seemed exciting and full of promise. Now he got himself out of his machinelike chair and came to stand by her. He did not touch her; but he would not have come at all if she had not been there. He supported himself with one big hand on the sill and looked out. She felt him take in a deep breath. She stood silent, feeling the life ebbing and coiling along the pavements and hoping he felt it. He let out his breath. She did not look at him. He took it in again. The hand trembled, then tensed, then set solid, a big, firmly made hand, with slightly freckled knuckles—its steadiness comforted her. It would be all right. Still without looking at his face, she kissed his cheek and turned away. He went back to his chair, she resumed her place on the blanket. The room was filling with dusk, the sky was greying, enormous, distant.

"You should get curtains, at least."

"I should be tempted to keep them drawn all the time."

"Why not, then, why not?" she insisted, feeling her eyes wet again. "All right, I won't cry," she said reasonably.

"Why not? If you feel like crying."

She no longer wept. But once, and not so long ago, she had wept herself almost to pieces over him, her, their closeness which nevertheless the cold third, like a cruel king, refused to sanction. She noted that the pulse moving in her ankle had the desperate look of something fighting death; her foot in the dusk was a long way off; she felt divided, not in possession of herself. But she remained where she was, containing her fragmentation. And he held out his fist, steady, into the glimmer of grey light from the sky, watching it exactly as she looked at her own pulse, the stranger.

"For God's sake turn the light on," she said, giving in. He put out his hand, pressed down the switch; a harsh saving light filled the room.

He smiled. But he looked white again, and his forehead gleamed wet. Her heart ached for him, and for herself, who would now get up deliberately and go away from him. The ache was the hurt of exile, and she was choosing it. She sat smiling, chafing her two ankles with her hands, feeling the warmth of her breathing flesh. Their smiles met and exchanged, and now she said: "Right, it's time to go."

She kissed him again, he kissed her, and she went out, saying: "I'll ring you."

Always, when she left his door shut behind her, the black

door which was exactly the same as all the others in the building except for the number, she felt in every particle of herself how loneliness hit him when she (or anybody) left.

The street she went out into was unfamiliar to her, she felt she did not know it. The hazy purple sky that encloses London at night was savage, bitter, and the impulse behind its shifting lights was a form of pain. The roughness of the pavement, which she knew to be warm, struck cold through the soles of her sandals, as if the shadows were black ice. The people passing were hostile, stupid animals from whom she wished to hide herself. But worse than this, there was a flat, black-and-white two-dimensional jagged look to things, and (it was this that made it terrifying) the scene she walked through was a projection of her own mind; there was no life in it that belonged there save what she could breathe into it. And she herself was dead and empty, a cardboard figure in a flat painted set of streets.

She thought: Why should it not all come to an end, why not? She saw again the potato face of Fred the vegetable seller whose interest in Ada's husband's illness was only because she was a customer at his stall; she looked at Ada, whose ugly life (she was like a heave of dirty earth or some unnameable urban substance) showed in her face and movements like a visible record of thick physical living. The pathos of the adolescents did not move her; she felt disgust.

She walked on. The tall building, like a black tower, stood over her, kept pace with her. It was not possible to escape from it.

Her hand, swinging by her thigh, on its own life, suddenly lifted itself and took a leaf off a hedge. The leaf trembled: she saw it was her fingers which shook, with exhaustion. She stilled her fingers, and the leaf became a thin hard slippery object, like a coin. It was small, round, shining, a blackish-green. A faint pungent smell came to her nostrils. She understood it was the smell of the leaf which, as she lifted it to her nostrils, seemed to explode with a vivid odour into the senses of her brain so that she understood the essence of the leaf and through it the scene she stood in.

She stood fingering the leaf, while life came back. The pulses were beating again. A warmth came up through her soles. The sky's purplish orange was for effect, for the sake of self-consciously exuberant theatricality, a gift to the people living under it. An elderly woman passed, mysterious and extraordinary in

the half-light, and smiled at her. So. She was saved from dead-
ness, she was herself again. She walked slowly on, well-being
moving in her, making a silent greeting to the people passing
her. Meanwhile the dark tower kept pace with her, she felt it
rising somewhere just behind her right shoulder. It was im-
mensely high, narrow, terrible, all in darkness save for a light
flashing at its top where a man, held upright by the force of his
will, sat alone staring at a cold sky in vertiginous movement.

# Notes for a Case History

●••●••●••●••●••●••●••●••●••●••●••●••●••●••●••●••●••●••●••●••●••●••●••●••●••●••●••●••●••●••●••●••●••●••●••●••●•

**M**aureen Watson was born at
93 Nelson's Way, N.1, in 1942. She did not remember the war,
or rather, when people said "The War," she thought of Austerity:
couponed curtains, traded clothes, the half-pound of butter
swapped for the quarter of tea. (Maureen's parents preferred
tea to butter.) Further back, at the roots of her life, she *felt* a
movement of fire and shadow, a leaping and a subsidence of
light. She did not know whether this was a memory or a picture
she had formed, perhaps from what her parents had told her of
the night the bomb fell two streets from Nelson's Way and they
had all stood among piles of smoking rubble for a day and night,
watching firemen hose the flames. This feeling was not only of
danger, but of fatality, of being helpless before great impersonal
forces, and was how she most deeply felt, saw, or thought an
early childhood which the social viewer would describe perhaps
like this: "Maureen Watson, conceived by chance on an unexpected granted-at-the-last-minute leave, at the height of the
worst war in history, infant support of a mother only occasionally upheld (the chances of war deciding) by a husband she had
met in a bomb shelter during an air raid: poor baby, born into
a historical upheaval which destroyed forty million and might
very well have destroyed her."

As for Maureen, her memories and the reminiscences of her
parents made her dismiss the whole business as boring, and
nothing to do with her.

It was at her seventh birthday party she first made this clear.
She wore a mauve organdy frock with a pink sash, and her

golden hair was in ringlets. One of the mothers said: "This is the first unrationed party dress my Shirley has had. It's a shame, isn't it?" And her own mother said: "Well of course these war children don't know what they've missed." At which Maureen said: "I am not a war child." "What are you then, love?" said her mother, fondly exchanging glances.

"I'm Maureen," said Maureen.

"And I'm Shirley," said Shirley, joining cause.

Shirley Banner was Maureen's best friend. The Watsons and the Banners were better than the rest of the street. The Watsons lived in an end house, at higher weekly payments. The Banners had a sweets-paper-and-tobacco shop.

Maureen and Shirley remembered (or had they been told?) that once Nelson's Way was a curved terrace of houses. Then the ground-floor level had broken into shops: a grocer's, a laundry, a hardware, a baker, a dairy. It seemed as if every second family in the street ran a shop to supply certain defined needs of the other families. What other needs were there? Apparently none, for Maureen's parents applied for permission to the Council, and the ground floor of their house became a second grocery shop, by way of broken-down walls, new shelves, a deep-freeze. Maureen remembered two small rooms, each with flowered curtains where deep shadows moved and flickered from the two small fires that burned back to back in the centre wall that divided them. These two rooms disappeared in clouds of dust from which sweet-smelling planks of wood stuck out. Strange but friendly men paid her compliments on her golden corkscrews and asked her for kisses, which they did not get. They gave her sips of sweet tea from their canteens (filled twice a day by her mother) and made her bracelets of the spiralling fringes of yellow wood. Then they disappeared. There was the new shop. Maureen's Shop. Maureen went with her mother to the sign shop to arrange for these two words to be written in yellow paint on a blue ground.

Even without the name, Maureen would have known that the shop was connected with hopes for her future; and that her future was what her mother lived for.

She was pretty. She had always known it. Even where the shadows of fire and dark were, they had played over a pretty baby. "You were such a pretty baby, Maureen." And at the birthday parties: "Maureen's growing really pretty, Mrs. Watson." But all babies and little girls are pretty, she knew that well enough. . . . No, it was something more. For Shirley was plump, dark—pretty. Yet their parents'—or rather, their mothers'—talk had made it clear from the start that Shirley was not in the same class as Maureen.

When Maureen was ten, there was an episode of importance. The two mothers were in the room above Maureen's Shop and they were brushing their little girls' hair out. Shirley's mother said: "Maureen could do really well for herself, Mrs. Watson." And Mrs. Watson nodded, but sighed deeply. The sigh annoyed Maureen, because it contradicted the absolute certainty that she felt (it had been bred into her) about her future. Also because it had to do with the *boring* era which she remembered, or thought she did, as a tiger-striped movement of fire. *Chance:* Mrs. Watson's sigh was like a prayer to the gods of Luck; it was the sigh of a small helpless thing being tossed about by big seas and gales. Maureen made a decision, there and then, that she had nothing in common with the little people who were prepared to be helpless and tossed about. For she was going to be quite different. She was already different. Not only The War but the shadows of war had long gone, except for talk in the newspapers which had nothing to do with her. The shops were full of everything. The Banners' sweets-tobacco-paper shop had just been done up; and Maureen's was short of nothing. Maureen and Shirley, two pretty little girls in smart mother-made dresses, were children of plenty, and knew it, because their parents kept saying (apparently they did not care how tedious they were): "These kids don't lack for anything, do they? They don't know what it can be like, do they?" This, with the suggestion that they ought to be grateful for not lacking anything, always made the children sulky, and they went off to flirt their full, many-petticoated skirts where the neighbours could see them and pay them compliments.

Eleven years. Twelve years. Already Shirley had subsided into her role of pretty girl's plainer girl friend, although of course she was not plain at all. Fair girl, dark girl, and Maureen by mysterious birthright was the "pretty one," and there was no doubt in either of their minds which girl the boys would try first for a date. Yet this balance was by no means as unfair as it seemed. Maureen, parrying and jesting on street-corners, at bus stops, knew she was doing battle for two, because the boys she discarded Shirley got. Shirley got far more boys than she would have done without Maureen, who, for her part, needed—more, *had* to have—a foil. Her role demanded one.

They both left school at fifteen, Maureen to work in the shop. She was keeping her eyes open: her mother's phrase. She wore a slim white overall, pinned her fair curls up, was neat and pretty in her movements. She smiled calmly when customers said: "My word, Mrs. Watson, your Maureen's turned out, hasn't she?"

About that time there was a second moment of consciousness. Mrs. Watson was finishing a new dress for Maureen, and the fitting was taking rather long. Maureen fidgeted and her mother said: "Well, it's your capital, isn't it? You've got to see that, love." And she added the deep unconscious sigh. Maureen said: "Well don't go on about it, it's not very nice, is it?" And what she meant was not that the idea was not very nice but that she had gone beyond needing to be reminded about it; she was feeling the irritated embarrassment of a child when it is reminded to clean its teeth after this habit has become second nature. Mrs. Watson saw and understood this, and sighed again; and this time it was the maternal sigh which means: Oh dear, you are growing up fast! "Oh *Mum*," said Maureen, "sometimes you just make me tired, you do really."

Sixteen. She was managing her capital perfectly. Her assets were a slight delicate prettiness, and a dress sense that must have been a gift from God, or more probably because she had been reading the fashion magazines since practically before consciousness. Shirley had put in six months of beehive hair, pouting scarlet lips, and an air of sullen disdain; but Maureen's sense of herself was much finer. She modelled herself on film stars, but with an understanding of how far she could go— of what was allowable to Maureen. So the experience of being Bardot, Monroe, or whoever it was, refined her: she took from it an essence, which was learning to be a vehicle for other people's fantasies. So while Shirley had been a dozen stars, but really *been* them, in violent temporary transmogrifications, from which she emerged (often enough with a laugh) Shirley—plump, good-natured, and herself—Maureen remained herself through every role, but creating her appearance, like an alter ego, to meet the expression in people's eyes.

Round about sixteen, another incident: prophetic. Mrs. Watson had a cousin who worked in the dress trade, and this man, unthought of for many years, was met at a wedding. He commented on Maureen, a vision in white gauze. Mrs. Watson worked secretly on this slender material for some weeks; then wrote to him: Could Maureen be a model? He had only remote connections with the world of expensive clothes and girls, but he dropped in to the shop with frankly personal aims. Maureen in a white wrapper was still pretty, very; but her remote air told this shrewd man that she would certainly not go with him. She was saving herself; he knew that air of self-esteem very well from other exemplars. Such girls do not go out with middleaged cousins, except as a favour or to get something. However, he told Mrs. Watson that Maureen was definitely model material, but that she would have to do something about her voice. (He meant her accent, of course; and so Mrs. Watson understood him.) He left addresses and advice, and Mrs. Watson was in a state of quivering ambitions. She said so to Maureen: "This is your chance, girl. Take it." What Maureen heard was: "This is *my* chance."

Maureen, nothing if not alert for her Big Chance, for which her whole life had prepared her, accepted her mother's gift of a hundred pounds (she did not thank her; no thanks were due) and actually wrote to the school where she would be taught voice training.

Then she fell into sullen withdrawal, which she understood so little that a week had gone by before she said she must be sick—or something. She was rude to her mother: very rare, this. Her father chided her for it: even rarer. But he spoke in such a way that Maureen understood for the first time that this drive, this push, this family effort to gain her a glamorous future, came from her mother; her father was not implicated. For him, she was a pretty-enough girl, spoiled by a silly woman.

Maureen slowly understood she was not sick, she was growing up. For one thing: if she changed her "voice" so as to be good enough to mix with new people, she would no longer be part of this street, she would no longer be "our Maureen." What would she be then? Her mother knew: she would marry a duke and be whisked off to Hollywood. Maureen examined her mother's ideas for her and shrank with humiliation. She was above all no fool, but she had been very foolish. For one thing, when she used her eyes, with the scales of illusion off them, she saw that the million streets of London blossomed with girls as pretty as she. What, then, had fed the illusion in herself and in other people? What accounted for the special time, the special looks that always greeted her? Why, nothing more than that she, Maureen, because of her mother's will behind her, had carried herself from childhood as something special, destined for a great future.

Meanwhile (as she clearly saw) she was in 93 Nelson's Way, serving behind the counter of Maureen's Shop. (She now wondered what the neighbours had thought—before they got used to it—about her mother's fondness so terribly displayed.) She was dependent on nothing less than that a duke or a film producer would walk in to buy a quarter of tea and some sliced bread.

Maureen sulked. So her father said. So her mother complained. Maureen was—thinking? Yes. But more, a wrong had been done her, she knew it, and the sulking was more of a protective silence while she grew a scab over a wound.

She emerged demanding that the hundred pounds should be spent on sending her to secretarial school. Her parents complained that she could have learned how to be a secretary for nothing if she had stayed on at school another year. She said: "Yes, but you didn't have the sense to make me, did you? What did you think—I was going to sell butter like you all my life?" Unfair, on the face of it; but deeply fair, in view of what they had done to her. In their different ways they knew it. (Mr. Watson knew in his heart, for instance, that he should never have allowed his wife to call the shop "Maureen's.") Maureen went, then, to secretarial school for a year. Shirley went with her: she had been selling cosmetics in the local branch of a big chain store. To raise the hundred pounds was difficult for Shirley's parents: the shop had done badly, had been bought by a big firm; her father was an assistant in it. For that matter, it wasn't all that easy for the Watsons: the hundred pounds was the result of small savings and pinchings over years.

This was the first time Maureen had thought of the word "capital" in connection with money, rather than her own natural assets: it was comparatively easy for the Watsons to raise money, because they had capital: the Banners had no capital. (Mrs. Watson said the Banners had had *bad luck*.) Maureen strengthened her will; and as a result the two families behaved even more as if the girls would have different futures—or, to put it another way, that while the two sums of a hundred pounds were the same, the Watsons could be expected to earn more on theirs than the Banners.

This was reflected directly in the two girls' discussions about boys. Shirley would say: "I'm more easygoing than you."

Maureen would reply: "*I* only let them go so far."

Their first decisions on this almighty subject had taken place years before, when they were sixteen. Even then Shirley went further ("let them go further") than Maureen. It was put down, between them, to Shirley's warmer temperament—charitably; for both knew it was because of Maureen's higher value in the market.

At the secretarial school they met boys they had not met before. Previously boys had been from the street or the neighbourhood, known from birth, and for this reason not often gone out with—that would have been boring (serious, with possibilities of marriage). Or boys picked up after dances or at the pictures. But now there were new boys met day after day in the school. Shirley went out with one for weeks, thought of getting engaged, changed her mind, went out with another. Maureen went out with a dozen, chosen carefully. She knew what she was doing—and scolded Shirley for being so *soft*. "You're just stupid, Shirl—I mean, you've got to get on. Why don't you do like me?"

What Maureen did was to allow herself to be courted, until she agreed at last, as a favour, to be taken out. First, lunch—a word she began to use now. She would agree to go out to lunch two or three times with one boy, while she was taken out to supper (dinner) by another. The dinner partner, having been rewarded by a closed-mouth kiss for eight, ten, twelve nights, got angry or sulky or reproachful, according to his nature. He dropped her, and the lunch partner was promoted to dinner partner.

Maureen ate free for the year of her training. It wasn't that she planned it like this: but when she heard other girls say they paid their way or liked to be independent, it seemed to Maureen wrongheaded. To pay for herself would be to let herself be undervalued; even the idea of it made her nervous and sulky.

At the end of the training, Maureen got a job in a big architect's office. She was a junior typist. She stuck out for a professional office because the whole point of the training was to enable her to meet a better class of people. Of course she had already learned not to use the phrase, and when her mother did, snubbed her with: "I don't know what you mean, better *class*, but it's not much point my going into that hardware stuck upstairs in an office by myself if I can get a job where there's some life about."

Shirley went into a draper's shop where there was one other typist (female) and five male assistants.

In Maureen's place there were six architects, out most of the time, or invisible in large offices visited only by the real secretaries; a lower stratum of young men in training, designers, draftsmen, managers, et cetera, and a pool of typists.

The young men were mostly of her own class. For some months she ate and was entertained at their expense; and at each week's end there was a solemn ceremony, the high point of the week, certainly the most exciting moment in it, when she divided her wage. It was seven pounds (rising to ten in three years), and she allocated two pounds for clothes, four for the post office, and one pound for the week's odd expenses.

At the end of a year she understood two things. That she had saved something like two hundred pounds. That there was not a young man in the office who would take her out again. They regarded her, according to their natures, with resentment or with admiration for her cool management of them. But there was nothing doing *there*—so they all knew.

Maureen thought this over. If she was not taken out to meals and entertainment, she must pay for herself and save no money, or she must never go out at all. If she was going to be taken out, then she must give something in return. What she gave was an open mouth, and freedom to the waist. She calculated that because of her prettiness she could give much less than other girls.

She was using her *capital* with even more intelligence than before. A good part of her time—all not spent in the office or being taken out—went in front of her looking glass, or with the better-class fashion magazines. She studied them with formidable concentration. By now she knew she could have gone anywhere in these islands, except for her voice. Whereas, months before, she had sulked in a sort of fright at the idea of cutting herself off from her street and the neighbours, now she softened and shaped her voice, listening to the clients and the senior architects in the office. She knew her voice had changed when

Shirley said: "You're talking nice, Maureen, much nicer than me."

There was a boy in the office who teased her about it. His name was Tony Head. He was in training to be an accountant for the firm, and was very much from her own background. After having taken her out twice to lunch, he had never asked her again. She knew why: he had told her. "Can't afford you, Maureen," he said. He earned not much more than she did. He was nineteen, ambitious, serious, and she liked him.

Then she was nineteen. Shirley was engaged to one of the assistants in her shop, and would be married next Christmas.

Maureen took forty pounds out of her savings and went on a tour to Italy. It was her first time out of England. She hated it: not Italy, but the fact that half the sixty people on the tour were girls, like herself, looking for a good time, and the other half elderly couples. In Rome, Pisa, Florence, Venice, the Italians mooned over Maureen, courted her with melting eyes, while she walked past them, distant as a starlet. They probably thought she was one. The courier, a sharp, young man, took Maureen out to supper one night after he had finished his duties, and made it clear that her mouth, even if opened, and her breasts, were not enough. Maureen smiled at him sweetly through the rest of the trip. No one paid for her odd coffees, ices and drinks. On the last night of the trip, in a panic because the forty-pound investment had yielded so little, she went out with an Italian boy who spoke seven words of English. She thought him crude, and left him after an hour.

But she had learned a good deal for her forty pounds. Quietly, in her lunch hour, she went off to the National Gallery and to the Tate. There she looked, critical and respectful, at pictures, memorising their subjects, or main colours, learning names. When invited out, she asked to be taken to "foreign" films, and when she got back home wrote down the names of the director and the stars. She looked at the book page of the *Express* (she made her parents buy it instead of the *Mirror*) and sometimes bought a recommended book, if it was a best seller.

Twenty. Shirley was married and had a baby. Maureen saw little of her—both girls felt they had a new world of knowledge the other couldn't appreciate.

Maureen was earning ten pounds a week, and saved six.

There came to the office, as an apprentice architect, Stanley Hunt, from grammar school and technical college. Tallish, well-dressed, fair, with a small moustache. They took each other's measure, knowing they were the same kind. It was some weeks before he asked her out. She knew, by putting herself in his place, that he was looking for a wife with a little money or a house of her own, if he couldn't get a lady. (She smiled when she heard him using this word about one of the clients.) He tried to know clients socially, to be accepted by them as they accepted the senior architects. All this Maureen watched, her cool little face saying nothing.

One day, after he had invited a Miss Plast (Chelsea, well-off, investing money in houses) to coffee, and been turned down, he asked Maureen to join him in a sandwich lunch. Maureen thanked him delightfully, but said she already had an engagement. She went off to the National Gallery, sat on the steps, froze off wolves and pickups, and ate a sandwich by herself.

A week later, invited to lunch by Stanley, she suggested the Trattoria Siciliana, which was more expensive, as she knew quite well, than he had expected. But this meal was a success. He was impressed with her, though he knew (how could he not, when his was similar?) her background.

She was careful to be engaged for two weeks. Then she agreed to go to the pictures—"a foreign film, if you don't mind, I think the American films are just boring." She did not offer to pay, but remarked casually that she had nearly six hundred pounds in the post office. "I'm thinking of buying a little business, sometime. A dress shop. I've got a cousin in the trade."

Stanley agreed that "with your taste" it would be a sure thing.

Maureen no longer went to the Palais, or similar places (though she certainly did not conceal from Stanley that she had "once"), but she loved to dance. Twice they went to the West End together and danced at a Club which was "a nice place." They danced well together. On the second occasion she offered to pay her share, for the first time in her life. He refused, as she had known he would, but she could see he liked her for offering: more, was relieved; in the office they said she was mean, and he must have heard them. On that night, taken home lingeringly, she opened her mouth for him and let his hands go down to her thighs. She felt a sharp sexuality which made her congratulate herself that she had never, like Shirley, gone "half-way" before.

Well, of course, girls were going to get married to just anybody if they let themselves be all worked up every time they were taken out!

But Stanley was not at all caught. He was too cool a customer, as she was. He was still looking for something better.

He would be an architect in a couple of years; he would be in a profession; he was putting down money for a house; he was goodlooking, attractive to women, and with these assets he ought to do better than marry Maureen. Maureen agreed with him.

But meanwhile he took her out. She was careful often to be engaged elsewhere. She was careful always to be worth taking somewhere expensive. When he took her home, while she did not go so far as "nearly the whole way," she went "everything but"; and she was glad she did not like him better, because otherwise she would have been lost. She knew quite well she did not really like him, although her mind was clouded by her response to his hands, his moustache, his clothes and his new car.

She knew, because meanwhile a relationship she understood very well, and regretted, had grown up with Tony. He, watching this duel between the well-matched pair, would grin and drop remarks at which Maureen coloured and turned coldly away. He often asked her out—but only for a "Dutch treat"—expecting her to refuse. "How's your savings account, Maureen? I can't save, you girls get it all spent on you." Tony took out a good many girls: Maureen kept a count of them. She hated him; yet she liked him, and knew she did. She relied on him above all for this grinning, honest understanding of her: he did not approve of her, but perhaps (she felt in her heart) he was right? During this period she several times burst into tears when alone, without apparent reason; afterwards she felt that life had no flavour. Her future was narrowing down to Stanley; and at these times she viewed it through Tony Head's eyes.

One night the firm had a party for the senior members of the staff. Stanley was senior, Maureen and Tony were not. Maureen knew that Stanley had previously asked another girl to go, and when he asked herself, was uncertain whether she could make it until the very last moment: particularly as his inviting her, a junior, meant that he was trying out on the senior members the idea of Maureen as a wife. But she acquitted herself very well.

First, she was the best-looking woman in the room by far, and the best-dressed. Everyone looked at her and commented: they were used to her as a pretty typist, but tonight she was using all her will to make them look at her, to make her face and body reflect what they admired. She made no mistakes. When the party was over, Stanley and two of the younger architects suggested they drive out to London airport for breakfast, and they did. The two other girls were middleclass. Maureen kept silent for the most part, smiling serenely. She had been to Italy, she remarked, when a plane rose to go to Italy. Yes, she had liked it, though she thought the Italians were too noisy; what she had enjoyed best was the Sistine Chapel and a boat trip on the Adriatic. She hadn't cared for Venice much, it was beautiful, but the canals smelled, and there were far too many people; perhaps it would be better to go in winter? She said all this, having a right to it, and it came off. As she spoke she remembered Tony, who had once met her on her way to the National Gallery. "Getting yourself an education, Maureen? That's right, it'll pay off well, that will."

She knew, thinking it all over afterwards, that the evening had been important for her with Stanley. Because of this, she did not go out with him for a week; she said she was busy talking to her cousin about the possibilities of a dress shop. She sat in her room thinking about Stanley, and when thoughts of Tony came into her mind, irritatedly pushed them away. If she could succeed with Stanley, why not with someone better? The two architects from that evening had eyed her all the following week: they did not, however, ask her out. She then found that both were engaged to marry the girls they had been with. It was bad luck: she was sure that otherwise they would have asked her out. How to meet more like them? Well, that was the trouble— the drive to the airport was a bit of a fluke; it was the first time she had actually met the seniors socially.

Meanwhile Stanley showed an impatience in his courtship— and for the first time. As for her, she was getting on for twenty-one, and all the girls she had grown up with were married and had their first or even their second babies.

She went out with Stanley to a dinner in the West End at an Italian restaurant. Afterwards they were both very passionate. Maureen, afterwards, was furious with herself: some borderline had been crossed (she supposed she still could be called a virgin?) and now decisions would have to be made.

Stanley was in love with her. She was in love with Stanley. A week later he proposed to her. It was done with a violent moaning intensity that she knew was due to his conflicts over marrying her. She was not good enough. He was not good enough. They were secondbest for each other. They writhed and moaned and bit in the car, and agreed to marry. Her eight hundred pounds would make it easier to buy the house in a good suburb. He would formally meet her parents next Sunday.

"So you're engaged to Stanley Hunt?" said Tony.

"Looks like it, doesn't it?"

"Caught him—good for you!"

"He's caught me, more like it!"

"Have it your way."

She was red and angry. He was serious.

"Come and have a bite?" he said. She went.

It was a small restaurant, full of office workers eating on luncheon vouchers. She ate fried plaice ("No chips, please") and he ate steak-and-kidney pudding. He joked, watched her, watched her intently, said finally: "Can't you do better than that?" He meant, and she knew it, better in the sense she would use herself, in her heart: he meant *nice*. Like himself. But did that mean that Tony thought *she* was nice? Unlike Stanley? She did not think she was; she was moved to tears (concealed) that he did. "What's wrong with him then?" she demanded, casual. "What's wrong with *you*? You need your head examined." He said it seriously, and they exchanged a long look. The two of them sat looking goodbye at each other: the extremely pretty girl at whom everyone in the room kept glancing and remarking on, and the goodlooking, dark, rather fat young accountant who was brusque and solemn with disappointment in her. With love for her? Very likely.

She went home silent, thinking of Tony. When she thought of him, she needed to cry. She also needed to hurt him.

But she told her parents she was engaged to Stanley, who would be an architect. They would have their own house, in (they thought) Hemel Hempstead. He owned a car. He was coming to tea on Sunday. Her mother forgot the dukes and the film producers before the announcement ended; her father listened judiciously, then congratulated her. He had been going to a football match on Sunday, but agreed, after persuasion, that this was a good enough reason to stay home.

Her mother then began discussing, with deference to Maureen's superior knowledge, how to manage next Sunday to best advantage. For four days she went on about it. But she was talking to herself. Her husband listened, said nothing. And Maureen listened, critically, like her father. Mrs. Watson began clamouring for a definite opinion on what sort of cake to serve on Sunday. But Maureen had no opinion. She sat, quiet, looking at her mother, a largish ageing woman, her ex-fair hair dyed yellow, her flesh guttering. She was like an excited child, and it was not attractive. *Stupid, stupid, stupid*—that's all you are, thought Maureen.

As for Maureen, if anyone had made the comparison, she was "sulking" as she had before over being a model and having to be drilled out of her "voice." She said nothing but: "It'll be all right, Mum, don't get so worked up." Which was true, because Stanley knew what to expect: he knew why he had not been invited to meet her parents until properly hooked. He would have done the same in her place. He *was* doing the same: she was going to meet his parents the week after. What Mrs. Watson, Mr. Watson, wore on Sunday; whether sandwiches or cake were served; whether there were fresh or artificial flowers—none of it mattered. The Watsons were part of the bargain: what he was paying in return for publicly owning the most covetable woman anywhere they were likely to be; and for the right to sleep with her after the public display.

Meanwhile Maureen said not a word. She sat on her bed looking at nothing in particular. Once or twice she examined her face in the mirror, and even put cream on it. And she cut out a dress, but put it aside.

On Sunday Mrs. Watson laid tea for four, using her own judgement, since Maureen was too deeply in love (so she told everyone) to notice such trifles. At four Stanley was expected, and at three-fifty-five Maureen descended to the livingroom. She wore a faded pink dress from three summers before, her mother's cretonne overall used for housework, and a piece of cloth tied round her hair that might very well have been a duster. At any rate, it was faded grey. She had put on a pair of her mother's old shoes. She could not be called plain; but she looked like her own faded elder sister, dressed for a hard day's spring cleaning.

Her father, knowledgeable, said nothing: he lowered the paper, examined her, let out a short laugh, and lifted it again. Mrs. Watson, understanding at last that this was a real crisis, burst into tears. Stanley arrived before Mrs. Watson could stop herself crying. He nearly said to Mrs. Watson: "I didn't know Maureen had an older sister." Maureen sat listless at one end of the table, Mr. Watson sat grinning at the other, and Mrs. Watson sniffed and wiped her eyes between the two.

Maureen said: "Hello, Stanley, meet my father and mother." He shook their hands and stared at her. She did not meet his eyes: rather, the surface of her blue gaze met the furious, incredulous, hurt pounce of his glares at her. Maureen poured tea, offered him sandwiches and cake, and made conversation about the weather, and the prices of food, and the dangers of giving even good customers credit in the shop. He sat there, a well set up young man, with his brushed hair, his brushed moustache, his checked brown cloth jacket, and a face flaming with anger and affront. He said nothing, but Maureen talked on, her voice trailing and cool. At five o'clock, Mrs. Watson again burst into tears, her whole body shaking, and Stanley brusquely left.

Mr. Watson said: "Well, why did you lead him on, then?" and turned on the television. Mrs. Watson went to lie down. Maureen, in her own room, took off the various items of her disguise, and returned them to her mother's room. "Don't cry, Mum. What are you carrying on like that for? What's the matter?" Then she dressed extremely carefully in a new white linen suit, brown shoes, beige blouse. She did her hair and her face, and sat looking at herself. The last two hours (or week) hit her, and her stomach hurt so that she doubled up. She cried; but the tears smeared her makeup, and she stopped herself with the side of a fist against her mouth.

It now seemed to her that for the last week she had simply not been Maureen; she had been someone else. What had she done it for? Why? Then she knew it was for Tony: during all that ridiculous scene at the tea table, she had imagined Tony looking on, grinning, but understanding her.

She now wiped her face quite clear of tears, and went quietly out of the house so as not to disturb her father and mother. There was a telephone booth at the corner. She stepped, calm and aloof, along the street, her mouth held (as it always was) in an almost smile. Bert from the grocer's shop said: "Hey, Maureen, that's a smasher. Who's it for?" And she gave him the smile and the toss of the head that went with the street and said: "You, Bert, it's all for you." She went to the telephone booth thinking of Tony. She felt as if he already knew what had happened. She would say: "Let's go and dance, Tony." He would say: "Where shall I meet you?" She dialled his number, and it rang and it rang and it rang. She stood holding the receiver, waiting. About ten minutes—more. Slowly she replaced it. *He had let her down.* He had been telling her, in words and without, to be something, to stay something, and now he did not care; he had let her down.

Maureen quietened herself and telephoned Stanley.

*All right then, if that's how you want it,* she said to Tony.

Stanley answered, and she said amiably: "Hello."

Silence. She could hear him breathing, fast. She could see his affronted face.

"Well, aren't you going to say anything?" She tried to make this casual, but she could hear the fear in her voice. Oh yes, she could lose him and probably had. To hide the fear, she said: "Can't you take a joke, Stanley?" and laughed.

"A joke!"

She laughed. Not bad, it sounded all right.

"I thought you'd gone off your nut, clean off your rocker. . . ." He was breathing in and out, a rasping noise. She was reminded of his hot breathing down her neck and her arms. Her own breath quickened, even while she thought: I don't like him, I really don't like him at all . . . and she said softly: "Oh Stan, I was having a bit of a giggle, that's all."

Silence. Now, this was the crucial moment.

"Oh Stan, can't you see—I thought it was all just boring, that's all it was." She laughed again.

He said: "Nice for your parents, I don't think."

"Oh they don't mind—they laughed after you'd left, though first they were cross." She added hastily, afraid he might think they were laughing at him: "They're used to me, that's all it is."

Another long silence. With all her willpower she insisted that he should soften. But he said nothing, merely breathed in and out, into the receiver.

"Stanley, it was only a joke, you aren't really angry, are you,

Stanley?" The tears sounded in her voice now, and she judged it better that they should.

He said, after hesitation: "Well, Maureen, I just didn't like it. I don't like that kind of thing, that's all." She allowed herself to go on crying, and after a while he said, forgiving her in a voice that was condescending and irritated: "Well, all right, all right, there's no point in crying, is there?"

He was annoyed with himself for giving in; she knew that, because she would have been. He had given her up, thrown her over, during the last couple of hours: he was pleased, really, that something from outside had forced him to give her up. Now he could be free for the something better that would turn up— someone who would not strike terror into him by an extraordinary performance like this afternoon's.

"Let's go off to the pictures, Stan. . . ."

Even now, he hesitated. Then he said, quick and reluctant: "I'll meet you at Leicester Square, outside the Odeon, at seven o'clock." He put down the receiver.

Usually he came to pick her up in the car from the corner of the street.

She stood smiling, the tears running down her face. She knew she was crying because of the loss of Tony, who had let her down. She walked back to her house to make up again, thinking that she was in Stanley's power now: there was no balance between them, the advantage was all his.

# To Room Nineteen

This is a story, I suppose, about a failure in intelligence: the Rawlings' marriage was grounded in intelligence.

They were older when they married than most of their married friends: in their well-seasoned late twenties. Both had had a number of affairs, sweet rather than bitter; and when they fell in love—for they did fall in love—had known each other for some time. They joked that they had saved each other "for the real thing." That they had waited so long (but not too long) for this real thing was to them a proof of their sensible discrimination. A good many of their friends had married young, and now (they felt) probably regretted lost opportunities; while others, still unmarried, seemed to them arid, self-doubting, and likely to make desperate or romantic marriages.

Not only they, but others, felt they were well-matched: their friends' delight was an additional proof of their happiness. They had played the same roles, male and female, in this group or set, if such a wide, loosely connected, constantly changing constellation of people could be called a set. They had both become, by virtue of their moderation, their humour, and their abstinence from painful experience, people to whom others came for advice. They could be, and were, relied on. It was one of those cases of a man and a woman linking themselves whom no one else had ever thought of linking, probably because of their similarities. But then everyone exclaimed: Of course! How right! How was it we never thought of it before!

And so they married amid general rejoicing, and because of

their foresight and their sense for what was probable, nothing was a surprise to them.

Both had well-paid jobs. Matthew was a subeditor on a large London newspaper, and Susan worked in an advertising firm. He was not the stuff of which editors or publicised journalists are made, but he was much more than "a subeditor," being one of the essential background people who in fact steady, inspire and make possible the people in the limelight. He was content with this position. Susan had a talent for commercial drawing. She was humorous about the advertisements she was responsible for, but she did not feel strongly about them one way or the other.

Both, before they married, had had pleasant flats, but they felt it unwise to base a marriage on either flat, because it might seem like a submission of personality on the part of the one whose flat it was not. They moved into a new flat in South Kensington on the clear understanding that when their marriage had settled down (a process they knew would not take long, and was in fact more a humorous concession to popular wisdom than what was due to themselves) they would buy a house and start a family.

And this is what happened. They lived in their charming flat for two years, giving parties and going to them, being a popular young married couple, and then Susan became pregnant, she gave up her job, and they bought a house in Richmond. It was typical of this couple that they had a son first, then a daughter, then twins, son and daughter. Everything right, appropriate, and what everyone would wish for, if they could choose. But people did feel these two had chosen; this balanced and sensible family was no more than what was due to them because of their infallible sense for *choosing* right.

And so they lived with their four children in their gardened house in Richmond and were happy. They had everything they had wanted and had planned for.

*And yet . . .*

Well, even this was expected, that there must be a certain flatness. . . .

Yes, yes, of course, it was natural they sometimes felt like this. Like what?

Their life seemed to be like a snake biting its tail. Matthew's job for the sake of Susan, children, house, and garden—which caravanserai needed a well-paid job to maintain it. And Susan's practical intelligence for the sake of Matthew, the children, the house and the garden—which unit would have collapsed in a week without her.

But there was no point about which either could say: "For the sake of *this* is all the rest." Children? But children can't be a centre of life and a reason for being. They can be a thousand things that are delightful, interesting, satisfying, but they can't be a wellspring to live from. Or they shouldn't be. Susan and Matthew knew that well enough.

Matthew's job? Ridiculous. It was an interesting job, but scarcely a reason for living. Matthew took pride in doing it well, but he could hardly be expected to be proud of the news-paper; the newspaper he read, *his* newspaper, was not the one he worked for.

Their love for each other? Well, that was nearest it. If this wasn't a centre, what was? Yes, it was around this point, their love, that the whole extraordinary structure revolved. For ex-traordinary it certainly was. Both Susan and Matthew had moments of thinking so, of looking in secret disbelief at this thing they had created: marriage, four children, big house, gar-den, charwomen, friends, cars . . . and this *thing*, this entity, all of it had come into existence, been blown into being out of no-where, because Susan loved Matthew and Matthew loved Susan. Extraordinary. So that was the central point, the wellspring.

And if one felt that it simply was not strong enough, im-portant enough, to support it all, well whose fault was that? Certainly neither Susan's nor Matthew's. It was in the nature of things. And they sensibly blamed neither themselves nor each other.

On the contrary, they used their intelligence to preserve what they had created from a painful and explosive world: they looked around them, and took lessons. All around them, mar-riages collapsing, or breaking, or rubbing along (even worse, they felt). They must not make the same mistakes, they must not.

They had avoided the pitfall so many of their friends had fallen into—of buying a house in the country *for the sake of the children*, so that the husband became a weekend husband, a weekend father, and the wife always careful not to ask what went on in the town flat which they called (in joke) a bachelor flat. No, Matthew was a full-time husband, a full-time father, and at night, in the big married bed in the big married bedroom (which had an attractive view of the river), they lay beside each other talking and he told her about his day, and what he had done, and whom he had met; and she told him about her day (not as interesting, but that was not her fault), for both knew of the hidden resentments and deprivations of the woman who has lived her own life—and above all, has earned her own living—and is now dependent on a husband for outside interests and money.

Nor did Susan make the mistake of taking a job for the sake of her independence, which she might very well have done, since her old firm, missing her qualities of humour, balance, and sense, invited her often to go back. Children needed their mother to a certain age, that both parents knew and agreed on; and when these four healthy wisely brought up children were of the right age, Susan would work again, because she knew, and so did he, what happened to women of fifty at the height of their energy and ability, with grownup children who no longer needed their full devotion.

So here was this couple, testing their marriage, looking after it, treating it like a small boat full of helpless people in a very stormy sea. Well, of course, so it was. . . . The storms of the world were bad, but not too close—which is not to say they were selfishly felt: Susan and Matthew were both well-informed and responsible people. And the inner storms and quicksands were understood and charted. So everything was all right. Everything was in order. Yes, things were under control.

So what did it matter if they felt dry, flat? People like themselves, fed on a hundred books (psychological, anthropological, sociological), could scarcely be unprepared for the dry, controlled wistfulness which is the distinguishing mark of the intelligent marriage. Two people, endowed with education, with discrimination, with judgement, linked together voluntarily from their will to be happy together and to be of use to others—one sees them everywhere, one knows them, one even is that thing oneself: sadness because so much is after all so little. These two, unsurprised, turned towards each other with even more courtesy and gentle love: this was life, that two people, no matter how carefully chosen, could not be everything to each other. In fact, even to say so, to think in such a way, was banal; they were ashamed to do it.

It was banal, too, when one night Matthew came home late and confessed he had been to a party, taken a girl home and slept with her. Susan forgave him, of course. Except that forgiveness is hardly the word. Understanding, yes. But if you understand something, you don't forgive it, you are the thing itself: forgiveness is for what you *don't* understand. Nor had he *confessed*—what sort of word is that?

The whole thing was not important. After all, years ago they had joked: Of course I'm not going to be faithful to you, no one can be faithful to one other person for a whole lifetime. (And there was the word "faithful"—stupid, all these words, stupid, belonging to a savage old world.) But the incident left both of them irritable. Strange, but they were both bad-tempered, annoyed. There was something unassimilable about it.

Making love splendidly after he had come home that night, both had felt that the idea that Myra Jenkins, a pretty girl met at a party, could be even relevant was ridiculous. They had loved each other for over a decade, would love each other for years more. Who, then, was Myra Jenkins?

Except, thought Susan, unaccountably bad-tempered, she was (is?) the first. In ten years. So either the ten years' fidelity was not important, or she isn't. (No, no, there is something wrong with this way of thinking, there must be.) But if she isn't important, presumably it wasn't important either when Matthew and I first went to bed with each other that afternoon whose delight even now (like a very long shadow at sundown) lays a long, wandlike finger over us. (Why did I say sundown?) Well, if what we felt that afternoon was not important, nothing is important, because if it hadn't been for what we felt, we wouldn't be Mr. and Mrs. Rawlings with four children, et cetera, et cetera. The whole thing is *absurd*—for him to have come home and told me was absurd. For him not to have told me was absurd. For me to care or, for that matter, not to care, is absurd . . . and who is Myra Jenkins? Why, no one at all.

There was only one thing to do, and of course these sensible people did it; they put the thing behind them, and consciously, knowing what they were doing, moved forward into a different phase of their marriage, giving thanks for past good fortune as they did so.

For it was inevitable that the handsome, blond, attractive, manly man, Matthew Rawlings, should be at times tempted (oh, what a word!) by the attractive girls at parties she could not attend because of the four children; and that sometimes he would succumb (a word even more repulsive, if possible) and that she, a goodlooking woman in the big well-tended garden at Richmond, would sometimes be pierced as by an arrow from the sky with bitterness. Except that bitterness was not in order, it was out of court. Did the casual girls touch the marriage? They did not. Rather it was they who knew defeat because of the handsome Matthew Rawlings' marriage body and soul to Susan Rawlings.

In that case why did Susan feel (though luckily not for longer than a few seconds at a time) as if life had become a desert, and that nothing mattered, and that her children were not her own?

Meanwhile her intelligence continued to assert that all was well. What if her Matthew did have an occasional sweet afternoon, the odd affair? For she knew quite well, except in her moments of aridity, that they were very happy, that the affairs were not important.

Perhaps that was the trouble? It was in the nature of things that the adventures and delights could no longer be hers, because of the four children and the big house that needed so much attention. But perhaps she was secretly wishing, and even knowing that she did, that the wildness and the beauty could be his. But he was married to her. She was married to him. They were married inextricably. And therefore the gods could not strike him with the real magic, not really. Well, was it Susan's fault that after he came home from an adventure he looked harassed rather than fulfilled? (In fact, that was how she knew he had been *unfaithful*, because of his sullen air, and his glances at her, similar to hers at him: What is it that I share with this person that shields all delight from me?) But none of it by anybody's fault. (But what did they feel ought to be somebody's fault?) Nobody's fault, nothing to be at fault, no one to blame, no one to offer or to take it . . . and nothing wrong, either, except that Matthew never was really struck, as he wanted to be, by joy; and that Susan was more and more often threatened by emptiness. (It was usually in the garden that she was invaded by this feeling: she was coming to avoid the garden, unless the children or Matthew were with her.) There was no need to use the dramatic words "unfaithful," "forgive," and the rest: intelligence forbade them. Intelligence barred, too, quarrelling, sulking, anger, silences of withdrawal, accusations and tears. Above all, intelligence forbids tears.

A high price has to be paid for the happy marriage with the four healthy children in the large white gardened house.

And they were paying it, willingly, knowing what they were doing. When they lay side by side or breast to breast in the big civilised bedroom overlooking the wild sullied river, they laughed, often, for no particular reason; but they knew it was really because of these two small people, Susan and Matthew, supporting such an edifice on their intelligent love. The laugh comforted them; it saved them both, though from what, they did not know.

They were now both fortyish. The older children, boy and girl, were ten and eight, at school. The twins, six, were still at home. Susan did not have nurses or girls to help her: childhood is short; and she did not regret the hard work. Often enough she was bored, since small children can be boring; she was often very tired; but she regretted nothing. In another decade, she would turn herself back into being a woman with a life of her own.

Soon the twins would go to school, and they would be away from home from nine until four. These hours, so Susan saw it, would be the preparation for her own slow emancipation away from the role of hub-of-the-family into woman-with-her-own-life. She was already planning for the hours of freedom when all the children would be "off her hands." That was the phrase used by Matthew and by Susan and by their friends, for the moment when the youngest child went off to school. "They'll be off your hands, darling Susan, and you'll have time to yourself." So said Matthew, the intelligent husband, who had often enough commended and consoled Susan, standing by her in spirit during the years when her soul was not her own, as she said, but her children's.

What it amounted to was that Susan saw herself as she had been at twenty-eight, unmarried; and then again somewhere about fifty, blossoming from the root of what she had been twenty years before. As if the essential Susan were in abeyance, as if she were in cold storage. Matthew said something like this to Susan one night: and she agreed that it was true—she did feel something like that. What, then, was this essential Susan? She did not know. Put like that it sounded ridiculous, and she did not really feel it. Anyway, they had a long discussion about the whole thing before going off to sleep in each other's arms.

So the twins went off to their school, two bright affectionate children who had no problems about it, since their older brother and sister had trodden this path so successfully before them. And now Susan was going to be alone in the big house, every day of the school term, except for the daily woman who came in to clean.

It was now, for the first time in this marriage, that something happened which neither of them had foreseen.

This is what happened. She returned, at nine-thirty, from taking the twins to the school by car, looking forward to seven blissful hours of freedom. On the first morning she was simply restless, worrying about the twins "naturally enough" since this was their first day away at school. She was hardly able to contain herself until they came back. Which they did happily, excited by the world of school, looking forward to the next day. And the next day Susan took them, dropped them, came back, and found herself reluctant to enter her big and beautiful home because it was as if something was waiting for her there that she did not wish to confront. Sensibly, however, she parked the car in the garage, entered the house, spoke to Mrs. Parkes, the daily woman, about her duties, and went up to her bedroom. She was possessed by a fever which drove her out again, downstairs, into the kitchen, where Mrs. Parkes was making cake and did not need her, and into the garden. There she sat on a bench and tried to calm herself looking at trees, at a brown glimpse of the river. But she was filled with tension, like a panic: as if an enemy was in the garden with her. She spoke to herself severely, thus: All this is quite natural. First, I spent twelve years of my adult life working, *living my own life*. Then I married, and from the moment I became pregnant for the first time I signed myself over, so to speak, to other people. To the children. Not for one moment in twelve years have I been alone, had time to myself. So now I have to learn to be myself again. That's all.

And she went indoors to help Mrs. Parkes cook and clean, and found some sewing to do for the children. She kept herself occupied every day. At the end of the first term she understood she felt two contrary emotions. First: secret astonishment and dismay that during those weeks when the house was empty of children she had in fact been more occupied (had been careful to keep herself occupied) than ever she had been when the children were around her needing her continual attention. Second: that now she knew the house would be full of them, and for five weeks, she resented the fact she would never be alone. She was already looking back at those hours of sewing, cooking (but by herself) as at a lost freedom which would not be hers for five long weeks. And the two months of term which would succeed the five weeks stretched alluringly open to her—freedom. But what freedom—when in fact she had been so careful *not* to be free of small duties during the last weeks? She looked at herself, Susan Rawlings, sitting in a big chair by the window in the bedroom, sewing shirts or dresses, which she might just as well have bought. She saw herself making cakes for hours at a time in the big family kitchen: yet usually she bought cakes. What she saw was a woman alone, that was true, but she had not felt alone. For instance, Mrs. Parkes was always somewhere in the house. And she did not like being in the garden at all, because of the closeness there of the enemy—irritation, restlessness, emptiness, whatever it was—which keeping her hands occupied made less dangerous for some reason.

Susan did not tell Matthew of these thoughts. They were not sensible. She did not recognise herself in them. What should she say to her dear friend and husband, Matthew? "When I go into the garden, that is, if the children are not there, I feel as if there is an enemy there waiting to invade me." "What enemy, Susan darling?" "Well I don't know, really. . . ." "Perhaps you should see a doctor?"

No, clearly this conversation should not take place. The holidays began and Susan welcomed them. Four children, lively, energetic, intelligent, demanding: she was never, not for a moment of her day, alone. If she was in a room, they would be in the next room, or waiting for her to do something for them; or it would soon be time for lunch or tea, or to take one of them to the dentist. Something to do: five weeks of it, thank goodness.

On the fourth day of these so welcome holidays, she found she was storming with anger at the twins; two shrinking beautiful children who (and this is what checked her) stood hand in hand looking at her with sheer dismayed disbelief. This was their calm mother, shouting at them. And for what? They had come to her with some game, some bit of nonsense. They looked at each other, moved closer for support, and went off hand in hand, leaving Susan holding on to the windowsill of the livingroom, breathing deep, feeling sick. She went to lie down, telling the older children she had a headache. She heard the boy Harry telling the little ones: "It's all right, Mother's got a headache." She heard that *It's all right* with pain.

That night she said to her husband: "Today I shouted at the twins, quite unfairly." She sounded miserable, and he said gently: "Well, what of it?"

"It's more of an adjustment than I thought, their going to school."

"But Susie, Susie darling. . . ." For she was crouched weeping on the bed. He comforted her: "Susan, what is all this about? You shouted at them? What of it? If you shouted at them fifty times a day it wouldn't be more than the little devils deserve." But she wouldn't laugh. She wept. Soon he comforted her with his body. She became calm. Calm, she wondered what was wrong with her, and why she should mind so much that she might, just once, have behaved unjustly with the children. What did it matter? They had forgotten it all long ago: Mother had a headache and everything was all right.

It was a long time later that Susan understood that that night, when she had wept and Matthew had driven the misery out of her with his big solid body, was the last time, ever in their married life, that they had been—to use their mutual language —with each other. And even that was a lie, because she had not told him of her real fears at all.

The five weeks passed, and Susan was in control of herself, and good and kind, and she looked forward to the holidays with a mixture of fear and longing. She did not know what to expect. She took the twins off to school (the elder children took themselves to school) and she returned to the house determined to face the enemy wherever he was, in the house, or the garden or—where?

She was again restless, she was possessed by restlessness. She cooked and sewed and worked as before, day after day, while Mrs. Parkes remonstrated: "Mrs. Rawlings, what's the need for it? I can do that, it's what you pay me for."

And it was so irrational that she checked herself. She would put the car into the garage, go up to her bedroom, and sit, hands in her lap, forcing herself to be quiet. She listened to Mrs. Parkes moving around the house. She looked out into the garden and saw the branches shake the trees. She sat defeating the enemy, restlessness. Emptiness. She ought to be thinking about her life, about herself. But she did not. Or perhaps she could not. As soon as she forced her mind to think about Susan (for what else did she want to be alone for?), it skipped off to thoughts of butter or school clothes. Or it thought of Mrs. Parkes. She realised that she sat listening for the movements of the cleaning woman, following her every turn, bend, thought. She followed her in her mind from kitchen to bathroom, from table to oven, and it was as if the duster, the cleaning cloth, the saucepan, were in her own hand. She would hear herself saying: No, not like that, don't put that there. . . . Yet she did not give a damn what Mrs. Parkes did, or if she did it at all. Yet she could not prevent herself from being conscious of her, every minute. Yes, this was what was wrong with her: she needed, when she was alone, to be really alone, with no one near. She could not endure the knowledge that in ten minutes or in half an hour Mrs. Parkes would call up the stairs: "Mrs. Rawlings, there's no silver polish. Madam, we're out of flour."

So she left the house and went to sit in the garden where she was screened from the house by trees. She waited for the demon to appear and claim her, but he did not.

She was keeping him off, because she had not, after all, come to an end of arranging herself.

She was planning how to be somewhere where Mrs. Parkes would not come after her with a cup of tea, or a demand to be allowed to telephone (always irritating, since Susan did not care who she telephoned or how often), or just a nice talk about something. Yes, she needed a place, or a state of affairs, where it would not be necessary to keep reminding herself: In ten minutes I must telephone Matthew about . . . and at half past three I must leave early for the children because the car needs cleaning. And at ten o'clock tomorrow I must remember. . . . She was possessed with resentment that the seven hours of freedom in every day (during weekdays in the school term) were not free, that never, not for one second, ever, was she free from the pressure of time, from having to remember this or that. She could never forget herself; never really let herself go into forgetfulness.

Resentment. It was poisoning her. (She looked at this emotion and thought it was absurd. Yet she felt it.) She was a prisoner. (She looked at this thought too, and it was no good telling herself it was a ridiculous one.) She must tell Matthew—but what? She was filled with emotions that were utterly ridiculous, that she despised, yet that nevertheless she was feeling so strongly she could not shake them off.

The school holidays came round, and this time they were for nearly two months, and she behaved with a conscious controlled decency that nearly drove her crazy. She would lock herself in the bathroom, and sit on the edge of the bath, breathing deep, trying to let go into some kind of calm. Or she went up into the spare room, usually empty, where no one would expect her to be. She heard the children calling "Mother, Mother," and kept silent, feeling guilty. Or she went to the very end of the garden, by herself, and looked at the slow-moving brown river; she looked at the river and closed her eyes and breathed slow and deep, taking it into her being, into her veins.

Then she returned to the family, wife and mother, smiling and responsible, feeling as if the pressure of these people—four lively children and her husband—were a painful pressure on the surface of her skin, a hand pressing on her brain. She did not once break down into irritation during these holidays, but it was like living out a prison sentence, and when the children went back to school, she sat on a white stone near the flowing river, and she thought: It is not even a year since the twins went to school, since *they were off my hands* (What on earth did I think I meant when I used that stupid phrase?), and yet I'm a different person. I'm simply not myself. I don't understand it.

Yet she had to understand it. For she knew that this structure—big white house, on which the mortgage still cost four hundred a year, a husband, so good and kind and insightful; four children, all doing so nicely; and the garden where she sat; and Mrs. Parkes, the cleaning woman—all this depended on her, and yet she could not understand why, or even what it was she contributed to it.

She said to Matthew in their bedroom: "I think there must be something wrong with me."

And he said: "Surely not, Susan? You look marvellous— you're as lovely as ever."

She looked at the handsome blond man, with his clear, intelligent, blue-eyed face, and thought: Why is it I can't tell him? Why not? And she said: "I need to be alone more than I am."

At which he swung his slow blue gaze at her, and she saw what she had been dreading: Incredulity. Disbelief. And fear. An incredulous blue stare from a stranger who was her husband, as close to her as her own breath.

He said: "But the children are at school and off your hands."

She said to herself: I've got to force myself to say: Yes, but do you realize that I never feel free? There's never a moment I can say to myself: There's nothing I have to remind myself about, nothing I have to do in half an hour, or an hour, or two hours. . . .

But she said: "I don't feel well."

He said: "Perhaps you need a holiday."

She said, appalled: "But not without you, surely?" For she could not imagine herself going off without him. Yet that was what he meant. Seeing her face, he laughed, and opened his arms, and she went into them, thinking: Yes, yes, but why can't I say it? And what is it I have to say?

She tried to tell him, about never being free. And he listened and said: "But Susan, what sort of freedom can you possibly want—short of being dead! Am I ever free? I go to the office, and I have to be there at ten—all right, half past ten, sometimes. And I have to do this or that, don't I? Then I've got to come home at a certain time—I don't mean it, you know I don't—but if I'm not going to be back home at six I telephone you. When can I ever say to myself: I have nothing to be responsible for in the next six hours?"

Susan, hearing this, was remorseful. Because it was true. The good marriage, the house, the children, depended just as much on his voluntary bondage as it did on hers. But why did he not feel bound? Why didn't he chafe and become restless? No, there was something really wrong with her and this proved it.

And that word "bondage"—why had she used it? She had never felt marriage, or the children, as bondage. Neither had he, or surely they wouldn't be together lying in each other's arms content after twelve years of marriage.

No, her state (whatever it was) was irrelevant, nothing to do with her real good life with her family. She had to accept the fact that, after all, she was an irrational person and to live with it. Some people had to live with crippled arms, or stammers, or being deaf. She would have to live knowing she was subject to a state of mind she could not own.

Nevertheless, as a result of this conversation with her husband, there was a new regime next holidays.

The spare room at the top of the house now had a cardboard sign saying: PRIVATE! DO NOT DISTURB! on it. (This sign had been drawn in coloured chalks by the children, after a discussion between the parents in which it was decided this was psychologically the right thing.) The family and Mrs. Parkes knew this was "Mother's Room" and that she was entitled to her privacy. Many serious conversations took place between Matthew and the children about not taking Mother for granted. Susan overheard the first, between father and Harry, the older boy, and was surprised at her irritation over it. Surely she could have a room somewhere in that big house and retire into it without such a fuss being made? Without it being so solemnly discussed? Why couldn't she simply have announced: "I'm going to fit out the little top room for myself, and when I'm in it I'm not to be disturbed for anything short of fire"? Just that, and finished; instead of long earnest discussions. When she heard Harry and Matthew explaining it to the twins with Mrs. Parkes coming in—"Yes, well, a family sometimes gets on top of a woman"—she had to go right away to the bottom of the garden until the devils of exasperation had finished their dance in her blood.

But now there was a room, and she could go there when she liked, she used it seldom: she felt even more caged there than in her bedroom. One day she had gone up there after a lunch for ten children she had cooked and served because Mrs. Parkes was not there, and had sat alone for a while looking into the garden. She saw the children stream out from the kitchen and stand looking up at the window where she sat behind the curtains. They were all—her children and their friends—discussing Mother's Room. A few minutes later, the chase of children in some game came pounding up the stairs, but ended as abruptly as if they had fallen over a ravine, so sudden was the silence. They had remembered she was there, and had gone silent in a great gale of "Hush! Shhhhhh! Quiet, you'll disturb her. . . ." And they went tiptoeing downstairs like criminal conspirators. When she came down to make tea for them, they all apologised. The twins put their arms around her, from front and back, making a human cage of loving limbs, and promised it would never occur again. "We forgot, Mummy, we forgot all about it!"

What it amounted to was that Mother's Room, and her need for privacy, had become a valuable lesson in respect for other people's rights. Quite soon Susan was going up to the room only because it was a lesson it was a pity to drop. Then she took sewing up there, and the children and Mrs. Parkes came in and out: it had become another family room.

She sighed, and smiled, and resigned herself—she made jokes at her own expense with Matthew over the room. That is, she did from the self she liked, she respected. But at the same time, something inside her howled with impatience, with rage. . . . And she was frightened. One day she found herself kneeling by her bed and praying: "Dear God, keep it away from me, keep him away from me." She meant the devil, for she now thought of it, not caring if she was irrational, as some sort of demon. She imagined him, or it, as a youngish man, or perhaps a middleaged man pretending to be young. Or a man young-looking from immaturity? At any rate, she saw the young-looking face which, when she drew closer, had dry lines about mouth and eyes. He was thinnish, meagre in build. And he had a reddish complexion, and ginger hair. That was he—a gingery, energetic man, and he wore a reddish hairy jacket, unpleasant to the touch.

Well, one day she saw him. She was standing at the bottom of the garden, watching the river ebb past, when she raised her eyes and saw this person, or being, sitting on the white stone bench. He was looking at her, and grinning. In his hand was a long crooked stick, which he had picked off the ground, or broken off the tree above him. He was absent-mindedly, out of an absent-minded or freakish impulse of spite, using the stick to stir around in the coils of a blindworm or a grass snake (or some kind of snakelike creature: it was whitish and unhealthy to look at, unpleasant). The snake was twisting about, flinging its coils from side to side in a kind of dance of protest against the teasing prodding stick.

Susan looked at him, thinking: Who is the stranger? What is he doing in our garden? Then she recognised the man around whom her terrors had crystallised. As she did so, he vanished. She made herself walk over to the bench. A shadow from a branch lay across thin emerald grass, moving jerkily over its roughness, and she could see why she had taken it for a snake, lashing and twisting. She went back to the house thinking: Right, then, so I've seen him with my own eyes, so I'm not crazy after all—there *is* a danger because I've seen him. He is lurking in the garden and sometimes even in the house, and he wants to *get into me and to take me over.*

She dreamed of having a room or a place, anywhere, where she could go and sit, by herself, no one knowing where she was.

Once, near Victoria, she found herself outside a news agent that had Rooms to Let advertised. She decided to rent a room, telling no one. Sometimes she could take the train in to Richmond and sit alone in it for an hour or two. Yet how could she? A room would cost three or four pounds a week, and she earned no money, and how could she explain to Matthew that she needed such a sum? What for? It did not occur to her that she was taking it for granted she wasn't going to tell him about the room.

Well, it was out of the question, having a room; yet she knew she must.

One day, when a school term was well established, and none of the children had measles or other ailments, and everything seemed in order, she did the shopping early, explained to Mrs. Parkes she was meeting an old school friend, took the train to Victoria, searched until she found a small quiet hotel, and asked for a room for the day. They did not let rooms by the day, the manageress said, looking doubtful, since Susan so obviously was not the kind of woman who needed a room for unrespectable reasons. Susan made a long explanation about not being well, being unable to shop without frequent rests for lying down. At last she was allowed to rent the room provided she paid a full night's price for it. She was taken up by the manageress and a maid, both concerned over the state of her health . . . which must be pretty bad if, living at Richmond (she had signed her name and address in the register), she needed a shelter at Victoria.

The room was ordinary and anonymous, and was just what Susan needed. She put a shilling in the gas fire, and sat, eyes shut, in a dingy armchair with her back to a dingy window. She was alone. She was alone. She was alone. She could feel pressures lifting off her. First the sounds of traffic came very loud; then they seemed to vanish; she might even have slept a little. A knock on the door: it was Miss Townsend, the manageress, bringing her a cup of tea with her own hands, so concerned was she over Susan's long silence and possible illness.

Miss Townsend was a lonely woman of fifty, running this hotel with all the rectitude expected of her, and she sensed in Susan the possibility of understanding companionship. She stayed to talk. Susan found herself in the middle of a fantastic story about her illness, which got more and more impossible as she tried to make it tally with the large house at Richmond, well-off husband, and four children. Suppose she said instead: Miss Townsend, I'm here in your hotel because I need to be alone for a few hours, above all *alone and with no one knowing where I am.* She said it mentally, and saw, mentally, the look that would inevitably come on Miss Townsend's elderly maiden's face. "Miss Townsend, my four children and my husband are driving me insane, do you understand that? Yes, I can see from the gleam of hysteria in your eyes that comes from loneliness controlled but only just contained that I've got everything in the world you've ever longed for. Well, Miss Townsend, I don't want any of it. You can have it, Miss Townsend. I wish I was absolutely alone in the world, like you. Miss Townsend, I'm besieged by seven devils, Miss Townsend, Miss Townsend, let me stay here in your hotel where the devils can't get me. . . ." Instead of saying all this, she described her anaemia, agreed to try Miss Townsend's remedy for it, which was raw liver, minced, between whole-meal bread, and said yes, perhaps it would be better if she stayed at home and let a friend do shopping for her. She paid her bill and left the hotel, defeated.

At home Mrs. Parkes said she didn't really like it, no, not really, when Mrs. Rawlings was away from nine in the morning until five. The teacher had telephoned from school to say Joan's teeth were paining her, and she hadn't known what to say; and what was she to make for the children's tea, Mrs. Rawlings hadn't said.

All this was nonsense, of course. Mrs. Parkes's complaint was that Susan had withdrawn herself spiritually, leaving the burden of the big house on her.

Susan looked back at her day of "freedom" which had resulted in her becoming a friend of the lonely Miss Townsend, and in Mrs. Parkes's remonstrances. Yet she remembered the short blissful hour of being alone, really alone. She was determined to arrange her life, no matter what it cost, so that she could have that solitude more often. An absolute solitude, where no one knew her or cared about her.

But how? She thought of saying to her old employer: I want you to back me up in a story with Matthew that I am doing part-time work for you. The truth is that . . . But she would have to tell him a lie too, and which lie? She could not say: I want to sit by myself three or four times a week in a rented room. And besides, he knew Matthew, and she could not really ask him to tell lies on her behalf, apart from being bound to think it meant a lover.

Suppose she really took a part-time job, which she could get through fast and efficiently, leaving time for herself. What job? Addressing envelopes? Canvassing?

And there was Mrs. Parkes, working widow, who knew exactly what she was prepared to give to the house, who knew by instinct when her mistress withdrew in spirit from her responsibilities. Mrs. Parkes was one of the servers of this world, but she needed someone to serve. She had to have Mrs. Rawlings, her madam, at the top of the house or in the garden, so that she could come and get support from her: "Yes, the bread's not what it was when I was a girl. . . . Yes, Harry's got a wonderful appetite, I wonder where he puts it all. . . . Yes, it's lucky the twins are so much of a size, they can wear each other's shoes, that's a saving in these hard times. . . . Yes, the cherry jam from Switzerland is not a patch on the jam from Poland, and three times the price . . ." And so on. That sort of talk Mrs. Parkes must have, every day, or she would leave, not knowing herself why she left.

Susan Rawlings, thinking these thoughts, found that she was prowling through the great thicketed garden like a wild cat: she was walking up the stairs, down the stairs, through the rooms into the garden, along the brown running river, back, up through the house, down again. . . . It was a wonder Mrs. Parkes did not think it strange. But, on the contrary, Mrs. Rawlings could do what she liked, she could stand on her head if she wanted, provided she was *there*. Susan Rawlings prowled and muttered through her house, hating Mrs. Parkes, hating poor Miss Townsend, dreaming of her hour of solitude in the dingy respectability of Miss Townsend's hotel bedroom, and she knew quite well she was mad. Yes, she was mad.

She said to Matthew that she must have a holiday. Matthew agreed with her. This was not as things had been once—how they had talked in each other's arms in the marriage bed. He had, she knew, diagnosed her finally as *unreasonable*. She had become someone outside himself that he had to manage. They were living side by side in this house like two tolerably friendly strangers.

Having told Mrs. Parkes—or rather, asked for her permission —she went off on a walking holiday in Wales. She chose the remotest place she knew of. Every morning the children telephoned her before they went off to school, to encourage and support her, just as they had over Mother's Room. Every evening she telephoned them, spoke to each child in turn, and then to Matthew. Mrs. Parkes, given permission to telephone for instructions or advice, did so every day at lunchtime. When, as happened three times, Mrs. Rawlings was out on the mountainside, Mrs. Parkes asked that she should ring back at such-and-such a time, for she would not be happy in what she was doing without Mrs. Rawlings' blessing.

Susan prowled over wild country with the telephone wire holding her to her duty like a leash. The next time she must telephone, or wait to be telephoned, nailed her to her cross. The mountains themselves seemed trammelled by her unfreedom. Everywhere on the mountains, where she met no one at all, from breakfast time to dusk, excepting sheep, or a shepherd, she came face to face with her own craziness, which might attack her in the broadest valleys, so that they seemed too small, or on a mountain top from which she could see a hundred other mountains and valleys, so that they seemed too low, too small, with the sky pressing down too close. She would stand gazing at a hillside brilliant with ferns and bracken, jewelled with running water, and see nothing but her devil, who lifted inhuman eyes at her from where he leaned negligently on a rock, switching at his ugly yellow boots with a leafy twig.

She returned to her home and family, with the Welsh emptiness at the back of her mind like a promise of freedom.

She told her husband she wanted to have an *au pair* girl.

They were in their bedroom, it was late at night, the children slept. He sat, shirted and slippered, in a chair by the window, looking out. She sat brushing her hair and watching him in the mirror. A time-hallowed scene in the connubial bedroom. He said nothing, while she heard the arguments coming into his mind, only to be rejected because every one was *reasonable*.

"It seems strange to get one now; after all, the children are in school most of the day. Surely the time for you to have help was when you were stuck with them day and night. Why don't you ask Mrs. Parkes to cook for you? She's even offered to—I can understand if you are tired of cooking for six people. But you know that an *au pair* girl means all kinds of problems; it's not like having an ordinary char in during the day. . . ."

Finally he said carefully: "Are you thinking of going back to work?"

"No," she said, "no, not really." She made herself sound vague, rather stupid. She went on brushing her black hair and peering at herself so as to be oblivious of the short uneasy glances her Matthew kept giving her. "Do you think we can't afford it?" she went on vaguely, not at all the old efficient Susan who knew exactly what they could afford.

"It's not that," he said, looking out of the window at dark trees, so as not to look at her. Meanwhile she examined a round, candid, pleasant face with clear dark brows and clear grey eyes. A sensible face. She brushed thick healthy black hair and thought: Yet that's the reflection of a madwoman. How very strange! Much more to the point if what looked back at me was the gingery green-eyed demon with his dry meagre smile. . . . Why wasn't Matthew agreeing? After all, what else could he do? She was breaking her part of the bargain and there was no way of forcing her to keep it: that her spirit, her soul, should live in this house, so that the people in it could grow like plants in water, and Mrs. Parkes remain content in their service. In return for this, he would be a good loving husband, and responsible towards the children. Well, nothing like this had been true of either of them for a long time. He did his duty, perfunctorily; she did not even pretend to do hers. And he had become like other husbands, with his real life in his work and the people he met there, and very likely a serious affair. All this was her fault.

At last he drew heavy curtains, blotting out the trees, and turned to force her attention: "Susan, are you really sure we need a girl?" But she would not meet his appeal at all. She was running the brush over her hair again and again, lifting fine black clouds in a small hiss of electricity. She was peering in and smiling as if she were amused at the clinging hissing hair that followed the brush.

"Yes, I think it would be a good idea, on the whole," she said, with the cunning of a madwoman evading the real point.

In the mirror she could see her Matthew lying on his back, his hands behind his head, staring upwards, his face sad and hard. She felt her heart (the old heart of Susan Rawlings) soften and call out to him. But she set it to be indifferent.

He said: "Susan, the children?" It was an appeal that *almost* reached her. He opened his arms, lifting them palms up, empty. She had only to run across and fling herself into them, onto his hard, warm chest, and melt into herself, into Susan. But she could not. She would not see his lifted arms. She said vaguely: "Well, surely it'll be even better for them? We'll get a French or a German girl and they'll learn the language."

In the dark she lay beside him, feeling frozen, a stranger. She felt as if Susan had been spirited away. She disliked very much this woman who lay here, cold and indifferent beside a suffering man, but she could not change her.

Next morning she set about getting a girl, and very soon came Sophie Traub from Hamburg, a girl of twenty, laughing, healthy, blue-eyed, intending to learn English. Indeed, she already spoke a good deal. In return for a room—"Mother's Room" —and her food, she undertook to do some light cooking, and to be with the children when Mrs. Rawlings asked. She was an intelligent girl and understood perfectly what was needed. Susan said: "I go off sometimes, for the morning or for the day—well, sometimes the children run home from school, or they ring up, or a teacher rings up. I should be here, really. And there's the daily woman. . . ." And Sophie laughed her deep fruity *Fräulein's* laugh, showed her fine white teeth and her dimples, and said: "You want some person to play mistress of the house sometimes, not so?"

"Yes, that is just so," said Susan, a bit dry, despite herself, thinking in secret fear how easy it was, how much nearer to the end she was than she thought. Healthy Fräulein Traub's instant understanding of their position proved this to be true.

The *au pair* girl, because of her own commonsense, or (as Susan said to herself, with her new inward shudder) because she had been *chosen* so well by Susan, was a success with everyone, the children liking her, Mrs. Parkes forgetting almost at once that she was German, and Matthew finding her "nice to have around the house." For he was now taking things as they came, from the surface of life, withdrawn both as a husband and a father from the household.

One day Susan saw how Sophie and Mrs. Parkes were talking and laughing in the kitchen, and she announced that she would be away until tea time. She knew exactly where to go and what she must look for. She took the District Line to South Kensington, changed to the Circle, got off at Paddington, and walked around looking at the smaller hotels until she was satisfied with one which had FRED'S HOTEL painted on windowpanes that needed cleaning. The facade was a faded shiny yellow, like unhealthy skin. A door at the end of a passage said she must knock; she did, and Fred appeared. He was not at all attractive, not in any way, being fattish, and run-down, and wearing a tasteless striped suit. He had small sharp eyes in a white creased face, and was quite prepared to let Mrs. Jones (she chose the farcical name deliberately, staring him out) have a room three days a week from ten until six. Provided of course that she paid in advance each time she came? Susan produced fifteen shillings (no price had been set by him) and held it out, still fixing him with a bold unblinking challenge she had not known until then she could use at will. Looking at her still, he took up a ten-shilling note from her palm between thumb and forefinger, fingered it; then shuffled up two half-crowns, held out his own palm with these bits of money displayed thereon, and let his gaze lower broodingly at them. They were standing in the passage, a red-shaded light above, bare boards beneath, and a strong smell of floor polish rising about them. He shot his gaze up at her over the still-extended palm, and smiled as if to say: What

do you take me for? "I shan't," said Susan, "be using this room
for the purposes of making money." He still waited. She added
another five shillings, at which he nodded and said: "You pay,
and I ask no questions." "Good," said Susan. He now went past
her to the stairs, and there waited a moment: the light from the
street door being in her eyes, she lost sight of him momentarily.
Then she saw a sober-suited, white-faced, white-balding little
man trotting up the stairs like a waiter, and she went after him.
They proceeded in utter silence up the stairs of this house where
no questions were asked—Fred's Hotel, which could afford the
freedom for its visitors that poor Miss Townsend's hotel could
not. The room was hideous. It had a single window, with thin
green brocade curtains, a three-quarter bed that had a cheap
green satin bedspread on it, a fireplace with a gas fire and a
shilling meter by it, a chest of drawers, and a green wicker armchair.

"Thank you," said Susan, knowing that Fred (if this was Fred,
and not George, or Herbert or Charlie) was looking at her, not
so much with curiosity, an emotion he would not own to, for
professional reasons, but with a philosophical sense of what
was appropriate. Having taken her money and shown her up
and agreed to everything, he was clearly disapproving of her for
coming here. She did not belong here at all, so his look said. (But
she knew, already, how very much she did belong: the room had
been waiting for her to join it.) "Would you have me called at
five o'clock, please?" and he nodded and went downstairs.

It was twelve in the morning. She was free. She sat in the
armchair, she simply sat, she closed her eyes and sat and let
herself be alone. She was alone and no one knew where she was.
When a knock came on the door she was annoyed, and prepared
to show it: but it was Fred himself; it was five o'clock and he
was calling her as ordered. He flicked his sharp little eyes over
the room—bed, first. It was undisturbed. She might never have
been in the room at all. She thanked him, said she would be returning the day after tomorrow, and left. She was back home
in time to cook supper, to put the children to bed, to cook a
second supper for her husband and herself later. And to welcome Sophie back from the pictures where she had gone with
a friend. All these things she did cheerfully, willingly. But she
was thinking all the time of the hotel room; she was longing for
it with her whole being.

Three times a week. She arrived promptly at ten, looked Fred in the eyes, gave him twenty shillings, followed him up the stairs, went into the room, and shut the door on him with gentle firmness. For Fred, disapproving of her being here at all, was quite ready to let friendship, or at least acquaintanceship, follow his disapproval, if only she would let him. But he was content to go off on her dismissing nod, with the twenty shillings in his hand.

She sat in the armchair and shut her eyes.

What did she *do* in the room? Why, nothing at all. From the chair, when it had rested her, she went to the window, stretching her arms, smiling, treasuring her anonymity, to look out. She was no longer Susan Rawlings, mother of four, wife of Matthew, employer of Mrs. Parkes and of Sophie Traub, with these and those relations with friends, school-teachers, tradesmen. She no longer was mistress of the big white house and garden, owning clothes suitable for this and that activity or occasion. She was Mrs. Jones, and she was alone, and she had no past and no future. Here I am, she thought, after all these years of being married and having children and playing those roles of responsibility—and I'm just the same. Yet there have been times I thought that nothing existed of me except the roles that went with being Mrs. Matthew Rawlings. Yes, here I am, and if I never saw any of my family again, here I would still be . . . how very strange that is! And she leaned on the sill, and looked into the street, loving the men and women who passed, because she did not know them. She looked at the downtrodden buildings over the street, and at the sky, wet and dingy, or sometimes blue, and she felt she had never seen buildings or sky before. And then she went back to the chair, empty, her mind a blank. Sometimes she talked aloud, saying nothing—an exclamation, meaningless, followed by a comment about the floral pattern on the thin rug, or a stain on the green satin coverlet. For the most part, she wool-gathered—what word is there for it?—brooded, wandered, simply went dark, feeling emptiness run deliciously through her veins like the movement of her blood.

This room had become more her own than the house she lived in. One morning she found Fred taking her a flight higher than usual. She stopped, refusing to go up, and demanded her usual room, Number 19. "Well, you'll have to wait half an hour, then," he said. Willingly she descended to the dark disinfectant-smelling hall, and sat waiting until the two, man and woman, came down the stairs, giving her swift indifferent glances before they hurried out into the street, separating at the door. She went up to the room, *her* room, which they had just vacated. It was no less hers, though the windows were set wide open, and a maid was straightening the bed as she came in.

After these days of solitude, it was both easy to play her part as mother and wife, and difficult—because it was so easy: she felt an imposter. She felt as if her shell moved here, with her family, answering to Mummy, Mother, Susan, Mrs. Rawlings. She was surprised no one saw through her, that she wasn't turned out of doors, as a fake. On the contrary, it seemed the children loved her more; Matthew and she "got on" pleasantly, and Mrs. Parkes was happy in her work under (for the most part, it must be confessed) Sophie Traub. At night she lay beside her husband, and they made love again, apparently just as they used to, when they were really married. But she, Susan, or the being who answered so readily and improbably to the name of Susan, was not there: she was in Fred's Hotel, in Paddington, waiting for the easing hours of solitude to begin.

Soon she made a new arrangement with Fred and with Sophie. It was for five days a week. As for the money, five pounds, she simply asked Matthew for it. She saw that she was not even frightened he might ask what for: he would give it to her, she knew that, and yet it was terrifying it could be so, for this close couple, these partners, had once known the destination of every shilling they must spend. He agreed to give her five pounds a week. She asked for just so much, not a penny more. He sounded indifferent about it. It was as if he were paying her, she thought: *paying her off*—yes, that was it. Terror came back for a moment when she understood this, but she stilled it: things had gone too far for that. Now, every week, on Sunday nights, he gave her five pounds, turning away from her before their eyes could meet on the transaction. As for Sophie Traub, she was to be somewhere in or near the house until six at night, after which she was free. She was not to cook, or to clean; she was simply to be there. So she gardened or sewed, and asked friends in, being a person who was bound to have a lot of friends. If the children were sick, she nursed them. If teachers telephoned, she answered them sensibly. For the five daytimes in the school week, she was altogether the mistress of the house.

One night in the bedroom, Matthew asked: "Susan, I don't want to interfere—don't think that, please—but are you sure you are well?"

She was brushing her hair at the mirror. She made two more strokes on either side of her head, before she replied: "Yes, dear, I am sure I am well."

He was again lying on his back, his blond head on his hands, his elbows angled up and part-concealing his face. He said: "Then Susan, I have to ask you this question, though you must understand, I'm not putting any sort of pressure on you." (Susan heard the word "pressure" with dismay, because this was inevitable; of course she could not go on like this.) "Are things going to go on like this?"

"Well," she said, going vague and bright and idiotic again, so as to escape: "Well, I don't see why not."

He was jerking his elbows up and down, in annoyance or in pain, and, looking at him, she saw he had got thin, even gaunt; and restless angry movements were not what she remembered of him. He said: "Do you want a divorce, is that it?"

At this, Susan only with the greatest difficulty stopped herself from laughing: she could hear the bright bubbling laughter she *would* have emitted, had she let herself. He could only mean one thing: she had a lover, and that was why she spent her days in London, as lost to him as if she had vanished to another continent.

Then the small panic set in again: she understood that he hoped she did have a lover, he was begging her to say so, because otherwise it would be too terrifying.

She thought this out as she brushed her hair, watching the fine black stuff fly up to make its little clouds of electricity, hiss, hiss, hiss. Behind her head, across the room, was a blue wall. She realised she was absorbed in watching the black hair making shapes against the blue. She should be answering him. "Do *you* want a divorce, Matthew?"

He said: "That surely isn't the point, is it?"

"You brought it up, I didn't," she said, brightly, suppressing meaningless tinkling laughter.

Next day she asked Fred: "Have enquiries been made for me?"

He hesitated, and she said: "I've been coming here a year now. I've made no trouble, and you've been paid every day. I have a right to be told."

"As a matter of fact, Mrs. Jones, a man did come asking."

"A man from a detective agency?"

"Well, he could have been, couldn't he?"

"I was asking you. . . . Well, what did you tell him?"

"I told him a Mrs. Jones came every weekday from ten until five or six and stayed in Number 19 by herself."

"Describing me?"

"Well, Mrs. Jones, I had no alternative. Put yourself in my place."

"By rights I should deduct what that man gave you for the information."

He raised shocked eyes: she was not the sort of person to make jokes like this! Then he chose to laugh: a pinkish wet slit appeared across his white crinkled face; his eyes positively begged her to laugh, otherwise he might lose some money. She remained grave, looking at him.

He stopped laughing and said: "You want to go up now?"—returning to the familiarity, the comradeship, of the country where no questions are asked, on which (and he knew it) she depended completely.

She went up to sit in her wicker chair. But it was not the same. Her husband had searched her out. (The world had searched her out.) The pressures were on her. She was here with his connivance. He might walk in at any moment, here, into Room 19. She imagined the report from the detective agency: "A woman calling herself Mrs. Jones, fitting the description of your wife (et cetera, et cetera, et cetera), stays alone all day in Room No. 19. She insists on this room, waits for it if it is engaged. As far as the proprietor knows, she receives no visitors there, male or female." A report something on these lines Matthew must have received.

Well, of course he was right: things couldn't go on like this. He had put an end to it all simply by sending the detective after her.

She tried to shrink herself back into the shelter of the room, a snail pecked out of its shell and trying to squirm back. But the peace of the room had gone. She was trying consciously to revive it, trying to let go into the dark creative trance (or whatever it was) that she had found there. It was no use, yet she craved for it, she was as ill as a suddenly deprived addict.

Several times she returned to the room, to look for herself there, but instead she found the unnamed spirit of restlessness, a pricking fevered hunger for movement, an irritable self-consciousness that made her brain feel as if it had coloured lights going on and off inside it. Instead of the soft dark that had been the room's air, were now waiting for her demons that made her dash blindly about, muttering words of hate; she was impelling herself from point to point like a moth dashing itself against a windowpane, sliding to the bottom, fluttering off on broken wings, then crashing into the invisible barrier again. And again and again. Soon she was exhausted, and she told Fred that for a while she would not be needing the room, she was going on holiday. Home she went, to the big white house by the river. The middle of a weekday, and she felt guilty at returning to her own home when not expected. She stood unseen, looking in at the kitchen window. Mrs. Parkes, wearing a discarded floral overall of Susan's, was stooping to slide something into the oven. Sophie, arms folded, was leaning her back against a cupboard and laughing at some joke made by a girl not seen before by Susan—a dark foreign girl, Sophie's visitor. In an armchair Molly, one of the twins, lay curled, sucking her thumb and watching the grownups. She must have some sickness, to be kept from school. The child's listless face, the dark circles under her eyes, hurt Susan: Molly was looking at the three grownups working and talking in exactly the same way Susan looked at the four through the kitchen window: she was remote, shut off from them.

But then, just as Susan imagined herself going in, picking up the little girl, and sitting in an armchair with her, stroking her probably heated forehead, Sophie did just that: she had been standing on one leg, the other knee flexed, its foot set against the wall. Now she let her foot in its ribbon-tied red shoe slide down the wall, stood solid on two feet, clapping her hands before and behind her, and sang a couple of lines in German, so that the child lifted her heavy eyes at her and began to smile.

Then she walked, or rather skipped, over to the child, swung her up, and let her fall into her lap at the same moment she sat herself. She said "Hopla! Hopla! Molly . . ." and began stroking the dark untidy young head that Molly laid on her shoulder for comfort.

*Well.* . . . Susan blinked the tears of farewell out of her eyes, and went quietly up through the house to her bedroom. There she sat looking at the river through the trees. She felt at peace, but in a way that was new to her. She had no desire to move, to talk, to do anything at all. The devils that had haunted the house, the garden, were not there; but she knew it was because her soul was in Room 19 in Fred's Hotel; she was not really here at all. It was a sensation that should have been frightening: to sit at her own bedroom window, listening to Sophie's rich young voice sing German nursery songs to her child, listening to Mrs. Parkes clatter and move below, and to know that all this had nothing to do with her: she was already out of it.

Later, she made herself go down and say she was home: it was unfair to be here unannounced. She took lunch with Mrs. Parkes, Sophie, Sophie's Italian friend Maria, and her daughter Molly, and felt like a visitor.

A few days later, at bedtime, Matthew said: "Here's your five pounds," and pushed them over at her. Yet he must have known she had not been leaving the house at all.

She shook her head, gave it back to him, and said, in explanation, not in accusation: "As soon as you knew where I was, there was no point."

He nodded, not looking at her. He was turned away from her: thinking, she knew, how best to handle this wife who terrified him.

He said: "I wasn't trying to . . . It's just that I was worried."

"Yes, I know."

"I must confess that I was beginning to wonder . . ."

"You thought I had a lover?"

"Yes, I am afraid I did."

She knew that he wished she had. She sat wondering how to say: "For a year now I've been spending all my days in a very sordid hotel room. It's the place where I'm happy. In fact, without it I don't exist." She heard herself saying this, and understood how terrified he was that she might. So instead she said: "Well, perhaps you're not far wrong."

Probably Matthew would think the hotel proprietor lied: he would want to think so.

"Well," he said, and she could hear his voice spring up, so to speak, with relief, "in that case I must confess I've got a bit of an affair on myself."

She said, detached and interested: "Really? Who is she?" and saw Matthew's startled look because of this reaction.

"It's Phil. Phil Hunt."

She had known Phil Hunt well in the old unmarried days. She was thinking: No, she won't do, she's too neurotic and difficult. She's never been happy yet. Sophie's much better. Well, Matthew will see that himself, as sensible as he is.

This line of thought went on in silence, while she said aloud: "It's no point telling you about mine, because you don't know him."

Quick, quick, invent, she thought. Remember how you invented all that nonsense for Miss Townsend.

She began slowly, careful not to contradict herself: "His name is Michael" (*Michael What?*)—"Michael Plant." (What a silly name!) "He's rather like you—in looks, I mean." And indeed, she could imagine herself being touched by no one but Matthew himself. "He's a publisher." (Really? Why?) "He's got a wife already and two children."

She brought out this fantasy, proud of herself.

Matthew said: "Are you two thinking of marrying?"

She said, before she could stop herself: "Good God, *no!*"

She realised, if Matthew wanted to marry Phil Hunt, that this was too emphatic, but apparently it was all right, for his voice sounded relieved as he said: "It is a bit impossible to imagine oneself married to anyone else, isn't it?" With which he pulled her to him, so that her head lay on his shoulder. She turned her face into the dark of his flesh, and listened to the blood pounding through her ears saying: I am alone, I am alone, I am alone.

In the morning Susan lay in bed while he dressed.

He had been thinking things out in the night, because now he said: "Susan, why don't we make a foursome?"

Of course, she said to herself, of course he would be bound to say that. If one is sensible, if one is reasonable, if one never allows oneself a base thought or an envious emotion, naturally one says: Let's make a foursome!

"Why not?" she said.

"We could all meet for lunch. I mean, it's ridiculous, you sneaking off to filthy hotels, and me staying late at the office, and all the lies everyone has to tell."

What on earth did I say his name was?—she panicked, then said: "I think it's a good idea, but Michael is away at the moment. When he comes back, though—and I'm sure you two would like each other."

"He's away, is he? So that's why you've been . . ." Her husband put his hand to the knot of his tie in a gesture of male coquetry she would not before have associated with him; and he bent to kiss her cheek with the expression that goes with the words: Oh you naughty little puss! And she felt its answering look, naughty and coy, come onto her face.

Inside she was dissolving in horror at them both, at how far they had both sunk from honesty of emotion.

So now she was saddled with a lover, and he had a mistress! How ordinary, how reassuring, how jolly! And now they would make a foursome of it, and go about to theatres and restaurants. After all, the Rawlings could well afford that sort of thing, and presumably the publisher Michael Plant could afford to do himself and his mistress quite well. No, there was nothing to stop the four of them developing the most intricate relationship of civilised tolerance, all enveloped in a charming afterglow of autumnal passion. Perhaps they would all go off on holidays together? She had known people who did. Or perhaps Matthew would draw the line there? Why should he, though, if he was capable of talking about "foursomes" at all?

She lay in the empty bedroom, listening to the car drive off with Matthew in it, off to work. Then she heard the children clattering off to school to the accompaniment of Sophie's cheerfully ringing voice. She slid down into the hollow of the bed, for shelter against her own irrelevance. And she stretched out her hand to the hollow where her husband's body had lain, but found no comfort there: he was not her husband. She curled herself up in a small tight ball under the clothes: she could stay here all day, all week, indeed, all her life.

But in a few days she must produce Michael Plant, and—but how? She must presumably find some agreeable man prepared to impersonate a publisher called Michael Plant. And in return for which she would—what? Well, for one thing they would make love. The idea made her want to cry with sheer exhaustion.

Oh no, she had finished with all that—the proof of it was that the words "make love," or even imagining it, trying hard to revive no more than the pleasures of sensuality, let alone affection, or love, made her want to run away and hide from the sheer effort of the thing. . . . Good Lord, why make love at all? Why make love with anyone? Or if you are going to make love, what does it matter who with? Why shouldn't she simply walk into the street, pick up a man and have a roaring sexual affair with him? Why not? Or even with Fred? What difference did it make?

But she had let herself in for it—an interminable stretch of time with a lover, called Michael, as part of a gallant civilised foursome. Well, she could not, and she would not.

She got up, dressed, went down to find Mrs. Parkes, and asked her for the loan of a pound, since Matthew, she said, had forgotten to leave her money. She exchanged with Mrs. Parkes variations on the theme that husbands are all the same, they don't think, and without saying a word to Sophie, whose voice could be heard upstairs from the telephone, walked to the underground, travelled to South Kensington, changed to the Inner Circle, got out at Paddington, and walked to Fred's Hotel. There she told Fred that she wasn't going on holiday after all, she needed the room. She would have to wait an hour, Fred said. She went to a busy tearoom-cum-restaurant around the corner, and sat watching the people flow in and out the door that kept swinging open and shut, watched them mingle and merge, and separate, felt her being flow into them, into their movement. When the hour was up, she left a half-crown for her pot of tea, and left the place without looking back at it, just as she had left her house, the big, beautiful white house, without another look, but silently dedicating it to Sophie. She returned to Fred, received the key of Number 19, now free, and ascended the grimy stairs slowly, letting floor after floor fall away below her, keeping her eyes lifted, so that floor after floor descended jerkily to her level of vision, and fell away out of sight.

Number 19 was the same. She saw everything with an acute, narrow, checking glance: the cheap shine of the satin spread, which had been replaced carelessly after the two bodies had finished their convulsions under it; a trace of powder on the glass that topped the chest of drawers; an intense green shade in a fold of the curtain. She stood at the window, looking down, watching people pass and pass and pass until her mind went dark from the constant movement. Then she sat in the wicker chair, letting herself go slack. But she had to be careful, because she did not want, today, to be surprised by Fred's knock at five o'clock.

The demons were not here. They had gone forever, because she was buying her freedom from them. She was slipping already into the dark fructifying dream that seemed to caress her inwardly, like the movement of her blood . . . but she had to think about Matthew first. Should she write a letter for the coroner? But what should she say? She would like to leave him with the look on his face she had seen this morning—banal, admittedly, but at least confidently healthy. Well, that was impossible, one did not look like that with a wife dead from suicide. But how to leave him believing she was dying because of a man —because of the fascinating publisher Michael Plant? Oh, how ridiculous! How absurd! How humiliating! But she decided not to trouble about it, simply not to think about the living. If he wanted to believe she had a lover, he would believe it. And he *did* want to believe it. Even when he had found out that there was no publisher in London called Michael Plant, he would think: Oh poor Susan, she was afraid to give me his real name.

And what did it matter whether he married Phil Hunt or Sophie? Though it ought to be Sophie, who was already the mother of those children . . . and what hypocrisy to sit here worrying about the children, when she was going to leave them because she had not got the energy to stay.

She had about four hours. She spent them delightfully, darkly, sweetly, letting herself slide gently, gently, to the edge of the river. Then, with hardly a break in her consciousness, she got up, pushed the thin rug against the door, made sure the windows were tight shut, put two shillings in the meter, and turned on the gas. For the first time since she had been in the room she lay on the hard bed that smelled stale, that smelled of sweat and sex.

She lay on her back on the green satin cover, but her legs were chilly. She got up, found a blanket folded in the bottom of the chest of drawers, and carefully covered her legs with it. She was quite content lying there, listening to the faint soft hiss of the gas that poured into the room, into her lungs, into her brain, as she drifted off into the dark river.

# An Old Woman
# and Her Cat

Her name was Hetty, and she was born with the twentieth century. She was seventy when she died of cold and malnutrition. She had been alone for a long time, since her husband had died of pneumonia in a bad winter soon after the Second World War. He had not been more than middleaged. Her four children were now middleaged, with grown children. Of these descendants one daughter sent her Christmas cards, but otherwise she did not exist for them. For they were all respectable people, with homes and good jobs and cars. And Hetty was not respectable. She had always been a bit strange, these people said, when mentioning her at all.

When Fred Pennefather, her husband, was alive and the children just growing up, they all lived much too close and uncomfortable in a Council flat in that part of London which is like an estuary, with tides of people flooding in and out: they were not half a mile from the great stations of Euston, St. Pancras, and King's Cross. The blocks of flats were pioneers in that area, standing up grim, grey, hideous, among many acres of little houses and gardens, all soon to be demolished so that they could be replaced by more tall grey blocks. The Pennefathers were good tenants, paying their rent, keeping out of debt; he was a building worker, "steady," and proud of it. There was no evidence then of Hetty's future dislocation from the normal, unless it was that she very often slipped down for an hour or so to the platforms where the locomotives drew in and ground out again. She liked the smell of it all, she said. She liked to see people moving about, "coming and going from all those foreign places." She meant Scotland, Ireland, the North of England. These visits into the din, the smoke, the massed swirling people were for her a drug, like other people's drinking or gambling. Her husband teased her, calling her a gypsy. She was in fact part gypsy, for her mother had been one, but had chosen to leave her people and marry a man who lived in a house. Fred Pennefather liked his wife for being different from the run of the women he knew, and had married her because of it, but her children were fearful that her gypsy blood might show itself in worse ways than haunting railway stations. She was a tall woman with a lot of glossy black hair, a skin that tanned easily, and dark strong eyes. She wore bright colours, and enjoyed quick tempers and sudden reconciliations. In her prime she attracted attention, was proud and handsome. All this made it inevitable that the people in those streets should refer to her as "that gypsy woman." When she heard them, she shouted back that she was none the worse for that.

After her husband died and the children married and left, the Council moved her to a small flat in the same building. She got a job selling food in a local store, but found it boring. There seem to be traditional occupations for middleaged women living alone, the busy and responsible part of their lives being over. Drink. Gambling. Looking for another husband. A wistful affair or two. That's about it. Hetty went through a period of, as it were, testing out all these, like hobbies, but tired of them. While still earning her small wage as a saleswoman, she began a trade in buying and selling secondhand clothes. She did not have a shop of her own, but bought clothes from householders, and sold these to stalls and the secondhand shops. She adored doing this. It was a passion. She gave up her respectable job and forgot all about her love of trains and travellers. Her room was always full of bright bits of cloth, a dress that had a pattern she fancied and did not want to sell, strips of beading, old furs, embroidery, lace. There were street traders among the people in the flats, but there was something in the way Hetty went about it that lost her friends. Neighbours of twenty or thirty years' standing said she had gone queer, and wished to know her no longer. But she did not mind. She was enjoying herself too much, particularly the moving about the streets with her old perambulator, in which she crammed what she was buying or selling. She liked the gossiping, the bargaining, the wheedling from householders. It was this last which—and she knew this quite well, of course—the neighbours objected to. It was the thin edge of the wedge. It was begging. Decent people did not beg. She was no longer decent.

Lonely in her tiny flat, she was there as little as possible, always preferring the lively streets. But she had after all to spend some time in her room, and one day she saw a kitten lost and trembling in a dirty corner, and brought it home to the block of flats. She was on a fifth floor. While the kitten was growing into a large strong tom, he ranged about that conglomeration of staircases and lifts and many dozens of flats, as if the building were a town. Pets were not actively persecuted by the authorities, only forbidden and then tolerated. Hetty's life from the coming of the cat became more sociable, for the beast was always making friends with somebody in the cliff that was the block of flats across the court, or not coming home for nights at a time, so that she had to go and look for him and knock on doors and ask, or returning home kicked and limping, or bleeding after a fight with his kind. She made scenes with the kickers, or the owners of the enemy cats, exchanged cat lore with cat lovers, was always having to bandage and nurse her poor Tibby. The cat was soon a scarred warrior with fleas, a torn ear, and a ragged look to him. He was a multicoloured cat and his eyes were small and yellow. He was a long way down the scale from the delicately coloured, elegantly shaped pedigree cats. But he was independent, and often caught himself pigeons when he could no longer stand the tinned cat food, or the bread and packet gravy Hetty fed him, and he purred and nestled when she grabbed him to her bosom at those times she suffered loneliness. This happened less and less. Once she had realised that her children were hoping that she would leave them alone because the old rag trader was an embarrassment to them, she accepted it, and a bitterness that always had wild humour in it only welled up at times like Christmas. She sang or chanted to the cat: "You nasty old beast, filthy old cat, nobody wants you, do they Tibby, no, you're just an alley tom, just an old stealing cat, hey Tibs, Tibs, Tibs."

The building teemed with cats. There were even a couple of

dogs. They all fought up and down the grey cement corridors. There were sometimes dog and cat messes which someone had to clear up, but which might be left for days and weeks as part of neighbourly wars and feuds. There were many complaints. Finally an official came from the Council to say that the ruling about keeping animals was going to be enforced. Hetty, like others, would have to have her cat destroyed. This crisis co-incided with a time of bad luck for her. She had had 'flu; had not been able to earn money, had found it hard to get out for her pension, had run into debt. She owed a lot of back rent, too. A television set she had hired and was not paying for attracted the visits of a television representative. The neighbours were gossiping that Hetty had "gone savage." This was because the cat had brought up the stairs and along the passageways a pigeon he had caught, shedding feathers and blood all the way; a woman coming in to complain found Hetty plucking the pigeon to stew it, as she had done with others, sharing the meal with Tibby.

"You're filthy," she would say to him, setting the stew down to cool in his dish. "Filthy old thing. Eating that dirty old pigeon. What do you think you are, a wild cat? Decent cats don't eat dirty birds. Only those old gypsies eat wild birds."

One night she begged help from a neighbour who had a car, and put into the car herself, the television set, the cat, bundles of clothes, and the pram. She was driven across London to a room in a street that was a slum because it was waiting to be done up. The neighbour made a second trip to bring her bed and her mattress, which were tied to the roof of the car, a chest of drawers, an old trunk, saucepans. It was in this way that she left the street in which she had lived for thirty years, nearly half her life.

She set up house again in one room. She was frightened to go near "them" to re-establish pension rights and her identity, because of the arrears of rent she had left behind, and because of the stolen television set. She started trading again, and the little room was soon spread, like her last, with a rainbow of colours and textures and lace and sequins. She cooked on a single gas ring and washed in the sink. There was no hot water unless it was boiled in saucepans. There were several old ladies and a family of five children in the house, which was condemned.

She was in the ground floor back, with a window which opened onto a derelict garden, and her cat was happy in a hunting ground that was a mile around this house where his mistress was so splendidly living. A canal ran close by, and in the dirty city-water were islands which a cat could reach by leaping from moored boat to boat. On the islands were rats and birds. There were pavements full of fat London pigeons. The cat was a fine hunter. He soon had his place in the hierarchies of the local cat population and did not have to fight much to keep it. He was a strong male cat, and fathered many litters of kittens.

In that place Hetty and he lived five happy years. She was trading well, for there were rich people close by to shed what the poor needed to buy cheaply. She was not lonely, for she made a quarrelling but satisfying friendship with a woman on the top floor, a widow like herself who did not see her children either. Hetty was sharp with the five children, complaining about their noise and mess, but she slipped them bits of money and sweets after telling their mother that "she was a fool to put herself out for them, because they wouldn't appreciate it." She was living well, even without her pension. She sold the television set and gave herself and her friend upstairs some day-trips to the coast, and bought a small radio. She never read books or magazines. The truth was that she could not write or read, or only so badly it was no pleasure to her. Her cat was all reward and no cost, for he fed himself, and continued to bring in pigeons for her to cook and eat, for which in return he claimed milk.

"Greedy Tibby, you greedy *thing*, don't think I don't know, oh yes I do, you'll get sick eating those old pigeons, I do keep telling you that, don't I?"

At last the street was being done up. No longer a uniform, long, disgraceful slum, houses were being bought by the middle-class people. While this meant more good warm clothes for trading—or begging, for she still could not resist the attraction of getting something for nothing by the use of her plaintive inventive tongue, her still-flashing handsome eyes—Hetty knew, like her neighbours, that soon this house with its cargo of poor people would be bought for improvement.

In the week Hetty was seventy years old came the notice that was the end of this little community. They had four weeks to find somewhere else to live.

Usually, the shortage of housing being what it is in London—and everywhere else in the world, of course—these people would have had to scatter, fending for themselves. But the fate of this particular street was attracting attention, because a municipal election was pending. Homelessness among the poor was finding a focus in this street which was a perfect symbol of the whole area, and indeed the whole city, half of it being fine converted tasteful houses, full of people who spent a lot of money, and half being dying houses tenanted by people like Hetty.

As a result of speeches by councillors and churchmen, local authorities found themselves unable to ignore the victims of this redevelopment. The people in the house Hetty was in were visited by a team consisting of an unemployment officer, a social worker, and a rehousing officer. Hetty, a strong gaunt old woman wearing a scarlet wool suit she had found among her cast-offs that week, a black knitted teacosy on her head, and black buttoned Edwardian boots too big for her, so that she had to shuffle, invited them into her room. But although all were well used to the extremes of poverty, none wished to enter the place, but stood in the doorway and made her this offer: that she should be aided to get her pension—why had she not claimed it long ago?—and that she, together with the four other old ladies in the house, should move to a Home run by the Council out in the northern suburbs. All these women were used to, and enjoyed, lively London, and while they had no alternative but to agree, they fell into a saddened and sullen state. Hetty agreed too. The last two winters had set her bones aching badly, and a cough was never far away. And while perhaps she was more of an urban soul even than the others, since she had walked up and down so many streets with her old perambulator loaded with rags and laces, and since she knew so intimately London's texture and taste, she minded least of all the idea of a new home "among green fields." There were, in fact, no fields near the promised Home, but for some reason all the old ladies had chosen to bring out this old song of a phrase, as if it belonged to their situation, that of old women not far off death. "It will be nice to be near green fields again," they said to each other over cups of tea.

The housing officer came to make final arrangements. Hetty Pennefather was to move with the others in two weeks' time. The young man, sitting on the very edge of the only chair in the crammed room, because it was greasy and he suspected it had fleas or worse in it, breathed as lightly as he could because of the appalling stink: there was a lavatory in the house, but it had been out of order for three days, and it was just the other side of a thin wall. The whole house smelled.

The young man, who knew only too well the extent of the misery due to lack of housing, who knew how many old people abandoned by their children did not get the offer to spend their days being looked after by the authorities, could not help feeling that this wreck of a human being could count herself lucky to get a place in this "Home," even if it was—and he knew and deplored the fact—an institution in which the old were treated like naughty and dimwitted children until they had the good fortune to die.

But just as he was telling Hetty that a van would be coming to take her effects and those of the other four old ladies, and that she need not take anything more with her than her clothes "and perhaps a few photographs," he saw what he had thought was a heap of multicoloured rags get up and put its ragged gingery-black paws on the old woman's skirt. Which today was a cretonne curtain covered with pink and red roses that Hetty had pinned around her because she liked the pattern.

"You can't take that cat with you," he said automatically. It was something he had to say often, and knowing what misery the statement caused, he usually softened it down. But he had been taken by surprise.

Tibby now looked like a mass of old wool that has been matting together in dust and rain. One eye was permanently half-closed, because a muscle had been ripped in a fight. One ear was vestigial. And down a flank was a hairless slope with a thick scar on it. A cat-hating man had treated Tibby as he treated all cats, to a pellet from his airgun. The resulting wound had taken two years to heal. And Tibby smelled.

No worse, however, than his mistress, who sat stiffly still, bright-eyed with suspicion, hostile, watching the well-brushed tidy young man from the Council.

"How old is that beast?"

"Ten years, no, only eight years, he's a young cat about five years old," said Hetty, desperate.

"It looks as if you'd do him a favour to put him out of his misery," said the young man.

When the official left, Hetty had agreed to everything. She was the only one of the old women with a cat. The others had budgerigars or nothing. Budgies were allowed in the Home.

She made her plans, confided in the others, and when the van came for them and their clothes and photographs and budgies, she was not there, and they told lies for her. "Oh we don't know where she can have gone, dear," the old women repeated again and again to the indifferent van driver. "She was here last night, but she did say something about going to her daughter in Manchester." And off they went to die in the Home.

Hetty knew that when houses have been emptied for redevelopment they may stay empty for months, even years. She intended to go on living in this one until the builders moved in.

It was a warm autumn. For the first time in her life she lived like her gypsy forebears, and did not go to bed in a room in a house like respectable people. She spent several nights, with Tibby, sitting crouched in a doorway of an empty house two doors from her own. She knew exactly when the police would come around, and where to hide herself in the bushes of the overgrown shrubby garden.

As she had expected, nothing happened in the house, and she moved back in. She smashed a back windowpane so that Tibby could move in and out without her having to unlock the front door for him, and without leaving a window suspiciously open. She moved to the top back room and left it every morning early, to spend the day in the streets with her pram and her rags. At night she kept a candle glimmering low down on the floor. The lavatory was still out of order, so she used a pail on the first floor, instead, and secretly emptied it at night into the canal, which in the day was full of pleasure boats and people fishing.

Tibby brought her several pigeons during that time.

"Oh you are a clever puss, Tibby, Tibby! Oh you're clever, you are. You know how things are, don't you, you know how to get around and about."

The weather turned very cold; Christmas came and went. Hetty's cough came back, and she spent most of her time under piles of blankets and old clothes, dozing. At night she watched the shadows of the candle flame on floor and ceiling—the windowframes fitted badly, and there was a draught. Twice tramps spent the night in the bottom of the house and she heard them being moved on by the police. She had to go down to make sure the police had not blocked up the broken window the cat used, but they had not. A blackbird had flown in and had battered itself to death trying to get out. She plucked it, and roasted it over a fire made with bits of floorboard in a baking pan: the gas of course had been cut off. She had never eaten very much, and was not frightened that some dry bread and a bit of cheese was all that she had eaten during her sojourn under the heap of clothes. She was cold, but did not think about that much. Outside there was slushy brown snow everywhere. She went back to her nest thinking that soon the cold spell would be over and she could get back to her trading. Tibby sometimes got into the pile with her, and she clutched the warmth of him to her. "Oh you clever cat, you clever old thing, looking after yourself, aren't you? That's right my ducky, that's right my lovely."

And then, just as she was moving about again, with snow gone off the ground for a time but winter only just begun, in January, she saw a builder's van draw up outside, a couple of men unloading their gear. They did not come into the house: they were to start work next day. By then Hetty, her cat, her pram piled with clothes and her two blankets, were gone. She also took a box of matches, a candle, an old saucepan and a fork and spoon, a tinopener, a candle and a rat-trap. She had a horror of rats.

About two miles away, among the homes and gardens of amiable Hampstead, where live so many of the rich, the intelligent and the famous, stood three empty, very large houses. She had seen them on an occasion, a couple of years before, when she had taken a bus. This was a rare thing for her, because of the remarks and curious looks provoked by her mad clothes, and by her being able to appear at the same time such a tough battling old thing and a naughty child. For the older she got, this disreputable tramp, the more there strengthened in her a quality of fierce, demanding childishness. It was all too much of a mixture; she was uncomfortable to have near.

She was afraid that "they" might have rebuilt the houses, but there they still stood, too tumbledown and dangerous to be of much use to tramps, let alone the armies of London's homeless. There was no glass left anywhere. The flooring at ground level was mostly gone, leaving small platforms and juts of planking over basements full of water. The ceilings were crumbling. The roofs were going. The houses were like bombed buildings.

But on the cold dark of a late afternoon she pulled the pram up the broken stairs and moved cautiously around the frail boards of a second-floor room that had a great hole in it right down to the bottom of the house. Looking into it was like looking into a well. She held a candle to examine the state of the walls, here more or less whole, and saw that rain and wind blowing in from the window would leave one corner dry. Here she made her home. A sycamore tree screened the gaping window from the main road twenty yards away. Tibby, who was cramped after making the journey under the clothes piled in the pram, bounded down and out and vanished into neglected undergrowth to catch his supper. He returned fed and pleased, and seemed happy to stay clutched in her hard thin old arms. She had come to watch for his return after hunting trips, because the warm purring bundle of bones and fur did seem to allay, for a while, the permanent ache of cold in her bones.

Next day she sold her Edwardian boots for a few shillings— they were fashionable again—and bought a loaf and some bacon scraps. In a corner of the ruins well away from the one she had made her own, she pulled up some floorboards, built a fire, and toasted bread and the bacon scraps. Tibby had brought in a pigeon, and she roasted that, but not very efficiently. She was afraid of the fire catching and the whole mass going up in flames; she was afraid too of the smoke showing and attracting the police. She had to keep damping down the fire, and so the bird was bloody and unappetising, and in the end Tibby got most of it. She felt confused, and discouraged, but thought it was because of the long stretch of winter still ahead of her before spring could come. In fact, she was ill. She made a couple of attempts to trade and earn money to feed herself before she acknowledged she was ill. She knew she was not yet dangerously ill, for she had been that in her life, and would have been able to recognise the cold listless indifference of a real last-ditch illness. But all her bones ached, and her head ached, and she coughed more than she ever had. Yet she still did not think of herself as suffering particularly from the cold, even in that sleety January weather. She had never, in all her life, lived in a prop- erly heated place, had never known a really warm home, not even when she lived in the Council flats. Those flats had electric fires, and the family had never used them, for the sake of econ- omy, except in very bad spells of cold. They piled clothes onto themselves, or went to bed early. But she did know that to keep herself from dying now she could not treat the cold with her usual indifference. She knew she must eat. In the comparatively dry corner of the windy room, away from the gaping window through which snow and sleet were drifting, she made another nest—her last. She had found a piece of plastic sheeting in the rubble, and she laid that down first, so that the damp would not strike up. Then she spread her two blankets over that. Over them were heaped the mass of old clothes. She wished she had another piece of plastic to put on top, but she used sheets of newspaper instead. She heaved herself into the middle of this, with a loaf of bread near to her hand. She dozed, and waited, and nibbled bits of bread, and watched the snow drifting softly in. Tibby sat close to the old blue face that poked out of the pile and put up a paw to touch it. He miaowed and was restless, and then went out into the frosty morning and brought in a pigeon. This the cat put, still struggling and fluttering a little, close to the old woman. But she was afraid to get out of the pile in which the heat was being made and kept with such difficulty. She really could not climb out long enough to pull up more splinters of plank from the floors, to make a fire, to pluck the pigeon, to roast it. She put out a cold hand to stroke the cat.

"Tibby, you old thing, you brought it for me then, did you? You did, did you? Come here, come in here. . . ." But he did not want to get in with her. He miaowed again, pushed the bird closer to her. It was now limp and dead.

"You have it then. You eat it. I'm not hungry, thank you Tibby."

But the carcase did not interest him. He had eaten a pigeon before bringing this one up to Hetty. He fed himself well. In spite of his matted fur, and his scars and his half-closed yellow eye, he was a strong healthy cat.

At about four the next morning there were steps and voices downstairs. Hetty shot out of the pile and crouched behind a fallen heap of plaster and beams, now covered with snow, at the end of the room near the window. She could see through the hole in the floorboards down to the first floor, which had collapsed entirely, and through it to the ground floor. She saw a man in a thick overcoat and muffler and leather gloves holding a strong torch to illuminate a thin bundle of clothes lying on the floor. She saw that this bundle was a sleeping man or woman.

She was indignant—*her* home was being trespassed upon. And she was afraid because she had not been aware of this other tenant of the ruin. Had he, or she, heard her talking to the cat? And where was the cat? If he wasn't careful he would be caught, and that would be the end of him. The man with a torch went off and came back with a second man. In the thick dark far below Hetty was a small cave of strong light, which was the torchlight. In this space of light two men bent to lift the bundle, carried it out across the dangertraps of fallen and rotting boards that made gangplanks over the water-filled basements. One man was holding the torch in the hand that supported the dead person's feet, and the light jogged and lurched over trees and grasses: the corpse was being taken through the shrubberies to a car.

There are men in London who, between the hours of two and five in the morning—when the real citizens are asleep, who should not be disturbed by such unpleasantness as the corpses of the poor—make the rounds of all the empty, rotting houses they know about, to collect the dead, and to warn the living that they ought not to be there at all, inviting them to one of the official Homes or lodgings for the homeless.

Hetty was too frightened to get back into her warm heap. She sat with the blankets pulled around her, and looked through gaps in the fabric of the house, making out shapes and boundaries and holes and puddles and mounds of rubble, as her eyes, like her cat's, became accustomed to the dark.

She heard scuffling sounds and knew they were rats. She had meant to set the trap, but the thought of her friend Tibby, who might catch his paw, had stopped her. She sat up until the morning light came in grey and cold, after nine. Now she did know herself to be very ill and in danger, for she had lost all the warmth she had huddled into her bones under the rags. She shivered violently. She was shaking herself apart with shivering. In between spasms she drooped limp and exhausted. Through the ceiling above her—but it was not a ceiling, only a cobweb of slats and planks—she could see into a dark cave which had been a garret, and through the roof above that, the grey sky, teeming with incipient rain. The cat came back from where he had been hiding, and sat crouched on her knees, keeping her stomach warm, while she thought out her position. These were her last clear thoughts. She told herself that she would not last out until

spring unless she allowed "them" to find her, and take her to
hospital. After that, she would be taken to a Home.

But what would happen to Tibby, her poor cat? She rubbed
the old beast's scruffy head with the ball of her thumb and muttered: "Tibby, Tibby, they won't get you, no, you'll be all right,
yes, I'll look after you."

Towards midday, the sun oozed yellow through miles of
greasy grey cloud, and she staggered down the rotting stairs, to
the shops. Even in those London streets, where the extraordinary has become usual, people turned to stare at a tall gaunt
woman, with a white face that had flaming red patches on it,
and blue compressed lips, and restless black eyes. She wore a
tightly buttoned man's overcoat, torn brown woollen mittens,
and an old fur hood. She pushed a pram loaded with old dresses
and scraps of embroidery and torn jerseys and shoes, all stirred
into a tight tangle, and she kept pushing this pram up against
people as they stood in queues, or gossiped, or stared into windows, and she muttered: "Give me your old clothes darling, give
me your old pretties, give Hetty something, poor Hetty's hungry."
A woman gave her a handful of small change, and Hetty bought
a roll filled with tomato and lettuce. She did not dare go into a
cafe, for even in her confused state she knew she would offend,
and would probably be asked to leave. But she begged a cup of
tea at a street stall, and when the hot sweet liquid flooded
through her she felt she might survive the winter. She bought
a carton of milk and pushed the pram back through the slushy
snowy street to the ruins.

Tibby was not there. She urinated down through the gap in
the boards, muttering, "A nuisance, that old tea," and wrapped
herself in a blanket and waited for the dark to come.

Tibby came in later. He had blood on his foreleg. She had
heard scuffling and she knew that he had fought a rat, or several,
and had been bitten. She poured the milk into the tilted saucepan and Tibby drank it all.

She spent the night with the animal held against her chilly
bosom. They did not sleep, but dozed off and on. Tibby would
normally be hunting, the night was his time, but he had stayed
with the old woman now for three nights.

Early next morning they again heard the corpse removers
among the rubble on the ground floor, and saw the beams of the
torch moving on wet walls and collapsed beams. For a moment

the torchlight was almost straight on Hetty, but no one came up: who could believe that a person could be desperate enough to climb those dangerous stairs, to trust those crumbling splintery floors, and in the middle of winter?

Hetty had now stopped thinking of herself as ill, of the degrees of her illness, of her danger—of the impossibility of her surviving. She had cancelled out in her mind the presence of winter and its lethal weather, and it was as if spring were nearly here. She knew that if it had been spring when she had had to leave the other house, she and the cat could have lived here for months and months, quite safely and comfortably. Because it seemed to her an impossible and even a silly thing that her life, or, rather, her death, could depend on something so arbitrary as builders starting work on a house in January rather than in April, she could not believe it: the fact would not stay in her mind. The day before she had been quite clearheaded. But today her thoughts were cloudy, and she talked and laughed aloud. Once she scrambled up and rummaged in her rags for an old Christmas card she had got four years before from her good daughter.

In a hard harsh angry grumbling voice she said to her four children that she needed a room of her own now that she was getting on. "I've been a good mother to you," she shouted to them before invisible witnesses—former neighbours, welfare workers, a doctor. "I never let you want for anything, never! When you were little you always had the best of everything! You can ask anybody; go on, ask them, then!"

She was restless and made such a noise that Tibby left her and bounded on to the pram and crouched watching her. He was limping, and his foreleg was rusty with blood. The rat had bitten deep. When the daylight came, he left Hetty in a kind of sleep, and went down into the garden where he saw a pigeon feeding on the edge of the pavement. The cat pounced on the bird, dragged it into the bushes, and ate it all, without taking it up to his mistress. After he had finished eating, he stayed hidden, watching the passing people. He stared at them intently with his blazing yellow eye, as if he were thinking, or planning. He did not go into the old ruin and up the crumbling wet stairs until late—it was as if he knew it was not worth going at all.

He found Hetty, apparently asleep, wrapped loosely in a blanket, propped sitting in a corner. Her head had fallen on her chest, and her quantities of white hair had escaped from a scarlet woollen cap, and concealed a face that was flushed a deceptive pink—the flush of coma from cold. She was not yet dead, but she died that night. The rats came up the walls and along the planks and the cat fled down and away from them, limping still, into the bushes.

Hetty was not found for a couple of weeks. The weather changed to warm, and the man whose job it was to look for corpses was led up the dangerous stairs by the smell. There was something left of her, but not much.

As for the cat, he lingered for two or three days in the thick shrubberies, watching the passing people and beyond them, the thundering traffic of the main road. Once a couple stopped to talk on the pavement, and the cat, seeing two pairs of legs, moved out and rubbed himself against one of the legs. A hand came down and he was stroked and patted for a little. Then the people went away.

The cat saw he would not find another home, and he moved off, nosing and feeling his way from one garden to another, through empty houses, finally into an old churchyard. This graveyard already had a couple of stray cats in it, and he joined them. It was the beginning of a community of stray cats going wild. They killed birds, and the field mice that lived among the grasses, and they drank from puddles. Before winter had ended the cats had had a hard time of it from thirst, during the two long spells when the ground froze and there was snow and no puddles and the birds were hard to catch because the cats were so easy to see against the clean white. But on the whole they managed quite well. One of the cats was female, and soon there were a swarm of wild cats, as wild as if they did not live in the middle of a city surrounded by streets and houses. This was just one of half a dozen communities of wild cats living in that square mile of London.

Then an official came to trap the cats and take them away. Some of them escaped, hiding till it was safe to come back again. But Tibby was caught. He was not only getting old and stiff— he still limped from the rat's bite—but he was friendly, and did not run away from the man, who had only to pick him up in his arms.

"You're an old soldier, aren't you?" said the man. "A real tough one, a real old tramp."

It is possible that the cat even thought that he might be finding another human friend and a home.

But it was not so. The haul of wild cats that week numbered hundreds, and while if Tibby had been younger a home might have been found for him, since he was amiable, and wished to be liked by the human race, he was really too old, and smelly and battered. So they gave him an injection and, as we say, "put him to sleep."

# Side Benefits of an
# Honourable Profession

O r rather, perhaps, a condition
of the mud which nurtures? Flowers, of course—but that isn't
the point. No, definitely not an effluent, a by-product. Accurate
as well as charitable to see it all as a kind of compost, the rich
mad muck which feeds those disciplined performances, exactly the same night after night, that we see and marvel at
and which might even cause us to exclaim—if we haven't
entirely lost that naivety which I for one maintain the theatre
needs as dreams need sleep, and could not exist without for
one moment: How *can* he/she bear to be someone else so entirely and devotedly every blessed night and two afternoons
a week for hours at a stretch! Even with intervals for orange
juice or Scotch. Possibly for months at a time. If the play finds
favour, as they say.

Those two, for instance: household names, or at least in
those households (one per cent of the population) which prefer
to give room to these rather than to the more vigorous performers, football players, or horses or dogs—those two, having
rehearsed for a month a play which called for a slow progress
towards a bed, made of the bed itself a stage for—not at all for
the guilt-ridden and eventually murderous lusts which the play
incorporated, but for innocence.

It was an innocence so immaculate that words like "mud"

and "compost" perhaps need looking at again. If, that is, we do not want to examine innocence.

It so happened—and no chance either, I feel—that both he (we'll call him John) and she (Mary will do) were involved during the period of rehearsal with some pretty savage moments in their private lives. He was in trouble with his marriage; and she, having been divorced, had reached that point with a possible new husband when she must decide whether to marry him or not. On the whole she felt not. At any rate, it wasn't at all that either could look forward, after a day of rehearsing passions not their own, to loving tranquillity. Far from it, and on the contrary, both returned to scenes, reproaches and torments not very different—and they even said so, with that appropriate good trouper's laugh used by actors to dismiss their private lives when engaged on their real business—from those they were developing during rehearsals. Well, one night Mary *found* herself, when everybody had left the darkened theatre, backstage and by the great bed which was such a feature of the play. It was made up, but for economy's sake not more than was essential. She sat by the bed on the little stool which was also part of the set and found herself shedding a tear, though for what she could not have said (her words when describing the experience). Through blurred vision she saw a figure approaching from the dressingrooms: no ghost or burglar, but the handsome John, whose feet, or at least, some impulse, had brought him here, also in the belief that the building was deserted. No need, she said, for words. He sat on the companion stool on the other side of the bed. He offered her a cigarette. Between them stretched the crumpled sheet on which they had spent at least four hours that day of steady, grindingly repetitive rehearsal locked in each other's arms, apparently in the extremes of passion. They left half an hour later, without even the casual theatre kiss that by custom they would have offered each other on parting. Next evening, and without arranging it, they met again. For a week these two rolled, morning and afternoon and some evenings, in torments of simulated lust and its associated emotions, and at night met, chaste and tender, for a half hour before returning to their tumultuous private lives. They were too shy, as she explained, to touch each other. As in a first love, the lighting of a cigarette, the accidental meeting of a hand, were exquisitely painful—indeed, more than enough.

That nightly half hour was filled with restoring breaths of air from lost horizons. Finally their *affaire* (so she always pronounced it) culminated in a kiss so delicate, so exquisite, that its poetry was enough to decide her not to marry her possible husband, and him to leave his wife. No, that kiss was not on the *first night*, but after the dress rehearsal. The first night being successfully accomplished in the usual ritual crescendo of shared tension, flowers, champagne, congratulations and the theatre emptying backstage into darkness as it had an hour ago in front, the two *found themselves* on their way out, by the bed, a slight detour and a temporary shedding of their first-night visitors being necessary. Looking at the pillow case, which should have been put on fresh for the just-completed performance, she noted a smear of lipstick—hers, from the dress rehearsal. "Really," she said, irritably, "I do think they might have remembered to put on a clean pillow case for the first night." "I quite agree," he said, cool, and with precisely the same degree of professional irritation at incompetence, "that lipstick must have been visible from half-way up the stalls." With which they kissed each other, comradely and brisk, as is customary, said goodnight, and parted, she to reaffirm to her lover that no, she would not marry him, and he to disagree with his wife, who was saying that really, as responsible and adult people, they should try again.

Or take that well-known playwright, now dead, whose dissatisfaction with his wives was not so much proclaimed—they were all damned fine women, he told the newspapers—as demonstrated by the fact that he dismissed them one after another, usually about four years after marrying them. He was on his sixth wife when she met, by chance, wives five and four, and confessed that things were not as they ought to be. Remarks were made that caused them to contact previous wives. Six women, five ex-wives and the present incumbent, met one afternoon—not, they said, in any spirit of anger, but from a scientific desire for psychological clarity. In each of this man's plays (we will call him John) appeared a woman, sometimes in a leading part, sometimes not, who was wise, witty, warm, tender, beautiful and all-forgiving, the last quality being the most valuable, in life if not theatrically, as each of these women had discovered. They were all actresses and all had played this woman, presented under different names, in different clothes and in different epochs. The first wife had played her in his first-performed play as a suburban school-teacher; the current wife had played her, evolved into full flower, four years ago in the shape of an Italian princess. They all had had the same experience, an uneasiness, which developed even during those first rapturous days of an at-last-discovered perfect love, that made them feel—and all of them said they had felt it—as if they were not themselves, as if, in life, they were being forced into a role, and even, as one of them put it, as if there were always a third person present—a ghost. The ghost, of course, of the stage woman. And each one had experienced that moment when, betrayed, wounded, knifed to the heart by reality, their John had shouted (and with such conviction of betrayal that there was nothing at all to be said): "Why don't you behave like . . . ? You aren't like *her* at all!"—using the name for whichever incarnation of his "she" that *she* had in fact played. And this was the moment when, giving her a look of disgusted dismissal, he had gone off into his study to begin the new play which would incorporate, in minor or major part, the new version of this woman who must continually be recreated in art since she did not exist in life. Which play, when it was put on, would infallibly lead to her—the present wife's—divorce. Because, although she did not know it, was perhaps still a half-tried girl waiting for her big chance, the new wife was already blue-printed, summoned. And from that moment, about a week after the rehearsals started, when she approached the great man shyly, her beautiful eyes shining with the effort it was costing her, and said: "I must say this, I really must, forgive me, but thank you for letting me play this beautiful part in your beautiful play"—nothing was more certain than that he would marry her, and then divorce her the moment he finally understood that she was, after all, only Mary, who might sulk, complain, or cry just like any woman.

Or take the case of Mary X—this time a female writer. It was when she was well on her career that her husband pointed out, and with rancour, that in almost everything she wrote occurred the same figure, male, though that was *not* the point, because he was for all practical purposes sexless, being a slight wry clown or harlequin figure, on whose face was printed the same grimace whatever he was actually doing, whether playing the flute, dancing, or being—apparently—a normal person, a smile that could not be distinguished from the contractions of the muscles which indicate pain or sorrow. Once having understood the truth of her husband's accusation, she searched through every word she had ever written. Sure enough, there he was, right from the beginning, even in those apprentice pieces written decades before and now filed away. The point was, who was he? Where did he come from? Her father? No. Her brothers? No. Her husband? Certainly not, nothing of the Petrouchka about him, and besides, the demon lover (her husband's name for him) had predated the husband by years. Her sons? She sincerely hoped not. Her mother, then?—since such figures from the underworld are no respecters of sex. No. Who? Who, possibly? No one. There was nobody she could think of, no matter how far back she went in her childhood, who could possibly have stood in for or inspired this ambiguously enticing wraith. But she did know, in the present, one, two, perhaps three of him. Pursuing this discovery, she made the new one that while until the performance of her first play, twelve years ago now, she had not met once, not once, any person, male or female, who incarnated the sad clown, since then and starting with the actor who had played the part (nicknamed Pierrot by the company even before her play was known by them) briefly, a friend before he had faded, as befitted his character, into a wry offstage existence on the fringes of her life, she had known several; she was never without him. The fact was, then, that the making flesh and blood of her— but her *what*? fantasy? a figure from her nightdreams?—on stage had had the power to bring him finally towards her? Well if so, it is not a thought a sensible person could enjoy. Particularly not a writer. She contents herself, when, meeting a man who turns that unmistakable face towards her, with saying to herself, never to her husband, who so strangely and obdurately resents this rival who could never be one, *Here he is again*, and with the secret contraction of the heart, the laugh that is half a shudder, which are the tributes we pay to the dark of our natures.

But to return to the light, the easily understood, with a man whom I once knew who claimed that his tragedy was that, while loving women, he was unable. He was always in our company, and taking us out, and being seen in public with us, but, when it came to the point—there it was, he said. Very well then. He was shooting a big film. During the course of this, it was necessary, he said, to make a screen test of the leading actor for another film, also to be shot by him, in which he, the actor, might again play the leading role. Reasonable enough—it was a very different film in which a handsome alçoholic eighteenth-century rake would endeavour, but fail, to rape a beautiful village girl in circumstances which would force her to become his mistress. In the film which was currently being shot, he was playing a lusty workingclass youth before whom women fell like cut grass. The scene was set for the test. In came the actor, transmogrified out of overalls and a cloth cap into aristocratic elegancies. It was about ten in the morning. The scene to be shot was the moment of the gentleman's failure with the lady—her lack of refinement and probably unwashed condition were responsible, the script suggested. Usually half a morning would have done for such a test. But for the whole of that day, hour after hour, the studio with its armies of hands, lighting experts, camera crews, makeup women, watched the mad director with the marvellous politeness of their most necessary discipline, while *he* watched the handsome hero attempt and fail, attempt and fail, and attempt and fail and fail, again and again, to have the beautiful and scornful girl. The great expanse of the harshly lit studio, the small area of especially focussed lights, the fourposter bed, and at least three hundred people standing about, if they were not actually assisting, forced to watch while the lusty young man who for weeks and weeks had been light-heartedly romping his way through at least a dozen women in one film, was reduced to public impotence for the benefit of another. Again and again. And again.

When it was all over, but not until five minutes before the trade union rules made it inevitable that the camera crews must go home to tea and their wives, the mad director said, addressing the by-now-exhausted young man: "Well, that'll do I think. But actually, love, I do think that X [another actor] could probably be better in this particular role. You are too earthy, darling, let's face it. He's more subtle."

Or the famous screen actress, American, well known for her fastidiousness about what she plays. Much dreaded is that moment when, surrounded by lawyers, agents, a husband and protectors of all kinds, she hands back a script with: "As it stands, it really is not for me—if we may suggest some changes . . ."

What, then, is for her? She has played, for some decades now, women in every kind of desperate situation, ex-jailbirds, betrayed lovers, doomed invalids, sorrowing mothers. But what can be the common denominator which causes her to say: "Yes, this is for me"? I once knew a man who worked, on a very humble level, in films she was starring in. What was she like? I wanted to know. It was offered that she was businesslike, adamant in her choices of co-stars, would not be photographed without the exact density of a piece of gauze being specified by lawyers, in triplicate, for certain revealing shots; that she could never be shot in such a way that her nose, not her best point, could emphasise itself . . . yes, but what is she *like?* "Good God!" said he, "you must have seen her in a hundred films."

She lives, has lived, a life of improbable probity, married to the same man, with never a breath of scandal; remains a lady who insists on maintaining what she describes as the high standards of Hollywood.

Not long ago, I heard, she turned down a part which would have involved her battering to death her husband (in such a way that it would look as if someone else had done it) so that she could benefit from his will. That was, she claimed, nothing but unmotivated nastymindedness. Soon afterwards she was pleased to play a part where she battered to death—but openly, as it were, nobly—a lawyer lover who had tricked her out of a fortune.

Fairly straightforward really, daylight stuff still, as is this . . .

A certain English gentleman, a sort of semi-lord, being a middle son (he refers to himself with a rather tetchy refusal to conform to current prejudices as well-connected), lives in a large country house but alone, as his wife died shortly after their marriage. Alone, that is, except for his manservant. Failing to remarry, the usual rumours gathered about him and his way of life, dark tastes of all kinds were hinted at, and the women who had not succeeded in marrying him allowed it to be understood that it was their discovery of his secret which had cooled their pursuit.

He had been a widower for more than a decade when he was taken to what he called "a show." He did not care for the theatre at all. There he saw Mary Griffiths, a woman who had been married twice but who had announced to everyone and even to the Press that she did not intend to remarry, she chose freedom.

She was an attractive blond woman, her stage personality formed in the Fifties to the formula of that time—casual, loud-mouthed, frank—and, as she insisted, as common as dirt. She took pains to conceal her middleclass origin—a handicap when she first started to act. She took care to play parts suited to this formula—mostly sad dishevelled girls doomed to disharmony. "A lost ugly duckling with moments of swan," as one critic put it. A *jolie laide*, said another, thus enabling Mary to describe herself as more laid than jolly, and to reap double benefit, when people protested the joke was not new, by claiming: "Well, I've never had an education—I've never pretended I did—have I, then?"

What the gentleman saw in her struck his friends into incredulity, and her into laughter, and then thought. She was the reincarnation, he said, of his grandmother, the best horse-woman in the county, the bravest woman he had ever known—and, but of course, a great lady.

Mary wondered for a while whether to take riding lessons, in case some play or film producer saw in her what her still unknown admirer saw, but decided against it. They were introduced, and he began to court her—the only word for it. She was living at the time with a fashionable dress designer, and it was hard to say which of the two, Mary or her lover ("boyfriend"), got more excitement from the ritual. John sent her flowers, formally charming notes, left visiting cards, took her to tea, drove her into the country in his Bentley—or rather, sat with her in the back seat while the manservant drove—took her to dinner. From each excursion Mary returned to mourn with her dress designer the sad lack of romance in modern life, and more than once they lay wrapped tearfully in each other's arms, because of the poetry their relationship lacked and must now always lack (there being a time and a place for everything) because for them flowers, formal notes, drives and long intimate dinners were simply impossible, out of key. Their fate had been to meet before a fitting-room mirror, to quarrel half an hour later, and to start living together a week after. Surely, they both wondered, it was not possible that gentleman John could be working up to a proposal of marriage? As Mary put it: "I know he's nuts, but he's not completely gone—me, his wife, he must be joking."

About six months went by, of a patient courtship conducted to rules invisible to Mary, but which she respected. Why not? As she said, she'd have time to fit in a dozen of such relationships concurrently, apart from acting in one play and rehearsing for another and keeping her boyfriend happy. What did those people *do* with themselves in those days, she asked, putting that time at about a hundred years back, while waiting for the moment of truth? Then, at last, John told her that he had decided she was the woman for him.

"You are the woman for him?" enquired her dress designer.

"That's what he said—I swear it."

Mary was then invited, and for the first time, to weekend at his house. Her lover made her some dinner dresses, romantic rather than frank, and the two of them considered her day clothes, since both felt strongly that she should be properly dressed for the occasion. But as at the time she was wearing very short skirts, if she wore skirts at all, and she was not prepared completely to lose her character, a trouser suit was concocted that was chiefly mink, which, worn with mink boots, made her look like a moon Eskimo.

Mary discovered that for the weekend there would be three people in the house: herself, gentleman John, and the manservant. She found the house charming. It fitted her like a glove, she insisted to disbelieving friends. In the afternoon she was taken for a drive, the manservant driving, drank sherry in the library before dinner, the manservant acting as butler, and ate a long and formal dinner, the manservant handing the dishes he had previously chosen. Then, intrigued to the point of hysteria, as she afterwards said, Mary waited for what surely must be a dishonourable proposal.

At eleven-fifty-five John leaned his handsome person towards her and said: "My dear, you must understand what my feelings towards you are, but before I could ask any woman to share my life, there is something I must do. If you like, you can call it a test."

Mary was willing for the test.

John then nodded at the servant, who went out of the room and came back a moment later wheeling a tall black coffin, upright. It had wheels at the feet-end, for manoeuvreability. This coffin was steered, upright, in front of a tall mirror. The servant, in his impeccable black clothes, stood as it were to attention, at one side of it. John, with a smiling nod of encouragement at Mary, went to the coffin, and stood inside it, his hands crossed on his breast, gazing into the mirror. Inside the black coffin, black-clothed John; beside it, the black-clothed servant.

Mary said afterwards that she was bothered because no gesture or pose that occurred to her seemed to be appropriate. So she rubbed out her cigarette, folded her hands in her lap, and remained silent, smiling. At the end of a long five minutes, her John stepped down from the coffin and nodded at the servant, who wheeled it away. He leaned intimately towards her.

"Brandy?" he enquired.

"Just a little, please."

Nothing more was said about the coffin. Soon after, he escorted her to her room. There, but outside it, he kissed her. "And not bad either," she said, describing the moment. "Not—bad—at all!" He said that she had passed every test, and with her permission he would like to ask her to marry him. She said she would think it over, and he kissed her hand and hoped that she would sleep well.

Still thinking it over, she returned next day to London, driven by the manservant, who offered not one word about the midnight ceremony. She had decided that she would be damned if she would ask him questions, but she cracked, and so found that the ceremony of the coffin took place every night of her John's life at midnight. "It's not every woman," said the servant, "who goes along with it. Some I've seen come and go who didn't take it as you did, madam."

Mary consulted with her lover, who designed her a bridal gown, inspired, he said, by a fifteenth-century French court dress—too way out for current fashions, but he had been dying to make use of the ideas it provoked.

The dress ready, Mary wrote to John saying that he could have his answer, but he must come around to the dressingroom after the performance one night. If she could forgive him, he replied, he would not actually watch the performance again; one show a year was really enough for him, though it went without saying, he hoped, that he respected her profession.

When he arrived at the dressingroom door, he was made to

wait. At last the dresser admitted him. He did not immediately know where to look—Mary was not there, it seemed, and since he had never been in an actress's dressingroom before, or, for that matter, backstage at all, the little room with its efficient mirrors, the cold strong working light, the surgical-looking appliances on the dressing-table, the clinical jars and bottles, were hostile to him. There stood the dresser, a small devoted grey figure, hands folded, her face saying nothing, in front of something that looked like—yes, she stood aside and there it was, a long black coffin, and in it, stretched out, dressed in the white wedding gown, eyes closed, hands folded around flowers, flowers all around her, lay his love Mary, dressed for a wedding ceremony, but most adamantly dead.

"As dead as blasted Ophelia," as she said, when describing the scene to her friends and her lover in their favourite restaurant later that night.

He stared, stiffened, and went white—all this from the dresser, because as Mary said, she was damned if she was going to open her eyes and spoil the performance. He then bowed, and went silently out, taking his dismissal like a gentleman.

The dress became a starry item in the designer's next collection, but by then he and Mary were no longer together. Discussing it in the friendly matter-of-fact way imposed on them by their style, or mode, they agreed there was something quite unassimilable about that wedding dress. Either she would put the bloody thing on and go to a registry office and be done with it, or they should call the thing off, with no hard feelings.

The dress then, *prêt à porter*, ready-to-wear, boutiqued, internationalised, led a thousand brides to the altar and the registrar's table.

Still quite straightforward, or at least, understandable. But now enters the dark—or, at least, the tale turns slightly to the moonlit side.

Mary had the dress hanging up in her cupboard for some months. She could not wear it, it was not her style, but she did not want, for some reason, to part with it. At last she wore it for a fancy-dress party, and became for one night a fifteenth-century court lady.

At the party were stage and film directors, as well as the cooks, dress designers, hair-dressers and pop stars who were the lions of the current fashionable scene. A director who had seen Mary a dozen times in her usual kind of role on stage or on television saw her now in a new light. A man with a fine nose for what was next, he wanted to make a large full-blooded film of a nine-teenth-century novel whose heroine was a headstrong aristocratic daughter in love with a revolutionary plebeian. He was dubious about Mary's voice, but it turned out her own voice did very well —he was the first person to have heard it for years. She got the part. She had to learn to ride. The film was shot in Somerset, where gentleman John had his country house.

For weeks she was riding across fields and woods where his grandmother, whose incarnation he had said she was, had won the admiration of a county. But gentleman John had gone abroad with his broken heart, taking the coffin and the manservant with him. Mary did not enquire, for to tell the truth, she hardly thought of him. As she said in a television interview, when she was emotionally involved in a part, she had no time for anything else. As for him, since he hates films as much as he hates the theatre, he will probably never see this film at all.

*But* she was observed, while taking a fence, by a local country squire. She married him, briefly—but as she said when it was all over, for long enough. She changed her style, on her way to becoming what every leading actress is doomed to become, a *grande dame* of the British theatre.

Which reminds me of the *grande dame* who was acting in what she critically described as a kitchen sink play—there were few of the other kind available at that time. Throughout the re-hearsals she complained of the disgusting immorality of the words she was forced to speak. At lunchtimes in the pub, at the top of a voice trained to carry, she described her views about current morality. At the top of the same voice she told the following story. She was on tour somewhere in the North. To her dressingroom came a man she did feel she had known. This feel-ing was so strong that she could not bring herself to say she had no idea who he was, and she agreed to go to dinner with him. Dinner over, she was still in the dark, although she hadn't been able to enjoy a mouthful for racking her brains for some clue. She at last confessed her predicament. He was rather put out, she said.

She didn't remember the restaurant, at least?

Well, there was something about it. . . .

"You don't remember that we came here every night for that

marvellous week before I robbed you of your ever-so-precious virginity, darling?"

"They must have redecorated it! Besides, that must have been 1935—I haven't been here since—I think. And besides, you must know that was *before* I became a Roman Catholic. . . ."

Which reminds me of that actress who, playing a nun in a stormily religious play, used to take the habit home with her—with the connivance of the dresser, who understood her feelings. The play, she explained, lacked a true Christian insight. She wore the habit for ironing, washing-up, rinsing out her underclothes—tasks which she called "my little hair shirts."

# A Year in Regent's Park

$L$ast year was out of ordinary from the start—just like every other year. What start, January? But January is a mid-month, in the middle of cold, snow, dark. Above all, dark. In January nothing starts but the new calendar, which says that the down-swing of our part of the earth towards the long light of summer has already begun, is already stimulating the plants, changing their responses. I would make the beginning back in autumn, when I "found myself possessor"— I put it like that because someone else is now in possession— of a wild, very long, narrow garden, between mellow brick walls. There was an old pear tree in the middle, and at its end a small wood of recently sprung trees, sycamores, an elder, an ash. This treasure of space was twenty minutes' strolling time from Marble Arch, on a canal. The garden had to be prepared for planting. By luck I found a boy up from the country to try his fortune in London, who hated all work in the world but digging. He chose to live in half a room, which he curtained with blankets, carpeted with newspapers, then matting, and wallpapered with his poems and pictures. He was, of course, in the old romantic tradition of the adventurous young, challenging a big city, but he saw himself and the world as newly hatched, let's say a year before, when he became twenty and discovered that he was free and probably a hippie. He lived on baked beans and friendship and, when he needed money, dug people's gardens. Together we stripped off the top layer of this potential garden, which was all builder's rubble, cans, bottles, broken glass. Under this was London clay. It is a substance you hear enough about; indeed, London's history seems made of it. But when you actually come on tons of the stuff, yards deep, heavy, wet, impervious, without a worm or a root in it, it is so airless and unused, you wonder how London ever came to be all gardens and woodland. I could not believe my gardening book, which said that clay is perfect potential soil for plants. I, friends, and the boy from the country, made shapes of the stuff, and thought it was a pity none of us was a sculptor—but that wasn't going to turn the clay into working earth. At last, we marked out flowerbeds, and turned over the clay in large clods, the weeds and grass still on them. The place looked like a ploughed field before the cultivators move in. But even before the first frosts, the soil between the flinty-sided miniature boulders was showing the beginning of a marriage between rotting grass and clay fragments. It had rained. It was raining. As London does, it rained. Going out to inspect the clods, each so heavy I could only pick one up at a time, I found they had softened their harsh contours somewhat, but I couldn't break them by flinging them down or bashing them with a spade. They looked eternal. Steps led up from the under-earth—the flat was a basement flat—and standing at eye-level to the garden, it all looked like a First World War film: trenches full of water, wet mats of the year's leaf, enormous clods, rotting weeds, bare trunks and dripping branches. All, everything, wet, bare, raw.

That was December. Around Christmas, after several heavy frosts, I went up to see how things went on, kicked one of the clods—and it crumbled. The boy from the country who, not being a farming boy, but a country-town boy, and who therefore had not believed the book either, saying the garden needed a bulldozer, came on my telephone call, and about an hour of the lightest work with a hoe transformed the heaving scene into neat areas of tilth mixed with dead grass. Not really dead, of course: but ready to come to life with the spring. But now we had faith in the book, and we turned the roots upwards to be killed by the frost. This happened. Each piece of stalk or root filled with wet, and then swelled as it froze, and burst like water mains in severe cold. Long before spring the earth lay broken and tamed, all the really hard work done not by the spade, or the hoe, or even the worms, but by the frost. The thing is, I knew Africa, or a part of it, and there you can never forget the power of sun, wind, rain. But in gentler England you do forget, as if the north-slanting sun must have less power than a sun overhead, as if nature itself is less drastic in her workings. You can forget it, that is, until you see what a handful of weeks of weather can do to smash a seventy-by-twenty-foot bit of wilderness into conformity.

It rained in January, and in February it did not stop. If I set one foot off the top of the steps that came up from the flat, I sank in clay to my ankle. The light was strained through cold cloud, but it was strong enough to drag the snowdrops up into it. I walked in Regent's Park along paths framed with black glistening twigs which were swelling, ready to burst: the shape of spring, next year's promise, is exposed from the moment the leaves fall. The park was all grey water, sodden grass, black trees, and the waterfowl had to contend for crumbs and crusts with the gulls that had come inland from a stormy sea. In March it rained, and was dull. Usually by March more than snowdrops and crocuses are showing from snow or mud; and already the paths are loaded with people staking claims in the spring. But it was a bad month. My new garden was calling forth derisory remarks from friends who were not gardeners and who did not know what a month's warmth can do for water-filled trenches, bare walls, sodden earth. April wasn't doing anything like what the poet meant when he said, "Oh, to be in England"—certainly he would have returned at once to his beloved Italy. April was not the beginning of spring, but the continuation of winter. It was wet, wet, wet, and cold, and it all went on the same, day after day. And in the park, where I walked daily, only the lengthening evenings talked of spring, for in spite of crocuses everywhere, the buds seemed frozen on the bushes and trees. It would never end. I don't know how they bear it in northern countries, like Sweden or Russia. It is like being shut inside a caul of ice, when the winter lengthens itself so.

And it was so wet. If you took one step off the paths you squelched. No air, you knew, could possibly remain in that sponge. There was so much water everywhere, tons of it hanging in the air over our heads, tons falling every day, lakes underfoot.

Suddenly there were some days of summer. No, not spring. Last year was without spring. In no other country that I know is it possible for things to change so fast. And when one state holds, then the one just past seems impossible. In the garden, from which baths of steam flew up to join the by-now-summer-like clouds, bluebells, hyacinths, crocuses and narcissus had sprung up, and if you turned the earth, the worms were energetically at work. Weeks of growth were being concentrated into each day; nature did overtime to catch up; and if things had gone on like that, we would have been precipitated straight into full summer, with fruit blossoms and spring flowers flying past as in a speeded-up film, but no, suddenly we were in a cold drought. And it went on for weeks. A cold sunless drought, a dry dull cold, with sometimes a cold withdrawn sun. In the garden the water sank fast in the newly turned, loose earth, and you could walk easily over the clay. The pear tree hung on the edge of blossom, but did not flower. The trees at the bottom of the garden had a look of green about them, but it was like the smear of moss on soil soaked and soaked again. When I turned a spade of earth, the worms were sluggish. The birds, dodging plentiful cats, snapped off each new blade of grass as it appeared, and slashed the crocuses with their beaks. In the park, the black boughs had frills of leaf on them, but walking along the shores you could see the ducks and the geese sitting on their eggs on leafless islands. The waters were still tenanted by adult birds, who converged towards their providers on the lakes' edges and climbed out on the banks with coloured beaks open, hissing and demanding. Soon, off the little islands would tumble nestfuls of baby birds, who would learn from their parents to follow the stiffly moving shapes along the banks with their expectations for bread. But not yet. And the blossoms were not yet. Everything was in check in that no-spring of last year where first it rained without sun, and then held a chilly drought for weeks. Yet we knew that spring must have arrived, must be here. Slowly, the chestnut avenue unfurled shrill green from each stiff twig's end. The catkins were dangling on branches inhibited from bursting into leaf. The roses had been pruned almost to the earth, but very late. The fine hair-lines of the willow branches trailing into the water had become yellow-green instead of wintry yellow-grey. And everywhere, on hawthorn and cherry, on plum and currant, on whitebeam and apple, the buds of that year's flowering stood arrested among leafbuds. The park's gardeners bent heavily sweatered over flowerbeds that had a cold dusty look, and the grass wore thin and showed the soil, as often happens in late summer after drought, but not often so early in the year. The evenings had already nearly reached their midsummer length—for just as spring stands outlined in black buds on empty branches in November, so the lengthening evenings of April, May, then June, spread summer light everywhere when the earth is still gripped with cold, and you are clutching at summer before it has begun, marking Midsummer Day as a turn towards the dark of winter before the winter has been warmed from the soil. The earth is tilted forward, dipped completely into light, light that urges on blossom, leaf, grass, light which is more powerful for growth even than warmth. The avenues are filled with strolling people until nine and after; the theatre is open; the swings in the children's playgrounds are never still. England's myriads of expert gardeners visit the rose gardens to match those paragons with the inhabitants of their own gardens —but last year found that the cold was still holding the roses, tightening their veins and arteries, and giving the long reddening shoots the pinched look of a person short of blood. And it all went on and on, the dry cold, just as, earlier, the wet winter had extended itself, and the park seemed like a sponge that could never dry.

And then, the year having swallowed spring whole, the sun and rain came together, and all at once, the whole park burst into flower, as did the pear tree in my garden, and the laburnum over the wall.

In each year, there is always a week which is the essence of spring, all violent growth, bloom, and scent, just as there is one week which is quintessential autumn, the air full of flying tinted leaves.

But last year, trees whose flowering is usually separated by their different natures, flowered at the same time; the cherries, currants, hawthorns, lilacs, and damask roses were out with bluebells, tulips, stocks, and there were so many different kinds of blossom that it seemed as if there must be hundreds of species of flowering tree instead of a couple of dozen. We walked over new grass under trees crammed with pink, with ivory, with greenish-white flower; we walked beside lakes where crowds of ducklings and goslings swam beside their parents, minute balls like thistledown tossing violently with every wind-ripple, and threatened all the time by the oars from rowing boats launched into the waters by spring. It was all spring and all summer at the same time, with flying, rolling, showering clouds, and lovers lay everywhere over the grass, rummaging and ravishing, while the squirrels leaped about like kittens after cotton reels, up and down the trunks of the chestnut trees that had belatedly achieved their proper summer shape, pyramidal green with pink-and-white candles. The squirrels were as fat as housecats, fed full from the litter baskets, and their friends' offerings.

From all the streets around the park, and from much further afield, came people with bread, biscuits, cake, each with a look of private, smiling pleasure. One woman, who had not the usual few bread slices or stale cake but a carrier bag full of food, confided to me as she stood surrounded by hundreds of pigeons, sparrows, geese, ducks, swans, thrushes, that her children had recently grown up and left home and her husband and herself were sparse eaters. Yet years of cooking for uncritically ravenous teenagers and their friends had got her used to providing and catering. She had found herself ordering much more food than an elderly couple could ever eat; she suppressed urges to create new and wonderful dishes. But she had found the solution. Each time the need gripped her to give a dinner party for twelve, or an informal party for fifty, she filled a bag and took a bus to Regent's Park where, on the edge of the bird-decorated waters, she went on until her supplies ran out and her need to feed others was done. The birds, having swum or flown along the banks beside her until they were sure she had no more food, turned their attention to the next likely provisioner, or floated and bobbed and circled to the admiration of humans who all around the shores were bound to be exclaiming: Oh, if only I could be a duck on a hot day like this, right in all that cool water—while these same waterfowl might quite reasonably be expected to be muttering: If only I could be a human, with naked skin for the wind to blow on and the water to touch, and not a bird encased in feathers in such a way that nothing but my poor feet can ever feel the air or water. . . . At any rate, these birds certainly have a fine sense of themselves, their function, their place. Accustomed to seeing them on the water, or tucked into neat shapes drowsing on the grass around the verges, I imagined that that was where they always stayed. But not so, as I discovered one very early morning when I got up at five to have—or so I imagined—the park to myself. There were five or six people already there, strolling about, talking, or at least acknowledging each other, in the camaraderie of those who feel themselves to be out of the ordinary. Meanwhile, the geese and ducks were all over the grass, and under the trees, where in the day they are never seen. Mother ducks and geese, each surrounded by their blobs of coloured down, were introducing these offspring to the land world, as distinct from the water world they inhabited when the park was busy. Greylag geese stood under the Japanese plums. Black swans were under the hawthorns. A squirrel came to investigate a duckling that was disconsolately alone under an arch of climbing rose. It was not six in the morning, but it seemed as if things had been busy for hours—as probably they had, now the nights were so short, and hardly dark at all from a bird's point of view, who probably can't tell the difference between dusk, dawn, or the shimmering dark of a summer's midnight. While people still slept, or were crawling out of bed, there was the liveliest of intimate occasions in the park, which the birds and animals had more or less to themselves.

The park changed as the gardeners arrived and the people walked through on their way to offices. The waterbirds decided to resume their correct places on the lakes—there is no other way to describe the way they do it, the mother birds calling their broods to them, and returning along the paths to the water's edge to leave the grass and paths and trees for humans. Again the waters were loaded with ducks and geese plain and coloured, dignified or as glossily extravagant as the dramatically painted and varnished wooden ducks from toy shops. It is exactly in the same way that the front of a theatre full of stage managers, assistants, prompters, directors, empties for a performance as the public come in. There was the land part of the park, with the usual sparrows and pigeons, and there the lakes so crowded it seemed there could not be room for one more bird—yet all the eggs were still not hatched on the islands which now were filled with green, so that the patiently sitting birds could no longer be seen through the binoculars of London's birdwatchers. And every day, while the earlier-hatched broods became gawky and lumpish attempts after the elegant finish of their parents, freshly hatched birds scattered over the water.

On an arm of the lake where a bridge crossed over, a water-hen was sitting in full view of everybody. The water is very shallow there. A couple of yards from shore, the waterhens had made a nest in the water of piled dead sticks. But not all the sticks were dead. One had rooted and was in leaf, a little green flag above the black-and-white shape of the moorhen who sat a few feet from the bridge. There she crouched, looking at the people who looked at her. All day and half the night, when the park was open to the public, they stopped to observe her. They did more than look. On the twiggy mattress that extended all around her were bits of food thrown by admirers. But these offerings caused the poor moorhens much trouble, because particularly the sparrows, sometimes thrushes and blackbirds, even ducks and other non-related moorhens, came to poke about in the twigs for food. The moorhen—male or female, it seemed they took it in turns to sit—had to keep rising in a hissing clatter of annoyance, to frighten them off. Or the mate who was swimming about to fetch morsels of food for the sitting bird came fussing up to warn off trespassers, but still the sparrows kept darting in to grab what they could, and fly off. Even the big swans came circling, so that the little moorhens looked like miniatures beside the white giants. Much worse than bread was thrown. All the lake under and around the bridge became laden with cans, bits of paper and plastic, and this debris lay bobbing or sagging on water which already, after only a few days of the powerful new summer, was beginning to smell. Now the summer was really here, and the park crowded, grass and paths were always littered, and the water smelled worse every day. Particularly where the moorhens were. That sitting of moorhen eggs must have been the most public in moorhen history. Yet they had chosen the site, had built the nest. And they went on with their work of warming the eggs, till it was done. Admirers loitered on the bridge through the last days, to shield the birds from possible vandals, and to prevent cans being aimed at the birds themselves, and also to catch, if possible, the moment when a moorhen chick took to the water. I am sure there were those who did see this, for the attention was assiduous. I missed it, but one hot afternoon when the bridge was more than usually crowded, I saw a minute dark-coloured chick floating near the nest, with a parent energetically foraging near it for bits of food. The sitting bird lifted itself off the twig mattress to stretch her muscles in a great yawn of wing, and there was a glimpse of white under her: an unhatched egg, and some shell. There was another chick there too, disinclined to join its sibling on the water. The swimming parent fetched slimy morsels for the one on the nest. He, or she, took the fragments and pushed them into the chick's gape. The swimming chick was crammed by the swimming parent. It looked as if the swimming bird was trying to måke the waterborne chick venture further from the nest. It kept heading off, in the energetic purposeful way of moorhens, and swinging around to see if the little chick had followed. But the chick had scrambled back to the nest, and disappeared under the sitting bird. The swimming bird went off quite a distance, and got onto the bank by itself. On the bridge was a threesome, a tall pretty girl with a young man on either side. They had been watching the moorhens. She said: "Oh, I know, he's gone off to see his mistress, and she is going to have to feed her babies herself." "How do you know?" asked one young man. The other laughed, very irritated. He walked off. The girl followed him, looking anxious. The young man who had said, "How do you know?" followed them both, hurrying.

All afternoon, the birds took turns on the nest, one swimming and fetching food for the other, and from time to time a chick climbed down off the great logs of the timber platform he had been hatched on, and bobbed and rocked on the waves. Meanwhile, all the surface of the lake around the nest was full of every kind of swimming bird, adult, half-grown, and just hatched. In such a throng, that one minute moorchick was an item, precious only to the guardian parents.

Moorhens are strict-looking tailored black-and-white birds among the fanciful ducks, the black swans with their red sealing-wax bills. They have a look of modest purpose, of duty, of restraint. And then one comes up out of the water to join birds crowding for thrown bread, and the exposed feet are a shock, being large, whitey-green, scaly, reptilian, as if they had belonged to half-bird half-lizard ancestors, and have descended unaltered down the chains of evolution while the birds modified above water into the handy, tidy moorhen shape—a land shape, it is easy to think. Yet the moorhen is more waterbird than any duck or goose. If you stand feeding a crowd of birds, and there are gulls there, they will swoop in and past, having caught bits of bread from the air as if these were leaping fish—

the gulls will get everything, if you aren't taking care of the others. A tall goose will stand delicately taking pieces from your fingers, like a well-mannered person, then turn to slash savagely another competing goose with its beak: after the gulls, the geese provide for themselves best. The ducks, apparently clumsy and waddling, are quick to snatch bits when the geese miss. But to try and feed the moorhens—for which, sentimentally, I have a fancy—is harder than to feed shyer deer in a zoo when the big ones have decided they are going to get what is going. First, the moorhens have to get up on the bank on those clumsy waterfeet. And then their movements are slower than the other birds; the moorhens are poking about after the bits when the others have swallowed them and are already crowding in for more. Yet, in the water, there is nothing quicker and neater.

That long public sitting succeeded, at last, in adding only one moorchick to the park's population. One afternoon there were two parents and two chicks, busy with each other and their nest among the crowds of birds; next afternoon there were two moorhens and one bobbing dark fluffball.

But the nest was there, with bits of bread still stuck in the twigs. And there it stayed all summer, and all autumn, and although the green fell off, or was pecked off the sentinel twig, nest and twig are there now, in winter—so perhaps in the coming spring the same or another pair of moorhens will bring up another family, in spite of the staring ill-mannered people and their ill-judged offerings, and their cans and their plastic and their smell. But the twig platform will certainly have to be refurnished, for as soon as the moorhen family had left it, it was found most convenient by the other fowl to sit on, and play around; and the twig that had rooted and stood up was a good perch for water-venturing sparrows. There never were so many sparrows as last year: you could mark the season's increase in population by the contrast between the young birds' tight shape and shiny fresh-painted look, and their duller shabbier parents. Where did they all hatch? Apart from those of the waterbirds, and a shallow fibre nest that was exposed when autumn came and stripped the chestnut avenue, woven on twigs not much higher above the path than a tall man's head, so that the sitting bird in its completely concealing clump of leaves must have been inches above the walking people—apart from these, I saw no nests save one on the ground, among blue-bells and geraniums and clumps of hosta. The bird was sleekly brown, and watching me, not over-anxiously, as I watched it from the path a yard or so away. She sat with her warm eggs pressed to her spread claws by her breast, and saw possible enemies pass and repass all day, for the days it took her to get the chicks out into the light. Yet, like the moorhen, she had chosen that exposed place to sit, near a path, just behind the Open Air Theatre. Perhaps, like the foxes that are coming in from the country, which hunts and poisons and traps them, to the suburbs, where they live off town refuse, some birds are coming to terms with us, our noise, and our mess, in ways we don't yet see. Perhaps they even like us? And not only people— a few yards from the sitting brown bird was a place where somebody was putting out food for stray cats. There were saucers of old and new food, and milk, and water, bits of sandwich and biscuit, under the damask roses all the summer, and the cats came to this food, and did not attack the sitting bird—who, perhaps, used this food when the cats were not there? It is possible that she put up with the amplified voices and music from the theatre because of its restaurant, not more than a few seconds' flight away, just the right distance for a quick crumb-gathering before the eggs had time to chill. There must have been many other nests in that thick little wood where the theatre is, and many birds calling that patch of the park theirs. Certainly each year's production of *Midsummer Night's Dream*, good, bad, or indifferent, offers marvellous moments that are not in the stage directions, when an owl hoots for Oberon, or swallows swoop over Titania's and Bottom's heads, or, while a moon stands up over the trees, making the stage seem small and insignificant, starlings loop and swirl past on their last flight before roosting. And all the time, while plays are being rehearsed and acted, the birds are building, sitting, feeding their young, and the fact that they choose this, the noisiest part of the park, surely says something about the way they view us. Or don't see us, don't regard us at all, except in association with food scraps? There's nothing odder than what is ignored, not seen, not noticed. Perhaps those moorhens chose that spot, the most public there is, because the water is the right depth there, and nothing else mattered; and they

were not aware of their audience on the bridge except as a
noisy frieze which emitted lumps of food and other objects.

The park holds dozens of self-contained dramas, human
and animal, in the space of an eye-sweep. On a Sunday afternoon in July, when the drought had held and held, and the
bushes under the tree-cover were wilting because what showers
that had fallen were not heavy enough to penetrate the thick
leaf-layers, the park was full, and coach-loads of people from
everywhere were visiting the zoo. There were queues at the zoo
gates hundreds of yards long, and inside the zoo it was like a
fair. There is a path down the west side of the zoo. It is tree-
shaded. A bank rises sharply to the fields used for football and
cricket. Being summer, and Sunday, it was cricket time, and
four separate games were in progress, each with its circle of
reserve players, friends, wives, children, and casual watchers.
This world, the world of Sunday cricket, was absolutely self-
absorbed, and each game ignored the other three. On the slopes
under the trees were lovers, twined two by two. At the end
where the Mappin Terraces are, four young people lay asleep.
They were tourists, and looked German, or perhaps Scandina-
vian. They all four had long hair. The two girls had long
dresses, the young men fringed leather. They owned four ruck-
sacks and four guitars. Most likely they had been up talking,
singing and dancing all night, or perhaps had not the money
to pay for a night's sleep. Now they slept in each other's arms
all day without moving. Quite possibly they never knew that
cricket was being so devotedly played so close, and that while
they slept the zoo filled and emptied again. From the slope
where they were, you can see nicely into the children's zoo, and
across the elephants' house. You can see, too, the goats and
bears of the terraces. Some people who had given up the effort
of getting into the zoo sat on the slopes near the four sleepers,
talking a lot, not trying to be quiet, and they watched the elephants showing off, poor beasts, in return for their little house
and the trench-enclosed space they have to live in. A woman
arrived with a plastic bag and sat on a bench, with her back
to the lovers and the sleeping young people, and fed sparrows
and pigeons, frowning with the concentration of the effort
needed to let the *poor* sparrows (who were so small) get as
much food as the (unfairly) large pigeons. And a little girl in

the children's zoo clutched at a donkey no higher than she was, and cried out: "It's getting wet, oh the donkey's getting wet." True enough, here came a small sample of the long-awaited rain. Not much. A brief sparkling drench. No one stopped doing anything. The cricketers played on. The woman frowned and fussed over the unfairness of nature. The lovers loved. The four sleeping young people did not so much as turn over, but a passing youth tiptoed up and covered the guitars with the girls' long skirts. And the little girl wept because of the poor donkey who was getting wet and apparently liking it, for it was kicking and heehawing. Where was her mamma? Where, her papa? She was alone with her donkey and her grief. And the rain pelted down and stopped, having done no good and no harm to anything. It was weeks before some real rain arrived and saved the brown scuffing grass; weeks before that moment of high summer which has nothing to do with gardener's calendar, or even the length of the days, shortening fast again, again the same number of hours as in the long-forgotten no-spring. But it is a moment whose quality is over-lushness, heaviness, fullness, plenty. All the trees are crammed and blowsy with leaf. They sag and loll and drag. The willows trail too long in the water, and then they look as if someone has gone around each one in a boat with shears, chopping the fronds to just such a length, like human hair trimmed around a pudding basin. The ducks and geese, who have been deli-cately, languidly, nibbling bits of leaf, and floating in and out through the trailing green curtains, now tread water and strive upwards on their wings to nip off bits of leaf. Perhaps it is the birds who have eaten the low branches away to an exact height all around? There are so many of them now, the chicks all having grown up, that everywhere you look are herds of geese, flocks of ducks, the big swans, moorhens. Surely the park can't possibly sustain so many? What will happen to them all? Will they be allotted to other less bird-populated parks, each bird conditioned from chickhood to regard every human being in sight as a moving bread fountain? Meanwhile, the rowing boats and the sailing boats have to manoeuvre through crowds of waterfowl, the sparrows are in flocks, the roses teem and mass, everything is at the full of its provision, its lushness. The hub of the park now is not the chestnut avenue, and the so English herbaceous border, but the long Italianate walk that has the fountain and the tall poplars at one end, the formal black-and-gold gates the other, the roses lining it all the way. A summer avenue, asking for deep blue skies and heat, just as the chestnut avenue, and the hawthorns, the plums, cherries and currants are for spring, or for autumn.

The summer gardeners all seem to be youngsters working with bare torsos, or bare feet. They cool off by standing in the fountain's spray as the wind switches it about. "They say" that the hippies have decided this work, summer gardening, is good for them, us, society. One evening I heard these sentiments offered to one gardening girl by another:

"There aren't any hangups here, you can do your own thing, but you've got to pull your weight, that's fair enough."

There is a different relationship between these summer amateur gardeners and the park's visitors, and between the visitors and the familiar older gardeners, these last being more proprietary. I remember an exchange with one, several springs ago, on an occasion when it had snowed, the sun had come out, and friends had rung to say that the crocuses were particularly fine. Out I went to the park and found that the new crocuses, white, purple, gold, stood everywhere in the snow. Each patch had been finely netted with black cotton to stop the birds eating them. I was bending over to see how the netting was done—a tricky and irritating job, surely?—when I saw that a uniformed gardener had emerged from his watchman's hut and was standing over me.

"And what may you be doing?"

"I am looking at your crocuses."

"They are not my crocuses. They are public property."

"Oh, good."

"And I am paid to watch them."

"You mean to tell me that you are standing in that unheated wooden hut in all this cold and snow just to guard the crocuses?"

"You could say that."

"Isn't this cotton any use, then?"

"Cotton is effective against bird thieves. I am not saying anything about human thieves."

"But I wasn't going to eat your crocuses!"

"I am only doing my job."

"Your job is, as it were, to be a crocus-watcher?"

"Yes, madam, and it always has been and my father before me. When I was a little lad I knew the work I wanted to do and I've done it ever since."

Not thus the youngsters, much less suspicious characters, understanding quite well how respectable citizens may envy them their jobs.

There was this incident when the geraniums had flowered once, and needed to be picked over to induce a second flowering. There were banks of them, covered with dead flower. I myself had resisted the temptation to nip over the railings and deadhead the lot: another had not resisted. With a look of defiant guilt, an elderly man was crouching in the geraniums, hard at work. Leaning on his spade, watching him, was a summer gardener, a long-haired, barefooted, and naked-chested youth.

"What's he doing that for?" said he to me.

"He can't stand that there won't be a second flowering," I said. "I can understand it. I've just deadheaded all mine in my own garden."

"All I've got room for is herbs in a pot."

The elderly man, seeing us watching him, talking about him, probably about to report his crime, looked guiltier than ever. But he furiously continued his work, a man of principle defying society for duty.

On a single impulse, I and the gardener parted and went in different directions; we were not able to bear causing him such transports of moral determination.

But, of course, he was quite in the right; when all the other banks of geraniums were brown and flowerless, the bank he had picked over was as brilliant as in spring.

By now it had rained, and had rained well, and just as it was hard to remember the long cold wet of the early year in the cold drought, and the cold drought in the dry heat, now the long dryness had vanished out of memory, for it was a real English summer, all fitfully showery, fitfully cool and hot. Yet it was autumn; the overfullness of everything said it must be. A strong breeze sent leaves spinning down, and the smell of the stagnant parts of the lakes was truly horrible, making you wonder about the philosophy of the parkkeepers—it was against their principles to clear away the smelly rubbish? They couldn't afford a man in a boat once a week to take it away? Or they had faith in the power of nature to heal everything?

In my garden last year's wasteland, so very soon to be left behind, the roses, the thyme, geranium, clematis, were all strongly flowering, and butterflies crowded over lemon balm and hyssop. The pear tree was full of small tasteless pears. The tree was too old. It could produce masses of blossom, but couldn't carry the work through to good fruit. At every movement of the air, down thumped the pears. All the little boys from the Council flats came jumping over the walls to snatch up the pears, which they needed to throw at each other, not to eat. When invited to come in and pick them, great sullenness and resentment resulted, because the point was to raid the big rich gardens along the canal, into which hundreds of gardenless people looked down from the flats, to raid them, dart away with the spoils, and then raid again, coming in under the noses of furious householders.

One afternoon I was in a bus beside the park, and the wind was strong, and all the air was full of flying leaves. This was the moment, the week of real autumn. Rushing at once to the park, I just caught it. Everything was yellow, gold, brown, orange; heaps of treasure lay tidily packed ready to be burned; the wind crammed the air with coloured leafage. It was cooling —the northern hemisphere, I mean, not the park, which of course had been hot, cold, and in between ever since the year had started running true to form, some time in July. The leaves were blown into the lakes, and sank to make streams of bubbles in which the birds dived and played. All around the moorhens' battered nest lay a starry patterning of plane leaves, in green and gold. You could see how, if this were wilderness, land would form here in this shallow place, in a season or two, how this arm of the lake would become swamp, and then, in a dry season, new earth, and the water would retreat. All the smelly backwaters were being covered over with thick soft layers of leaf, the plastic, the tins, the papers vanishing, as, no doubt, the parkkeepers had counted on happening when autumn came.

I walked from one end of the park to the other, then back and around and across, the squirrels racing and chasing, and the birds swimming along the banks beside me in case this shape might be a food-giving shape, and this food shape might have decided to distribute largesse around the next bend and was being mean now because of future plenty. There were many fewer birds. The great families bred that year off the islands had gone, and the population was normal again, couples and individuals sedately self-sufficient.

Only a week later, that perfection of autumn was over, and stripped boughs were showing the shape of next spring. Yet, visiting Sweden, where snow had come early and lay everywhere, then leaving it to fly home again, was flying from winter into autumn, a journey back in time in one afternoon. The aircraft did not land when it should have done, owing to some hitch or other, and luckily for us, had to go about in a wide sweep over London. I had not before flown so low, with no cloud to hide the city. It was all woodland and lakes and parks and gardens, and a highly coloured autumn still, with loads of russet and gold on the trees. All the ugly bits of London you imagine nothing could disguise were concealed by this habit of tree and garden.

In the park, though, from the ground, the trees looked very tall, very bare, and wet. The lakes were grey and solid. When the birds came fast across to see if there was food, they left arrow shapes on the water spreading slowly, and absolutely regular, till they dissolved into the shores: there were no boats out now, for these had been drawn up and lay overturned in rows along the banks waiting for spring.

And the dark had come down.

The park in winter is very different from high, crammed, noisy summer.

A long damp path in early twilight . . . it is not much more than three in the afternoon. Two gentlemen in trim dark suits and tidy, slightly bald heads, little frills of hair on their collars —a reminiscence of the eighteenth century or a claim on contemporary fashion, who knows?—two civil servants from the offices in the Nash Terraces, walk quietly by, their hands behind their backs, beside the water. They talk in voices so low you think it must be official secrets that they have come out to discuss in privacy.

The beds are dug and turned. New stacks of leaf are made every day as the old ones burn, scenting the air with guilt, not pleasure, for now you have to remember pollution. But the roses are all there still, blobs of colour on tall stems. All the stages of the year are visible at once, for each plant has on it brightly tinted hips, then dead roses which are brown dust rose-shaped, then the roses themselves, though each has frost-burn crimping the outer petals. Hips, dead roses, fresh blooms—and masses of buds, doomed never to come to flower, for the frosts will get them if the pruner doesn't. Pink Parfait and Ginger Rogers, Summer Holiday and Joseph's Coat are shortly to be slashed into anonymity.

For it will be the dead of the year very soon now; soon it will be the shortest day.

I sit on a bench in the avenue where in summer the poplars and fountain make Italy on a blue day, but now browny-grey clouds are driving hard across from the northeast. Crowds of sparrows materialise as I arrive, all hungry expectation, but I've been forgetful, I haven't so much as a biscuit. They sit on the bench, my shoe, the bench's back, rather hunched, the wind tugging their feathers out of shape. The seagulls are in too, so the sea must be rough today, or perhaps there is an oil slick.

Up against the sunset, today a dramatic one, gold, red, and packed dark clouds, birds slowly rotate, like jagged debris after a whirlwind. They look like rocks, but that's not possible; they must be more gulls. But it is nice to imagine them rocks, just as, on the walk home, the plane trees that are all bent one way by the wind, seem, with their dappled trunks, like deer ready to spring together towards the northern gates.

# Report on the
# Threatened City

*All co-ordinates all plans all prints cancelled. As of now condition
unforeseen by us obtaining this city. Clear all programmes all planners all forecasters for new setting on this information.*

*Base to note well that transmission this channel will probably be
interrupted by material originated locally. Our fuel is low and this
channel therefore only one now operative.*

## SUMMARY OF BACKGROUND TO MISSION

Since our planet discovered that this city was due for destruction
or severe damage, all calculations and plans of our department
have been based on one necessity: how to reach the city to warn
its inhabitants of what is to come. Observing their behaviour,
both through Astroviewers and from our unmanned machines
launched at intervals this past year, their time, our Commis-
sioners for External Affairs decided these people could have no
idea at all of what threatened, that their technology, while so
advanced in some ways, had a vast gap in it, a gap that could be
defined, in fact, precisely by that area of ignorance—not knowing what was to befall them. This gap seemed impossible. Much
time was spent by our technicians trying to determine what

form of brain these creatures could have that made this contra-diction possible—as already stated, a technology so advanced in one area and blank in another. Our technicians had to shelve the problem, since their theories became increasingly improb-able and since no species known to us anywhere corresponds even at a long remove with what we believed this one to be. It became, perhaps, the most intriguing of our unsolved problems, challenging and defeating one department after another.

## SUMMARY OF OBJECTIVE THIS MISSION

Meanwhile, putting all speculations on one side, attractive though they were, all our resources have been used, at top speed and pressure, to develop a spacecraft that could, in fact, land a team on this planet, since it was our intention, having given the warning, offered the information available to us but (we thought) not to them, which made the warning necessary, to offer them more: our assistance. We meant to help clear the area, transport the population elsewhere, cushion the shock to the area and then, having done what, after all, we have done for other planets, our particular mental structure being suited to this kind of forecasting and assistance, return to base, taking some suitable specimens of them with us, in order to train them in a way that would overcome the gap in their minds and, there-fore, their science. The first part we achieved: That is, we managed, in the time set for it, to develop a spacecraft that could make the journey here, carrying the required number of person-nel. It strained our own technology and postponed certain cherished plans of our own. But our craft landed here, on the western shore of the land mass, as planned, and without any trouble seven days ago.

## THE NATURE OF THE PROBLEM

You will have wondered why there have been no transmissions before this. There have been two reasons. One: We realised at once that there would be heavier demands on our fuel than we had anticipated and that we would have to conserve it. Two: We were waiting to understand what it was we had to tell you. We did not understand the problem. For it was almost at once clear to us that all our thinking about "the gap in their mental structure" was off the point. We have never understood the nature of the problem. So improbable is it that we delayed communicating until we were sure. The trouble with this species is not that it is unable to forecast its immediate future; it is that it doesn't seem to care. Yet that is altogether too simple a stating of its condition. If it were so simple—that it knew that within five years its city was to be destroyed, or partly destroyed, and that it was indifferent—we should have to say: This species lacks the first quality necessary to any animal species; it lacks the will to live. Finding out what the mechanism is has caused the delay. Which I now propose to partially remedy by going into an account of what befell us, step by step. This will entail a detailed description of a species and a condition absolutely without precedent in our experience of the inhabited planets.

## AN IMPOSSIBLE FACT

But first, here is a fact that you will find hard to believe. We did not find this out at once, but when we did, it was a moment of focus in our investigation, enabling us to see our problem clearly. *This city experienced a disaster, on a fairly large scale, about sixty-five years ago, their time.*

A thought immediately suggests itself: Our experts did not know about this past disaster, only about the one to come. Our thinking is as defective in its way as theirs is. We had decided that they had a gap, that this gap made it impossible for them to see into the immediate future. Having decided this, we never once considered another possibility, the truth—that they had no gap, that they knew about the threatened danger and did not care. Or behaved as if they did not. Since we were unable to conceive of this latter possibility, we did not direct our thoughts and our instruments back in time—their time. We took it absolutely for granted, an assumption so strong that it prevented our effective functioning as these creatures' assumptions prevent them from acting—we believed (since we are so built ourselves) that it would be impossible for a disaster to have occurred already, because if we had experienced such a thing, we would have learned from the event and taken steps accordingly. Because of a series of assumptions, then, and an inability to move outside our own mental set, we missed a fact that might have been a clue to their most extraordinary characteristic—the fact that such a very short time ago they experienced a disaster of the sort that threatens again, and soon.

## THE LANDING

Our unmanned craft have been landing on their planet for centuries and have taken various shapes, been of varying substances. These landings were at long intervals until one year ago. These intervals were because, except for its unique destructiveness and belligerence, this species is not the most remarkable or interesting of those made available to our study by our Technological Revolution in its Space Phase. But twelve times recently, each during a period when their planet was at full light potential, we have landed craft, and each time close to the place in question. This was easy, because the terrain is semi-desert and lightly populated. We chose material for the craft that would manifest as their substance light—which is why we always used maximum their planet light as landing times. These craft were visible, if at all, as strong moonlight. The craft we are using on this present mission, the thirteenth in this series, is of higher concentration, since it is manned.

We landed as planned. The sky was clear, the light of their moon strong. We knew at once that we were visible, because a herd of their young was near, some fifty or sixty of them, engaged in a mating ritual that involved fire, food and strong sound, and as we descended, they dispersed. Tapping their mind streams established that they believed our machine was extra-territorial but that they were indifferent—no, that is not an exact description, but remember, we are trying to describe a mind state that none of us could have believed was possible. It was not that they were indifferent to us but that indifference was generalised throughout their processes, felt by us as a block or a barrier. After the young creatures had gone, we surveyed the terrain and discovered that we were on high land rising to mountains, inland from the water mass on the edge of which stands the city. A group of older specimens arrived. We know now that they live nearby and are all some variety or other of agriculturalist. They stood quite close, watching the craft. An examination of their minds showed a different type of block. Even at that early stage, we were able to establish a difference in texture between their thought streams and those of the young, which we later understood amounted to this: The older ones felt a responsibility or a power to act, as members of society, while the young ones were excluded or had decided to exclude themselves. As this area of the planet turned into the sunlight, it was clear to us that our craft ceased to be visible, for two of these older creatures came so close we were afraid they would actually enter the concentration. But they showed an awareness of our presence by other symptoms—headache and nausea. They were angry because of this damage being done to them— which they could have alleviated by moving farther off; but at the same time, they were feeling pride. This reaction highlighted the difference between them and the young—the pride was because of what they thought we represented; for, unlike the young, they believed we were some kind of weapon, either of their own land mass or of a hostile one, but from their own planet.

## WAR-MAKING PATTERNS

Everyone in the System knows that this species is in the process of self-destruction, or part destruction. This is endemic. The largest and most powerful groupings—based on geographical position—are totally governed by their war-making functions. Rather, each grouping *is* a war-making function, since its economies, the lives of its individual members, its movements are all subservient to the need to prepare for or wage war. This complete domination of a land area by its war-making machinery is not always visible to the inhabitants of that area, as this species is able, while making war or preparing for it, to think of itself as peace-loving—yes, indeed, this is germane to our theme; the essence of it.

## RATIONAL ACTION IMPOSSIBLE

Here we approach the nature of the block, or patterning, of their minds—we state it now, though we did not begin to understand it until later. *It is that they are able to hold in their minds at the same time several contradictory beliefs without noticing it.* Which is why rational action is so hard for them. Now, the war-making function of each geographical area is not controlled by its inhabitants but is controlled by itself. Each is engaged in inventing, bringing to perfection—and keeping secret from its own inhabitants as well as from the "enemy"—highly evolved war weapons of all sorts, ranging from devices for the manipulation of men's minds to spacecraft.

## SUBSERVIENT POPULATIONS

For instance, recent landings on their moon, much publicised by the geographical groupings that made them and followed breathlessly by the inhabitants of the whole planet, were by no means the first achieved by the said groupings. No, the first "moon landings" were made in secret, in service of one grouping's dominance in war over another, and the slavish populations knew nothing about them. A great many of the devices and machines used by the war departments are continuously under test in all parts of the earth and are always being glimpsed or even seen fully by inhabitants who report them to the authorities. But some of these devices are similar (in appearance, at least) to machines of extraterritorial origin. Citizens reporting "flying saucers"—to use one of their descriptive phrases—may as well have seen the latest of their own grouping's machines on test as one of our observation craft or observation craft from the Jupiter family. Such a citizen will find that after reaching a certain level in the hierarchies of officialdom, silence will blanket him and his observations—he will in various ways be repulsed, ridiculed, or even threatened. As usually happens, a council of highly placed officials was recently ordered to take evidence and report on the by now innumerable sightings of "unidentified flying objects," but this council finished its deliberations with public words that left the situation exactly as it was before. The official report nowhere stated that there was a minority report by some of its own number. This is the level of behaviour in their public representatives that is tolerated by them. Large numbers, everywhere on the planet, see craft like ours, or other planets' craft, or war machines from their own or other geographical areas. But such is the atmosphere created by the war departments that dominate everything that these individuals are regarded as mentally inadequate or deluded. Until one of them has actually seen a machine or a spacecraft, he tends to believe that anyone who claims he has is deranged. Knowing this, when he does see something, he often does not say so. But so many individuals now have seen things for themselves that there are everywhere all kinds of dissident or sullen subgroupings. These are of all ages and they cut across the largest and most widespread sub-culture of them all, that of the young of the species who have grown up in a society of total war-preparedness, who are naturally reluctant to face a future that can only mean early death or maiming and who react in the way mentioned earlier, with a disinclination to take part in the administration of their various societies. The older ones seem much more able to delude themselves, to use words like "peace" when engaged in warlike behaviour, to identify with their geographical areas. The young ones are clear-minded, more easily see the planet as a single organism, but are also more passive and hopeless. We put forward the suggestion that the greater, or at least more purposive energy of the older ones may be because of their comparative narrowness and identification with smaller ideas. We are now able to explain why the young we met on the night we landed moved away. Some had already had the experience of insisting to the authorities that they had seen strange machines and objects of various kinds and of being discouraged or threatened. They would be prepared to publicise what they had seen in their own newssheets or to spread it by word of mouth; but, unlike their elders, most of whom seem unable to understand the extent to which they are subjugated to the need of war, they would never put themselves in a position where their authorities could capture or question them. But the older ones of the area who had seen our previous twelve craft, which had all landed there, had evolved a different attitude. Some had reported what they had seen and had been discouraged. One or two, persisting, had been described as mad and had been threatened with incarceration. But, on the whole, they had taken the attitude of the authorities as a directive to mind their own business. Discussing it among themselves, they had agreed to keep watch on their own account, not saying too much about what they saw. In this group are two spies, who report to the war departments on what is seen and on the reactions of their fellow agriculturalists.

## FIRST ATTEMPT AT A WARNING

Now we come to our first attempt to communicate a warning. Since the twenty or so elders were already on the spot and were unafraid, staying on the site where they believed we might redescend—they did not know it was only the strength of the sun's light that made us invisible—we decided to use them and again made contact with their thought streams, this time in an attempt to project our message. But there was a barrier, or at least something we could not understand, and it was time-consuming for us. We were already aware that we might run short of power.

## INCAPACITY FOR FEAR

Now, of course, we know we made a wrong assessment, for, expecting that the news of the expected disaster would jam their thought machinery in panic, we fed it in very carefully and slowly, taking an entire day and night. When we hit the block, or resistance, we put it down to fear. We were mistaken. This is perhaps the time to state a psychological law we consider basic to them: This is a species immune from fear—but this will be elaborated later, if the power holds. At the end of the day and night, still meeting the same resistance, we allowed ourselves another period of a day and a night to repeat the message, hoping that the fear—as we then saw it—would be overcome. At the end of the second period of transmitting, there was no change in their mental structure. I repeat, none. We know now what was far from our understanding then, that we were telling them something they already knew. As we were not prepared at that time to entertain that hypothesis, we decided that this particular group of individuals was for some reason unsuitable for our purposes and that we must try an altogether different type, and preferably of a different age group. We had tried mature individuals. We had already suspected what we since have confirmed, that in this species, the older they get, the less open they are to new thought material. Now, it so happens that the place where our craft descended is in an area much used for the before-mentioned mating rituals. Several times in the two day-and-night periods of our attempt with the older group, youngsters had arrived in various types of metal machines from the city—and had quite soon gone away, sensing our presence, if they did not see us. They all arrived in daylight. But on the third day, as the sunlight went, four young ones arrived in a metal conveyance, got out of it and sat fairly close to us on a small rocky rise.

## SECOND ATTEMPT AT A WARNING

They looked like healthy, strong specimens, and we began to transmit our information, but in greater concentration than we had used with the older individuals. But in spite of the increased power, these four absorbed what we fed into them and reacted in exactly the same way as their elders. We did not understand this and, taking the chance of setting them into a panic flight, concentrated our entire message (which had taken two entire days and nights with the mature group) into the space of time between the sunlight's going and its return. Their minds did not reject what we said nor jam up in fear. They were voicing to one another, in a mechanical way, what we were feeding into them. It sounded like this, over and over again—with variations:

"They say we have only five years."

"That's bad."

"Yeah, it's going to be real bad."

"When it comes, it's going to be the worst yet."

"Half the city might be killed."

"They say it might be as bad as that."

"Any time in the next five years, they say."

It was like pouring a liquid into a container that has a hole in it. The group of older ones had sat around for two days and nights repeating that the city was due for destruction, as if they were saying that they could expect a headache, and now these four were doing the same. At one point they stopped the mono-tone exchanges and one, a young female, accompanying herself on a stringed musical instrument, began what they call a song; that is, the vocalisations cease to be an exchange between two or more individuals, but an individual, or a group, very much enlarging the range of tones used in ordinary exchange, makes a statement. The information we fed into these four emerged in these words, from the young female:

> We know the earth we live upon
> Is due to fall.

*We know the ground we walk upon*
*Must shake.*
*We know, and so . . .*
*We eat and drink and love,*
*Keep high,*
*Keep love*
*For we must die.*

## PHASE I ABANDONED

And they continued with their mating rituals. We then discontinued the emission of thought material, if for no other reason than that we had already used up a fourth of our power supply with no result. This, then, was the end of Phase I, which was the attempt to transfer the warning material into the brains of selected members of the species for automatic telepathic transmission to others. We set about Phase II, which was to take possession of the minds of suitable individuals in a planned campaign to use them as mouthpieces for the warnings. We decided to abandon the first phase in the belief that the material was running straight through their mental apparatus like water through sieves because it was so foreign to the existing mental furniture of their minds that they were not able to recognise what we were saying. In other words, we still had no idea that the reason they did not react was that the idea was a commonplace.

## PHASE II ATTEMPTED

Three of us therefore accompanied the four youngsters in their machine when they returned to the city, because we thought that in their company we would most quickly find suitable individuals to take over—we had decided the young were more likely to be useful than the mature. The way they handled this machine was a shock to us. It was suicidal. Their methods of transport are lethal. In the time it took to reach the suburbs of the city—between the lightening of the dark and the sun's appearance—there were four near collisions with other, equally recklessly driven vehicles. Yet the four youngsters showed no fear and reacted with the mechanism called laughter; that is, with repeated violent contractions of the lungs, causing noisy emission of air. This journey, their recklessness, their indifference to death or pain made us conclude that this group of four, like the group of twenty older ones, was perhaps untypical. We were playing with the idea that there are large numbers of defective animals in this species and that we had been unlucky in our choices. The machine was stopped to refuel and the four got out and walked about. Three more youngsters were sitting on a bench huddled against one another, in a stupor. Like all the young, they wore a wide variety of clothing and had long head fur. They had several musical instruments. Our four attempted to rouse them and partly succeeded: The responses of the three were slow and, it seemed to us, even more clumsy and inadequate. They either did not understand what was being said or could not communicate what they understood. We then saw that they were in the power of some kind of drug. They had quantities of it and the four wished also to put themselves in its power. It was a drug that sharpens sensitivity while it inhibits ordinary response: The three were more sensitive to our presence than the four had been—they had not been aware of our presence in the vehicle at all. The three, once roused from their semiconsciousness, seemed to see, or at least to feel us, and directed towards us muttered sounds of approval or welcome. They seemed to associate us with the sun's appearance over the roof of the refueling station. The four, having persuaded the three to give them some of the drug, went to their vehicle. We decided to stay with the three, believing that their sensitivity to our presence was a good sign. Testing their thought streams, we found them quite free and loose, without the resistances and tensions of the others we had tested. We then took possession of their minds—this was the only moment of real danger during the whole mission. Your envoys might very well have been lost then, dissolving into a confusion and violence that we find hard to describe. For one thing, at that time we did not know how to differentiate between the effects of the drug and the effects of their senses. We now do know and will attempt a short description. The drug causes the mechanisms dealing with functions such as walking, talking, eating, and so on, to become slowed or dislocated. Meanwhile, the receptors for sound, scent, sight, touch are opened and sensitised. But for us, to enter their minds is in any case an assault, because of the phenomenon they call beauty, which is a description of their sense intake in an ordinary condition. For us, this is like entering an explosion of colour; for it is this that is the most startling difference between our mode of perceiving and theirs: The physical structure of their level appears in vibrations of brilliant colour. To enter an undrugged mind is hard enough for one of us; to keep one's balance is difficult. As it was, it might easily have happened that we were swept away in contemplation of vivid colour.

## NECESSITY TO CONDENSE REPORT, POWER FAILING

Although the temptation to dwell on this is great, we must condense this report if we wish to keep any use of this channel: the pressure of local material is getting very strong. In brief, then, the three youngsters, reeling with pleasure because of this dimension of brilliance which we of course all know about through deductions but which, I assure you, we have never approached even in imagination, shouting and singing that the city was doomed, stood on the side of the road until one of the plentiful machines stopped for us. We were conveyed rapidly into the city. There were two individuals in the vehicle, both young, and neither reacted in any way to the warnings we were giving them through the minds or, rather, voices of our hosts. At the end of the rapid movement, we arrived in the city, which is large, populous, and built around a wide indentation of the shore of the water mass. It is all extremely vivid, colourful, powerfully affecting the judgement, and it heightened the assault on our balance. We made a tentative decision that it is impracticable for our species to make use of this method: of actually possessing selected minds for the purpose of passing on information. It is too violent a transformation for us. However, since we were there, and succeeding in not being swept away into a highly tinted confusion of pleasure, we agreed to stay where we were and the three we were possessing left the vehicle and walked out into the streets, shouting out the facts as we thought them: that there was little doubt that at some moment between now and five years from now, there would be a strong vibration of the planet at this point and that the greater part of the city might be destroyed, with severe loss of life. It was early in the day, but many of them were about. We were waiting for some sort of reaction to what we were saying, interest at the very least; queries; some sort of response to which we could respond ourselves with advice or offers of help. But of the very many we met in that brief progress through the streets, *no one took any notice at all,* except for a glance or a short indifferent stare.

## CAPTURE BY THE AUTHORITIES

Soon there was a screeching and a wailing, which we at first took to be the reaction of these creatures to what we were saying, some sort of warning, perhaps, to the inhabitants, or statements that measures toward self-preservation must be taken; but it was another vehicle, of a military sort, and the three (we) were taken up from the streets and to a prison because of the disturbance we were making. This is how we understood it afterwards. At the time, we thought that the authorities had gathered us in to question us as to the revelations we had to make. In the hands of the guards, in the street and the military vehicle and the prison, we kept up a continuous shouting and crying out of the facts and did not stop until a doctor injected our three hosts with some other drug, which caused them instantly to become unconscious. It was when we heard the doctor talking to the guards that we first heard the fact of the previous catastrophe. This was such a shock to us that we could not then take in its implications. But we decided at once to leave our hosts, who, being in any case unconscious, would not be any use to us for some time, even if this method of conveying warnings had turned out to be efficacious—and it obviously was not —and make different plans. The doctor was also saying that he had to treat large numbers of people, particularly the young ones, for "paranoia." This was what our three hosts were judged to be suffering from. Apparently, it is a condition when people show fear of forthcoming danger and try to warn others about it and then show anger when stopped by authority. This diagnosis, together with the fact that the doctor and the authorities knew of the coming danger and of the past catastrophe—in other words, that they consider it an illness or a faulty mental condition to be aware of what threatens and to try to take steps to avoid or soften it—was something so extraordinary that we did not then have time to evaluate it in depth, nor have we had time since to do so, because—

. . . AND FINALLY, TO END THIS NEWS FLASH, A REAL HEART-WARMER. FIVE PEOPLE, NOT RICH FOLKS, NO, BUT PEOPLE LIKE YOU AND ME, HAVE GIVEN UP A MONTH'S PAY TO SEND LITTLE JANICE WANAMAKER, THE CHILD WITH THE HOLE IN THE HEART, TO THE WORLD-FAMED HEART CENTER IN FLORIDA. LITTLE JANICE, WHO IS TWO YEARS OLD, COULD HAVE EXPECTED A LONG LIFE OF INVALIDISM: BUT NOW THE FAIRY WAND OF LOVE HAS CHANGED ALL THAT AND SHE WILL BE FLYING TOMORROW MORNING TO HAVE HER OPERATION, ALL THANKS TO THE FIVE GOOD NEIGHBORS OF ARTESIA STREET—

. . . the expected interruptions on this wave length; but, as we have no way of knowing at which point the interruption began, to recapitulate, we left the doctor and the guards in discussion of the past catastrophe, in which two hundred miles of ground was ripped open, hundreds of people were killed and the whole city was shaken down in fragments. This was succeeded by a raging fire.

## HUMOUR AS A MECHANISM

The doctor was discussing *humorously* (note previous remarks about laughter, a possible device for release of tension to ward off or relieve fear and, therefore, possibly one of the mechanisms that keep these animals passive in the face of possible extinction) that for some years after the previous catastrophe, this entire geographical grouping referred to the great fire, rather than to the earth vibration. This circumlocution is still quite common. In other words, a fire being a smaller, more manageable phenomenon, they preferred, and sometimes still prefer, to use that word, instead of the word for the uncontrollable shaking of the earth itself. A pitiable device, showing helplessness and even fear. But we emphasise here again that everywhere else in the System, fear is a mechanism to protect or to warn, and in these creatures, the function is faulty. As for helplessness, this is tragic anywhere, even among these murderous brutes, but there is no apparent need for them to be helpless, since they have every means to evacuate the city altogether and to—

. . . THE NEW SUBURB PLANNED TO THE WEST. THIS WILL HOUSE
ONE HUNDRED THOUSAND PEOPLE AND WILL BE OPEN IN THE AUTUMN
OF NEXT YEAR FULLY EQUIPPED WITH SHOPS, CINEMAS, A CHURCH,
SCHOOLS AND A NEW MOTORWAY. THE RAPID EXPANSION OF OUR
BEAUTIFUL CITY, WITH ITS UNIQUE CLIMATE, ITS SETTING, ITS SHORE
LINE, CONTINUES. THIS NEW SUBURB WILL DO SOMETHING TO COM-
BAT THE OVERCROWDING AND—

## THE JETTISONING OF PHASES I, II, AND III

. . . In view of the failure of Phases I and II, we decided to
abandon Phase III, which was planned to be a combination of
I and II—inhabiting suitable hosts to use them as loud-speakers
and, at the same time, putting material into available thought
streams for retransmission. Before making further attempts to
communicate, we needed more information. To summarise the
results of Phase II, when we inhabited the three drugged young,
we understood we must be careful to assume the shapes of
older animals, and those of a technically trained kind, as it was
clear from our experience in the prison that the authorities disliked the young of their species. We did not yet know whether
they were capable of listening to the older ones, who are shaped
in the image of their society.

## INABILITY TO ASSESS TRUTH

While at that stage we were still very confused about what
we were finding, we had at least grasped this: that this species,
on being told something, has no means of judging whether or
not it is true. We on our planet assume, because it is our mental structure and that of all the species we have examined, that
if a new fact is made evident by material progress, or by a new
and hitherto unexpected juxtaposition of ideas, then it is accepted as a fact, a truth—until an evolutionary development
by-passes it. Not so with this species. It is not able to accept
information, new material, unless it is from a source it is not
suspicious about. This is a handicap to its development that is
not possible to exaggerate. We choose this moment to suggest,
though of necessity briefly, that in future visits to this planet,
with information of use to this species (if it survives), infinite
care must be taken to prepare plenipotentiaries who resemble
in every respect the most orthodox and harmless members of

the society. For it is as if the mechanism fear has been misplaced from where it would be useful—preventing or softening calamity—to an area of their minds that makes them suspicious of anything but the familiar. As a small example, in the prison, because the three young animals were drugged and partly incoherent, and because (as it has become clear to us) the older animals who run the society despise those who are not similar to the norms they have established, it would not have mattered what they said. If they had said (or shouted or sung) that they had actually observed visitors from another planet (they had, in fact, sensed us, felt us) as structures of finer substance manifesting as light—if they had stated they had seen three roughly man-sized creatures shaped in light—no notice at all would have been taken of them. But if an individual from that section of their society which is especially trained for that class of work (it is an infinitely subdivided society) had said that he had observed *with his instruments* (they have become so dependent on machinery that they have lost confidence in their own powers of observation) three rapidly vibrating light structures, he would at least have been credited with good faith. Similarly, great care has to be taken with verbal formulation. An unfamiliar fact described in one set of words may be acceptable. Present it in a pattern of words outside what they are used to and they may react with all the signs of panic—horror, scorn, fear.

## ADAPTATION TO THEIR NORM FOR THEIR DOMINANT ANIMALS

We incarnated as two males of mature age. We dressed ourselves with the attention to detail they find reassuring. An item of clothing cut differently from what is usual for older animals will arouse disapproval or suspicion. Sober tones of colour are acceptable; bright tones, except in small patches, are not. We assure you that if we had dressed even slightly outside their norm, we could have done nothing at all. It is the dominant males who have to restrict their choice of clothing. Women's garb is infinitely variable, but always changing, suddenly and dramatically, from one norm or pattern to another. The young can wear what they please as long as they are not part of the machinery of government. The cutting and arranging of their head fur is also important. Women and the young enjoy latitude in this, too, but we had to see that our head fur was cut short and kept flattened. We also assumed a gait indicating soberness and control, and facial expressions that we had noted they found reassuring. For instance, they have a way of stretching the lips sideways and exposing the teeth in a sort of facial arrangement they call a smile that indicates that they are not hostile, will not attack, that their intentions are to keep the peace.

Thus disguised, we walked about the city engaged in observation, on the whole astounded that so little notice was taken of us. For while we were fair copies, we were not perfect, and a close scrutiny would have shown us up. But one of their characteristics is that they, in fact, notice very little about one another; it is a remarkably unnoticing species. Without arousing suspicion, we discovered that everybody we talked to knew that a disturbance of the earth was expected in the next five years, that while they "knew" this, they did not really believe it, or seemed not to, since their plans to live as if nothing whatsoever was going to happen were unaltered and that a laboratory or institute existed to study the past upheaval and make plans for the forthcoming one—

. . . AT THE BASEBALL GAME THIS AFTERNOON, A PORTION OF THE SCAFFOLDING GAVE WAY AND SIXTY PEOPLE WERE KILLED. THERE HAVE BEEN MESSAGES OF SYMPATHY FROM THE PRESIDENT, HER MAJESTY THE QUEEN OF GREAT BRITAIN, AND THE POPE. THE MANAGER OF THE SPORTS STADIUM WAS IN TEARS AS HE SAID: "THIS IS THE MOST TERRIBLE THING THAT I HAVE EVER SEEN. I KEEP SEEING THOSE DEAD FACES BEFORE MY EYES." THE CAUSE OF THE ACCIDENT IS THAT BUILDING OF THE STANDS AND THEIR MAINTENANCE, AND THE PROVISION OF CRUSH BARRIERS, ARE SUBJECT TO MAXIMUM PROFIT BEING EARNED BY THE OWNERS. THE FUND SET UP AS THE CORPSES WERE CARRIED FROM THE STADIUM HAS ALREADY REACHED $200,000 AND MORE KEEPS POURING—

## THE INSTITUTE

We entered the Institute for Prognosis and Prevention of Earth Disturbance as visitors from Geographical Area 2—one allied at this time with this area and, therefore, welcome to observe its work.

A short description of this organisation may be of use: There are fifty of their most highly skilled technicians in it, all at work on some of the most advanced (as advanced as ours in this field) equipment for the diagnosis of vibrations, tremors, quakes. The very existence of this institute is because of the knowledge that the city cannot survive another five years—or is unlikely to do so. All these technicians live in the city, spend their free time in it—and the institute itself is in the danger area. They are all likely to be present when the event occurs. Yet they are all cheerful, unconcerned and—it is easy to think —of extreme bravery. But after a short time in their company, discussing their devices for predicting the upheaval, it is difficult to resist the conclusion that like the youngsters in the machine for transportation, who steer it in such a way that they are bound to kill or maim themselves or others, they are in some way set not to believe what they say—that they are in danger and will most certainly be killed or maimed together with the rest of the population—

. . . THE FIRE BROKE OUT AT DAWN, WHEN FEW PEOPLE WERE IN THE STREETS, AND WAS SO POWERFUL THAT IT REACHED THE FOURTH STORY FROM THE BASEMENT IN MINUTES. THE SCORES OF PEOPLE IN THE BUILDING WERE DRIVEN UPWARDS BY THE FIRE, A FEW MANAGING TO NEGOTIATE THE FIRE ESCAPES, WHICH WERE MOSTLY ENGULFED IN FLAMES. AN UNKNOWN MAN IN THE STREET PENETRATED THE BUILDING, IN SPITE OF THE SMOKE AND THE FLAMES, AND RESCUED TWO SMALL CHILDREN LEFT CRYING ON THE SECOND FLOOR. ANOTHER TWO MINUTES AND IT WOULD HAVE BEEN TOO LATE. HE INSTANTLY PLUNGED BACK INTO THE INFERNO AND BROUGHT OUT AN OLD WOMAN ON HIS BACK. IN SPITE OF PROTESTS FROM THE BY NOW LARGE CROWD, HE INSISTED ON RE-ENTERING THE FLAMING BUILDING AND WAS LAST SEEN AT A SECOND-FLOOR WINDOW FROM WHICH HE THREW DOWN A BABY TO THE PEOPLE BELOW. THE BABY WILL SURVIVE, BUT THE UNKNOWN HERO FELL BACK INTO THE FLAMES AND—

## A BASIC MECHANISM

. . . We believe we have established one of their mechanisms for maintaining themselves in impotence and indecision. It is precisely this: that they do continuously discuss and analyse. For instance, the technicians of this institute are always issuing warnings to the city's officials and to the populace. Their prognoses, one after another, come true—that minor vibrations are likely to occur in this or that area—yet warnings continue to be issued, discussion goes on. So accustomed have they become to this state of affairs that we found it was not possible to discuss active means for prevention with them. They would have become suspicious that we were some sort of troublemaker. In short, they do not find frightening discussion about the timing, the nature, the power of probable earth convulsions, but they are hostile to suggestions about the possible transfer of population or rebuilding of the city elsewhere. We have said that this is an infinitely subdivided society: It is the institute's task to warn, to forecast, not its responsibility to suggest solutions. But this mechanism—the role of talk—is merely part of a much deeper one. We now suspect that a great many of the activities that they themselves see as methods of furthering change, saving life, improving society are, in fact, methods of preventing change. It is almost as if they were afflicted with a powerful lassitude, a lack of vital energy which must resist change, because it is so easily exhausted. Their infinite number of varieties of oral, verbal activity are expenditures of vital energy. They are soothed and relieved by stating a problem, but, having done this, seldom have the energy left to act on their verbal formulations. We have even concluded that they feel that by stating a problem, it becomes in some way nearer solution—

. . . PROTESTS THAT THE THREE SKYSCRAPERS ON THIRD STREET ARE TO BE PULLED DOWN IN ORDER TO BUILD THREE MUCH HIGHER BUILD-INGS, INSTEAD OF PUTTING THE MONEY INTO PROVIDING LOW-RATE ACCOMMODATION FOR THE CITY'S POOR, OF WHICH RECENT SURVEYS REVEAL THERE ARE ONE MILLION OR MORE, NEARLY A QUARTER OF THE TOTAL POPULATION, AND ALL IN ACCOMMODATIONS SO IN-ADEQUATE THAT—

. . . for instance, debates, discussions, verbal contests of all sorts, public and private, continue all the time. All their ac-tivities, public and private, are defined in talk, public or private. It is possible that they are so constituted that for them an event has not occurred at all unless it has been discussed, presented in words—

. . . THIRTY-FIVE CONVENTIONS IN THE MONTH OF MAY ALONE TOTAL-ING SEVENTY-FIVE THOUSAND DELEGATES FROM EVERY PART OF THE CONTINENT, WHILE AT THE SAME TIME, THE TOURIST FIGURES FOR MAY TOPPED THOSE FOR ANY PREVIOUS MAY. THIS YEAR IS ALREADY A RECORD FOR CONVENTIONS AND TOURISM GENERALLY, PROVING

THAT THE ATTRACTIONS OF OUR CITY, ITS SITUATION, ITS CLIMATE,
ITS AMENITIES, ITS REPUTATION FOR HOSPITALITY, EVER INCREASE
IN EVERY PART OF THE CIVILIZED GLOBE. IT IS ESSENTIAL TO STEP UP
THE BUILDING OF NEW HOTELS, MOTELS AND RESTAURANTS AND TO—

. . . the one thing they do not seem able to contemplate is the
solution that has seemed to us obvious ever since we observed
their probable future and decided to devote so much of our own
planet's resources to trying to help our sister planet—to evacuate the city altogether. This is incredible, we know. Of course,
you will find it so.

## INDIFFERENCE TO LOSS OF LIFE

We can only report what we find—that at no point have the
inhabitants of this city even considered the possibility of abandoning it and moving to an area that is not absolutely certain
to be destroyed. Their attitude towards life is that it is unimportant. They are indifferent to their own suffering, assume
that their species must continuously lose numbers and strength
and health by natural disasters, famine, constant war. That this
attitude goes side by side with infinite care and devotion to
individuals or to small groups seems to us to indicate—

. . . THE DONATED SUM IS TO BE USED TO BUILD A MEMORIAL, TO BE
ERECTED IN THE SQUARE. IT WILL BE IN THE SHAPE OF A COLUMN,
WITH THE HEAD OF WILLIAM UNDERSCRIBE, THE DECEASED, IN RELIEF
ON ONE SIDE.

LAID TO REST

UPON THE BREAST

OF NATURE

GONE BUT NOT FORGOTTEN

WILL BE CARVED ON THE OTHER. JOAN UNDERSCRIBE, WHO LOST
HER HUSBAND FIVE YEARS AGO, HAS WORKED SEVEN DAYS A WEEK
FROM SIX IN THE MORNING UNTIL TEN AT NIGHT AT THE AVENUE
MOTEL TO EARN THE SUM NECESSARY FOR THIS SIMPLE BUT MOVING
MEMORIAL. SHE HAS JEOPARDIZED HER HEALTH, SHE CLAIMS. THE
FIVE YEARS OF UNREMITTING TOIL HAVE TAKEN THEIR TOLL. BUT
SHE HAS NO REGRETS. "HE WAS THE BEST HUSBAND A WOMAN EVER
HAD," SHE TOLD OUR REPORTER—

. . . on the point of deciding there was nothing we could do
against such total indifference to their condition; but since they
are at least prepared to talk about situations, we devised a
plan—

. . . THE BIGGEST ENTERTAINMENT EVER, COMBINING THE WORLD'S TOP CIRCUSES, ICE SHOWS, NONSTOP POP CONCERTS FOR THE ENTIRE WEEK, DAY AND NIGHT, NOT TO MENTION THREE OPERAS FROM THE WORLD'S GREATEST, THE BRITISH NATIONAL THEATRE COMPANY, IN THAT PERENNIAL ATTRACTION, THE INTERNATIONAL CULTURAL STAR ACE, "THE THREE SISTERS," WHICH WILL BE ATTENDED BY OUR OWN FIRST LADY AND HER CHARMING DAUGHTERS AND A GLITTERING ARRAY OF STARS, INCLUDING BOB HOPE—

. . . "calling a conference" is to gather a large number of individuals in one place, in order to exchange verbal formulations. This is probably their main anxiety-calming mechanism; they certainly resort to it on every occasion, whether under that name, called by governments, administrative bodies, authorities of all kinds, or under other names, for very often this procedure is social. For instance, a conference can be called a party and be for pleasure, but discussion on a theme or themes will be, in fact, the chief activity. The essential factor is that many of the creatures assemble in one place, to exchange word patterns with others, afterwards telling others not present what has occurred—

. . . THE CITY'S CONSERVATION YEAR IS OVER AND MUST BE COUNTED A REMARKABLE SUCCESS. IT BURNED AN AWARENESSS OF WHAT WE CAN EXPECT SO DEEPLY INTO ALL OUR MINDS AND HEARTS THAT INTEREST IS NOW NOT LIKELY TO FADE. A CONFERENCE TO—

## THEIR EDUCATION

The ability to define these, and to differentiate them from those of other people's, forms a large part of their education. When two of these creatures meet for the first time, they will set about finding out what opinions the other holds and will tolerate each other accordingly. Non-stimulating, easily tolerated opinions can also be called "received ideas." This means that an idea or a fact has been stamped with approval by some form of authority. The phrase is used like this: "That is a received idea." "Those are all received ideas." This does not necessarily mean that the idea or fact has been acted on nor that behaviour has been changed. Essentially, a received idea is one that has become familiar, whether effective or not, and no longer arouses hostility or fear. The mark of an educated individual is this: that he has spent years absorbing received ideas and is able readily to repeat them. People who have absorbed opinions counter to the current standard of ideas are distrusted and may be called opinionated. This description is earned most easily by women and young people.

By that time, we were well known to everyone in the institute as Herbert Bond, thirty-five years old, male, and John Hunter, forty years old, male. We had learned enough to avoid the direct "Why don't you take such-and-such steps?" since we had learned that this approach caused some sort of block or fault in their functioning, but approached like this: "Let us discuss the factors militating against the taking of such-and-such a step"; for instance, making sure that new buildings were not erected close to the area where tremors or vibrations must occur.

This formulation was initially successful, evoking the maximum amount of animated talk without arousing hostility. But very shortly, strong emotion was aroused by phrases and words of which we list a few here: profit motive, conflicting commercial interests, vested interests, capitalism, socialism, democracy —there are many such emotive words. We were not able to determine, or not in a way that our economic experts would recognise as satisfactory, the significance of these phrases, since the emotions became too violent to allow the conference to continue. The animals would certainly have begun to attack one another physically. In other words, the range of opinion (see above) was too wide to be accommodated. Opinion, that is, on matters to do with disposal and planning of population. Opinion concerning earth disturbance was virtually unanimous.

### BARBARIC METHOD OF TOWN PLANNING UNIQUE IN OUR SYSTEM, BUT SEE HISTORIES OF PLANETS 2 AND 4

It appears that their population disposal, their city planning, is not determined by the need of the people who live in an area but is the result of a balance come to by many conflicting bodies and individuals whose reason for participating in such schemes is self-interest. For instance: before the violence engendered by this subject closed the conference, we had gathered that the reason a particularly large and expensive group of buildings was built directly in the line of maximum earth disturbance was that that part of the city commands high "rents"—that is, people are prepared to pay more to live and work in that area than elsewhere. Nor can the willingness of the builders and planners to erect buildings in the maximum danger area be put down to callousness, since in many cases the individuals concerned themselves live and work there—

. . .THE EMERGENCY UNIT AT THE HOSPITAL IN WHICH A TEAM OF TEN DOCTORS AND NURSES WORKS AROUND THE CLOCK TO SAVE LIVES THAT WOULD HAVE BEEN LOST AS RECENTLY AS FIVE YEARS AGO—AND ARE STILL LOST IN HOSPITALS NOT EQUIPPED WITH EMERGENCY UNITS. THE PATIENTS ARE USUALLY THE VICTIMS OF CAR ACCIDENTS OR STREET FIGHTS AND ARRIVE AT THE UNIT IN A STATE OF SEVERE SHOCK. SINCE AS SHORT A DELAY AS FIVE MINUTES CAN MAKE THE DIFFERENCE BETWEEN LIFE AND DEATH, TREATMENT IS STARTED AS THE PATIENT IS LIFTED OUT OF THE AMBULANCE—

. . . as a good deal of the anger was directed against their own young, we left the institute and returned to the centre of the city, where we again made contact with the young.

## THE INSTITUTE FOUND NOT USEFUL

The young ones working at the institute in menial and assistive positions were all of a different subculture, patterned on the older animals in clothing and behaviour. The young animals we met in the city were in herds, or smaller groups, and not easily contacted by Herbert Bond and John Hunter, who, being older and dressed in the uniform of the dominant males, were suspected of being spies of some sort. We therefore reincarnated ourselves as two youngsters, male and female, having decided to spend a fourth of what was left of our supply of power in trying to persuade them to agree on one issue and to act on it. For, like their elders, they discuss and talk and sing endlessly, enjoying pleasurable sensations of satisfaction and agreement with others, making these an end in themselves. We suggested that in view of what was going to happen to the city, they, the young ones, might try to persuade all those of their age to leave and live elsewhere, to make for themselves some sort of encampment if to build a new city was beyond their resources, at any rate, a place in which refugees would be welcomed and cared for.

## FAILURE WITH THE YOUNG

All that happened was that a number of new songs were sung, all of a melancholy nature, all on the theme of unavoidable tragedy. Our encounter with these young ones was taking place on the beach and at the time of the fading of the sunlight. This is a time that has a powerfully saddening effect on all the animals. But it was not until afterwards that we understood we should have chosen any time of the day but that one. There were large numbers of young, many with musical instruments. Half a dozen of them converted the occasion into a conference (see above) by addressing the mass not as their elders do, through talking, but through singing—the heightened and emotional sound. The emotion was of a different kind from that at the conference at the institute. That had been violent and aggressive and nearly resulted in physical attack. This was heavy, sad, passive. Having failed to get them to discuss, either by talking or by singing, a mass exodus from the city, we then attempted discussing how to prevent individuals from massing in the most threatened areas (we were on one at the time) and how, when the shock occurred, to prevent mass deaths and injuries and how to treat the injured, and so forth.

## DESPAIR OF THE YOUNG

All these attempts failed. We might have taken a clue from the drugged condition of the three whose minds we at first occupied and from the indifference to death of the four in the metal conveyance. We have concluded that the young are in a state of disabling despair. While more clear-minded, in some ways, than their elders—that is, more able to voice and maintain criticism of wrongs and faults—they are not able to believe in their own effectiveness. Again and again, on the beach, as the air darkened, versions of this exchange took place:

"But you say you believe it must happen, and within five years."

"So they say."

"But you don't think it will?"

"If it happens, it happens."

"But it isn't *if*—it will happen."

"They are all corrupt, what can we do? They want to kill us all."

"Who are corrupt?"

"The old ones. They run everything."

"But why don't you challenge them?"

"You can't challenge them. They are too strong. We have to evade. We must be fluid. We must be like water."

"But you are still here, where it is going to happen."

"So they say."

A song swept the whole gathering. It was now quite dark. There were many thousands massed near the water.

> It will happen soon,
> So they say,
> We will not live to fight
> Another day.
> They are blind.
> They have blown our mind.
> We shall not live to fight,
> We live to die.

## MASS SUICIDES

And hundreds of them committed suicide—by swimming out into the water in the dark, while those who stood on higher ledges by the water threw themselves in—

. . . A DONATION OF $500,000 TO BUILD A BIRD SANCTUARY IN THE PARK. THIS WILL HAVE SPECIMENS OF EVERY KNOWN SPECIES IN THE WORLD. IT IS HOPED THAT SPECIES THREATENED WITH EXTINC- TION DUE TO MAN'S CRUELTY AND UNCONCERN WILL FIND THIS SANCTUARY A USEFUL BANK FROM WHICH THEY CAN REPLENISH AND STRENGTHEN VARIETIES UNDER THREAT—

. . . very low stock of power. We decided to make one last attempt, to concentrate our material in a single place. We decided to leave the herds of young and to return to the older animals, since these were in authority. Not to the institute, since we had proved their emotional instability. It was essential to choose a set of words that would not cause emotion—a received idea.

Now, the idea that the behaviour of an individual or a group can be very different from its, or their, self-description is already part of their mental furniture and is enshrined in many time-worn word sets. For instance, "Don't judge by what he says but by what he does."

We decided to reinforce this soothing received idea with

another of their anxiety-reducing devices. We have already noted that a conference is such a device. A variety of this is to put ideas into heightened or emotional sound, as was done by the young on the beach. We decided that neither of these was suitable for our last attempt. We considered and discarded a third that we have not yet mentioned. This is when disturbing or unpalatable ideas are put into ritual form and acted out in public to small groups or relayed by a technical device, "television," which enables visual images to be transmitted simultaneously to millions of people. A sequence of events that may fall outside their formal code of morality, or be on its borderline, will be acted out, causing violent approval or disapproval —it is a form of catharsis. After a time, these sequences of acted-out events become familiar and are constantly performed. This way of trying out, of acclimatising unfamiliar ideas, goes on all the time, side by side with ritual acting out of situations that are familiar and banal—thus making them appear more interesting. This is a way of making a life situation that an individual may find intolerably tedious and repetitive more stimulating and enable him to suffer it without rebelling. These dramas, of both the first and the second kind, can be of any degree of sophistication. But we decided on a fourth mechanism or method: a verbal game. One of their games is when sets of words are discussed by one, two or more individuals, and these are most often transmitted through the above-mentioned device.

We had reassumed our identities as Herbert Bond and John Hunter, since we were again contacting authority, and approached a television center with forged credentials from a geographic area called Britain, recently a powerful and combative subspecies, which enjoys a sort of prestige because of past aggressiveness and military prowess.

## LAUGHTER, FUNCTIONS OF, SEE ABOVE

We proposed a game of words, on the theme "Don't judge by words but by actions." The debate took place last night. To begin with, there was a good deal of laughter, a sign that should have warned us. This was not antagonistic, "laughing at," which is found disagreeable but which, in fact, is much safer a reaction than "laughing with," which is laughter of agreement, of feeling flattered. This second type is evoked by ideas that are minority ideas, when the minorities consider they are in advance of the mass. The aggressive and hostile laughter is a safer reaction because it reassures onlookers that a balance is being kept, whereas the sympathetic laughter arouses feelings of anxiety in those watching if the ideas put forward are challenging to norms accepted by them. Our thesis was simple and as already outlined: that this society is indifferent to death and to suffering. Fear is not experienced, or not in a way that is useful for protecting society or the individual. No one sees these facts, because all the sets of words that describe behaviour are in contrast to the facts. The official sets of words are all to do with protection of oneself and others. Throughout all this —that is, while we developed our thesis—we were greeted by laughter.

These games have audiences invited to the places where they are played, so that the makers of the ritual can judge the probable reaction of the individuals outside all over the city in front of their television. The laughter was loud and prolonged. Opposing Herbert Bond and John Hunter, professors of words from Britain, were two professors of words from the local university. They have rules of debate, the essence of which is that each statement must have the same weight or importance as the preceding. The opposing professors' statements, of equal length as ours, stated the opposite view and were light and humorous in tone. Our turn coming again, we proved our point by stating the facts about this city's behaviour in the face of a certain disaster—but we did not get very far. As soon as we switched from the theoretical, the general, to the particular, the laughter died away and violent hostility was shown. There is a custom that if people watching a ritual dislike it, they send hostile messages to the relay point. What Herbert Bond and John Hunter said caused so much violent emotion that the technical equipment used for listening to these messages broke down. While the two local professors maintained the calmness of manner expected during these games, they were nervous and, the ritual over, they said they thought they would lose their employment. They were hostile to us, as being responsible. They complained that as "foreigners," we did not realise that these rituals must be kept light in tone and general in theme.

When we two got to the door of the building, there was a mob outside, mostly of older animals, very hostile. The managers of the ritual game pulled us back and took us up to the top of the building and set guards on us, as apparently the mob was angered to the point of wishing to kill us—again, the focus of their anger was that we were foreign. We complied, since there was no point in creating further disorder and—

. . . BRING YOUR DECEASED TO US, WHO ARE FRIENDS OF YOUR FAMILY, FRIENDS IN YOUR DISTRESS. TREATED WITH ALL REVERENCE, CARED FOR AS YOU CARED WHEN MOTHER, FATHER, HUSBAND, WIFE, BROTHER, OR LITTLE SISTER WAS STILL WITH YOU, THE SLEEPING ONE WILL BE BORNE TO THE LAST HOME, LAID GENTLY TO REST IN A PLOT WHERE FLOWERS AND BIRDS WILL ALWAYS PLAY AND WHERE YOU CAN VISIT AND MUSE. . . . IN YOUR LEISURE HOURS, YOU WILL ALWAYS HAVE A HAVEN WHERE YOUR THOUGHTS CAN DWELL IN LOVING HAPPINESS ON YOUR DEPARTED FRIENDS, WHO—

. . . We are running very short of power. There is nothing more we can do. This mission must be regarded as a failure. We have been able to achieve nothing. We have also failed to understand what is the cause of their defectiveness. There is no species like this one on any other planet known to us.

As the guards on our place of detention relaxed their vigilance, we simply dematerialised and returned to the craft. They will think we escaped or perhaps were the subjects of kidnapping by the still-hostile crowd that we could see from the top of the building where—

. . . SHOCKING AND DISGUSTING PROGRAM THAT OFFENDED IN A WAY NO OTHER PROGRAM HAS IN THIS COMMENTATOR'S MEMORY. IT IS NOT WHAT WAS SAID BY OUR TWO VISITORS, IT WAS THE WAY IT WAS SAID. AFTER ALL, WE ALL HAVE TO LIVE WITH "THE FACTS" THAT THEY SO NAIVELY SEEM TO IMAGINE ARE A REVELATION TO US. FOR SHEER BAD TASTE, CRUDITY OF TONE, UGLINESS OF MANNER, AND INSENSITIVITY TO THE DEEPER FEELINGS OF THE VIEWERS, NOTHING CAN BE COMPARED WITH PROFESSORS BOND AND HUNTER LAST NIGHT.

## DEPARTURE FROM THE PLANET

We are now reassembled as our original six and will shortly be returning. We have a tentative conclusion. It is this: that a society that is doomed to catastrophe, and that is unable to prepare for it, can expect that few people will survive except those already keyed to chaos and disaster. The civil, the ordered, the conforming, the well-tempted can expect to fall victim at first exposure. But the vagabonds, criminals, mad, extremely poor will have the means to survive. We conclude, therefore, that when, within the next five years, the eruption occurs, no one will be left but those types the present managers of society consider undesirable, for the present society is too inflexible to adapt—as we have already said, we have no idea why this should be so, what is wrong with them. But perhaps concealed in this city are groups of individuals we did not contact, who saw no reason to contact us, who not only foresee the future event but who are taking steps—

*The West Coast Examiner*

Sam Baker, a farmer from Long Ridge, said he saw a "shining round thing" take off 100 yards away from his fence yesterday evening as the sun went down. Says Sam: "It rose into the air at such a rate it was almost impossible to follow it with my eyes. Then it disappeared." Others from the same area claim to have seen "unusual sights" during the past few days. The official explanation is that the unusually vivid sunsets of the past month have caused strong reflections and mirages off rocks and stretches of sand.

## MILITARY SECTOR III TO H.Q.
### (TOP CONFIDENTIAL)

The UFO that landed some time in the night of the 14th, and was viewed as it landed, remained stationary for the entire period of seven days. No one was seen to leave the UFO. This is exactly in line with the previous twelve landings in the same spot. This was the thirteenth UFO of this series. But this was rather larger and more powerful than the previous twelve. The difference registered by Sonoscope 15 was considerable. This UFO, like the previous twelve, was only just visible to ordinary vision. Our observer, farmer Jansen H. Blackson, recruited by us after the first landing a year ago, volunteered that this one was much more easily seen. "You had to stare hard to see the others, but I saw this one coming down, also lifting off, but it went up so fast I lost it at once." The suggestion from M 8 is that all thirteen are observation craft from the Chinese. The view of this section is that they are from our Naval Department 15, and it is our contention that as they have no right of access to this terrain, which is under the aegis of War Department 4, we should blast them to hell and gone next time they try it on.

## AIR FORCE 14 TO CENTER

The alightings continue—number thirteen last week. This was also unmanned. Confirm belief Russian origin. Must report also two further landings to the south of the city, both in the same place and separated by an interval of three weeks. These two craft identical with the series of fifty-five alighting to north of city last year. The two southern landings coincided with the disappearance of eleven people, five the first time, six the second. This makes 450 people gone without trace during the past two years. We suggest it is no longer possible to dismiss the fact that the landings of these craft always mean the disappearance of two to ten people with the word "coincidence." We must face the possibility that all or some are manned, but by individuals so dissimilar in structure to ourselves that we cannot see them. We would point out that Sonoscope 4 is only just able to bring these types of craft within vision and that, therefore, the levels of density that might indicate the presence of "people" might escape the machine. We further suggest that the facetiousness of the phrase "Little Green Men" might mask an attitude of mind that is inimical to a sober evaluation or assessing of this possibility.

Confirm at earliest if we are to continue policy of minimizing these disappearances. We can still find no common denominator in the *type* of person taken off. The only thing they all have in common is that they were, for a variety of reasons, somewhere in the areas in which these craft choose to descend.

### The West Coast Examiner

Our observer at filling station Lost Pine reports that groups of people are driving south out of the city to the area where the latest UFOs are known to descend and take off. Last night they numbered over fifty thousand.

## AIR FORCE 14 TO CENTER

In spite of Total Policy 19, rumors are out. We consider it advisable to cordon off the area, although this might precipitate extreme panic situation. But we see no alternative. The cult called Be Ready for the Day is already thousands strong and sweeping the city and environs. Suggest an announcement that the area is contaminated with a chance leak of radioactivity.

# Mrs. Fortescue

That autumn he became conscious all at once of a lot of things he had never thought about before.

Himself, for a start . . .

His parents . . . whom he found he disliked, because they told lies. He discovered this when he tried to communicate to them something of his new state of mind and they pretended not to know what he meant.

His sister, who, far from being his friend and ally, "like two peas in a pod"—as people had been saying for years—seemed positively to hate him.

And Mrs. Fortescue.

Jane, seventeen, had left school and went out every night. Fred, sixteen, loutish schoolboy, lay in bed and listened for her to come home, kept company by her imaginary twin self, invented by him at the end of the summer. The tenderness of this lovely girl redeemed him from his shame, his squalor, his misery. Meanwhile, the parents ignorantly slept, not caring about the frightful battles their son was fighting with himself not six yards off. Sometimes Jane came home first; sometimes Mrs. Fortescue. Fred listened to her going up over his head, and thought how strange he had never thought about her before, knew nothing about her.

The Danderlea family lived in a small flat over the liquor shop that Mr. and Mrs. Danderlea had been managing for Sanko & Duke for twenty years. Above the shop, from where rose, day and night, a sickly reek of beer and spirits they could never escape from, was the kitchen and the lounge. This layer of the house (it had been one once) was felt as an insulating barrier against the smell, which nevertheless reached up into the bedrooms above. Two bedrooms—the mother and father in one; while for years brother and sister had shared a room, until recently Mr. Danderlea put up a partition making two tiny boxes, giving at least the illusion of privacy for the boy and the girl.

On the top floor, the two rooms were occupied by Mrs. Fortescue, and had been since before the Danderleas came. Ever since the boy could remember, grumbling went on that Mrs. Fortescue had the high part of the house where the liquor smell did not rise; though she, if remarks to this effect reached her, claimed that on hot nights she could not sleep for the smell. But on the whole relations were good. The Danderleas' energies were claimed by buying and selling liquor, while Mrs. Fortescue went out a lot. Sometimes another old woman came to visit her, and an old man, small, shrunken, and polite, came to see her most evenings, very late indeed, often well after twelve.

Mrs. Fortescue seldom went out during the day, but left every evening at about six, wearing furs: a pale shaggy coat in winter, and in summer a stole over a costume. She always had a small hat on, with a veil that was drawn tight over her face and held with a bunch of flowers where the fur began. The furs changed often: Fred remembered half a dozen blond fur coats, and a good many little animals biting their tails or dangling bright bead eyes and empty paws. From behind the veil, the dark, made-up eyes of Mrs. Fortescue had glimmered at him for years; and her small old reddened mouth had smiled.

One evening he postponed his homework, and slipped out past the shop where his parents were both at work, and took a short walk that led him to Oxford Street. The exulting, fearful loneliness that surged through his blood with every heartbeat, making every stamp of shadow a reminder of death, each gleam of light a promise of his extraordinary future, drove him around and around the streets muttering to himself, brought tears to his eyes, or snatches of song to his lips which he had to suppress. For while he knew himself to be crazy, and supposed he must have been all his life (he could no longer remember himself before his autumn), this was a secret he intended to keep for himself and the tender creature who shared the stuffy box he spent his nights in. Turning a corner that probably (he would not have been able to say) he had already turned several times before that evening, he saw a woman walking ahead of him in a great fur coat that shone under the street lights, a small veiled hat, and tiny sharp feet that took tripping steps towards Soho. Recognising Mrs. Fortescue, a friend, he ran forward to greet her, relieved that this frightening trap of streets was to be shared. Seeing him, she first gave him a smile never offered him before by a woman; then looked prim and annoyed; then nodded at him briskly and said as she always did: "Well, Fred, and how are things with you?" He walked a few steps with her, said he had to do his homework, heard her old woman's voice say: "That's right, son, you must work, your mum and dad are right, a bright boy like you, it would be a shame to let it go to waste"—and watched her move on, across Oxford Street, into the narrow streets beyond.

He turned and saw Bill Bates coming towards him from the hardware shop, just closing. Bill was grinning, and he said: "What, wouldn't she have you then?"

"It's Mrs. Fortescue," said Fred, entering a new world between one breath and the next, just because of the tone of Bill's voice.

"She's not a bad old tart," said Bill. "Bet she wasn't pleased to see you when she's on the job."

"Oh I don't know," said Fred, trying out a new man-of-the-world voice for the first time, "she lives over us, doesn't she?" (Bill must know this, everyone must know it, he thought, feeling sick.) "I was just saying hullo, that's all." It came off, he saw, for now Bill nodded and said: "I'm off to the pictures, want to come?"

"Got to do homework," said Fred, bitter.

"Then you've got to do it then, haven't you," said Bill reasonably, going on his way.

Fred went home in a seethe of shame. How could his parents share their house with an old tart (whore, prostitute—but these were the only words he knew); how could they treat her like an ordinary decent person, even better (he understood, listening to them in his mind's ear, that their voices to her held something not far from respect)—how could they put up with it? Justice insisted that they had not chosen her as a tenant; she was the company's tenant, but at least they should have told Sanko & Duke so that she could be evicted and . . .

Although it seemed as if his adventure through the streets had been as long as a night, he found when he got in that it wasn't yet eight.

He went up to his box and set out his schoolbooks. Through the ceilingboard he could hear his sister moving. There being no door between the rooms, he went out to the landing, through his parents' room (his sister had to creep past the sleeping pair when she came in late) and into hers. She stood in a black slip before the glass, making up her face. "Do you mind?" she said daintily. "Can't you knock?" He muttered something, and felt a smile come on his face, aggressive and aggrieved, that seemed to switch on automatically these days if he saw his sister even at a distance. He sat on the edge of her bed. "Do you mind?" she said again, moving away from him some black underwear. She slipped over her still puppy-fatted white shoulders a new dressing-gown in cherry-red and buttoned it up primly before continuing to work lipstick onto her mouth.

"Where are you going?"

"To the pictures, if you've got no objection," she clipped out, in this new, jaunty voice that she had acquired when she left school, and which, he knew, she used as a weapon against all men. *But why against him?* He sat, feeling the ugly grin which was probably painted on his face, for he couldn't remove it, and looked at the pretty girl with her new hairdo putting thick black rings around her eyes, and he thought of how they had been two peas in a pod. *In the summer* . . . yes, that is how it seemed to him now; through a years-long summer of visits to friends, the park, the zoo, the pictures, they had been friends, allies; then the dark came down suddenly and in the dark had been born this cool, flip girl who hated him.

"Who are you going with?"

"Jem Taylor, if you don't have any objection," she said.

"Why should I have any objection? I just asked."

"What you don't know won't hurt you," she said, very pleased with herself because of her ease in this way of talking. He recognised his recent achievement in the exchange with Bill as the same step forward as she was making, with this tone, or style; and out of a quite uncustomary feeling of equality with her asked: "How is old Jem? I haven't seen him lately."

"Oh, Fred, *I'm late.*" This bad temper meant she had finished her face and wanted to put on her dress, which she would not do in front of him.

Silly cow, he thought, grinning and thinking of her alter ego, the girl of his nights; does she think I don't know what she looks like in a slip, or nothing? Because of what went on behind the partition, in the dark, he banged his fist on it, laughing, and she whipped about and said: "Oh, Fred, you drive me crazy, you really do." This being something from their brother-and-sister past, admitting intimacy, even the possibility of real equality, she checked herself, put on a sweet contained smile, and said: "If you don't *mind*, Fred, I want to get dressed."

He went out, remembering only as he got through the parents' room and saw his mother's feathered mules by the bed that he had wanted to talk about Mrs. Fortescue. He realised his absurdity, because of course his sister would pretend she didn't understand what he meant. . . . His fixed smile of shame changed into one of savagery as he thought: Well, Jem, you're not going to get anything out of her but *do you mind* and *have you any objection* and *please yourself*, I know that much about my sweet sister. . . . In his room he could not work, even after his sister had left, slamming three doors and making so much racket with her heels that the parents shouted at her from the shop. He was thinking of Mrs. Fortescue. But she was old. She had always been old, as long as he could remember. Sometimes other old women came up to see her in the afternoons; were they whores (tarts, prostitutes, *bad women*) too? And where did she, they, do it? And who was the smelly old man who came so late nearly every night?

He sat with the waves of liquor-smell from the ground floor arising past him, thinking of the sourish smell of the old man, and of the scented smell of the old women, feeling short-breathed because of the stuffy reek of this room and associating it (because of certain memories from his nights) with the reek from Mrs. Fortescue's room which he could positively smell from where he sat, so strongly did he create it.

Bill must be wrong: she couldn't possibly be on the game still, who would want an old thing like that?

The family had a meal every night when the shop closed. It was usually about ten-thirty when they sat down. Tonight there was some boiled bacon, and baked beans. Fred brought out casually: "I saw Mrs. Fortescue going off to work when I was out." He waited the results of this cheek, this effrontery, watching his parents' faces. They did not even exchange glances. His mother pushed tinted bronze hair back with a hand that had a stain of grease on it, and said: "Poor old girl, I expect she's pleased about the Act, when you get down to it, in the winter it must have been bad sometimes." The words *the Act* hit Fred's outraged sense of propriety anew; he had to work them out, thinking that his parents did not even apologise for the years of corruption. Now his father said—his face was inflamed, he must have been taking nips from the glass under the counter—"Once or twice, when I saw her on Frith Street before the Act I felt sorry for her. But I suppose she got used to it."

"It must be nicer this way," said Mrs. Danderlea, pushing the crusting remains of the baked beans towards her husband.

He scooped them out of the dish with the edge of his fried bread, and she said: "What's wrong with the spoon?"

"What's wrong with the bread?" he returned, with an unconvincing whisky glare, which she ignored.

"Where's her place, then?" asked Fred, casual, having worked out that she must have one.

"Over that new club in Panton Street. The rent's gone up again, so Mr. Spencer told me, and there's the telephone she needs now—well, I don't know how much you can believe of what *he* says, but he's said often enough that without him helping her out she'd do better at almost anything else."

"Not a word he says," said Mr. Danderlea, pushing out his dome of a stomach as he sat back, replete. "He told me he was doorman for the Greystock Hotel in Knightsbridge—well, it turns out all this time he's been doorman for that strip-tease joint along the street from her new place, and that's where he's been for years, because it was a night-club before it was strip-tease."

"Well there's no point in that, is there?" said Mrs. Danderlea, pouring second cups. "I mean, why tell fibs about it, I mean everyone knows, don't they?"

Fred again pushed down protest: that yes, Mr. Spencer (Mrs. Fortescue's "regular," but he had never understood what they had meant by the ugly word before) was right to lie; he wished his parents would lie even now; anything rather than this casual back-and-forth chat about this horror, years-old, and right over their heads, part of their lives.

He ducked down his face and shovelled beans into it fast, knowing it was scarlet, and wanting a reason for it.

"You'll get heart-burn, gobbling like that," said his mother, as he had expected.

"I've got to finish my homework," he said, and bolted, shaking his head at the cup of tea she was pushing over at him.

He sat in his room until his parents went to bed, marking off the routine of the house from his new knowledge. After an expected interval Mrs. Fortescue came in; he could hear her moving about, taking her time about everything. Water ran, for a long time. He now understood that this sound, water running into and then out of a basin, was something he had heard at this hour all his life. He sat listening with the ashamed, fixed grin on his face. Then his sister came in; he could hear her sharp sigh of relief as she flumped on the bed and bent over to take off her shoes. He nearly called out: "Goodnight, Jane," but thought better of it. Yet all through the summer they had whispered and giggled through the partition.

Mr. Spencer, Mrs. Fortescue's regular, came up the stairs. He heard their voices together; listened to them as he undressed and went to bed; as he lay wakeful; as he at last went off to sleep.

Next evening he waited until Mrs. Fortescue went out, and followed her, careful she didn't see him. She walked fast and efficient, like a woman on her way to the office. Why then the fur coat, the veil, the makeup? Of course, it was habit, because of all the years on the pavement; for it was a sure thing she didn't wear that outfit to receive customers in her place. But it turned out that he was wrong. Along the last hundred yards before her door, she slowed her pace, took a couple of quick glances left and right for the police, then looked at a large elderly man coming towards her. This man swung around, joined her, and they went side by side into her doorway, the whole operation so quick, so smooth, that even if there had been a policeman all he could have seen was a woman meeting someone she had expected to meet.

Fred then went home. Jane had dressed for her evening. He followed her too. She walked fast, not looking at people, her smart new coat flaring jade, emerald, dark green, as she moved through varying depths of light, her black puffy hair gleaming. She went into the underground. He followed her down the escalators, and onto the platform, at not much more than arm's distance, but quite safe because of her self-absorption. She stood on the edge of the platform, staring across the rails at a big advertisement. It was a very large, dark brown, gleaming revolver holster, with a revolver in it, attached to a belt for bullets; but instead of bullets each loop had a lipstick, in all the pink-orange-scarlet-crimson shades it was possible to imagine lipstick in. Fred stood just behind his sister, and examined her sharp little face examining the advertisement and choosing which lipstick she would buy. She smiled—nothing like the appealing shamefaced smile that was stuck, for ever, it seemed, on Fred's face, but a calm, triumphant smile. The train came streaming in, obscuring the advertisement. The doors slid open, receiving his sister, who did not look around. He stood close against the window, looking at her calm little face, willing her to look at him. But the train rushed her off again, and she would never know he had been there.

He went home, the ferment of his craziness breaking through his lips in an incredulous raw mutter: a revolver, a bloody revolver. . . . His parents were at supper, taking in food, swilling in tea, like pigs, pigs, pigs, he thought, shovelling down his own supper to be rid of it. Then he said: "I left a book in the shop, Dad, I want to get it," and went down dark stairs through the sickly rising fumes. In a drawer under the till was a revolver which had been there for years, against the day when burglars would break in and Mr. (or Mrs.) Danderlea would frighten them off with it. Many of Fred's dreams had been spun around that weapon. But it was broken somewhere in its black-gleaming interior. He carefully hid it under his sweater, and went up, to knock on his parents' door. They were already in bed, a large double bed at which, because of this hideous world he was now a citizen of, he was afraid to look. Two old people, with sagging faces and bulging mottled fleshy shoulders lay side by side, looking at him. "I want to leave something for Jane," he said, turning his gaze away from them. He laid the revolver on Jane's pillow, arranging half a dozen lipsticks of various colours as if they were bullets coming out of it.

He went back to the shop. Under the counter stood the bottle of Black & White beside the glass stained sour with his father's

tippling. He made sure the bottle was still half-full before turning the lights out and settling down to wait. Not for long. When
he heard the key in the lock, he set the door open wide so Mrs.
Fortescue must see him.

"Why, Fred, whatever are you doing?"

"I noticed Dad left the light on, so I came down." Frowning
with efficiency, he looked for a place to put the whisky bottle,
while he rinsed the dirtied glass. Then casual, struck by a
thought, he offered: "Like a drink, Mrs. Fortescue?" In the
dim light she focussed, with difficulty, on the bottle. "I never
touch the stuff, dear. . . ." Bending his face down past hers, to
adjust a wine bottle, he caught the liquor on her breath, and
understood the vagueness of her good nature.

"Well, all right, dear," she went on, "just a little one to keep
you company. You're like your dad, you know that?"

"Is that so?" He came out of the shop with the bottle under
his arm, shutting the door behind him and locking it. The stairs
glimmered dark. "Many's the time he's offered me a nip on a
cold night, though not when your mother could see." She added
a short triumphant titter, resting her weight on the stair-rail as
if testing it.

"Let's go up," he said insinuatingly, knowing he would get his
way, because it had been so easy this far. He was shocked it
was so easy. She should have said: "What are you doing out of
bed at this time?" "A boy of your age, drinking, what next!"

She obediently went up ahead of him, pulling herself up.

The small room she went into, vaguely smiling her invitation
that he should follow, was crammed with furniture and objects,
all of which had the same soft glossiness of her clothes, which
she now went to the next room to remove. He sat on an oyster-
coloured satin sofa, looked at blueish brocade curtains, a cabinet
full of china figures, thick creamy rugs, pink cushions, pink-
tinted walls. A table in a corner held photographs. Of her, so he
understood, progressing logically back from those he could
recognise to those that were inconceivable. The earliest was of
a girl with yellow collarbone-length curls, on which perched a
top-hat. She wore a spangled bodice, in pink; pink satin pants,
long black lace stockings, white gloves, and was roguishly pointing a walking-stick at the audience—at him, Fred. Like a bloody
gun, he thought, feeling the shameful derisive grin come onto
his face. He heard the door shut behind him, but did not turn,

wondering what he would see: he never had seen her, he realised, without hat, veil, furs. She said, pottering about behind his shoulder: "Yes, that's me when I was a Gaiety Girl, a nice outfit, wasn't it?"

"Gaiety Girl?" he said, protesting, and she admitted: "Well, that was before your time, wasn't it?"

The monstrousness of this second "wasn't it" made it easy for him to turn and look: she was bending over a cupboard, her back to him. It was a back whose shape was concealed by thick, soft, cherry-red, with a tufted pattern of whirls and waves. She stood up and faced him, displaying, without a trace of consciousness at the horror of the fact, his sister's dressing-gown. She carried glasses and a jug of water to the central table that was planted in a deep pink rug, and said: "I hope you don't mind my getting into something comfortable, but we aren't strangers." She sat opposite, having pushed the glasses towards him, as a reminder that the bottle was still in his hand. He poured the yellow, smelling liquid, watching her face to see when he must stop. But her face showed nothing, so he filled her tumbler half-full. "Just a splash, dear . . ." He splashed, and she lifted the glass and held it, in the vague tired way that went with her face, which, now that for the first time in his life he could really look at it, was an old shrunken face, with small black eyes deep in their sockets, and a small mouth pouting out of a tired mesh of lines. This old, rather kind face, at which he tried not to stare, was like a mask held between the cherry-red gown over a body whose shape was slim and young, and the hair, beautifully tinted a tactful silvery-blond and waving softly into the hollows of an ancient neck.

"My sister's got a dressing-gown like that."

"It's pretty, isn't it? They've got them in at Richard's down the street, I expect she got hers there too, did she?"

"I don't know."

"Well, the proof of the pudding's in the eating, isn't it?"

At this remark, which reminded him of nothing so much as his parents' idiotic pattering exchange at supper time, when they were torpid before sleep, he felt the ridiculous smile leave his face. He was full of anger, but no longer of shame.

"Give me a cigarette, dear," she went on, "I'm too tired to get up."

"I don't smoke."

"If you could reach me my handbag."

He handed her a large crocodile bag that she had left by the photographs. "I have nice things, don't I?" she agreed with his unspoken comment on it. "Well, I always say, I always have nice things, whatever else. . . . I never have anything cheap or nasty, my things are always nice. . . . Baby Batsby taught me that, never have anything cheap or nasty, he used to say. He used to take me on his yacht, you know, to Cannes and Nice. He was my friend for three years, and he taught me about having beautiful things."

"Baby Batsby?"

"That was before your time, I expect, but he was in all the papers once, every week of the year. He was a great spender, you know, generous."

"Is that a fact?"

"I've always been lucky that way, my friends were always generous. Take Mr. Spencer, now, he never lets me want for anything; only yesterday he said: 'Your curtains are getting a bit passé, I'll get you some new ones.' And mark my words, he will, he's as good as his word."

He saw that the whisky, coming on top of whatever she'd had earlier, was finishing her off. She sat blinking smeared eyes at him; and her cigarette, secured between thumb and forefinger six inches from her mouth, shed ash on her cherry-red gown. She took a gulp from the glass, and nearly set it down on air; Fred reached forward just in time.

"Mr. Spencer's a good man, you know," she told the air about a foot from her unfocussed gaze.

"Is he?"

"We're just old friends now, you know. We're both getting on a bit. Not that I don't let him have a bit of a slap and a tickle sometimes to keep him happy, though I'm not interested, not really."

Trying to insert the end of the cigarette between her lips, she missed, and jammed the butt against her cheek. She leaned forward and stubbed it out. Sat back—with dignity. Stared at Fred, screwed up her eyes to see him, failed, offered the stranger in her room a social smile.

This smile trembled into a wrinkled pout as she said: "Take Mr. Spencer, now, he's a good spender, I'd never say he wasn't, but but but . . ." She fumbled at the packet of cigarettes and he hastened to extract one for her and to light it. "*But*. Yes. Well, he may think I'm past it, but I'm not, and don't you think it. There's a good thirty years between us, do you know that?"

"Thirty years," said Fred politely, his smile now fixed by a cold determined loathing.

"What do you think, dear? He always makes out we're the same age, now he's past it, but—well, look at that, then, if you don't believe me." She pointed her scarlet-tipped and shaking left hand at the table with the photographs. "Yes, that one, just look at it, it's only from last summer." Fred leaned forward and lifted towards him the image of her just indicated which, though she was sitting opposite him in the flesh, must prove her victory over Mr. Spencer. She wore a full-skirted, tightly belted, tightly bodiced striped dress, from which her ageing bare arms hung down by her sides, and her old neck and face rose shameless under the beautiful gleaming hair.

"Well, it stands to reason, doesn't it," she said. "Well, what do you think then?"

"When's Mr. Spencer coming?" he asked.

"I'm not expecting him tonight, he's working. I admire him, I really do, holding down that job, three, four in the morning sometimes, and it's no joke, those layabouts you get at those places and it's always Mr. Spencer who has to fix them up with what they fancy, or get rid of them if they make trouble, and he's not a big man, and he's not young any more, I don't know how he does it. But he's got tact. Tact. Yes, I often say to him, you've got tact, I say, it'll take a man anywhere." Her glass was empty, and she was looking at it.

The news that Mr. Spencer was not expected did not surprise Fred; he had known it, because of his secret brutal confidence born when she had said: "I never touch the stuff, dear."

He now got up, went behind her, stood a moment steeling himself, because the embarrassed shamefaced grin had come back onto his face, weakening his purpose—then put two hands firmly under her armpits, lifted her and supported her.

She at first struggled to remain sitting, but let herself be lifted. "Time for bye-byes?" she said. But as he began to push her, still supporting her, towards the bedroom, she said, suddenly coherent: "But, Fred, it's Fred, Fred, it's Fred. . . ." She twisted out of his grip, fell two steps back, and was stopped by the door to the bedroom. There she spread her two legs under the cherry gown, to hold her trembling weight, swayed, caught at Fred, held tight, and said: "But it's *Fred.*"

"Why should you care?" he said, cold, grinning.

"But I don't work here dear, you know that—no, let me go." For he had put two great schoolboy hands on her shoulders.

He felt the shoulders tense, and then grow small and tender in his palms.

"You're like your father, you're the spitting image of your father, did you know that?"

He opened the door with his left hand; then spun her around by pushing at her left shoulder as she faced him; then, putting both hands under her armpits from behind, marched her into the bedroom, while she tittered.

The bedroom was mostly pink. Pink silk bedspread. Pink walls. A doll in a pink flounced skirt lolled against the pillow, its chin tucked into a white fichu over which it stared at the opposite wall where an eighteenth-century girl held a white rose to her lips. Fred pushed Mrs. Fortescue over dark red carpet, till her knees met the bed. He lifted her, and dropped her on it, neatly moving the doll aside with one hand before she could crush it.

She lay eyes closed, limp, breathing fast, her mouth slightly open. The black furrows beside the mouth were crooked; the eyelids shone blue in wells of black.

"Turn the lights out," she implored.

He turned out the pink-shaded lamp fixed to the head-board. She fumbled at her clothes. He stripped off his trousers, his underpants, pushed her hands aside, found silk in the opening of the gown that glowed cherry-red in the light from the next room. He stripped the silk pants off her so that her legs flew up, then flumped down. She was inert. Then her expertise revived in her, or at least in her tired hands, and he achieved the goal of his hot imaginings of these ugly autumn nights in one shattering spasm that filled him with no less hatred. Her old body stirred feebly under him, and he heard her irregular breathing. He sprang off her in a leap, tugged back pants, trousers. Then he switched on the light. She lay, eyes closed, her face blurred with woe, the upper part of her body nestled into the soft glossy cherry stuff, the white legs spread open, bare. She made an attempt to rouse herself, cover herself. He leaned over her, teeth bared in a hating grin, forcing her hands away from her body.

They fell limp on the stained silk spread. Now he stripped off the gown, roughly, as if she were the doll. She whimpered, she tittered, she protested. He watched, with pleasure, tears welling out of the pits of dark and trickling down her mascara-stained face. She lay naked among the folds of cherry colour. He looked at the greyish crinkles around the armpits, the small flat breasts, the loose stomach; then at the triangle of black hair where white hairs sprouted. She was attempting to fold her legs over each other. He forced them apart, muttering: "Look at yourself, look at yourself then!"—while he held in his nausea which was being fed by the miasmic smell that he had known must be the air of this room. "Filthy old whore, disgusting, that's what you are, disgusting!" He let his grasp slacken on her thighs, saw red marks come up on them as the legs flew together and she wriggled and burrowed to get under the cherry-red gown.

She sat up, holding the gown around her. Pink gown, pink coverlet, pink walls, pink pink pink everywhere. And a dark red carpet. He felt as if the room were built of flesh.

She was looking straight up at him.

"That wasn't very nice, was it?"

He fell back a step, feeling his own face go hot. That was how his mother corrected him: *That isn't very nice, dear*, in a long-suffering, reproachful voice exactly like Mrs. Fortescue's.

"That wasn't at all nice, Fred, it wasn't nice at all. I don't know what can have got into you!"

Without looking at him, she let her feet down over the edge of the bed. He could see them trembling. She was peering over and down to fit them into pink-feathered mules.

He noted that he was feeling a need to help her fit her pathetic feet into the fancy mules. He fled. Down the stairs, into his room, and face down onto his bed. Through the ceilingboard an inch from his ear he could hear his sister move. Up he jumped again, out of his box, and through his parents' room, which he hated so much he behaved as if it were a vacuum, and simply not there.

His sister was lying coiled on her bed, in her cherry-pink gown, painting her nails coral.

"Very clever, I don't think," she said.

He looked for the gun: it was on her dressing-table, in a litter of lipsticks.

He took up the gun and pointed it down at that woman his sister in her terrifying intimacy of warm pink.

"Stupid," she said.

"That's right."

She went on doing her nails.

"Stupid, stupid, stupid," she said.

"That's right."

"Then why?—oh do stop it, put that thing down."

He put it down.

"If you don't mind, I want to get into bed."

He said nothing, and she looked up at him. It was a long, hollow, upwards look that she had taken from an advertisement, probably, or a film. But then the look changed, and she was Jane. She had seen something in him.

His face had changed? His voice had changed? *He* had changed?

Triumph warmed his backbone; he smiled. He had regained his sister, he had made a step forward and come level with her again.

"Please yourself," he said, and went to the door.

"Ta-ta, goodnight, mind the bugs don't bite," said she, in a ritual of their childhood—of last year.

"Oh be your age," he said. He went through the loathsome dark of his parents' bedroom without thinking more than: Poor old things, they can't help it.

# An Unposted Love Letter

Y es, I saw the look your wife's
face put on when I said, "I have so many husbands, I don't
need a husband." She did not exchange a look with you, but that
was because she did not need to—later when you got home she
said, "What an affected thing to say!" and you replied, "Don't
forget she is an actress." You said this meaning exactly what
I would mean if I had said it, I am certain of that. And perhaps
she heard it like that, I do hope so, *because I know what you are*
and if your wife does not hear what you say then this is a smallness on your part that I don't forgive you. If I can live alone, and
out of fastidiousness, then you must have a wife as good as you
are. My husbands, the men who set light to my soul (yes, I know
how your wife would smile if I used that phrase), are worthy
of you. . . . I know that I am giving myself away now, confessing
how much that look on your wife's face hurt. *Didn't she know
that even then I was playing my part?* Oh no, after all, I don't
forgive you your wife, no, I don't.

If I said, "I don't need a husband, I have so many lovers,"
then of course everyone at the dinner table would have laughed
in just such a way: it would have been the rather banal "out-
rageousness" expected of me. An ageing star, the fading beauty
. . . "I have so many lovers"—pathetic, and brave too. Yes, that
remark would have been too apt, too smooth, right for just any
"beautiful but fading" actress. But not right for me, no, because
after all, I am not just any actress, I am Victoria Carrington, and
I know exactly what is due to me and from me. I know what is
fitting (not for *me*, that is not important but for what I stand

for). Do you imagine I couldn't have said it differently—like this, for instance: "I am an artist and therefore androgynous." Or: "I have created inside myself Man who plays opposite to my Woman." Or: "I have objectified in myself the male components of my soul and it is from this source that I create." Oh I'm not stupid, not ignorant, I know the different dialects of our time and even how to use them. But imagine if I had said any of these things last night! It would have been a false note, you would all have been uncomfortable, irritated, and afterwards you would have said: "Actresses shouldn't try to be intelligent." (Not you, the others.) Probably they don't believe it, not really, that an actress must be stupid, but their sense of discrepancy, of discordance, would have expressed itself in such a way. Whereas their silence when I said, "I don't need a husband, I have so many husbands," was right, for it was *the remark right for me*— it was more than "affected," or "outrageous"—*it was making a claim that they had to recognise.*

That word "affected," have you ever really thought why it is applied to actresses? (You have of course; I'm no foreign country to you, I felt that, but it gives me pleasure to talk to you like this.) The other afternoon I went to see Irma Painter in her new play, and afterwards I went back to congratulate her (for she had heard, of course, that I was in the auditorium and would have felt insulted if I hadn't gone—I'm different, I hate it when people feel obliged to come back). We were sitting in her dressingroom and I was looking at her face as she wiped the makeup off. We are about the same age, and we have both been acting since the year . . . I recognised her face as mine, we have the same face, and I understood that it is the face of every real actress. No, it is not "masklike," my face, her face. Rather, it is that our basic face is so worn down to its essentials because of its permanent readiness to take other guises, become other people, it is almost like something hung up on the wall of a dressingroom ready to take down and use. Our face is—it has a scrubbed, honest, bare look, like a deal table, or a wooden floor. It has modesty, a humility, our face, as time wears on, wearing out of her, out of me, our "personality," our "individuality."

I looked at her face (we are called rivals, we are both called "great" actresses) and I suddenly wanted to pay homage to it, since I knew what that scoured plain look cost her—what it costs me, who have played a thousand beautiful women, to keep my features sober and decent under the painted shell of my makeup ready for other souls to use.

At a party, all dressed up, when I'm a "person," then I try to disguise the essential plainness and anonymity of my features by holding together the "beauty" I am known for, creating it out of my own and other people's memories. Of course it is almost gone now, nearly all gone the sharp, sweet, poignant face that so many men loved (not knowing it was not me, it was only what was given to me to consume slowly for the scrubbed face I must use for work). While I sat last night opposite you and your wife, she so pretty and *human*, her prettiness no mask, but expressing every shade of what she felt, and you being yourself only, I was conscious of how I looked. I could see my very white flesh that is guttering down away from its "beauty"; I could see my smile that even now has moments of its "piercing sweetness"; I could see my eyes, "dewy and shadowed," even now . . . but I also knew that everyone there, even if they were not aware of it, was conscious of that hard, honest workaday face that lies ready for use under this ruin, and it is the discrepancy between that working face and the "personality" of the famous actress that makes everything I do and say affected, that makes it inevitable and right that I should say, "I don't want a husband, I have so many husbands." And I tell you, if I had said nothing, not one word, the whole evening, the result would have been the same: "How affected she is, but of course she *is* an actress."

Yet it was the exact truth, what I said: I no longer have lovers, I have husbands, and that has been true ever since . . .

That is why I am writing this letter to you; this letter is a sort of homage, giving you your due in my life. Or perhaps, simply, I cannot tonight stand the loneliness of my role (my role in life).

When I was a girl it seemed that every man I met, or even heard of, or whose picture I saw in the paper, was my lover. I took him as my lover, *because it was my right*. He may never have heard of me, he might have thought me hideous (and I wasn't very attractive as a girl—my kind of looks, striking, white-fleshed, red-haired, needed maturity; as a girl I was a milk-faced, scarlet-haired creature whose features were all at odds with each other; I was pretty only when made up for the stage) . . . he may have found me positively repulsive, but I took him. Yes, at that time I had lovers in imagination, but none in reality.

No man in the flesh could be as good as what I could invent,
no real lips, hands, could affect me as those that I created, like
God. And this remained true when I married my first husband,
and then my second, for I loved neither of them, and I didn't
know what the word meant for years. Until, to be precise, I was
thirty-two and got very ill that year. No one knew why, or how,
but *I* knew it was because I did not get a big part I wanted badly.
So I got ill from disappointment, but now I see how right it was
I didn't get the part. I was too old—if I had played her, the
charming ingenuous girl (which is how I saw myself then, God
forgive me), I would have had to play her for three or four years,
because the play ran for ever, and I would have been too vain
to stop. And then what? I would have been nearly forty, too old
for charming girls, and then, like so many actresses who have
not burned the charming girl out of themselves, cauterised that
wound with pain like styptic, I would have found myself playing
smaller and smaller parts, and then I would have become a
"character" actress, and then . . .

Instead, I lay very ill, not wanting to get better, ill with
frustration, I thought, but really with the weight of years I did
not know how to consume, how to include in how I saw myself,
and then I fell in love with my doctor, inevitable I see now, but
then a miracle, for that was the first time, and the reason I said
the word "love" to myself, just as if I had not been married twice
and had a score of men in my imagination, was because *I could
not manipulate him*, for the first time a man remained himself,
I could not make him move as I wanted, and I did not know his
lips and hands. No, I had to wait for *him* to decide, to move, and
when he did become my lover I was like a young girl, awkward,
I could only wait for his actions to spring mine.

He loved me, certainly, but not as I loved him, and in due
course he left me. I wished I could die, but it was then I understood, with gratitude, what had happened—I played, for the
first time, a woman, as distinct from that fatal creature, "A
charming girl," as distinct from "the heroine"—and I and everyone else knew that I had moved into a new dimension of myself;
I was born again, and only I knew it was out of love for that
man, my first husband (so I called him, though everyone else
saw him as my doctor with whom I rather amusingly had had
an affair).

For he was my first husband. He changed me and my whole

life. After him, in my frenzy of lonely unhappiness, I believed I could return to what I had been before he had married me, and I would take men to bed (in reality now, just as I had, before, in imagination), but it was no longer possible, it did not work, for I had been possessed by a man, the Man had created in me himself, had left himself in me, and so I could never again use a man, possess one, manipulate him, make him do what I wanted.

For a long time it was as if I was dead, empty, sterile. (That is, *I* was; my work was at its peak.) I had no lovers, in fact or in imagination, and it was like being a nun or a virgin.

Strange it was, that at the age of thirty-five it was for the first time I felt virgin, chaste, untouched, I was absolutely alone. The men who wanted me, courted me, it was as if they moved and smiled and stretched out their hands through a glass wall which was my absolute inviolability. Was this how I should have felt when I was a girl? Yes, I believe that's it—that at thirty-five I was a girl for the first time. Surely this is how ordinary "normal" girls feel?—they carry a circle of chastity around with them through which the one man, the hero, must break? But it was not so with me, I was never a chaste girl, not until I had known what it was to remain still, waiting for the man to set me in motion in answer to him.

A long time went by, and I began to feel I would soon be an old woman. I was without love, and I would not be a good artist, not really, the touch of the man who loved me was fading off me, *had* faded, there was something lacking in my work now, it was beginning to be mechanical.

And so I resigned myself. I could no longer choose a man; and no man chose me. So I said, "Very well, then, there is nothing to be done." Above all, I understand the relation between myself and life, I understand the logic of what I am, must be, I know there is nothing to be done about the shape of fate: my truth is that I have been loved once, and now that is the end, and I must let myself sink towards a certain dryness, a coldness of intelligence—yes, you will soon develop into an upright, red-headed, very intelligent lady (though, of course, affected!) whose green eyes flash the sober fires of humorous comprehension. All the rest is over for you; now accept it and be done and do as well as you can the work you are given.

And then one night . . .

What? All that happened outwardly was that I sat opposite a man at a dinner party in a restaurant, and we talked and laughed as people do who meet each other casually at a dinner table. But afterwards I went home with my soul on fire. I was on fire, being consumed. . . . And what a miracle it was to me, being able to say, not: That is an attractive man, I want him, I shall have him, but: My house is on fire, that was the man, yes, it was he again, there he was, he has set light to my soul.

I simply let myself suffer for him, knowing he was worth it *because* I suffered—it had come to this, my soul had become its own gauge, its own measure of what was good: I knew what *he* was because of how my work was afterwards.

I knew him better than his wife did, or could (she was there too, a nice woman in such beautiful pearls)—I knew him better than he does himself. I sat opposite him all evening. What was there to notice? An ageing actress, pretty still, beautifully dressed (that winter I had a beautiful violet suit with mink cuffs), sitting opposite a charming man—handsome, intelligent, and so on. One can use these adjectives of half the men one meets. But somewhere in him, in his being, something matched something in me; he had come into me, he had set me in motion. I remember looking down the table at his wife and thinking: Yes, my dear, but your husband is also my husband, for he walked into me and made himself at home in me, and because of him I shall act again from the depths of myself, I am sure of it, and I'm sure it will be the best work I can do. Though I won't know until tomorrow night, on the stage.

For instance, there was one night when I stood on the stage and stretched up my slender white arms to the audience (that is how they saw it; what *I* saw were two white-caked, raddled-with-cold arms that were, moreover, rather flabby) and I knew that I was, that night, nothing but an amateur. I stood there on the stage, *as a woman* holding out my pretty arms; it was Victoria Carrington saying: Look how poignantly I hold out my arms, don't you long to have them around you, my slender white arms, look how beautiful, how enticing Victoria is! And then, in my dressingroom afterwards I was ashamed; it was years since I had stood on the stage with nothing between me, the woman, and the audience—not since I was a green girl had I acted so—why, then, tonight?

I thought, and I understood. The afternoon before a man (a

producer from America, but *that* doesn't matter) had come to see me in my dressingroom and after he left I thought: Yes, there it is again, I know that sensation, that means he has set the forces in motion and so I can expect my work to show it. . . . It showed it, with a vengeance! Well, and so that taught me to discriminate; I learned I must be careful, must allow no second-rate man to come near me. And so put up barriers, strengthened around me the circle of cold, of impersonality, that should always lie between me and people, between me and the auditorium; I made a cool, bare space no man could enter, could break across, unless his power, his magic, was very strong, the true complement to mine.

Very seldom now do I feel myself alight, on fire, touched awake, created again by—what?

I live alone now. No, *you* would never be able to imagine how. For I knew when I saw you this evening that you exist, you are, only in relation to other people, you are always giving out to your work, your wife, friends, children; your wife has the face of a woman who gives, who is confident that what she gives will be received. Yes, I understand all that, I know how it would be living with you, I *know* you.

After we had all separated, and I had watched you drive off with your wife, I came home and . . . no, it would be no use telling you, after all. (Or anyone, except, perhaps, my colleague and rival Irma Painter!) But what if I said to you—but no, there are certain disciplines which no one can understand but those who use them.

So I will translate into your language, I'll translate the truth so that it has the *affected*, almost embarrassing, exaggerated ring that goes with the actress Victoria Carrington, and I'll tell you how when I came home after meeting you my whole body was wrenched with anguish, and I lay on the floor sweating and shaking as if I had bad malaria; it was like knives of deprivation going through me, for, meeting you, it was being reminded again what it would be like to be with a man, really with him, so that the rhythm of every day, every night, carried us both like the waves of a sea.

Everything I am most proud of seemed nothing at all—what I have worked to achieve, what I *have* achieved, even the very core of what I am, the inner sensitive balance that exists like a sort of self-invented super instrument, or a fantastically receptive and cherished animal—this creation of myself, which every day becomes more involved, sensitive, and delicate, seemed absurd, paltry, spinsterish, a shameful excuse for cowardice. And my life, which so contents me because of its balance, its order, its steadily growing fastidiousness, seemed eccentrically solitary. Every particle of my being screamed out, wanting, needing—I was like an addict deprived of his drug.

I picked myself off the floor, I bathed myself, I looked after myself like an invalid or like a—yes, like a pregnant woman. These extraordinary fertilisations happen so seldom now that I cherish them, waste nothing of them, and I both long for and dread them. Every time it is like being killed, like being torn open while I am forced to remember what it is I voluntarily do without.

Every time it happens I swear I can never let it happen again, the pain is too terrible. What a flower, what a fire, what a miracle it would be if, instead of smiling (the "sweetly piercing" smile of my dying beauty), instead of accepting, submitting, I should turn to you and say . . .

But I shall not, and so something very rare (something much more beautiful than your wife could ever give you, or any of the day-by-day wives could imagine) will never come into being.

Instead . . . I sit and consume my pain, I sit and hold it, I sit and clench my teeth and . . .

It is dark, it is very early in the morning, the light in my room is a transparent grey, like the ghost of water or of air; there are no lights in the windows I see from my own. I sit in my bed, and watch the shadows of the tree moving on the brick wall of the garden, and I contain pain and . . .

Oh my dear one, my dear one, I am a tent under which you lie, I am the sky across which you fly like a bird, I am . . .

My soul is a room, a great room, a hall—it is empty, waiting. Sometimes a fly buzzes across it, bringing summer mornings in another continent, sometimes a child laughs in it, and it is like the generations chiming together, child, youth, and old woman as one being. Sometimes you walk into it and stand there. You stand here in me and smile and I shut my eyes because of the sweet recognition in me of what you are. I feel what you are as if I stood near a tree and put my hand on its breathing trunk.

I am a pool of water in which fantastic creatures move, in which you play, a young boy, your brown skin glistening, and the water moves over your limbs like hands, my hands, that will never touch you, my hands that tomorrow night, in a pool of listening silence, will stretch up towards the thousand people in the auditorium, creating love for them from the consumed pain of my denial.

I am a room in which an old man sits, smiling, as he has smiled for fifty centuries, you, whose bearded loins created me.

I am a world into which you breathed life, have smiled life, have made me. I am, with you, what creates, every moment, a thousand animalculae, the creatures of our dispensation, and everyone we have both touched with our hands and let go into space like freed birds.

I am a great space that enlarges, that grows, that spreads with the steady lightening of the human soul, and in the space, squatting in the corner, is a thing, an object, a dark, slow, coiled, amorphous heaviness, embodied sleep, a cold stupid sleep, a heaviness like the dark in a stale room—this thing stirs in its sleep where it squats in my soul, and I put all my muscles, all my force, into defeating it. For this was what I was born for, this is what I am, to fight embodied sleep, putting around it a confining girdle of light, of intelligence, so that it cannot spread its slow stain of ugliness over the trees, over the stars, over you.

It is as if, since you turned towards me and smiled letting light go through me again, it is as if a King and his Queen, hand in hand on top of my mountain sit smiling at ease in their country.

The morning is coming on the brick wall, the shadow of the tree has gone, and I think of how today I will walk out onto the stage, surrounded by the cool circle of my chastity, the circle of my discipline, and how I will raise my face (the flower face of my girlhood), and how I will raise my arms from which will flow the warmth you have given me.

And so, my dear one, turn now to your wife, and take her head onto your shoulder, and both sleep sweetly in the sleep of your love. I release you to go to your joys without me. I leave you to your love. I leave you to your life.

# Lions, Leaves, Roses...

•••••••••••••••••••••••••••••••••••••••••••••••••••••••••••••••••••••••••••••••••••••••••••••

$A$s I went towards St. Mark's Bridge, where slow water drowned this summer's leaves, she accosted me, grinning, tugging with both hands at the ends of her red-spotted kerchief. "The sun always follows me," she said, looking at the midday sun, as brilliant as a sun in Italy, but lower in the sky, it being October and our end of the earth tilting back and towards the cold of the winter which would begin next day or next month. "Yes," she said, "the sun's always after me, yes and the moon too." She looked for the moon, not visible that day, while the sunlight lit all the sky, the shedding trees, the brilliant grass and us standing on the pavement by the bridge and the canal.

No moon, only one of her familiars present, and her face changed to suspicion. To save the moment from grief, I said quickly, "You're lucky to have the sun for your friend." Again her face spread in glee, she bent hooting, squeezing out triumphant laughter, and I walked on, envious of her whose cracked mind let the sunlight through. For I was walking that day to catch a fragment of late summer in this clouded year, to catch and have it, and for this purpose it was necessary to walk with emptied mind, and all senses awake, and thoughts, whether dragon-flies or blow-flies swatted well away.

The ornate bridge with its white pillars, its six iron lamp-posts, its balustrades, has at its ends flat oblong rectangles like pedestals, but empty. Here I paused to summon and set on watch my own personal lion. The way I see it, a park which has no extensions to or connections with the country, with un-

created wildness, has no rights; it has allowed itself to be enclosed and owned by houses. Already there are wild animals
caged there, and right in its centre the roses in their circle are
tamed and willing. The lion came off his dry hillside to crouch
on St. Mark's Bridge, facing inwards, a golden beast, his fore-
paws tucked under an eternal chest, his eyes green and solid,
the eyes of a man, but man much more than any we know. For
if I could walk through those eyes, like gates, into the region
between them, it would be into a form of understanding that
we hear only rumours about. I left him there, as patient under
the falling autumn leaves as on his rock on the slopes of (I
think) the Hindu Kush, eyes unblinking, with no need to swat
away thoughts, words, feelings, for he was everything he saw.

The avenue that runs from St. Mark's Bridge Gate to the
memorial to Sir Cowasjee Jehangir was silent with warm sun,
and full of people walking slowly to feel it, and through their
lungs, our lungs, sweetly fanned, sixteen breaths a minute, the
breath of trees whose long exhalation had begun at sunrise that
morning. The trees are big here, each one claiming attention,
and the air lies heavily, the felt essence of tree. Not only tree,
but goat too, a dozen or so white, smelling goats, and when they
are passed, the wire paddock, where wolves whose howls will
keep good people awake on the winter nights that are coming
play charmingly around a tree-trunk.

Almost, almost, I reach that moment when leaves, birds,
burn up separately one by one, but I fail, because of the urgency
that prompts: quick, this is the last day, probably the very last
before the thick cold grey fills the air between me, us, and the
sun; the last day when warmth lies about us like the slow support of warm water.

So nearly "almost" that it was a pain to come back to the
worry of separateness, the pain of not knowing, not being bird,
leaf, rose. But here I was, in the outer precincts still, with paths
and gates to cross, not even at

*This Fountain*
*Erected by the*
*Metropolitan Drinking Fountain*
*and Cattle Trough Association*
*Was the Gift of*
SIR COWASJEE JEHANGIR
(*Companion of the Star of India*)

*A Wealthy Parsee Gentleman of Bombay*
*As a Token of Gratitude to the People of England for the*
*Protection Enjoyed by Him and His Parsee Fellow Countrymen*
*Under British Rule in India.*
*Inaugurated by H.R.H. Princess Mary,*
*Duchess of Teck, 1869.*

Near this, my favourite zany monument, is a green wooden cross among shining green foliage which was attended by a small boy who leaned through railings to stick on it some half-penny stamps. His earnest tongue protruded, and over it, one after another, he wiped the orange stamps he then transferred to the cross.

A hundred yards down the avenue appear the Mappin Terraces, far away on the right in front of tall flats on Primrose Hill, so juxtaposed it seems that bears might climb from rock shelves to balconies among potted plants. Suppose I had just this moment descended from Mars, what could I make of this park, full of beasts and colours and creatures? What, my eyes just opening on newness, would I make of a tree? What had I made of it all those years ago, opening my eyes on the terrace in a dry hot plain between the snow mountains? Suppose that I, entertaining this being from Mars, had the task of explanation: Well, sir, *yes*—I do see . . . but not quite. The same general idea, I grant you (though *we* are smaller), sap runs, limbs branch, but wait a minute, *they* are fastened to the earth, they can't move . . . and besides, in every spring they suck in leaves from the soil and then every autumn spit them out again. What for? You do have a point, it is preposterous, when you think of it, tons and tons and tons of leaf, just think how many thousands of tons weighing the trunks and branches of this park alone, and all sucked up the trunks every year, then dropped again to make their own way back to the roots. Besides, *we* can think, yes.

In front of me now the chestnut avenue that has, half-way down it, the cruel white boy who so casually dunks the dolphin's head, and a few paces away the urn held by four grinning winged lions most of the year concealed by dripping leaves and petals. The chestnuts are blazing, are burning, orangy-yellow under the blue sky, and the earth is littered precisely, clearly, with solid, ribbed, curved leaves, green-gold, each one lying defined in its small shell of brown shadow. The long stretch of earth between the chestnut trunks and the sober wooden benches seems embossed with solid shapes of gold; it is all a glitter of blue and gold, and the distractions of the long avenue vanish as the light flares up, just for one moment, for one small moment, into the steady clarity of seeing what I want, then fades again, leaving me teeth-gripped, furious on behalf of us all who have so much around us that we cannot take in. I will do it, I swear, I *will*—and turn right between small neat trees whose trunks are marred brown satin, across the road of the Inner Circle, and in. Now I can turn left to the centre of roses (Queen Mary's—she again, metamorphosed now out of Princess- and Duchesshood) or go on past the big knobbed tree that says it is a manna ash, and on past the next which is a weeping elm, to the little hill still fragrant with herbs, although most of them are withering.

The herbs draw me, sniffing, the air being dry and sharp; unlike the slow breath in the avenue, here it is a quick air, a stimulant. And now, despite six stiff-uniformed park attendants sitting side by side on a bench to enjoy the sunlight, it is Italy, with tall aspiring trees around a five-jetted fountain, its white central plume a noble dropping curve. Towards it a path ascends, gently, in measured steps, with generously foliaged urns and sets of red roses and white roses; roses wild-fire coloured, and icy roses bedded in a blue haze.

Again it comes, or becomes: the fountains can never blow in any other shape, each leaf is self-contained, each rose perpetual, the sky blazes blueness into my brain, and as the moment swells up, I begin to exult, feeling that at last I know a hint of what the lion knows always, by nature, but snap!—what I feared happens, words came out of the silence though I had sworn, had promised, that for one day they would be held off.

"No matter how I stare with silent mind . . ."

Oh, quite so, quite so (even though the words do have the stiff lilt proper to a park which, I swear, is native of a century that would understand nothing at all of us), quite so, no matter what I do, it can be guaranteed that clouds of thoughts will come packing my mind, each one better known than the last, and that words will eat up the precious sharpness of feeling like packs of greedy dogs.

"No matter how I stare with silent mind . . ."

Mayakovsky said: "Not a man, but a cloud in trousers." Af-

fected, I used to think this; but I don't think so now. Today
I choose him, unlikely companion—what would he make of this
order, this urbanity?—for the long stroll down the descending
path, my back to the plumed fountain, past the six basking
attendants, past the working gardeners, past babies in prams
and women with reddening necks in hastily, that-morning-re-
sumed summer blouses. I walk, shut from the day inside a
whirling white or tinted, brownish or rainbow, cloud of thought.
Which nothing can dissipate or make silent.

At the foot of this descent are the big gilded gates and a
choice: left, past the ponds and the water-flowers and the rose
beds, to the circle of the rose garden; right, past the restaurant,
then down under trees so heavy and so huge their weight is a
silence, over the little bridge and then curving leftwards again
to the boats . . . past the boats, over more bridges and so to the
road of the Outer Circle and the long way around to the zoo,
where I'll see the four giraffes stretching their astonished heads
into the sky, rubbing their necks against a scratching post, four
giraffes with hides marked like the cracked mud at the bottom
of dried river beds. Or the elephants, swaying their trunks.
Suppose that man from Mars . . . ? Or suppose *I* had just that
moment jumped into this skin from another planet, what would
I think? Well, would a giraffe seem more extraordinary than a
tree, if you had never seen either, or elephants than roses?

I'll go back by the rose garden, to Madame Louis Laperrière,
Monique, and Rose Gaujat; Soraya and Helen Traubel; Rose
Hellène, Pink Parfait, Peace and Malagana. We sit on unob-
trusive benches, looking at the coloured roses under this foreign
sun, smiling at each other and at ourselves, and a woman sits
down and tells us all in confidence: "I've just seen a squirrel,
its tail was all shining, like a girl's hair, it's because of the sun
you know." A retired gentleman comes to claim his seat, opens
a newspaper, but is observed to let it fall again, where it lies
gently palpitating on his stomach, while his eyes blink slowly
and in wonder at the garden before they close.

It is slow here, a drugged place, where voices lower and
people walking through put out a finger to *almost* touch a petal.
When the shadows from the tall garlandlike climbing roses
have moved enough to make a different place of it, I leave, and
walk out of the great gilded gates to where a tree glitters, each
leaf shaking separately, in a million different rhythms. All my

resolves for the day have been stolen from me by the sweet delusions of the rose garden, so I tell myself stolidly that this frantic dance means no more than that the wind is there, and that a tree has no hands, nor eyes, nor wants them, and so I went retracing paths until towards the northeast exit a man shovelled leaves into a barrow so fast it seemed as if a continuous stream of gold showered from his spade.

The tall houses of the long terraces stood silent, their windowpanes on fire.

Since I had entered the park, the earth had spun a tenth of its way around itself and thousands of miles around the sun; and the sun had sped, dragging us with it, in an inconceivable curve towards . . .

As I walked past the shower of gold from the man's shovel, the wind swerved leaves off the barrow, tugged them off the trees, scattered the brilliant grass with copper and with gold.

Leaves, words, people, shadows, whirled together towards autumn and the solstice.

Outside the park, on the pavement, there she was. Still grinning, still tugging at her red-spotted kerchief, apparently brimful of glee, she stood near, or rather, under, a huge policeman who looked down at her, quite expressionless, his features determined to make no comment. But "Is that so?" his pose said, or even "Fancy that!" to her news of her relationship with the sun, the moon, and this our wet planet.

# Not a Very Nice Story

T his story is difficult to tell.
Where to put the emphasis? Whose perspective to use? For to
tell it from the point of view of the lovers (but that was certainly
not their word for themselves—from the viewpoint, then, of the
guilty couple) is as if a life were to be described through the
eyes of some person who scarcely appeared in it; as if a cousin
from Canada had visited, let's say, a farmer in Cornwall half
a dozen unimportant times, and then wrote as if these meetings
had been the history of the farm and the family. Or it is as if a
stretch of years were to be understood in terms of the extra
day in Leap Year.

To put it conventionally is simple: two marriages, both as
happy as marriages are, both exemplary from society's point of
view, contained a shocking flaw, a secret cancer, a hidden vice.

But this hidden horror did not rot the marriages, and seemed
hardly to matter at all: the story can't be told as the two betrayed ones saw it; they didn't see it. They saw nothing. There
would be nothing to tell.

Now, all this was true for something like twenty years;
then something happened which changed the situation. To be
precise, what happened was the death of one of the four people
concerned. But at any moment during those twenty years, what
has been said would have been true: conventional morality
would judge these marriages to have a secret face all lies and
lust; from the adulterers' point of view, what they did was not
much more important than sharing a taste for eating chocolate
after the doctor has said no.

After that death, however, the shift of emphasis: the long unimportance of the twenty years of chocolate-eating could be seen as a prelude to something very different; could be seen as heartless frivolity or callousness redeemed providentially by responsibility? But suppose the death had not occurred?

It is hard to avoid the thought that all these various ways of looking at the thing are nonsense. . . .

Frederick Jones married Althea, Henry Smith married Muriel, at the same time; that is, in 1947. Both men, both women, had been much involved in the war, sometimes dangerously. But now it was over, they knew that it had been the way it had gone on and on that had affected them most. It had been endless.

There is no need to say much about their emotions when they married. Frederick and Althea, Henry and Muriel, felt exactly as they might be expected to feel, being their sort of people—middleclass, liberal, rather literary—and in their circumstances, which emotionally consisted of hungers of all kinds, but particularly for security, affection, warmth, these hungers having been heightened beyond normal during the long war. They were all four aware of their condition, were able to see themselves with the wryly tolerant eye of their kind. For they at all times knew to a fraction of a degree the state of their emotional pulse, and were much given to intelligent discussion of their individual psychologies.

Yet in spite of views about themselves which their own parents would have regarded as intolerable to live with, their plans and aims for themselves were similar to those of their parents at the same age. Both couples wished and expected that their marriages would be the bedrock of their lives, that they would have children and bring them up well. And it turned out as they wanted. They also expected that they would be faithful to each other.

At the time these marriages took place, the couples had not met. Both Doctor Smith and Doctor Jones, separately, had had the idea of going into partnership and possibly founding a clinic in a poor area. Both had been made idealists by the war, even socialists of a non-ideological sort. They advertised, made contact by letter, liked each other, and bought a practice in a country town in the west of England where there would be many poor people to look after, as well as the rich.

Houses were bought, not far from each other. While the two men were already friends, with confidence in being able to work together, the wives had not met. It was agreed that it was high time this event should take place. An occasion was to be made of it. The four were to meet for dinner in a pub five miles outside the little town. That they should all get on well was known by them to be important. In fact both women had made small humorous complaints that if their "getting on" was really considered so important, then why had their meeting been left so late?

As the two cars drove up to the country inn, the same state of affairs prevailed in each. There was bad humour. The women felt they were being patronised; the men felt that the women were probably right but were being unreasonable in making a fuss when after all the main thing was to get settled in work and in their homes. All four were looking forward to that dinner—the inn was known for its food—while for their different reasons they resented being there at all. They arrived in each other's presence vivid with variegated emotions. The women at once knew they liked each other—but after all, they might very well have not liked each other!—and made common cause about the men. The four went into the bar where they were an animated and combative group.

By the time they moved into the diningroom, ill-humour had vanished. There they sat, with their wine and good food. They were attracting attention, because they were obviously dressed up for a special occasion, but chiefly because of their own consciousness of well-being. This was the peak of their lives; the long tedium of the war was over; the men were still in their early thirties, the women in their twenties. They were feeling as if at last their real lives were starting. They were all goodlooking. The men were of the same type: jokes had been made about that already. They were both dark, largely built, with the authority of doctors; "comfortable," as the wives said. And the women were pretty. They soon established (like showing each other their passports, or references of decency and reliability) that they shared views on life—tough, but rewarding; God—dead; children—to be brought up with the right blend of permissiveness and discipline; society—to be cured by commonsense and mild firmness but without extremes of any sort.

Everything was well for them; everything would get better.

They sat a long time over their food, their wine, and their happiness, and left only when the pub closed, passing into a cold clear night, frost on the ground. It happened that conversations between Frederick Jones and Muriel Smith, Althea Jones and Henry Smith, were in progress, and the couples, so arranged, stood by their respective cars.

"Come back to us for a nightcap," said Henry, assisting his colleague's wife in beside him, and drove off home.

Frederick and Muriel, not one word having been said, watched them go, then turned to each other and embraced. The embrace can best be described as being the inevitable continuation of their conversation. Frederick then drove a few hundred yards into a small wood, where the frost shone on the grass, stopped the car, flung down his coat, and then he and Muriel made love—no, that's not right, had sex, with vigour and relish and enjoyment, while nothing lay between them and their nakedness and some degrees of frost but a layer of tweed. They then dressed, got back into the car, and went back to town, where Frederick drove Muriel to her own home, came in with her for the promised nightcap, and took his own wife home.

Both married couples made extensive love that night, as the atmosphere all evening had promised they would.

Muriel and Frederick did not examine their behaviour as much as such compulsive examiners of behaviour might have been expected to do. The point was, the incident was out of character, unlike them, so very much *not* what they believed in, that they didn't know what to think about it, let alone what to feel. Muriel had always set her face against the one-night stand. Trivial, she had said it was—the word "sordid" was over-moral. Frederick, both professionally and personally, had a lot to say about the unsatisfactory nature of casual sexual relationships. In his consulting room he would show carefully measured disapproval for the results—venereal disease or pregnancy—of such relations. It was not a moral judgement he was making, he always said; no, it was a hygienic one. He had been heard to use the word "messy." Both these people had gone in, one could say on principle, for the serious affair, the deep involvement. Even in wartime, neither had had casual sex.

So while it was hardly possible that such extraordinary behaviour could be forgotten, neither thought about it: the incident could not be included in their view of themselves.

And besides, there was so much to do, starting the new practice, arranging the new homes.

Besides, too, both couples were so pleased with each other, and had such a lot of love to make.

About six weeks after that evening at the pub, Frederick had to drop in to Henry and Muriel's to pick up something, and found Muriel alone. Again, not one word having been said, they went to the bedroom and—but I think the appropriate word here is "screwed." Thoroughly and at length.

They parted, and again unable to understand themselves, let the opportunity to think about what had happened slide away.

The thing was too absurd! They could not say, for instance, that during that famous evening at the pub, when they first met, that they had eyed each other with incipient desire, or had sent out messages of need or intent. They had not done more than to say to themselves, as one does: I'd like to make love with this man, this woman, if I wasn't well-suited already. They certainly could not have said that during the intervening six weeks they had dreamed of each other, finding their actual partners unsatisfactory. Far from it.

For if these, Muriel and Frederick, were natural sexual partners, then so were Frederick and Althea, Henry and Muriel.

If we now move on ten years and look back, as the guilty couple, Frederick and Muriel, then did—or rather, as both couples did, ten years being a natural time or place for such compulsive self-examiners to make profit-and-loss accounts—it is only in an effort to give the right emphasis to the thing.

For it is really hard to get the perspective right. Suppose that I had, in fact, described the emotions of the two very emotional courtships, the emotional and satisfying affairs that preceded marriage, the exciting discoveries of marriage and the depths and harmonies both couples found, and had then said, simply: On many occasions two of these four people committed adultery, without forethought or afterthought, and these adulterous episodes, though extremely enjoyable, had no effect whatever on the marriages—thus making them sound something like small bits of grit in mouthfuls of honey. Well, but even the best of marriages can hardly be described as honey. Perhaps it is that word "adultery"—too weighty? redolent of divorces and French farce? Yet it is still in use, very much so:

it is a word that people think, and not only in the law courts.

Perhaps, to get the right emphasis, in so far as those sexual episodes were having an effect on the marriages, one might as well not mention them at all? But not to mention them is just as impossible—apart from what happened in the end, the end of the story. For surely it is absolutely outside what we all know to be psychologically possible for the partners of happy marriages, both of them founded on truth and love and total commitment, to have casual sex with close mutual friends—thus betraying their marriages, their relationships, themselves— and for these betrayals to have no effect on them at all?

No guilt? No private disquiet? What was felt when gazing into their loving partners' eyes, with everything open and frank between them, Frederick, Muriel, had to think: How can I treat my trusting partner like this?

They had no such thoughts. For ten years the marriages had prospered side by side. The Joneses had produced three children, the Smiths two. The young doctors worked hard, as doctors do. In the two comfortable gardened houses, the two attractive young wives worked as hard as wives and mothers do. And all that time the marriages were being assessed by very different standards, which had nothing to do with those trivial and inelegant acts of sex—which continued whenever circumstances allowed, quite often, though neither guilty partner searched for occasions—all that time the four people continued to take their emotional pulses, as was their training: the marriages were satisfactory; no, not so satisfactory; yes, very good again. It was better in the second year than in the first, but less good in the third than in the fourth. The children brought the couples closer together in some ways, but not in others— and so on. Frederick was glad he had married delightful and sexy little Althea; and she was glad she had married Frederick, whose calm strength was her admirable complement. And Henry was pleased with Muriel, so vivacious, fearless and self-sufficing; and Muriel was similarly glad she had chosen Henry, whose quietly humorous mode of dealing with life always absorbed any temporary disquiets she might be suffering.

All four of course, would sometimes wonder if they should have married at all, in the way everyone does; and all four would discuss with themselves and with each other, or as a foursome, the ghastliness of marriage as an institution and how it should be abolished and something else put in its place. Sometimes, in the grip of a passing attraction for someone else, all four might regret that their choices were now narrowed down to one. (At such times neither Frederick nor Muriel thought of each other; they took each other for granted, since they were always available to each other, like marriage partners.) In short, and to be done with it, at the end of ten years, and during the soul-searching and book-keeping that went on then, both couples could look back on marriages that had in every way fulfilled what they had expected, even in the way of "taking the rough with the smooth." For where is the pleasure in sweet-without-sour? In spite of, because of, sexually exciting times and chilly times, of temporary hostilities and harmonies, of absences or illnesses, of yearning, briefly, for others—because of all this they had enjoyed a decade of profoundly emotional experience. In joy or in pain, they could not complain about flatness, or absence of sensation. And after all, emotion is the thing, we can none of us get enough of it.

What transports the couples had suffered! What tears the two women had wept! What long delicious nights spent on prolonged sexual pleasure! What quarrels and crises and dramas! What depth of experience everywhere! And now the five children, each one an emotion in itself, each one an extension of emotion, claiming the future for similar pleasurable or at least sensational rivers of feeling.

It was round about the eleventh year that there came a moment of danger to them all. Althea fell in love with a young doctor who had come to help in the practice while the two senior doctors took leave: the two families usually took holidays together, but this time the men went off tramping in Scotland leaving the women and children.

Althea confided in Muriel. It was not a question of leaving her Frederick: certainly not. She could bear to hurt neither him nor the children. But she was suffering horribly, from desire and all kinds of suddenly discovered deprivations, for the sake of the young man with whom she had slept half a dozen times furtively—horrible word!—when the children were playing in the garden or were asleep at night. Her whole life seemed a desert of dust and ashes. She could not bear the future. What was the point of living?

The two young women sat talking in Althea's kitchen.

They were at either end of the breakfast table around which so many jolly occasions had been shared by them all. Althea was weeping.

Perhaps this is the place to describe these two women. Althea was a small round dark creature, who always smelled delightful, and who was described by her husband as the most eminently satisfactory blend of femininity and commonsense. As for Muriel, she was a strong large-boned woman, fair, with the kind of skin that tans quickly, so that she always looked very healthy. Her clothes were of the kind called casual and she took a lot of trouble over them. Both women of course often yearned to be like the other.

These two different women sat stirring coffee cups as they had done a hundred times, while the five children shouted, competed and loved in the garden, and Althea wept, because she said this was a watershed in her marriage, like eating the apple in Eden. If she told her beloved husband that she was—temporarily, she did so hope and believe—besottedly in love with this young doctor, then it must be the end of everything between them. But if she didn't tell him, then it was betrayal. Whatever she did would have terrible results. *Not* telling Frederick seemed to her worse even than the infidelity itself. She had never, ever concealed anything from him. Perfect frankness and sincerity had been their rule—no, not a rule, they had never had to lay down rules for behaviour that came so excellently and simply out of their love and trust. She could not imagine keeping anything from Frederick. And she was sure he told her everything. She could not bear it, would certainly leave him at once, if she knew that he had ever lied to her. No, she would not mind infidelity of a certain kind—how could she mind?—now that she forfeited any rights in the matter! But lies, deceptions, furtiveness—no, that would be the end, the end of everything.

Althea and Muriel stayed together, while one woman wept and talked and the other listened, stopping only when the children came in, for all that day, and all the next, and for several after that. For Muriel was understanding that it was the words and tears that were the point, not what was said: soon the energy of suffering, the tension of conflict, would have spent itself, making it all seem less important. But Muriel was determined not to listen for one minute more than was necessary.

And soon she was able to advise Althea, the tears having abated, not to tell her Fred anything at all, she would just have to learn to live with a lie.

And now of course she had to think, really to think, whether she liked it or not, about the way she had been making love— or sex—in a frivolous, and some people might say sordid, way with her best friend's husband. She was being made to think. Most definitely she did not want to think: it was extraordinary, the strength of her instinct *not* to examine that area of her life.

However, examining it, or rather, touching lightly on it, she was able to congratulate herself, or rather, both herself and dear Fred, that never had they in the presence of their spouses enjoyed that most awful of betrayals, enjoyment of their complicity while their said spouses remained oblivious. She could not remember ever, when together, their so much as looking at each other in an invitation to make love, or sex; she was positive they had never once allowed their eyes to signal: these poor fools don't know our secret. For certainly they had never felt like this. They had not ever, not once, made plans to meet alone. They might have fallen into each other's arms the moment the opportunity offered, as if no other behaviour was possible to them, but they did not engineer opportunities. And, having arrived in each other's arms, all laughter and pleasure, there was never a feeling of having gone one better than Althea and Henry, of doing them down in any way. And, having separated, they did not think about what had happened, nor consider their partners: it was as if these occasions belonged to another plane altogether—that trivial, sordid, and unimportant, that friendly, good-natured and entirely enjoyable plane that lay beside, or above, or within these two so satisfactory marriages.

It occurred to Muriel that its nature, its essence, was lack of emotion. Her feeling for Frederick, what Frederick felt for her, was all calm sense and pleasure, with not so much as a twinge of that yearning anguish we call being in love.

And, thinking about it all, as these long sessions with weeping and miserable (enjoyable miserable?) Althea had made her do, she understood, and became determined to hold on to, her belief that her instinct, or compulsion, never to examine, brood, or make emotional profit-and-loss accounts about the sex she had with Frederick was healthy. For as soon as she did put weight on that area, start to measure and weigh, all sorts of

sensations hitherto foreign to this relationship began to gabble
and gobble, insist and demand. Guilt, for one.

She came to a conclusion. It was so seditious of any idea held
in common by these four and their kind that she had to look at
it, as it were, sideways. It was this: that very likely the falling-
in-love with the young doctor was not at all as Althea was seeing
it (as anyone was likely to see it); the point was not the periods
of making love—love, not sex!—which of course had been all
rapture, though muted, inevitably, with their particular brand
of wry and civilised understanding, but it was the spilling of
emotion afterwards, the anguish, the guilt. Emotion was the
point. Great emotion had been felt, had been suffered. Althea
had suffered, was suffering abominably. Everyone had got it
wrong: the real motive for such affairs was the need to suffer
the pain and the yearning afterwards.

The two marriages continued to grow like trees, sheltering
the children who flourished beneath them.

Soon, they had been married fifteen years.

There occurred another crisis, much worse.

Its prelude was this. Due to a set of circumstances not important—Althea had to visit a sick mother and took the children; the Smith children went to visit a grandmother, Henry
was away—Frederick and Muriel spent two weeks alone with
each other. Ostensibly they were in their separate homes, but
they were five minutes' drive from each other, and not even in
a gossipy inbred little English town could neighbours see anything wrong in two people being together a lot who were with
each other constantly year in and out.

It was a time of relaxation. Of enjoyment. Of quiet. They
spent nights in the same bed—for the first time. They took long
intimate meals together alone, for the first time. They had
seldom been alone together, when they came to think of it. It
was extraordinary how communal it was, the life of the Joneses
and the Smiths.

Their relationship, instead of being the fleeting, or flighty
thing it had been—rolls in the hay (literally), or in the snow,
an hour on the drawingroom carpet, a quick touch-up in a
telephone booth—was suddenly all dignity, privacy and leisure.

And now Frederick showed a disposition to responsible feeling—"love" was the word he insisted on using, while Muriel
nervously implored him not to be solemn. He pointed out that

he was betraying his beloved Althea, that she was betraying her darling Henry, and that this was what they had been doing for years and years, and without a twinge of guilt or a moment's reluctance.

And without, Muriel pointed out, *feeling.*

Ah yes, she was right, how awful, he was really beginning to feel that . . .

For God's sake, she cried, stop it, don't spoil everything, can't you see the dogs of destruction are sniffing at our door? Stop it, darling Fred, I won't have you using words like "love," no, no, that is our redeeming point, our strength—we haven't been in love, we have never agonised over each other, desired each other, missed each other, wanted each other; we have not ever "felt" anything for each other. . . .

Frederick allowed it to be seen that he found this view of them too cool, if not heartless.

But, she pointed out, what they had done was to help each other in every way, to be strong pillars in a foursome, to rejoice at the birth of each other's children, to share ideas and read books recommended by the other. They had enjoyed random and delightful and irresponsible sex without a twang of conscience when they could—had, in short, lived for fifteen years in close harmony.

Fred called her an intelligent woman.

During that fortnight love was imminent on at least a dozen occasions. She resisted.

But there was no doubt, and Muriel saw this with an irritation made strong by self-knowledge—for of course she would have adored to be "in love" with Frederick, to anguish and weep and lie awake—that Frederick, by the time his wife came back, was feeling thoroughly deprived. His Muriel had deprived him. Of emotional experience.

Ah emotion, emotion, let us bathe in thee!

For instance, the television, that mirror of us all:

A man has crashed his car, and his wife and three children have burned to death.

"And what did you feel when this happened?" asks the bland, but humanly concerned, young interviewer. "Tell us, what did you *feel?*"

Or, two astronauts have just survived thirty-six hours when every second might have meant their deaths.

"What did you feel? Please tell us, what did you feel?"

Or, a woman's two children have spent all night exposed on a mountain top but were rescued alive. "What did you feel?" cries the interviewer. "What did you feel while you were waiting?"

An old woman has been rescued from a burning building by a passerby, but for some minutes had every reason to think that her end had come.

"What did you feel? You thought your number was up, you said that, didn't you? What did you feel when you thought that?"

What do you think I felt, you silly nit, what would you have felt in my place? What does everybody watching this programme know perfectly well what I felt? So why ask me when you know already?

Why, madam?—of course it is because feeling is our substitute for tortured slaves and dying gladiators. We have to feel sad, anxious, worried, joyful, agonised, delighted. I feel. You feel. They felt. I felt. We were feeling . . . If we don't feel, then how can we believe that anything is happening to us at all?

And since none of us feel as much as we have been trained to believe that we ought to feel in order to prove ourselves profound and sincere people, then luckily here is the television where we can see other people feeling for us. So tell me, madam, what did you *feel* while you stood there believing that you were going to be burned to death? Meanwhile the viewers will be chanting our creed: We feel, therefore we are.

Althea came back, the children came back, Henry came back, life went on, and Frederick almost at once fell violently in love with a girl of twenty who had applied to be a receptionist in the surgery. And Muriel felt exactly the same, but on the emotional plane, as a virtuously frigid wife felt—so we are told —when her husband went to a prostitute: If I had only given him what he wanted, he wouldn't have gone to *her!*

For she knew that her Frederick would not have fallen in love with the girl if she had allowed him to be in love with her. He had had an allowance of "love" to be used up, because he had not understood—he had only said that he did—that he was wanting to fall in love: he needed the condition of being in love, needed to feel all that. Or, as Muriel muttered (but only very privately, and to herself), he needed to suffer. She should have allowed him to suffer. It is clear that everybody needs it.

And now there was this crisis, a nasty one, which rocked all four of them. Althea was unhappy, because her marriage was at stake: Frederick was talking of a divorce. And of course she was remembering her lapse with the young doctor four years before, and the living lie she had so ably maintained since. And Frederick was suicidal, because he was not so stupid as not to know that to leave a wife he adored, and was happy with, for the sake of a girl of twenty was—stupid. He was past forty-five. But he had never loved before, he said. He actually said this, and to Henry, who told Muriel.

Henry, who so far had not contributed a crisis, now revealed that he had suffered similarly some years before, but "it had not seemed important." He confessed this to Muriel, who felt some irritation. For one thing, she felt she had never really appreciated Henry as he deserved, because the way he said "it had not seemed important" surely should commend itself to her? Yet it did not; she felt in some ridiculous way belittled because he made light of what had been—surely?—a deep experience? And if it had not, why not? And then, she felt she had been betrayed; that she was able to say to herself she was being absurd did not help. In short, suddenly Muriel was in a bad way. More about Frederick than about Henry. Deprived in a flash of years of sanity, she submerged under waves of jealousy of the young girl, of deprivation—but of what? what? she was in fact deprived of nothing!—of sexual longing, and of emotional loneliness. Her Henry, she had always known, was a cold fish. Their happiness had been a half-thing. Her own potential had always been in cold storage. And so she raged and suffered, for the sake of Frederick, her real love—so she felt now. Her only love. How could she have been so mad as not to enjoy being really in love, two weeks of love. How could she not have seen, all those years, where the truth lay. How could she . . .

That was what she felt. What she *thought*, and knew, was that she was mad. Everything she felt now had nothing, but nothing to do with her long relationship with Frederick, which was as pleasant as a good healthy diet and as unremarkable, and nothing to do with her marriage with Henry, whom she loved deeply, and who made her happy, and whose humorous and civilised company she enjoyed more than anyone's.

Frederick brought his great love to an end. Or, to put it accurately, it was brought to an end: the girl married. For a while he sulked; he could not forgive life for his being nearly fifty. Althea helped him come back to himself, and to their life together.

Muriel and Henry re-established their loving equilibrium.

Muriel and Frederick for a long time did not, when they found themselves together, make sex. That phase had ended, so they told each other, when they had a discussion: they had never had a discussion of this sort before, and the fact that they were having one seemed proof indeed that they had finished with each other. It happened that this talk was taking place in his car, he having picked her up from some fête given to raise funds for the local hospital. Althea had not been able to attend. The children, once enjoyers of such affairs, were getting too old for them. Muriel was attending on behalf of them all, and Frederick was giving her a lift home. Frederick stopped the car on the edge of a small wood, which was now damp and brown with winter: this desolation seemed a mirror of their own dimmed and ageing state. Suddenly, no word having been spoken, they were in an embrace—and, shortly thereafter, on top of his coat and under hers in a clump of young birches whose shining winter branches dropped large tingling lively drops tasting of wet bark onto their naked cheeks and arms.

But, the psychologically oriented reader will be demanding, what about those children? Adolescent by now, surely?

Quite right. The four had become background figures for the dramas of the young ones' adolescence; their passions were reflections of their children's; and part of their self-knowledge had to be that Frederick's need to be in love and the associated traumas were sparked off by the adults being continually stimulated by their five attractive offspring, all of whom were of course perpetually in love or in hate.

It goes without saying too that the parents felt even more guilty and inadequate because they worried that their lapses, past present and imaginary, might have contributed to the stormy miseries of the children. Which we all know too well to have to go through again—but what violence! what quarrels! what anguish! Adolescence is like this, we all know, and so do the children. The Jones and Smith youngsters behaved exactly as they were expected to. Oh the dramas and the rebellions, the leavings of home and the sullen returns; oh the threats of drug-taking, then the drug-taking and the return to caution; the near-pregnancies, the droppings out and in, the ups and downs at schools, the screamed accusations at the parents for their total stupidity, backwardness, thickheadedness and responsibility for all the ills in the world.

But just as the script prescribes crisis, so it prescribes the end of crisis. Those five attractive young people, with benefits of sound middleclass background and its institutions, with their good education, with their intelligent and concerned parents— what could go wrong? Nothing did. They did well enough at school and were soon to go to university. Could they have any other future beyond being variations on the theme of their parents?

Twenty years had passed.

There came an opportunity for the two doctors to join a large doctors' combine in London. It was in a workingclass area, but the senior doctors had consulting rooms in Harley Street. Doctors Smith and Jones had continued idealistic, conditionally socialist, and were shocked by the thought that they might also succumb to what they thought of as a Jekyll and Hyde existence.

The two families decided to buy a very large house in North London, and to divide it. That way they would all have much more space than if they each had a house. And the children were more like brothers and sisters and should not be separated by anything as arbitrary as a move to a new home.

Soon after the move to London Henry died. There was no sense in him dying in his fifties. He had thought of himself as healthy. But he had always smoked heavily, he was rather plump, and he had always worked very hard. These were reasons enough, it was thought, for him to have a stroke and for Muriel to be a widow in her forties.

Muriel stayed in the shared house with her two children, a boy of eighteen and a girl of fourteen. After discussing it thoroughly with Althea, Frederick made arrangements to help support Muriel, to be a father to the children, to support this other family as he was sure Henry would have done for Althea and the three children if it had been Frederick who had had

the stroke. As it might have been: Frederick's habits and constitution were similar to Henry's. Frederick was secretly frightened, made resolutions to eat less, smoke less, work less, worry
less; but he was doing more of everything because Henry had
gone.

In order to support his greater responsibilities, Frederick
attended two days a week and a morning in Harley Street—
Muriel acted as his receptionist there, and for the two other
doctors who shared his set of rooms. He also worked hard in
the combine's clinics, making up by evening sessions and night
visiting for time spent in Moneyland. So Frederick and Muriel
were now working together, as well as seeing each other constantly in the much-shared family life. Muriel was more with
Frederick than Althea was.

And now that Muriel was a widow, and the opportunities
were more, the sex life of the two had become as stable as good
married sex.

Muriel, thinking about it, had decided that it was probable
Frederick had deliberately "stepped up" his sexual life with
her because he knew she must be feeling sexually deprived.
This was very likely the kind of sexually friendly consideration
that would happen in a polygamous marriage? What made
her come to this conclusion was that now they would often
cuddle as married people do, for instance staying an hour or
so after time in the Harley Street rooms, their arms around
each other, discussing the day's problems, or perhaps driving
off onto Hampstead Health to discuss the children, sharing
warmth and affection—like married people.

For Fred could hardly be missing this sort of affection, far
from it, and that he was giving it to her must be the result
of a conscious decision, of kindness.

They sometimes did say to each other that what they all
had together—but only they two knew it—was a polygamous
marriage.

When in company, and people were discussing marriage, the
marriage problems of Western man, the problems caused by
the emancipation of women, monogamy, fidelity, whether one
should "tell" or not, these two tended to remain silent or to
make indifferent remarks that sounded in spite of themselves
impatient—as people do when entertaining inadmissible
thoughts.

Both of them, the man and the woman, had found themselves thinking, had even heard themselves exclaiming aloud
as the result of such thoughts: "What a lot of rubbish, what
lies!" meaning, no less, these intelligent and sensible ideas we
all do have about the famous Western problematical marriage.

Muriel had only understood that she was married to Frederick
when she started to think about marrying again: but it was
not likely that anyone would want to marry a forty-five-year-old
woman with children at their most demanding and difficult
time. She could not imagine marrying again: for it would mean
the end of her marriage with Frederick. This was probably
how they would all go on, into their old age, or until one of
them died.

This was Muriel's thinking on the situation.

Frederick: Muriel was right, he had indeed thought carefully about his old friend's loneliness. She would probably not
marry again; she was not after all of the generation where
there were more men than women. And there was something
too independent and touch-me-not about her. Her silences were
challenging. Her green eyes were outspoken. A tall rangy
woman with bronze hair (she dyed it), people noticed her, and
called her beautiful or striking: of her, people used the strong
adjectives. The older she got, the dryer and cooler became her
way of talking. Enemies called her unkind, or masculine;
friends, witty. *He* enjoyed these qualities, but would he if they
were not the other half, as it were, of Althea? Whom people
tended to call "little." So did he. Dear little Althea.

He would give Muriel as much warmth, as much sex as he
could, without, of course, giving any less to his wife. For years
his relations with Muriel had been all jam, nothing to pay, a
bonus. Now he felt her as part of his sudden increase in responsibility when Henry died, part of what he must give to
the two children. He was fond of Muriel—indeed, he was sure
he loved her. He knew he loved the children almost as well as
his own. It was an ungrudging giving of himself—but there
was something else in him, another worm was at work. For
what was strongest in Frederick now neither his wife nor
Muriel knew anything about. It was his longing for the girl
Frances—married with children. Neither of his women had
understood how deep that had gone. He had not understood it
himself at the time.

Now, years later, it seemed to him that his life was divided between dark, or perhaps a clear flat grey, and light—Frances. Between everything heavy, plodding, difficult, and everything delicious—Frances. Nothing in his actual life fed delight or sprang from it: somewhere else was a sweetness and ease which he had known once, when he had loved Frances.

By now he did know that Frances, a lovely but quite ordinary girl, must be a stand-in for something else. It must be so. No small human being could possibly support the weight of such a force and a fierceness of longing, of want, of need. From time to time, when he straightened himself morally, and physically, for it was like a physical anguish, from a pain that swept all through him, or when he woke up in the morning out of a dream that was all pain of loss to see Althea's sleeping face a few inches away on the other pillow, he had to tell himself this: It is not possible that I am suffering all this, year after year, because of a girl I was in love with for a few crazy months.

Yet that was how it felt. On one side was the life he actually led; on the other, "Frances."

His intelligence told him everything it ought, such as that if he had been fool enough to leave Althea for Frances, or if Frances had been fool enough to marry him, in a very short time Frances would have been a dear known face on a shared pillow, and what Frances had represented would have moved its quarters elsewhere.

But that was not what he felt. Although he worked so hard— it was virtually two jobs that he had now, one with the poor and the ignorant, for whom he remained concerned, and one with the rich; although he maintained with the most tender love and consideration the emotional and physical needs of the two women; although he was a good and tactful father for five children—he felt he had nothing, lacked everything.

Althea . . . we move into the shoes, or behind the eyes of, the innocent party.

These three people had all taken on loads with the death of Henry. With Muriel working, Althea's was to run all the large house, to do the shopping, to cook, to be always available for the children. She did not mind it, she had never wanted a career. But it was hard work, and soon she felt herself to be all drudgery and domesticity, and just at the time when, with the children older, she had looked forward to less. But this strain was nothing compared to the real one, which was that she had cared very much about being so attractive, and cherished for it. Cherished no less, she demanded even more of her vanishing looks. She could not bear to think that soon she would be elderly, soon Frederick would not want her. Comparing her tragic sessions in front of her mirror, and her feelings of inadequacy, with her husband's affection, she knew that she was unreasonable. Well, it was probably "the change."

She read many medical books and consulted another doctor —not one her husband knew—and got pills and came to regard her emotional state, all of it, everything she thought and felt, as a symptom without validity.

For she knew that her relationship with her husband was warm, good—wonderful. While other people's marriages frayed and cracked and fell apart, hers, she knew, was solid.

But when she looked at her life, when she looked back, she too divided what she saw into two. For her, the sunlit time lay on the other side of the affair with the young doctor. It was not the physical thing she regretted, no; it was that she had not told her husband. Time had done nothing at all to soften her guilt about it. Frederick and she had known a time of perfection, of complete trust and belief. Then she, Althea, had chosen to destroy it. It was her fault that he had fallen so much in love with the girl Frances. Oh, he was likely to fall in love with someone at some point: of course, everyone did—hadn't she? But so violently? That could only have been because of some deep lack between them. And she knew what it was: she had told him lies, had not trusted him.

She was left now with much more than she deserved. If she had to share him now—a little, with Muriel—then it was what she deserved. Besides, if she, Althea, had been left a widow, then she would have leaned as heavily on Henry. On who else?

Sometimes Althea had wild moments when she decided to tell Frederick about the young doctor; but that would be absurd, out of proportion. To talk about it now would surely be to destroy what they still had? To say: For more than a decade now I have been lying to you—she could not imagine herself actually doing it.

Sometimes she listened to other people talking about their marriages, and it seemed to her that they were able to take infidelities much more lightly. Lies, too. Althea kept telling herself that there was something very wrong in her, that she kept brooding about it, worrying, grieving.

For instance, there were these people who went in for wifeswapping. They thought nothing of making love in heaps and in bunches, all together. Some of them said their marriages were strengthened—perhaps they were. Perhaps if she and her Fred had shared each other with other couples . . . who, Muriel and Henry?—no, surely that could be too dangerous, too close? Surely they—the wife-swappers—made a rule not to get involved too close to home? But that was not the point at all; the point was, the lying, the deception.

The fact was, the only person in the world who knew all the truth about her was Muriel! Muriel had known about the young doctor, and knew about the years of lying. How odd that was, for your woman friend to be closer than your own husband! It was *intolerable*. Unbearable. Althea found it horrible to say to herself: I trust Muriel more than I do Frederick; my behaviour has proved that I do.

Of course she had sometimes had her thoughts about Frederick and Muriel. She had recently been jealous—a little, not much. This was because Muriel was working with Frederick now.

Often, when the three of them were together, Althea would look at those two, her husband, her closest friend, and think: Of course, if I died, they would marry. This was not envious, but her way of coming to terms with it. She even thought— though this was the sort of thing Muriel said, the kind of thing people expected from Muriel: This is a sort of group marriage, I suppose.

But Althea did not suspect a sexual tie. Not that he hadn't often said he found Muriel attractive. But one always could sense that sort of thing. Of course in all those years there must have been something: a kiss or two? A little more perhaps after a party or something like that? But not much more; these two would never deceive her. She could trust Muriel with anything; her old friend was a well into which confidences vanished and were forgotten; Muriel never gossiped, never condemned. She was the soul—if one could use that oldfashioned word—of honour. As for Frederick, when he had fallen in love, not only his wife, but the whole world had known of it: he was not a man who could, or who wanted to, conceal his feelings. But the real thing was this: the three of them had made, and now lived inside, an edifice of kindliness and responsibility and decency; it was simply not possible that it could harbour deception. It was inconceivable. So much so that Althea did not think about it: it was not sexual jealousy that she felt.

But she felt something else that she was ashamed of, that she had to wrestle with, in silence and in secrecy. She could not stop herself thinking that if Henry could die without warning, apparently in full health, then why not Frederick?

Althea was by nature a fussy and attentive wife, but Frederick did not like this in her. She longed to say: Take it easy, work less, worry less—relax. She knew he believed that he ought to be doing all this: duty ordained otherwise.

Often she would wake in the night out of dreams full of terror: if Frederick was on call, she would see the bed empty beside her, and think that this was what she could expect from the future. Then she would go to the stairs to see if Muriel's light was still on; it often was, and then Althea would descend the stairs to Muriel's kitchen, where they would drink tea or cocoa until Frederick came back. Muriel did not ask what drove Althea down the stairs so often at night, but she was always gay and consoling—kind. She was kind. Well, they were all kind people.

Sometimes, on those rare evenings when they could all be together, without pressures from Frederick's work, Althea, having cleared the table and come to join those two people, her husband—a large, worried-looking man in spectacles sitting by a lamp and piles of medical magazines, engaged on his futile task of keeping up with new discovery—and a lean restless woman who was probably helping one of the youngsters with homework, or a psychological problem—sometimes Althea would see that room without its centre, without Frederick. She and Muriel were alone in the room with the children. Yes, that is how it would all end, two ageing women, with the children —who would soon have grown up and gone.

Between one blink of an eye and another, a man could vanish, as Henry had done.

In the long evenings when Frederick was at the clinic, or on call, and it was as if the whole house and its occupants waited for him to come back, then Althea could not stop herself from looking across the livingroom at Muriel in the thought: *Coming events cast their shadow before. Can't you feel it?*

But Muriel would look up, smile, laugh, offer to make tea for them all, or would say that she heard Frederick's car and she was tired and would take herself to bed—for she was tactful, and never stayed on in the evenings past the time she was wanted.

But this is our future, Althea would think. Their future, hers and Muriel's, was each other.

She knew it. But it was neurotic to think like this and she must try to suppress it.

# The Other Garden

●··●··●··●··●··●··●··●··●··●··●··●··●··●··●··●··●··●··●··●··●··●··●··●··●··●··●··●··●··●··●··●··●··●··●··●··●··●··●··●··●··●··●··●··●··●··●··●··●··●

There were rumours another garden was hidden among trees.

Before finding it you speculate, make pictures of it in your mind. Perhaps it is hidden because it is so unlike everything else in the Park that it would strike people as discordant? And if it is unlike, or out of key, then in what ways? The Park already holds so much variety. The world's birds and animals are there. A tree will turn out to be an immigrant from Lebanon, another from Canada. Gulls come from the sea, migrating birds plane down to the many water surfaces on their way from one continent to another. There is wilderness near the canal where blackberries may be picked, there are fields of rough grass for lying on, or rolling on, or loving on, or running the dog or playing football and cricket. There are parts like Italy and parts that could not be anything but England. An island full of docketed plants for gardeners to bend over is reached by a little bridge that must have been copied from a teacup. Roses, miniature waterfalls, poplars, lakes, fountains, a theatre . . . what could possibly not be appropriate, be considered bizarre? A sand garden, as they have them in the East? But surely that would be hard to keep free of blown leaves. A garden of pebbles, coloured and matched? A sculpture garden, with metal and stone among gravel?

There is nothing you can't imagine the Park accommodating with no more of a jar than you get now, turning your eyes from oaks and beeches to bears on their rocky ledges or the head of a giraffe staring over a flowering bush, then to a small boy racing under a kite shaped like a yellow dish with a face on it.

Small children will take from their mother's kitchen a sprouting onion and a couple of carrots and, finding a few inches of bare soil in a corner, will plant them. Mother offers packets of seed and a garden fork and expertise, but the children fiercely guard their own conception: in the night the onion will make many, the carrots multiply. "No, no, this way, we want it this way, we don't want your old seeds. You say *a few weeks*? But that's for ever . . . we want them to grow *now!*" Perhaps this was man's first attempt to manipulate nature? No, you can't imagine that garden, but the houses of the gardeners and keepers are tucked away all over the Park and around these, probably, are samples of these embryo gardens. In a bombed building, rebuilt years ago new, a small girl used to dawdle on her way to school. She had made herself a house of a dozen bricks and some mortar rubble. Around the house she had a garden, spikes of wilting forsythia and blades of grass. Each morning she ran in with a new plant, a crocus pulled from her mother's garden, then a twig of cherry when it appeared in the spring. Everywhere was flowering growth, and the child came in daily in her purpose to make her own garden: a few square inches of dust with some withering fragments of plant. She scattered water on them from branches that had been rain-soaked in the night, she shaded them with a plank pulled from the debris of the building. Nothing helped, they had to die. So she brought shells, bits of glass and china, pebbles, beads, and made a pattern that said to her *garden*, one that would not die or dry out and vanish away.

Well then, if the other garden is not concealed because it is exotic, perhaps it is the quintessence of the Park, a concentrated statement of it? And so, at last, it turns out to be. Strolling in the Park, looking at trees and shrubs, you turn your head and see it. There it is.

It was a January day I saw it first. The night had been cold, the sky was chilly blue, full of racing cloud.

I was looking at a wide oblong of formal grass, with a deep border on either side. At the other end, shallow steps, almost the width of the grass, lifted the garden to its next level. The width of the steps, enough for a dozen or so to go up abreast, gives this reticent and secret place a look of welcome, as if it were waiting for guests. Yet there is no one in sight.

Of course, to see it in January means that you are imagining it in June; the dislocation you have suffered by seeing the garden there, where you didn't expect it, is sharpened by seeing two gardens at once, summer superimposed on this winter scene: easy, that morning, because of the sunlight everywhere, and the noise of the birds, bathing in it.

The grass of the lower garden, on its west side, and in shade, was filmed with ice that would not melt that day. The winter-flowering viburnum, pink crumblike buds, shed a faint sharp scent, like wind off snow.

The sound of footsteps is absorbed in grass: you walk in silence.

The steps are shallow and curved, and on either side are low pillars, and on them scrolls of stone, like frozen water-chutes. Above each scroll are shells, like those in Salamanca on that wall where people come to stand and watch the shadows move on dulled pink stone, the same colour of the stone that is used in the Cotswolds.

The green oblong of the pool of grass now lies behind, with its borders where the plants are all cut back. In spring, what will they be? And in summer? Of course, lavender and pinks, rue and rosemary, marjoram, thyme, catmint and peony. They will be scented, butterfly-filled, bee-visited, and people will stand hanging their noses over them, as drunk as the insects. The grass will be warm. Behind the borders now are stark bushes and trees, but when the leaves come this lower part will be enclosed twice, first by hedge, and then by a shimmer of green.

Even now, when you are well into the garden, on the steps, it is not possible to see the shape of the whole.

The second level has a fountain, as a centre to many roses—and grass, grass again, the roses will bloom over grass, not tarmac, and no footsteps will ever intrude here. A glossy black boy with a mermaid echoes the statue of the chestnut avenue, boy-with-dolphin, and also the spouting fishes of the poplar fountain. The water is frozen, but the ice has been broken for the birds. The thick water holds glassy plates that balance and slide, and on the coldly sunny edge a thrush and a blackbird wait for me to go so that they can drink.

Everywhere are birds. A blackbird uses his yellow beak in the soil under the roses. A fat pigeon holds his chest into the sun. Sparrows are quarrelling as if it were spring. Crows are making a fuss in some trees. And a squirrel, who surely ought to be hibernating, is watching what I shall do next.

At the edge of this round garden is another statue, of a girl holding a kid, its horns still in bud.

It is the kind of statue that can only arouse thoughts of the kind that true artists despise, such as: How the sculptor must have loved that girl!—She is beautiful, with a strong-boned face. Her hair looks wet. It is impossible not to imagine the sculptor saying: "Now wet your head. I'm going to do your hair today." And the owner of that face will surely have said at some point during the sitting, with the controlled commonsense that sounds like dry humour: "For goodness' sake, this statue is going to look as if the goat keeps turning its head to have a quick swig." But of course the artist went sternly on, ignoring her. The kid is tucked under one arm, very high, and close to her bare breasts.

It is the gentlest, most charming of statues, and it is

TO ALL THE PROTECTORS OF THE DEFENCELESS

It is in darkened bronze. The girl looks at the little animal, which is looking across to the shining black of the boy and mermaid rising out of the frozen water.

Some weeks later, on a day when the skies were low and dark, everything soaked and dismal, there was a wreath around the baby goat's neck. It was of daphne, fragrant pinkish-mauve on pale brown naked wood. Someone had reached up to garland the goat, and recently, for the flowers were fresh.

Soundlessly over grass into the next circle of this delicate garden, which is like a series of bubbles one above another. But you still can't make out the plan of the place; you can never see all of it at once. This "bubble" is smaller than the first. The person who said that this other garden was here said, too, that it was laid out in the shape of a man. This second bubble would be the chest.

It is like Queen Mary's rose garden, but an exquisite copy, segments of earth filled with roses in grass: these round gardens are like garlands laid on grass. It is enclosed by an espalier of limes, a lacing of black knobby branches that are horizontal and stiff on either side of the central stems. The black wood glistens and drips, the sunlight makes crystals of the scattering water. Each knob is already sprouting the yellowy shoots that when spring comes will make wands of green: the theme of garland will be repeated again.

A variety of birds sit on the cold wood, waiting for spring to start. The sky churns and tumbles.

At the very end of this series of grassy shapes is a very small circle or bubble—the head. Roses again. It is an intimate gay little place, and in summer it must be like being caught in a bunch of flowers and greenery. You look up into blue past black twigs, and out into the next bubble through the elegant bareness of the spreadeagled limes.

The design is still not evident, though you know it now: you are holding it in your mind, a tiny circle, a larger one, a larger one still, then the grassy oblong bordered and hedged on either side.

A small breeze lifts a dozen of last autumn's frozen leaves and clatters them on the icy film where the shadow is. In summer they will be butterflies and rose petals.

Silently back, over grass, with the blackbird hopping behind: you might be a gardener, and a gardener means turned soil. There is nobody else here, no one at all.

Back through one circle after another, then across the grass that lies beyond the steps. As you leave, the place draws itself in behind you, is gathered in to itself, like water settling after a stone has disturbed it. There it is, whole, between its hedges, its bare trees, repeating and echoing like a descant, using every theme that is used in the great Park outside, but used there roughly, in crude form.

A long way off now, the pigeon holds out its shining chest, and the blackbirds and thrushes probe the earth.

But the squirrel comes fast to the gate, and holds up its paws, as if it were begging; then it rakes my legs with its front paws like a cat wanting to be attended to, or to be fed.

Turn your back, turn a corner—it is all gone.

# The Temptation
# of Jack Orkney

Hhis father was dying. It was a
telegram, saying also: *you unobtainable telephone*. He had been
on the telephone since seven that morning. It was the housekeeper who had sent the telegram. Did Mrs. Markham not know
that she could have asked the telephone authorities to interrupt
his conversations for an urgent message? The irritation of the
organiser who is manipulating intractable people and events
now focussed on Mrs. Markham, but he tried to alleviate it by
reminding himself that Mrs. Markham was housekeeper not only
to his father but to a dozen other old people.

It had been a long time since he had actually organised something political; others had been happy to organise *him*—his
name, his presence, his approval. But an emotional telephone
call from an old friend, Walter Kenting, before seven that morning, appealing that they "all" should make a demonstration of
some sort about the refugees—the nine million refugees of
Bangladesh, this time—and the information that he was the
only person available to do the organising, had returned him to
a politically active past. Telephoning, he soon discovered that
even the small demonstration they envisaged would be circumscribed, because people were saying they could see no point in
a demonstration when television, the radio and every newspaper did little else but tell the world about these millions of
sufferers. What was the point of a dozen or twenty people

"sitting down" or "marching" or even being hungry for twenty-four hours in some prominent place? Surely the point of these actions in the past had been to draw public attention to a wrong?

Now the strength of his reaction to Mrs. Markham's inadequacy made him understand that his enthusiastic response to Walter so early that morning had been mostly because of weeks, months, of inactivity. He could not be so exaggerating details if he were not under-employed. He had been making occupation for himself, calling it stocktaking. He had been reading old diaries, articles of his own twenty or more years old, letters of people he had not seen, sometimes, for as long. Immersing himself in his own past had of course been uncomfortable; this is what it had been really like in Korea, Israel, Pretoria, during such-and-such an event: memory had falsified. One knew that it did, but he had believed himself exempt from this law. Every new day of this deliberate evocation of the past had made his own part in it seem less worthwhile, had diminished his purposes and strengths. It was not that he now lacked offers of work, but that he could not make himself respond with the enthusiastic willingness which he believed every job of work needed. Of his many possibilities the one that attracted him most was to teach journalism in a small college in Nigeria, but he could not make up his mind to accept: his wife didn't want to go. Did he want to leave her in England for two years? No; but at one time this certainly would not have been his reaction!

Nor did he want to write another adventure book; in such empty times in the past he had written, under *noms de plume*, novels whose attraction was the descriptions of the countries he had set them in. He had travelled a great deal in his life, often dangerously, in the course of this war or that, as a soldier and as a journalist.

He might also write a serious book of social or political analysis: he had several to his credit.

He could do television work, or return to active journalism.

The thing was that now the three children were through university he did not need to earn so much money.

"Leisure, leisure at last!" he had cried, as so many of his friends were doing, finding themselves similarly placed.

But half a morning's energetic organising was enough to

tell him—exactly as his mother had been used to tell him when he was adolescent: "Your trouble is, you haven't got enough to do!"

He sent a telegram to Mrs. Markham: *Arriving train early evening.* Flying would save him an hour; proper feeling would no doubt choose the air, but he needed the train's pace to adjust him for what was ahead. He rang Walter Kenting to say that with the organising still undone, urgent family matters were claiming him. Walter was silent at this, so he said: "Actually, my old man is going to die in the next couple of days. It has been on the cards for some time."

"I am sorry," said Walter. "I'll try Bill or Mona. I've got to go to Dublin in fifteen minutes. Are you going to be back by Saturday—oh of course you don't know." Realising that he was sounding careless or callous, he said: "I do hope things will be all right." This was worse and he gave up: "You think that a twenty-four-hour fast meets the bill better than the other possibilities? Is that what most people feel, do you think?"

"Yes. But I don't think they are as keen as usual."

"Well, of course not, there's too much of bloody everything, that's why. You could be demonstrating twenty-four hours a day. Anyway, I've got to get to my plane."

While Jack packed, which he knew so well how to do, in ten minutes, he remembered that he had a family. Should everyone be at the deathbed? Oh surely not! He looked for his wife; she was out. Of course! The children off her hands, she too had made many exclamations about the attractions of leisure, but almost at once she signed up for a Psychology Course as part of a plan to become a Family Counsellor. She had left a note for him: "Darling, there's some cold lamb and salad." He now left a note for her: "Old man on his way out. See you whenever. Tell girls and Joseph. All my love. Jack."

On that train he thought of what he was in for. A family reunion, no less. His brother wasn't so bad, but the last time he had seen Ellen, she had called him a Boy Scout, and he had called her a Daughter of the British Empire. Considering it a compliment, she had been left with the advantage. A really dreadful woman, and as for her husband—surely he wouldn't be there too? He would have to be, as a man? Where would they all fit in? Certainly not in that tiny flat. He should have put in his note to Rosemary that she should telephone hotels in S——. Would the other grandchildren be there? Well, Cedric and Ellen would be certain to do the right thing, whatever that was: as for himself, he could telephone home when he had found what the protocol was. But good God, surely it was bad enough that three of them, grownup and intelligent people— grownup, anyway, were going to have to sit about waiting, in a deathbed scene, because of—superstition. Yes, that was what it was. Certainly no more than outdated social custom. And it all might go on for days. But perhaps the old man would be pleased? At the approach of a phrase similar to those suitable for deaths and funerals, he felt irritation again; this would lead, unless he watched himself, to self-mockery, the spirit of farce. Farce was implicit, anyway, in a situation which had himself, Ellen and Cedric in one room.

Probably the old man wasn't even conscious. He should have telephoned Mrs. Markham before rushing off like—well, like a journalist, with two pairs of socks, a spare shirt and a sweater. He should have bought a black tie? Would the old man have wished it? Jack noted the arrival of an indubitably "suitable" phrase, and feared worse for the immediate future.

The old man had not worn black or altered his cheerfulness when his wife died.

His wife, Jack's mother.

The depression that he had suspected was in wait for him now descended. He understood that he had been depressed for some time; this was like dark coming down into a fog. He had not admitted that he was depressed, but he ought to have known it by the fact that what he had woken up to each morning was not his own expectation of usefulness or accomplishment, but his wife's.

Now, if Rosemary died . . . but he would not think about that; it would be morbid.

When his mother died, his father had made the simplest of funerals for her—religious, of course. All the family, the grandchildren too, had stayed in the old house, together for the first time in years. The old man had behaved like a man who knew that his grief ought not to be inflicted on others. Jack had not been close to his mother; he had not liked her. He was close to no member of the family. He now knew that he loved his wife, but that had not been true until recently. There were his beautiful daughters. There was his son Joseph, who was a chip off the old block—so everyone insisted on saying, though it infuriated Joseph. But they could not meet without quarrelling. That was closeness of a kind?

He ought to have been more attentive, when the mother died, to the old man, who had probably been concealing a good deal behind his mild dignity. Of course! And, looking back ten years, Jack knew that he had known what his father was feeling, had been sympathetic, but had also been embarrassed and unable to give anything of himself—out of fear that more would be asked?—had pretended obtuseness.

The old house was Church property, divided into units for old people who had been good parishioners. None had been friends before going to live there, but now it seemed that they were all close friends, or at least kept each other company in a variety of ways under the eyes of Mrs. Markham, who also lived there, looked after the house, after them. She put flowers in the church and mended surplices and garments of that sort —she was fifty, poor old thing. Jack now told himself that he was over fifty, although "the baby of the family," and that his sister Ellen, with whom he was to spend an unknown number of days, was fifty-five, while his boring brother Cedric was older still.

This train was not full and moved pleasantly through England's green and pleasant land. There were two other people in the compartment. Secondclass. Jack travelled secondclass when he could: this was one of the ways he used to check up on himself that he was not getting soft with success—if you could call what he had success. His brother and sister did, but that was the way they looked at life.

One fellow passenger was a middleaged woman, and one a girl of about twenty-three or twenty-four who leaned an elbow on the window ledge and stared at Buckinghamshire, then Berkshire, then Wiltshire, all green and soft on this summery day. Her face was hidden behind glittering yellow hair. Jack classed her as a London secretary on her way home for a family visit, and as the kind of young person he would get on with—that is, like his daughters rather than his son.

He was finding the company of his girls all pleasure and healing. It seemed to him that everything he had looked for in women now flowed generously towards him from Carrie and Elizabeth. It was not that they always approved him, far from it; it was the quality of their beauty that caressed and dandled him. The silk of their hair flattered, their smiles, even when for somebody else, gave him answers to questions that he had been asking of women—so it seemed to him now—all his life.

Though of course he did not see much of them; while living in the same house, upstairs, they led their own lives.

The woman, whom he disliked because she was not young and beautiful—he was aware that he should be ashamed of this reaction, but put this shame onto an agenda for the future—got off the train, and now the girl at the window turned towards him and the rest of the journey was bound to be delightful. He had been right—of course, he was always right about people. She worked in an office in Great Portland Street, and she was going for a visit to her parents—no, she "got on" with them all right, but she was always pleased to be back in her flat with her friends. She was not a stranger to Jack's world; that is, she was familiar with the names of people whose lives expressed concern for public affairs, public wrong and suffering, and she used the names of his friends with a proprietary air—she had, as it were, eaten them up to form herself, as he, Jack, had in his time swallowed Keir Hardie, Marx, Freud, Morris and the rest. She, those like her, now possessed "the Old Guard," their history, their opinions, their claims. To her, Walter Kenting, Bill, Mona, were like statues on plinths, each representing a degree of opinion. When the time came to give her his own name, he said it was Jack Sebastian, not Jack Orkney, for he knew he would join the pantheon of people who were her parents-in-opinion and, as he had understood, were to be criticised, like parents.

The last time he had been Jack Sebastian was to get him out of a tight spot in Ecuador, during a small revolution; he had escaped prison and possible death by this means.

If he told this girl about that, he knew that as he sat opposite her, she would gaze in judiciously measured admiration at a man retreating from her into history. He listened to her talk about herself, and knew that if things had been otherwise—he meant not his father's dying, but his recently good relations with his wife—he could easily have got off the train with the girl, and persuaded her to spend the rest of her holiday with him, having made excuses to her family. Or he could have met her in London. But all he wanted now was to hear her voice, and to let himself be stimulated by the light from her eyes and her hair.

She got off the train, with a small laughing look that made his heart beat, and she strode off across the platform with her banners of yellow hair streaming behind her, leaving him alone in the brown compartment full of brown air.

At the station he was looking for a taxi when he saw his brother Cedric. A brown suit that discreetly confined a small stomach came towards him. That suit could only clothe a member of the professional classes; it had to be taken into account before the face, which was, as it happened, a mild pale face that had a look on it of duty willingly performed.

Cedric said, in his way of dealing all at once with every possible contingency: "Mrs. Markham said it had to be this train. I came because Ellen has only just come herself; I arrived first."

He had a Rover, dark blue, not new. He and Jack, defined by this car and particularly accurately in this country town, drove through soothingly ancient streets.

The brothers drove more or less in silence to the church precincts. As they passed in under a thirteenth-century stone archway, Cedric said: "Ellen booked a room for you. It is the Royal Arms, and she and I are there too. It is only five minutes from Father."

They walked in silence over grass to the back door of this solid brick house which the Church devoted to the old. Not as a charity of course. These were the old whose own saved money or whose children could pay for their rooms and for Mrs. Markham. The poor old were elsewhere.

Mrs. Markham came forward from her sittingroom and said: "How do you do, Mr. Orkney?" to Jack, smiling like a hostess at Cedric. "I am sure you would like some tea now," she directed. "I'll bring you some up." She was like the woman on the train. And like Ellen.

He followed his brother up old wooden stairs that gleamed, and smelled of lavender and wax polish. As always happened, the age of the town, and of the habits of the people who lived in it, the smell of tradition, enveloped Jack in well-being; he had to remind himself that he was here for an unpleasant occasion. At the top of the stairs various unmarked doors were the entrances to the lives of four old people. Cedric opened one without knocking, and Jack followed him into a room he had been in twice before on duty visits. It was a smallish but pleasant room with windows overlooking the lawns that surrounded the church.

Sister Ellen, in thick grey tweed, sat knitting. She said: "Oh Jack, there you are, we are all here at last."

Jack sat. Cedric sat. They had to arrange their feet so as not to entangle in the middle of the small floor. They all exchanged news. The main thing that had happened to the three of them was that the children had all grown up.

The grandchildren, eight of them, knew each other, and had complicated relationships: they were a family, unlike their parents.

Mrs. Markham brought tea, of the kind appropriate to this room, this town: scones, butter, jam, comb honey, fruit buns, cherry cake, fruit cake. Also cream. She left giving the three a glance that said: At last it is all as it should be.

Jack asked: "Have you seen him?"

"No," said Cedric, a fraction of a second before Ellen did. It was clear that here was competition for the perfect disposition of his death. Jack was remembering how these two had fought for domination over each other, and over, of course, himself.

"That is to say," said Ellen, "we have seen him, but he was not conscious."

"Another stroke?" asked Jack.

"He had another before Christmas," said Cedric, "but he didn't tell us, he didn't want to worry us."

"I heard about it through Jilly," said Ellen. Jilly was her daughter.

"And I through Ann," said Cedric. Ann was his.

Jack had now to remind himself that these names represented persons, not samples of pretty infancy.

"He is very close to Ann," said Cedric.

"He is fond of Jilly too," said Ellen.

"I suppose there is a nurse in there?" asked Jack. "Oh, of course, there must be."

"There is a day nurse and a night nurse, and they change places at dawn and dusk," said Ellen. "I must say I am glad of this tea. There was no restaurant on the train."

"I wonder if I could see him?" asked Jack, and then corrected it: "I shall go in to see him." He knew, as he spoke, that all the way on the train he had in fact been waiting for the moment when he could walk into the little bedroom, and his father would smile at him and say—he had not been able to imagine what, but it must be something that he had been waiting to hear from him, or from somebody, for years. This surely was the real purpose of coming here? That what he had in fact been expecting was something like a "deathbed scene," with vital advice and mutual comfort, embarrassed him, and he felt that he was stupid. Now he understood that embarrassment was the air of this room: the combat between elder brother and sister was nominal; they skirmished from habit to cover what they felt. Which was that they were in a position not allowed for by their habits of living. Jack had a vision of rapidly running trains —their lives; but they had had to stop the trains, had had to pull the emergency cords, and at great inconvenience to everyone, because of this ill-timed death. Death had to be ill-timed? It was its nature? Why was it felt to be? There was something ridiculous about this scene in which he was trapped: three middleaged children sitting about in one room, idle, thinking of their real lives which stagnated, while in another room an old man lay dying, attended by a strange woman.

"I'm going in," he said, and this time got up, instinctively careful of his head: he was tall in this lowceilinged room.

"Go in without knocking," said Ellen.

"Yes," Cedric confirmed.

Jack stooped under the doorframe. An inappropriate picture had come into his mind. It was of his sister, in a scarlet pinafore and bright blue checkered sleeves, tugging a wooden horse which was held by a pale plump boy. Jack had been scared that when Ellen got the horse a real fight would start. But Cedric held on, lips tight, being jerked by Ellen's tugs as a dog is tugged by the other dog who has fastened his teeth into the bit of meat or the stick. This scene had taken place in the old garden, for it had been enclosed by pink hydrangeas, while gravel had crunched underfoot. They must all have been very young, because Ellen had still been the classic golden-haired beauty; later she became large and ordinary.

What he was really seeing was his father sitting up against high pillows. A young woman in white sat with her hands folded watching the dying man. But he looked asleep. It was only when he saw the healthy young woman that Jack under-

stood that his father had become a small old man: he had definitely shrunk. The room was dark, and it was not until Jack
stood immediately above his father that he saw the mouth was
open. But what was unexpected was that the eyelids had swelled
and were blue, as if decomposition had set in there already.
Those bruised lids affected Jack like something in bad taste,
like a fart at a formal meal, or when making love of a romantic
sort. He looked in appeal at the nurse who said in a normal
voice which she did not lower at all: "He did stir a moment
ago, but he didn't really come to himself."

Jack nodded, not wanting to break the hush of time that
surrounded the bed, and bent lower, trying not to see the dying
lids, but remembering what he could of his father's cool,
shrewd, judging look. It seemed to him as if the bruised puffs
of flesh were trembling, might lift. But his stare did not have
the power to rouse his father, and soon Jack straightened himself—cautiously. Where did the Church put its tall old people,
he wondered, and backed out of the room, keeping his eyes
on the small old man in his striped pyjamas, which showed
very clean under a dark grey cardigan that was fastened under
the collar with a gold tiepin, giving him a formal, dressed-up
look.

"How does he seem?" asked Ellen. She had resumed her
knitting.

"Asleep."

"Unconscious," said Cedric.

Jack asserted himself—quite easily, he saw with relief. "He
doesn't look unconscious to me. On the contrary, I thought he
nearly woke up."

They knew the evening was wearing on: their watches told
them so. It remained light; an interminable summer evening
filled the sky above the church tower. A young woman came
through the room, a coat over her white uniform, and in
a moment the other nurse came past them, on her way out.

"I think we might as well have dinner," said Ellen, already
folding her knitting.

"Should one of us stay perhaps?" corrected Cedric. He stayed,
and Jack had hotel dinner and a bottle of wine with his sister;
he didn't dislike being with her as much as he had expected.
He was even remembering times when he had been fond of
Ellen.

They returned to keep watch, while Cedric took his turn for dinner. At about eleven the doctor came in, disappeared for five minutes into the bedroom, and came out saying that he had given Mr. Orkney an injection. By the time they had thought to ask what the injection was, he had said that his advice was they should all get a good night's sleep, and had gone. Each hesitated before saying that they intended to take the doctor's advice: This situation, traditionally productive of guilt, was doing its work well.

Before they had reached the bottom of the stairs, the nurse came after them: "Mr. Orkney, Mr. Orkney . . ." Both men turned, but she said: "Jack? He was asking for Jack?"

Jack ran up the stairs, through one room, into the other. But it seemed as if the old man had not moved since he had last seen him. The nurse had drawn the curtains, shutting out the sky so full of light, of summer, and had arranged the lamp so that it made a bright space in the dark room. In this was a wooden chair with a green cushion on it, and on the cushion a magazine. The lit space was like the detail of a picture much magnified. The nurse said: "Really, with that injection, he ought not to wake now." She took her place again with the magazine on her lap, inside the circle of light.

Yet he had woken, he had asked for himself, Jack, and for nobody else. Jack was alert, vibrating with his nearness to what his father might say. But he stood helpless, trying to make out the bruises above the eyes, which the shadows were hiding. "I'll stay here the night," he declared, all energy, and strode out, only just remembering to lower his head in time, to tell his sister and his brother, who had come back up the stairs.

"The nurse thinks he is unlikely to wake, but I am sure it would be what he would wish if one of us were to stay."

That he had used another of the obligatory phrases struck Jack with more than amusement: now it was with relief as well. Now the fact that the prescribed phrases made their appearance one after the other was like a guarantee that he was behaving appropriately, that everything would go smoothly and without embarrassment, and that he could expect his father's eyes to appear from behind the corrupted lids—that he would speak the words Jack needed to hear. Cedric and Ellen quite understood, but demanded to be called at once if . . . They went off together across the bright grass towards the hotel.

Jack sat up all night; but there was no night, midsummer swallowed the dark; at midnight the church was still glimmering and people strolled, talking softly, over the lawns. He had skimmed through Trollope's *The Small House at Allington*, and had dipped into a book of his own called *With the Guerrillas in Guatemala*. The name on the spine was Jack Henge, and now he wondered if he had ever told his father that this was one of his *noms de plume*, and he thought that if so, it showed a touching interest on his father's part, but if not, that there must have been some special hidden sympathy shown in the choice or chance that led to its sitting here on the old man's shelves side by side with the complete works of Trollope and George Eliot and Walter Scott. But of course, it was unlikely now that he would ever know. . . . His father had not woken, had not stirred, all night. Once he had tiptoed in, and the nurse had lifted her head and smiled; clearly, though the old man had gone past the divisions of day and night, the living must still adhere to them, for the day nurse had spoken aloud, but now it was night, the nurse whispered: "The injection is working well. You try to rest, Mr. Orkney." Her solicitude for him, beaming out from the bright cave hollowed from the dark of the room, enclosed them together in the night's vigil, and when the day nurse came, and the night nurse went yawning, looking pale, and tucking dark strands of hair as if tidying up after a night's sleep, her smile at Jack was that of a comrade after a shared ordeal.

Almost at once the day nurse came back into the livingroom and said: "Is there someone called Ann?"

"Yes, a granddaughter; he was asking for her?"

"Yes. Now, he was awake for a moment."

Jack suppressed: "He didn't ask for me?"—and ran back into the bedroom, which was now filled with a stuffy light that presented the bruised lids to the nurse and to Jack.

"I'll tell my brother that Ann has been asked for."

Jack walked through fresh morning air that had already brought a few people onto the grass around the church, to the hotel, where he found Cedric and Ellen at breakfast.

He said that no, he had not been wanted, but that Ann was wanted now. Ellen and Cedric conferred and agreed that Ann "could reasonably be expected" never to forgive them if she was not called. Jack saw that these words soothed them both;

they were comforting himself. He was now suddenly tired. He drank coffee, refused breakfast, and decided on an hour's sleep. Ellen went to telephone greetings and the news that nothing had changed to her family; Cedric to summon Ann, while Jack wondered if he should telephone Rosemary. But there was nothing to say. He fell on his bed and dreamed, woke, dreamed again, woke, forced himself back to sleep but was driven up out of it to stand in the middle of his hotel room, full of horror. His dreams had been landscapes of dark menacing shapes that were of man's making—metallic, like machines, steeped in a cold grey light, and scattered about on a plain where cold water lay spilled about, gleaming. This water reflected, he knew, death, or news, or information about death, but he stood too far away on the plain to see what pictures lay on its surfaces.

Now, Jack was one of those who do not dream. He prided himself on never dreaming. Of course he had read the "new" information that everyone dreamed every night, but he distrusted this information. For one thing, he shared in the general distrust of science, of its emphatic pronouncements; for another, travelling around the world as he had, he had long ago come to terms with the fact that certain cultures were close to aspects of life which he, Jack, had quite simply forbidden. He had locked a door on them. He knew that some people claimed to see ghosts, feared their dead ancestors, consulted witchdoctors, dreamed dreams. How could he not know? He had lived with them. But he, Jack, was of that part of mankind delivered from all that; he, Jack, did not consult the bones or allow himself to be afraid of the dark. Or dream. He did not dream.

He felt groggy, more than tired: the cold of the dream was undermining him, making him shiver. He got back into bed, for he had slept only an hour, and continued with the same dream. Now he and Walter Kenting were interlopers on that death-filled plain, and they were to be shot, one bullet each, on account of non-specified crimes. He woke again: it was ten minutes later. He decided to stay awake. He bathed, changed his shirt and his socks, washed the shirt and socks he had taken off, and hung them over the bath to drip. Restored by these small ritual acts which he had performed in so many hotel rooms and in so many countries, he ordered fresh coffee, drank it in the spirit of one drinking a tonic or prescribed medicine, and walked back across sunlit grass to the old people's house.

He entered on the scene he had left. Ellen and Cedric sat with their feet almost touching, one knitting and one reading the *Daily Telegraph*. Ellen said: "You haven't slept long." Cedric said: "He asked for you again."

"*What!*" While he had slept, his energies draining into that debilitating dream, he might have heard, at last, what his father wanted to say. "I think I'll sit with him a little."

"That might not be a bad idea," said his sister. Was she annoyed that she had not been "asked for"? If so, she showed no sign of it.

The little sitting room was full of light; sunshine lay on the old wood sills. But the bedroom was dark, warm and smelled of many drugs.

The nurse had the only chair—today just a piece of furniture among many. He made her keep it, and sat down slowly on the bed, as if this slow subsidence could make his weight less.

He kept his eyes on his father's face. Since yesterday the bruises had spread beyond the lids: the flesh all around the eyes and as far down as the cheekbones was stained.

"He has been restless," said the nurse, "but the doctor should be here soon." She spoke as if the doctor could answer any question that could possibly ever be asked; and Jack, directed by her as he had been by his sister and his brother, now listened for the doctor's coming. The morning went past. His sister came to ask if he would go with her to luncheon. She was hungry, but Cedric was not. Jack said he would stay, and while she was gone the doctor came.

He sat on the bed—Jack had risen from it, retreating to the window. The doctor took the old man's wrist in his hand and seemed to commune with the darkened eyelids. "I rather think that perhaps . . ." He took out a plastic box from his case that held the ingredients of miracle-making: syringes, capsules, methylated spirits.

Jack asked: "What effect does that have?" He wanted to ask: Are you keeping him alive when he should be dead?

The doctor said: "Sedative and painkiller."

"A heart stimulant?"

Now the doctor said: "I have known your father for thirty years." He was saying: I have more right than you have to say what he would have wanted.

Jack had to agree; he had no idea if his father would want to be allowed to die, as nature directed, or whether he would like to be kept alive as long as possible.

The doctor administered an injection, as light and as swift as the strike of a snake, rubbed the puncture with one gentle finger, and said, "Your father looked after himself. He has plenty of life in him yet."

He went out. Jack looked in protest at the nurse: what on earth had been meant? Was his father not dying? The nurse smiled, timidly, and from that smile Jack gathered that the words had been spoken for his father's sake, in case he was able to hear them, understand them, and be fortified by them.

He saw the nurse's face change; she bent over the old man, and Jack took a long step and was beside her. In the bruised flesh the eyes were open and stared straight up. This was not the human gaze he had been wanting to meet, but a dull glare from chinks in damaged flesh.

"Ann," said the old man. "Is Ann here?"

From the owner of those sullen eyes Jack might expect nothing; as an excuse to leave the room, he said to the nurse, "I'll tell Ann's father."

In the livingroom sunlight had left the sills. Cedric was not there. "It's Ann he wants," Jack said. "He has asked again."

"She is coming. She has to come from Edinburgh. She is with Maureen."

Ellen said this as if he was bound to know who Maureen was. She was probably one of Cedric's ghastly wife's ghastly relations. Thinking of the awfulness of Cedric's wife made him feel kindly towards Ellen. Ellen wasn't really so bad. There she sat, knitting, tired and sad but not showing it. When you came down to it she didn't look all that different from Rosemary—unbelievably also a middleaged woman. But at this thought Jack's loyalty to the past rebelled. Rosemary, though a large, fresh-faced, greying woman, would never wear a suit which looked as if its edges might cut, or hair set in a helmet of ridges and frills. She wore soft pretty clothes, and her hair was combed straight and long, as she had always worn it: he had begged her to keep it like that. But if you came to think of it, probably the lives the two women led were similar. Probably they were all more alike than any one of them would care to admit. Including Cedric's awful wife.

He looked at Ellen's lids, lowered while she counted stitches. They were her father's eyes and lids. When she lay dying probably her lids would bruise and puff.

Cedric came in. He was very like the old man—more like him than any of them. He, Jack, was more like their mother, but when he was dying perhaps his own lids . . . Ellen looked up, smiled at Cedric, then at Jack. They were all smiling at each other. Ellen laid down her knitting, and lit herself a cigarette. The brothers could see that this was the point when she might cry. But Mrs. Markham came in, followed by a well-brushed man all white cuffs and collar and pink fresh skin.

"The Dean," she breathed, with the smile of a girl.

The Dean said: "No, don't get up. I dropped in. I am an old friend of your father's, you know. Many and many a game of chess have we played in this room . . ." and he had followed Mrs. Markham into the bedroom.

"He had Extreme Unction yesterday," said Ellen.

"Oh," said Jack. "I didn't realise that Extreme Unction was part of his . . ." He stopped, not wanting to hurt feelings. He believed both Ellen and Cedric to be religious.

"He got very High in the end," said Cedric.

Ellen giggled. Jack and Cedric looked enquiry. "It sounded funny," she said. "You know, the young ones talk about getting high."

Cedric's smile was wry; and Jack remembered there had been talk about his elder son, who had threatened to become addicted. What to? Jack could not remember; he would have to ask the girls.

"I suppose he wants a church service and to be buried?" asked Jack.

"Oh yes," said Cedric. "I have got his will."

"Of course, you would have."

"Well, we'll have to get through it all," said Ellen. It occurred to Jack that this was what she probably said, or thought, about her own life: Well, I've just got to get through it. The thought surprised him; Ellen was pleasantly surprising him. Now he heard her say: "Well, I suppose some people have to have religion."

And now Jack looked at her in disbelief.

"Yes," said Cedric, equally improbably, "it must be a com-

THE TEMPTATION OF JACK ORKNEY

fort for them, one can see that." He laid small strong hands around his crossed knees and made the knuckles crack.

"Oh, Cedric," complained Ellen, as she had as a girl: this knuckle-cracking had been Cedric's way of expressing tension since he had been a small boy.

"Sorry," said Cedric. He went on, letting his hands fall to his sides, and swing there, in a conscious effort towards relaxing himself, "From time to time I take my pulse—as it were. Now that I am getting on for sixty one can expect the symptoms. Am I getting God? Am I still myself? Yes, no, doubtful? But so far, I can report an even keel, I am happy to say."

"Oh one can understand it," said Ellen. "God knows, one can understand it only too well. But I really would be ashamed . . ."

Both Ellen and Cedric were looking to him, to add his agreement of which they were sure, of course. But he could not speak. He had made precisely the same joke a month ago, in a group of "the Old Guard" about taking his pulse to find out if he had caught religion. And everyone had confessed to the same practice. To get God, after a lifetime of enlightened rationalism, would be the most shameful of capitulations.

Now his feelings were the same as those of members of a particularly exclusive Club on being forced to admit the lower classes; or the same as the Victorian Bishop who, travelling to some cannibal-land to baptise the converted, had been heard to say that he could wish that his Church admitted degrees of excellence in its material: he could not believe that his lifetime of impeccable service would weigh the same as those of these so recently benighted ones.

Besides, Jack was shocked: to hear these ideas from Ellen, looking as she did, leading the life she did—she had no right to them! She sounded vulgar.

She was saying: "Of course I do go to church sometimes to please Freddy." Her husband. "But he seems to be losing fervour rather than gaining it, I am glad to say."

"Yes," said Cedric. "I am afraid I have rather the same thing with Muriel. We have compromised on Christmas and Easter. She says it is bad for my image not to be a church-goer. Petersbank is a small place you know, and the good people do like their lawyers and doctors to be pillars of society. But I find that sort of trimming repulsive and I tell her so."

Again they waited for Jack; again he had to be silent. But surely by now they would take his opinions for granted? Why should they? If they could become atheist, then what might he not become? The next thing, they'll turn out to be socialists, he thought. Surely all this godlessness must be a new development? He could have sworn that Ellen had been devout and Cedric correct towards a Church which—as far as Jack had been concerned—had been irritation, humiliation, tedium, throughout his childhood. Even now he could not think of the meaningless services, the Sunday school, the fatuity of the parsons, the social conformity that was associated with the Church, without feeling as if he had escaped from a sticky trap.

Ellen was saying: "As for me, I am afraid I find it harder to believe as I get older. I mean, God, in this terrible world, with new horrors every minute. No, I am afraid it is all too much."

"I quite agree," said Cedric. "The devil's more like it."

"Yes," said Jack, able to speak at last. "Yes, that's about it, I'm afraid." It was the best he could do. The room was now full of good feeling, and they would have begun to talk about their childhood if the bedroom door had not opened, and the Dean come out. The smile he had shed on the nurse was still on his healthy lips, and he now let it benefit the three, while he raised his hand in what looked like a benediction. "No, don't get up!" He was almost at once out of the other door, followed close by Mrs. Markham.

The look the three now shared repudiated the Dean and all his works. Ellen smiled at her brother exactly as—he realised in capitulation to a totally unforeseen situation—his own wife would have done. Cedric nodded private comment on the stupidities of mankind.

Soon Cedric went to the bedroom, to return with the report that the old man looked pretty deep in. Then Ellen went and came back saying that she didn't know how the nurse could bear it in that dark room. But as she sat down, she said: "In the old days, one of us would have been in there all the time?"

"Yes," said Cedric. "All of us."

"Not just a nurse," said Ellen. "Not a stranger."

Jack was thinking that if he had stuck it out, then he would have been there when his father called for him, but he said: "I'm glad it is a nurse. I don't think there is very much left of *him*."

Ann arrived. What Jack saw first was a decided, neat little face, and that she wore a green jacket and trousers that were not jeans but "good" as her Aunt Ellen used the word. Ellen always had "good" clothes that lasted a long time. Ann's style was not, for instance, like Jack's daughters', who wore rags and rubbish and cast-offs and who looked enchanting, like princesses in disguise. She kissed her father, because he was waiting for her to do this. She stood examining them with care. Her father could be seen in her during that leisurely, unembarrassed examination: it was both her right and her duty to do this. Now Jack saw that she was small, with a white skin that looked greenish where it was shaded, and hair as pale as her father's had been. Her eyes, like her father's, were green.

She said: "Is he still alive?"

The voice was her father's, and it took her aunt and her uncle back, back—she did not know the reason for their strained, reluctant smiles as they gazed at her.

They were suffering that diminution, that assault on individuality which is the worst of families: some invisible dealer had shuffled noses, hands, shoulders, hair and reassembled them to make—little Ann, for instance. The dealer made out of parts a unit that the owner would feed, maintain, wash, medicate for a lifetime, thinking of it as "mine," except at moments like these, when knowledge was forced home that everyone was put together out of stock.

"Well," said Ann, "you all look dismal enough. Why do you?"

She went into the bedroom, leaving the door open. Jack understood that Ann had principles about attitudes towards death: like his own daughters.

The three crowded into the room.

Ann sat on the bed, high up near the pillow, in a way that hid the old man's face from them. She was leaning forward, the nurse—whom Ann had ignored—ready to intervene.

"Grandad!" she said. "Grandad! It's me!"

Silence. Then it came home to them that the improbable had happened, that she had called up Lazarus. They heard the

old man's voice, quite as they remembered it: "It's you, is it?
It is little Ann?"

"Yes, Grandad, it's Ann."

They crowded forward, to see over her shoulder. They saw
their father, smiling normally. He looked like a tired old man,
that was all. His eyes, surrounded by the puffy bruises, had
light in them.

"Who are these people?" he asked. "Who are all these tall
people?"

The three retreated, leaving the door open.

Silence from the bedroom, then singing. Ann was singing
in a small clear voice: All Things Bright and Beautiful.

Jack looked at Cedric, Ellen looked at Cedric. He deprecated: "Yes, I am afraid that she is. That's the bond, you see."

"Oh," said Ellen, "I see, that explains it."

The singing went on:

> All things bright and beautiful,
> All creatures great and small,
> All things wise and wonderful,
> The Lord God made them all.

The singing went on, verse after verse, like a lullaby.

"She came to stay with him," said Cedric. "At Easter, I think
it was. She slept here, on the floor."

Jack said: "My girls are religious. But not my son of course."

They looked blankly sympathetic; it occurred to Jack that
his son's fame was after all circumscribed to a pretty small
circle.

"He takes after me," said Jack.

"Ah," said Cedric.

"A lot of them are religious," said Ellen, brisk.

"It's the *kind* of religion that sticks in one's craw," said
Jack. "Simple faith and Celtic crosses."

"I agree," said Cedric. "Pretty low-level stuff."

"Does the level matter?" asked Ellen. "Surely *c'est le premier
pas qui coûte?*"

At which Jack looked at his sister in a disbelief that was
meant to be noticed. Cedric, however, did not seem surprised:
of course, he saw Ellen more often. He said mildly: "I don't
agree. One wouldn't mind if they went on to something a bit

more elevated. It's this servants'-hall village-green mother's-meeting sort of thing. You spend a fortune trying to educate them decently and then it ends up in . . . My eldest was a Jesus freak for a few months, for example. After Winchester, Balliol, the lot."

"What is a Jesus freak?" enquired Ellen.

"What it sounds like."

Normally Jack would have cut out emotionally and mentally at the words "servants' hall," but he was still with them. He said: "What gets me is that they spout it all out, so pat and pretty, you know, and you get the feeling it might be anything, anything they had picked up or lay to hand—*pour épater le bourgeois*, you know." At this he had to think that the other two must be thinking, but were too polite to say, that his own socialism, a degree or two off full communism, when he was in his teens, had had no deeper cause. This unspoken comment brought the conversation to a stop.

The singing had stopped too. It was getting dark.

"Well," said Ellen, "I tell you what I am going to do, I am going to have a bath and then dinner and then a good night's sleep. I think Ann is meeting Father's requirements better than we could."

"Yes," said Cedric.

He went to the door, and communicated this news to his daughter, who said she would be fine, she would be super, she would stay with her grandad, and if she got tired she could sleep on the floor.

Over the dinner table at the hotel, it was a reunion of people who had not met for a long time. They drank some wine, and were sentimental.

But the little time of warmth died with the coffee, served in the hall, which let in draughts from the street every time somebody came in.

Jack said: "I'll turn in, I didn't sleep last night."

"Nor I."

"Nor I."

They nodded at each other; to kiss would have been exaggerated. Jack went upstairs, while Cedric and Ellen went to telephone their families.

In the bedroom he stood by the window and watched how the light filled the lime outside. Breaths of tree-air came to his face. He was full of variegated emotions, none, he was afraid, to do with his father: they were about his brother and his sister, his childhood, that past of his which everything that happened to him these days seemed to evoke, seemed to present to him, sharp, clear, and for the most part painful; he did not feel he could sleep, he was over-stimulated. He would lie on his bed for a rest. Waking much later, to a silence that said the night had deepened all around him, with the heaviness of everybody's sleeping, he started up into a welter of feeling that he could not face, and so burrowed back into sleep again, there to be met by —but it was hard to say what.

Terror was not the word. Nor fear. Yet there were no other words that he knew for the state he found himself in. It was more like a state of acute attention, as if his whole being— memory, body, present and past chemistries—had been assaulted by a warning, so that he had to attend to it. He was standing, as it were, at the alert, listening to something which said: Time is passing, be quick, listen, attend.

It was the knowledge of passing time that was associated with the terror, so that he found himself standing upright in the dark room crying out: "Oh, no, no, I understand, I am sorry, I . . ." He was whimpering like a puppy. The dark was solid around him, and he didn't know where he was. He believed himself to be in a grave, and he rushed to the window, throwing it open as if he were heaving a weight off himself. The window was hard to open. At last he forced it, leaning out to let the tree-air come to his face, but it was not air that came in, but a stench, and this smell was confirmation of a failure which had taken place long ago, in some choice of his, that he had now forgotten. The feeling of urgency woke him: he was lying on his bed. Now he really did shoot into the centre of the room, while the smell that had been the air of the dream was fading around him. He was terrified. But that was not the word. . . . He feared that the terror would fade, he would forget what he had dreamed; the knowledge that there was something that had to be done, done soon, would fade, and he would forget even that he had dreamed.

What *had* he dreamed? Something of immense importance.

But as he stood there, with the feeling of urgency draining away and his daytime self coming back, even while he knew, as powerfully as he had ever known anything, that the dream was the most important statement ever made to him, the other half of him was asserting old patterns of thought, which said that to dream was neurotic and to think of death morbid.

He turned on the light, out of habit, a child chasing away night-fears, and then at once switched it off again, since the light was doing its job too well: the dream was dwindling into a small feeling that remarked in a tiny nagging voice that he should be attending to something. And Jack was chasing after the dream: No, no, don't go. . . .

But the feeling of the dream had gone, and he was standing near the window, telling himself—but it was an intellectual statement now, without force—that he had had a warning. A warning? Was it that? By whom? To whom? He must do something . . . but what? *He had been terrified of dying:* he had been forced to be afraid of that. For the first time in his life he had been made to feel the fear of death. He knew that this is what he would feel when he was in his father's position, lying propped on pillows, with people around him waiting for him to die. (If the state of the world would allow his death such a degree of civilisation!)

All his life he had said lightly: Oh, death, I'm not afraid of death; it will be like a candle going out, that's all. On these occasions when, just like his brother Cedric, he checked up on himself for internal weakness, he had said to himself: I shall die, just like a cat or a dog, and too bad, when I die, that's that. He had known the fear of fear of course: he had been a soldier in two wars. He had known what it was to rehearse in his mind all the possible deaths that were available to him, removing pain and horror by making them familiar, and choosing suitable ways of responding—words, postures, silences, stoicisms— that would be a credit to him, to humanity. He knew very well the thought that to be hit over the head like an ox, stunned before the throat was cut, was the highest that he could hope for: annihilation was what he had elected.

But his dream had been horror of annihilation, the threat of nothingness. . . . It already seemed far away. He stretched his arms up behind his head, feeling the strength of his body. *His* body, that was made of fragments of his mother and his father, and of their mothers and their fathers, and shared with little Ann, with his daughters, and of course with his son— exactly like him, his copy. Yes, his, his body, strong, and pulsing with energy—he pushed away the warning from the dream, and switched on the light again, feeling that *that* was over. It was one in the morning, hardly the hour, in an English country hotel, to ask for tea, for coffee. He knew he would not dare to lie again on that bed, so he went down to let himself out. He was going to his father.

Ann was wrapped in blankets, lying on the floor of the living-room. He knelt by her and gazed at the young face, the perfect eyelids that sealed her eyes shut like a baby's, incisive but delicate, shining, whole.

He sat on his father's bed where Ann had sat, and saw that the old man was slipping away. Jack could not have said why he knew, but he did know the death would be this day: it occurred to him that if he had not had that dream, he would not have known; he would not have been equipped to know, without the dream.

He walked the rest of the night away, standing to watch the bulk of the old church dwindling down under a sky lightening with dawn. When the birds began, he returned to the hotel, bathed, and with confidence woke his sister and brother, saying that yes, they could have breakfast but should not take too much time over it.

At eight-thirty they arrived to find Ann again crouched up on the bed near the old man, crooning to him bits of hymn, old tunes, nursery rhymes. He died without opening his eyes again.

Cedric said he would deal with all the arrangements, and that he would notify them of the funeral, which would probably be on Monday. The three children of the old man separated in good feeling and with kisses, saying that they really ought to see more of each other. And Jack said to Ann that she must come and visit. She said yes, it would be super, she could see Elizabeth and Carrie again, how about next weekend? There was to be a Pray-in for Bangladesh.

Jack returned to his home, or rather, to his wife. She was out. He suppressed grievance that there was no note from her; after all, he had not telephoned. She was at another class, he supposed.

He went to see if anybody was in the girls' flat. Carrie and Elizabeth had made rooms for themselves on the top floor, and paid rent for them. They both had good jobs. There was an attic room used occasionally by Joseph.

Hearing sounds, he knocked, with a sense of intruding, and was bidden to come in by Carrie, who seemed in conflict at the sight of him. This was because she, like the others, had been waiting for his coming, waiting for the news of the death. She had prepared the appropriate responses, but had just finished cooking a meal, and was putting dishes on the table. A young man whose face he did not know was coming towards the table, ready to eat.

Carrie was flushed, her long dark hair fell about, and she was wearing something like a white sack, bordered with deep white lace.

"My father died," he said.

"Oh poor you," said Carrie.

"I don't know," said Jack.

"This is Bob," said Carrie. "My father. Dad, would you like to eat with us? It is a business lunch, actually."

"No, no," said Jack. "I'll see you later." She called after him: "Dad, Dad, I'm sorry about Grandad."

"Oh, he was due to go," Jack called back.

He cut himself bread and cheese, and rang Walter's office. Walter was back from Dublin, but had to fly to Glasgow that afternoon: he was to appear on television in a debate on the Common Market. He would be back by midday Saturday: the Twenty-four-Hour Fast would start at two o'clock Saturday. Thirty people were expected to take part. It was a good thing Jack was back: he could take over again.

But what was there to be done?

Nothing much, really; he should keep a tag on the names; some might decide to drop out again. Considering the scale of the horror at that moment taking place in India, the mass misery, it would be a surprisingly small turn-out—he was sorry, he had to leave, a car was waiting.

It is normal to feel, on returning to the place one lives in, after having been away, that one has not left at all: this is not what Jack was feeling now. Whether it was because he was so tired, or because he was more upset by his father's death than he knew, he felt at a distance from his commonplace self, and particularly at a distance from the Jack Orkney who knew so well how to organise a sit-down, or a march, or how to produce such occasions properly for the Press or television.

Walter's contrasting the numbers of the people involved

in the Bangladesh tragedy with the numbers who were prepared not to eat, publicly, for twenty-four hours in London, had struck him as bathos, as absurdity, but he knew that normally that was how he would be reacting himself.

Now he tried to restore himself by summoning well-tried thoughts. Every time the radio or television was turned on, every time you saw a newspaper, the figure *nine million* was used, with the information that these refugees had no future, or none of the normal kind. (India's short, sharp, efficient war that reprieved these same nine million was of course months in the future.) But there was nothing to be done; this catastrophe had the same feeling as the last, which had been Nigeria: a large number of people would die of starvation or would be murdered, but there was no power strong enough to stop this.

It was this feeling of helplessness that seemed to be the new factor; each time there was something of this kind, the numbers of people grew larger, and the general helplessness augmented. Yet all that had happened was that great catastrophes were being brought to general attention more forcefully than in the past. Not long ago, as recently as thirty years ago, it had been a commonplace for small paragraphs in newspapers to say that six, seven, eight million people had died, were dying of starvation, in China; communism had put an end to famine, or to the world's hearing about it. A very short time ago, a decade, several million might die in a bad season in India; the green revolution had (possibly temporarily) checked that. In Russia millions had died in the course of some great scheme or other: the collectivisation of the peasants, for instance.

The most shocking thing that had happened to his generation was the event summed up by the phrase "six million Jews." Although so many millions of people had been killed or had died in that war, and in a thousand awful ways, it was that one thing, the *six million*, which seemed worst. Because, of course, as everyone knew, it had been willed and deliberate murder. . . . Was it really any more deliberate than the *nine million* of Stalin's forcible collectivisation? And how about that *nine*, or *ninety million*, the figure for the deaths of black men in Africa caused by white men in the course of bringing civilisation to that continent? (This figure, whatever it was, never could accumulate about it the quality of senseless horror that had the figure for the death camps and gas chambers under Hitler. Why not?) During the next twelve months, between *twelve* and *twenty-four* million would die of starvation in the world (the figure depended on the source of calculation). The twelve months after, this figure would double—by the end of a decade, the numbers of people expected to die annually of hunger was beyond calculation. . . . These figures, and many more, clicked through his well-stocked journalist's head, and against them he heard Walter's voice, rather tetchy, critical, saying that there would only be thirty people for the Twenty-four-Hour Fast.

Yes, of course it was ridiculous to think on these lines and particularly when you were tired; he had been thrown off balance worse than he knew. He would sleep for a little—no, no, better not, he would rather not; he would not go to his bed unless Rosemary could be with him. Well, there were things that he ought to be doing, he was sure: for one thing, he had not read the newspapers for three days, nor listened to the news. He regarded it as his responsibility to read all the newspapers every day as if knowing what was bad could prevent worse. He did not want to read the papers; he wanted to sit down and wait quietly for his wife. This made him guilty, and he was associating his reluctance to plunge into the misery and threat of the newspapers with the brutalising of everybody, everyone's acceptance of horror as normal—well, it was, when had storms of blood and destruction *not* swept continuously over the globe?

His will was being attacked: he had no will. This was why he needed to see Rosemary. This thought, he knew, had put a small whimsical grimace onto his face; the grimace was for the benefit of an observer. The observer was himself; it was there for the sake of his pride—a very odd thing had happened between him and his wife. For a long time, in fact for most of the marriage, they would have said that they were unhappily married. It had been a war marriage of course, like those of most of their contemporaries. It had begun in passion, separation, dislocation. They had felt, on beginning to live together for the first time, when they had been married for nearly six years, that their good times had been stolen from them. Then three children: they had turned Rosemary into an obsessed complaining woman; so he had seen her, and so she now saw herself during that period. He was most often out of England, and had many affairs, some of them serious. He knew she had been in love with someone else; she, like himself, had refused to consider a divorce because of the effect on the children. There was of course nothing remarkable in this history; but some of the men he knew had divorced, leaving first wives to bring up children. He knew that many of his friends' wives, like Rosemary, had been obsessed with grievance at their lot, yet had been dutiful mothers.

Various unhappy balances had been achieved by himself and Rosemary, always regarded as secondbest. Best was in fantasy, or what other people had. Then the children grew up, and were no longer there to be cooked for, worried about, shopped for, nursed—suddenly these two people who had been married thirty years discovered they were enjoying each other. They could not use the words "a second honeymoon" because they had never had a first. Jack remembered that at the other end of what now seemed like a long tunnel of responsibility, worry, guilt—relieved by frequent exile, whose enjoyability caused more guilt—had been a young woman with whom he had been more in love than with anybody since. He relaxed into the pleasures of his home, pleasure with Rosemary, who, appreciated at last, took on energy and poise, lost her listlessness, her reproach, her patience under neglect.

It had been the completeness of her revival that was the only thing disturbing about their being in love again: Jack lived marvelling that so little a thing as his own attention should be enough to nourish this creature, to burnish her with joy. He could not help being guilty anew that so little an effort towards self-discipline would have produced the kindness which could have made this woman's life happy, instead of a martyrdom. Yet he knew he had not been capable of even so small an effort: he had found her intolerable, and the marriage a burden, and that was the truth. But the thought he could not come to terms with was this: what sort of a creature was she, to be fed and made happy by the love of a creature like himself?

And Rosemary was not the only woman he observed enjoying a new lease on life. At parties of "the Old Guard" it was enough simply to look around at the wives of the same age as his own wife, the women recently released from nursery and kitchen, to see many in the same condition, without having to ask if a second honeymoon was in progress—and here was another source of unease. He was not able to ask, to discuss frankly, or even to raise the matter at all, and yet these were friends, he had been with them, worked with them, faced a hundred emergencies with them—but they did not have with each other the friendship of the kind that would enable them to talk about their relationships with each other, with their wives, their wives with them. Yet this was friendship, or at least it was as close to friendship as he was likely to get. Intimacy he had known, but with women with whom he was having affairs. Intimacy, frankness, trust, had, as it were, been carried inside him, to be bestowed on loved women, and withdrawn when that love had ended because he was married. So it was not that he had not known perfect intimacy; it was that he had known it with several people, one after another. What was left now of these relationships was a simplicity of understanding when he met these women again—those that he did meet, for after all, many of these affairs had taken place in other countries. But even now he had to admit that this state had never been achieved with his wife, as good as their relation now was; for what he could not share with her was a feeling he could not control that he had to value her less for being so satisfied—more, fulfilled—with so little. Himself.

Yet, for all these reservations, the last two years had been better than anything he had expected with a woman, except in the expectations of his dreams about marriage so long ago. They went for holidays together, for weekends to old friends, to the theatre, for special meals at restaurants, and for long walks. They made little treats for each other, gave each other presents, had developed the private language of lovers. And all the time her gaiety and energy grew, while she could not prevent herself watching him—not knowing that she did it, and this humbled him and made him wretched—for the return of the old tyrant, the boor. Always he was aware that their happiness lacked a foundation.

But what foundation ought there to be?

Now he wanted to tell his wife the dream he had had about death. This is why he had been longing to see her. But he had not allowed himself to understand the truth, which was that he couldn't tell her. She dreaded change in him; she would feel the dream as a threat. And it was. For another thing, this new easy affection they had would not admit the words he would have to use. What words? None he knew could convey the quality of the dream. The habits of their life together made it inevitable that if he said: Rosemary, I had a terrible dream; well, no, that was not it, its terribleness is not the point, wait, I must tell you—she would reply: Oh, Jack, you must have eaten something. Are you well?—And she would run off to get him a glass of medicine of some sort. Her smile at him, while she handed it to him, would say that she knew, they both knew, that he didn't really need it, but she enjoyed looking after him when at last he was enjoying being looked after.

Tea time came. Jack watched the young man from upstairs walk away under the summer's load of leaf. The telephone rang twice, both times for Rosemary. He took messages. He saw Elizabeth come up the path to the side door, nearly called to her, but decided not. He sat on into the summer afternoon, feeling that it was appropriate to be melancholy: it was what was expected of him. But that was not it! It was as if he had no substance at all, there was nothing to him, no purpose, no worth. . . . Something was draining quietly away from him, had been, for a long time.

Elizabeth came running in, saying: "Oh, Father, I am so sorry, you must be feeling low." Caroline came after her. Carrie was now dressed in a purple shawl over tight red cotton trousers. Elizabeth, still in what she had worn to work, had on a dark green trouser suit, but her own personality had been asserted since she came home: she had tied her hair back with an exotic-looking piece of red material, and it was making a froth of gold curls around her face. His cold heart began to stir and to warm, and they sat themselves down opposite ready to share his grief.

Rosemary now came in, a large, tall woman, smiling and shedding energy everywhere.

"Oh, darling," said she, "you didn't telephone. I am so sorry. You have had tea, I hope?"

"He's dead," said Elizabeth to her mother.

"He died this morning," said Jack, not believing that it had been that morning.

Rosemary slowed her movements about the room, and when she turned to him, her face, like the faces of her daughters, was not smiling.

"When is the funeral?"

"I don't know yet."

"I'll come with you," said Elizabeth.

"I won't," said Carrie. "I don't like funerals. Not our kind of funeral."

"And I won't either, if you don't mind," said Rosemary. "That is, not unless you want me there." A glass and decanter had appeared beside him, and Rosemary was causing whisky to descend into the glass in a gold stream.

The whisky was not the point, the women's serious faces not the point, the funeral and who was at it, not the point.

"There is no need for any of you to come," he said. And added, as he had been afraid he might: "It wouldn't be expected of you."

All three showed relief, even Elizabeth.

Rosemary hated funerals: they were morbid. Carrie, being sort of Buddhist, believed, apparently, in putting corpses out for the vultures. Elizabeth's Christianity, like Ann's, was without benefit of church services.

"Oh no, I want to come with you," said Elizabeth.

"Well, we'll see."

He told them about the death—a mild and well-ordered affair. He said that Ellen and Cedric had been there, and watched for his wife's humorous glance so that he could return it: she wanted to convey sympathy for having to be with his family even for two days. Then he began speaking about the Twenty-four-Hour Fast. He did not ask if they would join him, but he was hoping they would.

Now, while Rosemary had early on been inculcated with his leftwing opinions, during all the years of their unhappiness his activities had been seen by her as being in some subtle way directed against her, or, at any rate, as depriving her of something. But recently she had several times gone with him to a meeting or a demonstration. Looking guilty, she said that she couldn't join the Fast, because she had a lecture on Saturday night on Stress in the Family. She made it sound funny, in her way of appearing like an intelligent child submitting to official pedantry; but there was no doubt she would be at the lecture. Carrie said nothing: she thought any kind of politics silly. Elizabeth said she would have joined the Fast, but she had a demonstration of her own on Saturday.

Jack now remembered Ann's programme, said that Ann was coming down at the weekend for a Pray-in. It turned out that this was the same as Elizabeth's. Both girls were pleased that Ann was coming, and starting talking about her and her relations with her parents. These were not very good: Ann found them materialistic, conventional, bourgeois. Jack was not able to be much amused; he found himself in sympathy with Cedric, possibly even with his sister-in-law. Probably Elizabeth and Carrie said to their friends that their parents were materialistic and bourgeois. He knew that his son Joseph did.

The girls had been going out for the evening, but because of the death, and wanting to cheer their father up, they stayed in to supper. Rosemary's new practice, now that the decades of compulsive cooking, buying, fussing, were done with, was to keep food to its simplest. She offered them soup, toast, and fruit. The girls protested: the parents could see that this was because they needed to do something to show their sympathy. Rosemary and Jack sat hand in hand on the sofa, while the girls made a long and delicious meal for them all.

They went to bed early: it was still not quite dark outside. But he needed to make love with his wife, feeling that here at least the cold which threatened him would be held at bay.

But the shell of himself loved, the shell of himself held Rosemary while she fell asleep and turned away from him. He was awake, listening to the tides of blood moving in his body.

He crept downstairs again. He read the newspapers—making himself do so, like a penance for callousness. He listened to the radio, avoiding news bulletins. He did not go to bed again until it was fully light, and was woken an hour later by Cedric: practical reasons had set the funeral for tomorrow, Saturday, at eleven.

Friday he spent in the activities that the journalist was so good at. Saturday was not a good day for train and air services: to reach S—— in time for the funeral, and to be back by two, would need luck and ingenuity. He checked the weather forecast: rain and mist were expected. Having made the arrangements, he rang Mona, since Walter was still in Glasgow. Mona was not only a wife of an "Old Guard," but one in her own right. It had been agreed that he, Jack, would be on the steps of the church at ten, to welcome the fasters as they arrived, and to see that the posters proclaiming the event were in place. He now asked Mona to do all this, explaining why.

"Oh dear," she said, "I am so sorry about your father. Yes, luckily I can do it. Who is coming?—wait, I'll get a pencil."

He gave her the names over the telephone, while she wrote them down.

They were the names of people with whom he had been associated in a dozen different ways, ever since the war ended; it seemed now as if the war had been an instrument to shake out patterns of people who would work and act together—or against each other—for the rest of their lives. They had not known about this process while it was happening, but that was when "the Old Guard" had been formed. The phrase was a joke of course, and for family use: he certainly would never use it to Walter, Bill, Mona and the rest—they would be hurt by it. Carrie had said one day, reporting a telephone call, "I didn't get his name, but it sounded like one of the Old Guard."

These names appeared constantly together on dozens, hundreds, of letterheads, appeals, protests, petitions; if you saw one name, you could assume the others. Yet their backgrounds had been very different, of all classes, countries, even races. Some had been communists, some had fought communism. They were Labour and Liberal, vegetarian and pacifist, feeders of orphaned children, builders of villages in Africa and India, rescuers of refugees and survivors of natural and manmade calamities. They were journalists and editors, actors and writers, film makers and trade unionists. They wrote books on subjects like Unemployment in the Highlands and The Future of Technology. They sat on councils and committees and the boards of semicharitable organisations; they were Town Councillors, members of Parliament, creators of documentary film programmes. They had taken the same stands on Korea and Kenya, on Cyprus and Suez, on Hungary and the Congo, on Nigeria, the Deep South and Brazil, on South Africa and Rhodesia and Ireland and Vietnam and . . . and now they were sharing opinions and emotions on the nine million refugees from Bangladesh.

Once, when they had come together to express a view, it had been a minority view, and to get what they believed publicised had sometimes been difficult or impossible. Now something had happened which not all of them had understood: when they expressed themselves about this or that, it was happening more and more often that their views were identical with conventional views put forward freely by majorities everywhere. Once they had been armed with aggressive optimistic views about society, about how to change it; now they were on the defensive. Once they had forecast utopias; now they forecast calamity, failed to prevent calamity, and then worked to minimise calamity.

This view of the Old Guard had been presented to Jack by his son, the chip off the old block.

When Jack had finished the list of names, Mona said: "Surely we can do better than that?" and he said, apologetically (why, when it was not his fault?): "I think a lot of people are feeling that the media are doing it for us."

Then he decided to ring his son, who had not yet heard about his grandfather. To reach Joseph was not easy, since he worked for a variety of "underground" organisations, slept in many places, might even be out of the country.

At last Jack rang Elizabeth, who was already at her place of work, heard where Joseph was likely to be, and finally reached his son. On hearing that his grandfather was dead, Joseph said: "Oh that's bad, I am sorry." On being asked if he and his friends "with nothing better to do" would like to join the Twenty-four-Hour Fast, he said: "But haven't you been reading the newspapers?" Jack did not want to say that he had not read them enough to know what his son's programme was likely to be, but it turned out that "all of us" were organising a Protest March for that Sunday.

In his son's briskness, modified because of the death, Jack heard his own youth speaking, and a sense of justice made him sound apologetic towards his son. He felt, too, the start of exhaustion. This was because his effort to be fair made it necessary to resurrect his own youth as he talked to Joseph, and it took the energy that in fantasy he would be using to bring Joseph around to see his point of view. He had recently been indulging fantasies of confronting Joseph with: Look, I have something of great importance to say, can you let me have an hour or two? He was on the point of saying this now, but Joseph said: "I have to rush off, I'm sorry, see you, give my love to everyone."

He knew exactly what he wanted to say, not only to his son—to his own youthful self—but to the entire generation, or rather, to that part of it which was political, the political youth. What he felt was, he knew, paradoxical: it was because his son was so much like him that he felt he had no son, no heir. What he wanted was for his son to carry on from himself, from where he, Jack, stood now: to be his continuation.

It was not that his youthful self had been, was, conceited, crude, inexperienced, intolerant: he knew very well that his own middleaged capacities of tact and the rest were not much more than the oil these same qualities—not much changed— used to get their own way; he wasn't one to admire middleaged blandness, expertise.

What he could not endure was that his son, all of them, would have to make the identical journey he and his contemporaries had made, to learn lessons exactly as if they had never been learned before.

Here, at precisely this point, was the famous "generation gap"; here it had always been. It was not that the young were unlike their parents, that they blazed new trails, thought new thoughts, displayed new forms of courage. On the contrary, they behaved exactly like their parents, thought as they had—and, exactly like their parents, could not listen to this simple message: that it had all been done before.

It was this that was so depressing, and which caused the dryness of only just achieved tolerance on the part of the middleaged towards "the youth"—who, as they themselves had done, behaved as if youth and the freedom they had to "experiment" was the only good they had, or could expect in their lives.

But this time the "gap" was much worse because a new kind of despair had entered into the consciousness of mankind: things were too desperate, the future of humanity depended on humanity being able to achieve new forms of intelligence, of being able to learn from experience. That humanity was unable to learn from experience was written there for everyone to see, since the new generation of the intelligent and consciously active youth behaved identically with every generation before them.

This endless cycle, of young people able to come to maturity only in making themselves into a caste which had to despise and dismiss their parents, insisting pointlessly on making their own discoveries—it was, quite simply, uneconomic. The world could not afford it.

Every middleaged person (exactly as his or her parents had done) swallowed the disappointment of looking at all the intelligence and bravery of his or her children being absorbed in —repetition, which would end, inevitably in them turning into the Old Guard. Would, that is, if Calamity did not strike first. Which everybody knew now it was going to.

Watching his son and his friends was like watching laboratory animals unable to behave in any way other than that to which they had been trained—as he had done, as the Old Guard had done. . . . At this point in the fantasy, his son having accepted or at least listened to all this, Jack went on to what was really his main point. What was worst of all was that "the youth" had not learned, were repeating, the old story of socialist recrimination and division. Looking back over his time—and after all recently he had had plenty of time to do just this, and was not that important, that a man had reached quiet water after such a buffeting and a racing and could think and reflect? —he could see one main message. This was that the reason for the failure of socialism to achieve what it could was obvious: that some process, some mechanism was at work which made it inevitable that every political movement had to splinter and divide, then divide again and again, into smaller groups, sects, parties, each one dominated, at least temporarily, by some strong figure, some hero, or father, or guru figure, each abusing and insulting the others. If there had been a united socialist movement, not only in his time—which he saw as that since the Second World War—but in the time before that, and the epoch before that, and before that, there would have been a socialist Britain long ago.

But as night followed day, the same automatic process went on . . . but if it *was* automatic, he imagined his son saying, then why talk to me like this?—Ah, Jack would reply, but you have to be better, don't you see? You have to, otherwise it's all at an end, it's finished, can't you see that? Can't you see that this process where one generation springs, virginal and guiltless— or so it sees itself—out of its debased predecessors, with everything new to learn, makes it inevitable that there must soon be division, and self-righteousness and vituperation? Can't you see that that has happened to your lot? There are a dozen small newspapers, a dozen because of their differences. But suppose there had been one or two? There are a dozen little groups, each jealously defending their differences of dogma on policy, sex, history. Suppose there had been just one?

But of course there could not be only one; history showed there could not—history showed this, clearly, to those who were prepared to study history. But the young did not study history, because history began with them. Exactly as history had begun with Jack and his friends.

But the world could no longer afford this. . . . The fantasy did not culminate in satisfactory emotion, in an embrace, for instance, between father and son; it ended in a muddle of dull thoughts. Because the fantasy had become increasingly painful, Jack had recently developed it in a way which was less personal —less challenging, less real? He had been thinking that he could discuss all these thoughts with the Old Guard and afterwards there could perhaps be a conference? Yes, there might be a confrontation, or something of that kind, between the Old Guard and the New Young. Things could be said publicly which never seemed to get themselves said privately? It could all be thrashed out and then . . . Meanwhile there was the funeral to get through.

That night, Friday, the one before the funeral, no sooner had he gone to sleep than he dreamed. It was not the same dream, that of the night in the hotel room, but it came as it were out of the same area. A corridor, long, dark, narrow, led to the place of the first dream, but at its entrance stood a female figure which at first he believed was his mother as a young woman. He believed this because of what he felt, which was an angry shame and inadequacy: these emotions were associated for him with some childhood experience which he supposed he must have suppressed; sometimes he thought he was on the point of remembering it. The figure wore a straight white dress with loose lacy sleeves. It had been his mother's dress, but both Elizabeth and Carrie had worn it "for fun." This monitor was at the same time his mother and his daughters, and she was directing him forward into the darkness of the tunnel.

His wife was switching on lights and looking at him with concern. He soothed her back to sleep and, for the second night running, left his bed soon after he had got into it to read the night away and to listen to radio stations from all over the world.

Next morning he travelled to the airport in light fog, to find the flight delayed. He had left himself half an hour's free play, and in half an hour the flight was called and he was airborne, floating west inside grey cloud that was his inner state. He who had flown unmoved through the skies of most countries of the world, and in every kind of weather, was feeling claustrophobic, and had to suppress wanting to batter his way out of the plane and run away across the mists and fogs of this upper country. He made himself think of something else: returned to the fantasy about the Conference. He imagined the scene, the hall packed to the doors, the platform manned by the well known among the various generations of socialists. He saw himself there, with Walter on one side, and his son on the other. He imagined how he or Walter would speak, explaining to the young that the survival of the world depended on them, that they had the chance to break this cycle of having to repeat and repeat experience: they could be the first generation to consciously take a decision to look at history, to absorb it, and in one bound to transcend it. It would be like a willed mutation.

He imagined the enthusiasm of the Conference—a sober and intelligent enthusiasm, of course. He imagined the ending of the Conference when . . . and here his experience took hold of him, and told him what would happen. In the first place, only some of the various socialist groups would be at the Conference. Rare people indeed would be prepared to give up the hegemony of their little groups to something designed to end little groups. The Conference would throw up some strong personalities, who would energise and lead; but very soon these would disagree and become enemies and form rival movements. In no time at all, this movement to end schism would have added to it. As always happened. So, if this was what Jack knew was bound to happen, why did he . . . They were descending through heavy cloud. There was heavy rain in S——. The taxi crawled through slow traffic. By now he knew he would not be in time to reach the cemetery. If he had really wanted to make sure of being at the funeral, he would have come down last night. Why hadn't he? He might as well go back now for all the good he was doing; but he went on. At the cemetery the funeral was over. Two young men were shovelling earth into the hole at the bottom of which lay his father: like the men in the street who continually dig up and rebury drains and pipes and wires. He took the same taxi back to the house in the church precincts where he found Mrs. Markham tidying the rooms ready to hold the last years of another man or woman, and his brother Cedric sorting out the old man's papers. Cedric was crisp: he quite understood the delay; he too would have been late for the funeral if he had not taken the precaution of booking rooms in the Royal Arms. But both he and Ellen had been there, with his wife and Ellen's husband. Also Ann. It would have been nice if Jack had been there, but it didn't matter.

It was now a warm day, all fog forgotten. Jack found a suitable flight back to London. High in sunlight, he wondered if his father had felt as if he had no heir? He had been a lawyer: Cedric had succeeded him. In his youth he had defended labour agitators, conscientious objectors, taken on that kind of case: from religious conviction, not from social feeling. Well, did it make any difference why a thing was done if it was done? This thought, seditious of everything Jack believed, lodged in his head—and did not show signs of leaving. It occurred to Jack that perhaps the old man had seen himself as his heir, and not Cedric, who had always been so cautious and respectable? Well, he would not now know what his father had thought; he had missed his chance to find out.

Perhaps he could talk to Ann and find out what the old man had been thinking? The feebleness of this deepened the inadequacy which was undermining him—an inadequacy which seemed to come from the dream of the female in a white dress? Why had that dream fitted his two lovely daughters into that stern unforgiving figure? He dozed, but kept waking himself for fear of dreaming. That he was now in brilliant sunshine over a floor of shining white cloud so soon after the flight through fog dislocated his sense of time, of continuity even more: it was four days ago that he had had that telegram from Mrs. Markham?

They ran into fog again above Heathrow, and had to crawl around in the air for half an hour before they could land. It was now four, and the Twenty-four-Hour Fast had begun at two. He decided he would not join them, but he would drop in and explain why not.

He took the underground to Trafalgar Square.

Twenty people, all well known to him and to the public, were grouped on the steps and porch of St. Martin's. Some sat on cushions, some on stools. A large professionally made banner said: THIS IS A TWENTY-FOUR-HOUR FAST FOR THE STARVING MILLIONS OF BANGLADESH. Each faster had flasks of water, blankets and coats for the night ahead. Meanwhile it was a warm misty afternoon. Walter had a thick black sweater tied around his neck by the sleeves. Walter was the centre of the thing; the others related to him. Jack stood on the other side of the road thinking that his idea of talking with these his old friends about a joint conference with "the youth" was absurd, impractical; now that he was again in the atmosphere of ordinary partisan politics, he could see that it was.

He was longing to join them, but this was because he wanted to be enclosed in a group of like-minded people, to be supported by them, to be safe and shielded from doubts and fears. And dreams.

By Walter was his wife, Norah, a small pretty woman whom he had always thought of as Walter's doormat. He had done, that is, until he had understood how afraid Rosemary had been of himself. Norah had once said to him after a meeting: "If Walter had been an ordinary man, I might have resented giving up my career, but when you are married to someone like Walter, then of course you are glad to submerge yourself. I feel as if this has been my contribution to the Movement." Norah had been a journalist.

Walter's face, usually a fist of intention and power, was beaming, expansive: they all looked as if they were at a picnic, Jack thought. Smug, too. That he should think this astounded him, for he knew that he loved and admired them. Yet now, looking at Walter's handsome face, so well known to everyone from newspaper and television, it had over it a mask of vanity. This was so extraordinary a metamorphosis of Jack's view of his friend that he felt as if an alien was inhabiting him: a film had come over his eyes, distorting the faces of everyone he looked at. He was looking at masks of vanity, complacency, stupidity or, in the case of Walter's Norah, a foolish admiration. Then Jack's sense of what was happening changed; it was not that he was looking through distorting film, but that a film had been stripped off what he looked at. He was staring at faces that horrified him because of their naked self-centredness: he searched faces that must be like his own, for something he could admire, or need. And hastily he wiped his hand down over his own face, for he knew that on it was fastened a mask of vanity; he could feel it there. Under it, under an integument that was growing inwards into his flesh, he could feel something small, formless, blind—something pitiful and unborn.

Now, disgusted with his treachery, but still unable to take his hand down from his face, unable to prevent himself from trying to tug off that mask fastened there, he walked over to his friends who, seeing him come, smiled and looked about them for a place where he could sit. He said: "I can't join you, I am afraid. Transport trouble," he added ridiculously, as first surprise, then incomprehension showed on their faces. Now he saw that Walter had already registered: *His father!* and saw that this born commander was framing the words he would use as soon as Jack turned his back: "His father has died, he has just come from the funeral." But this was no reason why he shouldn't be with them: he agreed, absolutely. Now he moved away, but glanced back with a wave and a smile; they were all gazing after the small drama embodied in: His father has just died. They looked as if they were hungry for the sensation of it—he was disliking himself for criticising people whom he knew to be decent and courageous, who, ever since he had known them, had taken risks, given up opportunities, devoted themselves to what they believed to be right. To what *he* believed was right. . . . He was also a bit frightened. Thoughts that he would never have believed he was capable of accommodating were taking root in him; he felt as if armies of others waited to invade.

He decided to walk down to the river, perhaps even to take a trip to Greenwich, if he could get on to a boat at all on a warm Saturday afternoon. He saw coming towards him a little procession under banners of: JESUS IS YOUR SAVIOUR and JESUS LIVES! All the faces under the banners were young; these young people were in no way distinguished by their clothes from the young ones he had watched marching, with whom he had marched, for the last fifteen years or more. Their clothes were gay and imaginative, their hair long, their faces all promise. He was smiling at Ann, who carried a square of cardboard that said: JESUS CARES ABOUT BANGLADESH. A voice said, "Hello, Dad!" and he saw his Elizabeth, her golden hair in heavy pigtails over either shoulder. Hands, Ann's and Elizabeth's, pulled him in beside them. In this way one of the most prominent members of the Old Guard found himself marching under a poster which said: CHRIST CAME TO FEED THE HUNGRY. REMEMBER BANGLADESH! Ann's little face beamed with happiness and the results of the exercise. "It was a nice funeral," she said.

"I was telling Liz about it. It had a good feeling. Grandad liked it, I am sure."

To this Jack found himself unable to reply, but he smiled and, with a couple of hundred Jesus-lovers, negotiated the Square, aided by some indulgent policemen. In a few moments he would pass his friends on the steps of the church.

"I shouldn't be here," he said. "False pretences."

"Oh why?" enquired his daughter, really disappointed in him. "I don't see that at all!"

Ann's look was affectionate and forgiving.

Around him they were singing Onward, Christian Soldiers. They sang and marched or, rather, shuffled and ambled, and he modified his pace to theirs, and allowed his depression to think for him that whether the banners were secular and atheist on principle, or under the aegis of Jesus, twenty-four million people would die in the world this year of starvation, and that he would not give a new penny for the chances of anybody in this Square living another ten years without encountering disaster.

He was now aware that Mona was staring at him: in her decisive face, in her unequivocal eyes, was not a trace of what he usually saw there—the reminder of their brief but pleasurable affair. She turned to tug at Walter's sleeve, in a way that betrayed panic—more than ordinary shock, anyway. Now they all turned to look at him; they were all blank, they could not take it in. He had a need to wave his arms and shout: Nonsense, can't you see that I am with my daughter and my niece? He felt he should apologise. He could not stand being condemned by them, his side, his family, but even as he nodded and smiled embarrassed greeting, he saw that Walter, whose mouth at first had really dropped open, had seen Elizabeth, whom of course he had known all her life. All was explainable! For the second time in half an hour Jack watched Walter framing words with which to exculpate him: Jack was with his daughter, that was it! After all, Jack was not the only one among them whose offspring had caught God in various extraordinary forms!

Jack entered the Square with the children, was informed that they would come to visit him later, and he left them singing energetic hymns by a fountain.

He took busses home. He was looking forward to letting the

false positions of the day dissolve themselves into unimportance while he laughed over them with his wife; but now he remembered that she would not be there, nor expect him to be.

There was a note, not to him but to Carrie, saying: "Please feed the cat, shall be very late, might stay at Judy Miller's, please lock all doors much love."

It was seven: it seemed like midafternoon. He drew the curtains to make a night, and sat in it with a glass of whisky. Later Ann came in to tell him about the funeral, about Jesus. He moved his position in his chair so that he could look at her shining eyelids. Carrie came in, and he looked at her, but her eyes were a woman's. He knew about her love life, because she talked freely to her parents about it, but if she had never said a word he would have known from her knowledgeable breasts, from the way the flesh was moulded to her eyeballs by kisses. She breathed tenderness, and care for him; he was happy she was there, but it was Ann he wanted to look at.

They discussed their respective faiths. Ann did not need to join a church because she had a direct relationship with Jesus, who loved her as she loved Him. Carrie defined her religion as "sort of Eastern, she supposed." No, she didn't think it was Buddhist so much as Hindu. She believed in reincarnation but could not see the point of cow-worship, though anything that made people be nice to animals was worth it, she thought. Had Ann read the Upanishads? That was what she believed in. She was taking it for granted that her father had not, and would not. She would like to be a vegetarian, but after all she shared a kitchen with Elizabeth, who would object. . . . Here Elizabeth came in, having bathed and put on an ancient peacock-blue lace dinner dress that had holes in the sleeves; Jack remembered Rosemary in it, twenty years before. Elizabeth was indignant, and said she would not at all mind Carrie turning vegetarian, she was ready to be one herself. But what would they feed the cat on? Were human beings going to kill all the cats and dogs in the world because they weren't vegetarian? Carrie got angry at this, and said: There you are; I told you, I knew you didn't want to be vegetarian! Ann restored good feeling by laughing at them both.

They went on discussing the exact nuances of their beliefs, *I* believe that, no, I don't agree with that, no I think it is more that . . . surely not, oh no, how can you believe that? An hour or so went by. Jack lifted the drawn curtain: there was a heavy golden light everywhere, thunder in the evening sky, the trees had damp yellow aureoles. He dropped the curtain, and they were in a small low lamplight, and the three girls were discussing Women's Liberation. Jack hated women talking about this, not because he disagreed with any of it, but because he had never been able to cope with it; it was all too much for him. He felt increasingly that he had reason to feel guilty about practically every relationship he ever had with a woman except for two or three special love affairs, which were outside ordinary categorisation, but did not know how to change himself—if, indeed, he wanted to. These three young women had different, but precisely defined, opinions about the roles of women, with Carrie representing an extreme of femininity, and Ann, surprisingly, militant. Elizabeth talked about the lot of working women and had no time for what she called "futile psychologising." This phrase made them quarrel, and for the first time Jack saw Ann strident. The quarrel went on, and then they saw that Jack was silent, and they remembered that his father was just dead, and they cooked for him, handing him many dishes, each as if it were a poultice for some wound he had suffered. Then, with an effort towards being reasonable, they went on discussing their ideological positions about Women's Liberation. Jack was again in the condition he had been in in the Square, when he had looked across traffic at his old friends. All he had been able to see there was a variety of discreditable emotions; all he could see in these charming faces was self-importance. What mattered to them was the moment when they said: I think so-and-so; no, I don't think that. He knew that what they believed was not as important to them as that they had come to an opinion and the reasons why they had reached that opinion. They possessed their beliefs or opinions; they owned them.

Now they were back to religion again: the other two attacked Ann for being Christian when Christianity's history in relation to women was so retrogressive. To which Ann said to Carrie: "You can talk, how about women in India?"

"Yes," said Carrie, "but then I don't believe in women being the same as men."

This started the quarrel again, and their voices rose.

He had to stop himself saying that they sounded like a Conference of World Churches debating doctrinal differences, because he knew that if it came to dogmas, and disagreements about historical personalities, then his faith, socialism, beat them all. He looked at, listened to, his daughters, his brother's daughter, and knew that in two, three, ten years (if they were all allowed to live so long) they would be laying claim, with exactly the same possessiveness, to other creeds, faiths, attitudes.

Again he felt like a threatened building, the demolition teams at work on its base. He was seeing, like a nightmare, the world like a little ball covered over with minuscule creatures all vociferously and viciously arguing and killing each other over beliefs which they had come to hold by accident of environment, of geography.

He told the girls he had not been sleeping well, must go to bed: he could no longer stand listening while they staked precise claims in fields of doctrine. They went off, kissing him fondly: he knew from the warmth of the kisses that they had talked about his reactions to Grandad's death; everything was bound to be much worse for him of course because he was an atheist and did not believe in survival after death.

They each had a different version of their futures. Ann for instance believed that she would sit up after her death, exactly as she was now, but better, and would recognise her friends and family, and Jesus would be there too.

Jack was thinking that his own attitude to life after death had been collected quite casually: when he was young and forming (or acquiring) his opinions, the people and writers he admired wore atheism like a robe of honour. Not to believe in an after-life was like a certificate of bravery and, above all, clarity of thinking. If he had been young now, he might have collected, according to the chances of his experience, and just as lightly, any one of a variety of opinions. Reincarnation? Why not? After all, as Carrie said, it was an optimistic and forward-looking creed. But when he was young he couldn't have taken to a belief in reincarnation, if for no other reason than that he never met anyone who had it. He had known that a few cranks believed in it, and people in India, but that was about it.

Now he made a ritual of going to bed. The sky was still full of light, so he made the room black. He drank hot milk. He wooed sleep, which he had never done in his life, and soon lay awake, hands behind his head. But he could not spend a third night reading and listening to the radio. Then lights crashed on and his wife was in the room. She was apologetic, and quite understood that he hadn't felt like joining the Fast. Her mind, he could see, was on her lecture and the friends she had met afterwards. He watched her dimming her vitality, damping her good mood, because she was afraid of it disturbing him. She lay in bed smiling, bright-eyed. She asked about the funeral, was sorry he had not reached it. Poor Jack! Smiling, she offered her arms, and grateful, he went into them. He would have gone on making love all night, but she went to sleep. In the close protective dark he lay beside his wife and in imagination saw the sky fill with dawn.

He fell asleep, he fell into a dream. In the dream he was thinking of what he had kept out of his consciousness all day, for to think of it was morbid. His father lay in a tight box under feet of wet soil. He, Jack, lay with him. He stifled and panicked, and the weight on him was as if he had been buried alive, in wet cement. He woke, and finding that although a cool damp light lay everywhere, and birds were at work on the lawn, it was only half past four; he went downstairs, turned on the radio, and made pictures in his head of the towns the stations were in, and lists of the people he had known in these towns, and then divided these into friends and enemies, and then, by a different classification, into the dead and the living, and so he returned in memory to the wars he had fought in or had reported, and relived, in a half-sleep, crisis-points, moments of danger, when he might have been killed, that now made him sweat and tremble but which he had simply lived through. When it seemed to him as if hours of a new day had already passed, he went back upstairs and got into bed beside his wife.

But at breakfast she betrayed that she had known he had not been beside her: she started to talk about the job in Nigeria. He knew that she did not want to go away for two years, leaving all her new interests, new friends, new freedom. There she would be back inside duties she had escaped from. There would be much social life. Yet it sounded as if she was trying to bring herself to believe she wanted to go if he did: she was worried about him.

He said, instead of replying about Nigeria, that he would like to go to church, just to see what it was like these days. She took in a puzzled but patient breath, let it sigh out of her, and looked at him with loving and respectful eyes—just like, he thought, the way Norah looked at Walter. She said: "Oh, I can understand why. You mean, you missed the funeral service?"

Perhaps it was because he had missed the funeral service. He put on a suit and she a dress, and they went to church together, for the first time, except for weddings. Carrie and Elizabeth went with them, Carrie because God was everywhere, Elizabeth because He was particularly in churches. Ann would not come; she had Jesus by the hand as she sat on the floor reading the Sunday newspapers.

He sat through the service in a rage; perhaps it was a retrospective rage; certainly this was what he had felt throughout years of compulsory attendance at Evensong and Matins, and Services Early and Late, at his public school. He did not mind that it was mumbo jumbo: it was bound to be! What he minded was that people voluntarily submitted themselves to the ministry of men palpably no better than themselves, men whose characters were written on their faces. This was perhaps what had first directed him towards socialism? He had not been able to stand that people submitted to being lied to, cheated, dominated by their equals? He was again afflicted by yesterday's disability: a film had rolled away from what he looked at. That man, wearing black with white lace and embroidery, and dangling strips of this and that colour—the sort of attractive nonsense that Carrie and Liz might wear—that man intoning and dancing and posturing through the service, had a face like Walter's. They were both public men, performers. Their features were permanently twisted by vanity and self-importance. Jack kept passing his hand across his own face, feeling the ugliness of the love of power on it. And Rosemary put her arm in his, asking if he felt well, if he had toothache? He replied with violence that he must have been mad to want to come; he apologized for inflicting it on her.

"Oh it doesn't matter for once," she said, with mildness, but glanced over her shoulder to see if Carrie and Elizabeth had heard: it was extraordinary how they all kowtowed to their children, as if they feared to offend them.

After the midday meal he felt as if he could sleep at last, and did so.

The dream pulled him down into itself as he rolled onto his bed in the sultry yellow afternoon light—and passed out. This time, as he sank down beside his father, who was very cold—he could feel the cold coming out and claiming him—the weight pressed them both down, right through the earth that was below the tight box. His father disappeared and he, Jack, quite alone, was rocking on a light blue sea. This too dissolved into air, but not before he had been pierced through and through with an extraordinary pain that was also a sweetness. He had not known anything like this before; in the dream he was saying to himself: That's a new thing, this sweetness. It was quickly gone, but astonishing, so that he woke up, pleased to wake up, as if out of a nightmare, yet what he had been happy to wake from was that high, piercing sweetness. Unhealthy, he judged it. It was not yet tea time; he had slept an hour and not been refreshed. He went down to be told as a joke by his wife that a journalist had rung that morning to find out his views on the Twenty-four-Hour Fast; did his not having been there mean that he was against it? Ann had answered, and had said that Mr. Orkney was at church. The journalist had seemed surprised, Ann said. She had had to repeat it more than once. Had she meant that Jack Orkney was at a wedding? At a christening? No, no, at church, at Sunday morning service.

Jack knew the journalist; they had been in several foreign fields together. Jack was now seriously worried, as a man is when faced with the loss of reputation. He said to himself: I was not worried what people thought of me when I was young. He was answered: You mean, you were not worried by what people said who were not *your side*. He said: Well, but now it is not a personal thing, criticism of me is a criticism of my side; surely it is right to worry about letting my own side down?

There was no answer to this, except a knowledge he was dishonest.

Rosemary suggested a long walk. He could see she had been thinking how to make him whole again—how to protect her own happiness, he could not prevent himself thinking. He was more than ready to walk as many miles away as they could before dark; when they had first met, before they married, one of their things had been to walk miles, sometimes for days on end. Now they walked until it was dark, at eleven o'clock; they worked out it was over fifteen miles, and were pleased that this was still so easy for them, at their age, and in the middle of their undemanding life. But the night now confronted Jack, a narrow tunnel at the end of which waited a white-robed figure, pointing him into annihilation. That night he did not sleep. The windows were open, the curtains drawn back, the room full of light from the sky. He pretended to sleep, so as to protect his wife from anxiety, but she lay alert beside him, also pretending sleep.

Next morning it was a week since Mrs. Markham's wire, and he became concerned for his health. He knew that not to sleep for night after night, as he was doing, was simply not possible. During the following days he went further into this heightened, over-sensitised state, like a country of which he had heard rumours, but had not believed in. On its edges his wife and daughters smiled and were worried about him. He slept little, and when he did he was monitored by the female figure in white, now a composite of his mother, his wife and his daughters, but quite impersonal; she used their features but was an imposter. This figure had become like an angel on a wedding cake, or on a tomb, full of false sentiment; its appearance was accompanied, like a strain of particularly nauseating and banal music, by the sweetly piercing emotion, only it was much worse now; it was the essence of banality, of mawkishness, like being rolled in powdered sugar and swallowed into an insipid smile. The horror of this clinging sickliness was worse even than the nightmare—he could no longer remember the quality of that, only that it had occurred—of the night in the hotel. His bed, the bedroom, soon the entire house, was tainted by this emotion, which was more a sensation, even like nausea, as if he could never rid himself of the taste of a concentration of saccharin which he had accidentally swallowed. He was all day in a state of astonishment, and self-distrust; he made excuses not to go to bed.

Walter came to see him. Unannounced. As soon as Jack saw him getting out of his car, he remembered something which told him why Walter had come. About four years before, Mona had reviewed a religious book, the memoirs of some sort of mystic, in a way which surprised them all. They would have expected a certain tone—light, carefully non-solemn, for it did not do to give importance to something which did not deserve it—not mocking, of course, which would have had the same result, but the tone you use to indicate to children that while you may be talking about, let's say, ghosts, or telling a story about a witch, the subject is not one to be taken seriously. But Mona had not used this subtly denigrating tone. Various of the Old Guard had commented on this. Then she had reviewed a book of religious poetry, which of course could not be dismissed in the light disinfecting tone, since poetry was obviously in a different category—but the point was that none of them would have reviewed it at all. For one thing no editor would think of asking them to. It was all very upsetting. There had been a party at Bill's house and Mona was not there. She had been discussed: she was at the age when women "get" religion. Jack, fond of Mona, offered to go and see her. His visit was to find out, as he put it to himself, if she was "still with us." He had found her amiable, and her usual self, helping to organise a conference for the coming week. He had probed—oh tactfully, of course. He mentioned an article in one of the Sundays about a certain well-known religious figure, and said he found the man a nauseating self-seeker. Mona had said that she was inclined to agree. He had said casually, "Of course I am only too ready to forgive somebody who can't face old age and all that without being cushioned by God." Mona had remarked that for her part she could not believe in personal survival after death. Well, of course not, but for years that she could not would have been taken for granted. He remembered feeling protective affection for her, as if he were helping to save her from a danger. Seeing Walter at a meeting to do with the Crisis in Our Communications a week later, he had said that he had made a point of visiting Mona and that she had seemed quite sound to him.

He knew now what to expect from Walter.

Walter was looking furtive. Of course Jack knew that this furtiveness was not anything he would have noticed normally: this state he was in exaggerated every emotion on other people's faces into caricatures. But Walter was playing a double part, almost that of a spy (as he had with Mona, of course, now he came to think of it), and Furtiveness was written large on him.

Walter mentioned the Fast—a success—and then made a clumsy sort of transition which Jack missed, and was talking about Lourdes. Jack wondered why Lourdes? And then he laughed: it was a short laugh, of astonishment, and Walter did not notice it. Or rather, had not expected a laugh in this place, found it discordant, and therefore discounted it, as if it had not happened. Walter was trying to find out if Jack's religious conversion—the rumour had spread that he went to church on Sundays—included a belief in miracles, such as took place, they said, at Lourdes. Jack said he had been to Lourdes once for the *Daily* . . . over some so-called miracles some years ago. Walter nodded, as if to say: That's right. He was already feeling relieved, because Jack had used the right tone. But he was still showing the anxiety of a priest who knew his beliefs to be the correct ones and was afraid of a lamb straying from the flock. He mentioned that Mona was suspected of having become a Roman Catholic. "Good God, no," said Jack, "she can't have." He sounded shocked. This was because his reaction was that she had been deceiving him, had lied. He sat silent, trying to remember the exact tones of her voice, how she had looked. If she was a Catholic, could she have said she did not believe in a personal survival? But he knew nothing at all of what Catholics thought, except that they did not believe in birth control, but did believe in the Pope.

Remembering that Walter was still there, and silent, he looked up to see him smiling with relief. The smile seemed to him extraordinary in its vulgarity, yet he knew that what he was seeing was the pleasure of a good comrade: Walter was happy that nothing was going to spoil their long friendship. The spontaneity of his reply over Mona had reassured him; now, mission accomplished, Walter was already thinking about the various obligations he had to get back to. But he stayed a little, to discuss some committee on pollution he was helping to set up.

He talked: Jack listened, wondering if this was the right time to raise the question of "the young." Walter's two sons were both classic revolutionaries and they despised their father for his success, his position in the socialist world, for "his compromises with the ruling class." Jack was thinking that of all the people in the world it was Walter, so like himself in experience, position and—he was afraid—character, with whom he should be able to talk about his preoccupation. But he was beginning to realise that there was a difference, and it was obviously an important one, between them. Jack was more on the outskirts of politics. He was more of a freelance, but Walter was always in the thick of every political struggle, always involved with the actual details of organisation. He never did anything else. And this was why he was so far from Jack's present vision of things, which saw them all—the people like them—continually planning and arranging and organising towards great goals, but fated to see these plans fail, or becoming so diluted by pressures of necessity that the results resembled nothing of what had been envisaged at the start. Sitting there, looking at his old friend's forceful and energetic face, it was in a double vision. On the one hand he thought that this was the one man he knew whom he would trust to see them all through any public or private tight spot; but at the same time he wanted to howl out, in a protest of agonised laughter, that if the skies fell (as they might very well do), if the seas rolled in, if all the water became undrinkable and the air poisoned and the food so short everyone was scratching for it in the dust like animals, Walter, Bill, Mona, himself, and all those like them, would be organising Committees, Conferences, Sit-downs, Fasts, Marches, Protests and Petitions, and writing to the authorities about the undemocratic behaviour of the police.

Walter was talking about some negotiation with the Conservatives. Normally, Jack would be listening to an admirably concise and intelligent account of human beings in conflict. Now Jack could see only that on his friend's face was a look which said: *I am Power*. Jack suddenly got up, with a gesture of repulsion. Walter rose automatically, still talking, not noticing Jack's condition. Jack reminded himself that in criticising Walter he had forgotten that he must be careful about himself: he had again, and suddenly, become conscious of the expressions that were fitting themselves down over his face, reflecting from Walter's, horrifying him in their complacency or their cruelty. And his limbs, his body, kept falling into postures of self-esteem and self-approval.

Walter was moving to the door, still talking. Jack, trying to keep his face blank, to prevent his limbs from expressing emotions which seemed to him appropriate for a monster, moved cautiously after him. Walter stood in the door—talking. Jack wanted him to go. It tired him, this self-observation he could not stop: there was his image at the door, oblivious to anything in the world but his own analysis of events. Yet at last, as Walter said goodbye and he saw Jack again—which he had not done for some minutes, being too self-absorbed—a worried look came into his face, and because of this look Jack knew that what Walter saw was a man standing in a rigid unnatural position who had his hands at his lower cheeks, fretfully fingering the jawbone, as if it were out of place.

Walter said, in a simple and awkward voice: "It's a bit of a shock when your old man goes. I know when mine died it took me quite a time to get back to normal."

He left, like a health visitor, and Jack thought that Walter had had to get back to normal when his father died. He was thinking, too, that the cure for his condition was activity. Walter was more sensible than himself: he filled every moment of his time.

He decided to go to the family doctor for sleeping pills. This was a house that self-consciously did not go in for pills of any kind. Or did not now: Rosemary, during what she now called "my silly time"—which after all had gone on for some years— had taken sleeping pills a lot. But that, even while she did it, had seemed to her a betrayal of her real nature. The girls went in for health in various ways—diets, yoga, homemade bread. His son was too strong—of course!—to need medicine. He smoked pot, Jack believed, and on principle—well, so would Jack have done at his age; the law on marihuana was absurd.

He told the doctor he was not sleeping well. The doctor asked for how long. He had to think. Well, for about a month, perhaps six weeks.

The doctor said: "That's not going to kill you, Jack!"

"All right, but before I get into the habit of not sleeping I'd like something—and *not* a placebo, please." The glance the doctor gave him at this told him that he had in fact been deciding to prescribe a placebo, but there had been something in Jack's voice to make him change his mind.

"Is there anything else worrying you?"

"Nothing. Or everything."

"I see," said the doctor, and prescribed sleeping pills and anti-depressants.

Jack had the prescriptions made up, then changed his mind; if he started taking these pills, it would be some sort of capitulation. To what, he did not know. Besides, he was thinking: Perhaps they might make it worse? "It" was not only the sweet mawkishness which threatened him at every turn, in a jingle of a tune for an advertisement on television, a shaft of light from behind a cloud at sunrise, a kitten playing in the next garden, but the feeling, getting worse, that he was transparent, an automaton of unlikable and predictable reactions. He was like a spy in his own home, noticing the slightest reactions of thought or emotion in his wife and daughters, seeing them as robots. If they knew how he was seeing them, how loathsome they were in their predictability, their banality, they would turn and kill him. And quite rightly. For he was not human. He was outside humanity. He even found himself walking abruptly out of rooms where he was sitting with Rosemary, or one or other of the girls; he could not stand his own horror and pity because of them, himself, everybody.

Yet they were treating him with perfect kindness. He knew that this was what it really was: even if he had to see it all as falsity, mere habits of kindness, sympathy, consideration, tact, which none of them really felt, wanting him to get back to normal, so that life could go on without stress. His wife particularly longed for this. While he took care that he did not betray the horror he was immersed in, she knew well enough their time was over—the gaiety and charm of it, the irresponsibility. Probably for good. Being what she was, thoughtful, considerate (taught by society to show thoughtfulness and sympathy when she wasn't really feeling it, he could not stop himself thinking), she was trying to decide what to do for the best. Sometimes she asked if he didn't think he should write another book—even if he would like to make a trip abroad without her; she talked about Nigeria. Each time Nigeria was mentioned his response to it was strong: it was the idea of forgetting himself entirely in an active and tightly planned life.

But he did not want to commit himself. He felt he would be losing an opportunity—but of what? And besides, how could he? He believed he was seriously ill, in some inconceivable, unprecedented way; how could he take a job when his energies had to go into presenting a bland and harmless surface to those around him, into preventing his hand rising furtively up to his face, to see if the masks of greed or power were fastened there, into watching the postures his body assumed, which must betray his vices to anyone looking his way—or would betray them, if everybody wasn't blind and deaf, absorbed in their kindness, their awful, automatic, meaningless "sympathy."

One night his son arrived upstairs. Joseph used sometimes to come, unannounced, and went up through the girls' room to the attic to sleep. He took food from his sisters' kitchen. Sometimes he brought friends.

About a year ago there had been a row over the friends. Feeling one evening as if the top part of his house had been invaded by a stealthy army, Jack had gone up and found a dozen or so young men, and a couple of girls, all lying about on sleeping bags and blankets under the rafters. They had moved in. A girl was cooking sausages in a frying pan that was on a camping stove; about a foot away was a drum that had written on it: PARAFFIN. INFLAMMABLE. The flame from the stove was turned too high, and showed around the edges of the frying pan. Jack jumped forward, turned it down, removed the pan, and stood up, facing them, the pan in his hand. His usual responses to his son—apology, or the exhaustion due to the effort to be fair, had been cut, and he asked: "What's the matter with you lot? What's wrong? You aren't stupid!"

Coming up the stairs he had been preparing a "humorous" remark—which he was afraid would sound pompous, to the effect: "How about introducing me to my guests?" Now he stared at them, and the young faces stared back. There was a half-scared smile on the face of the girl who had been cooking, but no one said anything. "I think you had better get out," said Jack at last, and went downstairs. Soon after he had watched the whole lot cross the garden like a tribe on the move, with their stove, their cartons, their paper-carriers, their guitars, their sleeping bags.

Now he came to think of it, this incident had been the beginning of his inadmissible depression. He had spent days, weeks, months, thinking about it. He felt there was a contempt there, in the carelessness, that went beyond anything he knew how to cope with; he did not understand it, them—his son. Who, meanwhile, had resumed his habits, and continued to drop in for a night or two when he had nowhere better to sleep. So it was not, Jack reasoned, that Joseph despised a roof over his head, as such? They had all been so stoned they had not known what they were doing? No, it hadn't seemed like it. They had not bothered to look at the drum, had not known it was full? But that was scarcely an excuse—no, it was all too much, not understandable. . . . He had not talked to his son since, only seen him go past.

The telephone rang from upstairs: Carrie said that Joseph would be down to see him in a few moments, if Jack "had nothing better to do."

Instantly Jack was on the defensive: he knew that Joseph

criticised him for having been away so much when the three
children were growing up. This message was a reference to that
—*again*? If it was simply careless, what had come into his head,
then that made it even worse, in a way. . . . Joseph came running lightly down the stairs and into the livingroom. A muscular
young man, he wore skin-tight blue jeans, a tight blue sweat-
shirt, and a small red scarf at his throat tied like a pirate's. The
clothes were old, but as much care had gone into their choosing,
preparation and presentation as a model getting ready for a photograph. . . . While Jack knew he had already begun the process
of comparison that always left him exhausted, he could not stop,
and he was wondering: Was it that we were as obsessed with
what we wore but I've forgotten it? No, it's not that: our convention was that it was bourgeois to spend time and money on
clothes, that was it, but their convention is different; that's all
it is and it is not important.

Joseph had a strong blue gaze, and a strong straight mouth.
The mouth was hidden under a wiry golden beard. A mane of
wiry yellow hair fell to his shoulders. Jack thought that the
beard and the long hair were there because they were fashionable, and would be dropped the moment they were not. . . . *Well,
why not? He wished very much he could have swaggered about
in beard and mane—that was the truth.*

This aggressively vivid young man sat on a chair opposite
Jack, put his palms down on his thighs with his fingers pointing
towards each other, and the elbows out. In this considering, alert
position he looked at his father.

Jack, a faded, larger, softer version of what he was seeing,
waited.

Joseph said: "I hear you have got religion."

"The opium," said Jack, in a formal considering way, "of the
people: Yes. If that's what it is, I have got it."

Jack felt particularly transparent, because of his son's forceful
presence. He knew that his posture, the smile on his face, were
expressing apology. He already knew the meeting was doomed
to end unpleasantly. Yet he was looking for the words to appeal
to his son, to begin the "real" talk that they should be having.
Joseph said: "Well, that's your business." He sounded impatient; having raised the subject, or at least used it as an opener,
now he was saying that his father's processes were of no interest
or importance.

"You've been following the Robinson affair?"

Jack could not remember for a moment which affair that was, but did not like to say no.

"We have to pay the defence lawyer. And there's the bail. We need at least three thousand pounds."

Jack did not say anything. It was not from policy, but inadequacy, yet he saw his son beginning to make the irritable movements of power, of confidence, checked and thwarted. It crossed his mind that of course his son saw him as powerful and confident, and this it was that accounted for the aggression, the hostility, the callousness. Into Jack's mind now came sets of words framed rhetorically; since this was not how he was feeling, he was surprised. "Why does it have to be like this, that more hate is used on people of the same side, thus preventing us ever from uniting in a common front, preventing us from bringing down the enemy?" These were words from the imaginary conversation with Joseph that he so often indulged in: only now did it strike him that he never had fantasies of a personal relationship —of their going for a holiday together, for instance, or just spending an evening, or walking for an hour or so. "Can't you see?"—the inner rhetoric-maker was continuing, "that the vigour of your criticism, your iconoclasm, your need to condemn the past without learning from it, will take you relentlessly to stand exactly where your despised elders stand now?"

It suddenly occurred to Jack, and for the first time, that he had repudiated his past. This so frightened him, leaving him, as it must, by himself out in the air somewhere, without comrades and allies—*without a family*—that he almost forgot Joseph's presence. He was thinking: For weeks now, ever since the old man's death—before, even?—I've been thinking as if I have abandoned socialism.

Joseph was saying: "I don't have to tell you what the conditions are like in that prison, how they are being treated."

Jack saw that the "I don't have to tell you" was in fact an admission that in spite of everything he said, Joseph saw him as an ally. "You've come to me for money?" he asked, as if there could be another reason.

"Yeah. Yeah. That's about it, I suppose."

"Why do you have to be American?" Jack asked in sudden real irritation. "You're not American. Why do you all have to?"

Joseph said, with a conscious smile: "It's a mannerism, that's all." Then he looked stern again, in command.

Jack said: "I'm one of the old rich lefties you were publicly despising not long ago. You didn't want to have anything to do with us, you said."

Joseph frowned and made irritable movements which said that he felt that the sort of polemic which abused people not standing exactly where he stood was rather like breathing, a tradition, and he genuinely felt his father was being unreasonable in taking such remarks personally. Then he said, as if nothing better could be expected: "Then I take it it is no?"

"No," said Jack, "I am sorry."

Joseph got up; but he looked hesitant, and even now could sit down—if Jack said the right things. If he could push aside the rhetorical sentences that kept coming to his tongue: how should they not?—he had spent many hours of fantasy ensuring that they would!

Jack suddenly heard himself saying, in a low, shaking, emotional voice: "I am so sick of it all. It all just goes on and on. Over and over again."

"Well," said Joseph, "they say it is what always happens, so I suppose that ought to make us feel better." His smile was his own, not forced, or arranged.

Jack saw that Joseph had taken what he had said as an appeal for understanding between them personally: he had believed that his father was saying he was sick of their bad relations.

Had that been what he was saying? He had imagined he was talking about the political cycle. Jack now understood that if in fact he made enough effort, Joseph would respond, and then . . . He heard himself saying: "Like bloody automatons. Over and over again. Can't you see that it is going to take something like twenty years for you lot to become old rich lefties?"

"Or would if we aren't all dead first," said Joseph, ending the thing as Jack would, and with a calm, almost jolly smile. He left, saying: "The Robinson brothers are likely to get fifteen years if we don't do something."

Jack, as if a button had been pushed, was filled with guilt about the Robinson brothers and almost got up to write a cheque there and then. But he did not: it had been an entirely automatic reaction.

He spent a few days apparently in the state he had been in for weeks; but he knew himself to have reached the end of some long inner process that had proved too much for him. This interview with his son had been its end, as, very likely, the scene in the attic had been its beginning? Who knew? Who could know! Not Jack. He was worn out, as at the end of a long vigil. He found himself one morning standing in the middle of his livingroom saying over and over again: "I can't stand any more of this. I can't. I won't."

He found the pills and took them with the same miserable determination that he would have had to use to kill something that had to be killed. Almost at once he began to sleep, and the tension eased. He no longer felt as if he was carrying around, embodied in himself, a question as urgent as a wound that needed dressing, but that he had no idea what the language was in which he might find an answer. He ceased to experience the cloying sweetness that caused a mental nausea a hundred times worse than the physical. In a few days he had already stopped seeing his wife and daughters as great dolls who supplied warmth, charm, sympathy, when the buttons of duty or habit were pressed. Above all, he did not have to be on guard against his own abhorrence: his fingers did not explore masks on his face, nor was he always conscious of the statements made by his body and his limbs.

He was thinking that he was probably already known throughout the Left as a renegade; yet, examining the furniture in his mind, he found it not much changed.

It occurred to him, and he went on to consider it in a brisk judicious way, that it was an extraordinary thing that whereas he could have sat for an examination at a moment's notice on the history, the ideas, and the contemporary situation of socialism, communism and associated movements, with confidence that he would know the answers even to questions on the details of some unimportant sect in some remote country, he was so ignorant of religious history and thought that he could not have answered any questions at all. His condition in relation to religious questions was like that of a person hearing of socialism for the first time and saying: "Oh yes, I've often thought it wasn't fair that some people should have more than others. You agree, do you?"

He decided to go to the British Museum Reading Room. He

had written many of his books there. His wife was delighted, knowing that this meant he was over the crisis.

He sent in his card for books on the history of the religions, on comparative religion, and on the relation of religion to anthropology.

For the first few days it seemed that he was still under the spell of his recent experience: he could not keep his attention from wandering from the page, and the men and women all around him bending over books seemed to him insane; this habit of solving all questions by imbibing information through the eyes off the printed page was a form of self-hypnotism. He was seeing them and himself as a species that could not function unless it took in information in this way.

But this soon passed and he was able to apply himself.

As he read, he conscientiously examined what he thought; was this changing at all? No, his distaste for the whole business could be summed up by an old idea of his, which was that if he had been bred, let us say, in Pakistan, that would have been enough for him to kill other people in the name of Mohammed, and if he had been born in India, to kill Moslems without a qualm. That had he been born in Italy, he would have been one brand of Christian, and if he had stuck with his family's faith, he would be bound to suspect Roman Catholicism. But above all what he felt was that this was an outdated situation. What was he doing sitting here surrounded by histories and concordances and expositions and exegetics? He would be better occupied doing almost anything else—a hundred years ago, yes, well, that had been different. The struggle for a Victorian inside the Church had meant something; for a man or a woman then to say: "If I had been born an Arab I would be praying five times a day looking at Mecca, but had I been a Tibetan I would have believed in the Dalai Lama"—that kind of statement had needed courage then, and the effort to make it had been worthwhile.

There were, of course, the mystics. But the word was associated for him with the tainted sweetness that had so recently afflicted him, with self-indulgence, and posturing, and exaggerated behaviour. He read, however, Simone Weil and Teilhard de Chardin; these were the names he knew.

He sat, carefully checking his responses: he was more in sympathy with Simone Weil, because of her relations with the poor, less with Teilhard de Chardin, who seemed to him not very different from any sort of intellectual: he could have been a useful sort of politician, for instance? It occurred to him that he was in the process of choosing a degree or class of belief, like a pipe from a display of pipes, or a jacket in a shop, that would be on easy terms with the ideas he was already committed to and, above all, would not disturb his associates. He could imagine himself saying to Walter: "Well, yes, it is true that I am religious in a way—I can see the point of Simone Weil, she took poverty into account. She was a socialist of a kind, really."

He bought more books by both Simone Weil and Teilhard de Chardin, and took them home, but did not read them; he had lost interest, and besides an old mechanism had come into force. He realised that sitting in the Reading Room he had been thinking of writing a book describing, but entirely as a tourist, the varieties of religious behaviour he had actually witnessed: a festival in Ceylon involving sacred elephants, for instance. The shape of this book was easy to find: he would describe what he had seen. The tone of it, the style—well, there might be a difficulty. There should not of course be the slightest tone of contempt; a light affectionate amusement would be appropriate. He found himself thinking that when the Old Guard read it they would be relieved as to the health of his state of mind.

Abandoning the Reading Room, he found that Carrie was becoming seriously interested in a young man met through her brother. He was one of the best of the new young revolutionaries, brave, forthright, everything a young revolutionary should be. Carrie was in the process of marrying her father? A difficulty was that this young man and Joseph had recently quarrelled. They had disagreed so violently over some policy that Joseph had left his particular group, and had formed another. Rosemary thought the real reason for the quarrel was that Joseph resented his sister loving his friend but did not realise it. Jack took his wife to task over this, saying that to discredit socialist action because it had, or might have, psychological springs was one of the oldest of reaction's tricks. But, said Rosemary, every action had a psychological base, didn't it, so why shouldn't one describe what it was? Jack surprised himself by his vehemence in this discussion—it was, in fact, a quarrel. For he believed, with Rosemary, that probably Joseph was reacting emotionally: he had always been jealous of his sisters. Whatever the truth of it was, Carrie was certainly forgetting her "Eastern thing." She was already talking about it as of a youthful and outgrown phase. Rosemary, in telling Jack this, kept glancing apologetically at him; the last thing she wanted to do, she said, was to disparage any experience which he might be going through himself. Or had gone through.

Had gone through.

There was a Conference on the theme of Saving Earth from Man, and he had been afraid he wasn't going to be asked. He was, and Mona rang up to say she would like to go with him. She made some remarks that could be openings to his joining her in a position that combined belief in God with progressive action; he could see that she was willing to lay before him this position, which she had verbalised in detail. He closed that door, hoping it did not sound like a snub. He was again thinking of something called "religion" as an area coloured pink or green on a map and in terms of belief in an after-life like a sweetened dummy for adults. In addition to this, he had two sets of ideas, or feelings, in his mind: one, those he had always held, or held since his early maturity; the other, not so much a set of ideas as a feeling of unease, disquiet, guilt, which amounted to a recognition that he had missed an opportunity of some sort, but that the failure had taken place long before his recent experience. Which he now summarised to himself in Walter's words as: It's a shock when your old man dies. His life had been set in one current, long ago; a fresh current, or at least, a different one, had run into it from another source; but, unlike the springs and rivers of myth and fairy tale, it had been muddied and unclear.

He could see that his old friends were particularly delighted to see him at the Conference, ready to take an active part. He was on the platform, and he spoke several times, rather well. By the time the Conference was over, there was no doubt he was again confirmed as one of the Old Guard, trusted and reliable.

Because of the attention the Conference got, he was offered a good job on television, and he nearly took it. But what he needed was to get out of England for a bit. Again Rosemary mentioned Nigeria. Her case was a good one. He would enjoy it, it was work he would do well, he would be contributing valuably. She would enjoy it too, she added loyally. As of course she would, in many ways. After all, it was only for two years, and when she came back it would be easy for her to pick up what she had dropped. And Family Counsellors would still be needed after all! Something that had seemed difficult now seemed easy, not much more than a long trip to Europe. They were making it easy, of course, because of that refusal to look at the consequences of a thing that comes from wanting to leave options open. Spending two years in Africa would change them both, and they did not want to admit that they had become reluctant to change.

On the night after he had formally agreed to go to Nigeria he had the dream again, the worst. If worst was the word?—in this region of himself different laws applied. He was dropping into nothingness, the void: he was fighting his way to a window and there he battered on panes to let in air, and as he hit with his fists and shouted for help the air around him thinned and became exhausted—and he ceased to exist.

He had forgotten how terrible—or how powerful—that dream had been.

He paced his house, wearing the night away. It was too late: he was going to Nigeria because he had not known what else it was he could do.

During that night he could feel his face falling into the lines and folds of his father's face—at the time, that is, when his father had been an elderly, rather than an old man. His father's old man's face had been open and sweet, but before achieving that goodness—like the inn at the end of a road which you have no alternative but to use?—he had had the face of a Roman, heavy-lidded, sceptical, obdurate, facing into the dark: the man whose pride and strength has to come from a conscious ability to suffer, in silence, the journey into negation.

During the days that followed, when the household was all plans and packing and arranging and people running in and out, Jack was thinking that there was only one difference between himself now and himself as he had been before "the bit of a shock." He had once been a man whose sleep had been—nothing, non-existent, he had slept like a small child. Now, in spite of everything, although he knew that fear could lie in wait there, his sleep had become another country, lying just behind his daytime one. Into that country he went nightly, with an alert, even if ironical interest—the irony was due to his habits of obedience to his past—for a gift had been made to him. Behind the face of the sceptical world was another, which no conscious decision of his could stop him exploring.

A NOTE ON THE TYPE

The text of this book was set on the Linotype in a new face called Primer, designed by Rudolph Ruzicka, who was earlier responsible for the design of Fairfield and Fairfield Medium, Linotype faces whose virtues have for some time been accorded wide recognition.

The complete range of sizes of Primer was first made available in 1954, although the pilot size of 12-point was ready as early as 1951. The design of the face makes general reference to Linotype Century—long a serviceable type, totally lacking in manner or frills of any kind—but brilliantly corrects its characterless quality.

Composed, printed, and bound by The Haddon Craftsmen, Scranton, Pennsylvania.

Typography and binding design by Camilla Filancia.